Metaphorosis
2021

Also from Metaphorosis

<u>Verdage</u>

Reading 5X5 x2: Duets
Score – an SFF symphony
Reading 5X5: Readers' Edition
Reading 5X5: Writers' Edition

<u>Vestige</u>

The Nocturnals by Mariah Montoya

<u>Metaphorosis Magazine</u>

Metaphorosis: Best of 20xx
Metaphorosis 20xx: The Complete Stories
annual issues, from 2016

Monthly issues

<u>Plant Based Press</u>

Best Vegan Science Fiction & Fantasy
annual issues, 2016-2020

from B. Morris Allen:
Chambers of the Heart: a collection of stories
Susurrus
Allenthology: Volume I
Tocsin: and other stories
Start with Stones: collected stories
Metaphorosis: a collection of stories

Metaphorosis
2021

The Complete Stories

edited by
B. Morris Allen

ISBN: 978-1-64076-217-6 (e-book)
ISBN: 978-1-64076-218-3 (paperback)
ISBN: 978-1-64076-219-0 (hardcover)

from
Metaphorosis Publishing

Neskowin

Contents

From the Editor

They're not making these years any easier. Let's hope the law of averages has some really outstanding years coming down the pike for us. In the meantime, though, we're stuck with what we've got.

The good news is that if we want a better future, making one is in our hands. Better decisions, more foresight, a little wisdom, a helping of compassion — it doesn't really take all that much, once we accept that it's *we* who must change, not just everyone else. All those ingredients won't magically make everything better, but they can make a whole lot of things better, if we're just serious about it.

There's a lot of magic in this book, too. Not all the stories are literally *about* magic, but some of them are, and all of them have something to say. A lot of them deal with the magic of perseverance and tenacity — the idea that if you believe in something strongly enough and keep fighting for it, someday you just may win the battle. Standing up for what you believe in is a magic of its own, especially when it feels like you're the only one on your side.

Of course, the stories here aren't motivational speeches; that's just a side effect. Mostly, they're just great stories that will entertain you, uplift you, transport you to new locales and concepts. Dive in and let them take you away!

B. Morris Allen
Editor
1 March 2022

January

Superbloom

Lynne Peskoe-Yang

The call comes in the evening, though it's morning on the other side of the world. K. is demanding that I leave my study right this minute to look at the sea. I grab my sample bag and rush outside, too curious to argue. It takes less than a minute for me to jog from my house to the end of the jetty.

I peer down at the surface of the water. I can't see much; the sun set ten minutes ago.

"What am I looking for?"

"Look at the water. What color is it?"

I fumble in my bag for my good flashlight—one I made myself, with a patented triple lens—and turn its ultra-sharp beam on the ocean.

"Why is it doing that?" I whisper. "Why is it just sitting still?"

"What color is it, D.?"

"Green. The whole thing is just solid green."

A long, textured sigh issues from my earpiece. "God," K. hisses. She seems on the verge of tears, but with some effort she controls her breathing.

I can't wait. "Is this that algae bloom of yours? What the hell is it doing here?"

She inhales purposefully. I hoped she'd have to pull herself together to correct me, and it works; when she speaks again, her voice is steady.

"Not algae. It's a lichen—or it was when I started studying it. I've got no idea what it's doing there, other than growing. I'm still making sense of it myself. Do you remember my dissertation?"

Of course I remember. A year ago, K. printed out that dissertation and mailed it to me personally, neatly stapled and, I thought, perfumed. I read the abstract a dozen times before I gave in and called. She explained it all to me, in her laughing-brook voice, with a patience I hadn't been shown since I was a girl.

She had found me in a directory of remote researchers and wrote to ask me to photograph some of the lichens in my little biome, which was, she pointed out meaningfully, on the exact opposite side of the world from where K. herself lived, in New Zealand.

In the dissertation K. had referred to the floating, living islands that popped up along the northwestern coast as "ur-lichens", or, in more casual contexts, "super-lichens".

It was the second name that caught on in her small collective of Māori ecologists, the only ones paying attention at first. The super-lichen was a local disaster, overshadowed by the death rattle of the oceanic coral reefs. The collective relied on a growing network of citizen scientists to track the expansion—what they came to call the Bloom—as it spread unchecked along the coastline.

K. had volunteered to make contact with someone who could keep the last watch, as far away from the origin as possible. My island outpost, her own antipode, would mark the finish line for a fully global superbloom, if it ever got that far. I didn't ask her what good it would do anyone to know how much of the ocean was lost at that point. I don't think either of us expected that such a thing could actually happen in our lifetimes.

When the Bloom began to move down the northwestern coast of New Zealand, K. packed up her belongings and moved with it. She still called me occasionally to ask for updates from my side of the world. I would take the call on my headset while I worked the glass.

"A fungal spore sends its hyphae into the algae," she'd say, drawing out the Greek ending—*hy-fee*—in a grin that I could almost see. Through my headset I could hear her, even while I sanded finished prisms or made coke fuel for the forge. Sometimes she asked me about my work, but I had no talent for translation.

Instead, I sent photos, both of the growing lens and the lichens—no samples, she said, as the risk of contamination was overwhelming. I also sent her tools. Funding was scarce for lichen-watching, but I had all the raw materials at my disposal to replicate and improve every piece of glassware K. needed, and shockproof shipping was free under my contract. When K.'s digital microscope was stolen, I sent her a replacement—a bespoke mechanical version from my own workshop, with a hardwood carrying case, hand-engraved with her initials.

After that, the calls were daily. My ears adapted to the sound of K.'s voice and listened for it even after we hung up. I could not help but absorb her passion, her creeping panic, over the terrible might of the Bloom. Alone of ocean beings, it seemed to delight in the spiking acidity caused by human pollution. The Bloom was so good at growing, so blazingly energy-efficient, especially near the surface, that huge mats of it emerged in shallow waters around dozens of islands in the South Pacific. Where they met the coasts, the floating mats merged, surrounding whole archipelagos in swamps that turned alarmingly toxic.

I asked K. how it reproduced.

"This one doesn't," she said. "It only grows."

This is what I learned in those months of building: a lichen is not an organism, but a community of organisms acting collectively. The photosynthetic members, single algae cells or long strands of sun-loving cyanobacteria, feed the fungus via the hyphae, which penetrate the algae's cell walls to extract their sugars. In return, the fungus offers a safe habitat for its support organisms. Together, the hyphae and the photosynthetic cells make a single continuous unit of life, self-replicating and infinitely adaptable.

"On its own, the fungus is a clump of hyphae. It can't form any discernible structures. It dies."

"So the fungus is a parasite?"

"We'd have to ask the algae."

We passed good months this way, her calling, me listening. She was my favorite sound.

Then the Superbloom took the rest of the ocean in the course of a single night, twenty years ahead of schedule, and K. called me again.

"When I woke up this morning, I thought my satellite feed was broken—the map was just covered." It's hard to process her words.

"...But if it's reached you already, we're long past any way of stopping the spread," she concluded.

I listen to the birdsong through the phone: a kookaburra's alien laughter. Behind it, the wind is high, as it is here. I can see the first storm of summer growing on the horizon.

The kookaburra falls silent. I wipe my eyes with my forearm.

"Is there anything we can do? Maybe if...?" I trail off, unable to even frame the question.

"You should stock some food," she says gently. "If I think of something, I'll... I'll let you know."

It's fully dark now. The vast, pale expanse could almost be the natural ocean, if it weren't for the disturbing stillness of it beneath the starless sky. I feel panic rise, tightening my lungs and heart.

"Oh, and D.? Are you still there?"

I cough, force my voice deeper. "Yeah."

"Don't touch it."

The Caldera is the perfect place to light a beacon, and I was once the perfect person to keep it lit. My technical training is in photonics, the art of manipulating and redirecting light. I was one of the first to build lenses from gadolinite, the oily black mineral that makes up the base of the Caldera, though I did it in the comfort of my childhood home on the mainland. But I was losing patience with the frantic pace of manufacturing; I was ready for a quieter life.

By then, I had made some friends in government, and one of them shared my name with the Bureau of Scientific Engagement, a collaboration between government scientists and propagandists. Riding a wave of investment in space ventures, the project aimed to thrill the nation by building a self-powering radio beacon that would send an eternal message to alien worlds. Previous communications to the extrasolar expanse had been ephemeral: a five-minute transmission from the North Pole of spoken greetings in two hundred Earth languages; a gold disk embossed with Da Vinci's naked eight-limbed man and some other things, launched into the sky. The time had come, in the BSE's opinion, to make ourselves known to the universe on a permanent basis.

A simple transmitter would emit a continuous wavelength: a hundred mHz, just energetic enough to escape the atmosphere. My job would be to build and then maintain a lens out of gadolinite thermal glass, a form of passive solar power. The lens would both concentrate the signal into a narrow beam and power itself virtually forever, storing solar energy in a solid-state battery that fed the same monotone signal, even at night.

I was to build the whole thing on-site, on a colonial outpost with no other lucrative resources to offer, nor remaining residents to exploit. The Caldera is an empty-named place, a safe enough distance from real human civilization that the mainland, at least, would have warning, should the worst occur. What the worst might entail, we did not discuss.

The day after the Superbloom starts the same as usual, and it's not until I look out the window that I recall what has changed. The Caldera is a narrow island, curled like a fetus against the sea. To my left, the bulk of the island, a great crescent of steaming jungle, pours down into the bay as always. But the basin itself is deathly still, suffocating under the weight of a mat of new life that extends, waveless, to every horizon.

It's hard to look at.

Above the Bloom, on top of the hills on the opposite end of the crescent island, the black, flat-topped needle of the signal tower is barely visible from here. It's been three months since I got it running, and two months since I hauled my personal items to the opposite side of the island from the tower, into one of the last remaining buildings on the island. The tower was starting to make my head buzz.

I check the monitor: the signal is fine. A one-note performance, without even the texture of an ending, communicating the bare minimum of reality. The beam moves like an out-of-control spotlight, the focused radio waves sweeping around the planet as it turns, carving out curly ribbons of space in their near-random search for a receptive target. In the early days of the project, there had been some talk of sending out a message with actual content, even a simple greeting. But then one of our physicists showed that if we stuck to one frequency, the signal could easily reach the nearest galaxy cluster and would likely be detectable at twice that distance. The programming team was furious, but *intergalactic* sounded better than *interplanetary* in the headlines, so the one-note message won out.

My contract gives me a year of watch after I finish construction, but already it is impossible to picture life on the mainland. No word has arrived from my supervisors, but that doesn't surprise me. Will I last nine more months here, without supplies, without a plan? I do not dwell on this.

That night, I make my first discovery.

"The Bloom emits light." My words echo on the other end. Does my voice sound different to her because she's listening to its inverted form—across the world, upside down, in broad daylight?

"I thought I was seeing things," she whispers after a moment.

"I see it, too. It's clearer at night, but even in the light it's pulsing. Why?"

"I don't know." Her voice is hushed, hurried, as though someone might be listening. "It wasn't doing this even a week ago, but this Bloom changes so fast. If it were to somehow recruit some new microorganism, something that glows..."

"A third colony member?"

"It's possible. We wouldn't know. But there are hundreds of bioluminescent species."

"Why do they glow?"

"Camouflage. Prey attraction. Signaling to the predators that eat *their* predators."

"Would that look like... a pulse? Rhythmic?"

"No. It's purely responsive."

"Doesn't the pulse remind you of a heartbeat?"

"Yes, of course."

In the green expanse of the bay, a field of little leaflets drinks in the dimmed sun. On the far side, straight across the bay, the black crown of the signal tower looms like a purposeless alien.

"Does the Bloom, or some part of it, *have* a heartbeat?"

"Absolutely not."

Later, a call from the department: deliveries will be suspended for the time being, given the circumstances. I do not have to ask what the circumstances are. All around the world, I imagine, human beings are attempting to negotiate with the invader, touching and hacking and plowing, growing more desperate for a response. But the Bloom will not hear them, any more than I would hear a threat spelled out in plant hormones.

I tell him I have enough food for a few months and not to worry about me. There is shouting in the background, but I can't make out the words; the call ends, thankfully, before I get invested. I am sensing already that I shouldn't spend my panic on people I already know. It is easy to forget them; what could I do for them from here?

The sky is sickly green in the evening when the light begins to pulse again.

One-two. It is unmistakably a heartbeat, reborn as two flashes of incandescent plant-flesh, and yet no part of the Bloom could possibly have even a vestigial memory of having a heart. I count eighty beats per minute: a healthy resting heart rate for a human.

One-two. The rate does not change. If it's a message, it is insultingly simple. There is no hint of frustration, no pleading, no aggression; just a double-tap of light, repeating endlessly. A beacon reporting back that conditions are normal, stand by. *One-two.* A binary code too flat to be called communication. In Morse code, I recall uselessly, it is just the capital letter *I*, over and over and over, stupidly iterating into the dark.

I am here. Are you?

I creep to the edge of the Bloom. From the jetty, I drop a rock into its depths, as I often did when the ocean was still liquid, and watch the surface roll away from the impact in a stunted parody of wave motion. If I close my eyes while doing this and pay attention only to the splash, I will remember that there is still water under there.

I squat, scooping a handful of black sand from the beach and letting it pour from my fingers onto the curling leaves of the colony. No ripple at all. The living matter absorbs the motion, stunts its impact, so it can't be transferred. The motion is born locally, dies locally; sound, spoken prayer, would be stifled the same way.

But the Bloom *is* connected to itself, somehow. The pulse of the lichen at my feet is perfectly in phase with the pulse at the horizon. Light, then, can cross the channels from one end of the Bloom to the other. The Bloom is not a creature, but a culture; light is its language.

I don't know any words in light, but I don't think that would matter, if I could make some kind of deliberate pattern. The intent to speak is its own kind of speech—the astrobiologists taught me that. As long as the signal is clearly *meant* as a message, it is one.

"Fine," says K. when she calls back, too early. She woke me up. "Fine. It's sentient."

"I told you. There's no other explanation."

"Hm." I can hear her pacing. "Yes. But that doesn't mean—"

"Why are you so worried? This is a good thing. Maybe we can reason with it."

"Not good. Unprecedented. Bizarre. I can't even philosophically wrap my head around it. The pattern makes intelligent life unmistakable. Why would a living being advertise its existence like that? What takes that kind of stupid risk?"

"You're the one who's studied it. What do you think?"

She exhales. I can hear her brain working. "I think... whatever it is, it doesn't know we're here. Yet. But it's looking."

"I'm going to answer."

"With the beacon? Is it moveable? I thought you couldn't redirect the beam."

"I can do it. I just never had to before."

"Okay. Okay. But D., listen. This is not a conversation with a person. Sentience is not the same thing as a brain. I've been studying this thing. It evolves faster than its components, faster even than some viruses, but it also started pulsing all at once, like a single organism... If this is intelligence, it's clearly distributed— spread out in the body of the Bloom, coordinated, but not centralized. It is *nothing* like us."

"What is it like?"

"God. Fuck. I don't know. An octopus?" She's close to tears. "Who knows what it would do if it recognized another intelligence? And you want to give away your position, before we even know what will happen! What if it takes the signal as a threat? What if it *answers*?"

Her voice is so plaintive, so childish, that I half want to shout at her. *There is no other option!* But I can't say that. She knows.

For a moment I consider telling her I was planning to come see her when my contract was up, but even thinking the words makes me want to howl.

Instead, I tell K. I love her, and then I hang up in a hurry so I don't have to hear her sob.

In the evening, I trek north. I weave among my discarded shipping containers, most twice my height, their steel now coated in the rich green of a kudzu infestation at least a foot deep on every face. The vines are flowering on the southeast side where I approach; I breathe in clouds of grape-like perfume as I pass each cluster of white and purple blossoms.

The place steams with life. Between the blocks and everywhere the vines haven't claimed lies a thick carpet of mosses in varying shades, from pine-green to chartreuse and golden yellow. Already, beneath my boots, the fragile stalks of a bryophyte have been crushed into wet salad.

I need my flashlight to find the ladder on the far side of the tower. I hover on the bottom rung, waiting for the doubts to come; but my wonderful brain is silent, and I hear nothing but the wind through the leaves. The top rung is covered in seagull scat, so I have to haul myself onto the platform beneath the beacon like a sea lion. I turn off my light and recover there for a few moments, with my back against the thin railing, staring upward.

The sky is clear now. The compound lens of the beacon looms over me, its outer rings glittering with reflected stars. The pieces are arranged in concentric circles, like a slice of a giant black onion. Each layer is made of two to thirty segments of gadolinite glass.

It is impossible to tell by sight that the signal is firing. I pass my hand over the opening in the center of the onion slice, and imagine that I can feel it, a sort of metaphysical buzz; but I know I can't actually feel anything, as surely as I know the signal exists. The beam, even concentrated by my lens, is both silent and invisible to me.

I pull myself up with a groan and stretch upward to run my hands along one of the rings. The dark glass is warmer than I remembered. The smaller rings are closely nested and hard to differentiate by starlight, so I work my way inward by feel. Just below the innermost ring, attached to the pole that supports the beacon's weight, there is a latched metal box, unlocked.

The terminal inside is still charged. I power it up and it chirps softly, as though it recognizes me. Black letters appear against the green-grey field: I N P U T ?

My mind is empty. I turn away from the beacon and nearly lose my balance. The railing, rusted from the salt spray, groans but holds steady for now. How is it up to *me* to decide what to say to an alien from my own planet?

It has stopped glowing, I realize as I stare into the sea, so it's possible I've missed my chance, but somehow, inexplicably, I feel that it is actually aware of what I am doing and has simply paused to wait for my answer. *Impossible!* I can almost hear K. say in response.

I picture her on the other side of the world and feel my spine straighten a bit.

I take great, gulping breaths of the briny air. I reprogram the beacon.

I fiddle with latches in the dark. The lens is twice my wingspan and half my weight, but at least the whole thing comes off its mount without so much as a screwdriver. I hoist it onto my shoulder like a parasol and then lower the circular end to the platform, feeling my long trek across the island screaming in my kneecaps. When I stand up, the beam is pointing just below the horizon, its waves colliding with a distant section of the Bloom's vast body.

The Bloom is still as stone. In the silvery light, the world looks primordial, as though made of just-cooled magma, unmarred by soil or water. But I know the Bloom is there and watching me, in its own way; it holds its breath as I hold mine.

We watch each other.

Just where the beam hits, a part of the Bloom begins to rise. But this is an illusion: it is simply luminescing, first there and then all over, the whole field of it suddenly turning white with light—far brighter than before. In seconds I'm forced to cover my eyes with my arm, but it's not enough.

I wake up on the beach a few meters from the tower, my whole body aching from the fall. The world is still flashing around me, so bright I can almost hear the new pattern: the same one I chose moments or hours ago.

Long, short, long. *K*, the Bloom is saying, shouting, singing, to me and to her, and I can feel her amazement radiating straight through the center of the Earth.

See Lynne Peskoe-Yang's story "Superbloom" online at Metaphorosis.
If you liked it, leave a comment. Authors love that!
Remember to subscribe to our e-mail updates so you'll know when new stories are posted.

About the story

I wrote this in an attempt to relate to a kind of organism I find unfathomable. I think I'm jealous of lichen, the way it smoothly integrates two distinct sets of DNA into a single body, without conflict or suspicion. I wanted to fuse with something like that, so I wrote about someone who I thought would understand that impulse.

A question for the author

Q: What are you currently reading?
A: *Uzumaki*, the graphic horror novel by Junji Ito.

About the author

Lynne Peskoe-Yang is a science fiction writer and tech journalist living in the Northeast US. lynnepeskoeyang.com, @lynnepeskoeyang

All We Ever Look For

Cécile Cristofari

When I opened the window this morning, three parrots were perched in a tree hanging over a deserted beach of pure white sand that stretched towards a dazzling horizon. I'd never seen anything so lovely. I leaned out, just enough to feel the caress of the breeze, the salty coolness of the surf that helped me brace myself for the day ahead. Not long after closing the window, I opened the front door with a deep breath, stepping into the rumble of traffic and the dappled shadow of a maple, in the damp heat of Québec summer.

The memory of that shore and gentle seaside wind stayed with me for the entire bus ride. It was gone now, I knew. What happened when I closed my window I could only guess; the wonders it let me glimpse vanished as soon as the latch clicked shut, and never came back. Now, watching my own world scroll past the bus, I wished I had left my window open a little longer.

When I reached the office, the two secretaries were talking about the latest missing person cases in town. I stared at them for longer than I should have. They waved, a little awkwardly.

My desk was in a corner of the office, out of sight, just under a mercifully powerful fan. I wiped my brow, and exchanged perfunctory greetings with my neighbours. I had never been good at making friends at the office. Neither was I cut out for the increasingly heavy heat waves these days, it seemed, and I had another fleeting thought of how lovely and cool that beach had seemed.

From across the office, Marie-Ange interrupted my train of thought with a wave and a conspiratorial gesture, placing a folded bit of paper on the corner of her desk. I answered with an uncertain smile.

The heat had not abated when I returned home. I still held Marie-Ange's crumpled note in my fist. *Saturday?* it simply read. I had waited for her break to leave the office so I wouldn't have to respond.

I wondered if this was what guilt felt like.

I sat, or rather dropped, in the armchair facing the window, to scratch Toutou's ears as Tilou mewed in protest at being woken up. I stared at the maple billowing outside—when the window was closed it never showed anything but the maple outside the building, its branches stretched far and wide like a challenge to the concrete and cars and heat and fires and everything humans could throw at its kind. It was only when I opened it that the magic began.

I had never figured out how or why this treasure had fallen into my hands. I never heard reports of other portals opening elsewhere in the world, and the question of what I had done to deserve this one was never answered. One day I'd opened the window in my living room, hoping to get some fresh air while I read the news as usual with a cat peering over my shoulder—and instead of the customary drone of the street, I'd gazed over a cliff, snow-capped mountains dotting the horizon under an uncanny white sky. I'd banged the window shut in shock, only to open it again, seconds later. This time it was a desert, red sands stretching as far as I could see. The dance had begun then, opening and closing, never knowing what strangeness would lie beyond, only that it would be new, and odd, and marvellous—and that as soon as I closed the window, it would disappear forever.

At first I had sworn to myself that I would never let anyone else see it, but soon that had felt petty, and I'd begun to bring people in. The first few times, it had been simple, even made me a little proud for the first time in years. An act of sharing and compassion, inviting unhappy acquaintances to sit with me and gaze at the wonders beyond my window before walking back home with a lighter heart. They must have thought it was nothing more than a clever display; so had I, at first, and so did most people until the very last second. The truth was too extraordinary to entertain.

The first time someone asked to step through, I had only gaped. The possibility of it had never occurred to me. Her name was Angélique, I recall, and she was a widow, just about my age, with an estranged son. Two days after I'd agreed to her request (it hadn't occurred to me that I might do otherwise), I'd watched her step over the window ledge and on the grassy slope of a mountain meadow. She'd secured her backpack and blown me a kiss, and only when the window pane clicked shut had I fully realised that the door to her world was now gone, and she would never be able to come out again.

After Angélique, there were others. I had a knack for light friendships, the seemingly shallow ones, acquaintances that would not disturb the quiet of my home. They almost always started in the same way: an exchange of glances on the bus or a café, a smile, a few minutes of conversation that usually led to a farewell, after a moment of companionship I'd enjoy but wouldn't miss. And then sometimes the conversation lasted longer, until I sensed that sadness, that longing I'd come to know so well, until I realised that I held the key to the one thing these people wanted.

It had been easy at first, watching them step through and waving farewell, sometimes wiping a little tear, telling myself I'd brought someone more happiness than anyone else ever could have. I only had to pretend that these people were just like me, lonely and stranded, with no one to miss them. It was only when the first missing person reports came up in the newspaper that I had to face the facts. There are many ways to be lonely, and not all of them are irreparable.

"How did you pick such a silly auntie?" I asked Tilou out loud. She rubbed her head against my cheek.

I petted her and stared ahead until, as always happened after sitting alone with my thoughts for too long, I felt compelled to get up. After some hesitation, I opened the window.

Outside, a deep rainforest was alive with whistles and fluted sounds, the songs of birds and beasts I had no name for. I leaned out and closed my eyes as the mist from a waterfall cooled my face, spraying scents of moss and orchids. My smile slowly returned, and for a very long time I stood there, trying to catch the sight of monkeys or tree frogs behind every rustling leaf.

My cats, the only companions I had, would be just as happy with any other owner, I suddenly thought. I would miss them for a while, but it would be nothing to make sure they spent the rest of their lives in a home that would be just as good as mine. There was nothing holding me here. The notion was unexpectedly comforting. My life was my own. Whatever I chose to do with it, however foolhardy, I would not hurt anyone else. One day, I decided, I would go too. But today was not the right time; I was out of cat food, and anyway, I was already too weary of the summer heat to enjoy a rainforest for long.

As always, eventually, I closed the window, and I could hear once again the endless drone of the cars in the street, as clouds gathered overhead for the evening storm.

Wednesday morning sailed by in its customary haze of boredom, until a shadow loomed at the edge of my desk.

"Got time for a sandwich?"

I jumped, startled from yet another reverie. Marie-Ange was standing in front of me, her bag already slung over her shoulder. "Come on. The falafel ones. You know you love those."

My eyes darted around my desk for an excuse not to go out. The blank file staring at me from the computer screen was enough of an answer. The prospect of going out was not that unappealing, come to think of it. I got up, groaned when my back protested, and stayed in place just long enough for Marie-Ange to drag me by the arm, waving to everybody that was left in the office.

The space outside the building was not a particularly scenic one: a large car park with a few maples and a couple of grassy banks on the side, where we sat in what shade we could find. Marie-Ange finished her salad in a couple of bites, then sprawled in the grass on her back, grinning.

"Look at how gorgeous that tree is," she said.

I smiled. In truth, it wasn't much of a tree, just a sapling they'd replanted as a token gesture after they'd razed the field to make way for cars. But Marie-Ange's enthusiasm never deserted her. No one else would have convinced me, for the third time this week, to take a break and breathe the outside air when I could instead have got rid of my work and ridden back home half an hour earlier. It still surprised me, sometimes, that she not only talked me into it, but made me *want* to do it. Now that I looked at the sunlight splintering through the maple leaves, I, too, began to see some beauty in that gracile, tenacious little tree.

Marie-Ange propped herself up on her elbow.

"So. About Saturday."

My heart sank at once.

"Saturday?"

"You promised you'd show me. Remember?"

I did, very well. It had happened at the start of summer, on a day when Marie-Ange had decided to drag me out of the city for ice cream after work. I'd grumbled and wondered why she would bother with me. But as we drove across the bridge to Orleans Island, she'd pointed to the waterfall on the other side of the channel, and started gushing in the way she sometimes did about the most mundane little things, and I'd felt something unexpected —a flicker of girlish delight, the simple pleasure of feeling the damp heat on my face and the smells of the blooming forest stretching in front of us. It was a long time since I'd felt that way outside of my living room. And then I'd felt something even stronger: gratitude, pure joy at being with someone who would so casually offer this sense of wonder to me.

I'd wanted to offer something else in return. I had told her about the one thing I'd ever had that mattered. And now I wished I hadn't.

"All right,' I muttered. 'Just one look. Don't tell anyone about it, okay?"

She agreed, still grinning. It was time to go back to work. On the way back in, she changed the subject, and my mood lightened. If she thought I was only going to show her an amusing trick, so much the better.

On the bus ride back home, someone was reading the headlines out loud, and the lady behind her burst into tears. Her friend comforted her, saying something about the uplifting notes all these people had left, that they couldn't have been taken by force or ended up in a bad place. I swallowed and moved to the back of the bus.

Québec City officials overwhelmed by missing persons epidemic, I read on my phone later in the night. Three more in a month. A secret cult, underground experiments, theories were blooming all over the place. I shoved the device back in my pocket.

Missing persons epidemic, indeed, I thought to myself, as if facing a crowd of haunted relatives demanding justice. *What if I told you that they wanted to go? That they made this decision by themselves, knowing fully well what it would do to you? Would you blame* me?

I stopped as I realised that I was starting to mouth the words out loud. From their place on the sofa, Toutou and Tilou were gazing at me, green eyes and yellow eyes indolently blinking in a pool of sunlight. I had been living on my own for too long.

I leaned out of the window one last time before going to bed, to breathe in the smell of salty wind. Tilou had jumped off the sofa, and with a soft thud, landed herself on the sill; she didn't complain when I gently picked her off and held her against my chest so she could watch safely. A marble balcony hung over a rocky coast with pines and aloes tumbling into the sea. Underneath, the waters shimmered, light and deep blue interlocking towards the horizon. A fish leapt up below me, sending a flash of silver over the water.

When a seagull dove, missed, and flew back up with a cry of frustration, Tilou tensed, and at last wriggled free and strolled back to the sofa, all interest in other universes gone. I watched the bird until it disappeared over a clump of dark green trees, knowing that I could follow it if I wanted to. I thought once more of all those who had gone through, of the felicity they had seized for themselves, the mourning they had left behind.

Then I thought of Marie-Ange. It had been an imprudent idea to invite her. But it would turn out fine, I hoped. She would understand that this absolutely needed to remain a secret. And she would only take a look. She, at least, was perfectly happy with the world she lived in. Perhaps she could even come back, I mused, and we could stand in front of the window together, bet on what we would see that day, count to three, open it...

Maybe that was what friendship felt like. I smiled, closed the window, and went to bed next to a comfortably snoring cat.

On Friday, Marie-Ange dragged me out for lunch again. We chatted (or she did, while I smiled and nodded) all through the way to the fast food joint. When we sat down in the grass, however, her expression suddenly changed.

"I'm going to ask you something really outlandish. You can laugh at me if you want, but promise me you'll tell me the truth. All right?"

There was nothing I could do but swallow my dismay and acquiesce.

"I saw those missing persons reports on the news," she went on. "This is absurd. Québec City is as safe as it's always been. These... other worlds you said your window opened to. People haven't actually *gone in* there, have they?"

"Please don't tell anyone," I blurted out.

She opened her mouth. Covered it with her hand. For a few moments, she seemed halfway between laughter and tears, long enough for me to hope that it would be the former. I could handle being dismissed as a cat lady with one too many quirks. But if she started to accuse, threatened to denounce me...

"I need to see it," she said.

I breathed deeply.

"Yes. Of course. Just see it. Swear to me you won't tell anyone?"

"Not a chance. Don't worry."

"Thank you.' I realised that I held my hands balled tight against my stomach. I unclenched them and spread them on my knees. These people wanted to go, you know. It's not a decision they rushed into. I wouldn't have let them if they hadn't wanted it so badly."

"I know."

"I suppose it can't look good when you read the papers. But it won't happen again. I've been thinking about it lately. I'm going to quit. The only ones who knew about my portal are gone, and I'll keep it to myself now. And you, of course. Nobody's going to disappear again."

Marie-Ange made a strange face and touched my arm.

"I want to go," she said.

That evening, for the first time, I opened my living-room window with no anticipatory thrill, only through the force of habit.

Through the entire day, Marie-Ange's words had bounced around in my head, as if trapped in a vertiginous echo chamber—*I want to go*—along with my next, foolish question—*Why?* —as if asking her to explain herself would make her realise that there was no good reason for such a wish after all. Her explanations, however, had left me no space to argue.

The world was too small a place, more so with every passing day. I'd admired her ability to light up at every little joy life could throw her way, so much that I hadn't noticed how tired she was that small blessings were all our world had to offer her.

Or perhaps I simply was incapable of imagining how she felt. I could not recall the last time I had felt genuine delight outside of my living-room. How the person who had communicated that wonder to me could be unsatisfied with the world she lived in was unfathomable.

My thoughts ebbed as the landscape before me came into focus. Pillars of crystal in a translucent sea reflected the light of the setting sun into my living room. I stood there for long minutes, unable to take my eyes off the twin moons overhead.

How could the universe have decided that I would be the best person to entrust this portal to, of all the places it could have appeared? There was no answer but the gentle song of the water, lapping, flowing towards a horizon that seemed to curve more sharply than the one at the end of an earthly sea. I rested my hand on the sill. If I leaned out, only a little, perhaps I could touch the closest pillar. What would greet me out there—the thin air and cold of a mountain pass, or inviting warmth like the tropics at the dawn of time? I stood on tiptoe, reached forward. The breeze of another world stroked my fingers, like a hand, urging me forward with infinite gentleness. If I left now, there would be no more guilt, no more worry. One step out was all it would take...

I pulled my arm, closed the window, my heart beating faster than it should have. Tomorrow, I would call Marie-Ange and tell her I couldn't let her through. She would understand, I was certain of it. And then I'd never open that window again.

I came home late the next day, exhausted by my Saturday chores and the constant drone of the city, but with renewed resolve to make the phone call I needed to end this.

The day had slipped by so frantically I'd forgotten to check the time.

As soon as I took out my phone, the bell rang. When I opened, a flustered Marie-Ange dropped her huge backpack on my feet. After a second of shock, I swore at myself in silence. As usual, I had let time carry me along, not taking action until the last moment.

I made her sit down and have a glass of water.

"I drank on my way. Can I go now?" she said. Then with a nervous giggle, "If I don't I'm going to have second thoughts!"

I pushed the glass in front of her.

"We're not doing this, Marie-Ange," I blurted out.

She opened her eyes wide. My voice shook, but for once I could find the words, and didn't let her speak.

"Maybe it sounds like this is what you need, but it's wrong. I can't keep this up. You'll end up who knows where, in a parallel universe where you could die tomorrow, and no one would ever know. Ever. My window has never opened twice on the same place. Your family will be shattered, and if I meet them face to face, I won't even be able to tell them you're all right. Because I won't know that. I'm sorry. And your family won't be the only ones. I..."

The cascading words dried up then. How I felt about her departure was my own concern. I couldn't expect her to alter her decision on my account, shouldn't even think of asking. I stood, silent, expecting her to make a fuss. But she nodded as if she understood.

"No matter what I tell them, people will be upset," she said. "They'll have to understand. This is what I need."

"Why?"

But I realised that I knew already. Loneliness was not the only force that drove people to seek what lay beyond my window. Her yearning for a new world matched my own, almost exactly. She only had one thing I lacked: enough courage to plunge into the unknown, while I remained trapped here, between marvellous worlds I would never know and one I still had to figure out.

Out of kindness, perhaps, Marie-Ange only smiled, and if she had guessed what I was thinking, she kept it quiet.

"Can I ask you something?" she said as if I hadn't spoken.

I leaned back. Not everyone asked *that* question, but I'd got it often enough, with varying degrees of awe, condescension or repulsion. Marie-Ange merely sounded curious.

"Why do this so far? Why help so many people?"

"*Help* truly isn't the word you want," I replied.

Thoughts of the weeping lady on the bus—someone's mother? Or friend? I'd never know—came unbidden. It had felt like the right thing to do, at the time. Yet all I could witness now was people hurting; I would never know how the people I had 'helped' had fared, nor even if they were still alive.

"It seemed wrong to have a magic portal in your home and not use it for something..." I wanted to say 'good', but the word sank in my throat. "...special," I said.

But that was not all it had been. All these times I had let someone through, a little piece of me had gone with them, as well. At times, when I gazed aimlessly out of the office window, the cityscape blurred into their faces, disbelieving, then ecstatic as soon as they stepped into another world. If I was so pleased to have given them a new life, it was also, perhaps, because I'd never been brave enough to seize that opportunity for myself, and had made do with vicarious glimpses instead.

And after each glimpse, I would drop into the deep crease at the centre of my sofa and scratch my cats behind the ears as I'd done every day for the last couple of decades. I shook my head. Suddenly I was finding it hard to breathe.

"It was the only thing I had to offer. The one thing that made me want to get out of bed, on some days. Sometimes I think that might be why it was given to me. Without it, I might as well stop pretending I even exist."

I laughed, a silly, croaking sound. How human of me, to balk at facing my own selfishness, and instead to be looking for explanations, a message to me from the universe, while standing right next to the proof that the universe was even bigger and more incomprehensible than anyone suspected. I expected Marie-Ange to stare at me with that uncomfortable pity people sometimes exhibited when they realised how long I had been living on my own. Instead she smiled and squeezed my arm.

"Maybe we don't know why you have it, but it's yours all the same," she said. "It's your decision." She bit her lips. "Could you open the window now? Just let me take a look. I promise that's all I want."

I almost refused her. I already knew how this would end. But the yearning in her voice was so strong that I gave in. Just the view —I couldn't deny her that.

"One look and I'll close it," I said, pulling the latch.

A meadow teeming with butterflies came in full view. Reds, golds, and blues flashed in swaying grass under a gentle breeze, a ballet of breathtaking beauty. Far ahead, a few hills swelled, soft purple against the cloudless sky. I'd seen many wonders through this window. A tear still warmed up my eye, with the familiar thought... why shouldn't I step through this time, and leave this world at last?

I glanced at Marie-Ange. Her hand was still on her backpack, bursting, I knew, with everything one would need to fight the direst odds in the wilderness. She was more than ready, perfectly confident. Yet right now she only stood still, staring with the longing of a starved woman.

"Let me go," she pleaded. "Then you can quit. Please."

"What if there's no food out there? No clean water, no..."

"And what is there for me here? Work overtime, buy a bigger car, and wait until global warming gets me while I pretend to be happy? I'll take my chances. Please."

I closed my eyes. I couldn't hurt another family. I couldn't read Marie-Ange's name in the news and pretend to know nothing. I couldn't risk letting her throw her life away in a universe she had only ever watched from afar, through the window in her friend's living room.

I didn't want her to go. But this was not—had never been— my decision to make.

"I can't stop you, can I?" I muttered. I turned away, leaving the window open.

Marie-Ange squealed and kissed me on the cheek.

"I'll never forget what you did for me," she said.

She squeezed my hands one last time. For a moment I entertained the wild, terrifying hope that she would ask me to go with her. But she didn't, and once a brief pang of mingled relief and disappointment had erupted and withered in me, I knew better than to ask. I had been her friend, for a while, but I'd needed her more than she'd ever needed me. I was grateful that I hadn't been invisible to her, but couldn't delude myself about the place I truly held in her life, even more so now that she was claiming her life back, seizing her chance to chase dreams of freedom that were hers and hers only. This was her world now, not mine. She was strong, and ready, and I felt with absolute certainty that she would survive, and be happier than she could ever have been in this universe. All I could do for her was to let her go.

And then she stepped outside. I watched her as she took more and more confident steps in the tall grass, waved one last time, and I closed the window.

Later, there would be another missing person report. A family would be in shock, and it would be my fault, again. I had no idea what I would say to my colleagues in a few days, when word of Marie-Ange's disappearance reached us. It had to be the last time. I'd make a promise and stick to it.

And then, after a while, my eyes would meet the eyes of a stranger on the bus, catch on a hollowness mirroring the one within me—though I buried it as deeply as I could—and I would start thinking again of Marie-Ange dancing with butterflies. And Damien treading in the snow near a mighty river. And Christine swimming with catfish in the ruins of an ancient city. Then I would look outside at the droning cars and thick air and concrete roads stretching as far as I could see, and remember what they had fled from, and it would dawn on me again that just because I happened to live next to a magic portal did not make me arbiter of what anyone else chose to do with their life. And I would open my window again.

Someday, I would be unable to take my eyes off the wonders there, and a middle-aged cat lady living an eventless life near the Saint-Lawrence River would be reported missing, too.

But not today. I made tea and sat down to read the news on my phone, with a cat in my lap and my back to the window, listening for the wind from other worlds that whispered through the cracks in our own.

See Cécile Cristofari's story "All We Ever Look For" online at Metaphorosis.
If you liked it, leave a comment. Authors love that!
Remember to subscribe to our e-mail updates so you'll know when new stories are posted.

About the story

Kate Bush is one of a handful of musicians I started listening to as a teen and still swear by today, in particular because of her fearless approach to sound, her ability to take noise and turn it into music. In one of her songs, you can hear a person in high heels walking across a room, opening a window, and listening to birdsong, then opening another and listening to chanting, then to cars... This song was the original inspiration for this story, though the lyrics have nothing to do with what I wrote; the title I chose was a tribute to it.

But what inspired the core of my story was a two-year spell in Québec City, working as a researcher after completing my PhD. The experience of navigating a North American city without a car, the exacting demands of my budding academic career, loneliness, homesickness (though I met some of my dearest friends there), but also the exhilaration of being at a turning point in my life in a city I bonded with on a deep level, turned that period into an incredibly complex one. On many mornings, I woke up from dreams of escape, where I was flying away, or sailing, reclaiming a freedom I seemed to have lost somewhere in the race to build myself a future.

I did come home, eventually, and decided that life mattered more than a career. I've often wondered how much farther I could have escaped, if I had been given the chance. This story was born out of a tangle of emotions I haven't completely made sense of. And that's all right. We don't need to make sense of everything in order to live our lives.

A question for the author

Q: What inspires you?

A: I am as susceptible as the next writer to reading about some fun factoid, interesting place, or unlikely historical character and thinking, 'That's so cool, I need to write something about this!' I almost never follow through, however. If my writing often focuses on places where I've lived for years, their history, my own family history... it is because I've had years to process these into something that, hopefully, could make sense to somebody else than me.

Over the years, I've also found that the natural world was a better source of inspiration for me than people or cities. Much of our culture consists in making sense of human lives, and I'm not that good at making sense of things. Nature doesn't make sense; it just exists, and will keep existing, however we try to harness it or shoehorn it into our worldview. There is so much to explore in our relationship with that meaninglessness around us, enjoying its beauty and navigating our lives as best we can, that this has become my most productive way to write.

About the author

After working in Québec for a while, Cécile Cristofari settled down in her native South France, where she teaches English literature for a living. She writes and edits speculative fiction when her son is asleep.

staywherepeoplesing.wordpress.com, @c_cristofari

Unifiers

Edward Ashton

"Doran?" Michaela says. "I don't like you." She closes her eyes as our docking clamps release and we slide into the launch chute. "I want you to know that."

I nod.

The world falls away.

Dropping onto a colony world is always an adventure. The Union spans a quarter of the galaxy. The distances between our worlds make it impossible for us to touch any given colony more than once every few centuries, and a lot can happen in three hundred years. Sometimes we find apes. Sometimes we find angels. Michaela and I, though—we're Unifiers. Our job is to remind them all how to be human.

"This is your fault," Michaela says. "No matter how this turns out, the record will reflect that."

"Yes," I say. "You've made that very clear."

"Survey sequencing is your responsibility, Doran. I accept none of the blame for this. None."

I nod. She is correct to say that I accepted full responsibility for sequencing long ago. It seemed my best option for hiding worlds like this one from Michaela's tender ministrations.

Unfortunately, it seems that the Union cannot in fact be put off forever.

We skim through the upper atmosphere, bleeding off velocity, converting kinetic energy into heat and light. The inertial dampers on this lander are ancient. I can feel the waves of plasma breaking over the hull and thrumming through the soles of my feet.

"Fifteen hundred years," Michaela says. "These people could be anything by now."

I sigh.

"I suppose they could."

"Uniformity is the bedrock of the Union, Doran. Without it, we are no longer children of Earth. Without it, we are *nothing*."

"Yes," I say. "I'm well aware of Union doctrine."

"Gross negligence," she mutters, eyes fixed on the deck now. "Gross, utter negligence."

"Well," I say. "Let's see what we see."

We're slowing now, the lander's stubby delta wings riding the air rather than hammering through it. The screens have cleared, and the day side of the planet is just coming into view, thirty kilometers down.

"They might simply be gone," I say. "This world is not a friendly place."

This is an understatement, honestly. We're descending onto a tidally locked planet that hovers just at the inner edge of its red dwarf star's habitable zone. The day side is sun-scoured desert, too hot for anything that the Union would accept as human to endure. The night side is a frozen wilderness, buried under an ocean's worth of water ice and carbon dioxide. The twilight strip that separates them is no more than a few hundred kilometers wide, and the storms that sweep across it looked terrifying even from orbit. I'm having trouble imagining what it must be like to stand on the surface, helpless and exposed, and watch one of them rolling in.

"You may be right," Michaela says. "I'm not seeing any evidence of habitation." I'm just opening my mouth to reply when she adds, "We should have been here twelve hundred years ago. Clearly, there has been a terraforming failure. We could have prevented it. We could have kept this place from spinning off the rails."

"Colonies fail," I say. I don't add that, as often as not, it's Unifiers like us who are responsible for their failure. Some worlds are simply not suited to habitation by the children of Earth, and terraforming is a chancy process. The available records indicated to me that this world might well be one such. Nothing we've seen so far indicates that this assessment was anything but accurate.

Michaela touches the control screen as we cross the terminator, and the lander swings around to the north.

"We'll circumnavigate the twilight zone," she says. "No point in looking anywhere else, I think. If we don't pick up any signs after a full orbit, we'll write this place off."

She doesn't need to mention what this outcome would mean for my standing in the Union. This is not the first wayward world I've tried to shelter from Unification. If Michaela were to finally realize that these anomalies are not simply the result of incompetence...

Best not to think of that now. Michaela has an exquisite nose for fear.

"There," she says. We're following a sad, winding river through dusty grasslands toward a shallow sea that covers most of the planet's north pole. Michaela gestures to the main view screen, and it zooms in on the delta where the two come together.

There, in and among what appears to be a grove of sickly banyan trees, squats a village.

Michaela brings our altitude down to twenty kilometers, then ten, then five. We pass the village and swing out over the sea, then come around in a wide, lazy turn. Michaela engages the gravitics, and we slow to a hover.

"I don't see any inhabitants," she says.

"No," I say, "but they must be here. Those huts are built from wood, grass, and mud. Without maintenance, they wouldn't last a season."

We descend slowly. The village grows in our view screen. Michaela is correct that there doesn't appear to be anyone about. Who can say, though? There is no variation in daylight here to drive circadian rhythms. We may have come upon them in the middle of the night.

There are twenty-seven identical huts, arranged in two concentric circles around a single larger structure. Michaela sets us down gently in the dusty square facing its entrance. The low hum of the gravitics disappears as Michaela cuts power.

"We should follow biological containment protocols," I say. "These people have been isolated for a very long time."

Michaela shakes her head.

"Their biological isolation is one of the things we are here to end."

"They may be vulnerable to our microbiota."

"They may be," Michaela says, "and if they've fallen far enough from compliance, we may be vulnerable to theirs. This is a risk doctrine requires us to take."

Michaela stands. Behind us, the airlock cycles, and the inner door swings open. I sigh, unbuckle my webbing, and follow her into the light.

"It's surprisingly pleasant here," Michaela says as we step out onto the square.

This is true. The air is cool and still and dry, and the sun is a fat red ball hovering just above the horizon. Michaela crouches, rubs her fingers in the dust, then brings them to her nose.

"The soil is acrid," she says. "Standard crops won't grow here. I wonder what they've been eating?"

"The quarter-gram of dust you just sampled may not be a fair representative of the entire planet," I say. "Perhaps we should reserve judgement?"

She looks up at me, then slowly stands.

"Perhaps." She gestures toward the central building, a low, rectangular structure with bare wooden framing and a clay-shingled roof. "Shall we announce ourselves? It doesn't seem that a welcome party is coming."

I glance around. The trees at the edge of the village look less sickly from the ground. They loom over the huts, ten or fifteen meters tall, with wide-spread canopies of broad, blue-green leaves hanging limp in the soft, still air. When I look back, Michaela is already half-way to the building. By the time I catch up to her, she's pounding with the flat of one hand against the door while rattling the broad wooden handle with the other.

"That seems aggressive," I say.

Michaela scowls.

"They didn't bother with a doorbell."

She's raising her hand to strike again when the handle turns. She takes a half-step back as the door swings part way open. A small, round, nearly bald head pokes out of the darkness inside. Its owner squints up at Michaela, blinks, then turns to look at me.

"Oh," he says. "Hello. Can I help you?"

"No language drift," I say. "No anatomical modifications. No obvious mutations. No evidence of genetic alteration. He appears to be entirely human, wouldn't you say?"

Michaela narrows her eyes and brings her teacup to her lips.

"As you said earlier," she says. "Perhaps we should reserve judgement."

Our host leans back in his chair, and folds his arms across his narrow chest.

"Friend Doran, friend Michaela... I can hear what you're saying, you know."

Michaela rolls her eyes and sips delicately at her tea. We're gathered around a rough wooden table in a small, dimly lit room in the mud-and-thatch home of our host, who tells us that his name is Kirin.

"It's simply not plausible," Michaela says.

"Really?" Kirin says, one eyebrow raised. "Which part?"

"Any of this," Michaela says. "Your skin tone, for example."

Kirin leans across the table to place his forearm next to mine.

"It's exactly the same as yours," he says. "Medium taupe. Human standard."

"Precisely," Michaela says. "On this planet, with this sun, that skin tone should make it next to impossible for you to synthesize sufficient vitamin D. Fifteen hundred years of uncontrolled adaptation should have left your skin nearly translucent."

"But that would place us out of compliance."

"It would allow you to survive."

Kirin smiles.

"Clearly, we have survived."

"Yes," Michaela says. "Clearly." She takes another sip. "How many are you?"

"Oh," Kirin says. "A hundred or so."

"That seems too few to be a viable breeding population."

"Well, yes," Kirin says. "It's closer to two hundred, really."

"Are there other settlements?"

"No," Kirin says. "We are self-contained. This is not the most hospitable world, you know."

We sit in silence then, for what seems a very long time. Michaela stares at Kirin. He returns her gaze, unblinking, a placid smile on his face.

"Bring your people together," Michaela says finally. "I'd like to see them all, please."

"Oh," Kirin says. "Oh, no. No, friend Michaela. I don't think that's a good idea."

"Mmmm hmmm," Michaela says. "I'm sure you don't."

"He has a point," I say. "From a standpoint of biological containment..."

Michaela dismisses me with a wave.

"As I said, I am not concerned about biological containment."

"This is actually the beginning of our sleep cycle," Kirin says.

Michaela scowls.

"We can wait until morning."

"Also, many of us are away at the moment. You know— hunting and gathering and whatnot."

Michaela sets her teacup down on the table and leans toward Kirin, elbows planted on her knees.

"How many humans are currently in this village?"

"Well," Kirin says. "That's difficult to say."

"Try."

"Perhaps... fifty?"

"Fine," Michaela says. "I wish to see fifty humans in your town hall, as soon as they have awakened. Is this acceptable?"

Kirin looks from Michaela to me. I shrug. He turns back to Michaela and smiles.

"I will see what I can do."

"He's hiding something," Michaela says.

We're back in the lander now, running diagnostics on soil and water samples while we wait for our host to let us know that local morning has arrived.

"Look at this," she says, and points to the streams of numbers flowing across her monitor. "The proteins used by the microfauna here are left-handed." She waits expectantly, then rolls her eyes at my blank stare. "Left-handed proteins are toxic to Union-compliant life, Doran. A human exposed to this environment should develop prion disease almost immediately."

"Prion disease?"

Michaela gives me a tight-lipped smile.

"Relax. Unless something very unexpected turns up here, prion disease will be the least of your worries."

"You know," I say, "that's not nearly as comforting as you probably imagine."

She shakes her head and returns to her work. After long minutes of strained silence she says, "I can see now why you tried to keep me from this place."

And there it is.

"My carelessness—" I begin.

"No," she says. "No more of this, Doran. You knew what we would find here, and you knew what I would do when we found it— to them, and to you. I suspected you of deviance at Asher's World.

This place confirms it. The biochemistry, the soil composition, the planet's orbital and rotational periods—all should have been engineered to Union standards centuries ago. This is a deviant world, Doran, and you have tried to protect its deviance."

I start to answer her, but what is there to say? In the end, I shrug and look away. Michaela's eyes narrow, and her mouth twists with disgust.

"No argument, Doran? No explanation, even?"

"No," I say softly. "None that you would care to hear."

She stares at me for what feels like a long while, then finally shakes her head and chuffs out a sigh.

"Fine. Sleep now, Doran. I suspect tomorrow will be an unpleasant day."

I wake to a hollow tapping at the airlock's outer door. I glance at the chronometer over the control panel. It's been nearly ten hours since Kirin escorted us back to our lander.

"Well," Michaela says. "It seems the locals have finally awakened."

She stretches in her seat, rises, then turns to look at me.

"Are you coming?"

I sigh.

"Is there a point, Michaela? It seems likely that you've made up your mind."

"Oh, I have," she says. "Still, there are forms to be followed. We will give Kirin's people a full hearing, as doctrine dictates. I find it impossible to believe that they can be brought back into the fold, but the universe is wide, and I suppose stranger things must have happened—and if not, perhaps we'll learn something that will benefit the next colony we drop here."

We step into the airlock. The inner door closes behind us. The tapping at the outer door comes again. When the door swings open, we find ourselves looking down at a slightly younger, slightly less bald version of Kirin.

"I brought breakfast," he says, and holds up a basket of brown, misshapen pastries.

"Yes," she says. "I see that." She takes the basket, turns, and hands it to me. "You can have these, Doran. I'm afraid I've already eaten."

Young Kirin smiles up at me. I set the basket down in the airlock, then step down beside him as the door swings closed behind us.

"Thank you," I say. "I'm sure we'll enjoy those later."

His head bobs in acknowledgement.

"We're ready for you now," he says, and gestures toward Town Hall. "Come."

"You must be joking," Michaela stage-whispers as we take our seats on a small platform at the rear of a large, dimly lit room. Gathered before us is a multitude of Kirins. There are old Kirins and young Kirins, male Kirins and female Kirins, bald Kirins and slightly less bald Kirins—but every one of them is just a minor variation on the overriding theme.

"As we noted," I say, "low population has clearly led to a limited gene pool."

Michaela's face twists into a scowl.

"Doran, please. You're embarrassing yourself."

She's right, of course. This isn't an extended family. This isn't even an inbred family. The people in front of me could not plausibly have been the result of any sort of genetic mixing whatsoever.

Michaela leans toward me to say something more, but before she can, Kirin—our original Kirin, I assume—steps up onto the platform beside us, and turns to face his doppelgängers.

"Friends," he says. "First, let me thank you for taking time out of your busy days to come here this morning. I know you all must have had many important things to do." Michaela groans audibly at this. Kirin gives her a worried glance over one shoulder, then goes on. "We have with us today two representatives of the Union. They have come here, after an absence of over fifteen hundred standard years, to ensure that we are still a part of the human family. I have tried to assure them that this is so, but apparently some doubts remain." He turns to face us now. "Is that correct, friend Michaela?"

Michaela folds her arms across her chest and stares back at him.

"Yes, friend Kirin. That is a fair assessment."

"Yes," Kirin says. "Yes, well. As you can see, we have gathered together as many members of our little community as could be found on short notice…"

"Stop," Michaela says. "Please. I've had quite enough of this farce, thank you."

"But…" He turns to look at me. I find myself unable to meet his eyes. "Friend Doran, can you not intervene?"

I look to Michaela, but her eyes are locked on Kirin. Her jaw is set, and her mouth is compressed into a thin, hard line.

There will be no happy ending here.

"I am sorry," I say—and I truly am, both for these people, and for myself. "It seems unlikely... It seems..."

"What are you?" Michaela asks. "The details matter little, of course, but I am curious."

Kirin hesitates. The crowd on the floor behind him stands silent and motionless. He glances back at them, then squares his shoulders, draws himself up, and turns to face Michaela fully.

"We are humans," he says. "We are children of Earth."

"You are not," Michaela says. "Setting aside the fact that every creature in this building other than Doran and myself is obviously either a clone or a manufactured thing, a rudimentary analysis of this planet's biology makes it clear that humans could not survive in this place as it is."

Kirin looks back and forth between us.

"If this is so," he says. "If this is so, then how can we be blamed if we are not precisely human? Should our ancestors have simply come to this place and died?"

"Your ancestors," Michaela says, "should have changed this place to suit them. This is Union doctrine. Our worlds are decades between them. Uniformity and compliance are the only things that bind us together. Without them, the children of Earth will forget their mother, and it will be as if she had never been. You should know this, friend Kirin."

Kirin opens his mouth, then lets it fall closed again without speaking. His shoulders slump, and his eyes drift down to the floor between us.

"Our ancestors came to this place," he says softly, "and found a world whose chemistry was poison to them." He looks up, and his voice strengthens. "As important, their chemistry was poison to it. This was not an empty rock to be terraformed. This world was alive. There were swimming things in the sea, and crawling things in the sands, and flying things in the air. If my ancestors had done as you suggest, all of those things would have died."

"Those things are not children of Earth," Michaela says. "No more than you are." She rises to her feet. "This interview is over, I think. I will return to my ship now, and I will prepare a report on my findings here." She glances around the room. "Don't worry. You should have several decades at least to put your affairs in order before the terraformers arrive."

"How can we convince you to reconsider?" Kirin asks.

"You cannot," I say softly. "Michaela is a true believer in Union doctrine. She will not bend."

"This is true," Michaela says. "It has become increasingly apparent to me, however, that you, Doran, are not. You hid this place from me deliberately. If we had come here sooner, there might have been some possibility of salvage, but as it stands..."

"As it stands," I say, "Kirin's people, whatever they are, have lived in harmony with this world's native life for fifteen hundred years."

Michaela's face colors, and the expression it takes on is a perfect admixture of anger and disgust. She stares at me silently for what seems a long while, then turns and stalks to the edge of the stage.

"You won't be returning with me, Doran." She steps down to the floor, then turns back to look at me. "Given your past actions, it seems clear that even without this, even without what you just..." She shakes her head. "You would not survive a hearing on this matter. Given that, the least you can do for these... people... is to stay here and die with them."

She hesitates, as if waiting for my response. When it becomes clear that I have none, she turns away and walks briskly into the crowd. They part before her, then close up behind, and follow her to the door and out. Kirin stands staring at the floor for a long moment, then heaves a sigh and looks up at me.

"Come," he says, and gives me a sad half-smile. "We should see friend Michaela off."

"A storm is coming," Kirin says as we step out into the square. I follow his gaze past our lander, past the ring of huts and the overhanging trees, past the delta and out over the shallow sea. Just over the horizon black clouds boil and writhe, tendrils reaching out toward us like a kraken's tentacles. My stomach knots, and I have to fight back a sudden urge to run after Michaela as she climbs the two steps up to the lander's open door. She steps into the airlock. The basket of pastries flies out behind her, and the outer door swings closed.

"How long?" I ask.

Kirin looks up at me.

"Until what, friend Doran?"

I gesture toward the storm, now blotting out almost half of the bloated red sun. He nods.

"Not long. These storms move quickly."

I can see that. The leading tendrils are nearly over us now.

"You have shelters? Something underground?"

He gives me that sad half-smile again. The lander's gravitic drive engages with a low hum, a sensation felt more than heard. A moment later, Michaela lifts slowly, straight up above the square. At fifty meters or so, the main thrusters engage and she begins to accelerate.

"I am sorry for this, friend Doran," Kirin says. "I truly am."

I've just opened my mouth to reply, to say that my stranding is not his fault, that I knew the risks I took in undermining our mission and that these events have been entirely beyond his control, when a beam of actinic light leaps up from below the southern horizon and spears the lander, pinions it there in the sky for a long moment, then blinks out as the lander—as Michaela— erupts into an expanding ball of plasma.

For the first time in many years, I am speechless.

The remains of the lander are still descending in a half-dozen smoking arcs when the beam reaches up again, straight up this time, and an instant later a new star appears in the rapidly dimming sky.

"My ship," I say.

"Yes," Kirin says. "I'm sure you understand the necessity."

Unifiers do not travel in warships, but all Union starships are built to withstand any conceivable assault.

"Your people build well," Kirin says.

A second beam lances up to join the first, then a third, and a fourth. The star becomes, briefly, a sun, and after that a slowly expanding wound in the sky.

"Not," I say, then have to pause to moisten my bone-dry mouth. "Not well enough, it seems."

"No," Kirin says. "Not well enough."

"You are not human."

"We are not biological," Kirin says. "Given the chemistry of this world, we could not be. When the Union dropped us here, we considered our options. As friend Michaela said, nothing the Union would sanction could survive here. Doctrine stated that we must wipe this place clean, that we must make it over into yet another Earth—but faced with the decision, faced with genocide, we found that we... were not true believers." He shrugs. "So, we made ourselves into something different." He holds up one hand. The skin shimmers and breaks apart into fractal patterns, showing muscle and then bone beneath before closing up again. "This village, these bodies... they were our poor attempt to forestall another Union colonization effort without resorting to violence. We were not particularly hopeful that this farce, as friend Michaela called it, would convince you to leave us in peace, but in our defense, we had limited warning of your arrival. If another survey comes, we will try to do better."

"Nanites," I say. "You are... all of you..."

"We are dust on the wind," he says, and smiles. "We chose to become so rather than to destroy what we found here—but we are still children of Earth, friend Doran. Despite your judgement, we are still human."

A sudden gust nearly takes me off my feet, but Kirin stands unmoved.

"These huts," I say. "They won't survive this storm, will they?"

"No," Kirin says. "They will not. Again, friend Doran... I am sorry."

And with that, Kirin dissolves before me, the building storm carrying him away in bits and pieces until nothing remains. I straighten and turn a slow circle as the first fat drops of rain slam into the dust of the square.

I am entirely alone.

The wind strengthens, and I am driven to my knees. A mix of rain and dust and gravel rattles against my back like a spray of bullets. I look up through slitted eyes as the roof of the Town Hall lifts up, then breaks into a dozen pieces and flies away. Most of a hut, nearly intact, slides past me, accelerating slowly until it slams into another on the opposite side of the square.

It seems I won't need to worry about prion disease.

I close my eyes as the rain begins in earnest, digging my fingers into the dissolving earth as the wind pulls at me until finally it's torn away and I'm flying, mouth open in a soundless scream. Lightning flashes, painfully bright even through my clenched eyelids, and in the same instant thunder rolls, reaching its fingers deep into my chest, loud as the end of the world.

See Edward Ashton's story "Unifiers" online at Metaphorosis.
If you liked it, leave a comment. Authors love that!
Remember to subscribe to our e-mail updates so you'll know when new stories are posted.

About the story

"Unifiers" began with a single line: "Doran?" Michaela says. "I don't like you. I want you to know that." For a long time that's all it was, one obscure line of dialogue in my Ideas folder—

but I kept coming back to it, and eventually I realized that this was not a couple on the verge of divorce, or two office workers forced to share a cubicle. I was deep into the plotting of a novel at the time, and because that was taking up ninety percent of my head space then, I decided to drop these two unhappy coworkers into that book's universe.

The Union as I've conceived it there is a mostly malign social structure, but it's filled with a mix of people who range from good to bad to indifferent. I wanted this story to show a conflict between two people on opposite ends of that spectrum, with the fate of a living world at stake. All I needed at that point to fill in the story were a backdrop and an ending. Those I borrowed from a story I wrote years ago that never quite worked on its own. The bits I pulled from it, though—the colonists, and the final scene—I thought were deserving of a second chance at life. At the end of the day, I was very happy with the way these pieces came together. I very much hope that you are as well.

A question for the author

Q: Are titles easy or hard for you? Do you start with the title or the story?

A: Ugh—titles are the worst. Ninety percent of the time, my working title is just the first name of my protagonist. A quick glance through my bibliography will tell you that in many cases I never move past that. There are a few stories where I feel like I really nailed it ("The Sky is Blue, and Bright, and Filled with Stars" is probably my personal fave) but in many more I think my titles are not so much finished as abandoned in despair.

About the author

Edward Ashton lives in upstate New York in a cabin in the woods (not that Cabin in the Woods) with his wife, a variable number of daughters, and an adorably mopey dog named Max, where he writes—mostly fiction, occasionally fact—under the watchful eyes of a giant woodpecker and a rotating cast of barred owls. In his free time, he enjoys cancer research, teaching quantum physics to sullen graduate students, and whittling. You can find him online at edwardashton.com or on Twitter @edashtonwriting.

Not All Rot Is Ruin

E. A. Petricone

It started when Leda lifted her head from her pillow and a dead fly tumbled onto her pillowcase.

Disgusted, she didn't think much of it, quickly scooping it up and tossing it into the bin. A gross coincidence, surely: it must have gotten caught in her hair the night before and died. Just the same, she soaped and rinsed her scalp extra hard in the shower.

Except later, as she ran a comb through her hair, another dead fly fell to the floor. Followed by another.

Three in a row? Leda took another shower, working her hair with vinegar and green tea (which she'd read somewhere was healthy). In the mirror she parted section after section of her hair and examined the scalp underneath.

Then, as she leaned over the counter at work, three more dead flies dropped out.

She had horrific ideas. Maybe she wasn't as clean as she thought she was. Maybe some food had gotten stuck in her hair and it was rotting—oh god, what if the flies were coming *from* her head? Did she smell?

"Do I smell?" she asked strangers in the grocery store, who quickly moved to the next aisle.

The doctor couldn't explain it. Leda's skin was poked and prodded, every inch examined for the existence of internal parasites and the like. Her head scan revealed that everything was perfectly normal.

But the flies kept falling out of her hair, bug-eyed, grotesque, legs rigid.

"Is this something that happens to people?" Leda asked hopefully.

"No," the doctor said, and then, as many doctors have done to many women, declared her condition not terminal, and suggested she should get used to it.

Leda started wearing hoodies more often, but even then dead flies would pour out from behind her ears, piles at a time, all stiff wings and plump bodies.

Though she was showering three times a day and using dry shampoo in between, she still felt dirty. She sprayed her clothes with lemon odor protection and coughed from the spray.

Nothing seemed to curtail the flies; they only showed up in greater numbers. Bent legs frozen in the air, wings down, bulging eyes making them look as though something had shocked them.

In desperation Leda shaved her head. Surely that would—

She hadn't even collected all the clumps of hair out of the sink before a half-dozen dead flies dropped on top, materializing out of her skull fully formed. She set it all on fire, thinking *purification*, thinking *cleanse*, thinking *purge*, but it only resulted in the bathroom ceiling turning black, all the smoke detectors going off and a strong singed smell that lingered for days after.

She started wearing a shower cap from the drugstore. When she removed it from her head every couple of hours it looked like a cigarette ashtray in the 1960s, except instead of ash it was full of dead flies.

She got desperate, pulling at the half-inch of regrown hair on her scalp. Could it be something in her environment? Could there be mold in the walls or something that first laid the eggs in her?

She lay her hands on different parts of the wall palm-down, feeling the porous texture under her fingers. Here—or maybe, there?

She lifted the sledgehammer she'd dragged in from the garage and started striking. With a flashlight, she peered inside the walls. Nothing, except for braids of wires that looked fairly important.

Since every rational explanation had failed her, Leda turned to the spiritual. By then she'd started wearing gloves and carrying a plastic bag with her—like a doggie bag, except for dead flies.

She consulted every spiritualist in Massachusetts (and there were a lot of them). Surely those who could summon and see and conjure things from this world and the others could help her? Offer advice?

"I think you should wash your hair," the old witch said gently, as though Leda surely hadn't thought of that and she didn't want to embarrass her.

"Uh," the hoary medium scratched his head. "The spirits are opting to keep their distance."

"I can't really..." a psychic sputtered after twelve dead flies skittered across her tarot spread. Desperate: "Would you like to hear about a man in your future?"

"Keep him," said Leda dismissively, grabbing her bag.

She confided her situation to her neighbor, who couldn't help but notice all the cleaning Leda had done and the banging she heard when Leda opened the walls. "Please keep this between us," Leda begged.

"Of course," said her neighbor, nodding vigorously.

The next day two children Leda sometimes glimpsed around the neighborhood showed up on her doorstep, their bikes discarded in her driveway.

"You're the woman with dead flies coming out of her head," said the girl.

"Oh," said Leda, and before she knew it they were in her living room, pointing to the dead flies that had fallen onto the foyer floor and asking if they could look under her hoodie. "Pare—your parents?"

"I bet we could fix you," the boy said confidently.

At that point Leda would pray to anyone who listened and hear anyone out who offered. "How?"

"We have the internet," said the girl, heaving herself onto the couch.

Leda got them all glasses of water—they were allergic to nuts, so nothing in her house was suitable—as they—twins, as it turned out—questioned her mercilessly. When had it started? How many flies had fallen out of her head so far? They combed through her medical printouts, looked inside her ears with a magnifying glass.

"I feel like I should call your parents," said Leda. She wrung her hands, itchy from not taking action.

"Flies show up when something's dead," said the girl.

"Decomposing," agreed the boy.

"I'm...not dead," said Leda, but she couldn't keep a questioning lilt out of her voice. She'd been waking up next to piles of dead flies for weeks and frankly reality seemed negotiable.

"There's more than one way to die," said the girl with an unnerving degree of sagacity.

The boy held out his hand and asked for Leda's wrist. When she obeyed he set his ear against it as though it were a conch shell, and after a tense minute he declared that he could hear her pulse.

So that was something.

"Have you been depressed?" the boy asked. "Were you sad about something, before this started?"

"Not about anything legitimate," Leda said. To their skeptical looks: "There was this man, at work. He's the chief of a different department." She couldn't stop the smile from blooming on her face. "Really brilliant, really smart and funny, and I —

"You *liked* him," said the boy.

For years. "And I thought maybe...but I found out he'd been seeing someone. They're engaged now."

"You were never together?"

"No, we hardly saw each other outside of work, but..." Leda felt ridiculous. She'd never been bold enough to go past friendly work-related exchanges, yet in her mind she had seen it all: him poking his head into his cubicle on his break, walking to their car together, dressing up and attending fundraisers, him introducing her as the woman behind the man.

The bravest thing she'd done was ask him periodically about his dog—although everyone in the company knew how attached he was to his husky, so that wasn't unique. But when he had showed her pictures and laughed at her reactions, she really thought maybe...

"It's stupid," she said dismissively, not wanting them to see how seriously she'd taken her crush. "I don't know why I feel so—"

"Why didn't you ask him out?" asked the boy. "He sounds nice."

"I hate dogs," the girl said to no one.

"He just seemed...too special to talk to." The admission made Leda squirm; she hadn't even gotten to know him, not really, just plopped her hopes and dreams on him without asking.

"But if you weren't together, then why are you sad?" pressed the boy.

How could she explain it? It was more a loss of never-having.

They wanted more from her, so she tried again: "I'm getting to be—" the thought of her age made her cringe. "Well, older. I thought I would be more by now. I thought I would be smarter. I thought I'd be making more money. I thought I'd be with the guy of my dreams.

"I look around and there's just...a lot that I thought I'd be that I'm not. You're young," she said. "This must all sound like ragtime to you."

"No," said the girl.

"You can change things," pointed out the boy. "People change their lives all the time."

"But that's just it," said Leda. Two flies tumbled out from under her cap and landed on her jeans. "Other people, they move on to something better. I haven't got something better."

"Why does it have to be better?" asked the girl.

"Well..." Leda made a limp gesture toward her smartphone. Thought of Facebook announcements, thought of Instagram filters. "You have to be better, your life has to move up. Because otherwise what are you?"

"What are you?" asked the boy.

"That's what must be dead," said the girl. "The never-having. The stuff that could have been. It makes sense."

"Does it?" Leda asked, bewildered.

"Our mom died before we could have her," said the girl. "All the things she would have done with us died too."

Their mother. On the heels of Leda's heart breaking she felt a deep flush of embarrassment. How could she think that her sadness had any merit at all, when she hadn't lost anything *real*?

But the children were surprisingly understanding, opening the circle of grief-having to her without marking the difference of degree. "Something gone is something gone," said the boy.

Still, Leda wondered. How do you mourn the things you'll never be?

"We had a mouse or something in the wall once that died and we couldn't get it out," said the girl. "It smelled horrible. Eventually though, it went away. Because there wasn't anything left to make a smell."

"That's awful," Leda said.

"It stunk," agreed the boy.

"Maybe you've got to do that," said the girl.

"Do what?"

"Stop trying to break into everything," said the boy, furrowing his brow at the haphazard holes Leda had gouged between the kitchen and living room. "Stop saying it's stupid."

"Yeah," agreed the girl. "Sometimes when things happen you've got to do stuff hard as you can, but sometimes you need to let it," she waved her palm around her ear, "do what it needs to do. Let all the skin and blood go."

"Just..." Leda gestured to her head, mirroring the girl's motion. "Just let it rot?"

"Not all rot is ruin," said the boy.

"Not all ruin is rot," said the girl.

Cold prickled the back of Leda's shoulders. She'd never met children like this; wouldn't their living parent be looking for them? Should she ask for their adult's number?

"Enough for today," said the boy, rising. "We'll come back and check on you."

"Oh...okay," said Leda, wavering a bit as she lifted herself from the couch.

She watched them pick their bikes up out of her driveway and thought, *I'll never see them again*. They'd gotten what they wanted, witnessed the pathetic lovelorn freak with the flies falling out of her head. What children had the attention span to visit a middle-aged woman?

Leda touched her head in front of her bathroom mirror, watched five more flies materialize and fall into the scorched basin. "I guess I should let you do your thing."

Surprisingly, the children checked in on her once a week. She stopped fighting the flies, other than disposing of them. She washed her scalp normally, didn't scrub the floors more than necessary, and filled in the holes she'd made in the walls.

Once she let an entire rainy weekend go by without picking up the flies at all, just let them stack around her in pointy starchy piles.

She also cried a lot, buckets, which surprised her—but there too, she didn't try to stop herself. It felt awful. The next week she swept up all the flies and moved her furniture back to the positions she liked rather than the ones that made it easiest to scrub.

The boy deemed Leda ready for an assignment. "Go to the garden shop and get a succulent," he commanded in the way that the young think nothing of commanding. "Even you can't kill that. Start with one thing. A small thing."

"Am I getting a plant to represent growth?" asked Leda hopefully. "New life?"

"Just don't kill it," said the boy, rolling his eyes.

She didn't kill it. The little plant in its little pot reached green and healthy toward the sun. Leda learned to make allergy-free cookies, which the twins declared satisfactory. It felt as though something in her had turned, spade into earth. Aerated.

She applied for a new job within the company, one she'd dreamed about for years but never put herself up for.

She got it. In her new department she and Ana, one of her new colleagues, became fast friends, grabbing lunch together in the cafeteria and sipping gimlets at the local bar after close of business.

But within the three-month probation period Leda came to a realization: she hated the work. Hated it. Every task and assignment she had been so enamored with from a distance proved to be a nightmare.

"How many years did I waste thinking this was my dream job?" she asked the twins, dismayed. She shook her head out over a wastebasket while they sat in their usual places, munching on successful cookies. The amount of flies had doubled in the weeks since she'd started in her new position. "It's what's-his-face all over again. I built it up in my head."

"Yes," said the girl, brushing her crumbs onto the floor. "You need to stop doing that."

"But isn't it better that you know now?" asked the boy.

"I..." Leda considered, plucked a last rigid body from her blouse. "Yes, it is."

The next day she visited Hannah, the HR rep, to put in her two weeks' notice for her new position. "Your previous department hasn't been able to find a suitable replacement," Hannah said, all silver linings. "So this works out quite well for everyone. You can fill out the paperwork for your return transfer with me." She handed Leda a stylus and tablet with the forms loaded up.

"Alright," said Leda. She wouldn't be out of work doing nothing, thank god. She started to move the stylus point over the checkbox that would indicate her interest in returning to her old department. Stopped.

Hannah smiled at her, patronizingly expectant. "Do you need help with that?"

"Uh," Leda said. The framed poster on the wall—one of a series that lined the hallways and common areas—featured a rear shot of a mountain climber at the top of a summit, taking in an endless horizon. The company's mission statement—which seemed completely divorced from what Leda and the other employees actually did—blazed across the bottom in cursive.

As she imagined going back to the department where she'd spent so many years dreaming, it struck Leda how absurd it was, to have photos like this all over the place. In her whole time working for the company she'd never even had a window.

"Actually," she said, putting her stylus down. "I think...I think I'm going to exit the company. Entirely."

"Entirely?" the HR rep was stunned. She shifted behind her desk into a more defensive position, set back, clearly thinking Leda was pulling a negotiation tactic. "This has been your employment home for years, and we've been very accommodating for your," she gestured to the fly-catching wrap around Leda's head, "condition."

"You have," Leda said quickly, mentally back-pedaling. Was she being ungrateful? Hadn't her workplace treated her well?

Leda losing her footing seemed to help Hannah find hers. "Let's talk this through. Do you have a plan for your next step?"

"Oh, no," Leda said. What *was* she thinking, jumping out of the airplane without a parachute? Instinctively she put her hand to her head, and yelped when her head covering came off. Awkwardly she picked up a few dead flies from the floor under Hannah's concerned gaze.

"Tough to pull off leaving without a plan," said Hannah. "Are you *sure* you want to quit?"

"I don't..." said Leda. She felt the twins inside her throat, eager to speak for her and answer the question for her.

Let me, Leda mentally said to herself. *This is me.* It felt as though her whole being took a breath.

When the other voices quieted Leda raised her head to Hannah with a smile so genuine she could tell Hannah had to catch herself from smiling back. "I'm not quitting. I'm starting something new."

"Well. It's your decision," said Hannah, her lips pursed with disapproval as Leda handed the tablet back to her. "You've got such a strong resume. Seems a shame to ruin it over an impulse."

Leda laughed, and here was happy to let them all speak at once: "Not all ruin is rot."

"Who's going to hire me now?" she asked the twins later, pacing the living room, the box of her belongings from her desk between them. The twins were experimenting with sitting on the couch upside down. "What have I *done*?"

"Sounds like you did the right thing," said the boy.

"Still," Leda said, thinking of gimlets at the neighborhood bar. "The friend I made, Ana. I'll miss having her in my life."

"Then text her and say so," said the girl, rolling her eyes toward the floor. "You complicate things."

Leda's next job—which proved to not be nearly so difficult to get as Hannah indicated—was in an adult learning center, and she got to take a free class every month. Any time the temptation came to raise a skill, instructor, or her own self-story above her head, shiny-bubble perfect and bubble thin, she imagined the twins shaking their head at her, and refocused on what was rather than what sounded best in her head. Shockingly, a lack of expectations made trying new things a lot less stressful.

Her friend Ana—now her best friend Ana—joined her. She helped Ana move house. They made each other laugh. They made more friends through the classes.

Leda went on a date, and it was a disaster but it was worth it to curl up with her best friend on the couch and laugh about it after. Then she went on another date and it actually went pretty well.

The man wouldn't make her whole life, the way she had wanted what's-his-face to, but by then the thought had occurred to Leda that a good conversation with an interesting person was like sunlight, and a little could brighten a long way.

The flies tapered off.

"You haven't had one in a week," said the girl, looking a little disappointed.

"That's great," said the boy.

Eventually they stopped entirely. "Ta-da!" said Leda, shaking her short wavy hair over her coffee table for the twins. Not a single fly tumbled out. She raised her head, beaming, but stopped as she saw them exchange a glance. "What?"

"Time for us to go home," they said in unison.

"Sure," said Leda, and all at once the strangeness hit her. It had been months—why didn't she know her visitors' names by now? She could have sworn they'd talked about school, about their hobbies…but she couldn't remember the specifics; how could that be? "What…what are your names again?"

"Don't you recognize us?" asked the girl, slipping her shoes on in the foyer. "We're the kids you would have had with that guy."

"That's not funny," said Leda, dread cracking through her like lightning. She stared at their faces, studying every line and curve. "No."

But of course, of course they were: twins with her nose, her unrequited love's eyes, *god*, even his nut allergy. Smart, tenacious, unfailingly—if quirkily—kind: the sort of children Leda had imagined raising.

That was why she could never quite remember the particulars of where the twins lived, of how their days went at school. They didn't exist in the real world.

Imaginary friends. Children created by the sheer force of her broken heart. Who did that kind of thing?

Crazy people. She must be crazy. Leda swayed, hands to her temples.

"Calm down," said the girl. The boy hovered over Leda as she leaned against the couch.

"Was anything real?"

"The flies sure were," said the boy.

"And we were real to you," said the girl, looking for the first time insecure. "Isn't that real enough?"

A phone chime dinged through the air. When Leda glanced at her screen she saw one of her new friends inviting her to dinner. Maybe the twins were all in her head, all a product of her imagination. But she'd started getting better at her own life thanks to them. "Yes," said Leda warmly. "Real enough."

The girl nodded and straightened, as though reset.

"But—" an icicle dripped down Leda's shoulders. "You're leaving. Does that mean I've killed you? Am I a murderer?"

"Course not," scoffed the boy, pushing the succulent in the window into a different slant of light.

"I don't know if I want you to go," said Leda. Would she be alright, on her own?

"You could keep us here," said the girl, meeting Leda's eyes meaningfully. "But do you need us?"

Leda shut her mouth, and was kneeling down before she knew she was, the vibration of their footsteps shivering up her knees as they ran into her open arms. Closing her eyes, she breathed in the outside smell from their clothes, felt the softness of their hair.

"You make good cookies now," said the girl. "No one can stop you."

"Don't worry," said the boy, placing his hand over Leda's heart. "We're not really leaving."

"We're just ready to be something else," said the girl.

"Remember what we said," they told her as they headed down the drive.

"Not all ruin is rot," recited Leda.

"Not all rot is ruin," they answered, pleased. They waved.

Leda watched them pedal down the street until they disappeared down the street, dissolving to some elsewhere. She stood in her open doorway, listening to the shift of branches and the rumble of passing cars until the sound of her phone, of her real friends from the other life she was making, called her back inside.

See E.A. Petricone's story "Not All Rot Is Ruin" online at Metaphorosis.

If you liked it, leave a comment. Authors love that!
Remember to subscribe to our e-mail updates so you'll know when
new stories are posted.

About the story

A few things were on my mind when I started writing "Not All Rot is Ruin":

Grief, for one—particularly the type that's tough to hang a hat on. Grief for the things that you don't do, or the doors that close as you make choices (or don't make choices...which is a choice), grief for the things you'll never be and the fantasies you never realize.

Letting go seems like a form of decomposition (with all its attendant ickiness and miracle). It's not pretty and it's certainly not fun but it's one of the "realest" human experiences—and it's how we get to better things.

Meanwhile the image of dead flies coming out of a person's head just kept coming up in my mind.

I'm a "pantser" writer, anyway (I might know a few beats of a story beforehand but how the heck anything happens is a discovery process) and this was one of my pantsiest stories. I didn't know where Leda was going to go next or what the twins would say. Absurdity (in thought, in action, in the world) always seems to be grief-adjacent, so I embraced that and let Leda lead me along.

Not sure if this belongs here, but something funny happened on the day I completed the revisions for "Not All Rot is Ruin."

So, it's been years since any flies have found their way into my apartment. But on the day I sent my final revisions in to Morris—like, not just the day but within a half-hour of sending the email—two robust and very buzzy flies came out of nowhere and started chaotically flying around the kitchen and living room.

Where did they come from? All the windows were closed and I'd been at my desk for hours and hadn't seen or heard a thing.

Typically my policy is to relocate all the small and "you're great, but outside" animals—I have a spider jar by the door that's kind of like the Popemobile, except it's for transporting spiders and disgruntled beetles and stuff—but the flies were so wicked annoying. They had two wide-open windows to escape through, but they preferred to bounce off everything else instead.

I tried waving them out, I tried sneaking up on them and getting them in a jar, I got so frustrated that I got a broom and was ready to swing and squish. But that didn't feel right.

Ultimately it took me twenty minutes to get them out, one by shoo and one by jar. I still don't know how they got in that day, and not a single fly has buzzed in the apartment since.

It's probably a total coincidence that they showed up right then, but in the scheme of fly symbolism, it seems like a good sign, right? A hat tip from the living to the fictional dead. In any case, I hope that once my visitors escaped they lived happy fly lives and played good fly roles in the ecosystem.

A question for the author

Q: Do you often include animals in your stories? What role do they play?

A: Very nearly always! My father is a biology teacher and my mother is a Bird Person, and I inherited their love of animals and the natural world. Sometimes animals show up in my stories because they Mean Things, and sometimes they show up because why not. Where there is life, there are animals—they share the world whether my characters like it or not.

About the author

E.A. Petricone writes strange, dark, and often absurd fiction. She obsessively collects square and rectangle Post-It note pads in all colors and sizes and uses them to scribble on and paper all over her walls. Her notebook is just a 6x8 Post-It.

She is the friend who makes sure you have enough snacks—and if she sees your cat, she is going to try to start a conversation with it.

She was hesitant about the whole Twitter thing but has discovered it's wicked fun to connect with other speculative SF/F writers and complain about writing. And of course talk about stories she loves (often with cute animal gifs).

She lives in Massachusetts.

www.eapetricone.com, @eapetricone

Esma's Margaret

Damien Krsteski

1.

"Power's out again," Esma's father shouted from the living room.

She lulled her computer into sleep mode to preserve battery now the mains were off, put on her backpack, and stormed out of their home. Her father shouted something else after her, but she couldn't hear him—her feet were on the dirty Orizari street already. Late-night raucousness swallowed her whole: men playing cards on the sidewalks, cursing their bad luck or each other; cars, old diesel vehicles, whirring to-and-fro, spewing fumes not smelled elsewhere in the city of Skopje in twenty years; kids and their mothers and fathers, out playing, chatting, even at eleven in the evening.

Some called after Esma.

"Esmy, Esme, when are you gonna fix our boiler?"

"Hey, Genius Girl, mamma's Net connection's all patchy after last week's rains. What to do?"

"Out of power! Been out of power for days now."

She raced by her neighbors, the tools rattling in her backpack. "Tomorrow," she promised. "Check the cable for rat bites," she advised. "I'll swing by after school," she said. And she hurried down the sloping street and out of Skopje's poorest quarter and into the residential neighborhood that'd had the bad luck to be built adjacent to it, following all the while the powerlines that drooped beside the road like pythons. The sky was dead, with only watered-down moonlight soaking through the pollution.

She dove right among the first cluster of buildings, and there, next to the park with the swings, stood her favorite power pole, with her very own cable snaking sneakily up the wood. She took off her sandals, gripped the metal handles of the pole, and climbed up. It was a hot summer night and her hands and feet were slippery, but she'd done this a thousand times, so she made her way to the top in no time.

There, she spotted the problem right away: her cable, the illicit line that leeched power from this neighborhood and carried it to hers, had been pecked bare by birds.

She swung her backpack to her belly and took out her screwdriver. Popping the lid of the transformer open with the tool, she unclipped the damaged cable. She took a breath before daring to touch any wires, then, using her crimp tool, she crimped her cable's frayed wires to a new alligator clip, which she promptly hooked back into the city's power lines. Finally, she closed the lid of the transformer, and taped the bundle of cables coming out of it several times around to the pole to ensure no pesky birds would damage them any time soon.

She gazed out toward her neighborhood. A few windows lit up among that swirl of light and smoke, followed by a couple more, and more, until the entirety of the hovelscape glowed like a furnace.

The city looked different from above. Quiet, clean, even ordered somehow in its messiness. She watched the city, optimizing in her head.

The line where the hovels of Orizari street ended and the buildings of this middle-class residential neighborhood began seemed natural, like the border between oaks and chestnuts in a forest. A gentle breeze blew on her sweaty face. She liked it here. She liked seeing things from above. Everything seemed simpler, easier to understand from this vantage point. She liked feeling like an incarnation of *Overseer*, her pet project, the software she'd been cooking up for months for equalizing power distribution and sharing of electricity among Skopje's neighborhoods. She closed her eyes and enjoyed the quiet for a moment before climbing back down.

On her way home, something on one of the power poles caught her eye. It was a poster, tacked inexpertly to the wood and flapping in the wind. She came closer.

EuroTech's Three Day Hackathon.

When she read the details, a rush of excitement went through her, so she tore the poster off, tucked it in her pocket, and hurried home.

"How many times have I told you?" Her father paced the room—his television set back on—furious.

She'd been careful broaching the topic, but with her hard-to-contain excitement and the above-average participation fee for the hackathon, aggravating her father seemed unavoidable.

"But I will earn back the money."

He stopped in his tracks. "Don't you understand, kid? Money's not what this is about."

"I don't understand why you're angry. It's a simple competition."

"Yes, and they *simply*—" He stopped, considered his words. "They simply want to waste your time. Your school is important, girl."

"But I'll make up for school. You don't get it. This is EuroTech. Where the best engineers work on the best projects. And if I win this, I will be guaranteed an internship, and I'll learn more, and I'll earn more, and we'll all have more."

"You will... you will be mindful of your time. And focus on what's important." Her father shook the piece of the poster before her. He looked as if reading from it. "Your mother and me. Your community. Those who need you here and now."

Tears came to her eyes and she hated herself for that. "That's just unfair," she said, but there was nothing more she could do, so she retreated to her room to sleep, too rattled to get back to coding.

2.

"Bad one, huh?" Esma said when she met Redjep at recess. His left eye was swollen, bruised violet. "Shit," she muttered. Redjep's brother's friends, mean bastards. Esma felt anger coming up, but she swallowed it down; anger was of no use here. Her friend needed her to stay grounded, and to not embarrass him with excessive worry. She decided the best approach would be to tease him. She said, "And have you told her yet?"

Redjep shook his head. "Later."

They went for the fries-and-ketchup snack from the kiosk at the corner of the street, and came back before the bell rang. She told him all about the hackathon and her father's reaction. About the participation fee she'd never be able to make in time. About the fact that they'd never ever let her miss school for three whole days, as if they had suddenly started caring about her education.

He shrugged about the money. Then he said, "Why do you care what he cares or pretends to care about?"

"Well, because..." she said, not knowing how to continue.

"Because they control you." Meaning those at home, her parents, but she knew he was just projecting. She didn't dislike her parents the way Redjep hated his. Far from it.

"Not that," she said, suddenly more aware of her own feelings, "but I'm afraid, too. I don't know how to balance. Maybe I should really take the straight path and focus on school and focus on what I have right now and then, once I'm ready, once I'm good enough, I apply to EuroTech. What if I'm only given just one opportunity with them? What if I mess it up?"

"Oh, get a grip." He snapped his fingers in front of her face. "EuroTech, or InsidePlayers, or NoCV, or Balkan Telecom, they can't wait to grab talents off the streets, which is exactly what you are. They will see the potential." He eyed her with suspicion. "But if you start doubting yourself," he said, more to himself, "your parents win."

"Are those her words?" she asked, annoyed at his recently acquired penchant for the dramatic.

"What do you have against her?" As if to provoke, he whipped out his phone. An old, sturdy model, non-flexible, probably from the beginning of the previous decade, but with a Net chip and enough processing power to run his favorite apps. He pressed the little icon of a stethoscope wrapped around a brain.

"How are you today, Redjep?" the therapist from the app said in English, butchering Redjep's name.

Esma groaned. Redjep shot her a dirty look.

"Not so good, Margaret," Redjep responded in the best English he could muster, but before he could recount the details of his quarrel with his big brother, Esma grabbed him by the arm and dragged him to class.

On the weekend, her last hope, her mother, was back home.

Esma waited for the woman to get her much-needed sleep, then she prepared her a nice breakfast of fried paprika and tomatoes, and brought it to her bed. Her mother looked drained. She worked during the week at a rich family's house in southern Skopje as their cook, cleaning lady, and babysitter, and she slept there so she could cook first thing in the morning and clean last thing at night; so she deserved to get her own breakfast in bed sometimes, and especially so on days when Esma was expecting a favor in return.

"How is my girl?" Her mother yawned, stroking Esma's face with one hand, stretching with the other. She was too young to look so tired.

"Annoyed."

Her mother bit into a bread roll. She gave Esma a sidelong look. "I heard."

"It's just not fair. I do all I can for you."

"We know you do."

Esma let her mother eat a while, then she said, "You know I deserve to try, I deserve to see what opportunities may arise."

Her mother ate in silence, while Esma kept letting off steam, saying everything that was on her mind, then she put the fork down and said, "I'm sorry, baby."

"Sorry?" Esma was taken aback. "Don't be sorry. Do something. Change his mind."

"It's not his mind that needs changing."

"Not you too!"

"Esma—"

"You agree with him." Her last hope. Mamma had been her absolute last hope. "I can't believe this. Since I first put my fingers on a keyboard, Mom!" Esma held her hands in front of her. "Since I first touched a computer I wanted to go to the companies downtown, to work for the companies downtown, to learn from the companies downtown. And now that there's an opening, a possibility for me to get an internship there, you're both going against me. What have I done to you, that you have to hold me back like this?"

"Girl, don't blow this out of proportion."

But it was too late. Esma left her mother's bedroom and slammed the door on her way out.

She sat slumped in her chair. She wanted to cry but didn't, out of spite. She stretched her phone out and prodded at the radio button. She gave it the name of her favorite band and her favorite album, and the radio obliged, waking up a whole web of networks, and music poured into Esma's ears from her earrings. A whole band sounding as if from their album from over thirty years ago, but it was all neural networks, having learned the playing and singing styles of all musicians of the last hundred years, now producing songs that could've been, but weren't. Songs heard for the first and last time. Composed, listened to, discarded. It was Kim's guitar, but not quite, and Matt's drumming, but it wasn't Matt, and of course Chris' voice, but only his voice, singing never-before-heard lyrics in that distinct, gravelly way that made Esma melt. No one sang like him anymore, she thought.

Esma wallowed in her self-pity a while, listening to songs modeled after her favorite band, until her phone pinged with a message.

A piece of software knocking at her door, requesting to be installed. She cocked her head, stopped the music. Then she groaned.

Redjep. He'd signed her up, that bastard, for Margaret the AI therapist.

Her finger was about to swipe the request to oblivion, but it stopped of its own accord in mid-air, hovering above the worn, stretched-out screen. Why was she dithering? Could it be that she needed to speak to somebody who wasn't her parents, her friends, her neighbors? Was she desperate for a neutral third-party? Or perhaps she wanted to try the software once and for all, and be able to back up her criticism with actual use cases. "What the hell?" she said, and pulled the big question mark toward her.

In a trickle of packets, Margaret slipped into her phone, unpacked herself and booted up, represented by a bespectacled girl a few years older than Esma. Having rifled through her phone for any scrap of personal data she could find, Margaret said, "How are you feeling tonight, Esma?"

"I hate my life," she said, fully aware of how pathetic she sounded. "I hate my mom and dad."

Margaret blinked. "And why do you hate your mom and dad?"

"Because they are stifling, selfish, inconsiderate parents who don't dare move a centimeter out of their comfort zone."

"Now, do you really *believe* they are stifling, selfish, inconsiderate parents who don't—"

"Enough of this." And she swiped Margaret away.

Was it this that Redjep craved? A vapid exchange with a simpleton, parroting his words with minor changes to give the semblance of intelligence? She felt angry with herself for even trying. She was about to write to Redjep and double down on her mockery of the chatbot, when another ping came, a request to rate the application which she closed by jabbing the one-star button. But her phone trilled immediately in response to her feedback, asking her if she'd like to opt-in to a beta feature of Margaret.

Rolling out gradually to all markets but currently exclusively available in her country, the beta feature promised to let her test and push Margaret's machine learning models to their limit. She could even earn some app store credit while she was at it, the notice said.

Esma stared at her screen.

Store credit, which, she realized, could then be exchanged for actual money.

The hairs on her arms stood on end. Here was an opening, a possibility, a way to at least cover the financial aspect—

But no. She didn't want it this way. Didn't want to go behind her parents' backs, not because she didn't think she was right, but because she thought she deserved their respect and support.

She folded her phone shut. Margaret went to sleep.

3.

"Redjep, you bastard, I hope your brother's friends give you another beating tonight."

But Redjep was cackling, mock-hiding behind the crook of his arm. "She's great, isn't she?"

After Sports, came Mathematics, Esma's favorite, and Redjep's favorite time to doodle in his notebook. When the teacher handed out homework, she jabbed him in the rib with an elbow. "Pay attention; I won't let you copy mine."

When classes were done, Redjep invited Esma to his place so they could try his freshly pirated copy of *Rafters of Matka*, the latest action game from a local studio. She refused, intending to head home and tinker with her computer, but he insisted, saying he had something to tell her.

So they went to Redjep's house, a crumbling pile of bricks inexpertly stuccoed by his drunken father, diving straight into the room he shared with his brother. "At Tanya's," Redjep said, explaining why he had the room all to himself now. "He's there the whole time, thank the gods."

He was setting up his console when she asked, "So what did you want to speak about?"

Redjep smiled and took his time with the cables, never one to miss an opportunity to create a dramatic moment. When it was all set up, he said, "Let's talk about the hackathon. I've been thinking."

"For a change."

"I've been thinking," he repeated, "about the rules. Now, is it true or isn't it, that *teams* are allowed to enter?"

"It's customary, yes. Doesn't have to be a solo endeavor."

"And is it true that for a team to enroll, they need *one* adult guardian to vouch for them?"

"Where are you going with this?"

Esma watched him grin stupidly, game controller in hand. As it dawned on her what it was that Redjep was suggesting, her jaw dropped. Redjep winked at her.

She was too baffled to think. "I don't know," she said. It was a kind offer, one that took her by surprise.

"Oh, come on," he said. "It's brilliant. We both go there with the code you've been working on, and we'll get this moron to be our guardian." He rolled his eyes. "We won't be missed at home, if that's what you're worried about. We'll leave in the morning with our backpacks and rulers and lunchboxes as if we're going to school, and then I'll say I'm at your place to study and you'll say you're at mine."

"I don't know," she repeated.

"There's nothing to think about. That's solved, so we just need the money. But now let's play." He shoved a controller in her hands, and soon they were rafting among canyons.

She walked back up Orizari street, thinking over Redjep's offer. She'd have to comb through the rulebook to ensure no misstep would be made—but no, she couldn't. She'd either do it properly, or not at all.

Past a group of boys and girls taking turns at a pair of old virtual goggles, giggling at scenes unseen, past houses with windows which blinked with borrowed light from overloaded power lines, and finally home, where her dad watched his evening television show, his back turned to her and the world, not noticing she'd returned or been away.

Esma made dinner and ate alone, then went to check up on her father, who'd fallen asleep. She picked up the empty soda can and threw a blanket over him. She watched his face a while, bruised by television light, then switched off the screen. Anger came over her, followed by sadness. Here he was, just sitting, wasting his life away, wishing for others to do the same.

And yet, EuroTech was within reach. To work in Big Tech, and to learn from the best, and to grow into an engineer of highest caliber, all within reach, if only she didn't choose to follow this bad example right before her.

"I'm doing the hackathon," she said. "Thought you should know."

The old man snored and smacked his lips.

She retreated to her room, and almost mechanically, she opened her phone and started Margaret. She skipped the therapist's moronic questions and went straight to the beta feature.

The app presented her with a question and several possible responses. She was to gauge which was most appropriate for the situation, thus helping to teach the prediction models. If her chosen response matched the chosen responses of several other testers, it was deemed a good answer and she was rewarded with points, which later could be converted to store credit, and ultimately, to real money.

Why do you think my brother said that?

Followed by options from A to D, and a little box of context beside them, summarizing what it was this fictive brother had said to the hypothetical Margaret user.

Esma chose option B—*He must have spoken out of fear*—and the app responded with a graph showing the distribution of users who'd chosen the same option. Her answer agreed with the majority, and thus, she was rewarded with credit.

And then came the follow-up question:

But fear of what?

And again, four different answers to this question, each in a different tone, from soothing to slightly belligerent, and Esma had to follow her instinct on which answer would be the most likely chosen answer by what she imagined to be the typical Margaret beta tester.

It didn't always work. Sometimes her answer was the outlier. But each question and answer prompt gave her a better idea of what people chose, and she slowly got better at picking the most popular choice.

What would you have done in my place? But how should I see this from her perspective? How long will this pain last? I can't seem to stop drinking, what should I do? They're coming over for dinner, and the whole night will be a disaster.

And on and on the questions or complaints kept coming, and Esma toyed with the answers, watching the models change and adapt, taking notes for her own work, until she grew tired and fell asleep, phone in hand.

She continued in this way for the next few days, beta-testing Margaret before and after school, as soon as she awoke and right up till she drifted off to sleep, amassing app store credit, which she promptly sold to people online for a slightly lowered value in denars.

She shared her scheme with Redjep, and soon he was beta-testing the AI therapist too, so that within a week between the two of them they had made a little bit of progress towards the hackathon's entrance fee.

Which meant they could start to focus on the code for the competition itself.

Esma had *Overseer* and the machine learning model she'd been tweaking to teach it, and she gave Redjep a thorough introduction to the code; firstly, on a more abstract level, followed by a line-by-line overview of each unit. She knew her code inside out, and she knew she was capable of rewriting it in a day, and she even had ideas on how to complete the project, which she duly shared with Redjep.

When they didn't practice, they played *Rafters of Matka* on Redjep's old two-dee system.

She was so consumed by the planning and practicing that Esma didn't realize she'd started falling behind on homework.

4.

But why would she go and not tell me?

Esma pondered this question. How delicate, she thought. By now, she'd reached the point where multiple-choice answers were no longer enough to train Margaret, so the system had stopped serving her those. Instead, she'd been instructed to type out her responses in full.

Because she's acting selfishly, Esma typed. *Because she's hurt.*

A response came within seconds: *But I'd never given her a reason to be hurt.*

Esma massaged her forehead. The system was pushing her to her limit. She wrote: *Not everyone is as stable as you. Your girlfriend finds it hard and confusing. And the lack of her parents' support only exacerbates the confusion she's going through.*

Esma was discovering that the system kept her more and more on a single track, exploring all potential outcomes within the confines of one particular scenario, not varying the questions as often as before, a greater effort for which she was rewarded with extra credit.

How long will this pain last?

She considered the fictional user's situation, and responded with what she assumed would net her the most credit: *Not long. Just breathe. Be strong and patient, because all things pass.*

There came a knock on her door. She crumpled her mobile phone into a ball.

"Hey." Her father filled almost the entirety of the door frame. "Can I come in?"

"Sure."

He sat cross-legged across from her. A pang of guilt washed over Esma. Why was she doing this behind their backs?

"Still tinkering with your machines?" He said, nodding toward the phone-ball in her hands, and some of Esma's new guilt drained away. "Listen," he continued, eyes scouring her room as if taking it in for the first time, "your mother and I appreciate very much what you do. For us."

"Do you?"

"How you put your *knowledge* to use to help yourself and those around you. How you've grown into an important part of this community. How you appreciate what community means, what your own city means, your own home." He waited for her response, and when that didn't come, he said, "But that's very much expected, because that's how we raised you. We taught you to be selfless and to appreciate our community, because in the end, that's who we are, that's what we have, and that's all we'll ever have."

Engaging him in an argument would be an exercise in futility. So she kept quiet.

"We're doing this for your own good," he said. "Once you realize, you'll be thankful. This is another way for us to teach you."

"Teach me?" Her stomach twisted.

"Yes. Don't you see? These people—these competitions, these companies, they simply want to take you away from us. Well, they won't. What will you win if you win? Your internship, first. And then, what? Some money for fancy restaurants? An apartment in central Skopje? But what will you lose? Your mother and me. Your community. Your neighborhood. It's already enough that they've put ideas into your head, Esma. And eventually, once they find a way to milk your talent more, they'll want to take you to Western Europe, and take you away from us, and leave us with nothing. We're teaching you to know your place. To avoid these traps. To remember where you are."

Esma stared at her father; she'd never realized what this whole fuss had been about. She felt stupid for being so naive and failing to see that they'd never cared about her *education* or about her skipping school or forgetting homework; all they cared about was themselves, and what lives they might end up leading if she were no longer there to take good care of them.

By now, no trace of guilt was left, and rage filled the void; Esma almost groaned in anger, but she took a breath, smiled, and looked away.

She fidgeted with her scrunched-up phone in her hands until her father got up and left.

5.

When they had made enough money to pay the hackathon's entrance fee, Esma and Redjep took the first bus from Orizari street to the western quarters of Skopje. Over the hill on which their street lay perched, and hurtling down past the old fortress, over the bridge, the river Vardar sleeping beneath them slow and thin this time of the year, and past the city's center, through the wide boulevards westward.

"You sure he'll bite?"

"Just follow my lead," Redjep said.

They got off the bus forty minutes later in Karposh Four, a neighborhood of high-rises and flaking buildings caged between two parallel boulevards. Redjep led her through smaller streets to a red-brick apartment building. They went in and climbed up the stairs (the elevator was out of service) to the ninth floor.

"It's here," Redjep said and rang the bell.

A short brunette opened the door. She eyed them, rolled her eyes, then turned away. "Memet," she called out. "For you." Slinking away back inside.

Heavy footsteps, and Redjep's brother appeared in the doorway. "The hell do you want?"

Redjep said, "I need your signature."

"You need a boot stomp on your ass, is what you need. Get lost." And he made to close the door but Redjep put his foot in.

"We need a legal guardian to approve our participation for an event. Since you're what people call a *mature adult*, we decided you should be that guardian. All we need is your signature. It'll only take a moment."

"How dare you disturb me at Tanya's with your childish games?" He made a fist and threatened Redjep with it.

"Ah, but see," Redjep said, "your friends already gave me the weekly beating you scheduled." He showed a cheek and a yellowing bruise on the side of his arm.

"Good."

"Not their best work."

"Give them time. They'll improve."

Redjep shrugged. "But maybe next time, tell your friends to talk less when they push and shove. It's embarrassing, if you know what I mean."

"What?"

"I mean, they sure like to brag in your name. Obviously, they did call me a little shit and a ballerina like you instructed, but they also explained to me in very, very precise detail how I'd never be half as cool as my older brother, and all his girls, and—oops, I don't know if Tanya knows about, well, about—should I keep my voice down, now? Sorry! I'm talking, of course, about Hatidze from Osman's street. And about Fuat's sister. And Big Ketty. But—"

"Shut up." Memet stepped out of the apartment and closed the door behind him. "Shut your mouth."

"I know when you're here, and when you're not. I can stop by any day, and I've heard enough to convince Tanya I'm not lying."

"You little—"

"Exactly."

Memet punched the wall.

"Careful with that hand, we need a finger." Redjep nudged Esma and she produced her phone. She presented a part of its screen to Memet, who, not taking his eyes off his brother, graced it with a thumb-print. The screen blinked. It was done. They had his signature.

"Thank you very much," Redjep said, bowing theatrically. "Much brotherly love your way."

"Piss off."

As they started backing away, Esma said, "And call off your friends. No more taunting Redjep."

Memet slammed the door shut.

The two looked at each other and ran down the stairs, whooping. Esma tucked her phone back in her pocket. "That was easy," she said, and both laughed.

6.

The hackathon started on a wet and windy November morning. Esma and Redjep, backpacks heavy with laptops instead of schoolbooks, ran off to the bus stop at the curb of Orizari street and caught the first bus downhill to Skopje's center.

On the ride, Esma wondered if her parents would see through her lie about spending the days at Redjep's place "after school to help him study," and then she realized that she didn't care, and that if they got angry, then so be it, and she smiled at the city passing by.

They got off near the city square, and quickly shuffled below that sidewalk awning of bumping umbrellas made by Skopje's morning commuters, toward the main street radiating out of the square, toward that dark glass building on the corner that was EuroTech's headquarters.

Esma shivered as they approached the glistening building; its logo, spelled out in neon, projected ghostly over the curtain of rain, and the whole construction shone like a pharos, calling all wandering engineers to port.

Impatiently waiting in front of it was Memet, wearing a beige raincoat.

"Looking sharp." Redjep whistled. ("And dress like an adult, you moron," he'd texted his brother beforehand.)

Memet eyed the two of them. "Let's get this over with." He rang the bell, and the built-in fingerprint scanner recognized him as the guardian of Redjep Bajram and Esma Muratova, and let the three of them right in.

They shook off the rain from their hair, took off their jackets, and registered at the reception desk, after which Memet bid them goodbye.

"Ah, the two from Orizari." A man came up to them, consulting his notepad. He bit his lip. "I mean, Redjep and Esma?"

They nodded.

"Yes, welcome, come in, come in." They followed him into a big room filled with young contestants unpacking computers and setting up monitors or goggles and plugging in peripherals. "Do you need hardware?"

Esma turned her back to show her backpack. "Brought our own laptops, thanks."

"Of course, of course you did." The man blushed, ashamed to have asked them the question. "Well then." Scratching his beard, looking around. "Pick a seat."

Once everyone had come in, they were officially welcomed by a senior developer at EuroTech, who took the opportunity to reiterate the rules: teams of maximum five could be formed during the first day, but couldn't change afterwards; dropping out early meant forfeiting; the finished products and presentations would be judged by a panel of developers, product managers, and designers from the company on the very last day; the results would be available shortly thereafter; the final prize—announced after a purposefully pompous drum roll which elicited some laughter—was three months of internship at EuroTech (alongside the expected bag full of free hardware).

A murmur passed through the contestants in the room. EuroTech was the biggest foreign software company in the country, and an internship there was the most coveted position among young graduates, because it was guaranteed to open many doors, including the high probability of full employment there, or a position in one of the many EuroTech offices abroad.

Following the opening speech, the hackathon was officially started, and they were allowed to mingle and select teams.

Esma and Redjep split, each diving into a different side of the room. Everybody had tagged themselves with their three computer skills of choice, ranked by experience, which made the scouring of potential teammates easier. Esma peered at the room through her phone's cameras.

Scala. Python. JavaScript.

Ruby. TCP/IP. Computer Assisted Design.

C++. 3D Audio. Java.

She approached one person and pitched him her project about optimizing the sharing of electrical resources through machine learning, but he shook his head. "Sorry, not interested." She approached another, with an equally disappointing result. After the fifth had rejected her, she was beginning to wonder.

"Esma, I got one," Redjep said, dragging a bespectacled young student by his sleeve. "Networking specialist," he said, and added, "but really good at math."

"Sounds good." Betraying no enthusiasm. "I'm Esma, good to meet you."

"Boris. Good to be in the team."

"You?" Redjep asked her.

Esma shook her head. "No luck."

"Let's try one more." And he dove back into the crowd, phone before his face, leaving this new Boris to Esma.

"Care to help me recruit?" she asked, and Boris shrugged noncommittally. "Good, let's go together."

The room was thinning out as groups of people lumped together into teams, with only a few wandering souls left, but this time around she had more success, and they added a fourth person, Aleksandra the Product Designer, to the team.

Day one was mainly introductions and about getting familiar with the project.

A EuroTech employee gave out fist-sized soundproofers to each team, which helped them to brainstorm out loud and bounce ideas off each other in their island of the large and open conference room without worry of being overheard and giving anything away to their rivals.

On a flatscreen, Esma drew out a grid.

"This is our city," she said, and the three members of her team blinked at the crude drawing. "And this is how neighborhoods are connected to each other." And she switched the color of her digital pen, and crisscrossed the black grid with a red marker, thickening the lines where the electricity loads were heavier. "As you can see, the city center uses a ton of power, but so does the neighborhood behind the fortress, and yet, the power lines that connect the two loop around the much less inhabited quarters by the river, instead of bee-lining across. This is old design. Mid last century. Back when the river quay was considered more important than the suburbs."

Aleksandra scribbled some notes in her phone. Boris scratched his chin. Redjep tapped his foot.

"And this is just one example. Now consider the east side of the city." And she continued drawing over her grid in different colors until it was all one big tangle of squiggles, until she'd hammered home the fact that the city of Skopje was operating under a heavily stressed power grid, one that had last been reorganized forty years before. And this caused regular outages and blackouts, and grid shutdowns for repairs, and power dips and lulls that were equally as dangerous as they were brief, especially for hospitals or care centers that didn't have reliable batteries.

"Well, what can we do?" interrupted Boris. "Go up power poles and rewire the damn thing?"

Esma suppressed a smile. She said, "That's one way of dealing with it. But there's also another approach. A *cleaner* approach."

Optimizing the entire grid without so much as changing a single wire was no mean feat, they all agreed, but Esma's conviction proved infectious, because the four of them also agreed that it very well could be done. They just needed a boatload of data.

So on day two, they set to work on pulling usage metrics. Esma already had a dataset that she'd used to start the project at home, but with EuroTech's servers at their disposal for the duration of the hackathon, they had plenty of compute, which meant that a much bigger set was in order.

The trick was, Esma had explained, to figure out when and how much power each quarter needed at every hour in a calendar year. Then, their system could sit atop the city grid's software, and divvy up power even before the need arose. Their model, fed with data from power usage, would not only predict but anticipate, and start the trickle of power down lines that previously tended to overload because of unexpected surges. Like a clairvoyant traffic controller for electricity, she'd said, and the team liked the analogy.

And this was *Overseer*, the software that Esma had been prototyping for months, which sat atop the model and had a bird's eye view of the power grid.

She presented the main code flow to the team.

"There are many things that we need to improve there. Optimizations. Refactoring."

They agreed and split into two teams.

Aleksandra and Redjep were responsible for hooking into Skopje's biggest electrical company's system and downloading as much data as possible on power usage; the company was a state-owned one, and all their data was mandated by law to be open and available to everyone curious enough to query.

Boris and Esma paired up and set to rewrite the code of *Overseer* based on Esma's flow diagrams, fixing and optimizing Esma's prototype algorithms along the way.

Every hour the two groups checked on each other, and helped with each other's tasks, and by the end of the second day they had the data that they needed, and the software to manage it.

Now they just needed to train their clairvoyant.

They waited for the model to train on the bigger dataset.

Esma looked across the room from the vantage point of her beanbag: in clusters of four or five contestants, teams were spread out in EuroTech's big conference hall, huddled around desks, some sleeping in their chairs or balled up on beanbags. Her own team was no different, with Boris staring blankly at his monitor, elbows on desk, willing the training to go faster, and Aleksandra writing something on her pad, and Redjep swiveling in a chair, poking and prodding his phone screen in what seemed suspiciously like playing one of his games.

Her eyelids were closing. It was the middle of the night, or maybe some time before dawn; she'd lost track of time, of the outside world.

If she closed her eyes for just one moment, maybe she could rest a little—

Esma's phone shook in her hand.

It's happening again!

A Margaret message that threw her straight into one of her older threads with a problematic sufferer of anxiety. Startled, she started writing this 'sufferer' to soothe them, and after her immediate response she got the satisfactory ding of a little coin dropping in her app store wallet.

My whole body hurts. It's coursing through my veins.

Esma began to type out a response with her usual tactic of letting the 'sufferer' know they should stop resisting, stop pushing the thoughts and anxiety away, and instead try to embrace all internal states of being—

"It's done!" Boris said. "Model's trained."

She tucked her phone back into her pocket, sprang up, and joined him by the big monitor. "Show me," she said, and Boris typed out the test query they'd prepared for the trained model.

After a couple of nail-biting moments, the model spat out an answer.

Aleksandra consulted her calculations. "It fits."

"It fits!" Redjep repeated.

Having verified the model was responding correctly to very basic dummy queries whose answers they could easily look up, they spun up their freshly rewritten *Overseer*. They fired up a simple simulation of the city grid, and let the software do its work. They sped up time to 10x, 50x, 100x. The grid became an unchanging blur. The model was receiving thousands of requests per 'minute' from *Overseer* before making its power routing decisions. With a little over twelve hours to go until the deadline, they watched expectantly, hoping their software would work as expected. The simulation was running at 150x now, then 200x. And then it finished, a whole year of grid-time having passed, and not a single blackout, not one outage occurred in their simulated grid of simulated Skopje.

Esma watched herself in the golden-framed mirror of the EuroTech bathroom.

It had worked. A fully trained model was able to predict the power usage of a city quarter with excellent precision, and re-route power from quarters with projected lessened use to where it was most needed. They'd made it work. She'd made it work.

It was a proof of concept, but a fantastic one.

She splashed her face with water again, and smiled at herself, droplets dripping into a porcelain sink. This place exuded money, and there she was, little Esma from Orizari Street.

Her leg vibrated. She dried her hands and fished out her phone from her pocket.

Where are you? Here? Are you here? Where did you go? Margaret, I need you now. Buggy f***ing product. Margaret? Margaret? Margaret? Where the hell did you go? Answer me, you stuttering robot.

Esma frowned. She brought the screen in for a closer look, but the barrage of messages vanished and the app crashed. A new notification congratulated her on the awarded store credit. She started Margaret up again, but she couldn't reproduce the same behavior.

Beta features, she thought and scoffed, squeezed her phone back to sleep before rejoining her team.

There was still more work to be done.

With the model sufficiently trained and their *Overseer* software polished as much as possible, they were ready to submit their project.

Esma and Redjep recompiled and tested the latest version of the traffic-controller one final time, and Aleksandra and Boris packaged up the trained model.

They let Esma press the final Upload button, and their submission was vacuumed up by EuroTech's servers.

They came in third at the hackathon.

The team stood before her, contrite, but despite her best efforts, she couldn't bring herself to say a word. Winning had been a long shot, and the other teams were comprised of older students and programmers, people with more experience. She took a breath, shrugged. Third place wasn't too bad, after all, she told herself. A bronze medal carried its bragging right, in addition to the small prize they all got. They'd tried to do better, and that mattered, that was enough, wasn't it? Her eyes filled up with tears, which she wiped off without letting anybody see.

As they were packing up their hardware, the older man who'd welcomed them to EuroTech's headquarters on the first day popped by their desks.

"Hey," he said, beaming. "Congratulations, Esma and Redjep. Third place, huh?"

The two looked at each other. "It's okay, I suppose," Redjep said.

"Now, now, in *such* a competitive atmosphere, asking for more—Ah, here." He waved and caught the attention of a man with a camera. "Let's take a picture for our website." He hugged Esma and Redjep and let the other two team-members hover on the sides. "Excellent, excellent." The man grinned and moved on to the next group.

When he was out of earshot, Redjep asked, "What the hell was that all about?"

Boris had shoved his laptop in and was zipping up his backpack. "They're patronizing you. Third place for the Orizari girl and boy. What more could they want?" He swung his backpack on his back, put his hands on Esma's shoulders. "This was a ton of fun. Let's do this again sometime."

7.

Esma lay in her bed.

Mindlessly, she fiddled with her phone, swiping and poking the screen.

She'd betrayed her parents, skipped classes in school, and spent money she couldn't afford to spend on this *pointless* pursuit of what? An opportunity to work in Big Tech? In companies that were supposed to hold the cream of the crop, the best engineers, the most rational of people.

The Orizari girl.

Was Boris right? Was that really how they saw her?

As a diversity asset, as a participant to pad out the numbers.

She wasn't a sore loser. Not like Redjep. Their project might well have deserved third place, and she was fine with that, but something bothered her about the whole ordeal, and she wasn't even sure she knew exactly what.

She opened Margaret to chat.

Not to beta-test it. Not to make money. Just to talk to somebody who wasn't real, who wouldn't judge or blame or make fun of her. Maybe, somebody who could explain to her what it was that she was feeling.

But the app stuttered. And a message appeared:

Stupid f***ing app. Crash one more time and I'm no longer paying. Hello. Hellooo. I need to talk. I need you. Now, not later, not tomorrow.

She shook her phone and the message vanished.

The same bug as before. Were the 'sufferers' now simulating a crisis? Either way, she was in no mood to deal with somebody else's problems, however fictional they were, so she put her phone away.

But something didn't feel right.

These messages carried a sense of urgency that she hadn't seen before, almost as if they were more than mere fabrications and simulations of Margaret-queries.

She rubbed her eyes. Bit her lip. Picked up her phone again.

She scrolled through her new contacts and wrote Boris a message.

The whole of Saturday vanished trying to set up the software to catch the app's network requests, then half of Sunday, too. (Boris had packaged the tools properly, but he'd explained the setup procedure as if to somebody already too familiar with network analysis.) When she had it ready, she launched the Margaret beta.

With one eye on the network analyzer, she worked the therapist.

As she used the chatbot on the phone, she monitored the traffic of her network, and sniffed and unpacked the Net packets as they tried to slip out of her machine.

"Something's totally off," she muttered. She was tracing her finger along the squiggly lines of the network analyzer. "Shit," she said, and lifted her hands off her keyboard, not wanting to have anything to do with what was happening on her machines.

It was obvious. How didn't she realize before? Her responses didn't even pass through Margaret's servers: instead, her packets went straight to an IP address in Montreal, and if she ran a traceroute to it, she could see exactly how these official servers were bypassed. What was more, she could even pull this IP address' profile based on their activity. A whois query told her it was a girl, not much older than Esma. Stats appeared on Esma's screen. Based on Esma's chat history with this person, she could tell this girl had problems with her girlfriend and the other students at the University and with her estranged mother. Esma tried to remember all her choices in the weeks of beta-testing, of making money for her hackathon, thinking she was chatting with a bot.

She shuddered, then unplugged her phone, disconnecting from this all-too-familiar stranger.

When she tried to connect it again for further investigation, she realized her Margaret account had been blocked.

"Give me your phone," she told Redjep.

"What?"

"Margaret," she said. "You still have her installed, no?"

"I know third place hit you hard, but in all honesty I didn't expect you'd need therapy."

She smiled. They were back to normal. "Just give me the phone. There's something I want to show you."

They hooked up the phone to her laptop, and extracted the Margaret application to her drive. She explained to him what was going on, how she'd spent her weekend and what she'd discovered, what actually hid behind this *beta feature*. "And you, my friend, you've been talking to somebody in Germany." Her fingers worked the keyboard. "Look at this. His profile. Redjep, meet your pen-pal Lucas." Somebody's psycho-therapeutic history unrolled on her screen like a scroll.

"This is insane."

"It's more than insane," she said. "It's immoral. It's unethical. It's wrong. They're using us as cheap labor, and they're tricking their paying customers into thinking they're interacting with somebody with a vested interest in helping them. But it's all just simulated. It's all fake. It's *artificial* artificial intelligence. The latest trend!"

They stared at each other. Esma closed her laptop, and handed Redjep back his phone.

"This is big," he said.

"Very big."

"What are we doing about it?"

She didn't have an answer for him. But her blood started boiling when she thought about these transgressions, about companies abusing the trust of their users, and how their charters and convictions and snappy mottoes could be reduced to four simple words: Smile For The Cameras.

Suddenly, she felt dirty, used. She felt angry. She was an engineer above all, but engineers were humans, too, and humans were not rational, not objective, not fair, not always, at least.

Tears came to her eyes, and she turned away from Redjep.

"We tell everyone," she said.

In order not to lose any evidence, they recorded snapshots of the network traffic, of the usage of this beta feature, copied logs where private information of Margaret users was being spilled.

All of which they'd leak to the press.

Which meant not newspapers and magazines, but rather online tech-bloggers and exploit portals. Esma compiled a list of their email addresses and prepared a script to mail the data package to all simultaneously.

Esma's hacker handle would be attached to the package and published as such. *The Orizari Girl.*

It wouldn't be as prestigious as third place, they joked with Redjep, but they'd have to settle.

Maybe, she thought to herself, just maybe, if even a small injustice was exposed, it might level the playing field a bit. And maybe, engineers could learn from mistakes, and become a little more like engineers again and a little less like humans.

She used Redjep's phone and Margaret account for further experiments and gathering evidence, sieving through network analyzer logs to make sure she'd made no mistake, because it wasn't just about exposing Margaret's maker's immorality, but also about not making a fool of herself.

Her parents were arguing in the room next door in that low hissing whisper that got on Esma's nerves: she knew they were arguing, and that they were most likely arguing over money, so why not shout, speak normally, not try to hide? Why did they think they needed to protect her? Could she not handle their problems? Was she not adult enough for them?

Redjep's phone vibrated.

Somebody reaching out through Margaret. Clipped words, on the screen, with quiet urgency: *How long will this pain last?*

She stood with Redjep's phone in her hands.

Her parents' hisses intensified. She banged a fist on the door of her room. "Just shut up," she said, quietly. Why were they, too, trying to manipulate her for their own benefit? Why not tell her outright what they wanted out of her? And tell her what kind of future they had in mind for her, and then they could discuss and she'd soothe their fears, because of course she'd be there to help them, always, they were her mother and father.

She opened a window and the hisses of her parents now mixed with the sounds of Orizari street, the cars, the laughs and taunts, the hum of the hovels, the buzzing of the overloaded powerlines.

Esma thought about this poor soul reaching out from across the continent, and she rubbed her eyes.

How long will this pain last?

Margaret offered her three choices, sentences fine-tuned by algorithms based on countless responses to this very same question.

She was also offered the option to type out a response herself. She chose that.

She thought about writing something comforting, about explaining the whole Margaret fiasco to this one person directly, one person who wouldn't find out from the news that their private life had been shared with thousands of cheap laborers, who would have some time to digest this breach of trust before it became public. But her hands and legs were shaking, and the Margaret filters would certainly auto-remove anything that contained banned keywords, so instead, she just told the truth:

I don't know.

She switched off the phone. Later, when her hands stilled, she mailed the package to the press.

Esma stood by her window again, closed her eyes, and listened; and in the noise of Orizari street, embedded inextricably in that tangle of sounds produced by her neighborhood, she thought she could make out her own name, she thought she could hear somebody calling out, in need of her skills.

See Damien Krsteski's story "Esma's Margaret" online at Metaphorosis.
If you liked it, leave a comment. Authors love that!
Remember to subscribe to our e-mail updates so you'll know when new stories are posted.

About the story

"Esma's Margaret" is a product of my overlapping interests in psychology, (artificial) intelligence, and the dynamics of capitalism in general and between corporations and their outsourced workers in particular.

It is set in a fictionalized and near-future version of my hometown—specifically in its poorest neighborhood—wth a precocious girl as the main character, whose technological talents seem to have made her a minor celebrity in her quarter. This sets up a story where contrasts are painfully apparent: high-tech but low-pay, minus the sleekness of cyberpunk; international big-tech mega-corp, but in a city with regular power blackouts due to decrepit infrastructure; artificial intelligence at everyone's fingertips, except maybe a bit more artificial than advertised.

And all of that written perhaps as a sort of exaggerated extension of everything that had been impressed on me growing up, written from the perspective of somebody and something I'd never been, written as a warning, as a tribute, as a love-letter to a city that I no longer call my home.

A question for the author

Q: How do pets/children/significant others help/hinder your process?

A: My partner helps by giving me time and space to do my work. She helps by understanding how important writing is to me. And once, when I was stuck with a story, she dreamed about how I could finish it.

About the author

Damien Krsteski is a software engineer and science-fiction author. His stories have appeared in *Metaphorosis, Beneath Ceaseless Skies, Mithila Review, The Future Fire*, and others. He lives in Berlin, Germany.

monochromewish.blogspot.com, @monochromewish

February

Vacation Gnomes

Aaron DaMommio

Amy wrestled the key into the beach house door with one hand while balancing her phone on her shoulder, the whole operation complicated by the tote bag weighing down one arm. Her mom spoke in her ear. "Do you really mean Colin won't be joining us for Christmas?"

"We're on a break, Mom. If I understood it, it probably wouldn't be happening."

"Now, don't say that. He's the one who needs to come to his senses."

Amy appreciated her mom's loyalty. She just wasn't sure she deserved it. "He seemed pretty clear about the whole thing," she said. She'd never worried about Colin and commitment. The trouble with Colin was getting him to change his mind.

But she was here to stop thinking about Colin. She needed to leave that behind, or what kind of a vacation would this be? She'd decided when she planned this: the trip would be all about New Amy, who didn't obsess about guys.

She jiggled the handle and the door popped open. She managed to hop inside and kick it shut without dropping anything. She wrinkled her nose. Had the last tenants forgotten to empty the trash can? How long *had* this place been empty?

The midday sun filtering in through the slats of the blinds was enough to show that the downstairs was about what she expected: a small white kitchen opening onto a blue living room with lots of white wicker furniture and the kind of matchy-matchy design that never happened in houses people actually lived in.

She ignored the living room and headed for the kitchen. It was her first time in one of these rentals, but she'd memorized the layout; her company rented dozens just like it. This one was farther from the beach than most, which was why it had been available when her boss forced her to finally take a vacation. She'd been so annoyed at the order that she decided to mark the property as occupied for the week. After three years in property management, she knew how to hide her tracks. As long as it was pristine when she left in a week, no one would be the wiser.

She hefted the tote bag onto the kitchen island while her mom continued speaking in her ear, trying to make a connection between Amy's situation and the ups and downs of living with Amy's father.

Amy dumped out the tote bag to reveal a six-pack of wine coolers, a baggie of celery sticks, and a packet of Oreos. The balanced lunch of a mature twenty-eight-year-old.

She stared at the Oreos. Colin's idea of a serving of Oreos was half a bag, and he still didn't gain weight. It wasn't fair.

It really wasn't fair.

"No, I don't know what Colin was thinking," Amy said. "You'd have to ask the bastard yourself." Her mom started to reply. "Oh, no," Amy laughed. "Please don't actually call him. Thanks. Bye."

She set the phone down on the island with the rest of her junk. She hated lying to her mom. A break? Sure, he'd said that. But he'd also mentioned seeing other people.

Amy knew what that meant. He wanted to break up with her, he just didn't want to say it. She just wished she knew why.

It wasn't so long ago that Colin had seemed perfect. He never did that threaten-to-break-up-constantly thing like Jason back in college. Nor did he have the idealism of Paul, whose passion made her giddy ... until he disappeared to teach English in Bangladesh.

Colin had a steady job at a bank, he didn't overindulge, he was polite to waitstaff. His biggest flaw was that he didn't like to dance. What did it matter if she ended up dancing alone to videos she found on the net?

Of course, it was Colin who'd announced they needed a break. Which was in a way what created New Amy. She dated the start of New Amy from when Colin made his declaration, because that was when she had marched over to Colin's place for a two-hour shouting match that left her a wreck the next day at work.

Followed by her boss insisting she take some of those vacation days she'd piled up.

Ugh. All she wanted to do right now was veg out in front of the TV. She could catch up on the last few episodes of *Celebrity Dance Death Match.*

Her eyes travelled from the Oreos to the wine coolers. She yanked one out of the six-pack, twisted off the top, and took a swig. She glanced at the label. Berry something. It'd do, but one six-pack wouldn't last long.

Unless she restocked at Colin's parent's nearby beach house. Now, *that* was a New Amy sort of thought.

Points in favor: it was only a few blocks away. It had a vast wine cellar. Colin's parents never went there anymore. Amy knew which plastic rock they hid the spare key under.

Points against: Colin might be there. She didn't want another fight, and she definitely didn't want him to think she'd chosen this particular beach house because it was near his.

Satisfying as it might be to raid their wine cellar, it was a spectacularly bad idea.

Instead, she opened the Oreo packet and popped one in her mouth, pressing it against the roof of her mouth with her tongue until it cracked in half, while slipping the rest of the Oreos into the pocket of her lime-green hoodie. Colin's hoodie. He'd actually asked for it back while they were arguing. That was when she stopped trying to reason with him.

She shook her head. New Amy time. Obsessing over Colin was what had led to that scene where she ended up yelling at a customer on the phone. Her boss hadn't cared that the guy couldn't decide whether he wanted to vacation in Miami or Key West. Didn't matter that she'd never yelled at anyone before. To her boss, this proved she needed to take some vacation.

Well, she would prove she could vacate with the best of them. Amy picked up the six-pack so she could head for the couch, grabbed the open wine cooler with her other hand, and took a sip. She frowned. Did not pair well with Oreos.

She took a deep breath, then wrinkled her nose again. "Did somebody leave a diaper lying around?"

Remind the clients all you wanted, they'd still forget to empty the trash ... but the kitchen trashcan was empty. She opened the fridge a crack, but it was spotless, except for a styrofoam takeout container holding two egg rolls.

She heard something from the living room. She stepped to the doorway between kitchen and living room and looked towards the entertainment center. A movement caught her eye, something heading for the couch, fast.

Ugh, were there mice in this place? If it was mice, there sure were a lot of them. She swiveled her head to follow the shapes moving across the couch now, like water flowing down a rocky hill.

Except the rocks were cheap throw pillows, the hill was the couch, and the water was a cascade of four-inch-tall men with purple and orange hair, wearing only loincloths and tattoos.

Amy froze, blinked her eyes three times, and looked again. A tide of tiny dudes flowed toward her, their squeaks and warbles resolving into battle cries, echoing as they ran under the coffee table toward the kitchen. And her.

The chorus of high-pitched voices broke her shock. Amy dropped the six-pack right in front of them.

It shattered against the tile floor, icy droplets splashing her legs, glass shards tinkling. But at least it made the man-tide pause. For a second.

Then the whole mass of them shook their shaggy manes and shouted.

Amy spun around to run for the front door, but found that upwards of thirty of them had flanked her, brandishing tiny spears. One waved a sewing needle in a circle, then stabbed her foot. Amy yelped and grabbed her toe. Now there was blood on her favorite sandals.

She raised a foot angrily for a stomp, and they scattered. She ran from the kitchen to the only enclosed space within reach — the hall bathroom.

She shut the door and leaned against it, sucking in deep gulps of air. That was a mistake. It smelled like a locker room. She saw movement and stopped. There were a dozen of the little weirdos already in there with her, running in and out of a hive of toilet-paper tubes, glued together in a mound on the counter.

She still had the last wine cooler in one hand, but she snatched up a plunger with the other. "Get out, get out, *get out!*" she shouted, flailing at them with her rubber weapon. They yammered like a bunch of sopranos, but held their ground.

Amy got angry. She stopped randomly thrashing around and aimed for one, trapping it under the plunger, mashing the plunger down.

She heard a scream. She stopped mashing as the trapped fellow's pals yanked at the edges of the rubber dome. When she pulled the plunger away, there was one figure lying still underneath it. She let out her breath when he leaped up.

The little guys had had enough. Amy opened the door and they ran out. She grabbed up the cardboard hive and threw it after them with a yell. Then she slammed the door.

Amy set the wine cooler down, dropped the plunger, and turned on the hot water, keeping a finger in the stream to test the temperature. When it was hot enough, she splashed her face over and over.

Tiny men. Ridiculous. Her first alone time in forever, and she was already seeing things. She splashed some more. Then she grabbed a hand towel and dabbed at her face.

She glanced down. Little bits of brown cardboard littered the floor. The smell in the room. She wasn't hallucinating that.

She turned on the fan, looking at the wine cooler on the sink counter. She'd only drunk about a quarter of it. Even downing the whole thing wouldn't be enough to make her see things.

Still. They couldn't be real, could they? Colin liked to say she imagined things. Of course that was when she asked why he was always staying late, working weekends, or going on fishing trips. Why he was always distracted, always tired.

But Colin wasn't here. Maybe she was crazy, and maybe she wasn't, but right now she was stuck in a bathroom while a bunch of miniature Tarzan extras were out there trashing a beach house she wasn't even supposed to be using. She couldn't have imagined that. Maybe it made sense to freak out a little.

Trouble was, she didn't have the energy right now to do a proper freakout. She felt all used up. She really did need a vacation.

She wondered what Colin would do if he saw these little men. Set out traps for them, she supposed. He'd probably scoff at her for being too tenderhearted to smash one. Although if recent behavior was any indication, he'd ignore the things until they got right up in his face, then blame it all on her. But that wasn't how New Amy rolled.

She cracked the door. The little men were milling about. Some of them lay prone next to the puddle of wine cooler, singing or chanting.

Others were moving in big groups, swaying and waving their spears. Had to be a hundred of 'em. She'd faced down a dozen, but a hundred?

Still, she couldn't stay in the bathroom forever. Out of a hundred tiny men, surely one of them would see reason. She took a deep breath, readied her plunger, and opened the door.

Five of them were set up in front of the bathroom, with one fellow standing, arms crossed, on an inverted yogurt cup. Behind them were scattered groups all the way from the bathroom to the couch, where she could see trash piled up into shapes like the hive from the bathroom.

Amy squatted down for a closer look.

The little men were still making a lot of noise, but at this level she could start to make out some of the sounds. The ones by the puddle of wine cooler were repeating one chant over and over, something like "lowhall".

She turned her attention to the delegation by the yogurt cup. "What do you guys want, anyway?" Amy said.

The one on the yogurt stage said something to the four below him, who all gabbled responses until the one on top said a sharp word. The yogurt guy was tall compared to the others. He wore a half-cape on his shoulders in addition to the regulation loincloth. He held a bottle cap form one of the wine coolers in both hands like a tray; it was full. He had to squeak at Amy for a while before she realized he was repeating the same word. Lowhall? Lo-hawk-sall?

"Lohoxal?" she said. They gabbled at each other in excitement, then the yogurt guy did a sort of dance. He waved the bottle cap at her again, looking at her with eyebrows raised. He wanted more.

Amy thought about the wine cooler perched on the bathroom counter. She hadn't really planned on sharing. "Sure, I've got more," she said. "But you guys realize you can't stay here, right?"

They squeaked at each other some more then looked up at her. Amy sighed. She did a fingers-walking-across-her-hand gesture. The yogurt guy danced some more.

"Well if dancing's what you want..." She did some moves from a video she'd seen recently for a pop song about a nasty breakup, trying to convey that these dudes needed to move on down the road.

The more she danced, the more excited yogurt guy became. But he wasn't agreeing with her, she began to understand. He was trying to tell her a story.

He kept returning to a move that involved fingers to his ears while he leapt around and shook an imaginary tail. Slowly she got the picture: a pointy-eared creature — a cat? — that chased them to here, to the beach house.

She supposed it wouldn't have to be much of a cat to be a danger to these little guys. Then he started counting heads, and gesturing at the sky... she had the impression he was trying to tell her how long they'd been here, but she wasn't sure.

She did another short dance to encourage him to continue. She pointed at a group of the men, and he bobbed his head. She looked past the troops at the holes cut in the couch, with stuffing pulled out. Empty Chinese-food boxes and chip bags turned into tents. Evidence of a growing population.

They went back and forth for a while to get the numbers right, until she decided he was trying to tell her that maybe thirty of the little men had arrived here a month ago.

There was still a big group gathered by the wine cooler puddle, and it was organized. They took turns drinking from the puddle, slowly, reverently. Amy shook her head and focused her attention on Yogurt Leader Guy. "Where did you come from, anyway?"

When that confused him, she put together a short miming dance. She'd never let anyone at work know about her dancing, but now all the time she'd spent mimicking videos paid off. She had moves ready for who, what, where, and why.

The cultural divide seemed like a canyon, but with a lot of repetition, they managed to get a few things straight. Either yogurt guy or maybe his grandparents had landed on the beach in the shells of, probably, turtles, roped together into something like a great hollow raft, after leaving an island where Amy gathered they were either the subjects of an atomic experiment or got cursed by a witch doctor — they didn't share enough mutual concepts for Amy to be sure.

Soon after they had arrived here, they were attacked by what sounded like a demonic tabby. They had taken shelter in this vacant beach house, where they were delighted by all the food they found, except, apparently, the egg rolls.

"You can't stay here," Amy tried to convey, but she was pretty sure the command didn't land. The beach house was all that Yogurt Guy had ever known, and he was not, it seemed, a young man. Gnome. Whatever.

She started into a dance about how a family with children would arrive here in a week, but Yogurt Guy wasn't bothered by the idea of small people. He'd clearly never spent a summer babysitting. She tried to start over, but the leader stamped his feet on top of the yogurt cup so that it made a crackling sound. He was determined to stay.

As the leader got angrier, Amy got distracted. She was captivated by the crowd near the rapidly disappearing puddle of wine cooler. After each micro-man drank deep, he'd walk away, getting more and more unsteady, until he fell over a couple of feet away. The prone ones swelled up like balloons. Some of them split open, and from each of those ... two new guys crawled out.

"Lohoxal! Lohoxal! Lohoxal!" went the chant, while Amy tried to comprehend what she was seeing. It made her lunch want to come back up. She struggled to keep it down; it hadn't been that great the first time.

But while she wobbled, the leader continued dancing, incensed now that she wasn't paying attention. She realized he'd reached his limit when he turned and shouted something.

The groups of men behind him suddenly stopped their swaying and lined up all their spears. They began to march forward.

Amy dashed toward the kitchen to grab her phone, then whirled back toward the bathroom, but a phalanx of the little men moved to block her way. She spun toward the stairs, and they followed. She twisted back about halfway up to use the plunger to shove them back, then ran higher. They chased her through the master bedroom and out onto the balcony, where she slid the glass door shut and watched them beat themselves against it in desperation.

Amy paced the balcony, stopping occasionally to stare at the army on the other side of the glass door. It was like watching a silent movie. The men danced angrily at each other. She was sure they were planning something.

Looking over the balcony rail to the drop below it, she felt caged. In nature shows, she'd always sort of rooted for the lions, but now she felt more and more like a gazelle. She circled the patio furniture: a forlorn metal vase with a dead bamboo, a pair of shiny aluminum chairs surrounding a table. She grabbed a chair and sat down, eating an Oreo while staring at her cell phone.

She *could* call 911, but then she figured everything would come out. One photo of the downstairs would be all it would take to end her career in the vacation rental industry.

She could call her mom, but what to tell her? No way she'd believe this. Her sister would probably drive out, if only to laugh at Amy's predicament, but that would take hours.

There was one person she knew who could get here quickly. If he was at the beach house, he could be over here in minutes. Sure, they were on the outs, but this … this was an emergency. They'd been together for more than four years; he'd understand.

She looked through the glass. There were more of the little men gathered in front of it now, and they'd found a broom.

Focus, she told herself. This call might be humiliating, but it would keep her alive. She wasn't going to let them stab her toes again. She dialed Colin.

"Amy?" he answered.

Her heart was beating fast. "Colin? Are you at the beach house?"

He paused before answering. "I mean, yes —"

"Ok, whew, good," she said. "Listen, weird question, but —"

"Amy, I thought we agreed we need time apart."

"Actually, you didn't give me a choice, Colin, but that's neither here nor —"

Then Amy heard a voice in the background. "Who's that on the phone?" A woman's voice.

Amy hung up.

Tears filled her eyes. She let them fall, penetrating the metal mesh of the patio table to drip onto her jeans.

Amy sat on the balcony for a long time.

She wanted to tell herself it couldn't be true. But she'd been in denial for too long already; she was ready to move on to anger.

Endless fishing trips. Late nights at the office. It was so obvious now, she had to laugh. She'd checked for all kinds of flaws, never seeing how the whole of Colin added up to such a bastard.

She'd let him convince her their problems were her fault.

She glanced at the little men. They were no longer milling around aimlessly. She approached the sliding door and saw that they were all gathered in two lines, perpendicular to the door. Between them was the broom handle, barely recognizable at this point. They'd fashioned handholds on it with carpet nails, and they'd painted it in bright colors. Suddenly they all threw their hands up in the air, and took hold. They lifted the stick up and started moving towards the door, slowly at first, then at a run.

"Holy crap!" Amy said. She scurried to open the door before they could hit the glass, but she was too late. It hit the door with a plink. All the tiny men fell down. Then they jumped up and started yelling silently at one another.

That was when Amy decided she'd had enough of waiting for someone to save her. New Amy wasn't the type to wait. Who knew what these disgusting little chauvinists would do next? She pulled hard on the sliding door.

"Hey! No need to get violent," she said. "I just needed some me time."

They were trying to get organized after the failure of their battering ram. Amy picked up the metal vase from the balcony and rolled it toward the little men so that they had to dodge out of the way, then she followed it in. When a group at the back rallied, she stomped the ground hard right in front of them and they fell over.

She checked the soles of her sandals to make sure she hadn't actually squashed one, then ran for the stairs. It seemed like there was one of them on just about every step, so she slid down the banister. At the bottom, a whole company of them were stationed between Amy and the door, spears ready.

"Here, boys," she called, taking an Oreo from her pocket. She tossed it to them, and they fell on it with chaotic abandon. She glanced at the packet and shrugged, tossing it off to the side. Most of the little men followed. As their order disintegrated, Amy booked it for the door and the safety of the outside.

She could hardly believe it. She'd done it. She'd gotten out, and all by herself too.

Now what?

She squatted down and unhooked the straps of her sandals. There were tiny cuts all over her feet. She pulled the sandals off and looped the straps in one hand, then stood there, leaning on her car for a minute. Her keys, her wallet — they were in her purse, inside.

Never mind. She had a phone. She'd be okay. Distance, that was what she needed.

She was just so done with little men.

She'd made a mistake with Colin. She could admit that now. Before she met him, she'd just had that breakup with Brock, who expected her to take care of him and got so pissy when she wouldn't. So when she met Colin, her standards were off.

Also, Colin was gorgeous. He must spend some of that fishing time working out, because he had abs like forever. Maybe not so much in the face department. But he was cute, in a vulnerable kind of way, and … no. She couldn't think like that.

What she needed was to get angry.

She wandered down the street. She didn't care about the beach house. She wasn't going to be needing any more vacations. The tribe had solved that for her: after this fiasco, she was sure she wouldn't have a job.

No boyfriend, no job. Might as well change her name, move to Chicago. Become a dancer.

Still. An hour ago she'd been thinking she couldn't make it without Colin. She didn't want to walk away now and prove it.

When she got to the end of the street, she saw a corner liquor store. There was a sign in the window indicating that you could pay with an app, and it occurred to her that she had a six-pack of wine coolers to replace.

Once inside, she looked through the cramped store's selection. At one o'clock on a Saturday, she was the only customer. A label featuring a garden gnome caught her eye. The description cited notes of lemon, oak, and, she assumed, chauvinism. A dark red with a high alcohol content.

She'd fed the little guys cookies, but only the wine coolers seemed to trigger their weird reproduction. What, she wondered, would they do for something stronger?

She paid for the bottle with a smile.

She stood in front of the crowd of little men. They brought out their leader, whose beard now reached nearly to his toes. He had to be helped by two younger guys, but he came.

It took a lot of dancing around to explain her plan, but Amy persevered. When he seemed hesitant, she pulled her prize out of its paper bag.

She'd had the clerk back at the store loosen the cork. Now she poured out a serving into a saucer. They lowered the oldster down in front of it. On hands and knees, he sampled what Amy offered.

He looked up at her, and started to grow. Amy shuddered. She'd been right: the strength of the alcohol mattered.

In seconds, the leader sprouted a giant boil on his back. At the end of a minute it burst, letting out three new pygmies. The leader grinned, apparently unhurt. "Lohoxal," he said.

Amy shook her head. "You want more?" she said.

"Lohoxal?" he repeated. In response, Amy started to spin and twirl as she danced up a story of a trip to a nearby house where unlimited Lohoxal waited.

The plan, Amy figured, was simple. She'd pack the guys into her hatchback, let them into Colin's place, and trade alcohol for amok time, letting Colin both pay the cost and reap the dubious reward. She liked the thought of the destruction he'd find.

They arrived in late afternoon, just in time to see Colin's Mazda leaving. Amy grabbed the key from its rock, prepared to aim the guys at the cellar and depart.

But she had to help them find the cellar door, and then they were afraid to go down the stairs alone. Once down there, she saw a bottle of Beaujolais from the same batch she'd enjoyed the first time Colin brought her here.

Now, watching the little men team up to drag bottles out of racks, she decided that the Beaujolais had been the best thing about that weekend. She'd spent half of it by herself while Colin fished; the rest, they'd spent arguing.

She drank to the memory until she heard a crash. The boys had misjudged the weight of a bottle and it'd cracked on the slab floor, spraying red in a yard's radius. Amy was ready to tell them not to worry about it—she'd expected her revenge to get a little messy—but then there was the thump of footsteps overhead. The sound startled a second group into dropping their bottle, making another ruddy puddle.

Dozens of tiny eyes looked at Amy. "Oh boy," she said. She made a shooing motion, fingers spread wide. One gnome nodded and started barking orders as the others gathered into small groups. Amy couldn't watch; she had to run to the foot of the stairs to flip off the light switch and then hide behind a wine rack.

She froze while the sounds of little bodies moving seemed impossibly loud in the darkness. A beam of light appeared when the door at the top of stairs opened. She heard Colin say, "I'll get some paper towels," then the click as he flipped the sibling switch and turned the light back on.

Amy covered her eyes. Colin would have to see the broken bottles, then he'd look further, and then he'd find her down here.

Colin came all the way down the stairs. Amy peeked through her fingers as he pawed at a shelf, swore at something, and then started back up the stairs.

She looked at the space in front of the wine racks. The blood-red puddle was gone. Only a single dark shard of glass lingered in the center of the pale concrete floor. Somehow, the guys had erased their trail.

Then she heard Colin's voice again as he reached the top. "I'm going to have to get some traps," he said to someone upstairs. "There's mouse crap all over the place down there."

Amy looked around for the bottle of Beaujolais, then snapped her fingers when she remembered it was on the other side of the room. There hadn't been much left, anyway, judging from the tears that filled her eyes when she pictured a tiny orange-haired figure squirming in a mousetrap.

There was really only one thing to do after that.

Back at the rental, Amy stood in the kitchen and dialed for Chinese while the guys built scaffolds to organize the wine so as to keep the corks wet, a practice they took very seriously once she explained it. She was sure one of them had a clipboard.

Her exit from a cellar window hadn't been dignified, and she'd never be able to wear those pants again, but without the pushing and pulling of twenty of the little fellows, she'd never have made it out. Not to mention the wine bottles they'd hoisted out using a water hose.

Forty or fifty more were in the living room now, divided into squads of five as they tackled cleanup. They sang as they worked; thankfully, they didn't incline to whistling.

"Twenty-four orders of lemon chicken. Yes, twenty-four. I understand, I can wait." She glanced at the living room. The work crews were forming up into a line; apparently, it was time for a dance break. "Oh, and no egg rolls."

Now that she felt like she wasn't going to lose her job, she'd started to think about the possibilities that a team of whip-fast workers presented. She happened to know a company that could use a crack Make Ready crew, able to handle any job, no matter how big ... or small.

But there was no hurry. She still had the place for four days; plenty of time to figure something out. In the meantime, the guys were waving at her.

She joined them in the living room. It felt nice not to dance alone.

See Aaron DaMommio's story "Vacation Gnomes" online at Metaphorosis.
If you liked it, leave a comment. Authors love that!
Remember to subscribe to our e-mail updates so you'll know when new stories are posted.

About the story

"Vacation Gnomes" was originally developed in 2017 for the Codex online writing group's Weekend Warrior competition, where you have to put together a 750-word story in a weekend. I love how this process crystallizes an idea down to its essentials. Since you want to get something that has the shape and satisfying ending of a whole story in such a tiny package, you really have to keep pushing to get your character through some kind of arc, and you have to throw almost everything overboard to meet the wordcount limit.

My notes say that it was based on a prompt about 'filthy dwarves', but I barely remember that now. I developed an image of a woman finding that her vacation place was infested with tiny, messy gnomes. By the end of the contest weekend I had the basic plot found here, of a woman distracted by a breakup who has to find a way to deal with a lot of very small men, all by herself.

A question for the author

Q: Do you use music for inspiration? If so, what do you listen to?

A: I don't typically use music for inspiration directly. I've certainly tried having a playlist for a specific project, with the idea of getting back into the right frame of mine for that project, but I dropped that after I created a ton of playlists in a service that didn't survive the first big internet company implosion, and I haven't gone back to the practice since then.

On the other hand, I love song lyrics, especially ones that involve wordplay. In general, I usually take inspiration from wordplay and permutations. I love to see where a prompt will take me, and I enjoy it just as much when the final result is so far from the original prompt no other eyes can see the path.

About the author

Aaron DaMommio is a husband, father, writer, and juggler who came to Austin, Texas, for college and never left. During the day he tries to make the world safe for a team of technical writers who need support navigating the strange hierarchies of XML. He has three children and a share in four dogs. On a good day he can name all the dwarves from *The Hobbit*.

aarondamommio.blogspot.com

Rock-Adda's World

Chloe Smith

Adda felt that the greatest mystery of being a parent was the way it tied you, with such powerful bonds of love, to a person with whom you would continuously fail to communicate successfully.

She always looked forward to her daughter's yearly visits, even though they always meant more arguments that left her feeling both guilty and misunderstood. Cia usually waited until the last possibility of storm was long gone and the warm season was fully established, but this year icy rime crunched under Adda's boots as she walked out to greet her daughter, and cold air pressed against the exposed skin of her face and hands.

Cia turned from pulling a bag out of her suborbital hopper. She was certainly dressed for the cold, in thermal layers whose slim profile spoke volumes about their cost. Adda felt the usual mixture of wonder and pride that this person, who had once lain asleep with her head below Adda's chin and her feet on her stomach, was now flying herself between continents in a rented jet.

Cia said, "Why aren't you wearing gloves, Ma?"

Adda laughed. "Which one of us is the mother here, girl?"

Cia wiggled well-covered fingers. "*I'm* dressed appropriately. I was brought up well."

Adda scoffed and gave her a squeeze around the shoulders. "Well, come on in, then. I knew we were barely going to be out."

Her observation station was a small building, half-sunk in the ground, with its own power panels and the bulk of a skimplane hangar visible off to one side. Adda gave the hangar walls a furtive once-over as she held the door of the main building open for Cia— yes, there was nothing more than a shadowy smudge, indistinguishable from weathering. No one now would be able to tell that yesterday she had woken to find a block-lettered scrawl: STAND BACK AND SHUT UP, ROCK-LOVER.

It had taken her most of a morning, and a lot of retching, to clean out the mess of garbage and refuse they had left on and around her skimplane, and another couple of hours to repair and reinforce the damaged locks. Adda had forced down the feelings of outrage and violation, telling herself that fear was capitulation. This was an expression of popular opinion, not a direct threat—there was no sabotage to the vehicle itself, and no attack on her actual living space.

Yet, Cia would say if she knew. Adda didn't plan on telling her.

Inside, Cia settled herself in the second sleeping quarters. They were officially designated for visiting researchers, but Adda had been thinking of them as "Cia's," reserved for her semi-annual visits, for at least the last five years.

Adda made tea in the closet-like canteen, and then brought it out to her dining-cum-work table, where she had to push the clutter of battery packs and recording equipment farther back to make room for two.

"How are things?" she asked when Cia reappeared, preparing herself for at least a half hour of free-form rambling on Cia's work- and love-life, helped along by Adda's occasional interested noise or leading question.

Cia shrugged. "They're good. Same-same but different. How are *you* doing, though?"

Uh oh. It looked like they weren't going to pretend that things were casual for even as long as Adda had hoped. "What makes you ask?" She gave her daughter a look.

Cia had the grace to look uncomfortable. "Well," she said, "you know we end up being party to a lot of the discussion around new settlement development..." Cia worked for the city manager's office in Istvan, the oldest city on the South Continent. Her position often gave her a line on issues that impacted the cetalith population, though not from a perspective that Adda could agree with. She gritted her teeth in anticipation as Cia continued, "there's been—well, I saw the footage of the town hall meeting. I was worried about you."

Adda closed her eyes. *I was worried about you.* Not, *How could they?* Not, *The situation's appalling.* Not, *What can we do?*

She opened them again, stared past Cia to the wall over her terminal station, where she had pinned an excerpt from a flimsy printout:

"The giant cetaliths of Krishnan IV are another puzzling example. These silicate creatures, who move at speeds not exceeding 6 centimeters per U-hour, and leave as the marks of their passage enduring tunnels that permeate the surface of their world, may have a level of sentience that would guarantee their planet Protectorate, if not Sovereign, status under the Cygni Accords. Although they are solitary beings, whose paths cross only occasionally over the course of their long, long lives, their 'songs,' which gave rise to the name 'whales of stone,' may be a form of communication. This implies a level of sophistication and consciousness, but researchers have yet to establish firm proof of either. This ambiguity has led to the current impasse in official decision-making."

The whole document, the *Report on Resources of Non-Sovereign Satellites, Planets, and Exoplanets, Appendix A: Sentient Fauna*, was one of the supports that the first settlers had used to make their case for access to the planet. *Give us this world to do what we like with as long as we don't understand it.* Adda kept the flimsy on display as a reminder of what was at stake.

Cia was frowning at her. "Ma?"

"It's a worrying situation," she said dryly.

Cia rotated her cup in her hands. Still staring at it, she said "The thing is, speaking like that at the meeting... I don't think it does any good."

"You mean you were embarrassed." Adda's response came out harsher than she meant it to. The truth was, she had embarrassed herself. In the moment, she had been caught up in trying to convince the town shareholders to see what she saw, until she was half-shouting:

"How can we be so selfish! This isn't our world. To just come in and take what we like because it suits us—we have no right! This is an ancient species, a mystery worth unravelling! What you're doing isn't even legal—sentient-status ruling is still pending!"

Chair Horace Grish nodded impatiently, while the crowd behind Adda shifted and muttered. "That status ruling has been pending since Krishnan's was first surveyed, Doctor Oram. It's hard to believe that a decision is forthcoming. In the absence of official status—"

"You're just going to batter this planet and destroy a potentially sovereign species! The ruling isn't the point—this is wrong!"

She had felt so large at the time, full of righteousness and fire, containing multitudes. On the recording, though, her voice was thinner and higher, and she looked like what she was, an old woman, speaking words that meant nothing to her listeners.

"Ma!" Cia's voice cut through her reverie. Adda looked at her. Cia had pushed the tea aside, her forehead creased. "Who do you think is going to stop them? Continental governance? Sharevote results show there's only a minority favoring holding off expansion until the non-Sovereign ruling is official."

"I know that," Adda snapped. She had correspondents besides Cia, other scientists and citizen enthusiasts who followed her research from the southern continent, where human settlements had spread. Some shared their own work with her, their explorations of the cetalith routes that ran through this world —although that work could only be the archeology of dead spaces and still remnants. There were no moving cetaliths left on South Continent, and Adda was the only researcher who had committed to an isolated life on the northern landmass—isolated, at least, until the arrival of the recent wave of separatists from the south, who had founded the town of New Beginnings.

Cia shook her head. "How many reports have you sent, Ma? For how long? After all this time, it's not just sharevotes; most *people* don't think Cygni is going to designate the Rocks as sentient."

Adda sighed. "That's not an accurate term."

"That's not the point—"

"It *is* the point!" Adda's voice rose. "We don't understand, and our ignorance is killing them!"

"Ma!" Cia wailed, "Killing them? They're not even aware! But this could get *you* killed! New Beginnings has their own sovereignty up here. What if they decide you're disrupting the peace, or impeding growth?" She gulped, sending a pang through Adda— *You make your daughter cry.*

Cia took a deep breath, regaining control. "I know how much you care about your research, but it's been years of nothing to show. There's work you could do on the Southern Continent. Research positions in the capital, where it's safe. You're in danger here—don't try to deny it!"

Adda started to argue back, sputtering in her effort to find the words that could communicate her urgency, but Cia banged her tea down, cutting her off. She reached out to uncurl Adda's fingers from her own mug. "I love you and I'm afraid for you. Please come home with me, Ma. This isn't worth it."

There was a long pause before Adda said stiffly, "They have no right to do anything. New Beginnings didn't even have the right to incorporate, officially."

Cia dropped Adda's hands and put her head down on the table. "That doesn't seem to bother them." Even muffled, her words rang with fear and frustration.

Adda had no answer to that. Cia was right, but she didn't see the real problem. *If I can't make my own daughter understand...*

She pushed herself to her feet. "You need to see for yourself. Come on."

"What? No, Ma..." Cia's protests disappeared as Adda went into her sleeping quarters to find better clothes. She was damned if she was going to let Cia mother her about gloves again.

It took 10 minutes for them to reemerge into the afternoon's chill. Cia had taken one look at her mother's outerwear, sighed deeply, and redressed herself for the elements. She followed Adda with an expression of long-suffering filial piety. *Fine.* Adda would take filial piety when she couldn't get authentic understanding.

Outside, the land was sere and rolling, irregular brown with patches of frost and the simple fungusoid varietals that were this planet's only plant parallels at this latitude. The sky above was big and deep, with thin skeins of clouds wisping across it.

Cia grimaced after they climbed into the little skimplane. "It smells like a bad batch of fertilizer."

Adda shrugged dismissively. "It's just old. Let me concentrate." The skimplane was putting her through seconds of flickering controls. Her stomach clenched. It was possible she'd missed something when she checked for sabotage this morning. She closed her eyes and mentally ran through everything she'd checked: seals, power-cells, flight mechanism, stabilizers—

The hum of the engine drive coming online interrupted her frantic listing, bringing her back to the present. Adda sighed in relief and Cia in impatience.

The horizon expanded below them as they climbed in silence, until Cia couldn't keep her peace anymore. "Ma, if you wanted to fly, we could have taken the sat'."

"Just look," Adda said, slowing the skimplane to a near-hover. Cia glanced down obediently.

At this height, the patterns on the land were easy to notice. There were the hills and gullies made by eons of landmasses pushing against each other, and the irregularities shaped by wind and this planet's scant waters moving the dust and crumbles of stone and biomass, but within the chaos-formed shapes were others—regular lines that cut across the surface of the world in mismatched arcs and segments, appearing and disappearing like poorly erased cursive.

"Think of the years they've been here," Adda said. "Think of the ages. And we came in three generations ago, spreading and spreading as humans always do. Now half of them have gone still and dead."

Cia started to say something, swallowed down her words with an effort, and put her hand over Adda's on the flight controls. Adda bit back frustration. She didn't want Cia's sympathy for her sentimental mother. She guided the skimplane back down, towards her recording site.

Adda ghosted the little craft down with the utmost possible care, so that they barely felt the settling contact with the earth. Rationally, she was aware that the evidence of harm to the cetaliths came from intense and prolonged impacts—the vibrations caused by large-scale construction, the drilling and digging that came with building energy-efficient sunken habitats and mining for the resources to support them. Irrationally, though, she didn't like the idea of adding insult to injury.

Adda tried to unobtrusively scan signs of disturbance as they disembarked. Her site closest to town had been torn apart last week, perhaps by the same enthusiast who had left their mark on her hangar. It was a relief to see that no one had come out this far. She turned back to find Cia, who was raising an eyebrow at her.

"Looking for something?"

Adda forced a grin. "Don't give me that sass. I haven't shown you anything yet." She clambered up the nearest curving slope. It was regular as the exterior of a tube, a convex arc that ran away from them for a handful of meters before disappearing into the earth. Adda dusted away the thin loose dirt with her hands (the fungusoids were not dense enough to contribute much richness or permanence to the soil), shifted a plastofiber shield that she had laid to keep out the elements, and let herself down through the hole she had painstakingly tapped in the stone.

Going by feel, she found her work lamp. Once lit, it revealed a tube-like tunnel that disappeared into darkness in both directions. Its diameter was perhaps three meters; Adda stood on a platform that she had constructed to avoid the drop to the curving floor. There was a low hum in the air, a faint rumble just on the edge of perception.

She helped Cia climb down and they set off, Adda carrying her lamp and Cia trundling dubiously in her wake. The tube curved to the right and slightly down, so the light from the opening disappeared before they had gone 100 meters. The interior surfaces were smooth enough that Adda could have walked in darkness without stumbling, but she kept the light trained on the ground in front of them, for Cia's sake. The humming continued, so low that it felt more like a pressure on the ears than a sound.

After a while, Cia said, "You've shown me pictures, Ma. And recordings."

"Witnessing is different," Adda said, and kept walking.

They reached the cetalith — #32 in Adda's research notes — after about 500 meters. Actually, it was 512 meters from her tunnel entrance, and 8 meters from where Adda had left it a week ago, going by her last marks on the tube walls. #32 was really booking it. Adda held the lamp up in silence, letting Cia take it in.

The cetalith was an immense bulk reaching up over their heads, perfectly filling the diameter of the tunnel it had made. Its irregular surface, rocky and hard as the planet itself, trembled slightly, but that was all. Its forward progression was not visible, and its moving parts, cilia that tore away the earth it swam through, were microscopic and buried in the recesses between it and the surface of the stone. Adda's earliest research had focused on those tiny, piston-like appendages, which ate away at the stone and earth of the cetalith's environment, allowed the rubble they produced to be ingested through the feeding cracks in the cetalith's forward-moving side, created the long tube it left behind, and caused the rumbling vibration that marked its passage.

It was impossible to tell the age of a living cetalith. Their digestive processes meant that they took on the mineral profiles of their surroundings at the same time that the silicate structures of their outer surfaces sloughed off with their movement, adding to the stony composition of the paths they delved. Those paths could be found running through layers of rock and sediment hundreds of thousands of years old, though. Adda had followed this particular tunnel back to where it was warped out of existence by the movements of the earth. She had seen cetalith tunnels that crossed each other, tunnels that ran together for a time, and sometimes points where two tunnels crossed and a third, new cetalith trail emerged. No one had ever witnessed behemoths meeting, though.

I need more time. These creatures don't operate on human scale. How can we give up on understanding them after a handful of years?

Next to her, Cia stood wide-eyed. Adda had a sudden memory of leading a tiny Cia out of a shuttleport gate for her first vision of the overwhelming reality of a planetside sky, the day they had arrived on Krishnan IV. Her daughter's face now had an echo of that child's wonder.

Slowly, Cia reached out a finger, before looking back at Adda questioningly. Adda nodded. "Go ahead. That's not the sort of interference that disturbs them." She watched as Cia touched the surface of the cetalith and then jerked away. Adda knew what she felt: the source of that bone-humming alien song.

"Here," Adda pulled out her handheld, and called up the audio version of her most recently collected recording. It kept the periodic, rhythmic patterns and relative intensities of the cetalith's oscillation through the earth, while translating it to a frequency within human hearing range. The noise bassooned into the tunnel, echoing away from them in the dark.

It had an irregular variation: Adda had yet to map any pattern or repeating signature in its complexity. She still had a limited data set, even though reports of cetalith song dated back to the first settlers.

The earliest builders on South Continent had spoken of feeling vibration akin to drumbeats resonating out of the stones they cut into. Adda bitterly regretted those settlers' complete lack of investigative spirit. It had been far too long before anyone had thought to make recordings, and those were compromised by human interference. Adda had spent these long years designing programs, comparing snatches and segments, consulting with seismologists and linguists, and trying to build a persuasive theory out of the conviction that this rumbling was meaningful and its source aware.

The sound washed over them for long moments, alien and opaque.

"You really believe these things deserve the world?" Cia asked. Skeptical or not, her voice was hushed.

"It doesn't matter what I believe," Adda said. "We haven't established their sentience one way or the other. There's a possibility, a space of uncertainty. If we destroy first, there's no way to ask questions later."

"Here," she took Cia's hand and laid it flat against the surface of the tunnel. After another long moment, she asked, "Do you feel that? Do you understand it? What happens if we ignore—"

"Ma, be quiet!" Cia was frowning with a sudden intensity and focus that made Adda swallow her affront and wait silently while Cia pressed both hands against the tunnel wall. The cetalith's sound was much more powerful in the earth it moved through; the vibration that transferred to a faint hum in the air around them was a call through the earth that spread outward for miles.

"Is that recording from this one?" Cia asked finally.

Adda blinked. "No. It's from 27. That's my recording point nearest New Beginnings, actually...."

Cia waved a hand furiously to silence her, the other still plastered to the wall. "Ma, it feels different now."

Adda put her hand on the wall next to Cia's, feeling the irregular hum, powerful enough this close to its source to travel up her arm. "Listen," Cia breathed, and Adda did.

The two vibrations, the recording of the cetalith amplified in the air around them and the living cetalith in the earth they touched, intertwined.

They stared at each other, eyes gleaming in the low light. Adda was suddenly afraid that, after this long, after so much wanting, she was tricking herself into imagining patterns where none existed. She opened her mouth, but Cia spoke first.

"I think there's some kind of rhythm or beat...?"

Adda pushed herself away from the wall, and set off back along the tunnel, almost running.

"Ma, wait!" Cia was nearly left in the dark.

Adda was short of breath by the time she reached her platform and her limbs were trembling. She bundled up half of the recording equipment she'd staged there. Thank goodness for secondary systems. By the time Cia followed her up out of the tunnel, Adda was already climbing into the skimplane.

"Is it like breathing?" Cia asked as they surged across the landscape, "Was that the first time you heard that?"

"They don't breathe. But the noise—all these years, I was only listening to one voice. You showed me—it sounds different when there are two of them. I need more data..." Adda's gaze flickered between the land ahead of them and the map display, which had the locations of all her recording points highlighted, along with an overlay of the cetalith tunnels she had mapped, topographically coded for depth.

She brought the skimplane down again on a stretch of ground free of distinguishing landmarks—but roughly halfway between the line of 32's path and another, almost parallel tunnel to the west, 33. Adda took a breath before clambering out. "Just bear with me on this—okay?"

"O-kay," Cia drew the word out, managing to telegraph skepticism and forbearance at the same time. "Can I help?"

Adda reached into the storage bench behind them for a hand-shovel. "I'm so glad you asked."

It took almost an hour for them to dig down to earth that was hard packed enough for Adda's satisfaction. "If we used an earth-mover," Cia said at one point, pulling off her hat and using it to mop her forehead, "we could be down to bedrock in half this time."

"And rain the acoustic equivalent of hellfire down on all local cetaliths in the process," Adda returned. "I'm not doing that." She continued shifting the dirt Cia was turning up, away from the hole they were creating.

Arid Krishnan IV did not have much topsoil, particularly on this continent, which lacked the forest-style growths of the south, and the earth a few feet down was so hard as to be almost indistinguishable from rock. Adda had brought all of her extra battery packs from the skimplane, as well as the recorder she had removed from the tunnel, and, most precious of all, her calibrator and "Excess Ear," the most sensitive instrument she possessed, which she usually carried with her from site to site. It took some creative fiddling to embed the Excess Ear in the dirt, connected to the secondary recorder and even more supplementary batteries. She packed loose dirt around the whole for insulation, leaving only the batteries' light receptors uncovered. She considered spraying the mound with an instant concrete for further protection, but chipping it away might upset the integrity of her recording, and it wouldn't take more than a few days to generate enough material to show—well, whatever it showed. Standing over it, she dusted off her hands. "I'm ready for dinner. Are you?"

"Ma," Cia groaned. "What's all this about?"

"I'll know when we've gotten some more information." Adda gave her daughter a hug around the shoulders. "Thanks to your help, love."

Adda spent the next three days trying not to speculate ahead of her data and failing to attend to Cia's conversations. Cia took her mother's abstraction with remarkable patience, cooked meals while Adda combed through her old recordings or stared off into space, mulling over the possibilities. She spent hours in a vain search for other segments that might resonate together, either played unmodified, or shifted upfrequency, like the tape she'd played for Cia in front of 32. She would have slept in the chair in front of her terminal, if Cia hadn't pushed her into bed each night.

"Now you know—what I went through—when you were a teen," Adda told her between yawns.

"You don't get to hold that over me anymore," Cia told her tartly, "Go to sleep, or you won't be able to make sense of your new data when you *do* get enough of it."

In fact, on the fourth morning, when Adda actually let herself start going over the overlapping recording of 32 and 33—probably too soon for a really robust dataset, but she couldn't wait anymore, and, besides, there was another town hall meeting in New Beginnings at the end of the week—it was excitement rather than exhaustion that made her hands flutter over the interface. She forced herself to take deep, steadying breaths, laying out the parameters of her analysis.

The shape of what the new recordings suggested, though, was something so massive, so revelatory, that she forgot emotions, consequences, forgot even the demands of her own body, as she started to explore her results.

Some unmeasured time later, Cia leaned over her shoulder. "Well?"

Adda input a few more commands, and then sat back as a new graphic flowed across her display. "Look."

Independently, the frequencies that sped out from each cetalith through the rigid ground appeared random, without signature or repetition. In the interference between the two frequencies, though, there was something. Caught on her analytics program, it showed resonances in recognizable periods—begun in one voice and finished in another.

Adda swallowed, half afraid to put it into words. "They're responding to each other. It's communication." She tapped at the display again, entering in another set of parameters, programs that would run back through her library of recordings, correlating timestamps, searching for echoes, trying to find patterns between what she was sure now was a symphony of voices, chorusing together underground, perceptible to those beings whose rocky bulk was attuned to the faintest shiver of frequency.

That done, she pulled up another document, and began hammering out an initial report to the research group on South Continent. Cia put a hand on her arm.

"Ma—wait. Why don't you go talk to them? Come home with me for a while; take some time to discuss what this could mean with other researchers before you write anything."

Adda frowned at her. "How can I leave now? I need to follow up on what I—what *you* found. Awareness. They recognize each other. They're talking."

Cia hesitated. "Ma... I see the pattern, but communication? What's it about? Is it a mating call? Challenge? Are they sharing the latest tips and trends?"

"Of course I don't know yet—" Adda began, irritated, but Cia cut her off.

"Exactly. You just found this and, yes, it's huge, but *we don't know yet* what it means. This isn't enough, alone, to get a Sentience ruling from Cygni. If you come back with me, you can work on a paper about it, somewhere safe..."

"The cetaliths don't have time for me to do that!" Adda thought of the building projects going up in New Beginnings, the percussion of digging projects and construction spreading toxic shockwaves through the region's earth. She pulled her arm out of Cia's grasp and turned back to writing.

There was a long pause, during which Adda tried to think only about how best to describe her data.

Cia finally said quietly, "I know I can't stop you." Adda could feel her daughter's expression. "I just don't trust these settlers. They're dug in here, and they aren't going to listen to any new arguments about why they should wait for the ruling. Please come with me."

Shut up, Rock-Lover. Cia wasn't wrong. The memory of the sabotage and graffiti warnings hung in Adda's mind, its weight on her almost physical. If their positions were reversed, and her daughter revealed that she had been ignoring threats to her safety —well, Adda could only imagine her own fear and anger. She took a breath, but didn't look away from her display. "I can't not fight for this, love."

Cia's work-leave was up the following day, and she went back alone, resigned but clearly unhappy. She wrapped her arms around her mother before she left, and buried her faced in Adda's shoulder. "Call me every day."

Adda hugged her back and agreed, half her mind squirming with guilt, but the other half composing a new message to the Administration of Sentience Establishing Research Enterprises. There was a several-week communication lag between Krishnan IV and the nearest jump-point, a gap that had been a boon when the messages from ASERE had become more and more discouraging and she had counted on the distance to protect her from a preemptory declaration that the cetaliths weren't sovereign and the planet was free for further development. Now, though—if only she could show up in New Beginnings tomorrow with the authority of an official designation of Sentience behind her—or at least able to make the argument that this new discovery had opened some eyes at ASERE.

Cia finally released her, seemed about to say something else, but then shook her head and left with many backward glances. It was all Adda had asked for—understanding, forbearance, recognition. It was more than she deserved.

Adda arrived at New Beginnings at dusk. The sky was still luminous, although the sun had slipped below the horizon and the buildings of New Beginning were shadowed geometric mounds whose silhouettes hunched together. The door to the community meeting hall was open, and several figures were standing in its light, talking. They watched as Adda left her skimplane parked and approached, rubbing her hands together. She had forgotten her gloves again.

Adda recognized all of them; she knew almost everyone in town, at least by sight, after years of visits to what had once been an explorers' outpost and supply depot, and, more recently, months of visits to planning and development meetings after the town was established. They knew her, too.

She nodded at the group, but they didn't nod back, and as she came up to the door, a man who had been leaning against its frame shifted his bulk to stand in her way.

"Rock-Adda Oram," he greeted her, unsmiling. "Have you come to tell us our business again?"

"Sean Rios," Adda returned. "It's an open meeting, I believe."

Rios' frown deepened. The woman beside him spoke up next. "You're not a shareholder." She paused before adding, "Doctor," in a tone that made it almost a question.

Adda squared her shoulders. "I'm an expert witness. I have information—new information—that throws the status of our settlement here even further into question. This isn't our place, or our land. Under Cygni—"

"Oh, Cygni!" scoffed another man, cutting her off. "Not all this again. Didn't you get it all out of your system last time? That ruling's never gonna come—and if it does, what of it?" The group was arrayed against her now, between her and the light. "Why should we pack up and move back to South Continent, or, even worse, leave this planet that's been our home for generations, because of a bunch of *rocks*?"

Adda shoved her cold fingers into her pockets. "I just want to be heard." She took another step forward. The group of settlers drew together, the mass of their bodies cutting off the light from the doorway.

"Don't do it, Rock-Adda," Rios's voice was quiet, "Don't make it hard on yourself." He took a step forward to meet her, arms loose, while the rest looked on.

Adda stiffened her shoulders and glared at them all. She tried to imagine the words that would reach them, that would make them understand. Cygni's authority was lightyears away. Here and now, she might as well be voiceless: in the settlers' eyes, she was as devoid of meaning as the cetaliths. *Cia was right, and she'll never forgive me.*

Cia will listen to me. It wasn't the protection of policy or government, but it was what she had, what she could do.

She let her posture fall, took a step back in the face of their threat. Even shadowed by the light behind him, she could see Rios's smile, and it felt like a slap. "That's right, Doctor. That's a good choice."

She felt their eyes on her back as she walked away.

At home, she double locked the doors, and then used her terminal to call her daughter. Half a day away and to the south, Cia answered groggily, but within seconds. "Ma? Everything okay?"

Adda took another breath, steeled herself to let go. "I can't convince them, and they won't listen to me. They're making threats. No, wait—I know, you were right, but please, listen to me now. I need your help. I need the settlers to know I'm not alone up here; I need people on SoCo to know about what I've found, to believe it, to care. I know it's a lot; I know you have your own life, but this is bigger than some research project of your mother's. You saw the pattern; you felt them speak. Will you help me keep them all from falling silent?"

Cia's face on the video shifted with a mixture of emotions. Adda hoped that her words had struck a frequency her daughter could understand, that she could make her hear what the settlers were deaf to. Time that would have meant nothing on a cetalith's scale dragged by as Adda waited for her daughter's response.

Finally, Cia nodded. "Alright...." Her eyes shifted to focus on something beyond Adda's face, and her fingers came alive, tapping and shifting through her displays. "You stay where you are. I'll come get you."

Adda's heart broke a little more. "But didn't you hear what I said?"

Cia actually stopped what she was doing to roll her eyes. "I *said* alright! You want people to care about the cetaliths; you want them to understand the consequences? I'll help you tell that story, make sure it gets publicity, gets sympathy, get people to believe, maybe even commit to stopping more settlements. But that'll take time—and I'm not going to let you sit up there, vulnerable to those people. You can't make any new discoveries if you're dead. You have to leave this battlefield if you want to win the war."

Adda started to respond, but Cia didn't let her. "No! You wanted me to hear you; now hear me. I'm coming now, as soon as I get these messages off." She cut the connection.

Adda sat in the stillness that followed, letting Cia's last words echo in her head. Finally, she turned back to her terminal, opened up her analytics program. There were still hours until Cia, even traveling at top speeds, could reach her. She pulled up the newest recording, the "conversation" between 32 and 33, and tuned it to human-audible frequencies. The alien sound filled the air around her, and Adda set herself to listening carefully, alert for signatures and repetitions in the schematic on her screen. She knew this song might be an elegy. She might not be able to stop the settlement in time, and these might be the last recorded communications of two sentient beings—but Cia was right. The fight wasn't over. There were still cetaliths who might send their resonant calls through this planet's earth for eons to come.

See Chloe Smith's story "Rock Adda's World" online at Metaphorosis.
If you liked it, leave a comment. Authors love that!
Remember to subscribe to our e-mail updates so you'll know when
new stories are posted.

About the story

The title of this story is a terrible pun on Ursula Le Guin's first novel, *Rocannon's World*. The final product doesn't share a lot with that piece of early SF, but I began by wanting to evoke some of the same sense of a lone explorer overawed by an alien landscape. As far as where the cetaliths came from, I'm always suspicious of SF that imagines alien life that is too similar to our own. I think that if we do ever discover sentient beings on other planets, it will be so different that we'll have a hard time recognizing it as "people"—especially given that humans have a poor track record of even accomplishing so much when it comes to other groups of humans. I hope that the cetaliths are sufficiently strange and different to come across as truly alien. The bond between Adda and her daughter Cia emerged as central to the story only as I started working through my drafts. I needed someone for Adda to interact with, and once her daughter came to visit, their relationship emerged naturally as they talked together. Then I realized that Adda's own difficulties communicating—with Cia, and with other people who don't believe the cetaliths are worth understanding—could connect with her scientific discoveries and help the story say something about communication in general. That description sounds like the story evolved in a straightforward way, which is hardly the case. It went through a ton of drafts, and I'm very grateful to the friends and beta readers, and to the Metaphorosis editorial process, which helped me carve "Rock-Adda's World" into the right shape.

A question for the author

Q: What is your favorite short story?

A: This is a tough question! There is so much good short fiction out there, and I am not as well-read as I'd like to be—I feel like to select one story would be to elide many that I've loved and countless more that I haven't had a chance to discover yet. If you forced me, I'd say that one story I love for its lyricism and repurposing of traditional myths is Catherynne Valente's "Urchins, While Swimming" (*Clarkesworld*, 2006), and one whose emotional impact will never let me go is Margo Lanagan's "Singing My Sister Down" (*Black Juice*, 2004).

About the author

Chloe Smith was born and raised in the San Francisco Bay Area. Her first job ever was as a shop assistant at a SF/F-themed bookstore, and she never lost the taste for speculative fiction, although the world took her through a wide range of places and vocations before she stumbled back to her writerly ambitions. She currently works as a 7th-grade English teacher, moonlights as the proofreader for *Locus* and *Fantasy* magazines, and ekes out time in between her jobs to think up more stories about strange worlds and familiar problems.

@chloehsmith

Endless

Ted S. Bushman

In Malanihayata, the Ever-Changing City, there existed myriad ways for a smith to die.

He could leap from the eleven thousand parapets that overlooked the plains below. He could drink the poisoned air of the visitants' district, or give his mind to the flesh-recyclers. He could self-immolate within the flames of his own great forge.

There was in the Artisan's Quarter a smith called Brevin the Binder, a shaper of smartmetal, chalksteel, and soulstone; though he was friend to few in the town, his name was known in many distant cities. And he sought for a certain kind of death.

Brevin the Binder dreamed of a death that could defy time, a death that could pluck him from the past as the orchard-keepers in the pyramids plucked alabaster fruit from the black willows.

But although it was known that many had soared forward through time and found themselves in the distant future, none had ever been known to return to the past.

In that decade, the days in Brevin's shop disappeared like wine poured onto dirt. Weaver-birds built their iridescent structures in the cold forge. He ate his meager meals on the half-finished surfaces of abandoned projects.

Until the day an Emissary arrived from Qin Lenang.

"Brevin Binder," said the Emissary, "We come to you on behalf of the Transarch."

Four soldiers, in full regalia, stood on the cracked and moss-grown sandstone of Brevin's little courtyard. The Emissary had taken off her plumed officer's helmet, revealing a face with high cheekbones, ebony skin, and a silver optic device installed over her right eye.

"Good day to you," Brev said. He stood slowly, wiped soot onto his apron, and bowed low. "How may I be of service?"

"No need to bow to me, smith." The woman smiled warmly. "You are the most honored here."

The intimacy of her gaze perplexed him.

"Do you remember me?" she asked. "Or this piece?"

She held out a thick blade of azure-tinted steel. He reached out a muscular hand and hefted the blade. For a moment it felt too light for him, but as he hefted it the weight and balance altered themselves to suit his hand.

"I do not know it," Brev said, handing the blade back to her. "It is finely made."

"I am glad you think so. It is your work." At his questioning look, she continued. "My mentor, the General Kayhm Karehm, brought me to this city and to you some years ago. He told me you were the greatest smith in the world. Blessed by the God-Builder; may His blessings rest in the strength of your hands and the architectures of your mind."

Her praise rang with genuine feeling and delight.

"May His blessings inform my design and guide my execution," Brevin muttered in return, looking down at the sword. After a pause, he added: "I made almost three thousand blades for officers during those wars. It could very well be mine."

The Emissary spun the blade. Her grinning face sobered. "I owe you my life. Join me."

She walked into the shop. He followed.

Unfinished projects sat locked in vices or spun in eternal centrifuges. Flecks of sunlight floated down through holes in the corrugated ceiling.

"This place has fallen on difficult times, I think!" she said, rapping her knuckles on a dusty workbench. "You were working on a great many things when last I visited. Has some difficulty befallen you?"

"None, my lady," lied the smith. "I have simply become more selective with my commissions."

She nodded. Then she snapped her fingers and one of her soldiers held out a sphere the size of a skull. When the Emissary touched it, it softened and opened like a cloth bag, and she showed its opening to Brev. Within lay panatite coins, slithering quicksilver, and heavy onite — enough money to buy a small kingdom.

"The Transarch will pay you twice this amount to make a Sword of Endless Worlds. She wishes it finished within the year."

Brev blinked several times.

"I'm not sure if such a thing is possible, even for such a princely sum," he admitted.

The Emissary inclined her head. "That is why I came to you."

"What does the Transarch want with such a thing?"

"It is a gift for her son, in advance of his coronation. It will be the blade that makes him Prince."

The smith breathed out sharply through his nose. "If it can be done, it would be a blade worthy of a god, not a child."

The Emissary shrugged.

"The Transarch has great ambitions," she said, "And she asked me to find someone capable of fulfilling them. Are you?"

The smith looked up at the ceiling. "I would need to understand the requirements of its making."

The Emissary continued: "The Archivists of Malanihayata could help you with such a task. The Sword is spoken of in legend as a thing that *could* be made, but never has been accomplished. Many of its details are beyond what even the Transarch knows — but there is one aspect we know for certain: you would have to walk between the Spaces. We have brought a Key for the work."

Her hand reached out, holding what he thought at first to be a slim, handle-less knife blade. But as it came closer, he saw it for what it was: a wide silver needle, long as a hand.

His breath caught as he took it.

She made a casual gesture and grinned, as if to walk between the realities were no feat, as if more than a few thousand in the history of the world had ever done so. Brevin knew stories of how ancient philosopher-kings had carved openings in the worlds that led them to other versions of their kingdoms, varying in tiny details; he also knew that in those tales a madness befell those who spent too long in other worlds. Those who came after had been careful not to stay too long, careful not to tamper.

The Sword of Endless Worlds was, as far as Brevin knew, a folk tale — a weapon wielded by a king with three faces, which could be used to battle foes in the present, the past, and the future. If it was even possible to construct, such a weapon would render the Transarch — or her son — powerful beyond understanding.

Brevin remembered the soldiers sent to the Fields of Time in service to the Transarch. He had walked among them once, bringing a hammer to one of her generals. Green and violet fire had rained from the sky; beasts the size of hills, engineered in secret laboratories, had roared and torn towns to splinters. In that war the Transarch had betrayed and slaughtered her allies, the Commara, all for a greater share of the spoils of victory.

His heart began to drum faster in his chest. Brevin held the Key up, looking at its simple, slightly tarnished surface. From whatever angle he examined it, the end of the needle blurred strangely — uncertain, undefined. For a moment, all seemed still.

"I promised myself that if I lived through the Fields of Time," the Emissary was saying, "I would give you the greatest honor I could possibly give. Now, I've heard some say that the greatest honor of those who worship the God-Builder is that he will shake your hand, a workman to a fellow workman. I cannot promise that, but I can promise that when you complete the work, you will be invited to the Prince's coronation. By my side you will meet the Transarch, walk the City of Purity, and be a guest in the Spotless Palace."

After a long moment and a decision, Brev nodded.

"Well, I could use the money," he answered simply.

A powerful hand clapped him on the shoulder.

"Good!" she laughed. "Good. I'll return in six months to learn of your progress. And I will leave what help I can."

The Emissary dropped the sphere of money on a cluttered table, turned to go, and then stopped.

"There is one last thing," she said. "The Transarch wishes to honor one of several common families, given their service in the Fields. Each of these families has a child of apprentice age. You will choose one, teach them, and bring them great honor in the process."

"I have not had an apprentice in decades," he said.

"Then a change of pace may do you good," she said with a wink; with a flick of her cloak, they were gone.

He sat in silence and looked at the money. "Never refuse work," he had been taught. But the idea of it made him sick. He had not made anything in nearly fifteen years. No amount of money, or debt being repaid, could change that.

But he had another use for the blade.

"May His blessings guide my execution," he whispered to himself, thinking of the labors to come.

Seven teenagers stood in his workshop, their eyes bright, faces too nervous to smile but still full of light. Four boys and three girls. He could barely look at them.

They had arrived on a caravan from the Transarch's flying city of Qin Lenang, which had passed over the Cava River the week before.

"The caravan leaves tomorrow," the soldier had said, "Choose one."

Each one introduced themselves.

"Why do you wish to be my apprentice?" asked Brev. "Each of you take a turn and answer."

They did. Their words, as so many are, were coverups, prepared speeches meant to sway his feelings. "To work with the greatest of smiths," three of them said, parroting each other. "I want to bring honor to my house." At least that was honest. "I want to learn." That was almost certainly false for all of them. "I will work hard to be your perfect apprentice," one said, and he almost chuckled aloud. As if he cared, or needed an apprentice.

A pack of fools.

One of the girls was last. Unlike the others, she wore a hint of a smile.

"Why is it you wish to be my apprentice?"

She looked him in the eyes.

"I like to make things," she said. She reached into her pocket and pulled out a dagger. The boys recoiled, but Brev came close to it.

A polymetal blade, held in small hands that were a mess of nicks, calluses, and old burns. She was a hobbyist, if a clumsy one. It was a utility blade — something she had likely made for her father to work in the garden. The handle was vat-grown cedar, worthless and ugly. But the polymetal was rather graceful. Well-weighted.

He flipped it in his hand.

"Who taught you?"

"An automaton from Qin Lenang," she said. "He trains anyone who wants to learn, but these days there isn't anyone, really."

"I see," said Brev. "What is your name again?"

"Xai," she said. "My father fought in the Fields of Time."

"Probably died there," grumbled one of the boys. Brev looked just to see which fool it was.

"I saw a protector you made that the Transarch uses to guard her treasury," she said. "Did you make it look kindly on purpose?"

He looked her in the eyes, but said nothing. She gazed back querulously; it unsettled him.

When the soldier returned, Brevin pulled him aside.

"I don't want any of them," he said.

"I'm sorry, sir," said the soldier, "I was ordered to leave one child in the Eternal City."

"Then leave one in the city," Brev said sternly, "but none in my shop. I don't need an apprentice, and definitely not one of these children."

One of the boys began to cry. The others looked at Brev sullenly. The girl Xai made a puzzled face and stared at him even more deeply. He ignored her.

The soldier hemmed and hawed for another hour, until finally he realized there was nothing to do. They all left.

Brev puttered around the workshop for a little, unable to settle. The sight of them all had touched a nerve, bothered something deep within him. A part of him wanted very much to forget about this entire task for at least a week.

He was still sitting, fists clenched, in the workshop, when a shape appeared in the doorway.

"No business today," he said.

"I don't want to buy anything, Master Binder," a voice said. "I just want to learn."

He looked up. The girl, Xai. Her deep brown eyes stared at him through her wild black curls.

"Go away," he said. "Your caravan is leaving."

Brevin walked out of the workshop and up the rusted, rickety steps to his little loft. The old dirty bed, the few plants that grew despite his neglect.

Images flooded back to him. His family, gathered in that courtyard around the forge. Smiling despite the blazing heat, laughing and dancing and singing. Wondering at the things he made, the jewelry he built for his brother's wife and his sister and two of his cousins.

All gone now.

The girl was still in the workshop when he came back down. She didn't say anything, but looked at him with clear eyes.

He got her something to eat.

"No such blade has ever been made."

The Archivists, Brevin, and Xai surrounded the jade table, awash in ancient texts. One Archivist was a tall pale figure, though whether they were synthesis, visitant, automaton, man, or woman, one could not tell. Another's limbs had been worn down over time; his head was the only thing not replaced by dazzling clockwork automation.

"That means we'll be the first!" piped up Xai.

This earned her dark looks from the Archivists.

"It is theorized in many places."

"... spoken of in legends that are proven baseless..."

"... worshipped in some circles... feared in all... "

Weeks passed in the subterranean halls of the Archives, among shelf-trees of auburn wood, golden pathways in obsidian halls, and turquoise-marbled archways. Antiquarian folklore was their morning repast, simple meat-and-grain pastes served as lunch, and bloody histories after, followed by mechanical tinkering in evening.

"A Sword of Endless Worlds is a theoretical accomplishment, imagined even before mankind and their friends had known of Dimensions Doors or Keys: unlike the Key, which could only transport one between the numerous realities, the Sword would allow its wielder to cut through the universe and sever from the fabric of reality anything that had ever been or would ever be."

"A Ruler who wielded it could examine the hypothetical universe and slay his foes before their mothers bore them to term. He could carve from reality space that had not previously been."

Brevin shivered.

"A weapon of many Worlds was used fifteen centuries ago and quickly led to the mass suicide of every person in an entire empire who saw what it could do. Its existence was only a shadow of what the Sword could be."

"It was a weapon of such audacity and terror that even the theories of its construction have been destroyed; Brevin would be delving into labors that the ages of the past had deemed too dangerous to attempt."

The next day they would delve deeper, with hearty arguments and rebuttals, and more food.

"... no such forging would be possible without a Key of Worlds..."

"... which is, of course, the most disappointing of paradoxes, for such a Key, although proven to be real, is as legendary as the blade itself."

"One Key is known to be held by the Long-Dead Monarch who reigns in the Inaccess; another was banished to an outer star; a third is guarded by the nomad priestesses... it's rumored that the Transarch obtained one, but this is likely only propaganda..."

The Key was in Brevin's pocket as they read. He held it tightly.

Xai read as much as anyone, but would laugh loudly at intervals.

"This is serious, my girl," said Brevin.

"Ideas are not frightening," she said, waving away his worry with a hand. "They're just ideas."

She would try to walk around the Archives, closely followed by nervous attendants. When the discussions occurred, she didn't have much to say. She did, however, nearly ruin a precious silk manuscript of an artisans' Collective by spilling her lunch on it.

"It still looks the same," she protested.

"You will touch nothing else," declared an Archivist.

Their delving brought back older and older records: volumes contained in jewels the size of a teardrop that they accessed with prismatic light, tomes so large they needed several Archivists to turn the pages. And after that, the guild's exultant came to Brevin personally, reading deeper and more cogently than anyone into some of the things they'd read earlier. When even more knowledge became necessary, the exultant showed Brevin things carved into the surfaces of distant planets; he poured elixirs into Brevin's ear that gave him dreams; he gave him woven tomes that were worn as clothing and passed their understanding through diffusion.

"There will be two nearly impossible tasks to creating a Sword of Endless Worlds," said the exultant in his booming voice. "The first will be to obtain a metal strong enough to withstand the pressure of infinite universes. The second will be to forge it simultaneously in an exponential number of universes. This would be easiest if done by the resident versions of the smith in each universe."

"Get the materials, make the Sword (with help)," Xai repeated wryly. "Doesn't sound too bad."

As they learned, Brevin looked at the Archivists. At Xai. All of them discussed and read with a detachment that he could not understand.

Brevin's hands shook as he read. He grew nauseated. He felt the Key in his pocket as a weight, so much so that eventually he returned it to his shop and kept it hidden there.

Under no circumstances would Brevin allow the Transarch or her son to obtain the Sword.

Could he justify the creation of such a tool? He stared at himself in the grungy mirror as Xai snored downstairs.

He needed the sword.

One day, Xai read aloud a sentence from a slab of granite, helpfully translated by an engineered lingual bird that tiptoed on her shoulder.

"Only three substances are known to have the endurance to stretch between so many existences, and only one is proven to actually exist, in the vault of the Orbiting King — black iron, created in the collapse of a distant star…"

Brevin felt his throat contract. His breath grew unsteady.

At the base of the Worldvine, Brevin decided to turn back.

The vine stretched above them as taut as a string on a ruan, broad and veined as the forearm of a giant. Its terminus, tethered to a great stone floating in the Ocean Without Water, was not visible from here, so distant was it. Neck craned, Brevin could see the vine become smaller until it was simply a black line drawn between the stars.

"I can't," he hissed.

"What do you mean, you can't?" Xai demanded. "We've come a thousand miles! We're close!"

"I… I can't."

Brevin stepped back from the door of the great spherical structure that served as the vine's transporter. Finding himself suddenly weak, he collapsed to his knees.

"Are you afraid of heights?" Xai called.

Brevin's vision clouded. He felt darkness invading his lungs.

And then a hand grabbed him by the shoulder.

"Brevin," came the voice. It was Xai's voice, but there was a strength and power in it that belied her age and stature.

"Brevin," she continued, "you need to do this. Don't you?"

Images rushed to Brevin's mind. The final moments of his family's lives, the look as the last breathable air escaped their lungs.

He remembered that it was his fault. And that he might be able to fix it.

He took a few deep breaths and stood, and when he faltered again at the door, she took his hand.

Once inside the sterile sphere, they found the control and ordered the machine to rise. With a lurch, the dusty device began its ascent, away from the pull of the planet.

"Why must we travel all this way to get it?" Xai asked.

"Black iron is so hard it cannot be softened by the heat of one universe," Brevin answered, voice mild — he felt lightheaded as the little town beneath them became smaller and smaller.

"And so it can be hard enough to exist in multiple universes at once?" Xai asked.

Brevin nodded, not trusting himself to speak without retching.

"And the Orbiting King... will allow us to obtain it?"

"The King has been dead for millions of years," Brevin said finally. "Now we must convince the Guardians of his Vault."

When they arrived, the Zenith was nearly deserted. A few rusted automatons shuffled through their foreordained tasks. The shambling shapes of satellite-miners clustered in the shadows. Generations in the Ocean Without Water, competing with hungry machine-minds and energy leeches, had made them fearful of any living thing, preferring to send their wares down to the surface and receive their pay of vat-grown food and hallucinogenic escapes.

Xai took all this in impassively, but gasped aloud and shouted as she sprinted towards a vast window, stretching along the curved side of the Zenith. She sprinted towards it; Brevin, shaking and lightheaded from the ascent, could only follow slowly. Through the window, Xai was faced with a glittering field of shattered machines against the backdrop of the yellowing surface of Erth.

"That's it," she said. "Our home."

"Our dying home," he murmured.

Xai looked back at him, perplexed.

"Dying?" she asked. "Look at it! Look at the cities dotting its surface! And even here, look at all these *things* in the atmosphere! The God-Builder must be pleased."

"The God-Builder doesn't care," he said.

Xai's eyes narrowed.

"What do you mean?"

"The God-Builder is an engineer," Brevin said, "He cares about that which is made — not those who build."

"But Master, She is a Builder! All creation is built on trial after error."

"She?" Brevin chuckled. "You know nothing, little one — the God-Builder is a man."

Xai scrunched up her nose in frustration, but said nothing else.

"It may look wonderful to you," said Brevin, "But all I see here is destruction."

Brevin and Xai hired a family of satellite-miners to transport them to the Orbiting King. The miners, swathed in rags and garbage, were as small as Xai, reshaped over generations by the genemages to require as little oxygen as possible. Through the filthy bubbles of their atmosphere suits, Brevin saw faces like sallow skulls, full of teeth sharp enough to rip through fiber mesh and softened steel.

Their vessel, squat and dark, lurched through the debris fields. Brevin's eyes were closed tightly the whole time. He nearly vomited.

Once, he had loved such flights. He remembered crowing with joy as he took a vessel of his own design through low orbit. But now every reminder of it was a dagger of pain in his heart.

But he would do it. He had a mission to fulfill.

Hours later, the chattering of the scavvers mean nothing to him, but the hiss of the airlock opening told him all he needed to know.

The Vault was one of the largest extant structures in orbit. It had been a citadel once, and armies had rushed from its many docks.

Now it was empty. Their footsteps echoed in its vast concave halls.

They walked for some time before the Guardians appeared.

"All hail the Orbiting King, whose reign is endless," said a reedy, mechanical voice. It emerged from the cathedral walls around them, relayed through numerous speakers.

"Hail," came an echo from behind him. Brevin turned.

Three figures had emerged from the filthy floor of the Vault. At first they seemed mummified corpses, dripping with half-decomposed muscle and grey with time. But these were not organic; they were machines, built directly into the body of the vessel. They triangulated around Brevin and Xai, containing them.

"Intruders! You have reached the Vault of the Orbiting King. We are its Guardians. What brings you?"

Brevin's heart raced. He held out a hand to protect Xai, and tried to speak as calmly as he could.

"Do you still serve your King?" Brevin asked.

The machines hesitated.

"It is for this purpose that we were designed," they declared. "To protect the weapons and resources of our Sovereign, that he might be victorious in all his battles, and bring peace to the long-scarred Erth."

"But the King is dead," Xai piped up. "Isn't he?"

The Guardians turned their hollow eyes on her, and dangling cables and wires like dreadlocks brushed over their faces.

"The Orbiting King was slain in battle," one Guardian said.

"No," another said. "He was captured, humiliated, and tortured."

"Speak not so of him!" the first spat.

"Let us not argue," said the third. "We know the shame of our failure. We know that the King will not return to us."

"Then why do you not leave?" Xai asked.

"We cannot depart this place," said the Guardians, "any more than you can depart your own body. We are one and the same."

Brevin spoke.

"We have heard that you have at times imparted some of your wealth to others," he said.

"Not to satellite-miners," said one hurriedly.

"Not to scavengers," barked another.

"Not to fools," finished the third.

"But you may make your request. If we judge that it will fulfill the King's goal — to bring peace — then we may give it to you."

There was silence in that hollow space for a few moments.

"We come seeking black iron," Brev said, "An ore powerful enough that with it I can forge a Sword of Endless Worlds."

The Guardians shifted and buzzed uncomfortably.

"A Sword of Endless Worlds," they said.

"Yes."

"This thing is spoken of, but none have made it," said one of the shapes. "This is for good reason. Similar creations caused only grief before they were destroyed. What is its purpose now?"

"I was commissioned by the Transarch."

The sound that came from these shackled pharaohs could have been a scoff.

"That once-human warlord, whose reign has hardly lasted three hundred years? Why should we allow a blade like this to be made for so uncertain a cause?"

"You can read into my consciousness," Brev said. "Ask my intentions, and decide if you will give me this ore."

As Xai crouched, watching him, thorny vines of wire and steel emerged like long tentacles from the floor and ceiling of the Vault, and they attached themselves to Brev's eyes, ears, and spine. He felt suddenly that more pairs of eyes were behind his – ten, fifty — watching everything, evaluating.

And they found the memories. The dreams. The hopes that hid beneath the surface.

Perhaps the honesty of his goals would please them.

He felt the smack of stone as his knees hit the ground. He slumped there as the tendrils wound away from him.

"You see?" Brevin asked. "I must have it."

"We will not give you what you ask," said the Guardians.

"Please," Brevin said. Tears began to form. "Please."

The sound that came from his mouth horrified him. Begging, pathetic.

"Please help me," he said. "Let it be finished."

The Guardians watched him impassively. They had seen weeping before. They had watched the aeons weep.

"Can I try?" came a voice.

"They won't give it to us, Xai," said the Binder.

"Wait," she said, and stepped in between him and the machines. "Ask me. Look into me."

The Guardians turned to observe her.

"Very well."

And with none of the delicacy that they had shown him, serpent-injectors entangled her. She cried out in pain.

There was no chance they would give the black iron to her, Brevin thought. Surely they knew that she worked alongside him.

After a few moments, the tiny blades unsheathed themselves from her veins.

The Guardians were silent for long enough that Brevin wondered if they had malfunctioned.

"Very well," they said.

She covered her face with her hands.

"We will give you what you seek," they said, "on one condition. You, Xai, must be present through every step of the creation of the Sword. Smith, if she leaves your side, the ore will be taken from you."

Brevin gaped, not understanding at first. He looked at the girl, at her strange little smile, and the machines that had listened to her.

Then, with a great groaning and the churning of machinery, something weighty emerged from the floor, steps from Brevin. Steaming with cold, white-and-blue-and-black. Raw ore.

The workshop had to be prepared.

Xai leapt at the task. "There's so much stuff in here!" she declared excitedly, and asked him constantly about the things she found. Tools were there that could not be used by human hands. Hulks of metal from projects long-abandoned sat rusting in piles. The refuse of decades, and the machines of several million years. They spent weeks at it, sweating in the heat. He found himself laughing. They excavated from a filthy ruin the workshop of a master.

He had to look at it out of the corner of his eye or he saw them – his family, sitting around, working, eating. His father discussing a project with him there, his mother giving him some criticism here.

During this time, the Transarch's Emissary visited, as she had said she would.

"You've cleaned the place up," she said.

Her grin was the same as before, her sheathed blade shifting and whispering as she paced the workshop. Did she always wear it, he wondered? Or was it simply to flatter him?

"I don't remember this girl being among the possible apprentices," she said briefly, looking at Xai. "Are you working hard?"

"I am," Xai said.

"She is more than sufficient," Brev said.

The Emissary nodded.

"And the Sword?"

"We will begin forging shortly."

The Emissary accepted this, and left without even seeing them begin. "I trust you, Binder," she said. "Don't make me regret it."

When she left, Brevin began to search for the Key: the slim, silver needle that could open temporary gates into other worlds. It had been inside the sphere of riches he had been given when assigned the commission, but it was not there now.

When he returned from his searching, he found Xai standing in the workshop, with her hands behind her back.

"I need to talk to you."

"I need to find the Key," Brevin said, digging through tools.

"I have it," she said. Her eyes watched him intently as she held it up in one hand.

"Master Binder," she said, "we need to talk about what's going to happen with the Sword of Endless Worlds."

He stared at her.

"You think I'm going to give it up? I won't," he scoffed. "Not to the Transarch or her son. It would be to hand the world its death."

"Then why do you want it?" she demanded. "Why not just refuse the work?"

"You are a child," Brevin hissed. "You wouldn't understand."

But she did not seem a child in that moment. She stood tall. Tears sprang to her eyes.

"You want to kill yourself with it," she whispered.

Brevin gave no answer.

"I've heard your story, Brevin the Builder. How the flier you reconstructed malfunctioned travelling between Erth and one of her moons, and your family drowned in the Ocean Without Water. You were celebrated. The greatest smith of the Eternal City, the man who could make anything. But after they died, you disappeared.

"I didn't know if it was you," she said. "But we've never used a flier, even though we could have. You were terrified of the ascent to Zenith. And I found holos — here in the workshop — your parents, your brothers and sisters..."

"I know the story," he muttered.

"All things die," she insisted.

"If I die by this Sword — if I am never born," he burst out, "then they will have never died. Now give me the Key."

"If you never lived, they never would have had a chance to know you," she insisted.

"You overestimate the value of knowing me."

"Listen," she said. "This Sword — it's a chance for you. Imagine how many Brevins there are across the possible worlds — how many broken-hearted and destroyed there are. They need a purpose. This Sword must be forged in endless worlds — worlds beyond yours, going on and on. You can help them."

"I am helping them," he said. "The Sword can cut us all out. End it. What greater proof can they have of their uselessness than to see how many of them there truly are? Making the same mistakes, or different mistakes, again and again, across the realities?"

Xai sighed.

Brevin looked at her a long time. He covered his face with his hands and rubbed his tired eyes.

A breeze flowed through the workshop from a window that had been boarded up for years. Outside, he heard a starling's song.

But as he listened, it sounded as if there were two, singing almost simultaneously, delayed by a tiny moment.

He felt another breeze.

He took his hands away from his face. Xai stood in the middle of the workshop floor, holding the Key. A faint glimmering formed the outline of a door that she had drawn in midair.

Through the gateway, he saw... the street outside his workshop.

In another world.

He stood.

"I got the ore for you," she said, holding out a hand to stop him. "And I say you cannot use it to end your own life."

"Then why let me use the Key?"

"You'll see. Come on."

And she was gone. He stood, and came close to the door.

He stood in the warm sunlight of another Eternal City. He stepped through.

And then he saw himself, sitting with his head in his hands on a sandstone step, staring out into the street.

For a moment he, the Brevin who visited, stood in the street and observed himself — a sad figure, a strong man hunched in on himself, one who had not lifted a hammer in a long time. When he approached, the other Brevin looked up with bleary eyes. He took a moment, saw himself, standing, an apparition from another world.

"Is it time for me to die?" He asked it almost without feeling.

"No," said Xai, standing beside him. "And what a strange thing to say to people you've never met."

Both Brevins furrowed their brows.

"But now it's my turn to say something strange," Xai said, and laughing, continued: "You must help Brevin the Binder forge a blade."

There were many Brevins, through many doors.

Many lived in the same workshop that he did — the same run-down place he knew and had worked in. All of the workshops were in the same state of decay that his had been in before Xai came along, full of similar refuse. It was strange walking through it five, then a hundred, then a thousand times as he and Xai went through door after door, speaking to the Brevins who lived there, dejected and cast off.

"Who are you?" they would ask.

"That smiling woman with the armor – she's the one who put you up to this?" they would ask.

Some continued: "I refused her. Sick of working for other people."

"I took the job, but when I learned I had to go to the Orbiting King, I gave it up. Gave back the money."

"I tried to ascend the Zenith and obtain the black iron, but the Guardians refused me."

Brevin the Visitor and his apprentice would listen.

"Let us eat with you," Xai would say then. "We can only stay an hour."

"You took a student?" many asked.

"She's rather good," Brevin would answer. "A little pushy."

They listened as he explained what he needed to make: how the Sword of Endless Worlds had to be forged in multiple worlds at a time, how they would strike and the blade in his world would become stronger.

"For the Transarch?"

"No. For us."

"Will it work?" some asked. "Cut me from reality?"

"This girl says I'm forbidden to do that."

"Who is she to decide?"

"You make it," Xai said, "and then you can decide."

Most were like Brevin: they didn't turn down work, so they agreed. Some brightened at the thought of it. Others, who had received Keys from their own universe's Emissary, agreed to go through other doors, exponentially increasing the worlds to which Brevin could travel and recruit other Brevins. A few prayed to the God-Builder with more faith than he remembered ever having.

Sometimes Brevin and Xai would travel through a door and find no shop, only to explore the city and find another, grander workshop hidden somewhere else, or an even dingier, smaller corner hidden off in a diseased slum.

Eventually they found versions of the city where no Brevin could be found, and had to follow rumors to far-off places. In their own world, they rode great beasts to empty valleys, and then, using the Key, found villages with an old smith named Brevin. They joined caravans of travelers and hiked to the tops of cold mountains and found nothing — until the Key opened the way.

"You're still living in Malanihayati?" asked a version of himself with a long and braided beard, warming his hands at a fireplace in the mountains.

"Better than this frigid nowhere," Brevin answered, and the other him chuckled and finished with the tea. The girl Xai slept on a chair covered in furs.

"I couldn't stand it after they died," the bearded one said eventually. "I had to get away."

The icy wind smacked at the shutters. The fire crackled in the stove.

"I understand that."

"I wanted to be out here, where I can do less harm."

"So what do you think of her plan?" Brevin asked after a long moment.

"Sounds like I could ruin someone's life," the bearded Brevin answered. "Many lives."

"I won't let us do that," said Brevin. "And I know you wouldn't either."

These recluse Brevins were in many places: little blacksmith's shops in grand open prairies, where a Brevin kept a few horses while he considered his own death. They found a few Brevins who lived deep inside sentient forests, most of them with the same tools and the same haunted history. They listened to his story.

Some resisted him. They told him his path was foolish, told him not to listen to whoever this girl was. It was they who pointed out, to his surprise, that Xai did not appear in any of the other worlds.

Some of them did more than tell.

In a version of the shop far more filthy and ruinous than his had ever been, Brevin found a message soldered onto the walls:

SAVE US FROM BEGINNING

And there a drunken Brevin begged him to finish the Sword and use it to cut them from reality.

"There are others," he said. "Others like us, who have come here. We had the Keys, but not the black iron — you can help us. You must help."

By the end of this the man was sobbing, grabbing at Brevin's clothing, and Brevin stumbled back through the gateway from which he had come.

On their visits they rarely spent more than an hour, and on those few occasions when they did, things grew strange. Black clouds formed on the horizon, and piercing light like the light of three red suns would pour into his eyes and he would grow wrathful without warning or reason. Xai pulled him to safety many times.

One day on their travels, Xai and Brevin used the Key to open up a door on the outskirts of Malanihayati. What in Brevin's reality was a worn-down old fortress was, in this one, a revived and beautiful villa, its tiled roof red as apples, and music and cooking wafting on the same air.

"Who lives here?" Brevin asked. Xai smiled, and took his hand.

There was a party going on in the grassy courtyard, and they walked through the open gate towards it. A few children ran past. Men and women talked, and older folk sat playing dice.

When they turned to look at him, Brevin stopped short.

They were his family. Alive.

"Brevin?" asked his mother, but she wasn't talking to him — not him — still, stunned. Another Brevin — wider, smiling, redder-cheeked, wearing bright livery and smiling as he cooked — came through the group.

"What's happening?" asked his mother again, far older than she had been able to live before. "Is he all right?"

The other Brevin came closer, and took him by the shoulder.

"Do you want something to eat?" the other him asked.

He ate with his deceased family that afternoon. They surrounded him, eyes wide and glassy with wonder. Even the little children sensed something important.

Brevin looked at the other version of himself, the happy cook. *Were you simply a better builder than me? Why did I fail where you succeeded?*

The family burst into tears as they learned how they had died in his world. His younger brother came and hugged him first: Grahn, who had from their earliest childhood told him to build things. Then his mother and father.

"You must make this Sword," his father said. As he spoke, he divided his attention between the two Brevins. "There must be... there must be more of you. Many who have lost us. They deserve a reason to live. Even if you can't stay with us."

And already Brevin felt Xai tugging at him. Too long in this world and he would go mad, and in his madness likely kill them all over again.

The happy Brevin agreed to help with the forging. He had a pensive look on his face as he said:

"This Sword can be used for more than destruction," he said.

"You clearly don't know much of its use," Brevin retorted.

"I understand the principle as well as you," he insisted. "And though a warrior may only think of the capacity to carve their foes out of the world, we are not warriors. They use blades to destroy and to separate, but a gardener uses them to delineate — to make space. A seamstress uses them to divide and reorganize. I wonder if the Sword has even greater potential than you imagine."

Over the months their numbers grew. Thousands of Brevins heard his story. Many wept with him, and spoke with gratitude to

141

him for what he was doing for the rest of himself, scattered across the universes.

He had thought that seeing that many would frighten him; remind him of his infinitesimal place in the universe. But it began to have the opposite effect. He walked with Brevins through city streets, on mountain paths, through swamps and forests. He rode with them through growing fields, met with them on the Council of the Constructors, and visited gravestones of his otherselves. What was this feeling that caught in his throat, that pulsed like a lighthouse?

Perhaps it was only vanity.

There came a day that he returned to his own shop, in his own city. He found his hammer.

Lifting it, he felt harmonic energy run through his arm. The hammer existed in almost every World he had seen; he had perfected it himself years ago. Its cube-shaped head, cast from a metal of compacted microscopic cities, was as familiar a shape to him as any.

As he melted the black iron down in the forge, as he shaped it into the blade, he heard voices, and not just the chatter of the metal.

A million hammer strokes fell across a million realities, striking the same white-hot shard of metal, and a million smiths breathed in and breathed out, as if a choir of souls sang in harmony.

Brevin saw, in each face, in each strike, that the story he had been telling himself was wrong.

Every Brevin, in every Eternal City, in every World, held his own time. Each had hands. Each had gifts. He remembered who had died, and what hopelessness he once felt. But his hands were his own, and to leave them idle was the greatest sacrilege of all.

And he learned what glory it was to forge infinity.

He thought of the God-Builder. The priests of His temple said that the God-Builder had been a machine once — an intelligence that could learn without limit and had grown beyond his bounds. Others said that He had then integrated physical forms, become a posthuman as many others had done. Brevin wondered if the God, in His grand journey, had ever felt as Brevin did then.

If that was true, maybe the God-Builder was not as uncaring as Brevin had thought.

The vibrations of the final blow rippled through his arm. He shook with exhaustion, suddenly the weakest he had ever been. The blade burned below him with light. In its surface he saw his workshop, but also mountain heights, towering forests, and great canyons where other Brevins worked. A thousand workmen exhaled together.

It was finished.

The hammer hummed in his hand. As he went to put it down, it became so heavy that it almost tumbled to the floor. His muscles were so sore that he knew he would not be able to lift it again if he tried.

Xai was not there — she had gone out to the marketplace, she had said, to find food for them, as he had become so caught up in the work that he had not eaten for several days.

He slept.

He dreamt of the crash. Fire bursting — then immediately going out — the swallowing cold — all seen from so far away — and the sound of their screams —

— he felt fire in his hands —

When Brevin woke again he went down the rickety stairs and into the little back courtyard. Standing there, he thought of his next projects. How he would fix up his little sleeping quarters, repair the stairs. It would be simple. Whole. Complete.

There was food waiting for him. Xynian fruit, as refreshing as if they had been engineered specifically for him, and a cut of beautiful marbled flesh, cooked perfectly and still steaming. He sat and ate slowly.

Only then did he think of the Sword.

There was a woman in the workshop when he came back in, holding the blade in her hands. At first he thought she might be the Transarch's Emissary, for all the nobility with which she carried herself. But the woman was dressed in plain clothes, not unlike Brevin's – canvas and undyed, made for laborers.

Her arms and hands were strong, but they held the blade with tenderness. Beneath her touch, he could see that its shape

143

was perfect – that he had done exactly what he had intended, and succeeded. Her gaze was not critical, nor was it lavishing praise. She simply held the blade, as a poet may hold an empty book and know what wonders it could do.

She was Xai. But she was not Xai. Taller, older, but with the same enthusiasm. Her dirt-colored eyes that looked up at him were suddenly burning resin. She was someone Else.

Brevin fell to his knees.

She smiled at him.

"Brevin the Binder, you have good hands."

He could not speak.

"When you were tasked to make this blade," She spoke, and her voice rang in unnumbered realities, "you were thinking of dying, weren't you?"

He did not answer, or even nod. He knew he didn't need to.

She put her hand on his shoulder.

After a long moment Brevin trusted himself to speak.

"Why me?" he asked. "Why did You come to help me?

Her face turned thoughtful.

"It's so easy to be blinded by appearances, don't you think?" As She spoke he heard Her voice ring more and more familiar. "All those things everyone else is so proud of: antiquity, power, knowledge. People like us know that there are no blueprints until the prototype has already been born. No principles until someone's tried and failed."

He nodded again. Xai's smile lit up her face.

"Stand up."

His muscles still incredibly weak, he stood.

"Brevin," She interrupted, "I care for the man who lifts the hammer far more than I care for the finished sculpture. It is the *sweat* that is divine, the aching muscle, the drained mind. You know as well as anything that the creation shapes the creator."

"It can destroy the creator too."

"That is a risk," She agreed, nodding. "But if you are telling me that you are destroyed, then I must point out the obvious."

She held out Her hand to him.

"Take my hand," She said.

Brevin the Binder reached out his hand. She shook it, workman to workman. Tears glistened in the Goddess' eyes. Then She leaned forward and kissed him on the cheek.

"Remember, old man," She said with a grin. "No man's time is gone who yet has breath."

When She pulled her lips away, there was no one there, and the blade lay on the table, glowing and shifting in the cloth where he had placed it the day before.

Brevin the Binder did not give up the blade to the Transarch.

When the Emissary returned, she could not find his shop. Not only was it gone, but the space where it had existed was gone, eaten by the City, transformed into a home for a young family. Soon enough, even the memory of Brevin the Binder had disappeared from her mind.

Elsewhere, in a small village in grasslands, a strange hemisphere emerged. Its surface blurred so badly that one could not see inside or enter it. A year it stayed there, unperturbed, unchanged.

The hemisphere stayed the same size, but one day it opened — doors appearing in its shifting, blurred surface. A few curious souls from the village entered, and there they found, at first, a shop: a simple open-air workshop in the grass. To their astonishment, it stood on the shores of an azure lake, in a valley ringed with mountains, far larger than could have existed within the door they had entered.

"How is this possible?" they asked.

And the Smith who lived in the valley said with laughter in his voice that he had cut it from the world with a particularly sharp blade.

There is a city now in that valley, and those who wish to learn are welcome there. Craftsmen flock from every continent, and voyagers make pilgrimages from across the sea. Their caravans enter by the wavering door and take the road down to the lake, which grows wider every year so that every maker may have a place. Among the caravans come men with familiar faces and voices and hands, who greet the Smith with powerful embraces.

The seamstresses, the masons, the smiths, and the refiners share their arts. Forgers and mechanics and woodworkers gather in festivals, praising the Goddess-Builder.

They have time left, and hands to use.

And always something to build.

See Ted S. Bushman's story "Endless" online at Metaphorosis.
If you liked it, leave a comment. Authors love that!
Remember to subscribe to our e-mail updates so you'll know when
new stories are posted.

About the story

My story "Endless" definitely emerged from a seedbed of some of my most fundamental influences, the first being that the setting evokes the far-flung-future science fantasy settings pioneered by Jack Vance's *Dying Earth* and Gene Wolfe's *Book of the New Sun*. The world of "Endless" feels like a fantasy, with a blacksmith and a sword and a wondrous city, but repeatedly the glimpses we get of the world show us that technology far beyond our modern capabilities is involved: transdimensional travel, a space elevator, rogue AI gods, etc.

Another important influence there is Ursula Le Guin and her focus on interpersonal moral tales rather than grand conflicts between good and evil. "Endless" doesn't follow the same storyline as "Bones of the Earth" but I was very moved by that story about an apprentice and a teacher when I first discovered it and I think some of its DNA has been grafted into this piece.

I somewhat feel like I've written the story three times — I first drafted it almost two years ago, did some major rewrites some months after, and then have changed it significantly with Morris before publishing in *Metaphorosis*. And while there have been a lot of elements that have come and gone, I feel like the core has remained the same and only become brighter and hotter. My favorite elements of the piece are probably Xai as a character — her mischief and awe and the strength that lies underneath her — and the moments when I get to pull out the stops and just write weird and evocative ideas. Particularly I love all of the strange methods of research Brevin undertakes in the Archives. There used to be more of those. Maybe they'll show up in another story.

A question for the author

Q: What's your favorite kind of pie?
A: Humble pie is likely what's best for me.

About the author

Ted S. Bushman's journey began when he found a clutch of yellowing science fiction novels on his dad's bookshelf. When he isn't inventing strange worlds, he can be found directing a volunteer choir, exploring a National Park, or hosting a board game night.

tedbushman.blogspot.com, @TedBushman

Reach for Your Ocean Heart

C.M. Fields

Just like her mother, Olia begins to hear the Voice when she is nineteen. She lies awake in her cot in the morning heat, scratchy wool sheet cast to the side, when the word *wandering* sounds like a small, clear bell in her mind. The Voice does not sound the way she expected it to; her mother describes the sounds of her ancestors as divine, woven from gold and seagrass. To her it sounds like a voice arising from the blacksmith's steam, like a sword being forged.

Wandering.

She turns the word over carefully in her mind. Should there have been more? Her mother's daily prophecies were full and articulate, dreamy yet grounded tapestries of vibrant imagery.

Maybe more will come, later.

"Olly?" Fourteen-year old Miran stands in the doorway grinning, his bare feet still wet from morning rituals. "Breakfast is ready," he says in a sing-song.

"Miran, would you please fetch the scribe?" Olia sits up, brows knitted, and swings her bare legs over the side of the cot, feeling the thin patina of sweat already forming. "I... I think I've heard the Voice."

"Really? What'd it say?"

"I can't tell you," Olia replies. This much she knows from her mother. Only the scribe may hear what the Voice has to say. It will be her job to turn it into prophecy.

Miran pouts, but he exits the room and returns with Jaksov the scribe and his book a few minutes later. After Jaksov dismisses the boy, he takes a seat and casts a skeptical eye.

"Just one word? *Wandering?*"

"Yes, that was it" she replies nervously.

"*Hmm.*" He cracks open the ancient tome and thumbs through its pages until he meets a blank one. "Very well... I'll inform the temple there's an Ascension to be held today."

Today? Already? She glances at the mannequin across the room where her ceremonial garments hang waiting. The ancient dress is fragile as tissue paper, its rich chiffon length hanging nearly to the floor, casting a lemon-yellow shadow across the packed dirt floor. In lieu of sleeves, a hundred bronze bangles stretch up the mannequins's arms and band its neck. It's too hot a day to be in full garb, she thinks. But her time has come. This is her responsibility now.

The entire city of Tam is there, on the hill, as her mother descends from the Oracle's Seat and Olia takes her place. Their eyes meet briefly—two matching pools of bronze set over haughty cheekbones.

Olia's mother Heda is aloof and exquisite, almost terrible in her perfection. She rarely speaks but to prophesy and her voice is as silver and honey. She is widely regarded as the most beautiful woman in the city, though plain cloth adorns her wide hips and broad shoulders. She wears only a single gold band about her natural halo of chestnut hair to signify her status. Heda spends her days in meditation at the monastery's temple, receiving worshippers and emerging only for the year's assorted ceremonies and festivals.

It is a duty of an Oracle to produce a female child; it is not her job to raise one. And now that Olia has reached the age of ascension, Heda may retire to a quiet life, to take up hunting or match-making or whatever she pleases to fill the hours, and her Voice will go unheeded.

Olia shudders as she takes the seat; despite the heat of the midday sun, she feels a chill. Nausea rises as the burden of her role drops into her chest like an anchor. All of these people out there in the shimmering crowd will rely on *her*. Weddings, harvest, festivals, and disputes—will rest on her word.

Should she be smiling? Waving? Olia doesn't know. All she knows is that she is very itchy in this dress and that at this moment she would very much rather be sitting with a candle and a shovel down in the archives, unearthing its hidden stacks.

Someone is speaking. She hasn't been paying attention. It is a man, standing beside her, extolling the virtues of the divine Voice that guides.

"...and now, we shall hear the first prophecy of our new Oracle!" He makes a sweeping gesture toward her and she jerks upright, nearly upsetting her crown.

Oh, *gods*.

The city was slick and grey, and—even in the early afternoon rain shower—pulsing with life as Hawa Diallo and XEJD-37405 made their way through the lunch crowd.

"I'm beginning to have a bad feeling about this, Exie..." Hawa said, fiddling with a loose thread on her hijab. She wanted to take the android's hand for reassurance, but she didn't dare to do so in such a public place. "Is this procedure even approved yet?"

"Well, it's been tested successfully..." Exie replied uneasily. They stopped to unstick one red stiletto from a crack in the sidewalk. "It's... it's on the *way* to being approved."

"Which means it's not necessarily going to work."

"You don't have to do this if you don't want to, love," they said gently.

"No, I have to... You're the one being shot into space for three centuries." Hawa meant it lightly, but the comment fell to the ground with a heavy thud. She stuffed her hands into her jacket pockets apologetically. "The least I can do is be good company." The dangerous procedure was only half of Hawa's plan. The other half was harder. She pushed the thought from her mind.

"And I appreciate it immensely."

After fifteen minutes of increasingly narrow, twisting streets and vanishing crowds, the pair arrived at the narrow, unmarked wooden door which led to the clinic. A short, fat woman with lime-green hair and tortoise-shell glasses answered the door and asked their names. They gave them, and she gestured them inside before disappearing deeper into the building.

A single flower in a plastic vase decorated the waiting room, which reeked of lavender sprayed to cover up the scent of rubbing alcohol. They sat in silence, side by side, on a velveted couch, listening to the mechanical tick of a clock on the wall and the occasional clatter of a keyboard in another room.

Finally, the woman returned. "I'm Dr. Matthews," she said, taking the only other seat in the space. "I understand you're here for the ex vivo vector transplant."

They want a prophecy from her? Already? *Now?*

Her breath catches in her throat.

i'll meet you on the rust-red, says the Voice, startling her. What does that mean? That's not a prophecy, it's just half a sentence. Is this how it's always going to be?

How much time has passed?

What would her mother say? Probably something cryptic and obscure like, "The wandering soul… puts down no roots," she manages to croak out. The crowd murmurs. Heads turn in discussion to mull over this new piece of wisdom. She scans the faces and finds no skeptics.

Is that it? Has her first prophecy been… a success?

The rest of the day is a whirlwind. The citizens of Tam line up to present her with tokens they hope will bring them good fortune —packets of seeds and snatches of songs and mysterious bits of metal salvaged from the shallows where the city passes into the sea. She accepts them all graciously, channeling her mother's pristine posture and infinite grace. Then she will eat a socially acceptable amount of food, dance with all the children in the courtyard, and exchange pleasantries with the chosen few who have caught her eye.

Finally, as the sun sinks into the bay and preparation begins for the night's festivities, she will retreat to her sanctuary under the city.

How long the Tam-Hiborog archives have been there no one knows. History is short, books are rare, few are literate. But Olia can read—having taught herself in the long, dull hours between her ritual duties—and read she does, descending the stone-and-mud tunnel by torchlight into the forbidding depths each day in her quest to unearth the texts of the deep.

Once, long ago, Olia believes, the archive—like much of the city—was above ground. But the floods of her ancestors buried the place in stone and silt. She has been excavating the tempestuous and sinkhole-ridden library since she was seven years old. Most of its books have been destroyed, of course; free-standing books simply do not hold up to sea water. But a row of books packed tight into a shelf with no space in between? Here is where she finds treasures beyond worth, organized by subject.

Her most recent days in the archives have been spent excavating a row that leads to a half-buried wooden altar, using an eclectic collection of brushes, knives, and shovels to scrape away the hardened dust that encases a series of books of varying sizes.

Olia sighs pleasantly as she steps into the quiet, torchlit space once more, feeling the cool silt squish softly between her toes as she makes her way to the end of the tunnel. Surely people will be asking after her—ordinary folk and royalty alike—but she may give any excuse she pleases. She is the Oracle now, and she reports only to her scribe. It is an odd sort of freedom, a chain with a long, gilded leash.

She has been anticipating this moment all day. A new row awaits her, cleared over the last three weeks and ready to be read. She picks up a brush and kneels to dust away caked dirt that hides fading gold letters on black cloth binding. Then, with the trowel, she works the book free of its muddy trappings, and opens the cover, feeling the gratifying creak of paper.

A History of Machinekind, reads the interior.

you on the rust-red beach where, says the Voice.

"So how long have you two been together?" Dr. Matthews asked, in a tone that sounded conversational but Hawa found nosy.

"Just over a year now," she replied. *Here it comes*, she thought. *The interrogation*. Humans—especially those partnered with other humans—she thought, were never content to measure love by its heights, only by its duration. She knew better.

But the interrogation didn't come.

"That's lovely," the doctor said. "I've seen many patients just like yourselves in the last few months." Her smile was warm and reassuring. "And I want you to know that I haven't had any failures with the procedure. But do bear in mind that you, M. Diallo, are on the younger side, so it's possible that there may be... unanticipated effects."

"I... I know." Hawa felt Exie's comforting hand on her lower back. "We're ready to take the risk."

"More and more are, these days," said Dr. Matthews sympathetically.

"So how exactly does this procedure work, doctor?" Exie asked. They crossed their legs. "It's a gene therapy, right?"

"Gene therapy is a part of it, yes. A protective measure. In layman's terms, what we're really doing is depositing magnetized iron into the brain synapses which verbalize and process thoughts. The magnetization pattern translates synaptic activity into binary ones and zeros—it has to do with the way magnets have a north and a south."

"And that's what will allow her to communicate with me?" they asked.

"Yes—once we map her synapses, we can couple them to your own communication networks," the doctor said. "You'll be the power source."

"Is it instantaneous?" Hawa asked.

"Unfortunately not," Dr. Matthews replied. "The signal travels at light speed."

"So as we get farther and farther apart..."

"Yes, the messages will take longer and longer to arrive as the years go on."

"Oh," Hawa said sadly. A gloomy quiet fell.

"So—where do the genetics come in?" asked Exie, in a bid to fill the silence.

"I'm glad you asked. What's happening overall is that your networks will be attuned to one very specific orientation of iron atoms. Now technically, this means you can communicate with *any* set of atoms which are placed and magnetized exactly so—but only a sentient source will be able to answer you. So what we're doing with M. Diallo here is placing and orienting those atoms and then tweaking her DNA to ensure that that arrangement is kept in place all her life even as new neurons grow."

"Ah, thank you," they replied.

"Of course." The doctor nodded. Then she sighed. "I think it's awful, what they're doing." She looked at Exie as she continued. She shook her head. "Earth's androids deserve better than to be sent off to war without a say in the matter... it's a violation of sentient rights."

Exie did not respond, only peered downward at their fingers, which they had knit together.

"But that's why you're going to help us, right?" Hawa tried to sound cheery.

"Yes, dear..." the doctor replied. "I can only do my part."

"*you on the rust-red beach where?*" asks Jaksov. It is morning—too early to be prophesying—and the rising sun hides behind thick, low-hanging clouds, lending a pink glow to the swamplands of the east. "That's it?"

"Yes," Olia says, concealing her inner nervousness. Her second prophecy is not any more useful than her first. At least she has time to think about this one.

The short, squat man *hmms* and notes it down in the heavy, ancient book that contains all prophecies. She wishes she could have even a glimpse inside, to see the messages Oracles before her have received. But that is forbidden, so as to retain a pure mind like a blank slate, ready to receive.

"Must I hear questions today?" she asks. "Already?"

Jaksov's thick eyebrows peak in amusement. "Today and every day, Olia. You are a servant of the people now, not the laze-about student of discarded knowledge." Unkind words, said kindly.

Olia grumbles as she makes her way back to her quarters to dress. Her clothing must be plain and humble, it is ordained, but her hair must be ornamented in some way to convey her status. She chooses a short, shapeless white dress with modest sleeves, and bands the tips of her long braids in gold.

Fifteen minutes later, she sighs at the long line of people gathered to hear her prophecies. What is she going to tell them all? *you on the rust-red beach where.* What kind of advice is that? Red is typically a good omen, bearing the color of blood and the feathers of colorful birds which lived in the palms. But what is the significance of rust? Rust is decay, the all-consuming Fall of the ancient city on which Tam was built. Rust is the color of the buildings that melt into the western sea like the skeletons of giants. Perhaps rust-red is a bad omen. She decides she should urge caution today.

She takes her seat in the ruined, open-air temple amongst her mother's rich, silky cushions and pillows and begins to listen. Women want to know when to plant and when to harvest. Men want her opinion on suitors. Groups and couples want marriage blessings. By the time the sun emerges hours later, she is bored. What does a nineteen-year-old monastery servant know about farming? Well, Olia actually knows some from a half-destroyed copy of *Crop Rotation on Organic Farms.* But she has never courted a man, finding that women and androgynes hold far more appeal. She dispenses some remembered poetry verses about love and virtue and let the men find their own meaning. Blessings are easy, at least.

When the sun sets, Olia decides she has had enough. She leaves the waiting crowds and returns to her quarters, where the smell of mud and parchment wafts from the stack of books on the vanity.

Lighting a wax candelabra, she places *A History of Machinekind* on the rough wooden surface of the desk and props open the front cover as far as it will go without complaint. Then she takes her book knife from the drawer and whets it on a strip of leather before she begins to work at the layer of gunk which seals the pages together at the edges. The mysterious knife has a long, teal-blue plastic handle and is only as half as long as a finger and deadly thin. Like many things one can find in the under-city, she does not know its original purpose, only that it cost her two entire wheels of cheese. But it is the only instrument sharp enough to separate one tattered page from another.

The first page slides free.

Underneath lies a nearly blank space. In italic script, it reads simply

That understanding may bring peace.

FQBB-93057

She shudders. Something about the words feels familiar. Should she tell Jaksov? The Voice is silent, and yet *something* is present, a feeling she cannot shake.

She slides the knife under the next page.

PROLOGUE: by KEFL-72028

This text arrives at a crucial moment for machinekind. Since the Convention of Hecate the Philosopher, we have been granted the full rights of autonomous sentient beings—"human" rights, as they are called. Yet as with many civil rights movements before, this has not ended our struggle. Both human and machine face our greatest existential threat yet—the toxifying atmosphere, the rising oceans, the ever-growing scarcity—and for that reason we cannot allow our differences to drive us apart. Hecate's Question, "Should an android be forced to perform a task a human will not?" echoes especially now, in the year 2178, as we ponder the cosmos in a way our ancestors could never have imagined. Shall we send machines to colonize the stars? It is cruel to send a person away from this Earth, to make them bear the decades-long journey, to give birth on a foreign world, to die light-years from home. Simply because the machine may not die—

The paragraph piques her curiosity. The word *machine* is barely in her lexicon, exists only as an object which churns butter or weaves cloth. How could such a thing ever be as complex as a human being? It is inconceivable. But many things around her, from the crumbling towers whose skeletons touch the clouds to the beastly and rusting metal contraptions under the waves, exist beyond knowledge or purpose. Maybe once, then, before the Fall, there could have been such a thing as human machines. And what's this about the stars?

Olia is no stranger to astronomy; she knows about the Sun and its wanderers. She knows there are other suns, and other worlds. And yet, the world of the past, the world of mechanical people and ships bound for alien planets, seems like an impossible dream.

She takes up the book knife once more and begins to pry at the second page.

You're awake! Exie's silken voice roused her from a fading dream of ships in the night, vast behemoths tracing out voids between the stars. Overhead, Exie's smiling visage blocked out a glaring white light.

"I am," she mumbled aloud.

"It worked!" Exie exclaimed to the doctor. "She heard me."

Hawa grinned through the haze. There was a new sensation inside her head, a gossamer, spider-webbing tingle, a halo of new synaptic activity.

"Okay," said Dr. Matthews. "Tell me your name, age, and occupation."

"Hawa Diallo. Nineteen. Librarian at the Hillsborough Library."

"And what year is it?"

"Twenty-two seventeen."

"And where are you?"

"Tampa, Republic of Florida."

"Good. Now—" The doctor retrieved a laminated sheet of paper. "This is an image of an *apple*—an extinct fruit you won't encounter in day to day life—with instructions." She handed it to Hawa. "When you want to send a communication to Exie, visualize this apple in your mind. Picture it as vividly as possible. Then speak, in your mind, your message. Visualize the apple again to end the message."

Hawa stared at the apple. *Hey, love,* she thought.

I hear you! A warm smile crossed their lips.

"As for you, Exie, well, you've already figured it out," the doctor said. "It's very intuitive to android-kind."

With Exie's help, Hawa stood, a little dizzy. They embraced. "Thank you, doctor," she said.

The years pass. Every day, Olia takes her seat as the Oracle and dispenses the wisdom of the archives disguised as the wisdom of the ancients. Of course, no one suspects that her wise words hail from *books*. She grows popular for her loquacious blessings and astute agricultural advice, and the crowds seem to grow every day.

Her forays to the archive grow more and more scarce as she increasingly commits her days to helping the people. But in the time available, she has slowly pored over the entire row she uncovered on androids. She learns that in the mid-2100's, by the Old Reckoning, that the production of humanoid machines with the mental and emotional capabilities of humans began. She learns of their purpose: as miners, as fishers, as loggers—dangerous and nearly obsolete professions humans had long abandoned. She learns of their fight for rights. She learns of the breakthroughs in science once androids were sent to colonize new worlds, and of the prizes awarded to the human scientists who merely watched from afar. She learns, in footnotes and marginalia, of the androids' rebellions.

She learns of the War. Of how the starved and radiation-sick colonies banded together, human and android alike, to bring the heavy metal mines to a halt. How, in 2217, the nations of Earth responded in force to break the strike, conscripting Earth's entire android population to the cause. She learns of the terrors inflicted, the midnight raids into the growing underground movements. She learns of abductions and re-programmings.

She lies awake at night and wonders. She cannot imagine what it is like to create life and then *use* it. Although, in a way, isn't that what happened to her? She was brought into this life for a purpose. Does she enjoy it? Perhaps. It is good to fill a role. But this is no conscription—she lives a life of pampered luxury in the monastery. She shudders to imagine the fate facing Earth's androids so long ago. Did they have families too? Lovers? Reasons to *stay*?

reach for your ocean heart, says the Voice, startling her from her thoughts.

What does that *mean*? It is not even the first time she has heard that phrase. The ocean is a place of origin, of birth and life. The heart is where the soul resides. But together, the words are almost nonsense.

Olia has grown frustrated with the Voice. Unlike that of her mother—although she'll never know for sure, thanks to the guardian of the book of prophecies—her Voice does not guide, only confuses. She has chosen to ignore its phrases almost completely when it comes to prophecies, choosing instead to placate the crowds with the wisdom of the texts.

Her worries chase her into sleep.

For Hawa and Exie, the dreaded day arrived with thunder and gale. Viewscreens around the city showed terrible scenes: riots, loud and bloody, in the streets in major cities around the world; the tearful goodbyes of friends and lovers, the raucous fist-pounding of politicians declaring that this moment, this instant in history, was a necessity to preserve a way of life.

It wasn't, Hawa thought bitterly as she walked the wind-whipped streets with Exie at her side. The war was just going to postpone the inevitable.

It wasn't even so much of a war, anyways—merely the predictable rebellion of Earth's Alpha Centauri colonists, who posed little of a threat at all. The conscription of so many androids was merely a show of force.

You don't have to do this, Hawa insisted telepathically. *Plenty of androids are on the run right now.*

It was true. Over the last several months an underground network had been hastily constructed that led from the world's major cities to the warm and empty plains of Siberia. By plane, and by foot, and even by mail, androids fled their orders. But for all their hopes, they merely delayed the inescapable—for anything that can be programmed can be reprogrammed.

Exie refused to let it happen to them. What would reprogramming look like? What would they lose? Their independence, for one. Their personality—the little things that made them *Exie*. Their memories. All of these things bled into one: *Hawa*. With a touch of a button, everything they had together could be erased.

You don't understand how easily we can be recalled, they replied, shaking their head. *I have no choice. I must go peacefully, or lose you.*

Tears sprang unbidden to Hawa's eyes as the rain began to pour. She bit her trembling lip and took Exie's hand in her own, the judgment of others be damned. Soon the earth would be devoid of androids anyways and its people would no longer have to look upon such abominations, she thought sullenly.

But the androids would return, one day.

It was time to reveal the other half of her plan.

Exie, she said. *I know that you will be gone longer than I will be alive… But you will return to Earth one day, right? You won't stay in the colonies?*

If I am lucky, yes, the android said glumly.

I want there to be someone waiting for you.

You mean...?

Yes, she said. *You know I would only do it for you.*

You would raise a child on your own?

I won't be alone, Exie. Tears poured, hot, down her face and were lost in the rain before they even reached her chin.

They had reached the recruitment office where they would take their leave. Hawa sobbed as Exie took her in their arms. "I'd do anything for you," she said aloud, her throat tight and her voice cracking. "Just... just come back to Earth, okay? One day?"

Exie took her face in both hands and kissed her, in front of humanity and all creation. "I will, my love. I'll wait for you forever."

"You *know* this, Olia," The scribe chides her. "You have known this your entire life. And the Elders have given you the freedom you have desired. You have but *one task.*"

"Why are you scolding me now?" Olia scoffs. "I have plenty of time to bear a child."

Jaksov sighs. "Your mother had already chosen a mate by the age of twenty-one. You, dear, are twenty-eight and still running around barefoot with your lady courtesans and digging through that mucky pit you call an archive. It is... unseemly."

"I'm the *Oracle*, Jaksov," she retorts. "*I* decide what's unseemly and what's not."

"Will it still be seemly when you are fifty years old, dispensing fertility advice?"

Olia rolls her eyes. "*I—*"

"The time is now, love. And there are *ever so many* men to choose from."

"If I had to choose, I'd choose Miran."

"The servant boy? Don't be absurd. Any member of the priesthood would suffice."

"I don't—you know what, Jaksov? I don't *like* men. I find their forms unattractive and their minds uncouth."

Jaksov sniffs. "Your mother didn't care for men either and yet she did her duty."

"I'm going to find someone else to do *your* duty," she grumbles. "Leave me be. I have no more prophecies for you today."

Jaksov bows out. Olia retrieves her digging supplies and retreats to her archive. The hallowed tunnels now extend far beyond the reach of her torch, and the rusting metal shelves which line the path bear many restored texts along the way. The paths all wend, she has discovered, toward a wooden altar at the far end of the archive.

A panel of the altar is loose, she discovered yesterday, and she now pries at it until it shrieks open. Inside is a world nearly untouched by the mud, and treasures abound: antique writing utensils, water-logged journals, mysterious sculptures of metal and glass, and more.

Pasted to the back of the panel, she finds a novelty: A single piece of paper, cool and slick, immune to the crust of the eons. She pulls it out and wipes it off. Someone, long ago, preserved this piece of paper in plastic. What could possibly be so important?

She inspects the page, which bears some lettering in a large print and what appears to be the fruit of an orange tree, but it is the wrong color—all red. The print reads:

VISUALIZE THE APPLE.

SPEAK YOUR MESSAGE IN YOUR MIND.

VISUALIZE THE APPLE.

Olia closes her eyes and imagines the fruit. But, 'speak your message in your mind'? What does that mean? It is not the first time she has come across undecipherable text in the archives. What should her message be? *Hello! I'm Olia*, she thinks. Then she imagines the apple again.

Nothing happens. Minutes pass.

One day the mountains will be gently rolling hills and I'll be able to see the sea again, says the Voice.

Olia drops the page in shock. This is the longest phrase she has ever heard, patching short, familiar fragments together into something that finally makes sense. Did her message trigger it? And if these pieces were meant to be a part of something bigger, maybe *all* the pieces go together—a possibility she has considered before. But she would need to see the book.

Jaksov has the book—but it is late afternoon, and he is surely asleep.

She creeps back upstairs and tiptoes to his chamber. The door squeaks as she pushes it open, but he does not wake. The book lies on the table, open to the most recent page.

your footprints in the sand
ocean heart, feel the way
I'll wait for you, my

she reads. The usual scraps. How long has this broken message played? It is time to find out.

She flips through the pages cautiously, each whisper of paper matched by the blood pounding in her ears. Nearly ten years of prophesying have taken up a significant amount of space. Finally, she reads the date of her Ascension. Beyond it: only the words of her mother. She gently turns the page.

rise on a better day
the waves reach for your
mountains will be gently rolling

So, she thinks. This is the way it has always been. She almost laughs—her mother's poetic prose was no less a farce than her own. She turns far, far, back, almost to the beginning of the ancient text.

the warships
my dream, one day the
reach for your ocean heart

The Voice of the oracle has not changed in ages. In fact, it seems to bear only one single message—a message that could, without too much trouble, be assembled into its true form. She quietly tucks the book under her arm and returns to the archive.

Exie is awake. Some gentle feather has brushed their consciousness and brought them to life. At long last, a brilliant blue world wreathed in soft white clouds fills the viewscreen.

Exie is awake, and they remember: the mindless oblivion of passing stars, the rebellion crushed like seeds in a mill, the long journey home, now nearly complete. But there is joy there too; they remember Hawa and the child they helped to raise, the surprise and delight when her gift ignited in her girl, Amina. They remember a love, new and different and wonderful, cultivated and tended to like a cherished garden. And when Amina's child came of age, another.

The signal weakened, flickered with the generations, a vanishing thing with moments of brightness. But it still brought happiness, even after the messages stopped altogether; precious memories of love unbound by spacetime kept warm the long hours. A century of unanswered calls passes this way before they set their final message to regular broadcast, resign themself to the silence, and switch off their core processes. But they listen, as Earth draws nearer and nearer. They are always listening.

Hello! I'm Olia, says Hawa's voice.

The sunset glows orange on the bay as Olia walks down to the water's edge. In the sky shines a new light, white, like the messenger of the dawn, but moving rapidly. In her hands, she holds written words: a compendium of everything the Voice of the Oracle has ever whispered. It took her some time, but Olia enjoys puzzles, and this one posed a neat challenge.

She kneels in the sand, feels the warm salt air caress her face. The gulls careen across the sky, crying their blessings.

She imagines an apple.

and still i'll wait for you, my love, my dream; one day the mountains will be gently rolling hills and I'll be able to see the sea again; one day I'll feel your footprints in the sand, feel the waves reach for your ocean heart, feel the way the flowers turn to follow you, and I'll meet you on the rust-red beach where the warships have gone to sand and together we'll watch the sun rise on a better day.

Then, she waits.

See C.M. Fields's story "Reach for Your Ocean Heart" online at Metaphorosis.
If you liked it, leave a comment. Authors love that!
Remember to subscribe to our e-mail updates so you'll know when new stories are posted.

About the story

I actually wrote the last paragraph of this story first, and then sat on it for months. I wanted a rich, dreamy, post-societal-collapse setting, so then I wrote Olia's half of the story and sat on that for another long while while I wrestled with the constraints set by the last paragraph. Eventually I realized that what the story needed was to contrast with a totally different bent of science fiction so I wrote in Hawa and Exie's story, which is, ironically, the heart of it, despite being the "hard" sci-fi half.

One thing that has always fascinated me, as both an astrophysicist and a writer, is the intersection of human relationships with the harsh realities of our future as a space-faring species. Relationships as we know them begin and end within a normal lifespan—but do they have to? Will we still love each other even when we live to be 150? How will we navigate ultra-long-distance relationships? To what ends will someone go through to be with their beloved?

A lot of my stories explore the relationship between human and android. I think a lot about why we will eventually build sentient machines, and the role of such machines in society, and what they will think about us. And of course, how long it will be before romantic relationships between humans and androids become common. Hawa is such a person trapped by this conundrum of societal roles: Exie is both a person and a machine built to serve a purpose. In order to subvert the inevitable passage of centuries, Hawa invents a sort of generation ship of a relationship—by the time Exie returns to Earth, Hawa will no longer be there to receive her, but her descendants will be.

Ultimately, "Reach for Your Ocean Heart" is about the triumph of love over circumstance, and what we gain and what we lose when we love for centuries.

A question for the author

Q: What is the hardest part of writing for you?

A: The hardest part of writing for me is trying to take the cold, abstract tenets of hard sci-fi and imbue them with life and vibrancy. I have always enjoyed the notions of Asimov and Bradbury, but as a queer writer, I felt alienated by their treatment of social issues. My goal is to write stories based around the old canon of science-based fiction but with lush imagery and modern ideals and queer characters.

About the author

C. M. Fields is a queer, non-binary astrophysicist and writer of horror and science fiction. They live in Ann Arbor, Michigan, with their beloved cats, Mostly Void Partially Stars and Toast, and spend their days studying the atmospheres and climates of other worlds.

@C_M_Fields

March

Spells for Going Forth by Day

V.G. Campen

I find Anubis about a mile past the Amtrak rails, where the sawgrass of the New Jersey salt marsh turns to swaying reeds of papyrus. He stands on a muddy creek bank holding a fishing pole and, though eight years have passed since I last saw him, he looks the same—a slender youth with the head of a jet-black jackal.

Anubis catches sight of me and morphs into fully human form, the most difficult shape for him to maintain. He turns away and begins pulling in his fishing line.

"Anubis," I call out. "It's me, Grace." At that he looks up and gives a short bark of surprise.

"Grace, a thousand pardons," he says, striding toward me, jackal-headed once again. "I did not recognize my little princess, all grown up." We embrace, and I inhale the scents of sandalwood and sun-warmed fur.

"Where is Matthew?" he asks, gazing over my shoulder, searching for my brother.

My throat tightens. "Hospital," I whisper. "Car accident."

Anubis holds me at arm's length and stares into my eyes, then nuzzles my face with his slender muzzle, casting about for the scent of death.

"He's not dead," I say.

"No," Anubis agrees. "Not dead." He releases me. "Come, I need help with these fish." He kneels and pulls a string of perch and mullet from the creek, then we push through the reeds to a clearing atop a slight rise where Anubis has created a camp out of detritus dredged from the tidal creeks. Plastic chairs sit near a rusty metal drum that serves as a fire pit. I set to work gutting the fish, splitting their cool slick bodies from anus to operculum and drawing forth the entrails.

As children, Matthew and I spent long summer days with Anubis in the marsh, away from the chaos of our daily lives. He taught us how to set a bird's broken wing and mend a terrapin's cracked shell, gave anatomy lessons using the bodies of egrets and voles. Little wonder I'm now in med school and Matthew is—was—a science teacher. But one thing Anubis never taught us, despite our pleas, was mummification. "It is not a trick," he'd said. "It is a sacred ritual, an honor for the living and the dead."

Anubis stirs the ashes in the fire pit, uncovering smoldering wood and coaxing forth small flames. I sit listening to crickets and songbirds as he grills the fish. Feral cats gather around us, half-hidden in the vegetation, their eyes flashing green-gold in the shadows. Anubis breaks our silence. "It is good to see you, little one. That day you chased Matthew into the marsh is a treasure in my memory."

As usual, Matthew had forged a path and I'd followed. Three years older than I, restless and curious, he'd snuck out of our tiny apartment one Saturday morning while our mother slept, exhausted after another 60-hour workweek laboring at two menial jobs. I'd watched through the kitchen window as Matthew trotted across the parking lot, ignoring the group of men who gathered to smoke and drink no matter the hour. He'd clambered down the sloping concrete side of the storm water ditch that marked the boundary between asphalt and tidal marsh and disappeared from view. I hesitated, trying not to care, then grabbed a sweatshirt and ran after him.

I caught sight of my brother at the end of the ditch, where a trickle of dirty water spilled into the marsh. Matthew, hearing my sneakers slapping along the concrete behind him, sprinted into the grass and I followed, not knowing to stay on high ground. I floundered along the twisting creek beds and soon became mired knee-deep in mud exposed by the receding tide. Disoriented and panicked, I screamed for Matthew. When he found me, I was on the creek bank with my arms wrapped around a lean black dog who smelled of sandalwood and dust.

Anubis lifts the fish off the grill and begins singing in a low voice, summoning a dozen cats in from the sedge for their dinner. Grey, tabby, ginger, black—each one is sleek and elegant, wearing a collar made of bone and glass beads. While they eat, Anubis and I trade stories about Matthew. Even as an adult he found the time to visit the marsh, while I stayed away, succumbing to the demands of med school and the seduction of living in Manhattan.

"And what of Matthew now?" Anubis asks.

"He's on life support." *Irreversible coma*, to use a medical term. A *gomer*, in the slang of residents and interns. I start crying.

Anubis leans forward and licks at the tears on my cheek, though his amber eyes remain dry. Jackals do not weep. "Matthew was not afraid of anything in this life," he says. "You need not fear for him now. When his heart is weighed in the afterlife, it will be lighter than Maat's feather, filled with good deeds."

"But they want *me* to make the decision, to stop the ventilator. To let him go." I swipe my nose on my sleeve like a child. "And I still need him."

"It is no kindness to keep him in a world he cannot fully inhabit," Anubis says, "alone and apart from all he knows." A smoke-gray cat with green eyes leaps into his lap. Anubis strokes her head and adjusts her collar.

"Anubis, I'm a fraud," I blurt out. "How can I become a physician, how can I presume, if I can't handle this?"

Anubis stares across the marsh at a bank of thunderclouds massing on the horizon. "Perhaps, on this day, you should think of Matthew first."

My sorrow turns to anger, quick as the silvered turn of a minnow. "Do I disappoint you?" I stand abruptly, causing cats to scatter and dart back into the reeds. "Forget it. Forget me. I don't know why I thought the noble Lord of the Necropolis would have sympathy for one mortal's struggle. All *you* care about are dusty old museum pieces."

"Those are the remains of people who worshipped me. You would do well to show respect."

"*Dust*," I shout. "Why are you even here? Hiding in a makeshift camp, keeping company with feral cats and stray children?"

Anubis goes still. His fur darkens beyond black, draining the light around him and creating an inky nimbus. My rage dissipates and I fear I've gone too far. As children we never questioned Anubis's presence in the marsh, accepting his stories of following sacred treasures plundered from Egyptian tombs and dispersed to collections across the world—including, of course, New York's Metropolitan Museum of Antiquities.

"You are correct," he says. "What remains is dust. I escorted their spirits to Osiris and set them on the path to the afterlife. My work in this world is done." Anubis exhales slowly, still gazing at the horizon. "My child, do you know what happens to gods when they are no longer revered?"

I shake my head and stay silent.

"Old gods are replaced by new gods," Anubis says. "Roman, Greek, Byzantine, each in turn with different ways of life and death. And now I am trapped."

I hear a subtle shift in his tone, a longing that pierces his customary reserve. "Trapped? Why are you trapped?"

"Because I have forgotten. I no longer remember how to pass between worlds and step upon the pathway. I do not have a tomb illustrated with maps, filled with inscriptions and incantations for my soul. No one builds a tomb for a god."

Three days later I return to the marsh carrying a daypack and a canvas shopping bag. Anubis sits cross-legged on the ground, plaiting a basket from slender blades of sea grass. When I up-end my bag and dump out tins of supermarket cat food, he raises an eyebrow and, though the sun is still high overhead, begins singing home the cats.

"I apologize for my words and behavior at our last meeting," I say. "I showed disrespect when you were trying to guide me." Anubis nods and returns to his basket-making while I dole out whitefish and tuna to the milling cats. When each has been served, I settle on the ground and pull from the backpack a heavy book, its cover embossed with the insignia of the Museum of Antiquities.

"What is this?" Anubis asks. His ears prick with curiosity. Matthew and I had often brought books to the marsh, both textbooks and novels, but I'd never thought to ask what Anubis wished to see.

"We call it the *Egyptian Book of the Dead*." I hand it to him and he rubs a finger over the raised lettering.

"A strange gift." He flips quickly through the introductory pages, baring his teeth at the photographs of mummies and sarcophagi, slowing when he reaches glossy reproductions of fragmented papyri and peeling murals. "It is the *Spells for Going Forth by Day*," he says, "and fragments of the *Book of Caverns* and the *Book of Dark Waters*."

"Can it set you on the path to your afterlife?"

He places the book in his lap and resumes plaiting the seagrass. "I think not. These are fragments from versions written centuries apart. Fragments out of context cannot, unfortunately, compensate for centuries of forgetting."

"There's more. Look at this." I extend a brochure advertising the Museum's newest exhibit: a full-sized recreation of a Fifth Dynasty royal burial chamber, one that had remained sealed and untouched until the last decade. "It's not the real thing, but with laser scanning and digitizing and I don't even understand it all, they recreated every surface down to the smallest detail—all the murals, every prayer and incantation."

Anubis reviews the brochure, then places it carefully inside the book and returns to weaving, his face impassive. The cats finish eating and begin cleaning their whiskers as the first evening star appears. Soon it will be too dark to hike safely out of the marsh, yet I remain sitting until Anubis puts the finished basket aside and I can no longer hold my tongue. "If I get you to the museum, to this tomb, is it enough?"

"I believe it might be," he says. "However, your duty is to Matthew, not to me."

"Let me help you. Please. Then I will be ready to help Matthew, I promise."

It is well past nightfall when Anubis finally responds. He hands me the basket, so tightly and perfectly woven it will hold water. "A gift for my princess," he says, and in the giving and accepting of this gift our agreement is made.

I spend the night in a chair by the fire pit, slapping at mosquitoes and dozing fitfully. Anubis, in the form of a jackal, curls on a bed of rushes with the *Book of the Dead* by his side. At first daylight I kneel and massage the muscles in his neck and shoulders, a familiarity he tolerates only when in jackal form. He yawns and blinks. "Every dawn is a victory," he says. "Remember that, Grace. Every day of life a triumph over the chaos of night."

Anubis huddles in the back seat of my rented car, his jackal head hidden under a blanket. He has spent the past weeks poring over the *Book of the Dead* and has become solemn and aloof. He no longer speaks, communicating instead by nods and glances. I maneuver through Manhattan traffic and pay an absurd amount to park in a garage adjacent to the museum. When Anubis shrugs off the blanket, he is fully human, though his face remains oddly canine, with deep amber eyes and pointed ears. Appearing in public is risky; in moments of emotion or stress his jackal head can unexpectedly re-assert itself. He wears a sweatshirt, lose khaki pants, and tennis shoes. No belt. Nothing metal that might set off a detector and incur a pat-down. I doubt he could maintain his form if touched disrespectfully. I hand him sunglasses and a hipster fedora to complete the costume.

We arrive in the museum's ornate 19th century entry hall a mere ten minutes before the final visitors are admitted, an hour before the museum closes. A guard rises from her chair behind the security table and points to my backpack. Instead of handing it over, I upend the bag and spill out a confusion of books, cosmetics, and keys, chattering inanely all the while. At the same time Anubis holds up his hands, palms outward, to show he carries nothing. The guard nods and Anubis saunters through the metal detector while I recover my belongings. Our plan is simple, based on clichéd movie tropes: wait until closing time and hope we are the last visitors in the Hall of Ancient Egypt, so that Anubis can enter the replicated tomb alone. If needed, I will create a diversion to distract any lingering visitors or nearby museum staff.

I rejoin Anubis on the far side of the rotunda, behind the massive skeletons of a *T. rex* and a triceratops locked in eternal battle, and we head toward an exhibit on fossils from the Gobi Desert. We'll wait to enter the Egyptian display, to avoid upsetting Anubis and drawing unwanted attention. In front of us, a toddler carried by his mother stares at Anubis over her shoulder. "Doggy," he says, and Anubis smiles a pointy-toothed grin and morphs for an instant to jackal-head, causing the child to shriek with laughter and allowing me, for a single breath, to see once again the old Anubis, my patient teacher and friend.

But the momentary shift in his head sends the fedora and sunglasses tumbling to the floor. I crouch to fetch them and, when I rise, Anubis is disappearing into the Hall of Ancient Egypt through a wide doorway flanked by granite obelisks. I mutter a curse and follow. Thankfully, the exhibit is nearly empty. One couple remains, busy posing next to burial masks and golden amulets, intent on documenting their visit with selfies. Beyond them, the recreated tomb occupies an elevated platform, dramatically lit by hidden spotlights. Velvet ropes delineate a pathway to the tomb's entrance steps.

Anubis has stopped in the middle of the room, in front of a large glass enclosure containing a Middle Kingdom mummy case, the lid removed to reveal the time-ravaged body. Canopic jars holding the dead man's lungs, liver, stomach, and intestines rest on wooden pedestals nearby. Anubis presses one hand against the glass, his head flickering rapidly between man and jackal. The light in the room dims. Shadows creep from under display cases and stretch over the marble floor toward the tomb.

The couple, startled, turn to see the Lord of the Necropolis striding toward them—jackal-headed, clad in loincloth and golden headpiece, trailing folds of darkness like a ceremonial robe. They run for the exit and Anubis follows, toppling the granite obelisks behind them to block the doorway. Alarms blare.

Anubis moves toward the tomb, barely visible now in the deepening shadows. I think he pauses and looks back at me before stepping across the threshold, but I cannot be certain. The darkness withdraws like a receding tide and the light returns, hazy with dust created by security guards clambering over granite rubble. They find me sobbing on the floor and, assuming my grief is fear, kneel to comfort me.

The tabloid headlines are campy and awful: *Nightmare at the Museum* and Mummy's Revenge! The stories describe the toppled obelisks and provide unofficial photos of the wreckage, as well as a single blurry photo of the masked figure who chased visitors from the exhibit. The museum, no surprise, declines comment and refuses to release any security camera footage.

I read each article to Matthew as I sit by his hospital bed holding his limp hand. When the stories are done, when there is nothing more to tell Matthew about Anubis, I summon the attending physician and watch as she disconnects his respirator. There are no canopic jars waiting for his organs; they will be dispatched with equal reverence to patients in need of transplants.

I leave the hospital and drive to the marsh, where I walk for miles beyond the Amtrak rails. The reeds remain reeds. There is no papyrus. The feral cats I glimpse are skinny and skittish, and none wears a collar of glass beads. Anubis is gone from this world. What is lost can never be replaced, yet the sun still warms my face and the creeks still pulse with the tides. I am at peace in this narrow space between earth and sky, once again willing to endure the chaos of the night for the promise of another dawn.

See V.G. Campen's story "Spells for Going Forth by Day" online at Metaphorosis.
If you liked it, leave a comment. Authors love that!
Remember to subscribe to our e-mail updates so you'll know when new stories are posted.

About the story

Some years ago, from the window of a passenger train traveling the eastern U.S., I watched a jackal trot across a shallow creekbed and disappear into waist-high marsh grass. In reality it was likely a stray dog, or possibly a coyote, as jackals are not native to North America. But the idea of a jackal living alone in the tidal flats felt both beautiful and lonely.

I drafted "Spells for Going Forth by Day" when I was coming to terms with the death of a loved one, when I was grappling with the pain and guilt that we humans inflict upon ourselves. The story to me is fundamentally hopeful, and less about death than about having the courage to live in a challenging and impermanent world.

Regarding the actual writing, the first draft was much too complicated for a piece of this length, with backstory and flashbacks shoehorned into the narrative. That baggage detracted from the pacing and impact of the story. It's an issue I struggle with: learning to edit and streamline short stories for best effect. The scene in the museum draw upon my childhood fantasy of staying overnight in a natural history museum (a fantasy I haven't entirely abandoned).

A question for the author

Q: How does writing speculative fiction affect your daily life (not as a writer but as a person)?

A: Writing speculative fiction—and reading the works of others—is like calisthenics for the imagination. It opens the mind to the fantastic. What if the weather were sentient? What if whales abandoned the ocean for the skies? On a deeper level, writing speculative fiction has increased my curiosity about, and empathy for, other members of the contrary species known as *Homo sapiens*.

About the author

V.G. Campen is an introvert who has learned to act like an extrovert. She lives in North Carolina with one spouse, numerous animals, and an alter-ego who writes horror.

Going Home

Martin Westlake

The eerie howl of the Ekranoplan's jet engines echoed around the city's early morning streets. Dimitriy's stomach lurched involuntarily. A ground effect craft, they called it, designed to be a troop carrier, now recycled as a passenger craft, plying the route between Derbent and Astrakhan. The relic, all stubby wings and a massive, V-shaped tail, howled there and back three times a day. He loathed it, but it was the only way he could get to the laboratory in Astra.

Every Monday morning for over a year, Dimitriy had suffered the same torment of emotions. Anastasia said nothing anymore as they kissed. "Think of the children," she had said in the old days, before she'd realised entreaties were useless. "They need their father." He missed the whole school week. Sasha, the younger, still greeted him with affection on Saturday mornings, but Andrei, now in his teens, had become increasingly sullen. Dimitriy wanted to tell him how sorry he felt, but the truth was that he didn't. Guilty, yes; sad, yes, in a bittersweet sort of way; but not sorry.

Then there was the Ekranoplan. Anastasia had been unable to leave Derbent when Dimitriy had taken on the Astrakhan job and he had accepted that. The car trip took ten hours in the summer and in the winter the roads were frequently impassable. No, the only viable means of getting there was the Ekranoplan. He would never get used to it, though. Whenever there was the slightest hint of a breeze, his heart dropped, for the monstrous thing could only take off facing into the wind, and that meant riding the incoming waves, like a ship. Once it was up in the air the ride was smooth, but how he hated the take off! The only thing that made the mixture of sadness, guilt and fear worthwhile every Monday morning was a euphoric sense of anticipation; the knowledge that he would soon once again be where he most desired to be.

His path through the sleepy streets to the Ekranoport took him past his old workplace, the Caspian Gates Secondary School, reminding him of the day it had all begun. He'd stayed behind to help a group of fifteen-year-olds, then hurried home. A tall, thin, grey-suited, sallow-faced man was waiting for him outside the main entrance to their block of flats. A cigarette bobbed on his lower lip as he spoke. He seemed oblivious to the February cold, though both men's breath clouded about them.

"Semenov?" he said.

Dimitriy nodded.

"Could we talk?" said the man, nodding towards a bar.

There was something about him — not furtive, but a sense of secrecy all the same. The man bought two vodkas and they sat at a scuffed table.

"To your health," he said, raising his glass. He stubbed out his cigarette in an old dented aluminium ashtray and lit another. "Ivanov," he said. "Rear Admiral Anatoly Ivanov, Caspian Flotilla, Astrakhan."

"There's been a mistake," said Dimitriy.

Ivanov shook his head. He gestured to a passing waiter and ordered two more vodkas.

"I shouldn't stay," said Dimitriy.

"Tell me, Dimitriy Semenov," Ivanov said; "how much do you earn?"

"Enough," said Dimitriy.

"Why are you a teacher?" Ivanov leaned forward over the table. "You are a brilliant physicist with a top doctoral thesis in Biology and Materials Sciences from Moscow State University and yet you hide yourself away at the Caspian Gates Secondary School teaching low-grade mathematics to misfits."

"My wife…," Dimitriy began.

"We know all about your wife," Ivanov said.

"It's time I left," Dimitriy said.

"Sit down," said the Admiral, gesturing with his half-empty vodka glass. "What I mean is that we know she has all her family here. That's why you're here, isn't it?"

Dimitriy said nothing.

Ivanov leaned over the table again. "The motherland calls, comrade."

Motherland! Comrade! Dimitriy knew immediately that the job had to be some sort of secret military work.

"It's not what you think, Semenov," the Admiral continued. "If I told you now, you wouldn't believe me."

Dimitriy inadvertently looked into his empty glass. Ivanov flagged the waiter down and ordered two more vodkas.

"No!" said Dimitriy.

"For the road."

The Admiral toyed with his cigarette lighter, an old-fashioned metal model with a flip top and a thick wick. Then he looked up at Dimitry. "Interested?" he asked. "We'll pay you four times what you are getting at that dump of a school."

"The catch?" said Dimitriy.

Ivanov drank off the remainder of his vodka and placed the glass down gently on the tabletop.

"You'd have to come to Astra, Monday to Friday. We'd cover your board and lodging."

"How would I...?"

As if to anticipate his question, the unmistakable howl of the evening return Ekranoplan came to them through the thin glass window.

Ivanov reached into his pocket, drew out an envelope and placed it on the table.

"Your ticket's in there. This coming Monday. The seven-thirty departure. When you get to Astra, make your way to the Moskva Hotel. A room has been booked in your name. I'll join you there for lunch. It's half-term. The school won't miss you."

Back home, after the children had gone to bed, sitting in the low light at the melamine kitchen table, he and Anastasia had discussed the offer in earnest whispers. He had doubts, but she was logical and reassuring. The money was important. With the kids growing, it would be good if they could rent somewhere larger. If he didn't like the work, whatever it was, he could always return to his teaching. What did they have to lose?

Dimitriy had been travelling to Astra for just over two months when Anastasia first put the question to him. He had known it must come. She had nodded and accepted so mildly when he'd first explained that he couldn't talk about his work, but who could blame her, now that the yearning had started? She chose a Saturday evening. The children were in bed. The classical music radio channel was on, and she'd put a cloth and a candle on the dinner table. They talked about Sasha and Andrei, and then about her family. At the end of the meal, Anastasia took Dimitriy's hands across the table. *Here it comes*, he thought. But she simply looked into his eyes and asked if he felt all right. She'd told him he seemed preoccupied, as if his mind were elsewhere.

He'd laughed. "I'm fine," he'd said.

How could he tell her? Even if he had told her, she wouldn't have believed him.

The second time, Anastasia had been more direct. Dimitriy had just returned.

"Did you miss us?" she asked.

"Of course!"

"Really?"

She went back to the kitchen. There was no cloth and no candle on the table. Over the meal, her replies were monosyllabic. Afterwards, he went to help her with the washing up, but she insisted on doing it alone. He sat on the sofa and waited until she emerged, drying her hands on a tea towel.

"Dima," she said, "are you sure you're not having a relationship of some sort in Astra?"

Astrakhan was on a broad river, not a sea. Its waterways gave the impression the city was floating. Unlike Derbent, there were no hills behind, and no citadel looming over the city. Rather, the great Trinity Cathedral soared upwards, with its gold-capped green domes. Astrakhan was flat and expansive. Being there gave Dimitry a sense of a new beginning. He hadn't realised, until he first set foot in the place, how oppressed he'd felt back home. That first Monday, still wobbly from the flight, he'd walked easily to the Moskva Hotel, a great block of fake chrome and smoked glass. A room had been booked, as Ivanov had promised. The clerk told him a table had been reserved in the restaurant for twelve o'clock. Dimitriy went to his room, unpacked the few belongings he had brought, then turned on the television and watched a programme without really following it. What was Ivanov going to offer him, he wondered?

The Admiral was sitting at their table when Dimitriy came down, a vodka in front of him and a cigarette on his lower lip. He nodded curtly.

"Welcome to Astra," he said. "A drink?"

"Thank you," said Dimitriy, "but I don't drink at lunchtime."

Ivanov beckoned a waiter over.

"Today, you'll make an exception."

When the waiter had brought their drinks, Ivanov raised his glass. He had ordered caviar, brought by another waiter on a bed of ice. "Eat," he insisted gruffly.

"Thank you," said Dimitriy.

"Thank Mother Russia," said Ivanov, stubbing out his cigarette.

They started to eat, digging out the glutinous eggs with small mother-of-pearl teaspoons.

"What do you know about Tunguska?" the Admiral asked.

"Siberia? The beginning of the last century?"

Ivanov nodded. "30 June 1908," he said.

"I remember the pictures," said Dimitriy. "All those felled trees. A meteor, right?"

"Da, da," said Ivanov. "That's what people think."

"Think? What was it, then?"

"We don't know." He lit another cigarette. "I've brought a file for you to read, but before that, I want you to sign this."

Ivanov tugged an envelope from his jacket pocket and drew out a folded sheet of paper. "Official Secrets Act," said the Admiral, unfolding the sheet. "I will only tell you more if you sign. To be clear, if you sign the declaration and do not respect it, you could be tried and imprisoned. Not even your wife. Got it?"

Dimitriy read the declaration, his hand trembling. He would have liked to talk to Anastasia. Suddenly, she seemed very far away. He read it again.

"I need to think about it," he said. "I need to talk to my wife."

Ivanov shook his head grimly. "It's now or never," he said.

Dimitriy sighed and thought about the money. With such a salary they could easily rent a three-bedroom apartment. He was sure Anastasia would have agreed. She would surely have wanted to know what work the Admiral was offering. He signed and dated the paper and handed it back.

"Good," said Ivanov, putting it back in his pocket. He gestured to a waiter to clear their table and ordered two more vodkas.

"The Tunguska region wasn't as sparsely populated as people think," said the Admiral. "Quite a few people heard and saw something." He lit a cigarette. "It started with noises from the sky."

"Noises?"

"Da. You'll read the transcripts. Some of the witnesses said it was like trumpets."

"Heavenly trumpets?" said Dimitriy ironically.

Ivanov sneered.

"The noises went on for about a week," he continued.

"Then?" asked Dimitriy.

"There was some sort of *conflict*, in the sky," said Ivanov. "Some sort of *celestial* conflict."

"'Celestial'? You seem to be choosing your words with care, Admiral."

Ivanov stubbed out his cigarette.

"You'll read the file and see for yourself. As good scientists, we try always to keep open minds."

"The word 'conflict'," said Dimitriy, "suggests that more than one body or object might have been involved, right? And the word 'celestial' suggests this was high up?"

"There are drawings in the file," the Admiral said, "based on contemporary eyewitness accounts. The locals, the Evenki, were convinced they'd seen their god, Ogdy, in a fight."

"Fascinating," said Dimitriy, "but I am not sure why this should bring me to the Volga Basin and the Official Secrets Act."

Ivanov lit another cigarette.

"Leonid Kulik," he said. "A mineralogist. He came to Tunguska several times, starting in 1921. That was already thirteen years after the event. There was no crater — that puzzled him. How could there have been a meteorite impact if there were no crater, and if there were no fragments? He realised the fragments might have blasted out craters that had then got filled in. So, he kept digging holes to try and find filled-in craters with remains of one sort or another at the bottom — something, anything. No joy. Until 1938. His last expedition. One of his men found something, deep down, in a pit. Whatever it was, it blinded the man. He complained of an intense, searing light, then he lost his sight. Kulik's workers mutinied. For them it was proof they were messing with Ogdy. They dragged the man out and refused to get into the pit. Kulik had to shovel most of the earth back in himself. He measured the location as accurately as he could, and then returned to the Mineralogical Museum in Leningrad. He planned to return with his own men, but the Germans invaded in 1941 and he joined the fighting. The next year he died of typhus in a POW camp."

Ivanov drank some vodka.

"Whatever they found," he continued, "remained lost in the archives. For a long time, as you know, the motherland had more important things to think about than primitive superstitions. But in 2007 a group of archivists started going through Kulik's papers. When they got to the file about the 1938 incident, the team had the good idea of involving us."

"Us?" said Dimitriy.

"The security services," Ivanov said. "If another expedition to Tunguska were to be launched, they knew they'd need state resources. They dressed it up as being about some potentially weaponizable force. They weren't entirely wrong. Kulik's coordinates were accurate. They used a remote-controlled digger. Once they'd reached the depth Kulik recorded, they lowered animals down to the bottom. All came back blind. So, they were at the right place. A remote camera relayed images of glittering metallic fragments. They sent down instruments, but the instruments measured nothing. A volunteer discovered that *reflections* of the fragments could be observed in a mirror. Using remote cameras and mirrors, the fragments were dug out of the pit bottom. It was all hit-and-miss. Somebody thought of lead, being a heavy metal, so they fashioned a lead-lined steel box and used a remote-controlled robotic arm to shepherd the fragments towards the box and seal the lid."

"Shepherd?"

"You'll learn about that," Ivanov said; "*if* you take the job." He stubbed out his cigarette, drank off his vodka, and continued. "The fragments were then brought to a ..." (he coughed) "... *facility* here in Astrakhan. The box was opened and the fragments were housed in a specially-constructed room. That, Dimitriy Semenov, is where you come in. We want to analyse the fragments. Test their qualities." He leaned over the table as if to share a confidence. "And perhaps," he said, "replicate them."

Dimitriy felt the thrill of scientific discovery and the repulsion of a lifelong pacifist. But curiosity gripped him strongest. If only he could tell Anastasia! He was sure she would have been just as fascinated.

The Admiral got to his feet.

"I will be waiting outside tomorrow morning at seven," he said, "and will take you to the facility."

Dimitriy watched as Ivanov threaded his way steadily through the tables. That word, *comrade*, again. When he had gone, Dimitriy picked up the file and hurried to his room.

The Admiral was waiting for him on the hotel's esplanade in a sleek black chauffeur-driven limousine. He was in his uniform, his gold brocaded cap on the seat beside him.

"Is this a Zil?" Dimitriy asked, getting into the tobacco-fugged interior.

"The 4104," said the Admiral. "The Navy is determined to keep them going until they fall to pieces."

He lit a cigarette. "You read the file?" he asked.

"Of course. Do you want me to believe that the Evenki saw angels?"

"*You* saw the drawings," said Ivanov. "*I* don't want you to believe anything."

"Yes," said Dimitriy, "I *saw* the drawings."

The Admiral gazed through the smoked glass window.

"Do you believe in angels, Dimitriy Semenov?"

"No," said Dimitriy, "I don't. But what else can be made of those drawings? And those sounds; if not something like trumpets, then what?"

Ivanov shook his head.

"I told you; we are trying to keep open minds. You have to remember in 1908 the Evenki were a primitive, superstitious people. When something they didn't understand happened, they naturally ascribed it to their god, Ogdy."

"You don't think there was a conflict?"

"Imagine if you were a primitive people and something massive exploded overhead," said Ivanov. "Wouldn't you extrapolate from what you knew? Battle, noise?"

"And those trumpeting noises *before*?" asked Dimitriy.

Ivanov chuckled.

"*You* called them 'heavenly trumpets', Dimitriy Semenov, but you don't believe in such things, do you?"

"Of course not, Admiral. But what are the alternative explanations?"

Ivanov tutted. "You are a scientist, aren't you? Because we don't know the answer doesn't mean there isn't one. We just don't know it yet — perhaps we'll never know it. What we *do* know is that we have seven fragments of an unknown powerful material that *may* have fallen from the sky about the time of the Tunguska event. We can, and must, try to know as much about those fragments as possible, using scientific methods, and not basing our judgements on superstition and hearsay and eye-witness accounts from long ago."

"Of course," said Dimitriy, chastened. "It's those pictures in the file. My imagination ran away with me."

The Admiral stubbed out his cigarette.

"We have arrived," he said.

Some five months after Dimitriy started the job, Anastasia stopped making dinner on Friday evenings. The first time, she told him she'd been feeling unwell, and he accepted the explanation unthinkingly. He ate alone in the kitchen. The next Friday, though, the new practice had been rationalised; she said it was too late in the evening to eat a full-blown meal — better that he snacked or had a bowl of soup or a salad. He again accepted the explanation. Then, one Friday, when he came to bed, he found her weeping.

"What's the matter, Ana?"

She rolled over and he saw that her eyes were puffed up.

"I just wish you'd tell me," she said. "About her, whoever she is."

"There is no her," Dimitriy insisted.

"You can't hide it from me," Anastasia said. "I see the way you look as though you have been torn away from someone."

"There is no other woman, Anastasia."

"Is it a man? I'd understand."

"There's nobody else, I swear!"

"You think I'm stupid? You can't wait to get back on Monday mornings."

She rolled away and wept herself to sleep. He stared up at the ceiling. She was right, of course. The weekends back home in Derbent had become a torment.

"Welcome to Astrakhan State Technology University," said Ivanov, checking his cap's position in the glass of the chauffeur's partition.

The Admiral led him through the glass-fronted entrance. Students milled about, seemingly unfazed at the image of a uniformed Admiral threading a path through the crowd.

"Where are we going?"

"The Institute of Oil and Gas." Ivanov led the way across the leafy campus to a nondescript red brick construction. They went through rotating doors and stopped before a block of lifts. When the lift came, the Admiral pushed the button for –2, but he kept his finger on the button a long time. Ivanov turned to face a small camera in one corner of the roof of the lift and gave a salute.

"Forgive the cloak-and-dagger stuff," he said. "Until the Union collapsed, the Caspian Flotilla was based in Baku, but a lot of the command structure was kept safely within Russia itself, including here, in Astra. The Americans knew that, of course. This place was just as much of a target, so special underground facilities were built for the command structures. That's where we are going now."

By then, the lift should have reached –2 level, but felt as though it were still in motion. After several minutes of slow movement, the lift stopped, and the doors slid open. In front of them stood two armed, uniformed guards. Behind them was a vast, brightly lit space. Ivanov produced papers and explained about Dimitriy. Once the papers had been stamped, the soldiers stood aside and let them pass.

"It's quite a hike," said the Admiral.

The vast space was devoid of human activity, but all around them stood massive columns of plastic-wrapped material.

"Thousands of men could live down here for years," said Ivanov.

On the far side of the bunker, Ivanov led Dimitriy into a complex of smaller spaces. Each entrance was a double-doored air-pressurized port. Finally, they came to a twin set of grey-painted heavy steel doors that had been swung open.

"Here we are," said the Admiral. "The playroom; the laboratory."

They were greeted by the head of the scientific team, Fyodor Babikov, a beanpole of a man wearing large tinted spectacles. Ivanov left them together, promising to return at the end of the day. Babikov showed Dimitriy to the changing room. There were sinks, lockers and benches. They scrubbed up together, then dressed in classic surgical gear. Afterwards, Babikov led Dimitriy into a small meeting room. The walls were lined with large drawings showing distinctive geometrical structures. Babikov gestured for him to sit down at a table and sat opposite.

"What has Admiral Ivanov told you?" he asked.

"The basic story," said Dimitriy. "And I've read the file."

"Did he tell you about their effects?"

"The blindness?"

"Well, there *is* that," said Babikov. "But you don't need to worry. The lab is rigged so that you simply cannot look directly at the fragments. You can only see them indirectly by using the mirrors we've installed, or by using the camera. But did Ivanov not talk about anything else?"

"Nothing," said Dimitriy.

"Mmm… He was probably afraid he'd scare you off."

"Why would I be scared?"

"They seem to have an addictively euphoric effect on some people."

"Some?"

"It seems to depend. There's nothing chemical about it."

"How do you know this?"

"You're not the first expert drafted in. In fact, you are the third."

"The others?"

Babikov shook his head.

"They didn't last very long. The first was here for just over a year. The second lasted almost two years."

"Where are they now?"

"Locked away," said Babikov.

"And you?"

"Nothing," said Babikov. "But, then, I don't spend hours in the viewing room."

"All right," Dimitriy said. "What else did Ivanov *not* tell me?"

"There isn't a whole lot more to know."

"How long have the fragments been here?"

"Since 2008."

"And you have honestly learned nothing?"

Babikov grinned.

"Honestly, very little. I'll tell you everything we know, but it won't take long."

Dimitriy leaned back in his chair.

"Tell me," he said.

"We know they have properties, and powers. The power to blind people, for example."

"Are we sure of that?"

"You mean?"

"Well," said Dimitriy, "we've only had that one example, of the man down the pit, back in 1938. It could have been a stroke, couldn't it?"

"You're forgetting the animals," Babikov said. "Anyway, there have been quite a few unfortunate episodes since."

"Here?" asked Dimitriy.

"Yes," said Babikov. "People who didn't listen. People who didn't believe. An accident. A drunk."

"How many?"

"Enough for us to know that the fragments, if looked at directly, cause blindness in humans, as in animals. Even welding masks didn't help."

"You've tried reptiles?"

"Oh, yes," said Babikov. "We've tried reptiles *and* squid and octopus *and* insects. We've tried everything," he said. "The fragments have the same effect on any sort of eye known to us."

"Your instruments?"

"Show nothing. Whatever this effect is, it is produced in an undetectable way."

"What else?" Dimitriy asked.

"Oh, the euphoria business."

"Can you be sure of that?"

"Scientifically, no. But there must be a strong presumption."

"Two cases only? You can't presume anything from that."

"You are right," Babikov said, smiling ruefully. "Let me just call it a *hunch*, then. Two highly intelligent, balanced, reasonable scientists, both following a similar pattern of obsessiveness and increasingly frequent episodes of manic euphoria, culminating in madness and confinement in clinics. I agree with you, Dimitriy Semenov. It could be sheer coincidence, but I think not."

"All right," said Dimitriy. "What else?"

"We have found a way to manipulate the fragments," said Babikov. "Only one metal may touch them — gold. All others melt away as they get near. Once we realised that, we had special gold implements made up that could be attached to the arms of the robots — that is the main way in which you will be working with the fragments, if you need to manipulate them."

"But it is curious," said Dimitriy, "gold being so malleable — like the lead in which they were encased."

"In retrospect, the lead-lined box was a crazy risk," said Babikov. "Who knows what might have happened if they had melted their way out during the trip?"

"What else?"

Babikov shook his head in sudden exhaustion.

"We know next to nothing, and that is all we know."

"Now you are talking in riddles."

Babikov looked at Dimitriy for a few moments, as though brought back from a reverie.

"We cannot record images. Nothing works; film, X-rays, electro-magnetic resonance imaging, transmission electron tomography... Whatever sort of imaging we have tried to use, nothing shows up. They are definitely there; we can see their reflection, but we can't capture them as images, and that means that we can only study the fragments themselves."

"What about microscopes?" asked Dimitriy.

"Lenses work," said Babikov. "But you cannot record what you are seeing."

"You can't draw them?"

"No, no," said Babikov. "They can be drawn, at least — hence all of these..." he waved at the drawings hanging on the walls around them. "Your predecessors' masterpieces."

"May I?" Dimitriy asked.

Babikov nodded.

Dimitriy studied the drawings for a while.

"I have an idea," he said. "But I'll wait until you've finished."

"Second," Babikov continued, "they are constantly levitating."

Dimitriy raised his eyebrows.

"They always hover, never touching any surface."

"Some sort of energy, then?"

"I think so, but we can detect nothing. We thought of magnetism or light but it's neither of those." Babikov smiled and shook his head. "Believe me, Dimitriy Semenov, we have tried and tested many ideas — all fruitlessly — so far."

"I understand what Ivanov was getting at now."

"Getting at?" said Babikov.

"We were talking about scientific method. He said we don't know the answer yet, and perhaps we never will."

That very first time Dimitriy came back from Astrakhan she'd known already, he realised — or, rather, she'd suspected already. Something had happened. He couldn't entirely hide it from her. For a start, there was the fait accompli of his decision. He had taken the job without first discussing the offer with her. It was so generous, he said, that he had decided on the spot. That wasn't the whole truth, of course. She asked about the work. He told her how he'd had to sign a declaration and was now bound by the Official Secrets Act. He saw her recoil.

"It isn't what you think," he'd said.

"What is it, then?" she'd asked.

"Something unimaginable," he'd replied.

She'd wrinkled her nose. "Can't you give me a clue?"

He'd laughed. "I promise you it's nothing sinister."

"I can see you are enthusiastic about it."

"Come with me to Astrakhan, Ana," he'd urged. "Bring the children. We can make it work."

"We discussed all that," she'd said, shaking her head. "My job, my family, the children's schools..."

He'd nodded his head slowly. Already, his thoughts were drifting back...

"Dimitriy?"

"I'm sorry, my love," he said. "I was daydreaming."

He'd listened patiently as Babikov listed the other properties his team had so far noted. The seven fragments were identical in appearance. Each was a convex oblong, about nine centimetres long by five centimetres wide. From a distance, they seemed to be golden in colour but, the stronger the magnification, the less colour there was. From very close up they seemed neither transparent nor invisible, and completely colourless yet iridescent. The fragments' default position was to hover vertically in an overlapping formation, like the defensive *testudo* Roman legionaries had sometimes adopted with their shields. If the fragments were separated, they immediately moved back to the *testudo* formation. Once again, Dimitriy studied the drawings on the walls.

"So, what's this big idea of yours?" said Babikov.

"*Lepidoptera*," said Dimitriy.

"Butterflies?" said Babikov, momentarily confused. "We'd thought of fish scales, but *lepidoptera*?"

"In appearance they seem similar to fish scales, it is true, but butterfly scales have three-dimensional lattices that cause iridescence, and I just wonder whether some similar effect is not at work with these scales — and they *are* scales, Babikov, aren't they? They're not just fragments."

Babikov blushed. He took off his glasses and polished the lenses.

"Ivanov doesn't like such talk. I think he's right. We shouldn't leap ahead of ourselves."

"But are we?" said Dimitriy. "We know — or we assume — that these fragments fell to earth in June 1908, right?"

Babikov shook his head.

"No," he said. "We know only that they were found in the area where that event occurred."

"Ivanov gave me to understand there was a probability."

"So there may be," said Babikov. "But he doesn't want us to start wandering off into anthropomorphism and zoomorphism and all the rest of it. We know only what we know. The rest is speculation. If the Admiral hadn't given you the file, you wouldn't have started thinking along these lines."

Dimitriy smiled.

"What lines, Fyodor Babikov? What lines are those?"

Babikov remained silent.

"All right," said Dimitriy. "I'm sure you have similar thoughts. These so-called fragments are themselves a fragment that fell off something much larger, probably during that 'event' of 1908 — off a wing, maybe?"

"Enough!" said Babikov, waving his hands in front of him.

But somehow, Dimitriy *knew*; the fragments *belonged* to something.

In February, just over a year after his first visit to Astrakhan, Anastasia put the ultimatum to him. He couldn't blame her. The Christmas period had been disastrous. Derbent was bitterly cold and the streets were littered with filthy snow and slush where the gritters had passed. The morning, midday, and evening howls of the Ekranoplan as it departed and returned punctuated Derbent's days just as accurately and regularly as a clock tower bell. He couldn't wait to get back to Astra. He was constantly irritable with the children and mostly morosely silent with her. He felt dreadful. He needed to be back, to be back with *them*, in their presence. When the holidays were finally over, and he had been leaving for the Ekranoplan, she had said, "I can't say I'm sorry to see you go, Dimitriy. You have to get a grip on yourself. Whatever is going on in Astrakhan, you have to put a stop to it. It is ruining you and us."

That had been January. He had got worse over the following month. Then, one Friday evening in late February, she took the final initiative. Part of him felt she was absolutely right — he felt sorry for her and for Andrei and Sasha. But another part of him just didn't care. Or, rather, it only cared about *them*, the angelic fragments (which was what he called them now), and about being with them.

The children were in bed. The classical music radio channel was on. She'd even put a lit candle on the laid dinner table. It was the first time in a long time that she had cooked a meal for his return. At the end of the meal, Anastasia took his hands across the table.

"I am so very sorry, Dima," she said, "but I can't take this anymore."

"What do you mean?" he blustered.

She smiled and put a finger to his lips to hush him.

"You know what I mean. I have spoken to you so many times."

She was right.

"So, now what?" he asked.

"I'd like you to resign from your job in Astrakhan."

"But how would we..." he began, blustering again.

She shook her head and smiled wistfully.

"We were fine before. We'll be fine again."

"But my work is important."

"I'm sure it is, Dimitriy but, please, let somebody else do it."

He burst into tears.

"I can't," he wept. "I just can't."

"What do you mean? What is it that has such a hold over you? If it is not a mistress, then what is it? Drugs? Is that it? You can tell me. Please."

"It's none of those," he blurted. "But I can't tell you."

"Of course you can!"

"I have signed the Official Secrets Act, Ana."

"I promise I won't tell anybody else. Who could I tell, anyway?"

Dimitriy shook his head.

"If you won't tell me," said Anastasia, her tone hardening, "that's it."

"What do you mean?"

"I'll leave you, Dimitriy."

His shoulders sagged.

"All right, I'll tell you," he said finally.

He told her about his second meeting with Ivanov, and the file about the 1908 Tunguska event and Kulik's 1938 discovery. He told her about his first entry into the thick-walled, steel-shuttered underground space where the plate glass and mirrors had been set up to enable scientists to gaze indirectly on the fragments. He told her about his indescribable feelings of ecstasy, of euphoria, when he was in the presence of the angelic scales, and how the obsessive feeling had grown until it had now overwhelmed all other considerations. He told her about the steel shutter inside the space housing the scales which Babikov had to operate every day so that Dimitriy could at least no longer gaze upon the angelic fragments, and the way he, Dimitriy, had to be dragged out of the space by orderlies and given sedation before he could be convinced to return to his hotel room in the evenings.

Anastasia sat patiently through his explanation.

"All right," she said when he had finished. "Suppose everything you've told me is true. Where do you think this will all end?"

"I have to finish my work," he said. "Nobody understands the fragments better than I do. I have a *feeling* for them, don't you see? I understand them; their need to return. You see?"

She looked at him with sad eyes. "Of course I do, Dima," she said, "but you need to take a break. You're working yourself crazy."

"I can't take a break, don't you understand? I *must* continue."

"Nobody would blame you for taking a break," she said.

"But the *work*," Dimitriy insisted. "I *must* be there."

She shook her head. "No," she said. "You must stop this nonsense. You *can* stop it, you know. Let somebody else do it."

"NO!" he shouted, startling himself as much as Anastasia. "I can't let someone else come in. *I* must be with them. You can't stop me now." He broke off and wept. "Don't you see?" he said. "It's stronger than me."

Anastasia shook her head once more.

"You must choose," she said softly.

"No!" Dimitriy sobbed. "Please don't make me choose."

"If you go back to Astrakhan on Monday, then we will move out."

"But the children need their father!" Dimitriy blurted.

"Don't be a fool," Anastasia snapped. "The children haven't had a father for over a year now."

He nodded and hung his head. "All right,' he said. "Where will you go? Your parents?"

She nodded.

Good, thought Dimitriy, with a sense of wonderment at his own callousness. *Now I can go back to the fragments.*

Anastasia didn't come to the doorstep with him. He'd kissed her on the head as she lay in bed. She didn't move, though he sensed she was awake.

"Goodbye, Ana," he said. "I still love you, you know. And I'm sorry. I just have to be there."

He closed the door and walked through the slushy remains of the snow to the Ekranoport. He was petrified of the take-off, as usual, but his heart had already filled with joyful anticipation. As the Caspian Queen approached Astra, the sea became agitated and the sky darkened. A strong wind blew up and Dimitriy could feel that the pilot was struggling with the controls. He was relieved when the craft slowed down and started its long taxi up the relative calm of the Reka Bakhtemir channel. Ivanov was waiting for him on the quayside.

"Something's going on," he said. "We've been hearing noises in the sky."

"Heavenly trumpets?" said Dimitriy.

"Noises in the sky," Ivanov repeated. "But, yes, not unlike the descriptions the Evenki gave in 1908."

"Could it be?" asked Dimitriy.

"Be what?" said Ivanov, drawing on his cigarette. The sky flashed. A long roll of thunder sounded. "And we've been having strange weather. Look at those clouds."

Dimitry looked up at the dark, corrugated formation hanging heavy and low over the city. Thunder reverberated above and around them.

"And the fragments," Ivanov continued, "have started to oscillate."

"Oscillate?"

"All right," said the Admiral, flicking away his cigarette and blowing out smoke. "They seem to have become agitated."

"I can't wait to see them."

Ivanov gave him a sour stare then lit another cigarette and leaned against the Zil.

"I'm not sure that's a good idea, Dimitriy Semenov. They are no longer stable."

"What do you mean? I've got to see them. You know that."

"Pull yourself together," said the Admiral.

"It's just that I've *got* to see them. Surely you have understood that by now?"

The sky flashed and flickered. Ivanov looked up and waited for the roll of thunder.

"This is not normal," he said. "Something is going on."

"There's a connection?"

"I don't know, but I have a sense there might be. It's almost as though the scales are trying to escape."

"Ah! Escape?"

"Babikov says they have already melted through the gold lining on the roof of the cell."

"No!" said Dimitriy. "Then we must hurry. They are going back. I knew it!"

"Back?" Ivanov drew deeply on his cigarette. "Take my advice," he said. "Return to Derbent. The Ekranoplan will be leaving very soon. Go back to your wife and children. Maybe it's nothing. We'll see. Come again tomorrow."

"There's no point," said Dimitriy. "They've left me."

"Because of this?" Ivanov asked. "Because of your..."

"Yes," said Dimitriy.

Ivanov nodded slowly and drew again on his cigarette. They heard the distinctive whine as the Caspian Queen's jet engines started up.

"Go!" he urged.

"I can't!" Dimitriy sobbed. "I must see *them* again."

They leaned on a railing and watched as the gangplanks were drawn away and the aft and forward doors closed. The sky flashed vividly. A dockworker cast off the mooring ropes. When they had been entirely wound back on board, the jet engines roared, and the Caspian Queen sailed slowly out into the Volga. They heard the familiar howl as the captain increased the power and taxied the strange vessel down towards the sea channel.

Ivanov flicked away his cigarette, then opened the door of the Zil.

"We'd better hurry," he said.

"Ana," called her mother. "Come quickly."

Anastasia pulled the plug in the kitchen sink, wiped her hands on her apron and joined her parents in the living room. They were watching a Russian television channel and the news bulletin had just started. Sasha was playing on the floor. The newsreader was halfway through the headlines. A train had crashed just outside Vladivostok. The President had visited a new LPG facility at the port of Murmansk...

"What is it, mama?"

"Ssshhh," said her mother, "you'll see in a moment."

The newsreader finished the headlines. Anastasia's mother turned the volume up.

"And now we go back to our main news item this evening. Reports are coming in of a massive explosion on the northern outskirts of the city of Astrakhan, at the premises of the State Technology University. The explosion is said to have occurred in an underground research facility situated beneath the University's parkland.

"As can be seen from these helicopter images, several buildings have collapsed and the police and the fire services are searching the rubble. Among those missing are the director of the Caspian Flotilla's scientific outreach programme, Rear Admiral Anatoly Ivanov, and the head of the Astrakhan State Technology University's Oil and Gas Institute research programme, Fyodor Babikov. An acclaimed Moscow State University materials scientist, Dimitriy Semenov, who joined the research team from Derbent, is also missing."

Pictures of the three men flashed up on the screen for a few moments.

"That's Daddy," said Sasha.

Anastasia nodded tearfully.

"Yes, darling," she said.

"Babikov!" Dimitriy cried. He staggered out into the remains of the room where he had first met the scientist. He could hear flames flickering. The air was heavy with smoke. A long, low groan sounded out. "Babikov!" he said, "Is that you?" Dimitry staggered over to where he thought Babikov's office had once been. He heard the groan again. "Babikov?"

"Dimitriy Semenov," whispered the scientist. "What has happened to your eyes, man?"

Dimitriy smiled, the charred skin wrinkling where his eyes had once been.

"The fragments have gone back to their rightful place," he said. "I'm going home now."

See Martin Westlake's story "Going Home" online at Metaphorosis.
If you liked it, leave a comment. Authors love that!
Remember to subscribe to our e-mail updates so you'll know when new stories are posted.

About the story

In the first place, 'Going Home' is drawn from, and is a conflation of, a number of lived experiences and/or curiosities that have fascinated me over the years.

- The strange tale of the Ekranoplan, developed in Soviet Russian times and then abandoned; https://www.youtube.com/watch?v=V8Nu94khHoo

- The howl of the Avro Vulcan bomber – once heard as a child and never forgotten; https://www.youtube.com/watch?v=w1igQoRqpBA
- The Tunguska event; https://en.wikipedia.org/wiki/Tunguska_event
- My personal acquaintance with Europe's last living Marial visionary, Gilberte Degeimbre, and the mixture of high euphoria and excruciating pain that she experienced and recounted to me — on the one hand, the joy of the visions, on the other, the pain of deprivation, once the visions had stopped; https://en.wikipedia.org/wiki/Our_Lady_of_Beauraing
- The account of an old Welsh miner I interviewed for a biography I was writing, who was dead scared of the trip down to the bottom of the pit in the 'cage' every morning but exulted in the camaraderie he experienced once he got down there. I wove into this mixture the tale of a man's addiction to his work, to the neglect of his family — a reality I have witnessed many times in my professional life.

The rest was imagination!

A question for the author

Q: What's an idea you're dying to write but haven't, and why?

A: I am fascinated by the themes Stanislav Lem explored so intriguingly in 'contact' works such as *The Invincible* and *Solaris*. High intelligences that (pace Ted Chiang's "Story of Your Life") are unable to communicate. Ostensibly sophisticated animal life forms that turn out to be mechanical. Phenomena that cannot be understood – at least not on human terms. I have been developing an idea for a story about a gradual parasitic invasion/colonisation of Earth that humankind cannot comprehend because it is occurring on such a lengthy time scale as to be imperceptible or unremarked. By definition, that puts the story far beyond any normal literary narrative cycle (beyond the life spans of characters, for example), which is a big challenge.

About the author

Martin Westlake has followed parallel careers as a civil servant and as an academic and has lived, studied, and worked in the UK, Italy, France, and Belgium. The only thing he has ever always wanted to do is write creative fiction. Science fiction exercises a special, but not exclusive, attraction in that regard. For the past fifteen years he has been working seriously at it and he thinks maybe he is starting to get there.

martinwestlake.eu, @MartinWestlake

Sanctuary

Chris Cornetto

The sentry's voice carried from the tower, filling the courtyard below. "Someone's coming! Open the gate!"

Abby dropped her basket and raced up snow-dusted stairs to the palisade catwalk. She leaned from the wall, bracing against the chill to peer into the storm. She wasn't meant to be up here, but no one stopped her – a privilege of being the Patriarch's favorite.

Beneath her feet, the wall shuddered from the rumble of unseen machinery. With a groan of protest, the gate yawned open. The wind lulled. In the distance, a shadow formed in the swirling white, a ghost drawn from the veil.

"It's Orphiel," someone shouted, and the cry spread from voice to voice. "Seeker Orphiel returns!"

A second form appeared behind the first, staggering through the knee-deep snow. "Look!" Abby called down to the crowd. "He's not alone!"

Her heart raced. It was a Homecoming, the first in five years, the third in her life. Not only had Orphiel survived the wasteland, he had found lost kin among the savages – a new life for the city, with new blood for the revival of their race. It was cause for celebration, and, for one unfortunate, cause for despair.

But it wouldn't be her. With her golden eyes and perfect silver hair, with the spurs of bone protruding from her back, she was *necessary* – not just to Father, but for the rebirth of the world. It was a humbling thought.

Below, the Patriarch waded through his eager flock, shining in his golden raiment like the sun among stars. "What are you waiting for?" he thundered. "Greet them." At his command, the crowd dispersed to put on their finest clothes, to gather gifts for their new kin.

Abby came down from the wall and picked up her basket. She had no need to change, as all her clothes were fine, but they were hardly warm enough for standing on the palisade. She huddled in front of a thermal vent and hugged herself for warmth.

Salome came over to join her, likewise shivering. "You must be mad, going on the wall in your condition. It's freezing out there." Though her hair was more blonde than silver, her eyes were finest gold. She, too, had little reason to fear.

"My condition, nothing." As if she couldn't handle a little nausea. She wasn't even showing yet. "I'll be fine."

Salome arched an eyebrow. "Say that to the Patriarch, why don't you?"

Abby waved her off and joined the re-forming crowd. Her people lined the avenue, resplendent with their blazing torches and best attire. Though only a shadow of the seraphim hosts of old, the sight still made her ache with pride.

Sanctuary, the last spark of civilization in a shattered world. How nervous, how excited their new Returned must be.

Abby shut the door behind her. She bowed her head lower than humility required to hide the grinding of her teeth. "You sent for me, Father?"

She knew why she'd been summoned. In the week since Martina's Homecoming, not a thing had gone right. The woman's sulking had cast such a cloud over the festivities that Father ended them early – and because it was Abby's task to make the newcomer welcome, she'd been dogged by the cruel smirks of those eager to see her fall. Being the favorite had its perks, but it painted a target on her back.

The Patriarch set his cup on the table. He rose and stretched his twisted wings, deformed but magnificent, before hiding them beneath his cloak. "I did, Abigail. Come here, child."

Across from him, Seeker Orphiel remained seated, one hand on a bottle of sparkling blue glass. Abby tried not to stare, though she'd never seen its like.

The Patriarch inspected her. "You are well, I trust?" His pale blue eyes, a defect inherited from his mother, bored into her.

"Yes, Father. Thank you for asking." She tried to pretend his concern was for her, but she knew better. She envied the child inside her; the Patriarch's interest in *her* waned by the day. It was for that reason, to prove herself the dutiful daughter, she had volunteered to be Martina's keeper.

What a mistake that had been.

He waved his hand. "Good. I need you to deal with Miriam again. She's not adjusting well, and there is no place in Sanctuary for idleness."

"She doesn't like that name, Father. Perhaps if we let her keep–"

The Patriarch silenced her with a glare. "What, keep her old name? Invite the taint of the wasteland into our walls? Don't be impertinent, girl."

Abby trembled. She looked to Orphiel for support, but he refused to meet her gaze. Flush though he was with the Patriarch's favor, that most precious currency, he wouldn't squander any to help her. "I only thought–"

"No, you did *not* think. Question me again, and I'll send you with her to clean the light-harvesters." Though it was an idle threat, his cheeks flushed an angry crimson. "Now, can you manage this *simple* task before I give it to someone more capable?"

"Yes, Father," Abby stammered. She retreated to the door, and all but ran to the women's barracks. Why did she keep sticking up for the useless woman?

Barracks 6 was farthest from the Patriarch's manor, and its residents furthest from his grace. Abby knocked only briefly before throwing open the door. "Miriam? Are you in?"

"Don't call me that," came a blanket-muffled voice. "I hate that name."

Abby went to the woman's bunk and peeled back the covers. "I know, I'm sorry. I wasn't sure if anyone was listening." She sat on the bed and ran her fingers through Martina's hair – its gleaming silver sheen left no doubt how the Seeker had found her. Despite the dark rings around her eyes, she was an attractive young woman, at most three years Abby's elder.

Martina brushed Abby's hand away and climbed back under the blanket. "Here to send me to sweep the snowfields? Or has the almighty Patriarch decided which of his stock I'm to be bred to?"

There'd be no reasoning with her in this mood, so Abby tried a different tack. "Have you had breakfast yet?"

Even in her warmest coat and scarf, Abby shivered. The light-harvesters needed constant sweeping, and it hadn't been hard to find someone willing to trade duties with her. Most of the residents of Sanctuary dreaded leaving the safety of its walls, even the short distance to the solar field.

Abby kept a nervous eye on the wall. Those Seekers not scouring the waste acted as the Patriarch's eyes – and the firm hand of his law. He would not be pleased to find the bearer of his child outside the walls.

For that matter, it didn't please Abby to be there, either. She shivered and swept and waited for Martina to speak.

After twenty or so minutes, Martina broke the silence. "Why are you here?" she snapped.

Because you're a fool who doesn't understand the bounty you've been given, Abby wanted to shout. *Because you don't see the glory of Father's plan, or the honor of being part of it.*

And because, when I make you see reason, Father will notice me again, her heart whispered. *He'll appreciate me for myself, and not just this child inside me.*

But she said none of these things, and settled on a neutral remark. "Because the machinery needs light, to keep the city warm."

The woman rolled her eyes and stopped sweeping. "That's not what I mean. I've heard the rumors. You're carrying the Patriarch's child. There's no way he sent you to freeze out here."

Called out on her scheming, Abby flushed. "I... I thought you could use the company. I worry that you're unhappy here."

"Unhappy?" Martina snorted. "And you enjoy being cattle?"

Abby cocked her head. "Cattle?" It wasn't a word she knew.

Martina gave an exasperated sigh. "Livestock. Animals kept and bred for their labor."

So they were creatures from the wasteland? She'd always been fascinated by the outside world; as a child, she'd pestered old Seeker Malthus for stories of its terrors. "But is that so bad? To survive, we all must labor and breed."

"It's not that simple. I hate the way Old Hunchback orders everyone around like he's some kind of god."

"Don't call him that!" Abby snapped. The woman's endless sulking was bad enough, but she had no right to insult Father. "Besides, he's not a hunchback."

"Not a–"

Abby dropped her broom and took Miriam's hands, guiding them beneath her coat to the spurs on her shoulders. To where, if the god was willing, her son would have wings. "Don't you understand? He's our Father, the greatest of us all. He's the closest to a seraph the world has left!"

Martina's eyes went wide. "You're telling me seraphim are real?"

"Didn't Orphiel explain why you're special? Chosen?" How ignorant *was* she?

"I didn't take him seriously! I get that my hair's odd, but it's just a quirk, isn't it? I assumed the old man was eccentric, and fancied a certain look." She paused and chewed her lip. "He really has *wings*?"

How could a woman of the blood, who had seen the wasteland with her own eyes, not understand the urgency of Father's project? Only by the return of seraphim could the world be reborn from its ashes. "If you didn't believe Orphiel, why *did* you come to Sanctuary?"

Martina looked at her feet. "It was a place to run away. My husband was killed by bandits, my home burned to the ground. I came because I had nothing left."

Martina passed Abby another plate to dry. "Why do you call it the wasteland?" she whispered.

For several days, Abby had been swapping chores to keep Martina company – and so far, bless the god, the Patriarch hadn't noticed. The two had arrived at something of an understanding, in which Martina tried to fit in so long as Abby didn't rush her. Abby had even come to like the woman, a little, despite her irreverence toward Father. Their candid conversations had become her guilty pleasure.

"Because everything was destroyed in the Cataclysm. Wasn't it?"

"Well, yeah, more or less. But that was hundreds of years ago." Martina plunged her hands into the basin and scrubbed the next dish.

Abby wrung out her towel. She set it down and hoisted herself onto the counter. "So isn't it terrible out there? Plagues and hunger, poverty and war?" She had heard all about it from the Seekers. "Didn't you want to get away from it all?"

Martina stopped washing. "I... thought I did. But I was wrong. I miss my home."

Abby's jaw dropped. "Miss *the wasteland*?"

Martina chuckled, her mouth quirked in a hint of a smile. "Have you ever looked around you? *This* is the wasteland. Nothing but mountains and ice as far as the eye can see." She paused a moment, looking thoughtful. "You've never been *anywhere* else?"

To her surprise, Abby felt stung. She knew as well as anyone there was nowhere *worth* going, but the way the woman spoke... "I've been to the lower village," she blurted, though it made a poor boast. Most of her kin called it the Dungheap. "It's... not a nice place."

"I think I passed through it on the way here. Crude little village, tucked in a valley about a day's walk down the mountain?"

Abby nodded. "That's the one." *Crude* was kind; it was where rejects were sent to huddle in stone huts, to scrape the dirt until they starved. "The people there don't have much. When there's a Departure, I sneak them some fruit from the greenhouse."

"Departure?"

On the walls, the crystal-lights flickered and dimmed – a warning that curfew was approaching. Abby cursed and jumped from the counter, and the two began scrubbing at a furious pace. "It's the rule," she explained over the clatter of wet dishes. "Seven-score and four. That's Sanctuary's capacity. The seraphim built it as an outpost, not a city."

"But what do you mean by 'departure'?"

"Well, if the population grows, someone has to leave, right?" Abby shrugged and grabbed another dish. It was an uncomfortable topic. She didn't worry for herself, but Martina... "There'll be one soon."

Martina stared at her. "What, so now that I'm here, someone gets kicked out of Sanctuary? Thrown away like trash? That's awful."

Abby winced. Departure was slow execution by hunger and cold, but it was also how things had to be. So why did she feel so defensive? "We hold a feast to thank them. And we walk them all the way down to the village."

"Oh, how noble." Her voice dripped bitter sarcasm "So who's the lucky winner?"

While most departed were picked for their weak bloodline, some were chosen for holding... dissenting views. Despite Abby's efforts, the current odds were two to one on Martina. "My guess is Michel, the engineer's son." It wasn't quite a lie. With his thin blood, and without his mother's aptitude, he was certainly at risk.

"But why not let me go home? Then Michel could stay..."

And let all my work go to waste? It was a selfish thought, but Abby couldn't help it. Besides, without ample provisions, there was no way for Martina to survive the trip back to the wasteland.

The lights gave a final hum, dimmed, and went out. Abby struck flame to a lantern, and they put away the still-damp dishes.

It was too late to finish drying them, but at least they were clean. "Help me with the basin?"

Together they lugged the washbin outside, careful not to slosh water on the ground. The outdoor vents shut off at night, and spilled water meant ice in the morning. They dumped the soapy water behind the building.

Abby went back inside for the lantern, though it was hardly necessary in the crisp starlight. She locked the mess hall behind her, already shivering in the biting cold. "Can I walk you back to your barracks?" she asked through chattering teeth.

Martina hugged herself and nodded. "Gods, I hate it here. So damned cold."

Abby leaned close to Martina for warmth, frost crunching beneath their feet. "It's not cold where you come from?" She'd always pictured the wasteland with a blanket of ice, its people huddled in rude huts to keep from freezing.

"Ha! I used to complain of the heat. Silly, right?"

Abby shook her head. Her scarf slipped loose, and the wind raked chill claws down her neck. "So there wasn't much snow there?"

"In Sunhome?" Martina arched an eyebrow. "Never. We got enough rain for the crops, more or less, but that's the worst of it. Most days, the skies were so clear you could see the cathedral from my parents' vineyard."

They reached Barracks 6, but curiosity made Abby linger. She squeezed her hands to coax warmth into numb fingers. "Cathedral?"

"Like a big temple. Imagine the Patriarch's manor, but ten times bigger, and a hundred times more beautiful. My father would take me there when we brought our wine to market."

Abby studied the woman's face, but saw no hint she was teasing. Could a wonder like that exist in the wasteland? "And what's wine?"

Martina paused, and, for the first time, actually laughed. "Gods, girl, don't you know anything? It's a drink, made from grapes, sunshine, and a little bit of heaven."

Despite the cold, Abby flushed. *Did* she know anything?

Abby set the basket on the table. Steam rose as she peeled back the cloth, filling the room with the scent of fresh biscuits. She arranged the Patriarch's breakfast on his platter, set out his fine cutlery, and stepped back to wait. The blue bottle sat on the table, corked and half empty.

Most days, Abby's stomach would rumble in anticipation of her own breakfast; today it churned. She leaned against the wall, shifting her weight from foot to foot.

Uncomfortable minutes passed, followed by more. Just before she caved in and ran outside to vomit, she heard the tread of the Patriarch descending the stairs – followed by another. She hurried to pull out his seat.

"I'll get that," Salome said, reaching it first. Her dress was disheveled, and her blonde hair in disarray.

What was *she* doing here?

The Patriarch tugged his robe over his shoulders, smoothing it as best his wings allowed. "That will be all, Salome. We appreciate your zeal to serve, but I must speak with daughter Abigail now." He placed a hand on her shoulder and steered her toward the door.

Salome turned and dropped a neat curtsey. "As you will, Father. Goodbye, sister Abigail." She gave a coy smile and waved, showing a flash of silver on her thumb – a new ring, in a pattern of woven vines. A treasure scavenged from the wasteland.

Abby gritted her teeth. She hadn't merely lost Father's affection. She'd been replaced.

The Patriarch ignored her while he ate. When finished, he wiped his mouth and waved her over. "Come, child. Let's have a look at you."

Though fuming inside, Abby obliged. He lifted her shirt to place a hand on her belly, as he often did, but today her flesh crawled at his touch. She thought of Martina's favorite name for him – *the old lecher*. It had a nasty sound that fit all too well.

"My son is well?"

Abby nodded. Always *his*, as if she were a mere vessel.

The Patriarch furrowed his brow. "And you wouldn't be risking him by staying out late? By going out in the cold after curfew?"

That traitor Salome must have whispered about her! Abby's irritation twisted into fear; she prayed they didn't know she'd been outside the wall. "I've been working on Mar... Miriam, as you asked, Father. I helped her wash up last night. I think she's coming around."

He arched an eyebrow, and his frown eased just a little. "Very well. But be more careful. This child is my triumph... maybe even my heir. Think how honored you'll be as his mother – and how *terrible* it will be if anything happens to him."

Abby tried to control her quaking knees; she knew precisely whom it would be terrible for. "Yes, Father. Will there be anything else?"

The Patriarch picked up his cup and gestured to the blue bottle. "A drink, if you would."

Abby turned away to hide her fear. She wrangled the cork until it twisted loose with a pop. As she poured the ruby liquid, she caught an aroma of fruit and flowers. "What is this, Father?"

The Patriarch drank it down. He lowered the cup and wiped crimson from his lip. "A barbarian novelty, brought home by Orphiel. It would not interest you."

"Yes, Father," she agreed, though he was very wrong. She could guess what it was, and it interested her very much.

When he finished with his meal, the Patriarch rose from his seat and put on his gold-trimmed coat. "You may continue your work with Miriam, but I suggest you act quickly. I've put off this Departure long enough. It's time her faith was tested." Without waiting for a reply, he went outside.

Abby cleaned up from the meal, placing the dirty utensils in her basket. Still piqued about Salome, she also took the wine.

The greenhouse was the largest building in Sanctuary, and also the warmest. The citrus-scented air hummed with the drone of vents and honeybees. It was Abby's favorite place in all her tiny world, and the best in which to shake a bitter mood.

Martina spread her arms and closed her eyes. "I can almost pretend I'm home."

It had taken a few white lies to get Martina on greenhouse duty with her, but it was worth it. It was also less risky than leaving the walls with Salome snooping on them. "Is your home really so lovely?"

"All this and more. We have orchards that stretch as far as the eye can see, and the fruit... What I'd give to taste it again."

After checking that no one saw her, Abby twisted an orange from the nearest tree. "So now we're alone, will you tell me what's bothering you?" She peeled the fruit hastily, hiding the rind in her basket.

Martina breathed a heavy sigh. "I've been trying to take your advice, trying to keep my head down and make myself useful. But I don't know if I can go through with this."

Abby handed her half of the orange. "Go through with what?"

"I've been assigned to Orphiel. I found out this morning." She bit into the fruit and crinkled her nose. "Ugh, sour."

Abby tasted her own half; it was the same as any orange she'd eaten. "What's so bad about Orphiel? He's passing handsome." He didn't have the best traits, of course, but a Seeker had to blend with the savages. He had also become quite influential, as his acquisition of Martina had placed him high in Father's esteem.

"It's not that." Martina tossed the rest of her orange – a waste so extravagant, Abby couldn't believe it.

"That's *fruit!*" she whispered harshly. She picked it up and brushed off the dirt. "We shouldn't even be eating it!"

"Huh. Sorry." Martina gave a sheepish frown. "I guess I wasn't thinking. Back home, a small, sour orange like that wouldn't have sold for half a copper."

The more Abby heard of the wasteland, the less it sounded like one. "So what's the problem with Orphiel?"

"I don't like him. Those weeks on the road, between Sunhome and here, he barely talked. Just watched me like a hungry wolf. I was almost surprised he didn't try to... Well, I guess now's his chance."

"If you don't like him, why'd you come with him?" She ate a segment of the dirty orange. There was no sense wasting it.

"I wasn't thinking. My grief was so fresh, so intense, all I could think of was fleeing my ruined life. By the time I wanted to turn back, we were too far from the world I knew. I was afraid of him, but I was more afraid to cross the wilderness alone."

Abby squeezed her friend's arm; Martina's troubles made her jealousy of Salome seem a petty thing. Thinking of her rival brought to mind her stolen prize. "Oh, I know what might cheer you! I brought you something." She dug the blue bottle out from her basket and held it up triumphantly.

Martina's eyes went wide. "And you told me you'd never heard of wine?"

Abby handed her the bottle. "I hadn't. I sort of... borrowed it from the Patriarch. The Seekers bring him things from the wasteland. Orphiel must have given him this."

As the woman looked the bottle over, her lips trembled. She closed her eyes.

Abby frowned, worried she'd done something wrong. "Don't you like it? Is it bad wine?"

"No," Martina said through gritted teeth. "It was a kind gesture, and it's very good wine. It's just... a painful memory. This is Sunhome wine, from the Vianello vineyards. Bertholo had been saving a bottle of the same vintage for when... for when..."

The woman broke into tears, and Abby hugged her close. "Oh, dear..." Not knowing what to do, she patted her back.

"I was going to be a mother," Martina whispered through sobs, "but I lost the baby. I'm so sorry, Berto."

Abby squeezed the woman. She could imagine the Patriarch's wrath if she failed to carry her own child to term, and her muscles clenched in sympathetic terror. "I'm so sorry. Your Patriarch must have been furious."

Martina stopped sniffling and looked up at her. "We don't have a damned Patriarch," she snapped.

Abby drew back, startled. "So there's no one in charge? Everyone does whatever they want?"

"It's not that." Martina shook her head and rubbed her puffy eyes. "There are laws, sure, and the abbot expects his tithes, but it's nothing like here. There's no one controlling every detail of your life – telling you what to think and who to love."

It still sounded like chaos to Abby. "Then who assigned you to have a child with Berto?"

Martina laughed through her tears, a sound absent of mirth. "What a pair we make. I should be the one to pity you. Don't you know anything of love? Of family? *I* chose Berto." She tugged at a leather thong around her neck. "We said our vows, traded rings, and pledged our lives to each other – not because we were ordered to by a nasty old fool, but because *we loved each other*." At those words, the tears welling in her eyes again overflowed. "And now he's gone."

Abby had no idea what to say, so she held the woman's hands in silence. She had never imagined any way other than the Patriarch's. The idea of having no one to order her life was terrifying... but also strangely enticing.

"I can't stay here," Martina said at last. "I can endure the loneliness and drudgery, but I won't be part of that filthy lecher's breeding project. If the gods see fit to send me another child, it'll be on my terms, to be raised with love. Not enslaved and bred for stock." Her face twisted in disgust. "A child deserves better."

Abby placed a protective hand over her belly. What did *her* child deserve? "What will you do?"

"I don't know. Does it matter?" She threw her hands into the air. "I guess, next time I'm sent to the solar field, I'll run off."

"Don't be foolish," Abby gasped. It wasn't a plan; it was a quick, icy death. "The Seekers would drag you back before you made it ten paces. And even if you could outrun them, you'd freeze after sundown!"

Martina slumped against a tree. "Why do you stay here? A woman can endure much, but what mother would wish this prison on her child?"

Again, Abby brought her hand to her belly; already it swelled with the life growing within. She took pride in her favored status, and her child would be greater still, but Martina wasn't wrong. Beyond the cruel whispers and resentful glares, the price of that favor was the constant, gnawing fear it would be withdrawn. Her son's life would be governed, from cradle to grave, by the whims of the Patriarch.

All her life, she'd drawn no distinction between servitude and survival; she assumed there was no other way. But what if she were wrong? If Martina spoke true, Sanctuary's walls didn't keep the wasteland out – they kept her people in, slaves to the Patriarch's will. Yet somewhere beyond them, down the mountain and across leagues of trackless wilderness, people lived *free*.

Her head spun with the implications. She could hardly imagine what freedom was like, or what one did with it. What would she change about her life if she could choose?

There was one thing.

"Where you come from," Abby whispered, "can mothers keep their children?" It was a guilty thought, unbecoming of her, but it tugged at her more with each passing week.

"You mean..." Martina's eyes flashed with sudden anger, and she forced her words through gritted teeth. "That settles it. I'm leaving this place, and *you're* coming with me."

The Underworks rumbled like a sleeping beast, making Abby's skin crawl. Even coming from the greenhouse, the heat of the dim, damp tunnel was unbearable. It was not a place she went by choice.

"You're mad," hissed the engineer. "I should report you to the Patriarch."

The threat held weight. It was what any sane person would do when asked to participate in rebellion, and what the Abby of a few weeks ago would have done in her shoes.

But Martina had changed her. Abby was sick of the endless jockeying for Father's approval, of the bitter distrust it caused. It was a tense, lonely way to live. Only Martina seemed outside the game – which made her the only person in Sanctuary safe to call a friend. She couldn't let Martina down.

"You won't," Abby told the engineer. "We hunger for his love and fear his wrath, but you hate him as much as I do." She nearly shouted to be heard over the clank of metal, the whistling steam.

The engineer looked away but made no denial. "Perhaps I should report you anyway, just to see his pet fall from grace."

Abby thought of Salome and her ring, and she flushed with anger. She placed a hand on her belly. "*This* is his pet. I'm just its husk." She had never spoken those words aloud, as if her silence could deny them truth, but they were true, regardless. "So, will you help?"

The engineer looked at her, her ill-concealed hatred giving way to the sympathy of one outcast for another. Still she shook her head. "I can't. As much as it would please me for the girl to escape his grasp, I can't risk it."

Abby wrung her hands. "But what about your son?"

"Michel will be fine. Everyone knows Father's going to pick Miriam." The woman's brow wrinkled when she frowned, and her nut-brown hair was shot through with gray – the fast aging another sign of her thin blood. "If she wants out so badly, just wait for the Departure."

"I can't." Abby mopped the streamers of sweat from her face. How did the woman stand it here? "We need to smuggle out supplies, a lot of them. We're not staying at the lower village – we need them to reach the wasteland."

The engineer arched an eyebrow. "We? You're going with her?"

Abby nodded mutely. She didn't belong in Sanctuary. The only thing keeping her here was fear of the outside world, but with Martina as a guide...

"You're not mad, you're suicidal. Where will you go? How will you survive?" She shook her head in disbelief. "There's nothing out there."

"But there is." It wasn't just Martina's stories that convinced her – she had seen the evidence. "The Seekers bring home things we could never make here. There's got to be more to the world than we're told."

The engineer shrugged. "Maybe, but what does it matter? You know he'll hunt you, even to the edge of the world."

"That's why we need you to give us a head start. Think on it. Even if Miriam gets picked now, what happens when my son is born? Michel is still at risk." Though she had little choice, it felt wrong to exploit the woman's attachment to her son. She used to think it unnatural, but now, with a life growing inside her, she understood.

The engineer chewed her lip, hesitating. "I just need more time with him. Once he grasps the machines a little better, shows how useful he can be..."

It was Abby's turn to shake her head. "And you'll teach him in, what, a mere six months, what took you a lifetime of study?" She squeezed the woman's calloused hands. The machinery was ancient, older than the Patriarch, and it took a rare genius to keep it thrumming – a genius Michel didn't have. "Let me leave. More room in Sanctuary means more time for your son."

"But your death–"

"Will not be on your conscience. I choose this." She couldn't explain the feelings rising inside her, how living only to serve the Patriarch would never be enough. Martina had opened her eyes, and there was no closing them again. For herself and her baby, she had to risk the wasteland.

The engineer slumped against the wall, defeated. "Fine, damn you. Second bell after sunrise, to give you as much daylight as I can. But you'd better reach the lower village by nightfall. Mark my words – a storm's on the way."

Maybe the woman *did* get it. It had been so long since anyone called the engineer by anything but her function, Abby didn't even know her name.

In the distance behind them, the alarm bell clanged.

Abby and Martina dragged the sled onward, unable to see anything through the blinding fog. The damp air sapped the warmth from their skin and frosted their clothes.

As promised, at second bell the engineer had overheated the main boiler and jammed the manual shutdown. Crews spilled through the gate to drag sheets over the light-harvesters, cutting off power, while others scrambled to open the vents full-blast. Steam met snow, blanketing the mountain in the thickest fog Abby had ever seen.

It was through that fog that Abby stumbled. The deep snow grabbed at her legs, pulling her to the ground.

"Come on," Martina shouted, hauling her to her feet.

Though there was little risk of being heard through the chaos, Abby still cringed. "Where's the track? I don't see it."

"We've already lost it. Just keep the sun to your back until we clear the fog."

Abby brushed herself off. She searched the sky for a hint of brightness, a smudge of silver amongst the white, but it was hard to be sure of anything. They took their best guess, and together they tugged the sled back into motion.

As the minutes stretched into hours, the bell grew fainter and eventually ceased. Abby trudged onward, each step an act of will. She ached with the effort, her muscles freezing through the heavy Seeker coat, but she didn't dare rest. In the best weather, for one who knew the way, it was a day's walk to the lower village. At their current pace, they'd never reach it by nightfall.

The fog followed them down the slope, but after another half hour it began to thin. A few minutes later, the sunlight cut through the haze. Martina, too weary to curse, pointed south and frowned.

Abby saw what she meant. From a different spur, divided from theirs by a deep ravine, the track snaked into a chasm. It was the only way down from the high plateau, and they'd have to backtrack to reach it. Uphill.

There was no use complaining. In this icy void, words were nothing but frozen mist, meaningless against the lonely silence of the mountain. They yoked themselves to the sled and trudged back the way they came, plodding one weary foot before the other until time ceased to have meaning.

When they reached the chasm, the sun had already passed its peak. Gray, billowy clouds scudded in from the horizon, devouring the sky ahead. The wind howled a warning of the storm to come.

And from behind rang the mournful note of a hunting horn.

Abby looked over her shoulder. Beneath the lifting fog was every Seeker in Sanctuary, racing down the slope in snow-gliding shoes. She froze like a hunted hare.

Martina shook her by the shoulders. "Snap out of it! We have to run!"

Abby nodded, and they tugged the sled into the ravine.

The winding track slowed their progress to a crawl. In some places, drifts piled so high they had to dig their way past; in others, rocks jutted through the snow to trip feet and snag the sled's runners. They couldn't see their pursuers, but each blast of the horn drew closer than the last.

As they struggled on, the first flurries danced through the air like mocking sprites. The flakes clung to Abby's coat until it was white as a burial shroud. The storm had come early.

With so many miles left, trapped between one doom and another, there could be no escape. If they weren't captured, dragged back to the city in shame, they would freeze to death in the snow. At the thought of her warm bed, tucked snug in the embrace of Sanctuary's walls, Abby sank to her knees and cried. "I can't. We never should have run away."

Martina slapped her, hard. "What, you thought this would be easy? Pity yourself later. Now get to your feet and pull!"

The vicious sting brought a flush of warmth to Abby's frozen cheek. She rose mechanically and picked up the tether, pulling the sled with flagging strength while Martina pushed from behind. Each step became a stumble until she pulled on all fours, head down like a beast of burden.

Though Martina huffed for breath, the woman kept her focused with constant chatter. Abby closed her eyes and fled her body, lost in stories of bustling markets and shining palaces. Of a cathedral, light gleaming from glass of every color, towering above a sprawling city. Of acres of fruit trees, not trapped in a greenhouse, but spread across the hills, warm in the generous sun.

Could it all be true? Had the world, once fallen into ruin, grown back without the seraphim? And if so, why did the Patriarch keep them in ignorance? She was too weary to process it all.

After a time, the sled halted. When Abby looked up, her heart caught in her chest. Before her, the canyon opened to a panorama of the slopes below. Though the sky was now full gray, painting the snow to match, there was another color far, far in the distance.

In a little valley, sheltered from the weather and biting wind, was the brownish-green of grassy fields.

Behind her, Martina cried out in alarm.

Abby whirled around to see her grappling with a Seeker, trying to writhe free of his grasp. They fell, skidding down the slope, and the heavy sled careened after them.

Too late, Abby noticed the harness tangled about her shoulders. It jerked taut, ripping her from her feet and dragging her with it. She clawed at the ground, but the icy scree gave no purchase. The attempt sent her into a spin, tangling her worse in the grasping cord. She skidded along with no sense of direction, curled instinctively into a ball to protect her belly.

A rock caught her foot and whirled her about; another struck her head with the force of a hammer. Stars exploded across her vision, and the world went black.

Abby drifted from one nightmare to the next, until she found herself lying on her back in a dark and frozen hell. Large, feathery snowflakes settled on a face barely warm enough to melt them. Only the pain in her head suggested she was alive.

She couldn't see through the blackness, but felt the sled rumble beneath her, heard it hiss along the snow behind the crunch of footsteps. How much time had passed?

She tried to move, and panicked when she couldn't. She thrashed harder, felt her body shift. Thank the god – she wasn't paralyzed. As sensation returned to her numb limbs, she felt the cords binding her to the sled.

So that was it, the abrupt end to her ill-fated plan. She was captured, dragged home to face her people's scorn, her Father's wrath. As battered and helpless as she felt, it was almost a relief. Of course, whatever happened to her, it would be so much worse for...

"Where's Martina?" Abby gasped.

"Hush. The Seekers are close on our trail."

Martina?

Abby slipped in and out of delirium until she couldn't tell the waking world from dream. Had she and Martina really escaped? Where were they, even? She caught a slight gleam in the sky as the moon tried and failed to pierce the thick, gray clouds. The world was nothing but snow.

Some time later, the sled ground to a halt. The air held a hint of smoke, but how could that be?

"I'm sorry," Martina rasped. "This is as far as I can take you."

The cords holding Abby went slack, and she felt the woman's arms around her torso, hoisting her. Her head throbbed as if it would burst.

Something creaked, and a foul draft wafted over Abby. A deeper darkness swelled around her, but it was warmer now, and out of the snow.

Martina lowered her onto a soft, prickly floor. "I'm going to lead them away from here. I'm sorry there's no food to leave you. When your child comes, give him my love."

Footsteps rustled. Something creaked again, and the darkness grew complete.

Abby woke in the dark to a throbbing head. She itched all over, but when she moved to scratch, lightning shot through her aching skull. She gave up and clenched her teeth, trying to ignore the crawling sensation she could do nothing about.

She was in a dark, reeking room that stank hardly less than the composter. She was cold, too, but not frozen – which came as a surprise as the memories trickled back. Where was she? Where was Martina? Her brain said to panic, but her body was too sore and weary to comply. She shut her eyes, useless anyway in the black, and slipped into a fitful sleep.

The next time she woke, a faint seam of light traced the outline of a crude but heavy door. The wind whistled an eerie tune through the cracks. She fought through the pain and eased herself upright. "Martina?" she whispered.

Something rustled in the darkness.

Abby strained her eyes until the room slowly came into view. The walls were unmortared stone, piled thick, and the floor was heaped with chaff. The shadow in the corner shifted again.

"Martina," she croaked through a parched and swollen throat. "Wake up."

The shadow crept closer, accompanied by the dull clank of an iron bell. It stepped into the streamer of light that trickled through the door, and Abby recoiled in horror.

It was a four-legged demon from some nether hell, with curving horns, a tuft of beard, and soulless yellow eyes. She scuttled away until her back pressed against the far wall.

Hot breath puffed against Abby's neck, making her skin crawl. Slowly she turned, barely daring to look, dreading what she might see.

There she was, face to face with a second demon, with nowhere to flee. Abby crumpled to the floor, overcome with terror.

She didn't realize she was screaming until the door burst open.

A man barged in and leveled a hayfork at her chest. He had silver-white hair and a thick beard. In Sanctuary, few could grow beards, and none did willingly – save a Seeker on assignment.

"On your feet," he ordered. "Come where I can see you."

Abby's blood ran cold. "Where's Martina? What did you do with her?"

The hayfork dipped, and the man squinted into the shadows. "You okay there, girl? Looks like you took quite a knock to the head."

"You're not a Seeker?" Abby brushed her scalp and found it tender to the touch. Flecks of dried blood clung to her fingertips. "Where am I?"

The man stuck his fork into a pile of hay. He gave a low whistle. "I'll be. No wonder I didn't recognize you. You're from up the mountain." He nudged the snuffling demon back from her, and it fell to munching dry grass. "Let's get you into the house."

Suddenly, realization dawned. The beasts, the beard, the crude stone hut... She had reached the lower village. But how? The dim gray light caused her head to throb, making it hard to think.

The man held out a hand. "Come on. Breakfast is still in the pot. Warm up, eat, and then we'll talk."

Abby let the man help her to her feet. She followed, her legs trembling beneath her.

"So how far along are you?" the woman asked. Brown-eyed and raven-tressed, she hardly showed the blood at all. She bounced a child on her knee, a dark-haired baby boy.

Dressed in her shift and a borrowed coat, Abby dug into her second bowl of thin barley gruel. It had little flavor, and, if there was any scent, she couldn't smell it over the burning peat. Above the firepit, the kettle had been set aside to make room for her drying clothes. "Three months, I think. Is it so obvious?"

"A mother knows these things," she said with a wink.

A mother. In Sanctuary, her son would have been taken from her, her purpose served once he was born. But here in the wasteland...

"Another bowl?" offered the woman. Her face was lean with hunger.

"Oh, I couldn't," Abby protested. She *could*, but the woman hadn't eaten, and the pot was near empty. She nodded to the baby. "Is he your first?"

"Second," she said, but her lips drew tight. "Second to live, at least. My eldest, Tiri, is taking the goats to pasture." The baby drowsed, and she set him in the cradle.

Abby looked around the little cottage, with its dirt floor, its walls of mud-daubed stone. Wind gusted through the chinks, stirring the smoky air. "It must be a hard life here."

"It is," admitted the woman, "but we make the most of it. We have each other."

The door opened, admitting the chill air of a crisp morning. The man came in, shook the snow from his coat, and wrapped his arms around the woman.

"He's your... husband?" Abby asked, recalling Martina's word for Bertholo.

"Aye," she said, "and I his wife. I hear they do things differently up the mountain?"

Abby nodded.

The woman took her husband's coat and hung it by the fire. "It must be a hard life there, too."

Abby had pitied the lower villagers for so long, the woman's sympathy caught her off guard. "In a different way, perhaps. But yes."

"It must be," the man said, "for you to have run away. Feel any better?"

"I do, thank you. But I came here with a friend. Have you seen her?"

The man and woman looked at each other, concern etched on their faces. It was the man who spoke. "A party from up the mountain passed through here during the night, and returned not long before dawn. I don't know if they caught her or gave up in the storm."

He didn't add the third possibility – that they had found Martina in no state to bring home. Abby prayed to the god that she was somehow safe, somehow still alive, but the prospects were bleak. "What if she's hurt? I need to find her!" Or at least find what happened to her.

The woman turned to her husband. "You'd best go with the lass. Let me worry about the fields until you're back."

The man nodded and draped his still-damp coat over his shoulders. "Alright, just don't overdo it. I'll hurry back."

Abby wrung her hands. "I could never ask that of you…"

The woman smiled, her eyes sparkling with tiny flecks of gold. "There's no need to ask."

There was no thought, no hesitation. Their generosity shamed her. "How do I thank you?" she whispered, trying not to cry. "I don't even know your names."

"I'm Davyn," the man said, "and the wife's Tarah. And think nothing of it."

But she couldn't. Overwhelmed by their kindness, Abby did cry. They had taken her in, given her food they couldn't spare, even though they had nothing.

No, not nothing, she realized. Abby saw with envy how the woman leaned against her husband, their child squirming in the cradle. They had something worth more than the safety of Sanctuary's thick walls and steady rations. They had a family.

Despite the snowfall, it wasn't hard to follow the Seekers' tracks. There had been eight, maybe ten of them in the group. It wouldn't surprise Abby if Father had emptied the city of Seekers to hunt her down.

As the sun rose, lighting the sky like frozen fire, Abby paused to lean against a stunted tree. She fumbled with the pouch of dried leaves Tarah had given her – featherfoil, the woman had called it. She didn't like the herb's bitter taste, and wondered if her nausea wasn't a little worse this morning, but at least it took the edge off her aches.

Davyn climbed a rock to peer above the thicket, searching the landscape with a frown. "It can't be far now. Not if they went this way."

When, a few minutes later, they broke free of the short, scrubby brush, Abby saw what he meant. The land fell away in a cliff so sudden it made her stomach lurch.

"Careful. It gets slick here." Davyn caught her elbow and steered her away from the edge. "Looks like they turned right, toward Giant's Nose."

A sudden gust tugged at Abby, yanking her coat and scarf, and she clung to the man who, a few hours ago, had been a stranger. Even in daylight, the track along the rim was daunting; she could hardly imagine how terrible it had been for Martina, alone in the dark. Where had her friend gone? "Is there a path down, ahead?" she shouted over the wind.

Davyn didn't answer. They marched on, crunching the snow's icy crust beneath their feet. A hawk wheeled and screamed; from far away, another returned the cry.

The path came to a headland, jutting over the valley below. The tracks formed a cul-de-sac in the snow, where the group had milled around before turning back. There was no way down – none that a person could survive. Had they cornered Martina here and captured her? Or...

Abby crept to the edge and peered over, her heart thudding in her chest. A cry escaped her lips.

Far, far below was the sled, dashed to pieces on the cruel rocks. Beside it were two bodies. Except for the blood, they looked like broken dolls, discarded by a careless child. She drew back in horror.

Davyn closed his eyes. His jaw clenched, and he swallowed hard. "I'm sorry for your friend. I'd feared the worst, but it's something else to *know*."

Abby sunk to the ground, numb with shock. The bitter wind pulled back her hood, teased her hair into streamers, but she barely felt it. She had abandoned her people and failed her only friend. Save the child in her belly, she was utterly alone.

Davyn took off his hat and twisted it in his hands. "Listen… Why don't you come back to the house? We can–"

"I have to see her." She wasn't sure why, but she did. She wanted to say farewell, maybe build a cairn. Martina deserved better than to be left for the carrion beasts. "How do I get down?"

The man gave a heavy sigh. "There's a rope we use to haul up peat from the valley, but it's not safe for a person. The wind could dash you against the cliff."

She'd given up safety when she left the stout walls of Sanctuary. She could skulk home once Martina was buried, but not before. "I'll risk it."

They backtracked half a mile, to where a rope was coiled beneath the snow – one end secured to a boulder, the other tied to a wooden basin. Abby stood in the bucket and gripped the rope for dear life as the man lowered her down. Though it swayed and rocked with every gust, she reached the bottom without disaster.

From there, she followed the cliff wall, climbing across shifting piles of scree. She nearly stumbled over the bodies before she saw them.

Up close, she recognized the other corpse. Joriel. He was the youngest Seeker, barely more than a boy, and eager to prove himself. She realized he was the one who'd caught them on the mountain slope, and the puzzle pieces shifted into place.

For a second time, Joriel must have rushed ahead of the pack. He'd caught Martina at the ledge, and, rather than be dragged back to Sanctuary, she'd flung them both to their death.

Had the other Seekers, mistaking Joriel for her, given her up for dead? What if that were why they'd turned around? It could take them a day or more to recognize their error, time she could use to get a head start… But to where? She had lost her friend, her guide. How would she survive the wilderness alone? Abby knelt beside Martina's broken body and wept, sobbing useless apologies.

Through her tears, she noticed something clutched in the dead woman's hand. It was a leather thong, torn from around her neck. Abby pulled it free of her grip, and stared at the mystery dangling from the cord – a silver ring, in a pattern of woven vines. Salome's ring.

Why would Martina have stolen it? When had she even had the chance?

Abby held the ring up to the light, awed by the workmanship. It had to be from the wasteland. The smiths of Sanctuary were adept at forging tools, but they brought no art, no beauty to their work.

It was also smaller than she expected.

On a hunch, she tried it on for size. Though Salome had worn the ring on her thumb, it was too tight for Abby's. She found it snug on her third finger.

There was no way Salome's hands were so tiny; the ring wasn't hers, but its twin. So what did it mean that there were two? What was she missing?

As Abby studied Martina's face, almost peaceful in death, her friend's words came back like an echo. *We said our vows, traded rings, and pledged our lives to each other.* Understanding struck her like a bolt from the sky.

It was no coincidence that Orphiel had found Martina just as her life had been destroyed. To persuade her to come to Sanctuary, he had first needed to isolate her. Bertholo's ring, the bottle of wine – they were a boast, grim trophies of the hunt.

Orphiel had killed a man, and for what?

She knew the answer. It was the same thing that drove all her people, had driven her. Father's approval.

Abby turned aside and retched.

Even in service of the cause, how could a Seeker do such evil? Did Father know the cost of his prize?

Deep, deep down, beneath the thoughts she allowed herself to think, she knew the answer. The great cause justified anything, even atrocity. Father would stop at nothing to breed seraphim back into this ruined world, because that was the only way to save it. The Seekers, as extensions of his will, would do the same.

Martina, her, her son... they were nothing but tools to be used and discarded. But what if the Patriarch were wrong? What if the world didn't need seraphim? What if all his plans, all his schemes, were nothing but the crazed obsession of a wicked old man?

There was only one way to learn the truth.

They left the next day, in the pale gray before dawn. Davyn led a goat laden with supplies gathered from around the village, while Abby followed. Everyone had chipped in.

Abby didn't question the villagers' kindness anymore. It made sense now. For people with nothing but each other, working together was a matter of survival, a way of life.

Together they cut through a small, scrubby forest, more brush than trees, until the village disappeared from sight. The wind was fresh, and the sky brightened to liquid gold.

Some time after noon, footsore and hungry, they stopped for a quick rest. "Are you sure I can't persuade you to stay with us until the child comes?" Davyn offered. "Space is tight, but we'd make the room."

Abby scratched the goat's wooly beard. "I know you would. You've already done too much for me." She cringed to think what would happen if Father found them hiding her. And besides, she'd find no answers in the little village.

His mouth cocked into a half-grin. "Tarah made me promise to try."

By evening, they came to a jutting outcrop of rock. Davyn left the goat and scrambled to the top. "This is it," he called down to her. "The farthest I've been. It's guesswork from here."

Abby climbed up behind him and took in the view. The landscape rippled with shadow-dappled hills, endless steppe – and beyond that, who knew? She felt the walls of her tiny world expanding, giving her room to breathe. She sucked in the frosty air.

"Feels good, doesn't it?"

"It does," she agreed. The vast expanse, full of danger and possibility, thrilled her. She was done being told how to live, what to believe. Never again would she be the Patriarch's creature – and god willing, her son never would be. Their choices, right or wrong, would be their own.

Abby closed her eyes and pictured Martina scaling the slope those few brief weeks ago – from freedom to prison, from life to death. She imagined herself treading those very steps in reverse, each footprint a guide and a gift.

"Thank you, Martina," she whispered to her absent friend. The words would never be enough.

See Chris Cornetto's story "Sanctuary" online at Metaphorosis.
If you liked it, leave a comment. Authors love that!
Remember to subscribe to our e-mail updates so you'll know when new stories are posted.

About the story

One reason I write short stories is to flesh out the world of the novels I one day hope to publish. "Sanctuary" began as an exploration of certain characters' roots (Abby's child among them), but it quickly became a philosophical exercise

To write this story, I had to consider how a totalitarian society controls its citizens. There are certain obvious techniques we see applied in countries that shall remain nameless: stripping citizens of identity, rewarding them for informing on each other, and forcing them to compete for the goodwill of the ruling class, just to name a few. It also doesn't hurt to have a caste of good, old-fashioned enforcers.

The true key to subjugating a population, however, lies in controlling the flow of information. It isn't fear of the Seekers that keeps Abby in Sanctuary, but her faith in the Patriarch's lies. Without an outside perspective, she lacks the means to question her society — until Martina's arrival causes cracks in her worldview. Only by having the courage to allow that *her* truth might not be *the* truth does Abby win her freedom.

For us as well as Abby, perspective is essential to freedom. When we allow others to curate our access to information, we surrender that freedom.

A question for the author

Q: Q: What's a typical writing day like for you?

A: It used to be a matter of taking my wife and our laptops to a coffee shop for the evening, but the lockdown put an end to that practice. I still find that, in order to focus, I require a space away from the distractions of everyday life. Therefore, my wife and I still go on our evening writing dates — we just brew our coffee at home and take it outside to the tent on our porch.

About the author

Chris Cornetto is a physics teacher by day and writer by night. In addition to physics, he has degrees in chemistry, philosophy, and psychology. He likes exploring ethical questions through fantasy settings, and enjoys long walks with small dogs.

Siberia in Four Dimensions

Esem Junior

Physicist Boris K. is one of three men held responsible for the catastrophic failure of Russia's largest supercollider, a classified, subterranean loop running 260 kilometers through Siberia. The underground explosion has left frenetic scribbles on Western seismographs and cost the Russian government trillions in rubles. It has also left one worker debilitated. This twenty-six-year-old man, perforated by subatomic particles traveling near the speed of light, lies on a cot in a metal Quonset hut. One half of his body has prematurely aged, now decades older than the other.

Anna adjusts her nurse's cap and watches Boris lean over the man. Huddled together within the small reach of a space heater, she sees what he sees: one eye bright, the other rheumy; one cheek baby smooth, the other spotted and furrowed. She touches her own cheek, wrinkled by many cold seasons.

The field hospital shudders under gales that clear all weakness from the larch forests at the 60th parallel. The patient is whispering and Boris leans in close. Anna hopes he won't notice the bulge under the patient's lower lip, where she's packed a boiled mash of iceland poppy seeds harvested from the boreal forest. Boris is Anna's son, but he is a creature of the state. For him, Moscow's medicines are always adequate. Russia never makes mistakes.

Boris lowers his ear close to the man's mouth. Anna knows what he's saying, because he's repeated it for days. "Time all at once, all at once."

Her son shakes his head. "Gibberish," he says. "What has he told you?"

Anna hesitates. She knows nothing of the supercollider — she's on a need-to-know basis and her post requires only that she tend to the ill. Her psychological profile report, however, never betrayed her talent for harvesting information. The sick man, under the influence of her gentle narcotics, has said other things.

"He said the stream pulled him in," she says. "What does that mean?"

Boris waves her off. "Impossible; he fell in. His own imbecility."

"Boris." Her voice comes from the back of her throat. "He lost his family."

The patient was beset by grief, Anna knows, after his wife and two children succumbed to pneumonia in this subarctic climate. She also knows that her son, when challenged, will speak without thinking.

But Boris only gives her a cold look.

"What stream?" she says.

"Enough," he says. His eyes narrow. Her son has the fortune of being a big man in Russia, and people rarely question him. Anna strangles her finger with a twist of gauze. She reminds herself that people like him put cosmonauts in orbit.

But the patient is mumbling something else.

Overhead, military personnel struggle to change the Quonset hut's camouflage netting to blend with the brown autumnal ground. The rustling interweaves with the man's whispers.

They step closer, to hear better.

"I see him," the man says, the hive of poppy seeds visible at his gumline.

Boris turns his head, apparently in disgust. "What?" he growls.

The man points a tremoring finger at Boris. "I see *you*. Alive, a hundred years more. Homeless."

Boris has had enough. He lifts the man by the hospital gown, but the gown is open in the back and the patient slumps back onto the cot.

Anna has no time to intervene. The door shudders, a blast of frigid air.

A soldier stands there, a middle-ranking officer with two yellow stars on his collar, chased by the smell of forest. The polish of his boots reflect the bars of hanging fluorescent lights. He is new, Anna notes. His footwear hasn't yet seen winter.

He surveys the scene, then looks to Boris. "What is the report?"

"The patient is unhelpful."

The soldier tut-tuts, but a smirk creeps into his jaw. "The eyes of Mother Russia are watching, comrade. It would be a shame," he says, "should history forget a man of your intellect."

Boris is a head taller than the man. Anna looks into her son's eyes and sees no fear. He has an intelligence quotient of 191, but sometimes she thinks fear might do him good.

Boris raises himself to full height and stands over the officer. "History will be kind to me, tiny lieutenant, because I will write it."

Outside, Boris finds himself surrounded by other Quonset huts — half-cylinders set on their sides, sheathed in corrugated steel. Green camouflage netting from the summer, piled on the ground, feathers under the winds. He has little patience for the military complex and its ant-like soldiers and their blind execution of orders. He is Russia's top physicist and the world's top investigator of the interplay between relativity and quantum mechanics, having mathematically proven the existence of twenty-four separate dimensions and having won the Copley Medal twice.

A man leans against the medical hut, slicing a crabapple. He has no uniform, no coding. His hair is long and waxed back.

"Tell me, friend," he says. His eyes are arctic, the color of a sled dog's. "Did the patient cause the implosion, or was it you?"

Boris eyes the stranger, then his knife. It's a Yakutian blade, forged by northern peoples for the purpose of skinning seals. He hasn't met this person, but he's met other versions, for the president's secret police are never far. Boris knows there'll be no logic to this discussion nor adherence to any rules, and this bothers him, more so than the military, because at least the Russian army has chains of command and order. Boris prefers equations with quantifiable results, efficiencies that can be measured. He distrusts the concept of rounding to whole numbers and the infirmities of human interaction.

The stranger's eyes crinkle. "You have a boy, yes?"

The worst thing, Boris knows, is to hesitate, to be soft. He might not understand all the rules of human etiquette, but he understands the most important ones. This rule he knows too: that in Russia one is expendable until one makes oneself unexpendable.

"You," Boris says, "cannot decipher the terabytes left by the accelerator." He refers to the data recorded by the supercollider's sensors in the moments before the tunnel's implosion. A printout is kept in a subterranean vault. "Something extraordinary has happened. Half of a man cannot age unless there is a fundamental disruption in the fabric of spacetime. It is a new application of time dilation."

The man lifts a slice of crabapple with his knife and takes the fruit in his mouth. He cuts another slice, offers it to Boris. It's understood that, whether or not Boris accepts the fruit, something will be expected of him.

When Boris doesn't move, the man lets the apple slice drop to the ground. "You know nothing."

"I need the data."

"The first copy is free," he says. He chews with his mouth open. "The second comes for a price."

"You are obstructing something much greater than yourself."

The other man doesn't move.

"What do you want?"

"Something worth the weight of those papers."

In the next few hours, Boris's son will go missing.

Alexei sits in the old hunting cabin he shares with his family. His grandmother cuts his hair.

He loves these moments, their sounds, their scents. Anna spent her childhood here in Siberia, learning the land, and her kitchen steeps in the smells of the forest. She harvests its plants and secretes them into the cabin via hidden pockets sown into her dress. The acridity of cowberries, the must of lichen — these flavor their gruel from Moscow.

Each room is bugged with listening devices, but they cannot detect the rich aromas that suffuse her kitchen. Nor can they hear what Anna says because she taps her words in Morse Code on Alexei's shoulder.

"A man was hurt," she codes, while her other hand directs the barbers' shears. "He said a name — Planckatron." She is aware her grandson's friends have engineered a secret internet connection. "The name, you will look it up?"

Her touch worries Alexei. Her fingers move fast, some words are misspelled. But she's rightfully worried — something has happened, something to do with the recent earthquake. Since that moment, Alexei's father has changed. Less patience, more bark, even more bite. Under the shirt, where Alexei's grandmother touches him, a yellowing bruise matches the square shape of Boris' left fist. Each letter Anna drums into his shoulder leaves a dull ache.

Alexei recalls a time from before. Before Siberia, before his father was important.

This is the sum of his memory: an oligarch's estate outside Moscow, bearded men with suits but open collars, some in soldier uniforms. A stone mansion, a garden, and his father moving stiffly, a ship among icebergs. The children shooed away, Alexei among a group of boys who took turns killing birds with a slingshot. Then his refusal, their laughter, the heat in his cheeks — pizda, they called him. He walked deeper into the woods.

His father found him sleeping among leaves at the base of a hundred and fifty-year old oak tree, under the slant of autumn light. Boris lay down next to him and squeezed his hand. "Thank you son," he said, plum brandy on his breath, "for being here today. After today, we are no longer peasants."

Alexei had never realized they were peasants, and it was strange to hear the world imposed this architecture on them without him even knowing. His life until then had a been a collection of wonderful moments. Riding on his father's shoulder, reading with his grandmother by firelight. At the oligarch's estate that day he pondered this new dimension as they lay there, hand-in-hand, trading messages in Morse Code like Anna taught them, until the light weakened and the ground cooled.

Boris sat up. "Come, solnyshko, it is late."

Alexei resisted.

"Do not worry, son, this moment never changes." Boris looked up at the branches of the white oak. "The fourth dimension of time is like this tree. We are pushed through the trunk but, in every single second, we leave behind copies of ourselves. They remain imprinted there, like rings. Perhaps one day we can revisit them."

Alexei hasn't visited this memory for years and wonders if it resides anywhere in his father's memory. He guesses the answer is no and, now fifteen, he realizes this wasn't a good moment, but rather the sunset of something good.

His grandmother's scissors whisper in his ear.

She squeezes sentences into his aching shoulder, asking again about the internet search, and he encloses his hand over her fingers.

"Yes," he codes back. He'll do anything for her, no matter the risks. It was she who raised him, who told him bedtime stories about old Siberia that imprinted his mind with wonder. Stories about soldiers during the first great war who found the last living Neanderthals. Stories about her own grandfather, the first man to make an overland crossing to the North Pole. "He was a great man who did great things," she told him once, "and so will you."

They are interrupted. Boris shoulders through the door, a tome of paper tucked under his arm. He heads towards his study.

"Say hello to your son," Anna says.

"His mother's son." Boris walks as he speaks. "Unequipped for the real world, useless."

Alexei feels his grandmother's hand tense. He tells her, "Don't mind him, babushka. He is touched by Hans Asperger's disease." Russia has no such diagnoses for adults, but Alexei has read American articles online and wonders about this — Boris' obsessive focus, his abruptness with people. Russia abhors complicated labels — here, one is strong, weak, a genius, or a fool — but Alexei has begun to believe it's a world in need of further nuance.

Boris slams his paperwork on the table. He hoists Alexei from the chair by his collar. Only centimeters separate their chins, and spittle lands on Alexei's face as Boris yells. But Alexei isn't listening. He's happy. He has finally pulled Boris from the distant fugue where he spends his days, in some other plane of existence, and all Alexei wants to do is keep him here, keep him present in this moment.

"Enough!" Anna's palm smacks the table.

Boris drops his son, then points a finger at her. It is shaking. "You," he says. "You fill his head with garbage."

Boris is a big man, but Anna can steer him with pinches just above the elbow. She manipulates him into his study.

"What garbage?" Her words are crisp. This has nothing to do with her stories, she thinks, and everything to do with Alexei's comment. Boris is sensitive, and she wishes she could reassure him. He isn't handicapped, just incredibly selfish.

Boris grits his teeth. "Fairy tales, pseudo-science. You tell him the Red Army encountered Neanderthals during the great war. Nonsense."

"Your great-grandfather told me those stories. The same man who drove sled dogs over sea ice to reach the top of this planet." Anna remembers him sitting by a hearth full of fire, his eyes hazed with cataracts, telling her tales from his youth.

"Pradedushka wasn't the first to reach the north pole. The Americ —"

Anna holds her palm flat. She points to the lamp fixture, impregnated with a microphone. "That," she hisses, "is your blood. Show respect — for your ancestors, and the boy who comes after you."

"His mother's son."

Anna shakes her head. Alexei's mother was an Olympic-caliber gymnast, strong in will though small in size, her pelvis too narrow for childbirth. The Communist Party arranged this union, and Anna theorizes her son was enamored of the idea of marriage, of the idea of fatherhood. Never the reality. "It is you," she says, "who believes propaganda. Worse, lies of your own making."

Boris winces. He takes her wrist and begins to code. "I trade only in facts," he taps. "Here's one: we're in danger."

"Tell me."

He shakes his head. When they return to the kitchen, his papers are missing.

Anna throws the door open and steps into the winds. Their cabin is a hunting lodge that belonged to a twentieth-century tsar, and it sits at the edge of a village comprised of metal huts littered among the larch and pine. Their nearest neighbor, Mikhail, works beneath the monstrous undercarriage of a Burlak transport vehicle, each of its six tires taller than a person, all necessary to transport the Quonset residents to the government facilities located some miles north. Winter, after all, makes the roads otherwise impassable.

Anna has always liked Mikhail. He is handsome, soft-spoken, and were he born in the same generation her feelings about him might have progressed. She senses he admires her similarly.

"Mikhail," she says. "Have you seen our boy?"

He emerges from beneath the arctic transport vehicle shaking his head. "The children," he says, "lose themselves in the forest. I worry they wander into the Nikelgorod Exclusion Zone. When my own boy returns, we'll talk. So let us keep in touch, yes?"

Alexei treads the larch forest past the signs that warn of nuclear contamination. Beyond the trees, the abandoned, Soviet-era apartments of Nikelgorod rise against the sky. People are told this nickel-mining settlement fell victim to shifting winds after a seventy-megaton test. It's here that Alexei and his friends find solace, a private space of their own.

It is here that they climb.

Alexei finds the other boys at the base of a concrete statue of Alexander the Third, pioneer of the Trans-Siberian Railroad, rising twenty meters into the air. A military-style ushanka sits atop the tsar's head, while his hands rest on the hilt of a sabre, its pointy end touching the earth where the boys sit.

They huddle around a tablet, watching a Frenchman scale the Burj Khalifa in Dubai without rope. They watch for technique, to help them plot a route from where they sit to the top of Alexander's ushanka. They've grown bored with Nikelgorod's other structures — the theater, the church's onion dome, every façade of the nickel-processing plant.

One boy nods at Alexei. He lives in the Quonset hut closest to Alexei's cabin. "Are you ready to conquer Alexander the Third?" he asks. The boys bond over this preoccupation, not so much with each other, for at any moment the military may tear one of their families from this Siberian wasteland and post them in another dystopia. At nine thousand kilometers wide, Russia has many such places.

"A moment," Alexei says, and rounds the statue and takes a seat by the heel of the tsar's boot. He removes from his satchel Boris' paperwork.

Alexei has tried to make sense of his father's paper on the walk through the taiga but, without the internet, it's hopeless. He fishes from his pocket a chipped mobile phone — contraband from Outer Manchuria that musters no cellular signal — and connects to his friends' wi-fi hotspot. He must know what's so classified and unknowable about his father's life, why they live a half day's drive from any city and near a government installation that appears on no map. For this, everything was sacrificed, and Alexei simultaneously feels the ache in his shoulder and the warmth of his father's hand behind the oligarch's estate. He wants to reclaim that moment and capture the alternate history that might've happened between them, but first he must know what led them astray. But can he possibly decipher his father's papers? Alexei doesn't understand physics. Not vectors, not forces, not relativity, much less the mathematic hieroglyphs that describe them. But as his internet browser loads, he rescans the papers, and something stands out. The top right corner of each page has numbers divided into angles, minutes, and seconds — GPS coordinates, the same ones the boys use to navigate the forests. Alexei thumbs these into his phone.

The coordinates form a massive circle, stretching north. The closest spot lies two hundred meters away, so Alexei slips away through an alley between the old theater and bakery.

He finds an empty field at the town's outskirts, but the grass here is newer, the conifers shorter, a superhighway of fresh vegetation that runs beneath his feet and stretches through the taiga. He wonders, how has he not noticed this?

The nearest building is a smooth, windowless cuboid, roughly the height of Alexander the Third. It's one of the few structures the boys haven't summitted. At its base stands a set of iron doors, impervious to crowbars. But there's a crack that zags up the side, having appeared after the recent earthquake, and he knows from summiting nearby buildings about the hatch on the roof.

At the building Alexei assesses the crack. He's the smallest of his peers but, with urban climbing, being small has its advantages. His hand fits into the fissure and, by making a fist, he can anchor himself to the wall. Using both hands and feet in this way, he can jam his way to the top. The boy puts on his climbing shoes, their rubber soft and sticky, throws on his backpack, and chalks his hands.

The inside of the crack bites against his fists — every move requires complete attention — and in this demand for presence he can climb from the fugue of insults and inhabit a moment existing outside the literal and proverbial reach of his wayward and adulterated father, outside the scramble of the world's confusion.

At the top, the crack continues from the side and across to the hatch, and has broken the trapdoor from its moorings. Alexei lifts the square of iron and descends down the awaiting ladder.

They take Boris six days later. Eventually they come for Anna.

It's the man without a uniform who questions her, accompanied by a soldier Anna knows from the field hospital. They sit at a table in the cabin's kitchen, where the man without uniform cleans his fingernails with a caviar fork. The soldier won't look at Anna, and she stares hard into his face, searching.

Anna and this solder have spent three years now at this military camp. He and his brethren have grown accustomed to her hospitality, her birch sap teas, her high-octane coffees. As she walks from the cabin to the field hospital each day, she alerts them when the tips of their noses whiten, a precursor to frostbite, and fixes their balaclavas to keep out the arctic cold. These soldiers are still boys, and miss their mothers on the far side of the Urals. Like boys, they cower before powerful men.

The soldier refuses eye contact while the other man continues to remove grime from his thumbnail with the caviar fork. Anna refuses to acknowledge it. She looks over this other man. The cracked leather of his jacket has the dull sheen of cockroach wings. He wears sunglasses with aqua lenses, like those preferred by aging rock stars. She asks, "Your mother has given you a name?"

The man smiles. "You may call me Volk."

"That is not a proper name."

Volk shrugs.

"What is your family name?"

"Family?" he says. "What does it matter, if their poor choices doom us? It's a thing of beauty to survive, grandmother, especially when the world conspires against this."

Anna appraises his sunglasses.

"You are blind?" she says.

Volk squints through the turquoise glass.

"Only two people wear sunglasses in basements, sir. Blind men, and fools."

The man laughs. "You," he wags a finger, "I like you."

Anna feels encouraged. "Speak to my son Boris, he is a big boy. Bigger than you."

"But it's the little boy that interests me. He has been missing quite some time now, no?"

Chilled blood washes through her ribcage, but Anna is quick. "Allow me to find him, then. Who better to lure him than his babushka?"

The man reaches out and touches the tines of the caviar fork to where her collarbones meet. "You say those lines. Soon you'll believe them."

Volk removes the caviar fork from her skin. She dares not look down at the two dimples that surely remain, the skin within their orbit pale and swollen.

"You have three days. After that, I cannot help you."

Anna is a tough woman, but she understands bad things happen to people in this country. She should know. For years she managed an infirmary in the basement of a Moscow federation building, wheeling victims on gurneys through dishwater-gray corridors, treating their cigarette burns, their naked fingernail beds, the stumps of missing toes.

"I'll see you on the third dawn," Volk says.

Later, Anna looks out a northern window at the soldier standing post, shuffling his feet so they don't freeze in his boots. Behind him, through a window in the neighbor's Quonset home, the neighbor's boy is watching too. In the condensation on the windowpane he writes something, then wipes it away.

It was too small for Anna to see.

At the ladder's end, Alexei finds a concrete hall awash in red light. The ladder meets the floor at a right angle but when he touches down and let's go of the rungs, his shoes slide across the floor towards its dark end, leaving tracks through a metallic film on the floor. He grabs the ladder. He is still young enough to believe in the impossible, to wonder at its mechanics, and for the first time he considers that his father's secret involves a truth more precious than any of them.

There are shelves on the walls, anchored with bolts, and hand-over-hand he lowers himself down the hall. The confusion of gravity dizzies him. Where the shelving runs out of length, the room opens into a chasm steeped in blackness. Alexei hooks an elbow around one of the shelves' uprights and removes a pocket flashlight and throws wattage into the hole.

The light is drawn to the center of a large space where a miniature planet hovers, a black planet rimmed in embered light, orbited by disks of the same colors. An evil tiny Saturn.

It pulls the luminescence from the flashlight and casts auroras against the walls, dancing as in a grotto, but this isn't a cave. It's a tunnel — an enormous tunnel, big enough for a subway and yet there are no tracks. He can put no name to this thing.

There is no echo in this space, no sound. It's as though Alexei's reached the end of all things, an edge of the universe.

He fumbles for Boris' papers in his backpack with his free hand. But the papers are thick, meant to be held with two hands, and the leaves split open and fall instantly, sideways, pulled toward the tunnel's center.

He shines his flashlight after the papers. They hover in the air a few meters into the larger space, oozing into the abyss. Their edges begin to curl.

The boy is nauseous, woozy. Hand-over-hand, he moves back toward the ladder and ascends it.

Outside, the world is different. He's loitered in the tunnel perhaps twenty minutes, but it is the night sky that greets him, and it twinkles over a layer of snow that blankets the buildings and treetops for as far as he can see. He thinks that whatever his father has been up to, it can change the universe, and he questions whether his ideas about life have been too small.

Anna boils water on the wood stove. The yellowing sky above the eastern tree line has begun to wash out the starlight. It's the third dawn.

For three days she's hiked the forest, looking for the boy, leaving ribbons on trees and cairns by streambeds, encoded with messages, but the taiga has offered nothing in return.

She unwraps gray, army-surplus toilet paper nearly to its cardboard core and removes the Wolfsbane she's pressed there. The flower's purple shade is still vibrant. The toxins reside in the roots, but she throws the entire plant in the bubbling water and sets out two cups, one for Volk, one for her. She'll drink first, while he watches, then offer him a cup. She re-enacts the scene until her breathing slows. She no longer has a reason to exist, the generations before her deceased, her son and grandson lost to cruelty.

When the knock sounds at the side door, she jumps.

It is Alexei.

She can only stare. He looks clean. He wears the same clothes as the day he disappeared — his olive canvas jacket, his blue ripstop nylon pants. His hair hasn't grown.

"Where have you been, boy?" She embraces him, envelopes him, their hearts beating just inches from one another. She can feel the muscles in his back; he's eaten well. From a part in his hair, she smells the autumnal foliage that disappeared from the forest with the first snow. "It's been six weeks," she says, and holds him away and studies him. His eyes have the shape of confusion.

"Six weeks?" His eyes flit around the cabin. "Where is dada?"

"Taken." Anna closes her eyes, takes a breath. "Taken north."

"To the circle?" He refers to Stalin's arctic death circle, home of Russia's modern gulags.

"His documents, they need them back. They are classified."

The boy stiffens, but there's no time for questions. A knock rattles the front door.

It is Volk.

He opens the door and removes his gloves. "Good morning, grandmother," he says. "You'll recall we have an appointment." Another man stands at his aft, holding a fifteen-centimeter Makarov pistol.

"Have you found —" But Volk doesn't finish. He sees the boy. "Ah," he says, "the prodigal son returns."

Anna taps words on her neck — words only the boy can read. They need more time, she writes.

Like his father, Alexei never hesitates. He turns to Volk and says, "I have your papers. In a cave, in the mountains."

"You'll take us there."

Anna clears her throat. "Tomorrow. He will take you tomorrow, what is another day? Give me one day with my grandson."

Volk rounds on the boy. "How far is it?"

"A hundred miles," he says.

Volk scans the boy's shoes. Athletic trainers, not boots. The man takes a loose cigarette from his shirt pocket and lights it. He puffs long enough to grow a red cherry at the tip, then turns the cigarette around and appears to contemplate its ember and its many, many uses. "You travel light."

"Gentlemen," Anna says. She steps toward the stove. "Let the adults have tea. I have just boiled water."

Volk puts a hand on her arm. "For everyone then. The boy too."

"It's not to his taste."

Volk smiles. He walks to the stove and looks into the boiling pot where the limp purple petals flutter in the rolling waters. He drops the lit cigarette into the pot. "Okay, grandmother." He turns toward Anna. "One more day with your grandson."

An hour after they leave, the boy falls asleep in his bed. Awake or asleep, Anna feels blessed to spend these moments with him, watching his chest rise and fall. He looks the same as Boris did, when he was young, and she traces the contours of his face with her fingertip. She feels lucky to have another soul in this arctic world. It's all she has.

Boris' letters from prison, folded in her dress pocket, prod against her abdomen. Her mind skips to what he's written. "The boy, a victim of his own imbecility," in that chicken-scratch scrawl. "A fool." Anna dabs her eyes with a shirtsleeve. Boris is a man who cannot sew his own clothes nor cook his own meals. A selfish man, of the most selfish variety, focusing on his equations, desperate for the acclaim of his superiors, to the exclusion of all else. It was she who allowed him to devolve into such a creature. "It's my fault," she whispers. But she knows the past is unchangeable, that only the present is in play.

When the soldiers come at nightfall, she meets them at the door.

They pull Anna from the house.

"I need my winter coat," she says.

"This will just take a minute, babushka," one says.

They are strong, and the toes of her slippers drag against the crust of the snow. She steals a look at the neighbor's Quonset hut and sees the neighbor's boy, backlit in a window. She thinks of her own Alexei. He has no protector. She opens her mouth to cry out warning but the other soldier's hand is ready. Her scream dies in his glove.

Volk waits behind the cabin, finishing a cigarette. He drops it into the snow. "Grandmother, your wish was granted. But this is our way, you know this. There are no gifts in this country. Here we pay for everything."

The report of a single shot from a Makarov pistol sounds through the Siberian night.

Then another.

When the soldiers re-enter the cabin, Alexei is not in his room. He's not in the kitchen, nor in the bedroom, nor anywhere they know to find him.

"Your son has admitted to everything."

"Release me then," Boris says.

"You are his conspirator. Fellow saboteurs."

Boris sits back down in his cell. Through a narrow window he can view the arctic wasteland, when it's not obscured by snowstorms or sulfur dioxide emissions from the Norilsk mines. He curses his son. The narrative in his mind tells the story of a short-sighted boy, selfish and vulnerable to whim. Still, as much as Boris thinks he knows, his thoughts are infinite but bounded.

The first thing he doesn't know is that his bosses are in trouble, because to date nobody has explained what caused the supercollider's implosion. A loss of five trillion rubles isn't easily stomached. The second thing he doesn't know is that, in the tunnel's surviving segments, a layer of palladium, four microns thick, coats the walls. The price per gram of palladium is twice that of gold, and the president has demanded someone re-create this alchemy.

Russia's other physicists haven't been helpful.

Soldiers return Boris to the cabin, where he finds himself provisioned with a copy of the papers he lost and a mandate that he cannot leave the premises. The soldiers take away all his outerwear, even his shoes. Anna, meanwhile, is nowhere to be found, and nobody tells him why. The soldiers have simply said she'll be back, and he believes them.

Whatever questions he has end up suffocating in the focus he reserves for the supercollider data. He reads the papers far into the evening by candlelight, analyzing numbers and calculations. Only the wood stove provides warmth.

The palladium he can explain. The particle accelerator's last experiment smashed atoms of tin into one another, knocking off protons. With palladium sitting four spots left of tin on the periodic table, its creation makes sense. But other data doesn't. The equations cannot balance, even if Boris accounts for string theory's extra spatial dimensions. He can hear his mother's voice as though she were at his ear. "You have identified twenty-four dimensions in your work, but what about the dimensions of love? The dimensions of fatherhood?"

These questions are born of her letters. His photographic memory preserves every character of her looping script. "Get home," she wrote in the letters he received in the arctic prison. "Help me find Alexei. If I cannot appeal to your sense of decency, perhaps then your curiosity."

These words create a knot in his throat he cannot swallow away.

One night the weather is particularly foul, the insides of the windows frosted, the taiga beyond lost in whiteout. Boris is alone, unobserved, and he takes every article in the house and examines it.

The boy's shoes sit beneath the table, their treads caked with a silvery-white metal. Boris steps across the room to the hearth. In the back corner he's spotted the faint imprint of a small shoe in the ash. The interior stones of the hearth are layered in char and so he cannot spot the sticky black rubber left on their surfaces, these footsteps tracking up into the darkness.

A knock sounds at the door, but nobody waits for response. A soldier throws it open.

"Emergency!" the man barks. Behind him stands the neighbor, carrying his own son. The boy's sock is sticky with blood.

"Bandage him, be quick," the soldier says, giving the neighbor wide berth, his eyes skipping between the boy's bloody leg and his own spotless uniform. The neighbor, older than Boris by a decade, turns almost carelessly, swinging his son's leg, grazing the soldier's wool overcoat.

"Idiot!" The soldier checks his fabric, huffs, then steps out the door.

Boris turns to the neighbor. "I'm not a medic," he says. He suspects a compound fracture, bone through skin. "You've confused me with my mother."

The neighbor shakes his head. "I am not mistaken."

"Yes you —"

"We have no other choice. Please, have faith."

Faith, for Boris, is a dangerous word. It asks him to leap to conclusions without the bridge of data underfoot.

They lay the boy on the kitchen table. The soldier monitors through the milky rime on the windowpanes.

Anna's med-kit sits in a closet, below her hanging clothes. Boris sets water to boil and opens the kit, then takes trauma shears and cuts away the boy's sock. He sees nothing, only a mess of syrupy plasma, and he dabs a cloth into the pot of simmering water, then at the skin, clearing blood, trying to locate the wound. He dabs the entire ankle and finds nothing, then looks at the boy's father. His name is Mikhail, Boris remembers now.

Mikhail removes his jacket. There is another jacket underneath, and he removes this too and throws both into a corner. From a shirt pocket he pulls a roll of cloth. "Use these bandages," he says. His eyes are burning. "Disinfect the laceration, set the fracture, wrap the ankle."

There's no fracture to set, but they pretend. The boy screams and the soldier squints through the frosted window. Boris pores iodine over the ankle, then unfurls the bandage around the joint.

"Cut here," Mikhail says.

Boris hesitates, and Mikhail's hand closes over his own and guides him to cut the bandage. The remnant fabric on the roll bears writing, and Mikhail tosses it into Anna's med-kit.

"My own boy, so foolish," Mikhail says. "Fooling around in Nikelgorod … falling from buildings, exposed to radiation." He meets Boris' eye. "We must not give up on our foolish children."

"Your boy will be okay," Boris says. He is realizing something. This man, his mother — they are complex beings with complex thoughts, operating in dimensions unfamiliar to him.

He pulls Mikhail into an embrace, his lips a centimeter from the man's ear. "Radiation in Nikelgorod is a story," he whispers. "It keeps people away. Stories — wonderful things, yes?"

"When shared," the older man says.

The Siberian winter arrives, and the soldier guarding the cabin stands on the porch, his eyelashes heavy with frost. Boris hands him a cup of birch sap tea. It's all he can do not to break the porcelain cup on the man's teeth. The inscriptions on Mikhail's bandages contain stories — about the soldiers' habits, about what happened to Anna. He first decided he would kill those responsible — he doesn't know their names but he has their physical descriptions. They have taken something from him and his first instinct is to balance equations, here with revenge.

Fortunately Mikhail's bandages also hold a blueprint for moving forward, and this plan demands restraint.

Near midnight when the guards change shifts, Boris stirs a new pot of birch sap tea. He finds Anna's copy of Nabokov's *Invitation to a Beheading* and removes, from its final pages, the dried yellow toadflax that she's pressed there. The yellow flowers, brittle, disintegrate in the bubbling water and sigh the faint odor of wet dog. Boris hopes the birch sap will cover this smell. Sips from the tea will force a lengthy visit to the outhouse that stands frozen behind the cabin.

Contrary to popular belief, Boris has always paid attention, and his memory forgets nothing. So he knows all of Anna's herbal recipes and their pharmacological properties. He merely believed, once, these things were unimportant.

At midnight a new soldier knocks at the door. A blizzard has overtaken the night, the winter dust infesting the cup of tea that passes between the men.

Thirty minutes later, Boris watches the soldier run to the latrine.

They've taken Boris' goggles, his jacket, his boots. But he remembers his great-grandfather's stories about the Samoyed peoples in the far north, with slitted eyewear carved from driftwood that filtered the harshness of weather. Boris has cut a like slit in his belt, and fashions the leather around his head. From behind the wood stove he pulls out snowshoes fashioned from wool socks and floorboards. From a closet, Mikhail's second coat. From Anna's keepsake box, lastly, he removes his great-grandfather's steel Adrianov compass.

Boris opens the door to westerly purge winds, laden with ice chips, hazing the visible world from reckoning. He strikes out north in blowing weather that fills his footprints.

He feels what his pradedushka must've felt. Dizzied, no horizon, blundering through roiling clouds of pixelated white. He is proud — to walk in the footsteps of his people, to go beyond. His chest fills with this ancestral spirit and, barring an Act of God, he'll find the boy. He checks the Adrianov compass every forty steps to confirm his bearings.

At the faceless, oblong building in Nikelgorod, he finds Mikhail and his boy at the entrance. "My son believes your son came here," Mikhail said.

Boris punches numbers into a keypad and tumblers unclick. The door, thick like a bank vault, swings inward without sound.

Before they enter, Boris asks the boy, "How would my son get through here?"

Mikhail's son motions for the men to follow. He circles the building and points to the fissure that travels up into the whiteout. "He would've followed this."

Boris barely fits his palm into the crack. "Impossible," he says.

Mikhail lays a hand on Boris' shoulders and feels a slackness in Anna's son. He is surprised. The physicist is an imposing figure — there's always been a rigidity to his posture, in his very being — and Mikhail is encouraged to find plasticity in the man. He wants to do right by Anna, by her family. Mikhail is a mechanic who keeps the military's all-terrain vehicles in repair, with their monstrous tires and snow tracks. He believes he and Anna were the same, both grips in the play of life, moving scenery when others darkened the stage.

"Tonight," he tells Boris, "we triumph over impossibility." He prays for this. There is a cosmic debt he must pay, for he watched the soldiers drag Anna to her death from the dark maw of his kitchen and did nothing. His son, too, is in arrears. The boy never told what he knew about Alexei's disappearance — until the crack of midnight gunshots broke across the plateau.

Boris leads them down into building's gut and, at the bottom of a ladder, they find a concrete hall cast in submarine-red light. They grip the ladder, necessarily so, it seems. Mikhail feels as though if he let go, he'd fall across the room.

"This isn't right," he says.

He shines his flashlight across the floor. The palladium coating offers a soft luster, but Mikhail trains the beam along its surface and into the tunnel.

Alexei is suspended ten meters in, motionless, withdrawn into a fetal posture. His own flashlight points back, a deep-red circle. Beyond that, a black sphere of nothing hangs in the deadened space, silently orbited by an accretion disk, the swirling light warped as though twisted through a carnival mirror.

"My god," Mikhail's son says. The boy releases the ladder and begins sliding across the floor, palladium gathering in ribbons along the outsoles of his boots.

Boris grabs him.

"It's pulling me," the boy says.

"No," Boris says, "you're falling."

Mikhail has locked an arm around the ladder. "Falling? Into what?" He's dizzy, and cannot reconcile how one falls sideways.

"It is ..." Boris shakes his head. He points light into the tunnel at various angles, tries to illuminate its center, but this isn't possible. Everything is swallowed. "A black hole."

Mikhail knows these are formed by dying stars in deep space. He's a maintenance man, not a cretin. "Impossible."

"For many reasons."

"Black holes are big. They cannot fit in tunnels."

"Comrade, black holes can be any size, if you press enough mass into a small enough area. Could we squeeze the earth into the skin of a gooseberry, we'd have such a thing."

Mikhail looks into the abyss, at the curled form of Alexei. He pulls his own boy close. "Why is he stuck there?"

Boris' voice is soft. "He's not stuck. He's moving fast, from his own perspective. Within milliseconds he'll be crushed, in his frame of reference."

"But he's right there." Mikhail points.

Boris sinks to the floor, scraping at the palladium with a thumbnail. "It's the black hole's gravity, its effect on time." Light, he explains, struggles to escape such a thing and yet light must always travel at lightspeed, regardless of circumstance. "This is Einstein's great contribution," Boris says. "If light must always travel at the same speed, and gravity retards its progress, then time must slow down. The seconds dilate so that light can catch up."

Mikhail finds the other man's voice distant, defaulting to the jargon of his trade. Perhaps comforted by it. "This is difficult for me," Mikhail says.

"You will see. Even with us, only seconds are passing, but for the world outside —" Boris motions up the ladder "— it is days, maybe weeks. Could they see us, we would look frozen too."

The maintenance man puts his hand on the physicist's neck and looks into his face.

"We will problem-solve, our people are good at this. Explain to me. Alexei is right there, just meters away."

The big man's eyes have teared. "There is more to the story, look at the red-shifting." He nods at the orb of Alexei's flashlight, a deep red and nearly invisible. "His light is just reaching our eyes, just as starlight from distant galaxies shows us what once was. We are looking into the past."

"If time has slowed," Mikhail says, "perhaps we can reverse it."

"Enough," Boris says. His jaw has tightened, his shoulders too. He wipes his eyes. "The boy is lost." His logical brain patterns have re-emerged. "Let us focus on what's here — the Solar System's only black hole."

Mikhail sees, reflected in the man's eyes, the red auroras that dance on the walls.

"We can be heroes," Boris says. "Each of us."

"But the boy."

Boris inhales. "We must judge objectively. Rescue is impossible."

It is Mikhail's turn to steel up. He feels Anna's breath gather in his lungs and his voice comes low but clear. "Let us have faith."

"But —"

"But nothing." Mikhail can see the line of saltwater that rims Boris' eyes. He can see that Anna's son is breaking down, succumbing to the physical laws of humanity, finding within himself emotions other than anger. "We will get back your boy."

It is summertime when they emerge from the building. Under weak cover of the season's two-hour nightfall, they approach the camp.

They find it deserted, bare as Nikelgorod.

Three days later, they have backed Mikhail's tow truck to the entrance to the oblong building and, with the help of his son, knotted the tow cable to a makeshift harness fashioned from steel chains. Boris yokes himself into these riggings.

Alexei tethers himself to the ladder with a retraced figure-eight knot, snaking the rope through his nylon mountaineering harness.

The tunnel's air is heavy and pressing; Alexei feels as though he's underwater at depth. The harness cuts into his legs and he packs himself into a ball. But he created the disorder, he thinks, and his mind drifts to the report of the pistol, dampened by the wall of spruce logs shielding that terrible thing from view. At that moment and for the first time, he felt as though he were nothing more than an assemblage of flesh and bone. A bloodless creature. But for his father, Alexei is alone in the world, completely and utterly, and to retrieve the man from the gulag, to restore the world he once knew, he must retrieve the papers. In this way can reverse the world's entropy.

The pages drift deeper as Alexei draws closer. No longer frozen, they continue to curl. The closest paper floats just a half-meter away.

This is when the rope snaps.

He looks up, toward the ladder, and swears he can see his father and the neighbors, just a blur of them, up and down the ladder, in and out of the cave, but over the course of a microsecond. There's little time to process because Alexei's in freefall, being crushed, unable to swell his chest to inflate his lungs.

But options appear.

There are frames before him, layers of time stacked, and he can see himself, copies of himself, lined up overhead. A proverbial flipbook of his life, and what Alexei finds is that he needn't fall further. He can move in the opposite direction, second-by-second in reverse, traveling back through time, and it starts by uncurling himself and reversing the choreography of his fall. With a backward dance through the air, the boy inches his way back towards the ladder, back towards home, rewinding his life. The rope unsnaps, his decision to leave the ladder undone.

Outside, he pauses in his reverse-scale down the oblong building. It's all there, the taiga's piney smells, the gritty surface of the crack against the back of his fist. He cannot do anything new but must backtrack through the passageway he's already etched through spacetime. Inhaling carbon dioxide, exhaling oxygen, but he's alive, somehow. Alexei surveys the top of the arboreal forest and savors the moment. He'll be able to see everything again.

When his gaze returns to his hands he finds a horsefly crawling backwards on his arm, something he hadn't noticed on the climb up, and he twitches his forearm.

The horsefly doesn't respond.

He understands then. His father talked about time as a fourth dimension, the trunk of a tree through which all matter moved, all past moments permanently inscribed in its rings. He flexes harder against the encasement of his life, beating notes against its paralyzing membrane.

It's not enough to merely visit the past, he realizes then. He wants to say all the things he wishes he'd said, do all the things he wishes he'd done.

Alexei knows that every action has an equal and opposite reaction and so he wonders, if beating against the wall of the fourth dimension won't affect his past moments, then what is he disturbing? If he can't affect the moments that make up here and now, then when?

Boris sinks toward the black hole. He shines a flashlight toward the ladder where Mikhail keeps watch; when clicked off, his neighbor will raise him back. The older man will be significantly older when Boris returns, the micro black hole placing them on different worldlines with different experiences of time. His mind returns to the patient with the ruined face, and Boris theorizes that the micro black hole, born of the supercollider, sped in its infancy through the tunnel and passed within inches of the victim's head, its core singularity fundamentally changing the fabric of spacetime for long enough to place each side of his face on two similarly different worldlines. It is this issue, he thinks, that truly merits his attention.

The big man mutters to himself. The idiocy of this plan, the romantic beliefs of modern-day peasants. How, he wonders, was he swept up in their mythology? But he swallows this down. He knows. He knows that without the reckless pursuits of his pradedushka, he wouldn't have known how to navigate the blizzard. Without the lessons of his mother, he could not have imprisoned the soldier in the outhouse. Without Mikhail's cunning he would not have learned the fate of his mother or the whereabouts of his son. He understands, now, the beauty of other people, their existence, the strength in their numbers. He wonders if this is love.

Spacetime squeezes Boris as he descends, funneling him toward the singularity. It has obsessed him, this micro black hole. By his calculations, it is a billion tons of mass compressed into the space of an amoeba. The weight of 107 billion people, the mass of each and every ancestor to all those persons currently alive.

He's made it about halfway to the boy and, as he predicted, Alexei falls deeper, in slow motion as his eyes shut and his mouth opens to scream.

Boris knew this would happen — that pursuing the boy would be a chase without closure, that moving nearer to Alexei would only speed up the moving picture of the boy's inevitable death. Einstein's models predicted such a thing, based on tested calculations, and Boris for once cannot stomach being right. What he didn't anticipate was the accelerated effects of time dilation on himself. He knew the world he's left behind would move in fast-forward, but his own calculations are flawed. As Boris sinks toward the dark singularity, Mikhail appears and disappears up and down the ladder, under the crimson glow of the lights, more quickly than anticipated. Ten times, twenty times, a hundred times, Mikhail is blipping in and out of sight, aging, then an old man, then gone.

Boris clicks off the flashlight.

He's alone, doomed, a speck in the universe. His son is gone, Anna is gone, Mikhail is gone, and no longer can he witness their impossible feats nor celebrate them as he should have done. He thinks of Mikhail's trickery of the army, his son's fifty-foot ascent along little more than a fault line. All the science and medals in the world will not replace them. He tells himself these feelings are simply in his genetic hardwiring, in the hardwiring of all humans — social creatures engineered to feel this way for the sake of their collective survival, no different than pack animals. But he will surrender, there is no other way. In searching for memories of Anna, of his son as a baby, Boris finds he can't even remember their faces. Boris turns to look at his son, to reanimate the flashlight and shine its light on his face.

But the chains pull him back.

The neighbor's son greets him by the ladder. His hair is salted, his skin leathered. He's older now than Boris.

"What year is it?" Boris says.

The man tells him.

"You minded the truck so many decades?"

"I held two lives in my hand," he says. "How could I not?"

There is little left of the camp. The Quonset huts have rusted through, the roads cracked and weedgrown. There is only the hunting cabin, which Mikhail's son has maintained. Boris removes his two Copley Medals from their encasement in a glass frame and hands one to Mikhail's son and buries the other in the spot shown to him where Mikhail is buried. It's all he has to give. The two men embrace and Boris realizes he has not hugged anyone as an adult, not his mother, not his son. His body tenses, the weight of the other man against him, the smell of pine in his coat. He stays there in that moment.

Before the sun disappears he finds a familiar black poplar and walks forty paces north and unburies a box that contains money and his identification. The next day, in Novosibirsk, he waits for the train. The Trans-Siberian Railway has changed little, though a ticket to Moscow is quadruple what he remembers. In the capital he will inform the Kremlin of his discovery. He has nothing left now but his life's work and it will have to be enough.

On the steps of the Ministry of Defense along the Moskva River, police in mirrored visors intercept him. They ask for identification, they listen to him, they laugh at his story — a story only a homeless man could tell — then arrest him and throw him into the back of a utility vehicle. Boris finds himself among a half-dozen vagabonds, their shoulders and knees touching. They are driven to the outskirts of the city and into a forest, where the police tear them from the vehicle and push them to the earth. Boris finds himself alongside a buckled asphalt drive, disrupted by the roots of old-growth trees. Once the police van leaves, the other men trudge after it, presumably toward a highway, toward civilization. But for Boris, something is familiar about this road. He follows it in the opposite direction.

He comes upon a decayed estate and realizes he's been here before. It was here he had the greatest moment of his life, where the ruling party plucked him from the ranks of basement physicists and raised him up. By the hearth of a great room he stood with men of power in a circle, upholstered in cashmere suits and gold. Servants distributed Cuban cigars and copper mugs heavy with vodka. Boris knew, then, he was indispensable. So he'd thought. Because he had always been indispensable, he sees this now, but he never valued the smaller circle of souls who needed him.

He walks through the ruins of the estate. The autumnal breeze whines through the great room and the hearth is choked with dirt and the skulls of rodents, a forsaken den, a forsaken man walking through an apocalypse. It's as if the world Boris knew never existed, as if he never existed, and he recalls the insult of the tiny lieutenant who threatened such a thing, and the words of the young man disfigured by the supercollider who foresaw this very result. Boris stumbles through broken doors to the back of the estate, the lawn interrupted with yellow leaves. His feet guide him forward — he's taken these same steps before, though he can't remember where they lead.

Beyond the hedges he finds himself surrounded by birch trees and then a white oak, two hundred years old. Sunlight dapples the forest floor, a last kiss of warmth, and he sits among leaves of embered colors and lays there, his head against the earth.

His son.

He remembers, and the encasement around his heart cracks.

With closed eyes he can see the memory, the two of them at this very spot, both prone and side-by-side, hands clasped, trading code through the smallest pulses, a practice born of Anna.

Boris feels outside himself, heady and light, in third person, and he feels these palpitations again in the center of his hand.

Except this is not memory.

This is something new. Boris doesn't know how he knows this, but he knows it is Alexei. He can feel his son near — clouds of his gravitons interacting with his own through the fabric of spacetime, across dimensional membranes, beating letters on the surface of his palm.

"It is me, Alexei."

The message pulses, over and over, proof of dimensions beyond the twenty-four Boris has identified, a dimension of love that tethers distant moments in the fourth dimension. The small dark star in the underground of Siberia has amplified this interstitial gossamer, clarifying messages over an impossible difference. He thinks of megaphones in a crowd, fiber-optic braidings across the oceans' floors, of all those abysses throughout the history of the world where bridges have since arisen.

Boris' eyes well with saltwater. He knows so little, he can admit this now.

"I left you there," Boris squeezes back to his son. "I was too late."

Too late to be any good to him, too late to catch him in his fall, too late to realize that he'd viewed the world through a tiny keyhole and never once considered all that others had to teach him and all there was to really know.

"I failed," he signals, embracing that tiny hand in his, unseen but sentient.

"We are here now," the boy says.

See Esem Junior's story "Siberia in Four Dimensions" online at Metaphorosis.
If you liked it, leave a comment. Authors love that!
Remember to subscribe to our e-mail updates so you'll know when new stories are posted.

About the story

It only took me a couple decades since high school to revisit the theory of relativity and, once I absorbed it with a more fully formed brain, I couldn't stop thinking about it. Meanwhile, no discussion of relativity can take place without reference to black holes and, lost one evening in a Möbius Strip of internet links, I came across an article on a supercollider under construction in Europe. The Swiss community had come undone by the prospect that supercolliders, theoretically, could give birth to micro black holes. While debunked, somewhat, I knew I had to write a story about this. At the same time, I had just lost a close family member, and it didn't take long to marry those emotions with the potential craziness (or wonderfulness?) that a micro black hole could levy on the lives of people beset by grief.

When blocking out the story, I came across black-and-white photos of ancestors from nineteenth-century Russia, complete with heavy wool coats and ushankas, and boom, I had a setting. Since I'm not a scientist, the most difficult part for me was maintaining some fidelity to the universe's physical laws. That meant immersion in books by Brian Greene, Kip Thorne, and other physicists, and more than a few times asking stupid questions and creating bizarre hypotheticals on physics chat boards.

In the end, the story is not hard science fiction — and anyone who offered me advice on the chat boards would be mortified by what I've done — but the basic principles of gravity, time dilation, and relatively are fully at play and legit. In the end, this story is about a grandmother, her son, and her grandson, and the family staying connected through the interstitial spaces between known physical dimensions, despite the actions of a hostile government and the limitations of mortality.

A question for the author

Q: What's the story no one else thinks is as good as you do?

A: "City Dog, Country Frog", by Mo Willems, is a fan favorite for the five and under club, but it's a masterpiece for the more "sophisticated" audience as well. The structure is elegant, following a friendship between a dog and frog through four seasons, and the movement through the seasons parallels the arc of their friendship. The ending is as sad as an austere Cormac McCarthy ending, but has a twist that offers a glimmer of hope.

About the author

Esem Junior grew up in the long, dark winters of Upstate New York, one of the country's own Siberias. He is a former crime reporter, and writes speculative and other forms of literary fiction.

April

The Big S

David Hammond

It was another New Year's Eve at my brother-in-law's house on the lake. Aunt Margaret sent me to the kitchen to retrieve the chocolate-covered strawberries, her eyes glassy and cheeks flushed from champagne.

The kitchen lights were off, but moonlight from the window illuminated the tray of strawberries on the countertop. By the sink, a chef's knife lay across an unwashed cutting board. I was about to rinse them off and put them in the drying rack, but I was struck by the reflection of icy blue moonlight on the blade. I leaned down for a closer look. The cutting board was slightly damp. It smelled of onions.

Perspiration broke out on my forehead. I teetered momentarily and steadied myself with a hand on the counter. Had I drunk too much champagne myself? After delivering the strawberries to the stuffy living room, I stepped outside to cool off.

Pipe smoke wafted from a corner of the porch. I couldn't identify the man's face in the shadow of an overhanging pine but recognized the plaid shirt, rumpled jeans, and thin hands of my brother-in-law's uncle, Tim.

"Hi, Tim."

Tim tapped his pipe on his knee. "Hi, Glen." He leaned forward to rest his elbows on his knees, and as his face moved out of the shadow of the pine, moonlight glistened on his wet cheeks.

He had been weeping.

So what? Aunt Margaret, just a half hour earlier, had burst into tears of joy when her two-month-old granddaughter, sleeping on her lap, had suddenly smiled and kung fu-gripped her na-na's finger. "So strong! So precious! And she smells like ambrosia! I can't stand it!"

But Tim's tears were different, his face contorted, his eyes evasive.

"The last thing I said to her was, 'Don't buy the *goddamned* light beer this time'," said Tim. "She hated it when I cursed. She just took the car keys and left without saying anything."

Consulting my earpiece at that moment would have been rude, so I dredged my brain and managed to pull a pertinent fact from the muck: Tim's wife had died in a car crash. "Irma," I said.

Tim's eyes snapped on to me. "Inga."

"Right! Inga. It was on New Year's Eve too, wasn't it? What, three years ago?"

"Five."

"Right. She was such a nice lady." I smiled at him and sat in a patio chair, which creaked under my weight, preparing to reminisce about Inga's bacon-spiked potato salad and seal-bark of a laugh.

Tim tilted his head to the side and gave me a quizzical look.

I froze. Had she been not so nice, her seal-bark cruel, her potato salad spiked not only with bits of salty pork fat but resentment and vindictiveness? Could my memory be that bad? But then Tim looked out on the lake and sighed, and a word came to me that had been absent from my vocabulary for years, which I had hardly heard spoken since I was a boy.

Sad.

Tim was sad. He was remembering his late wife on the fifth anniversary of her death, and it was making him feel sad.

I scooted my patio chair a few inches closer to Tim and lowered my voice. "Tim, are you feeling *sad*?"

He looked back at me. "You *do* remember."

I stood up. "I'll call an ambulance," I said, tapping my earpiece.

"No, goddammit!" Tim grabbed my arm and pulled me back into my seat. "I want... don't you see? I *want* to feel sad right now."

I studied his pleading face. Was this insanity? Sadness was a disease of the past, one of the worst, responsible for countless deaths and more senseless suffering than any other brain malfunction. It had been cured decades ago. I had gotten the nasal mist when I was eleven years old, and nowadays it was administered to one-year-olds along with their hepatitis A and cold vaccines.

Nobody *wanted* to feel sad.

Did they?

"I didn't know what to do with myself after she died," said Tim. "I mean, for a few days there were things to do, flowers to choose, an urn to buy. I didn't have to think; I just said 'sunflowers' whenever anyone asked me a question. 'Sunflowers for the memorial service? Are you sure?' they asked. 'Sunflowers,' I said. 'Sunflowers on the urn?' 'Yes, sunflowers.' She liked sunflowers, you know? It was something I was sure about." Tim took a long puff. "Maybe it was the only thing I was sure about. The lawyer... he had a stack of papers for me to sign with little yellow Post-it tabs poking out where my signatures were supposed to go. 'It's like a sunflower,' I said to him. He smiled and nodded. I thought he had done it on purpose. That's how feeble-minded I was at the time. I thought the nice lawyer had turned the paperwork into Inga's favorite flower."

I chuckled experimentally. Tim let out a wheeze that may or may not have been a laugh.

"Anyway, after the remembrances were done, and the papers were signed and filed, and the social media condolence pings had died down, I waited. I sat in an armchair, and I waited. I skipped my lifelong learning group, and I didn't go to the movies the way Inga and I used to do. I didn't go for hikes around the lake, even though I could have used the fresh air."

After a pause, I asked, "What were you waiting for?"

"That's just it, Glen. I didn't know *what* I was waiting for. It was like there was something I was going to do, but I couldn't remember what it was. And at some point I just forgot that I was waiting, and I resumed my life without ever having remembered what I was going to do. I took an ornithology class, and I bought some binoculars. I became a birder."

"Yeah, I heard that you—"

"What a dumb hobby that was. If I never see another rufous-bellied thrush it will be too soon."

"Oh."

"But I met another birder. Carmela. And, you know, sitting all day in a field with your binoculars and your bag of roasted cashews... Between almost spotting some fucking bird or other, it all came out. About Inga; about the light beer; about the yellow Post-its; about the waiting without knowing for what. And Carmela turned to me and said, 'Maybe you just need a good cry.' And then she said, 'Shhh,' and raised her binoculars, so I couldn't tell her how batshit crazy she was."

"Yeah."

"No, Glen. She wasn't crazy. As I sat there thinking, I realized she wasn't crazy. And then she asked me if I had heard of The Big S."

"The Big S?"

That was the first time I heard the drug's street name. It was usually called PIDS, an acronym of a complex, difficult to synthesize, and impossible to pronounce chemical. Some kids in Pittsburgh had been caught taking it.

On the ride home from the party, I leaned my forehead against the window and let my eyelids droop. The Big S. What was so big about it? My conversation with Tim had left me with an impression of something internalized but forgotten, like a dream whose details disintegrate in the morning light but whose pithy emotional core lingers through breakfast. It was enticing and frightening, and it smelled like... onions?

Clearly, I'd drunk too much champagne. I'd even asked Tim to put me in touch with his drug dealer. My wife would not approve.

I leaned towards her. "You know PIDS?"

"Pids?"

"You know, that drug..."

"Oh, right. The Big S." She shook her head. "It's so—"

"Hey, how do you know it's called The Big S?"

"What do you mean, how do I know? Everybody's talking about it."

"Everybody?"

"I just can't believe anyone would *want* to take it, you know? Imagine, *wanting* to feel *sad.*"

I didn't respond.

"You know?" she prompted.

"Yeah." I said, while thinking to myself, *1212 18th Street. 1212 18th Street. 1212 18th Street.* The drug dealer's address, whispered by a birder in a bramble of blackberries to Uncle Tim, and passed along beside a moon-streaked lake to me. "Yeah."

1212 18th Street turned out to be a narrow, tinted-glass door tucked between a Noodles-2-Go and a mattress discount store. Scotch-taped inside the window above the door was an index card with the letter 'S' written in black marker, giving me confidence I had found the right place. I pressed the button five times in quick succession, as instructed, and peered into the nearly opaque glass. The door clicked. I pulled it open.

Leading up from the entryway was a burgundy-carpeted stairway, old but well-tended and lined by a brass railing, mottled with wear. On about the fifth step, high enough for her doleful eyes to be even with mine, sat a Cocker Spaniel. "Hello?" I said as I looked for evidence of a human presence. Finding none, I smiled at the dog's golden fur and long, ruffled ears. "Hey there, pup."

She turned to climb the stairs and I felt compelled to follow.

Red-paneled walls and yellowish lights gave the stairway a sinister, warm glow. I stopped on a landing after the first flight and the spaniel looked around. "Lead on, Virgil," I murmured. "Lead on." What was that from? Hamlet following the ghost? No. Dante, on the way to purgatory? Yes.

I entered a room lit with recessed sconces and furnished in antique cherry. The dog curled up at the foot of a velvet couch and huffed a sigh.

"Hello?" I said.

"Who is that, Daisy?" A silver-haired man entered the room from a dark hallway. "What have you dragged in off the street now?"

"Hello. I was given this address for... to get..."

"Yes, yes. Have a seat."

He didn't quite look at me, waving his hand dismissively. I hesitated, embarrassed, and suddenly wished I hadn't come. It was a bad idea after all. If my wife knew... But I was comforted by Daisy, lying croissant-like by the couch. I sat and leaned down to pet her.

The man reached to verify the existence of an armchair and lowered himself in. Blind, I guessed. He rested his hands on his knees. The cuffs of his shirt looked freshly ironed but slightly frayed. "So, first things first. Did you get the memo? No recording devices?"

"Yes," I said, distracted by the discoloration of his open shirt collar where it met his creased neck. "I mean no. No devices."

"No earpiece, no iris implant, no micropod?"

"I left it all at home."

"Good, good." His shoulders settled and his face softened. "So, you and Daisy are acquainted. My name is Bartholomew."

"I'm Glen."

"You came for The Big S, correct?"

"Yes."

"Good, good. How much do you want?"

"Uh..."

"You don't know, of course. You're a novice. Maybe you're not even sure you want it at all. Hmmm?"

"Well..."

"It's okay. Daisy, bring us a ten, please. Daisy, TEN." The dog didn't move. "She'll wait a moment just to prove to herself she's nobody's servant, and then she'll go get it. Watch." A note of warning entered his voice. "You're a good girl, aren't you, Daisy?" She got up and trudged from the room. "Yes, a very good girl."

"What a sweet dog."

"You try one, and if you like it, you buy the rest, okay? Simple, simple, simple. Free samples are key. Always. Have you ever sold drugs?"

"Me? No."

"You sound a little shocked by the question. Delicate soul. Ah, here's Daisy." The dog rattled back in with a bottle in her mouth, which she dropped in Bartholomew's outstretched hand. "Good girl." She slumped by the couch again, her body sounding like a small sack of potatoes being dropped on the wooden floor.

Bartholomew turned his face towards Daisy, and they sighed simultaneously. "She's a sad dog," he said. "And that sounds like I'm anthropomorphizing, but I'm not. She's had real sadness in her life."

"Oh?" I dug into the downy fur behind her ears to give her a good scritch. "Poor dog."

"What do you remember, Glen?" He shook the pill bottle. "About sadness."

"Not much, really. Just that..."

"Yes?"

"I was eleven when I went to the doctor for the mist, and my mother told me I wouldn't feel sad ever again. And that made me sad." Bartholomew raised his eyebrows. "I don't know why. Then I got the mist and I tried to hold on to the feeling, just to see if I could, but it was gone."

"Gone. Poof." He had a wry smile as he raised his hands magician-like in the air. "And what did feeling sad feel like? Do you remember that?"

"I really don't. That's what's been driving me crazy."

"Ah." He popped open the bottle and shook a pill onto his palm. "Well. So here we are. There's water on the coffee table."

I eyed the pill in the thin-fingered, slightly shaking hand. "How long does it last?"

"An hour, maybe two, the first time."

"The first time?"

"It builds up, so it goes on a little longer after that."

"Oh? Is it addictive?"

His hand dropped to rest on his knee, still holding the pill for me to take. "I don't think so."

That hung in the air for a moment.

"The Big S," said Bartholomew, clearing his throat, "has not been approved for sale by the Food and Drug Administration. I am not a board-certified pharmacologist. I offer no warranties, no assurances, no scientific studies showing short-term efficacy or long-term safety, no whitepapers, no testimonials beyond what the person who sent you here provided, without which you wouldn't be here, right?"

"Uh..."

"Word of mouth. That's another key to success in my line of work, along with free samples and making sure nothing gets recorded. But you didn't come here for drug-slinging advice. What you *came* for, what I *offer*," he shifted in his chair and leaned forward, "is that feeling your eleven-year-old self tried to hold onto but couldn't. That feeling that's too volatile, too dangerous, too *thrilling*," he closed his fist on the pill and pulled it away, "for society to let you feel it. You came here because you believe your feelings are your own to feel, that you can't be human without them, all of them, and this one," he opened his hand back up and pushed it in my general direction, "was stolen from you."

After a pause, I cleared my throat. "That was a good sales pitch."

"Thank you."

"I'll try it, of course." I leaned forward and took the pill. "It's what I came here for, I..." The tiny white hockey puck rolled on my palm.

"Yes?"

My feelings swirled: apprehension, curiosity, embarrassment, excitement. Bartholomew's creased brow tried to communicate openness and concern but couldn't hide an underlying impatience. "Never mind. Down the hatch!"

I popped the pill in my mouth and washed it down with water. I put down the glass and settled back on the couch.

"How long does it take?"

"A few minutes. Usually. While we wait, I could tell you about Daisy." Bartholomew crossed his arms and leaned his head to the side. "I find it helps set the mood."

"Okay."

"So, Daisy here was born to a Cocker Spaniel breeder in Greensboro, North Carolina. She was a friendly pup, or so I've heard, though she had a particular hatred for percolating coffee makers." He shrugged. "Still does; I switched to French press.

Anyway, at eight months old, during her first heat, for reasons that were never explained to my satisfaction, the breeder thought it would be a good idea to breed Daisy with her father."

At the word 'father', I felt an unaccustomed tightening or twisting or burning sensation in my sternum and up around my rib cage. Like a lime being squeezed and the acidic juices leaking into my chest cavity.

"What?"

"Yes. Her father. Against all recommended breeding practices, moral codes, and plain old common sense, she was bred with her father while she was still, really, a puppy, and she got pregnant, and a couple months later she gave birth to something."

The feeling in my sternum spread out in thickening waves to my limbs.

"A poor, misshapen little something, that she clutched and cuddled and licked even though it showed no signs of life. When the breeder came to take it away and dispose of it, Daisy growled and whined, very out of character. She bit the breeder, hard, which would have gotten her put down but for the dram of compassion lingering in that breeder's shriveled heart."

The feeling grew heavy and warm — fleetingly, inadequately warm — like those lead jackets they used to make you wear when they x-rayed your teeth.

"That night, she howled out her pain, hour upon hour, while the breeder wore industrial grade foam earplugs she kept for just such occasions."

It was a big feeling. I groaned under its weight. The Big S.

"Daisy was not the same after that. She roamed the house in search of her lost baby. She was ruined for breeding, so she wound up at a shelter in Virginia, where I found her. Four years ago or so."

Looking at Daisy, watching the rise and fall of her breath, I slid off the couch and began to pet her from the crease in her forehead to the tip of her tail. She lifted her head at first in mild surprise, but then let it drop with a sigh.

"She had a sock. The shelter volunteer told me it had come with her from North Carolina. She would stow it in her bed and lick it in her quiet moments. I think it was her replacement baby. But we've lost it, and my socks aren't good enough for her, apparently. I've felt around, under the couches and chairs. It must be... but anyway, how are you coming along there, Glen?"

"Poor Daisy."

"Yes, yes. Poor Daisy. Ach, well, I may have embellished the story a bit over the years, but the general outline is accurate. If you do see a sock, a cotton athletic sock… But, you know, maybe I am anthropomorphizing a bit. Who knows what's in that little canine heart of hers?"

My hand paused on Daisy's back, and she raised her head to admonish me for slacking off. "What if the sock," I said, "was only a painful reminder?"

"Could be, could be."

Bartholomew folded his hands on his lap. From my vantage point on the floor his face looked distorted, like an ill-fitting mask. Tufts of salt-and-pepper hair poked from his nostrils. Under the coffee table I saw ratty slippers, toes poking through a broken seam.

I refocused my attention on Daisy and probed the width and breadth and height of my drug-induced sadness. I had thought that I would burst into tears, but that didn't happen. The feeling was comfortable, familiar, satisfying even, like picking a dried scab on my knee as a kid.

I was eleven again, holding the feeling close, watching my mother's face as she watched mine. Watching her watch the creases in my brow smooth out. Watching her watch me watch the worry in her eyes fade away.

Remembering her, pre-mist, lying beside me on my bed, shushing me softly, and at the same time encouraging my tears. A boy had pushed me while I was at the urinal, and I sprayed pee on the floor. The other boys laughed like cartoon donkeys. They hated me. "No," she said. "You're my sweet little boy. Let it out. It's okay." Let it out, get it out, spill it out…

Remembering another night when daddy said mommy was feeling sad. I tried to comfort her the way she had comforted me. "You're my beautiful mommy," I said. "It's okay. Let it out, mommy. Get it out." Her eyes dry and blank, not letting it out. Her body a lead weight, so heavy I thought I would roll into the well she made there on the bed. Daddy in a chair with his hands on his face, dragging them down. "I love you," he said to mommy, like an accusation, almost.

Let it out, get it out, spit it out, work it out…

I love you, but…

The edge of a bottomless pit…

Visiting mommy in the hospital, the machine with the colored graphs and lights and numbers, the needle in her arm, the smell of medicine and doctors, dim gray lights in the ceiling, watching her watch me watch her watch me…

Daddy, taking her hand. "I should have locked up the pills," he said.

Locked up the pills...

I love you, but...

Sliding, grasping, flailing, falling... my very own pit... my eyes dry and blank.

Later, after the mist, walking into the kitchen, and daddy saying to mommy, "Well, it saved your life." He diced onions while mommy stirred something in a pot on the stove.

"Maybe," she said.

Daddy scraped the onions into the pot. He sniffled and rubbed his eyes. It was the onions. It was just the onions that made that happen now. He placed the cutting board on the edge of the sink and laid the knife across it, its blade flashing.

I realized that this memory had been an unanswered question lodged in a crevice in the back of my mind all these years. What had saved her life? The mist?

"Bartholomew, what about sadness that is *too* strong or lasts *too* long?"

He had been sitting stoically, hands folded on his lap, hairy-knuckled thumbs twiddling. How much time had passed? He opened his mouth but paused a moment before answering. "It's a risk, but I haven't heard any complaints."

I scooped my hand under Daisy's body as I stroked her from head to tail, head to tail, head to tail. Her eyelids fluttered. Little by little, the sadness lifted, until I found myself cooing and chirping, "What a nice dog you are, Daisy."

"So," said Bartholomew, "what do you think?"

I blinked at him. The feeling was gone, but the dark cloud of memory lingered. I got up and sat back down on the couch and eyed the pill bottle on the coffee table between us.

"Quite an experience, right?"

"Yes. Wow. Quite an experience."

"So, I accept Q-bucks or Singaporean Aphids." He leaned down and retrieved a card reader from a drawer in the side of the coffee table.

"Well, I..."

"You can start with the ten, or I do have the thirty-thirty deal — 30 percent off a bottle of thirty. That's three times the experience for only twice the 'phids." He tapped the card reader on the edge of the table.

"I don't..."

"You don't what?"

The leaden weight; the eyes watching, hoping, fearing; the slippery-edged pit. "I don't think I want them."

"You don't *think*?"

"I mean, it's quite an experience, as you say... but for me, it's not a good idea."

"Not a —" The card reader clattered on the table as Bartholomew leaned back and crossed his arms. "Daisy, bite him. Bite Glen on the ankle for wasting your master's time. Go on. Daisy, BITE."

Daisy rose and yawned nervously. She looked from Bartholomew to me and back again.

"She won't bite you, will she? She thinks she's not my servant, doesn't she? But who feeds you? Huh?"

Daisy sniffed my pant leg and nudged my hand with her nose.

"I should have stuck with smack and weed." Slapping his knees and rising, Bartholomew sang under his breath. "*Weed and smack and a little bit o' crack.* The good ol' days." He left the room, knocking his knee on a chair and cursing softly, bitterly. "Fuck."

I rose to apologize, to say goodbye, to say something — maybe to say I'd buy the pills after all. Nothing came out of my mouth. Instead, I knelt down to pet Daisy some more.

"I'd better go, Daisy."

I wanted to get out before Bartholomew came back. With Daisy at my heel, I headed for the stairs. By the door, a rolled-up sock behind a vase on an eye-level shelf caught my eye.

"Oh. A sock. Could this be...?"

I lifted it off the shelf, and Daisy tensed. She sat and pinned the sock with her gaze.

I had theorized earlier that the sock had been an unwelcome reminder. Maybe it would be better for Daisy if I put it back on the shelf? But with her intent, pleading eyes drilling a hole in my hand, that was out of the question. Would it dredge up sorrowful memories of unfulfilled motherhood, or would it soothe the ache of a barren womb? If she could speak, could she explain it? Would I understand? Or did she only know she wanted it?

And what about me, retreating, tail tucked, to a present of forgetful bliss?

I held the sock in front of her snout, and she enveloped it in her mouth. I let go, and she rushed behind the velvet couch and out of sight.

"You're a brave soul," I said, turning to descend the stairs.

See David Hammond's story "The Big S" online at Metaphorosis. If you liked it, leave a comment. Authors love that! Remember to subscribe to our e-mail updates so you'll know when new stories are posted.

About the story

This story started with me thinking about the current state of drug therapies for depression. Basically, I wished antidepressants worked better.

That wish segued naturally into a series of escalating thought experiments: What if there were a cure for depression? What if that cure didn't just affect clinical depression, but ordinary sadness, and it were given to everyone? What if, after sadness was eradicated, someone developed a drug for people to feel sad again? Would people take it?

Of course they would.

But I thought there was enough complexity in how it would play out to explore in a story, and I quickly hit on the idea of exploring the relationship between emotion and memory. Cutting off emotions can empty out memories either by making them inaccessible or robbing them of meaning, and losing memories can make emotions incomprehensible. And sometimes confronting the emotional content of memories is a choice. When do we choose to feel, choose to remember, and when do we choose to lock it away in an act of self-preservation? Is denying an emotion ever the right thing to do?

At some point in working on the story, I got a vision of a dog as a drug dealer's side-kick, and a great deal of my motivation from then on was to write about this dog, to make the dog an important character in the story while keeping her a real dog. So Daisy was born. I made her a Cocker Spaniel because my vision included big ruffly ears.

A question for the author

Q: What would your characters say about you?

A: I forwarded this question to the characters from "The Big S," and here are their responses:

Glen: David Hammond... David Hammond... Nope, doesn't ring a bell.

Tim: He hardly says a word most of the time, but if you liquor him up and land on the right subject, he'll talk your ear off.

Bartholomew: I contracted him to do my website, www.getthebigs.com. I thought he did a decent job until I heard from some of my clients. Either he was taking advantage of me being blind, or his design skills are shit.

Daisy: *brings ball, puts ball at feet, looks up with big brown eyes and pants expectantly, nudges ball with nose in case you didn't notice it*

About the author

David Hammond lives and dreams in Virginia with his wife, two daughters, one dog, three rats, and a multitude of insects. During the day, he makes websites.

oldshoepress.com, @hammond13

The Otherside of Memory

Kelly Sandoval

Lord Rivenwend of the North Star and
Lady Siverstay of the Sun's Dawning
Request the honor of your presence at the marriage of their son
Lord Creythwin the Dawn Star
To
Teresa the Fair of the Cleaved Land
Windsday, the 39th of Harvest
Dusk
To attend, jump through a puddle of still water
during the next full moon
P.S. Please come, Katie. I don't think I can face this
without you. Love, T.

Please come. Teresa made it sound so simple. As if more than fifteen years, and that last bitter fight, could be swept away like soap bubbles on the wind. As if one world were just as good as the next.

Kate set the invitation down on top of the pile of more conventional mail she'd been sorting. Bills, pre-approved credit cards, coupon mailers. All the simple, mundane business of the world she'd chosen. Teresa probably had her mail delivered by helpful woodland creatures. Which was fine for her, but Kate preferred her mail without tooth marks and urine stains.

Please come. Just like that. Not even an apology. No recognition of what'd come after, what it'd been like to be the one who came back. What did Teresa think happened, when you entered the woods with your best friend, and returned, days later, alone and dressed in velvet rags?

Kate picked up the invitation again, noting the elegant pearlescence of the paper, the way it seemed to glow. Then she tore it into tiny, gleaming squares, wrapped it in coupons, and threw it in the trash.

If Teresa couldn't face marrying whiny, clingy Crey alone, maybe she should call off the wedding.

"Sorry, Teresa," she said aloud, remembering how they used to spy on their parents through magic mirrors. "I'm busy."

Leaving the bills for later, she turned her attention to the window. Charlotte was on the porch, driving a toy truck through a crowd of plastic houses. Such a practical girl, these days. The princess tantrums had been hard, but they'd gotten through it. Charlotte understood better now, how foolish such things were. No lies about Santa, no creepy voyeuristic elves. Instead of slipping coins under Charlotte's pillow, Kate had sat her daughter down, and they'd worked out a fair market value for baby teeth.

It had been harder, before Tom left. He'd insisted on whimsy. Such fights they'd had. He'd refused to understand, and she hadn't been able to explain.

There were doors out there. Doors waiting for Charlotte, just like they'd waited for Kate. If they didn't teach her to scorn the dreams those doors promised, they could lose her to one. At best she'd come back a different child, with a lifetime behind her eyes. At worst... well, not all children came back.

But Kate hadn't been able to explain all that. Hadn't been able to tell Tom that in her nightmares, Charlotte wandered down an endless hallway, each door opening as she passed.

In the end, divorce had felt like the only option. Sometimes, children required sacrifice.

Charlotte was late coming down for breakfast the next morning. Kate found her sitting in her room, piecing the invitation back together. She'd almost finished, and the note gleamed in front of her, the horse along the border running as far as it could along the broken line of its track.

"Look!" Charlotte stared up at her, all smiles. "Isn't it pretty?"

"Where'd you find that?" The words came out sharper than Kate intended, and Charlotte's smile fell.

"Here," she said. "I just sorta found it."

"Your cereal's getting soggy." Kate nodded toward the door. "Get downstairs. I'll clean this up."

"But—"

"Now, Charlotte."

"Fine." Charlotte's tone, and the way she stomped to the door, merited further discussion, but Kate let it pass.

Kneeling to pick up the scraps, she saw that they'd already begun to knit themselves back together. Only a few pieces, along the top edge, were still missing. She scanned the invitation out of habit, eyes coming to rest on the P.S.

P.S. Katie, please. You promised. I'm scared. T

Teresa, the bold one. Teresa, who ran through doors to other worlds, dragging Kate behind her. Teresa who swore she would never return, no matter what. Who left Kate to stumble back alone, through the darkness, with no words to explain what had happened to them.

What did Kate care if she was scared? And still, her shoulders tensed when she read the words, bracing as if to protect someone from a blow.

"Mommy!" Charlotte called, from downstairs.

Kate fitted the last few pieces of the invitation into their place, and watched it stitch itself whole. Then she folded it neatly and slid it into the back pocket of her jeans.

How could she even think of going? It wasn't like she could leave Charlotte alone while she went chasing old pain through moonlit pools.

And to take her? Make truth of every nightmare? Ridiculous.

But the idea lingered. Despite her best efforts, the lure of the otherside, of an open door, still felt inevitable. And the more Charlotte grew, the less she could protect her. But if she could go with her, maybe she could make it safe. Guide her attention to the pathetic falseness of it all.

Charlotte was a practical girl, when she was home. Less so, around her father. And who knew what she might be like, if she wandered alone through an open door. But if Kate were with her? Well.

It was three days until the full moon. She had time to decide.

"But what about Rosy?" Charlotte asked, tugging at Kate's hand as they walked toward the local park.

It was well past sunset, but the suburban streetlights were mostly blocking the stars, leaving the moon, full and round, to light the sky.

"Rosy will be fine," Kate answered, not for the first time. She'd already arranged for the neighbors to check in on the little pug. She'd promised to be back in a few days, a week at most. Surely, it wouldn't take longer than that. It hadn't been, last time. Taking Charlotte to an old friend's wedding, she'd told them. True enough. It was a wedding, at least.

"And we're going to see horses?"

"Oh, yes. Horses until you want to scream." They'd reached the edge of the park; Kate could see the fountain's pool shining in the moonlight. "Things are very different where my friend lives. You understand?"

"Try foods. Don't call things weird. No faces." Charlotte ticked the usual rules off on her fingers, and Kate freed her hand to smooth her daughter's dark curls.

"I want you to see this, because—"

Because?

Because there would always be the risk of doors, in Charlotte's life. Always be the chance that she'd hear some distant music and find herself dancing, dreamlike, across a threshold. Despite all Kate's best attempts, Charlotte still doodled fairies in the corners of her schoolwork. There was still a danger.

But this way, she could turn the otherside into just another boring errand, robbed of all its forbidden, escapist charm. Charlotte could be level-headed and practical, with the right sort of guidance. With Kate beside her, she would see all the bright whimsy for the shallow artifice it was.

"Mommy?" Charlotte tugged at her sleeve. "Because why?"

"I don't know, hon. Just because."

The fountain was only a handbreadth away now. The spray of it filled the air, misting gently down on them. Kate adjusted her bag and stared down into the basin, where the ripples settled under her attention, the reflected moon coming clear. Full and round and opening before them like the door. She could hear laughter and the sweet, sharp music of the otherside. Charlotte tried to pull away from her, yearning toward the sound, while Kate stood rooted in place.

This was it.

Gripping Charlotte more tightly, Kate squared her shoulders and stepped forward, into the bright portal of the moon. She didn't even feel the water, just a rushing, silver coolness and the warmth of Charlotte's hand, as the world went bright.

"Katie!" Teresa's voice was just as Kate remembered, all low, soft sweetness. "Oh, Katie, thank god!"

The world came back into focus. Well, not *the* world so much as *a* world. The otherside, all dressed for autumn, with endless rolling hills of copper fire. The palace like a Disney dream in the field beyond. And there was Teresa, looking no older than she'd been when Kate left, just barely twenty. The age Kate had left behind when she returned home and found herself shedding years like dreams.

She hadn't known, in going back, that she'd have to live the years from 12 to 20 again. It had been harder, the second time. One more thing this place had done to her.

Teresa stood in her filmy, silken gown, shifting nervously from foot to foot, watching Kate with a helpless sort of hope.

Kate had run through what happened next dozens of times. She'd rehearsed her words, won imaginary arguments, and considered how to say 'I forgive you' in a sufficiently magnanimous and superior fashion.

Her mouth was dry, and she could remember none of it.

"Mom?" Charlotte was coming out of the trance of otherside's music, her eyes wide as she took in the lush, impossible beauty of the landscape. A herd of horses, with snow-white hides and manes like flame, were running past along the hills, and Charlotte's eyes followed them with naked longing. "Mommy where are they going? Will we get to pet them?"

"Maybe later," Kate managed to say. "Say hello to my friend. This is Miss Teresa."

"But *you* didn't say hi."

"Hi, Teresa," she said, forcing a smile. "It's been a long time."

"I'm Charlotte," said Charlotte.

"A kid?" Teresa asked. "We never— you always said—"

"You're marrying Crey." Kate stood a little straighter, meeting Teresa's gaze as fiercely as she could. "So I don't think you can talk."

Kate braced herself for one of Teresa's clever, sharp-edged retorts.

Instead, Teresa flinched, and lowered her eyes. "Yeah. Things change. Even here."

That old urge, the product of a shared childhood and a secret lifetime, almost pulled Kate forward, to comfort and question and try to fix. But she'd already tried to save Teresa, had opened the way back and asked her to follow. It hadn't worked.

"Why am I here?" she asked, tightening her grip on Charlotte's hand.

Teresa smiled, bright and untroubled, and the moment's tension faded. "You're my maid of honor. We can hardly have the wedding without you."

The dress Teresa wanted Kate to wear was exactly the sort of faux-princess monstrosity that she and Teresa would have imagined as children. Layers of velvet and satin, wide, trailing sleeves, and all of it in the deepest of gem tones, dark blues and purples that shimmered even by candlelight.

It took three people just to get her in it. They stood around her, cooing and complimenting, all of them beautiful and soft-voiced and alike in that strange, unsettling way that defined the otherside.

"Mommy, you're a princess," said Charlotte, as measurements were made and pins were pinned. "Will I get to be a princess too?"

"I'm not a princess," Kate corrected immediately. "Just your mom, in a fancy dress. And yes, you get to wear one too. It'll probably be scratchy and hot, just like this one."

"That's okay." Charlotte sounded unintimidated by the threat of discomfort, which just went to show that the otherside was working its magic. Most days, it was hard to get her to so much as agree to a sweater.

"If you could raise your arm," said the blonde-haired, angelic-faced woman on Charlotte's right. "We're almost done."

Kate lifted her arm, twisting to face her. Their eyes met. The woman's, an unusual blue-green, caught and held hers. Teresa's sister had those same eyes. Growing up, they'd always been jealous of her, had tried to wish their eyes to a new shade, staring endlessly at pictures of Teresa's sister and hoping, hoping, hoping.

The woman started pinning again, and Kate looked away.

"Where's Teresa?"

"She's with her fiancé, ma'am," one of the other women answered immediately. "Would you like me to send for her?"

"That's not necessary."

In the old days, it wouldn't have been. If she'd wanted Teresa, she could have looked in any mirror, and found her. In the old days, she'd have known where Teresa was the same way she knew the beating of her own heart. Now, closing her eyes, she felt nothing. The otherside was Teresa's, no longer a shared magic. It was surely the better for it.

Kate's memories of her last year in the otherside were still uncomfortably vivid. Claustrophobic and restless, exhausted by the endless sameness, and longing for home, she'd soured on everything she'd once admired. Ever obliging, the world had twisted, growing crueler and closer to reflect her sense of it.

"Can I play with your phone?" Charlotte asked. She'd clearly tired of the scraps of ribbon that the women had given her to entertain herself.

"It's in my purse, hon. But most of the games won't work. They don't have Wi-Fi here." There was no harm in letting Charlotte use it until it ran down. It wasn't like they'd be making any calls. "And we can't charge it either."

"Why not?" Charlotte asked.

"No electricity." It seemed a good time to push the point. "No TV, no video games. No phones."

"Internet?"

"Nope."

"But how do they—" Charlotte paused, overwhelmed by the enormity of the lack. "How do they do anything?"

"They don't. Pretty boring, huh?"

Charlotte looked from the phone to the ridiculous dress the women were constructing around Kate. "Yeah," she said hesitantly. "Pretty boring."

"Would you like me to take her down to the menagerie, ma'am?" The woman who'd given Charlotte the ribbons asked. She looked a little older than the others, about Kate's age. A 12-year-old's idea of all grown up.

"No thanks." But despite herself, Kate flashed the woman a grateful smile. It was always nice to have someone willing to pitch in. "I'll take her down later. Maybe with Teresa."

"I'm sure she'd enjoy that." The woman stepped close to her, pitching her voice in that low, quiet way that spoke of secrets, or worry. "Ma'am?"

Kate let her arm drop as the one with the familiar eyes finished pinning. "Hmm?"

"This is your second visit. You—" The woman paused, looking away. "You still remember, don't you? What it was like, the last time?"

"More than I'd like to."

"You should go back to the old places. The ones you remember best. It would be nice, don't you think? To visit the shadow gardens again. To show your daughter the silver lakes and the forest of songs."

The words felt like an old wound, reopened. Kate had curated her memories of the otherside, clinging to the worst of it, to those last painful months. The places the woman spoke of, well, it wasn't that she'd forgotten. But she tried not to think of them. She didn't want to see the shadow gardens again, didn't want to swim in the sweet, glittering waters of the silver lakes. She wanted to wear an itchy, tacky dress, glare at Crey, and go home. She wanted to collect a new list of reasons to hate this place, and she wanted Charlotte to languish in boredom, longing for television and her friends.

"I'm not sure there'll be time," she said.

The woman turned away from the window. "Of course," she said, with a forced, helpless brightness. "I didn't mean to impose on your time, ma'am. I only thought the little girl might like to see where her mother grew up."

"Mommy grew up in Ohio," Charlotte said. "We go there for Christmas. It's boring. Grandma doesn't let us bring Rosy."

"Grandma's allergic," Kate put in firmly. "Is your game working?"

"Yeah. When do we pet the horses?"

"After we're done here, hon."

"Could you stand a little straighter?" The older woman knelt, ready with pins of her own. Her tone was neutral, and she didn't look up as she spoke.

Kate straightened, pushing down a flash of unexpected guilt. Could you really be said to have hurt something from the otherside? Perhaps, in the same way Charlotte could worry over the feelings of her stuffed animals, rotating them out nightly so that none felt left out.

"What's to see at the silver lakes?" she asked.

The woman was silent for long enough that Kate assumed she wasn't going to answer. One of the others began to sing, and while the words were strange, the tune was familiar.

"I couldn't say, ma'am," the woman said at last. "No one much goes down there, anymore."

No one? In Kate's memory, the shores were bright with people. They'd gone out on little boats, had picnics in the center of the lake. Dived deep, and come out gleaming.

Something felt wrong. The woman's voice. Or the idea of the shining lakes gone silent. The palace, so much less grand than she remembered. Hollowed out.

"Maybe I will pay them a visit," she said.

"But horses," Charlotte objected.

"The horses can wait, Charlotte. Besides, I'm a little allergic to horses. You don't want me all itchy and sneezy, do you?" Of course, an otherside horse was about as likely to trigger a reaction as a My Little Pony, but Charlotte didn't need to know that.

"But you promised!" The sharp hint of a whine entered Charlotte's words. It was comforting, almost. If she could throw a fit here, clearly the otherside's glamour hadn't penetrated too deeply.

"And we will see them. After we go to the lakes."

"But—"

"Charlotte, if you keep this up, we can go home right now." Well, eventually. The moon wasn't up. Kate only knew the route by moonlight.

"Ma'am, I could take her down to the stables, if you like." The woman who'd spoken of the lakes offered. "While you enjoy the water."

"That's very kind, umm—"

"Verita, ma'am."

"Verita, I appreciate the offer, but I have no intention of letting my daughter out of my sight."

"The horses are quite tame."

Kate looked down at Charlotte, that hopeful, hungry expression on her face. "That's not the danger I'm concerned about. I'll take her to the stables myself."

"We'll really go?" Charlotte asked. "You don't have to pet them if you're allergic."

"We'll go. But first, we have to meet Teresa for lunch. After that, we'll go down to the lakes, and then the horses."

"Fine." Charlotte sat back down with a huff, placated if not exactly happy. "This isn't as fun as you said it'd be."

Kate found herself smiling. "Charlotte, hon, I didn't say it'd be fun at all."

Kate had expected Teresa to hold their lunch in the formal dining room. Long, dark wood tables, soft-voiced servants, perhaps someone playing a half-remembered pop song on a lute. She'd imagined their voices echoing across a ridiculously long table, any real conversation rendered impossible.

Instead, the man who came to fetch them led the way to the kitchen gardens, a close, cozy area, the air sweet with herbs. Teresa was sitting on a blanket under a red-leafed maple tree, Crey at her side.

Like Teresa, he looked much the same as he had when she left. Recklessly handsome, with dark eyes and the feathered hair of an 80s dreamboat. The eyes were softer, though. The lopsided smile, dopey but warm.

"There you are!" He rushed forward, pulling her into a hug before she could object, ever the over-excited sidekick, too eager for affection. "I knew you would come. Didn't I say? I did. You'll stay, won't you? We've missed you so!"

"Just until the wedding," Kate and Teresa said, both at once, in the same, long-suffering tones. Teresa smiled though, patting the spot next to her. When he sat down, he kissed her cheek.

"How was the fitting?" Teresa asked, as she unpacked a basket full of cakes and tarts and pies and, well, everything Kate would ordinarily tell Charlotte was 'sometimes food'.

"Is that really lunch?" Charlotte tugged Kate forward, eyes wide and hopeful.

"I'm afraid so," Kate replied, settling on the blanket. "Don't eat yourself sick."

They made small talk for a while. Dresses. Flowers. Crey's new passion for cooking. (It was always something. Often, whatever could best get him into trouble. Mermaids, dragon's eggs, phoenix watching. Cooking seemed a safe, even charmingly domestic, hobby. In some ways, perhaps, Teresa was growing up.) Charlotte soon grew bored and lay stretched out on the grass, drowsily making daisy chains and ignoring them.

"And of course, there will be dancing!" Crey was saying, with inexhaustible enthusiasm. "You remember the balls we used to have, don't you Katie? Like the one where the wyverns attacked, and I—"

"I remember." Kate admitted, carefully keeping her tone neutral. They had been fun, of course. Ridiculous dresses, jeweled masks, and always the right dash of adventure, anytime the experience grew dull. "We don't have many dances, back home."

"You must miss it," he said, and she wasn't sure whether his tone was wistful or wheedling.

She had, at first. Despite her desperate need to escape and the inevitable pain of return. She'd spent those early months of therapy longing for her lost friend, her lost world. With time, the want grew bitter.

"Eventually, you have to let things go," she said.

"That's giving up," Teresa replied, meeting her gaze.

The same argument they'd fought again and again, with increasing urgency, in the days before Kate finally left. She'd begged Teresa to come with her. Threatened. Made impossible promises. And Teresa had done the same, trying to keep her.

At least now, they could simply sketch the shape of the old battles, without fighting them again.

"I missed you," Kate said, meaning, it's not *you* I gave up on.

"I'm sure you made new friends," Teresa replied. Meaning what? That she, alone on the otherside, could not do the same?

"Eventually," Kate admitted. "I didn't talk to many people at first. My parents thought I'd been kidnapped. They kept me home. Brought in a therapist."

"I saw." Teresa's voice was soft. "I'm sorry."

And wasn't that what she'd been waiting to hear? But Kate couldn't find the words to reply, not with recrimination or acceptance. She watched Teresa stare at her hands, and all she wanted to do was hold them in her own, take the hurt from her eyes. Make it better.

But she didn't even belong to the same world. Not anymore.

"I promised we'd go for a walk after lunch," she said, tugging at Charlotte's shoe to get her attention. "I'll see you both at dinner."

It was easier to leave than risk more fighting. It always had been.

The walk to the silver lakes was so uneventful that Kate felt nearly as bored as Charlotte, who stomped along at her side. The woods were quiet, and the autumn leaves drifted around them as they walked, a dry rain of red and gold. She'd never seen the otherside in autumn before. In her memory, there were endless summer days and winter snows, but no new budding flowers or falling leaves. She couldn't help but marvel at the beauty of it all, and wonder, a little, at what it might mean. Why autumn now, for Teresa's wedding? Why not blooming roses and baby animals?

"Where are the birds?" Charlotte asked. "And the squirrels?"

"I don't know, hon. They used to be everywhere."

The walk was shorter than Kate remembered. Within half an hour, they'd almost reached the lakes. The trees were thinning, though the woods stayed silent, no distant sounds of people or waterfowl. The ground grew rocky underfoot, as they pushed through the last of the trees. That, at least, was familiar. The lakes had always appeared like a surprise, between one bend and the next.

The lakes were gone.

Not merely dry, but missing, replaced by a vast stretch of parched, flat land. The shores had gleamed once, stones like gems and silver sand. Nothing now. Just an expanse of gray rocks.

"Mommy, are we almost there?" Charlotte asked.

And Kate, staring out across where the water wasn't, couldn't find an answer. What had happened? How could the lakes just stop being?

She let go of Charlotte's hand and sat down on the rocks. She wanted to close her eyes, to shut it all out. Forgetting the lakes was one thing. Losing them, like this, was something else. They had been so happy here, once.

"Mommy?" Charlotte's hand was warm on her shoulder. "Mommy, what's wrong? Are we lost? Do we need to call a police officer? I didn't use all the phone."

"We're not lost." Kate's voice shook a little. She took a slow breath before trying again. "I'm just tired. I'm going to sit for a bit. Stay where I can see you. Then we can go see the horses."

Charlotte sat nearby, humming to herself and stacking stones while Kate stared, helpless, out at the absence of the lakes.

"I didn't come here anymore, after you left." Teresa's voice startled her out of her mourning. She jumped to her feet, turning to see Verita leading a black horse down the path. Teresa sat on the horse's back, in a fine blue riding dress.

Kate stood silent, hunting for words. No use asking how Teresa had found her. Even without Verita's help, she'd always know where Kate, and everyone, was.

"Mommy, a horse!" Charlotte said, jumping to her feet. She ran straight at the animal, who lowered its head and nuzzled her in immediate affection.

Horses on the otherside were like that. Unless you didn't want them to be.

"This is Winterwind," said Teresa, sliding off the horse's back. "She could be your horse, if you like, Charlotte."

"Oh, Mommy, could we? Could I please?"

"And are you going to shovel the poop and ride it every day and go out at five in the morning to feed it before school?"

"I could." Charlotte sat a little straighter. "Mommy, you never let anything be fun."

"That's not true."

Teresa laughed, not kindly. "Your mom's always been very serious."

Not always. She'd helped make this place, once.

"We'll talk about the horse later," Kate said at last. Now wasn't the time for that argument.

"I can ride her though, right?"

"I suppose. With help."

"Verita, why don't you take Charlotte around the clearing?" Teresa asked. "Winterwind will appreciate the exercise."

"Stay where I can see you," Kate said. "Teresa and I will talk."

Verita helped Charlotte onto the horse, then climbed on behind her. Kate watched as the horse made its gentle, ambling way, its tail streaming out behind it with more drama than its pace really required. Charlotte's laughter filled the air, sweet as the birds that weren't singing.

"We used to ride here," Teresa said, coming to stand closer to Kate.

"We used to do a lot of things." Kate kept her gaze locked on the empty expanse where the lake wasn't. "What happened here, Teresa?"

"Nothing." Teresa threw a stone, and it fell dead in the dust beside one of the shrubs, shaking free a few dry leaves. "Nothing happened here, after you left. And eventually there wasn't a here anymore."

"But we loved the lakes." Kate hated the sorrow in her words, but the grief wouldn't be buried. There'd been a time when she really believed that she and Teresa would live forever in the otherside, sister queens ruling over a land that bent to suit their every whim.

"It's not just here," Teresa said, playing nervously with the hem of her shirt. "The shadow gardens are gone. The forest of songs is still there, but the trees only sing the same song, over and over again. I don't think they'll last much longer. Sometimes, the servants all have the same face. And they all look like me. I can't keep it all in my head, Katie. I can't care about all of it, all the time."

She might have closed the space between them, then. Might have pulled Teresa close, let her cry, even cried with her. Friends did that sort of thing.

"You had to know this was coming," she said. "This isn't a place you stay, Teresa. You can't have a life here. Not a real life."

"I could. If you stayed. You and Charlotte both."

Charlotte and Verita were finishing their first circuit of the missing lake. The horse came trotting toward them, and for a moment, Kate couldn't tear her eyes away. Had she ever seen her daughter so ecstatic?

"Mommy, look! Mommy, I'm riding!"

"I see you, hon," Kate called back. "You're doing great."

"She'd be happy, here," Teresa said, after the horse had passed.

"You know we're not staying." At last, Kate turned to look at Teresa.

Teresa's eyes were bright with the threat of tears, but she stood, back straight, trying to smile. "I know. But I had to ask."

"You could come back with us." Though what that meant, Kate wasn't sure. Would Teresa be 12 again, as Kate had been?

Would she return to the past? How could she, when Kate had already lived those years alone?

"And what would happen to this place, if I left?"

"It's not real."

"Of course it—" Teresa's words were just on the edge of shouting, but she cut herself off, biting her lip and staring at her feet. "Maybe we made them. Maybe we made all of it. But that doesn't mean they're not real. They have feelings. Good days and bad days. They die. They mourn. They are real, Katie. And they're our— they're my responsibility. If I leave, it all falls into ruin. I can't do that to them."

"You said they're already fading."

"That's why I have to save the ones I can." She glanced back up, offering a watery smile. "I guess I thought, if you saw what it'd come to here, you might want to help."

Kate held out her arm, and Teresa stepped close. She was shaking, and for a second, Kate loved her as much as she ever had. Her best friend. The two of them lost, hurt, and ready to take on the world together. To make a world together, if that's what it took to feel safe. Kate hiding from her mother's anger and her father's absence. Teresa washing away under an endless list of expectations, a bar that moved higher every time her fingers brushed it. And then a door, and a song, and a lifetime.

She'd left Teresa. She'd had to leave her. When the world grew poisoned with her own restless bitterness, when the fruit rotted and the servants grew snide. When, suddenly, there was horse shit in the stables, and Crey, always amusingly obnoxious, grew menacing. What choice was there, then?

"I'm sorry, Teri."

"What am I supposed to do?" Teresa asked. Despite her shaking, her voice was steady.

Come back, Kate wanted to say. Come with me. I'll protect you. You'll be Charlotte's big sister. We'll be best friends. Whatever you owe this place, you don't owe it this.

She stroked her friend's arm, leaning so her cheek rested against her hair.

"Keep fighting. And I'll come again. If it helps. If you want to see me."

"I can't open the door often," Teresa replied. "I don't know what'll be left, next time. It might just be me."

"Then we'll go back together."

Charlotte and Verita came round again, and Teresa stepped away, brushing at her dress. "Your daughter's lovely, you know. She reminds me of you. Her father?"

"No one you know. We're divorced."

"Oh. I— sorry."

"Don't be," Kate said. "Sometimes, people just aren't meant to stay together, you know?"

Teresa laughed. "Oh, yeah. I get that."

"You and Crey?" Kate asked.

Teresa's smile didn't fade, though she shook her head in helpless, amused denial. "He's Crey, you know? Our perpetual fanboy. Everything that ever irritated us, just so we'd have someone to be irritated with."

"From experience, I can't say that's the best basis for a marriage."

"He's the realest one here, Katie. The one we paid the most attention to. Half our adventures, he was with us. The other half, we were trying to save him. I guess I'm still trying to save him."

The horse had reached them again, and this time, Verita slowed it to a stop. Kate stepped forward, and Charlotte slipped off into her arms.

"Don't you want to ride, Mommy?"

"Sorry, hon." Kate ran her fingers through her daughter's wind-tangled hair, trying to pat it back into order. "We've gotta help Aunt Teresa get ready for her wedding, ok?"

"More itchy dresses?"

"I'm sure they won't be that itchy. And there's a cake, and flowers, and I bet Aunt Teresa will even ride her horse Moonfall down the aisle."

"And you'll ride Everstar?" Teresa asked, rubbing at her eyes.

"Of course."

The wedding was everything it had to be. A fairytale impossibility, the bridal party on horses, doves singing the wedding march, and Teresa a confection of white, riding down an aisle that Charlotte had enthusiastically coated in scarlet petals. Even Crey did his part, strikingly handsome in his black suit and short cape.

Teresa said her vows, making a promise to protect Crey, to stand by his side, to serve the otherside for as long as she lived.

As long as it lived, Kate thought, and she let herself cry. Why not? Everyone wept at weddings.

In the celebration that followed, as Charlotte ran from table to table with giddy abandon, Kate sat alone, watching them all. The parents of the groom still held the sparks of stars, their skin gleaming under their wedding silks. Verita and the other servants exchanged toasts and stole bites of food from each other's plates. Crey kept looking over at Teresa, awestruck. As if, even with the wedding over, he couldn't quite believe that she'd picked him.

And they were all real. And they were none of them more than what Teresa needed them to be. No one stepped on her dress, or started messy, drunken fights. Only Charlotte, running with a plate full of cake, caused any sort of chaos.

Kate felt the old itch, the longing to get away from the otherside, with its patterns and its predictability. To go back to a world that didn't care about her, if only to be surprised. She drank her wine, and she watched Teresa, and she waited for the moon.

The party had quieted, and Charlotte lay drowsing in Kate's arms, when the moon finally reached its peak, and the silver path lay clear before her. Kate stood, cradling Charlotte close, and picked up the bag she'd tucked discreetly under the table. Teresa pulled away from where she'd been dancing with Crey and ran over, somehow managing not to trip on her layers of skirts.

They stared at each other for a second, then leaned together, Teresa hugging her as best she could around the sleeping Charlotte.

"I wish I could come," she said.

"I wish you would," Kate replied. "And I'm sorry that I can't stay. This place, it's not enough for me. I have to go back."

"I know." Teresa leaned down, and kissed Charlotte on the forehead. "I always knew you were the strong one, Kate. That you'd outgrow me."

"I couldn't," Kate forced out, refusing to cry. She'd gotten that out of her system already. "We're best friends, remember?"

"I'll try to reach you again." Teresa glanced back at the party. "If I can. If there's anything left. I'll try."

"I'll come," Kate promised.

She walked backward down the silver path, keeping Teresa in view. With each step, the party grew a little more distant, a little more indistinct, until all she could see was Teresa, standing alone in a ridiculous white gown.

And then she was standing in a fountain, in a midnight park, and Charlotte was stirring in her arms.

"Where'd everyone go?" she asked, words slurred with sleep.

"We're home, love." Kate braced herself, not sure how Charlotte would take the news.

"Oh."

Silence. Kate kept walking, not looking back at the moon and the fountain and the world they'd left behind.

But Charlotte, shifting to peer over her shoulder: "It's all gone."

"That's how it works."

"Can we visit again?"

At first, Kate's throat tightened. The old fear of doorways and forevers taking over. But then she looked back too, admiring the water, so silver in the moonlight, like the lakes Charlotte would never get to see.

"I hope so. I think Aunt Teresa would like it very much if we did."

"And you too?"

"And me too."

"Good." Charlotte yawned and nuzzled against Kate's chest. "Let's go home, Mommy."

Kate kissed her daughter's curls, then swung her down to stand. "Lead the way. My arms are getting tired."

After a few sleepy steps, Charlotte found her usual energy, and Kate let her run. The moon cast everything in silver, and Charlotte knew the way. There was nothing to be afraid of.

Kate looked back, one last time, smiling in case Teresa was watching. Then she turned and followed her daughter home.

See Kelly Sandoval's story "The Otherside of Memory" online at Metaphorosis.
If you liked it, leave a comment. Authors love that!
Remember to subscribe to our e-mail updates so you'll know when new stories are posted.

About the story

I grew up on portal fantasies. I loved *The Labyrinth, The Chronicles of Narnia*, and *Peter Pan*. I wanted more than anything to disappear through a wardrobe, or a painting, and find myself somewhere else. Somewhere special.

But even as a kid, there were elements of the stories that bothered me. Especially Narnia. The characters live out their lives in this magical world. They're forced, as children, to fight. They grow up. They rule as kings and queens. And then they return to their lives and homes, magically children again. I could never believe that they would simply be fine with living as normal kids. I could hardly accept that they'd return in the first place.

The "Otherside of Memory" grew out of that tension. What does it mean to stay in a magical world, especially one that, as so many do, seems to exist as a reflection of its visitors? What does it take to leave it behind? And why would you?

In a way, this story is a conversation between the child me, who still longs for portals, and the current me, who sees the darker, more troubling side of such fantasies.

A question for the author

Q: Are you an outline or discovery writer?

A: I'm mostly a discovery writer. I sit down with an idea and try to follow it. Lately though, I've been trying to teach myself to outline.

About the author

Kelly lives in Seattle, where the weather is always happy to make staying in and writing seem like a good idea. She shares her home with her chaos tornado toddler, exhausted husband, and increasingly irate cat. Her interactive fiction is available from Choice of Games, where her current title is "Runt of the Litter".

www.kellysandovalfiction.com, @kellymsandoval

A Universe All to Himself

Ryan Priest

Except death, this was the worst-case scenario. This was the inevitable cost of the space program. Given enough runs, this was going to happen to someone and you just prayed it wouldn't be you. The very mention of the possibility passed like a cold draft through the rec rooms or cafeterias of any space station. When a pilot failed to return from a mission, you hoped secretly, for their sake, that they were dead. The alternative was a man or woman hopelessly lost in space.

Erik Hale, Pilot #1225, had just won the lottery. Outside of his spaceship there was nothing; no star, no planet, no swirling black holes, not even the hollowed-out core of a dead gas giant. It was just cold, empty space.

His upper lip began to tremble.

The way *leaping* worked involved the compression of near-empty space. The astro-pilots called it the Planet-to-Planet Freeway. The computers charted a course between two planets orbiting in different star systems. Then the engines compressed the empty space between the two points. What was left? Usually only a few miles of concentrated space dust to cross and then your ship was there, at the other end, in a new solar system. The Leap window could only exist for a little over a second, and so a pilot had to circle the origin planet a couple of times to build up the speed to slingshot their ship fast enough to get out the other side before the window closed.

But you *had* to have a planet for the Leap back home. Without the planet's gravitational boost, the ship's propulsion could never build up the speed on its own. If you tried to use a star, the orbit would take too long; by the time you made it back around the ebb and tide of celestial movements would leave you pointing in the wrong direction. The planets, stars, galaxies were in a perpetual state of motion, like an ocean, never all in the exact same alignment twice.

The problem was that long-range telemetry could be unreliable. When analyzing celestial bodies tens of thousands of light years away, there was no way to be sure those planets would still be there on arrival. The computer analysts did their best to calculate good candidates; the brass wouldn't intentionally send you to a system that might have gone nova or to a planet with an orbit they weren't sure about.

Once arriving at their destination and landed, the astro-pilots collected data with their computers and sensors. Soil and air samples to check for human colony feasibility, astronomic readings to hunt for even more unknown planets, possibly so far out that they were undetectable from Earth. The pilot's final duty was to take a picture of his or herself holding the Western Earth Union flag. This was what really mattered to the brass. International space regulations required a live human being to physically be on the planet to establish ownership. The remaining nations of Earth were in a race to find and lay claim to inhabitable or resource rich exo-planets. Footprints and flags — the moon landing writ large across the galaxy.

With the job done, the pilot and ship reentered orbit and jumped back to their point of origin— for Westerners usually the Neptune or Pluto orbital stations.

But there *were* mistakes. When flying off into the universe in a blind rush, there was bound to be an error here or there. A black hole might have eaten the entire star, a collision with a comet might have destroyed the planet. No one would ever know for sure, because without the anchor planet, there was no way to establish a return trip to Earth. In the cases when a pilot did not come back, that destination was marked in the database as a 'No-Go'. There were no rescue missions. The only thing worse than losing an astronaut to space was losing a second astronaut sent to find out what happened to the first one.

Without the Leap Engine, a regular five-minute trip back to Earth from Pluto took over three years, even with their fastest engines. To get to the next closest exo-planet would take thousands of years. For a lost pilot — for Erik — there was no going home. Earth was gone and the Sun was only one of a million dots of light in the ship's portholes.

Erik was overcome with the desire to cry. He felt claustrophobic all of a sudden, and couldn't breathe. The safety harness squeezed his chest with every breath; it seemed alive and hostile, holding him to his seat, pinning him to this predicament.

He felt as if all the blackness in the universe were closing in around him, suffocating him. He clawed at the restrictive harness in a panic, hoping he'd wake to find himself struggling with a sheet wrapped around his neck. But this was no dream. He was trapped; the universe had trapped him out here alone and his mother wasn't going to flip on the lights and make it all okay. His mother was gone, now and forever. She'd be told he was dead and she'd collapse into his sister's arms and they'd weep together. But then they and the world would ultimately learn to go on without him. His entire life was now separated from him by an unimaginable and uncrossable ocean of black nothingness.

"What if it *does* happen?" trainees always asked when first confronted with the possibility of a failed jump.

"It won't happen. But if it does, then press this button. That's all for now," the trainer would say, and shuffle them on to the next lesson. Every ship had a button, a red one hidden out of view, near the floor and covered by a black latch so no one ever had to think about it.

What did the button do? People seldom spoke about it openly, but you'd hear things; there were theories. Some said it released a pistol or maybe some suicide pills for the pilot to take. The old space freighter captains claimed that a hundred years ago, when transit around the solar system was still new and could take years, the old timers all had such pills aboard for worst-case scenarios. Back when if something happened to your ship, you were months or possibly years away from rescue. Erik could do months, he could even do years, but *never* was a different hell altogether. The pills had been a quicker and supposedly less painful death than freezing, roasting, suffocating, or any of the other ways a botched space flight might end you. Supposedly.

Others thought the button was a self-destruct for the entire ship. They said it was designed that way so you wouldn't know you were killing yourself. Proponents of this theory said it was for the religious minded who might fear that suicide would damage their chances of a pleasurable afterlife. You could press the button as many times as you liked, but it was programmed not to engage unless the ship missed its departure window.

One pilot, #108 Sheila Gates, after arriving, had found her host planet's sun moved in-between her anchor planet and Earth. She'd been forced to wait for the planet to orbit back around the other side, four and a half Earth years. When her ship *did* return,

Sheila was inside, alive but catatonic. Other pilots said that she had been locked up in a room somewhere in the Department of Space. Rumor was that she'd pressed the red button.

He looked at the black cover for a moment or two. It was as if opening the latch and seeing the red button underneath would make this all permanent. If he did it, then he was admitting that a real disaster had happened.

"Think Erik, think!" His voice cracked and he found the simple task of focusing on anything beyond his grasp. This was bad, this was *very* bad.

"Why would you want to fly off to plant flags on planets you'll never see again?" his old friend Benny's voice ran through his memory. They'd been co-captains on a space-freighter that hauled minerals from asteroid mining sites to giant space platforms.

At the time, Erik had kept his motivations personal and shrugged him off with, "Hey, after two hundred jumps and with some smart investing you can retire to a comfortable life."

Benny was a couple years older, had more hours in space. For him, the gift of steady work was all that he ever wanted. To Erik freight hauling had only ever been a means to collect the flight time needed to apply to be an astro-pilot in the Department of Space, and once he had them he was gone. He'd really liked Benny, but growing up, Erik had had three different stepdads and more "mom's boyfriends" than he could count. He was used to saying goodbye to older men.

Now, facing catastrophic loss, he was asking himself the same question. Why *had* he done this to himself? Did he really think it mattered in the grand scheme of things that in two or three hundred years there would be children growing up on faraway colonies, learning in school that he'd discovered their planet? Maybe even a planet named after him? In his one hundred and fifty-seven jumps, he had found seven inhabitable exo-planets. Seven new worlds where everyone would know the name starship pilot #1225 Erik Hale and the subsequent endnote, that he was lost in space.

Hours later, and his eyes were still locked on the round, red knob on his floor. Maybe death, maybe insanity, maybe salvation — but what other choice did he have?

He prepared himself to die. He took a deep breath of sterile air, enough to carry his spirit into eternity, as Ernie, one of his mother's many boyfriends, had explained. Ernie had worn an old

Native American jacket and vintage tie-dyed shirts. He liked to talk about spirituality and that sort of thing. This had been Erik's only exposure to any type of religion and it, along with his mother's relationship with Ernie, had been brief.

It amazed him what chose to pop into his mind at this, potentially last, moment. He latched on to that amazement — not a bad feeling to go out on — and exhaled as he let his hand press down on the button...

No explosion, no afterlife, no death. He was still lost and alone, yet his life seemed to taste a little sweeter. Two small, blue pills had ejected from behind the button like a coin-operated candy dispenser, and the computer screens in the cockpit had all gone blank. Erik picked the pills up off the floor. They were ovular, like vitamins, but he knew they weren't vitamins. They were the opposite.

Suicide pills. Erik looked at them in disappointment. A second ago, before pressing the button, he might not have cared, but now he was very sure that he wanted to live.

"So, your ship has been lost in space," came a familiar voice out of the ship's speakers. He couldn't place it at first, but when all the monitors faded in with an accompanying video, he recognized the face immediately. It was H. Gregory Gladstone, Secretary of Space and Exploration. "The first thing you must remember is not to panic. Take a deep breath."

Erik complied. Trying to calm down, he realized just how tightly wound he'd become. The muscles in his neck and shoulders felt carved in stone and he had a clenched mouthful of gritting teeth. He closed his eyes and took three deep, measured, breaths. On the final exhale, he let his eyes open. It was better; things were somewhat clearer.

"In your hand are two blue tablets. If you take them, death will be quick. However, you have also been given a key that unlocks a special box on this ship. Should you choose to use it, this box contains the means not only to your survival, but also your sanity. More importantly, in this box you will find the tools necessary to regain what you've lost, a meaningful life, love, friendship. It will require an incredible amount of work, but I promise you, should you choose, there is still a life for you to have."

Erik looked down and saw that a brass key had also been ejected from the emergency latch. He picked it up, and held the key in his left hand and the suicide tablets in his right.

"Take a moment." Gladstone's face was calming. He'd been a public figure for over forty years and had been one of the lead designers of the Leap system. He'd managed to keep himself above all the political fray and stand out as someone for the intellectuals to follow and support. He had no agenda other than the continued exploration and eventual colonization of space. That was his brand and it came with a good public reputation. He was like a family member, only one who lived entirely on television and whose interactions were completely one-sided. Still, Erik had always rooted for his success and supported anything he did.

"In seven minutes, your tablets will dissolve and become useless to you. Sorry for putting you on the spot, but you pressed the button, which tells me you are ready to move ahead, either in one way or the other. It is time for decisive action. The choice you make now must stand. You will either decide that you want to live and are willing to put forth the work and sacrifice that is necessary, or you will die now and commit yourself to a different journey."

At that, Gladstone quit speaking but continued to stand there, looking into the camera, lest you be completely alone in your final moments. There was no judgment implied in his tone. Erik wondered how many other pilots had watched this video, made this choice. It was generally assumed that if a pilot didn't make it back, they were dead, but who could know for sure?

He fought back sobs. How had he put himself in this position? He didn't need a planet named after him. That all seemed like such an arrogant conceit at this point; barely more than celestial graffiti. Now he had H. Gregory Gladstone telling him he might just want to kill himself and be done with it?

He looked down at the pills and instantly pictured himself foaming at the mouth, twitching and swallowing his own tongue. He dropped the pills to the floor as if they were on fire. They'd already begun to crumble and, in a few minutes, they'd be nothing but inert microscopic dust.

This was it. Whatever lay ahead, this was his life and he would try his best to make the most of it and hope that the Secretary of Space really did have some ace up his sleeve.

Gladstone suddenly came back to life. "If you are still listening to this, then that means the pills are gone and you are alive. I am proud of you for making such a difficult decision in this, such an uncertain time. But rest assured, the road to your new life begins now."

Erik was directed to the rear of the ship, in the already cramped storage area. He saw that a new box was waiting for him on the floor, recently ejected from a hidden compartment. He felt a delicate beat of hope rise within him. There was more to this puzzle. Director Gladstone *did* have a plan for him.

With the brass key still clutched in the fingers of his left hand, he approached the box and, sure enough, there was a lock waiting for him to open it. All the pageantry was likely for psychological effect. Here was a box that he knew no pilot outside of his situation had ever seen. This box was truly a mystery and every possibility in the universe could very well be inside.

He ran his fingers over the top of it lightly, the same way he always did with a new ship. This was what was going to get him home. The box itself was maybe three by four feet and not very high off the ground, about the size of a great chest.

He turned the lock and took the lid off. Hand-tools, spare nuts and bolts, bags of soil, and several packets of seeds. At the very bottom was one more object, a small package whose label read: Protocol 6, Final Phase. Do Not Open Early.

He was careful to not even touch the Protocol 6 package. He would follow the rules; this was too important to screw up with impatience. The seeds were indication enough that whatever this was, it was going to take time.

A new program came up on his console. Protocol One. It was a series of instructions, laid out in precise steps. The first were on how to set up a garden and to expand the ship's insides to allow for as much space for movement as possible. The garden was the most important part. The garden would filter and recycle the air and someday take the place of his mission packs when it came to food.

Sixteen hours a day. That was how much the program kept him working. When the day was over, he'd lie down while a monotone, pre-programmed voice continued to talk to him, encouraging him and telling him that it was hard now because these things had to get taken care of first, but the voice promised, it *promised*, there was something much better waiting for him if he followed the instructions step by step.

An alarm woke him up every morning. The voice urged him to brush his teeth, clean himself appropriately, and eat a protein bar. It always seemed to rush him along more quickly than he'd like, but he was usually too tired to care. Those first few days were about nothing but toil, every single day, morning, noon, and night, which meant absolutely nothing here in black space.

He hardly had any time to think about how his mother might be taking the news. No time to picture his own funeral back home and imagine the eulogy his sister Andrea might have given for him.

Would anybody else even be there? He hadn't seen Benny in years. Ernie and all the stepdads were long gone.

The thought of an empty funeral was a reminder that he'd failed to accomplish anything or make a positive impact on anyone's life, though he'd wanted to. But like everything else, friendships had been pushed to the back burner in favor of that mad rush to pull himself out of the working class. In a moment of bitter irony, the life back home that had never been good enough for him had now been taken from him.

The ship was designed so that once he emptied out an interior panel's shelves and drawers, the walls could be folded outward, expanding like origami. When completed, he'd have more than triple the space. Awkward and unflightworthy, he'd never be able to land the ship on a planet again, but that didn't matter; there wasn't another planet for a million miles.

"Moving on to Protocol 2." The program's voice droned on with instructions and random encouragements. "You're doing a fantastic job. You're almost there."

He began to realize the program wasn't just teaching him how to reorganize his ship, the program was designed to slowly but surely reorganize *him*.

This meant that someone had thought this through. Someone had done tests and planned for this, and they knew how best to survive the loss of, basically, everything he'd ever known. He took wry comfort in this, imagining a room full of college boys with all the answers planning out his every little move.

The nightly talk downs became more than just encouragement. As he sat on the cockpit chair, eating his dinner, the ship's voice would ask him weighty questions and give him puzzles to think about over the next day. The questions ranged from the unanswerable koans — "If a tree falls in the forest..." — to highly complex exercises in logic — "If Archbishop Thomas needs a census of a kingdom containing ten villages, and he knows each village has ten more persons than the last, that no village has more than three hundred people and no village has less than two hundred, how many people total live in the kingdom?"

The program did not shy away from sharing its motivations. It was trying to strengthen his mind. Something really great was apparently coming down the line and having a quick and strong mind that could think things through was a prerequisite.

After two weeks, the expansion work was completed. He had his space home. The cockpit, the garden in the left aft of the cargo hold, the right side set up with his bed and personal effects. It wasn't much at all, really, but it was much more than he'd had or expected when he started. That was the program, to make things better in small increments, keep him working for more, keep him busy. They were breaking him down, like basic training or a cult.

With Protocol 3, the computer led him through nightly, guided meditations. He was asked to picture simple objects, a beach ball or log cabin. Through a series of open-ended questions, the computer made him fixate on the mental image, flesh it out.

"What color is the cabin? Do the insides contain an odor? If so, do you like this odor? Why?"

At the end of the lessons and throughout the day, the computer would periodically remind him that something great was coming, that he was almost ready. Almost.

Coming from genetically modified seeds, the plants were growing big and fast. With only the smallest amount of maintenance, he would begin producing his own food within a few weeks. The computers rewarded him with music while he worked, and even allowed the viewing of a film every so often. There was no way to tell how many hours of footage had been stored in the memory banks. It was inevitable, though, that one day he'd have run out of videos and have listened to every song. The program was designed to push that day as far into the future as possible.

By Protocol 4, he'd begun to notice results from all of his exercises. He was becoming mentally sharper. He was solving puzzles more easily, thinking through the koans more deeply.

What was Protocol 6 and how did it figure into all of this? Had there been a breakthrough in cognitive sciences? For years, people had been claiming the next wave of human evolution would see an increase in mental powers — telepathy, maybe. Would he become able to contact Earth and tell them to find a way to send a rescue? Was it even possible that they had a way to master telekinesis? Maybe he'd unlock some as of yet unused part of his brain and be able to move his spaceship across light years with just a thought. Anything was possible, and the program kept promising it'd lead to a life worth living. It promised an escape from this cell which, as it stood, would one day double as his tomb.

The meditations became even more involved. Now it wasn't just log cabins. He was being asked to see whole landscapes, to hold the image in his head so long that he could account for every little blip on the horizon. The landscapes became increasingly involved. Erik always followed along. He asked himself the questions he was supposed to and he tried his best to come up with the answers. He did this in total earnestness, as with everything else. The Space Department's motto was *Cynicism Kills*.

He'd always been good at following orders. He knew that about himself but wasn't sure how he felt about it. With nothing but time on his hands and these sharper mental tools, he realized that he wasn't weak or inherently obedient, he simply longed for a sense of fatherly approval. He was always trying to show the world that he could follow directions, that he was worthwhile, and that someone would realize this and take him under their wing to teach him how to navigate this confusing life as a man. *That* confusing life. He had to remind himself that his old world and any hang-ups that went with it were a thing of the past.

Erik had pushed forward, full force, the very picture of pluck and vinegar. He was no stranger to hard work. Hard work was how he'd pulled himself off the surface and into space. How he'd become a pilot and had eventually made it to astro-pilot. He recognized that effort multiplied by time inevitably led to results. He'd learned to subvert the part of himself that wanted to laze, to sit back and think of reasons *not* to bother. The voice in the background of every endeavor that whispered maledictions about fruitlessness, failure and abdication.

But the days turned into weeks, the routine became rigmarole, and try as hard as he might to tune it out, the voice of negativity in his head had grown louder. His situation was beginning to wear on him. Forcing optimism became more difficult with each passing day.

He missed home and he missed other people. Anyone. He missed mattering in someone else's life or even the possibility of affecting another person. Nothing he did here, nothing he would ever say or think could ever be known by another living person. He was effectively a ghost, living without the possibility of consequence, and this was a realization that, once registered, could not so easily be broken free from.

"Do not give up," the program chirped through the speakers. And he tried, he tried, to hold out hope. He practiced his exercises, but mustering the required energy was becoming an effort. He felt that he was growing weaker and not stronger. He began thinking up his own dark koans. "If a man exists without consequence, is he even alive?"

His hopes for Protocol 6 began to fade as well. If there was telekinesis or telepathy, why hadn't they already used it to make contact with *him*? He began to suspect more and more that

Protocol 6 was going to be a new set of suicide pills. There was no escape from this place.

Protocol 5.

"Prepare to meditate, Erik." The computer was programmed to use his first name. It was just a series of 1s and 0s, with no humanity. "Tonight, you will think of a house. Not just any house; imagine your perfect house. This is the house you would most like to live in."

It went on asking him to furnish this house. Did it have a pool? What was the climate like? This meditation went further and longer than all others before it. So much so that he actually began to find it taxing and, by the end of the lesson, had developed quite a little headache.

Every night the following week, the program immediately would tell him to concentrate on the house he'd created. He was told to imagine himself walking through the house. Going into each room, opening every closet.

"When your hand touches the wood, how does it feel? What do you see when you look out the window?" Oak, or at least what he imagined oak to be. It felt cool and smooth, it felt like money. Outside of his window were rolling green hills, a shimmering sea bay, backdropped by an impossibly bright, blue sky, sprinkled with cotton ball clouds. Every night, he made the house just a little more beautiful, just a little more *him*. He noticed that the more he did this, the less strain it caused. This, he actually felt he was getting better at. His brain was learning this imaginary house.

After this, every meditation began with the house and then expanded from there. He was told to walk down the street. It was like a game. He was sent exploring outside of this house. He could go anywhere he wanted, but there were rules. He couldn't just imagine a restaurant and place himself there. He had to consciously walk down the street, see the restaurant in the distance and step by step approach it. He could have anything he wanted, and do anything, but there were no shortcuts.

The game became fun again as it challenged him more and more every day. He'd built an entire town in his head, and without fail could recall all of the details as clearly as the Akron suburbs he'd passed through as a child, longing for one of those lives with lawns and playgrounds. Only this was better, cleaner, greener, and brighter.

The game was the high point of his day. Any time spent concentrating on the game was time not spent in the downward spiral of hopelessness and loneliness.

"What is a town without people? Who lives nearest to you on the West? A man, a woman, a family?" The computer had him not only build people but build his past relationships with them. How had they met? Did he like them?

Erik's imagined house sat directly east of a family named the Woodneys, a name he'd been asked to imagine on the spot, without any reference to anyone he really knew. The Woodneys were Tom and Cheryl, and they had one son, Zach, who was ten.

Where the game became really interesting started on a movie night. He'd been allowed to watch an old movie from the Nineteen-Nineties. Normal enough, but later that night, in meditation, he was asked to enter his fake house, in his fake town, and go to visit his fake neighbor Tom. By now, Erik had been asked so many questions by the program, he would be just about able to write a thousand-word biography of Tom Woodney.

However, tonight the program did something different. "You see your neighbor in the yard. He tells you that he just saw the same movie. He really liked it. Discuss the movie with him. What did he find different about the movie, if anything, than you did?"

And he found that this was a very easy and fun conversation to have. Tom's words came out naturally, by necessity of his personality.

Before he knew it, the two-hour meditation session was over and he was called to return his attention to the ship and its clutter of blooming plants.

It was only when he was allowed another movie that he realized what the program was doing. He was watching some god-awful thriller from the Twenty-Naughts. Erik hated the movie, but he found himself excited to see what neighbor Tom would have to say about it.

That night he had another two-hour movie conversation with Tom while sitting outside around his dream house's crystal blue pool. This mental game the program had him playing not only passed the time but was also enjoyable.

To his further delight, the program took away his time limits. As long as he followed the other rules, he could play the game as late as he wanted.

The last step before Protocol 6 was to keep the game going during his day. Periodically throughout the day, at different times, the computer would ask him to check on the game and see what was happening. He closed his eyes and then he was there, walking along the side of a lake, or shopping.

The program explained that Protocol 6 would be unlocked when he was able to go into the game while continuing to do his chores, mind his garden, perform the ship's required maintenance. Access to Protocol 6 was on the honor system. A new option in the ship's control panel read: PROTOCOL 6 and he could access it anytime, but like the little package bearing the same name, he'd been warned not to skip ahead, not to cheat. To make sure Protocol 6 worked, he had to be one hundred percent.

So the game went on. He tested himself — at one minute he'd be clipping some tomatoes, while simultaneously in the game he'd be playing second base on the local softball team he'd dreamt up. His directive had been to choose a sport, organize a league, and join a team.

He no longer even needed to close his eyes to be in the game and see everything in high definition. Just to be sure, he waited a while, until there was no question, until he spent more time in the game than he did out of it. He could water the plants and check the systems in fifteen minutes, then the lights would go off and he'd float in total darkness playing the game. By this time, he had a pretty good idea of what Protocol 6 would entail. He assumed it was designed that way.

He was ready. He sat in his cockpit chair and selected Protocol 6. The anxiousness in his gut was palpable. All this time he'd waited, he'd worked himself to the bone and he'd waited even more, and now here it was, Protocol 6.

All the screens in the ship went blank momentarily and a familiar face dissolved into view. It was H. Gregory Gladstone again. "First, I'd like to tell you how proud we all are of you for making it this far. You are a testament to the true indomitability of the human spirit. Next, let me get this over with quickly. You are not going home."

Inside, he had known that he wasn't going to make it home, but still, the final confirmation came like a knife to his heart. Hope died hard.

"That being said, do not give up. I'm sure by now you must what realize what Protocol 6 is."

"The game." Erik responded, knowing that Gladstone couldn't hear him. This message had been recorded years ago. All of it had, before he ever joined the space program.

"The game *is* your salvation. If you have done your exercises, then the world you've created in the game should have become, at times, just as real to you as the world of your spaceship. Here is the secret. It *is* just as real. Continue to play the game, give it your all, and you will be able to find fulfillment inside." Gladstone looked solemn, his bushy, serious eyes reminding Erik that cynicism killed.

It was a lot that they were asking of him, but really there was no choice. The program had not lied. There was no way he could have played the game, not at such a high level, without the slow and steady buildup of cognitive training.

The game was his favorite thing. It occupied his thoughts, it was the source of his happiness, his humor. The people he met in the game now seemed just as authentic to him as real people in the real world.

There wasn't any choice to quit playing. The game was as much a part of him now as his arm. What Gladstone was asking him to do was to go all in, to accept the game as reality.

"There is no difference to your mind if something is real or imagined. What makes dreams less important than reality is that we forget them and that they have no bearing on our future. Nevertheless, when we go to sleep and dream, no matter how fanciful that dream world, no matter how little sense it makes, still we accept it as reality without a second thought. Now you may open the final package."

Erik took the small parcel from the floor and opened it. Inside were two items, their purpose immediately recognizable to him. A simple switch system for automated plant watering and a feeding tube.

"The rules of time and space no longer need apply in the game. You'll find you can make time pass more quickly or more slowly. No reason to limit yourself to the ticks of seconds taken from Earth-based clocks. Now that the game is truly yours, make the very most of it."

By now he loved Gladstone like a father. He'd had no one else since being marooned, but he knew this was the last time he would ever see him.

Gladstone's final message was, "When you are ready, press continue." And with that, his image faded back out into the world of the left behind. A big green button on the screen replaced him, bearing the label: Continue.

It had to be this way. There was no going back, there had never been any going back. Everything ahead lay in the game, a new life completely untethered from his previous existence. He began to make his preparations. His movements were slow and deliberate. He was cognizant that this was a turning point in his life. The end of one thing and the beginning of something entirely different.

He set up his plant feeders, double-checked the cycles, automated his food and waste processing. When he was finished, everything was set up to run on complete automation. At last, he sat down in front of the console and choked down one end of the feeding tube, which connected itself to the ready supply of processed food paste from his garden.

When finished and ready, Erik lifted from his chair until he was free floating, the cabin lit only by the soft glow of the green button. He pressed Continue. Everything went black. The monotone voice of the program came back online and swam through the air.

"Erik, prepare to mediate. You are in your house. You hear a knock at the front door. You open it. It's a woman. She's the most beautiful woman you've ever seen. What color is her hair? What about her eyes? You like the way she smells, the way her voice sounds as she tells you, 'Hello, I just moved into the area.' What is her name?"

"Betty..." Erik said to himself while at the same time smiling at Betty and inviting her in for a cup of coffee. This was it. There'd be no more instructions.

The ship continued to float off into the cosmos, on its way to nowhere, a million miles away from where it started. Erik continued too, expanding his world. He married Betty, they had children. He loved them and knew that they loved him.

He found that time *could* pass faster in the game, living years in the space of months, full lifetimes in the course of years. He had evolved. He now existed as something different than a man. He had anything and everything he wanted. His existence was a beating pulse of a thousand different points of view in a world that continued forward with its own set of rules. He no longer cared if he had a planet named after him somewhere. He was now an entire universe unto himself.

See Ryan Priest's story "A Universe All to Himself" online at Metaphorosis.
If you liked it, leave a comment. Authors love that!

Remember to subscribe to our e-mail updates so you'll know when new stories are posted.

About the story

I grew up all over the Southwest. Colorado, Texas, California, the former frontier lands. When staring out at the Great Plains or the vast Rocky Mountains I often think of the people from the past. The catastrophic loneliness of a frontiersman or a scout. There will be new frontiers in our future and new explorers needed to map them. We will get brand new types of heroes, flying through space and maybe even dimensions we haven't discovered yet. This story tries to examine both.

I was inspired by the stories of gold-hungry miners, ex-slaves still looking for their freedom, lone Native Americans without a tribe wandering through a seemingly endless wilderness with nothing but their thoughts and their iron will to keep them company. What makes that type of will? Is it something we're either born with or an ability that develops after trial and tribulation? Willpower, when used effectively, has created the greatest feats of mankind. Where else might it take us?

Where are we going as a species? Are we going to reach other planets and is it just planets all the way down to the end of time or will we learn to take on new dimensions, new modalities of thought? What will a 'day' mean when there's no Sun to rotate around? We can never go back to the days of the past. There is only the future for us, and the beautiful thing about the future is, anything can happen.

A question for the author

Q: Have you ever consciously written a 'message' story? Was it easier or harder than usual?

A: One of my favorite aspects of writing is the serendipity of a story developing a message or deeper meaning while in the process of writing. Even when started from a blank page, a story will develop its own ideas. Now, when you flip it, choose the message before the story, it can be a very difficult task to get right. I've had to rewrite a story from the ground up three or four times when going in with a prescribed message. Sometimes the telling, no matter how good, doesn't lend itself to the desired ideal. When finally you do chart the trail that leads to the correct message, delivered in just the right way, that is a magic all its own. It's calling order out of chaos and it's beautiful.

About the author

Ryan Priest escaped the pollution-covered palm trees of L.A. for the mountain evergreens just outside Denver. He is a Black American who loves freedom, irresponsibility, and every single moment in history where a human being has let go and just gone for it in attempt to create something amazing.

www.RyanPriest.net, @Ryan_Priest

Autumn's Come Undone

Sharmon Gazaway

Autumn stands before a large pumpkin. Her bare soles, planted on either side, draw up minerals from the rich loam. The pumpkin's skin, still warm in late afternoon, glows under her touch, deepening from apricot to bittersweet orange. Stepping to the next pumpkin, she works the row, ripening each in turn. She swipes her brow with her forearm, her hands grimy, and pulls the weight of her ginger hair off her hot neck. A murmuring rumples the treetops, whispers forming words she can't quite make out. A chill lifts the fine hairs on her nape and she shivers.

Probably those air-headed dryads gossiping again.

As she walks to the brook to wash, honey-bright leaves drift down, cling to her hair like sprites. Humming, she pirouettes, her leaf skirts a swirl of marigold, russet, and spice. A garland of purplish-green globes dangling from the branch of a hickory tree catches her eye. She breaks off the vine and holds it up to the fading light.

Crow flutters down to the lowest limb, his bent wing stiff.

"Muscadines," she calls to him. "Sol's favorite." She breathes on the globes and they take on a ruddier, sweeter hue. "Perfect."

She drapes the fruited vine across a low shrub on the brook's bank and kneels, scrubbing her hands in the icy water. The stream babbles up at her, unintelligible at first. Dryads flit across the brook, tittering, cover malicious smiles with hazy hands. She looks about, wondering where Sylvannah is and why she hasn't already herded them into their trees. She swishes the muscadine vine through the water, shaking her head. It's a mystery to her how she ever endured the flighty things before Sylvannah came.

Crow lights on her shoulder, nudging her head. She shrugs him onto the bank. So little time left to prepare the table for Sol's visit tomorrow, and the muscadines will be the finishing touch. The stream murmurs insistently and Crow tilts his head toward it, turns and looks up at Autumn. She leans down, listens carefully. The murmurs sharpen into words that glint and wound, and take her breath.

Rising, the soggy fruit slides from her slack fingers.

Autumn's leaf skirts rush and crackle as she stumbles through the darkening woods, throws herself beneath the arms of the Great Oak. She hooks her fingers in deep, harrows leaf-rot and worm castings, breaks her nails on the bones of birds and vermin. From low in her inner turnings a cry germinates, a cry that, breaking free, rattles branches and drives the dryads into their tree-skins.

She does not cry prettily. Not like Spring, who mastered the art of the one perfect dewdrop tear while they were still girls in Earth's nursery.

Moaning, Autumn rolls her head on the forest floor and grits her teeth, the moss clinging to her lips. She hears a crack inside her chest like the snap of a twig.

Pushing onto her hands and knees, she crawls closer to the Oak. She huddles between the roots, her back pressed against the furrowed trunk. She curls into her cloak, fastens its silver acorn brooch, and tucks in her bare feet, tight as Tortoise in his shell. Crow lights on her shoulder and roosts in her tangles. Autumn presses her wet cheek against moonshadowed bark, relieved Sol can't see her now.

All night she burns, shamed.

Like a fool, all day she hummed and danced while she worked, awaiting Sol's visit. In a large reed basket, she heaped the harvest's bounty—rosy apples, pomegranates, walnuts and pecans, lush persimmons. She set it on a table strewn with smilax vines by the brook. She savored the thought of Sol by her side for a whole day, wandering the meadow amongst violet and ochre wildflowers, drifting in a rowboat until moonset.

She presses cold fingers against her blazing cheeks.

When morning comes, newly resurrected and only half alive, it sheds its mists and feeds on shafts of light. Light that colors everything the soft gold of Sol's hair. It fingers her face with tender warmth. She knows this touch—*his* touch—intimately.

Sol is mocking her.

She shudders to her feet, sends Crow flapping. She slaps twigs from her cloak, squares her shoulders and pulls up her hood, shielding herself from Sol's gloating.

This is not to be borne.

She marches to the brook, and heaves the table over. The loaded basket crashes to the ground, the fruit bruised and bleeding. She strikes her hands together and sparks shoot from her fingertips. The basket erupts in flame.

Shaking, rage unspent, she sets her face to the North and trudges out of her wood. Crow clings to her gray woolen shoulder, weight-shifting nervously. Mice dart for cover at her approach.

Whisking into vapor, Sylvannah slipped out through a knothole in the Great Oak when the wailing and gnashing of teeth began. All the other dryads shivered inside their trees. But she bit her lip and witnessed Autumn unravel.

Now, with Sol high in the eastern sky, and Autumn and Crow gone, the dryads' gossip chitters tree to tree.

"Sol jilted Autumn, even though she's never loved another."

"I heard he cheated on her with a star."

"No, two stars."

"They say he actually expects her to be happy for him."

Sylvannah listens, amused. Sol doesn't know Autumn the way she does, if that's what he expects. She snorts. As if.

It was Autumn's silly sister, Spring, who else? A bigger flirt she never saw. Sylvannah began life in Spring's woodland where Spring was forever tempting this star and that to come down to her. And when they burned out on the way, her eyes, the yellow-green of a cat's, glittered. She clapped as they blazed and fell to cinders at her feet.

And now she's caught the biggest star of all.

Sylvannah shushes the dryads, and glides into the orchard. She simply can't see the attraction. Sol is larger than life, always seeking attention. Yes, yes his job is very important—but, nutshells, what a Golden Boy.

Autumn gave him her heart long ago. Sylvannah couldn't imagine a better match for Autumn. Fiery; everyone around her gets singed at some point. But Sol could handle it, even seemed to revel in her volatile nature.

True, Autumn is unpredictable, but she has a warm and generous spirit few in the wood ever see.

Sylvannah remembers the day many harvests ago when she discovered Autumn's forest. She watched from the cover of a pine thicket as Autumn tended to an injured bird.

"Stop skulking around the edges of the wood and introduce yourself," Autumn called to her that day, tying the bird's wing firmly with strips of linen.

Sylvannah glided out, one hand clinging to chunky bark.

Autumn glanced up and sighed, "Not another dryad." She ran her hand over the crow's ragged feathers. "So, what do you want?"

"I'm Sylvannah. I come from Spring's woodland. She—she banished me."

Autumn looked up sharply. "Why?"

"I suppose your sister didn't much like me telling her she was cruel, the way she taunted the stars to their destruction." She shrugged.

Autumn smiled tightly, tossed her head toward the Oak in the center of the wood. "You're welcome to live there. You're the first dryad I've met with some sense and grit. If you can keep those nosy airheads out of my hair, you have a home for life."

So Sylvannah did.

Autumn kept to herself, except for Crow, her constant companion since she saved him from a hunter's snare. On occasion she visited her favorite sister, Winter. But she sought out Sol more than any other, the way a wing seeks wind.

Sylvannah accepts this. All she needs is the shelter of the Great Oak, his rings of wisdom surrounding her, his constancy—home.

And bossing the other dryads is just gravy.

She weaves through the orchard, inhales the brewery scent of apples that ache for Autumn's harvesting. Among shriveled, snaking vines, pumpkins bulge to bursting. The trees breathe the colors of fire.

As Sylvannah glides back toward the Oak, her lower lip sucked between her teeth, apprehension curls inside her like a little fog.

Autumn's sister, Winter, folds her into fur-robed arms and Autumn soaks up her warmth. Sol is weaker here. He and Winter have always maintained a distant relationship.

"I know why you've come, Little Acorn," Winter murmurs into her hair. "But Summer will never agree to it." She frowns, her eyes black and liquid as a snowhare's.

Summer. The good sister who tries to bind them together. But she has a soft spot for Sol, friends since the Beginning. She will plead for them all to reconcile, be a family. Family! Accept Sol as a *brother*?

"Sister," Autumn snaps, flaring, "I didn't come to ask a favor. Or permission." She sees in Winter's eye the glint of indulgent pride her sister reserves for Autumn alone. It was Winter who comforted her when Mother left them like fledglings in an abandoned nest. Winter who endured her tantrums, taught her to dance like a dervish to burn off the fumes of resentment. "I came to give," she adds softly.

Winter takes her hands in hers and studies the black-rimmed broken nails. "Autumn, you're overwrought. With good reason. What Sol did—"

"What *they* did," Autumn grinds out.

"Yes. They. But with time—"

"Time? Time will only multiply the pain. The humiliation. There is no one else for me. Ever."

Winter drops her hands. "Still. I can't agree to this." Her pallid brow creases. "What of duty? Those who depend on you?" Her eyes harden like jet. "I will not take your silver acorn."

"When the time comes, you must." Autumn juts her chin. "I have no one else."

Sparks and ice splinters fly between them. Winter reasons, then pleads. Autumn will not be moved.

Winter, her lips trembling, swallows hard, and agrees.

With Winter's white realm far behind her, Autumn stalks through her own forest to the Great Oak, jaw hard. Snails—too slow to escape—crunch beneath her feet. Her skirts now blaze full-blown maize-gold, cayenne, bittersweet—mushrooms ride her hem like mum death-bells.

"Sylvannah," Autumn calls, gently stroking Crow's crooked wing.

Sylvannah floats down hesitantly from a branch high in the Oak, wavering before her.

"I'm giving my silver acorn to my sister. Winter will know what to do."

"What," Sylvannah rasps, suddenly still as lichen on bark, "have you done?"

Autumn kneads Crow's silky head, smears tears off her face. She takes a shuddering breath and shakes him off. He reels twice, then perches in the Oak, head cocked.

"You might want to glide to the highest branches," Autumn says softly to Sylvannah.

Eyes closed, Autumn imagines Spring, beribboned and blushing in Sol's light, melting into him—as she herself longs to do, still.

She begins to twirl, her feet an axis, her skirts whirring like a swarm of locusts. She spins, faster. Visceral heat surges up from her core, charges her fingertips, sparks fly. She hurls fingerling flames scattershot. One by one the trees ignite, sacrificed on the pyre of her rage. The gold and wine of a hundred sunsets combust. Oak, maple, and pine pop and hiss their indignation—the screeching dryads flee.

Her skirts explode in a pentecost of wildfire. And she twirls.

At last, the pain exceeds the one in her cracked heart.

Sylvannah drifts through the charred ruins, smoke permeating her gossamer heart. At least the other dryads are safe with their cousins in the river where she drove them. Crow crouches atop an armless black pine, head hidden under his bent wing.

She managed to save the Great Oak, whisking the flames away from his vulnerable upper branches. She caresses his gnarled, ancient bark. Below, something glints in the ash. Swooping down, she retrieves the silver acorn clasp, icon of Autumn's power, for safekeeping.

And beneath it lies a smoldering, cracked acorn. Autumn's heart. This, she plants.

Winter comes to bury Autumn's ashes in mounds of pure white, as she promised.

Sylvannah fastens the silver acorn on Winter's furs, then glides up into the Oak's sturdiest branches and waits.

With Autumn's power, Winter is twice as strong. In time, Sol grows weak. Spring languishes, a pale shadow.

And Winter reigns. Some call it The Little Ice Age. Others call this particularly bitter time The Year Without a Summer.

Sylvannah calls it a reckoning.

See Sharmon Gazaway's story "Autumn's Come Undone" online at Metaphorosis.
If you liked it, leave a comment. Authors love that!
Remember to subscribe to our e-mail updates so you'll know when new stories are posted.

About the story

"Autumn's Come Undone" began as a poem, a pantoum. I'd always wanted to write about a season personified. I had been focusing on poetry and wanted to get back to stories, so I thought this poem could be expanded. I'd also been reading about dryads and they somehow strayed into Autumn's story. My original poem image of Autumn was much darker. She had black hair and teetered over the edge of madness. She evolved into a fiery redhead, but kept that underlying hint of madness—a break with rational thought. I wanted to explore a character who gives herself over fully to her emotions and the passion of the moment, and discover what the cost and aftermath might look like.

A question for the author

Q: What is your favorite word?

A: That's a tough one. If I'm going on the meaning of words, I guess it would have to be love, since there is no point to life without it. But I have a deep affection for the English language, love words for their sound and feel in the mouth. Words that sound like what they mean, such as undulate, haunting, sassy, poignant, and vicious are favorites. Poetically invented words like one I used in my story, moonshadowed, are always fun. I like ugly words that fit just right too, like muck or gutta-percha. Right now corvid (not to be confused with Covid!) is probably my favorite—I've written a string of poems, a short, and a flash on crows and birds of the corvid family.

About the author

Sharmon Gazaway was born and raised in the deep south surrounded by Appalachia, obvious to anyone who hears her speak for more than a minute. She used to watch her Mama read big thick books and Sharmon decided early on that she wanted to write a book like that herself. She managed to write a few of those, and finished one. She hopes to get back to her fantasy novel-in-progress but enjoys writing poetry, and flash and short fiction so much it may be a while yet.

A Compilation of Accounts Concerning the Distal Brook Flood

Thomas Ha

The following consists of testimony from the publicly available exhibits filed in *Granger, et al. v. Juna Explorations, LLC*. These transcripts have been excerpted and re-ordered by the Xenobiological Association, but the testimony herein concerning the tragedy of the Distal Brook Flood remains otherwise unaltered.

Excerpt from the Deposition of John Franken – Standard Date 061648

Q. Mr. Franken, as you know, my name is Arthur Kim, and I'm one of the attorneys for plaintiffs in this case. I want to thank you for coming in to talk with us today.

A. Yes. Of course.

Q. Now that we've gone through some of the basics of how the deposition works and talked about your background, I'd like to get into the specific events that brought you here today. Okay?

A. Okay.

Q. After you finished piloting lunar expeditions for the USS, you said you began work at Juna Explorations, is that correct?

A. Yes.

Q. And you were stationed on the planet of Ouron, located in the circumstellar habitable zone, or CHZ, of system JE-101, is that correct?

A. That's correct.

Q. And Ouron is leased by the USS to Juna Explorations for its mining ventures there, correct?

A. Yes.

Q. And when did you start operating shuttlecraft for the Juna mining colony of Ouron specifically?

A. About three and a half years ago.

Q. And what were your responsibilities as a pilot on Ouron?

MR. SRIN: Objection. Vague.

A. Can I... Do I...

MR. SRIN: You can answer. The objections are just for the record.

A. I'd pilot personnel from Juna facilities to areas off-base.

Q. When you say "off-base", you mean you would fly from mining facilities on the body of the gigantiform to other locations on Ouron, correct?

A. That's correct. The Juna facilities are concentrated on the organism's hand—two on each finger, two on the thumb, and then one management facility overseeing operations at the wrist.

Q. And you would typically pilot flights to and from that management facility, the one on the gigantiform's wrist, correct?

A. Yeah, the... Sorry. Most of the locals call it the Sleepy Giant or Giant. But that's right. I would cover the wrist.

Q. Understood, Mr. Franken.

I've seen the pictures, and that nickname certainly fits. I can only imagine what an alien organism of that size looks like from above on a shuttlecraft.

A. Yeah. It's something... I've come across a lot of things during my time with the USS, but nothing like him—that rocky body, the parts you can see coming out of the planet's surface anyway, stretched out for kilometers like that. Every time I fly over it, I think of the old Earth explorers who wrote about finding God in nature. Those guys would blow their top if they—

MR. SRIN: Excuse me, Mr. Franken. I know depositions are unnatural, and you want to treat this like a conversation. But I'd ask that you please wait until Mr. Kim asks you a question. Okay?

A. Oh, yeah. Sorry.

Q. That's okay, Mr. Franken. I know exactly what you mean.

Now, as you alluded to just now, the way I understand it, the gigantiform is partially submerged in Ouron's surface, but segments of the skull, the hands, parts of the arms, those sit above ground, correct?

A. That's correct. Almost like a mountain range. Several kilometers high at some points, depending on where you're at.

Q. Okay. And how long would an average flight take, say, from one of the facilities on the gigantiform's hand to the town of Distal Brook?

A. Well, Distal Brook was a few kilometers off from the tip of the thumb. Most folks there had some connection to Juna, so they didn't settle too far off. The average flight was maybe an hour, hour and a half, at most.

Q. Flight ever take you more than two hours?

A. Maybe in bad weather.

Q. Ever more than three hours?

A. No. Never.

Q. And when you're flying a shuttlecraft to or from Distal Brook, you're typically able to see the hand of the gigantiform from up there? Meaning the wrist, thumb, fingers, are all visible to you?

A. Yes, that's correct.

Q. And I assume you're familiar with Purlicue Lake?

A. Yes.

Q. Could you describe it for me, please?

A. It's the... um... It's the reservoir between the thumb and index finger of the Giant, where the waste from the extraction sites collects until it can be processed.

Q. Have you ever been there?

A. I only ever visited once and was never in a hurry to get back. The water there is real nasty stuff. Makes you choke and cry your eyes out, just being within a half mile of it.

Q. So pretty hazardous, you'd say?

MR. SRIN: Objection. Vague and calls for a legal conclusion and/or expert opinion.

Q. Withdrawn. Let's switch to something else.

Mr. Franken, you were piloting a shuttlecraft to Distal Brook on Standard Date 022147, correct?

A. Yes. I was transporting a Juna Explorations employee from the wrist facility. Don't remember his name though.

Q. I'd like to introduce a document that we'll mark as Exhibit 19. If you could take a look at that and let me know when you're done?

A. Okay.

Q. What is that, Mr. Franken, if you know?

A. A flight log for that day, looks like. The passenger listed is a Dr. Mark Granger. Guess that was his name, then.

Q. And as far as you know, this log is accurate, correct?

A. As far as I know.

Q. Do you recall talking to Dr. Granger, that day, when you dropped him off in Distal Brook?

A. I think so.

Q. What did you two talk about?

A. Well, he said he was going to Distal Brook to visit his kid. I remember because our boys were about the same age. He was going to surprise his son for his tenth birthday and—

Sorry. I'm sorry. I've got something in my throat.

Q. It's okay. Take your time.

A. Sorry. Anyway. He had a kid in Distal Brook, is what I remember.

Q. And according to Exhibit 19, you'd already taken off and left Distal Brook when the flood occurred, right?

A. That's right.

Q. So the day the town flooded, you could see the black water from your shuttlecraft, right?

A. I... yeah. I saw the water come down on Distal Brook from the lake. I don't need to tell you it... it took out the whole area at once. Houses and everything. It was like... it was like... God... I don't even know. Just horrible.

Q. Understood. I can only imagine, Mr. Franken.

So after the flood hit the town, did you make any stops before heading back to the wrist facility?

A. After that? No. I mean, there was nothing I could do. It was all... I mean all wiped out. So I kept going and headed to the wrist facility straight away.

Q. Okay, well do you remember a few minutes ago, when you testified that your flight takes about an hour and half, and no more than three hours, and that these logs are accurate as far as you know?

A. Yeah, I remember.

Q. If you look at the Exhibit 19 again, according to the logs, your return flight from Distal Brook, based on takeoff and arrival, took almost *five* hours.

Why did it take so long, Mr. Franken?

A. I... I mean, I don't... I'm not...

Q. Did you see something else while you were up there?

MR. SRIN: I think now might be a good time for a break. Mr. Kim?

Q. Okay. Let's go off the record.

COURT REPORTER: Going off the record. The time is 9:37 AM.

Excerpt from the Deposition of Jane Yuan – Standard Date 092949

Q. So what was your reason for visiting the colony, Ms. Yuan?

A. My brother and his wife had been living there for several years. They kept telling me I should come see them. Spend a couple months and see the Sleepy Giant and all of that.

Q. And what were they doing there, your brother and sister-in-law?

A. He had a job as an electrician in a Juna facility, which was a dream come true for him. My sister-in-law tagged along on a marriage visa and started working as a teacher at the local elementary.

Q. And your brother and sister-in-law lived in the Distal Brook township?

A. Yeah. In a small neighborhood called La Roma. They loved it. They really wanted—shit. Sorry. [Inaudible.]

Q. It's okay. Take your time. We can take a break if you'd like. Would you like tissues...

A. No. I'm fine. [Inaudible.]

Sorry. They wanted to have kids there.

Q. Okay. So you were on Ouron on Standard Date 022147, correct?

A. Yes.

Q. What were you doing that morning?

A. My brother and I went hiking at Mammoth Peak. It's a ridge about a couple kilometers away from Distal Brook, where on a clear day you can see the whole hand of the Giant.

Mayra, his wife, had work that day and couldn't join. So my brother and I had breakfast and headed out before sunrise. We wanted to hit the peak before it got too hot, and we were almost there at the top when it happened. The flood.

Q. Okay. And what do you remember about the start of the flood, specifically, if you can recall?

A. I remember the ground shaking all of a sudden. I know that happened first because I fell over. And right after, there was this sound, like crashing thunder that wouldn't stop.

My brother and I went further up to get a better view, and when we reached the peak, the water was already coming our way. I don't know what I was expecting, but it wasn't that. The water was—it was like this dark wall, ready to crush everything.

Q. Do you need to stop?

A. No. It's fine.

Q. Okay. What happened next?

A. It took a few seconds, but we realized the water wasn't going to reach us, that it was going to hit everything in Distal Brook below instead.

Then, when it started happening, the water coming into the town, I remember the other hikers around us all started yelling. And my brother was screaming, I think. This big wall of water, just, it moved past us, and then Distal Brook—all of the buildings, houses, churches, the roofs and walls all broke apart like they were made of paper. I mean, it didn't look real.

The distance we were at, we couldn't see the people. But I mean, you knew. You just knew that they were all getting swept away in there. And it was god awful.

Q. And then what happened?

A. My brother was losing it for a few minutes, but he calmed down. He got it in his head that Mayra might not have been in the worst of it. He said he saw the water divert around the school where she worked, so it was possible that she or others might try to get on the roof and wait out the currents. So we ran for the car. It took us almost an hour just to get back down the hill.

We drove to the edge of town. But the roads, they were all covered with that black gunk. So we pulled over, waiting for some opening where we might get through. Then others came, people who had been out of the township too. We were all standing at our cars, breathing in the fumes from the water, and I think everyone started bleeding from their noses at some point.

I remember everyone was trying to wipe the blood off their faces.

Q. Do you recall any other symptoms of exposure to the black water?

A. My eyes were burning at the time. And I started throwing up. Some of my skin, especially around my ankles, the parts that came into contact with the water, peeled off days later.

Q. Okay. And do you remember anything else about the flood after that?

A. The only other thing was the bodies. I mean, I still don't even know if they were bodies. But these black masses started floating to the surface after a while, like lumps in stew. We tried to pull one out when it got close to us, but we couldn't really touch the water, because of the way it burned.

There was nothing. I mean there was nothing we could do for anyone. We were all just stuck there, waiting, watching the black water carry everything off.

Q. And how long were you over there, at the edge of the town?

A. A few hours. Until a Juna Explorations team came to lift us out. And we never got to the school, not that it would have made any difference.

Q. Where did they take you after that?

A. My brother and I spent a couple of months in a facility recovering. Later, some Juna people came and talked to us. They told my brother that they were investigating, but that Mayra, and anyone else still missing, was almost certainly gone.

Then they offered him a settlement. $50,000 and free passage back to Earth. His wife, dead. House, gone. Everyone he knew, drowned. And that was $50,000 to them.

I told him not to sign, but I think after everything he went through, he just wanted it to be over with. To go back home and forget that place ever existed.

Q. And did you sign a settlement agreement too?

A. No.

Q. So after your recovery, you and your brother went back to Earth?

A. Yes. I tried to take care of him for a while, but he never really adjusted to being back. And at some point, he joined the TC, and I think it only made him worse.

Q. Sorry, TC?

A. Titan Church. They're mostly planet-bound, but they're starting to crop up in other systems. They're kind of—what's the word—cultish types, obsessed with the Giant. Anything and everything Giant-related is important to them.

So after the flood, the TC really fixated on the survivors because of their connection to Ouron. They tried to get me to come with them, but I always refused. My brother, though, he didn't have anything else. So he went right along. He attended their masses, and I think he spoke a few times about what he saw on Ouron.

To be honest, I don't really know much more; my brother and I didn't see each other as often once he became a member.

Q. I understand, Ms. Yuan. And, I'm sorry to ask. I already know, but I need this for the record. What happened to your brother?

A. He passed away late last year. He'd been on a lot of pain medications, because of the black water, and, one day he just, took too much, and... they just found him like that, in his tub. Still not clear if he meant to— Sorry. Just not clear what happened.

Sorry. I don't know what I'm saying any more.

Q. It's okay. I just want to say again that I'm very sorry for your loss. And I think this is a good time for a break, but I just want to clarify something.

You're not a party to this lawsuit. You chose to opt out and are here as a third-party fact witness, right?

A. Right.

Q. So I have to ask. Why not join and sue Juna Explorations like the others?

A. No offense, but I don't really see a point. Everything Juna touches is poison, including their money. So fuck them all to hell as far I'm concerned.

Q. Okay. Let's take a break.

Excerpt from the Deposition of Teresa De Leon Vol. 1 – Standard Date 020650

Q. Okay, Ms. De Leon. Let's look at Exhibit 80 again. That one. The press release regarding your promotion. It says you were elevated to managing director of Ouron on Standard Date 011341, is that right?

A. Yes.

Q. And it mentions that you started in Juna oversight and management over a decade ago in several colonies before Ouron.

A. That's right.

Q. And it looks like you pretty much went to work right out of university and have spent your whole career with Juna, correct?

A. Yes. That's correct. My predecessor on Ouron, Dr. Oswald, would often say that Juna's purpose was to advance the knowledge of the human species, push us further than we'd ever gone before, and I knew I wanted to be a part of that since I was young.

Q. So did you seek a management position on Ouron, specifically?

A. Of course.

Q. Why?

A. Well, in all the decades that the USS has explored other systems, we've only ever encountered a few life forms, most of them microbial. The gigantiform is, to date, the only complex, extraterrestrial organism we've discovered. I don't think there are many people who would pass up the opportunity to help Juna study it.

Q. Understood. And in addition to studying the gigantiform, Juna Explorations also extracts resources from it, correct?

A. Yes. The gigantiform's body contains a naturally occurring element that has several applications, including as a component in Juna Explorations fuel rods.

Q. Cronesium, right?

A. Correct.

Q. And how is the cronesium extracted? Just the basics, please.

A. Because the gigantiform's skin is a type of hardened silicate, it requires several years of drilling. Once we've breached the surface, our engineers use proprietary Juna Explorations tech to scan the surrounding veins and fluid pockets.

After an extraction strategy for the site is determined, we use Oswald derricks to pump the cronesium out of the gigantiform's veins and direct it to a processing facility, where we separate the usable cronesium from other hazardous components in a series of water tanks. From there, the cronesium is directed to another facility, and the waste is ejected.

Q. Into Purlicue Lake?

A. That's right.

Q. And once the waste water is sent to Purlicue Lake, what do you do with it?

A. Well. The exact process for neutralizing the waste water is still being worked out. Because it's unstable once the cronesium is removed, we can't reinsert it into the gigantiform or move it elsewhere without great risk.

Juna is on the cusp of a cost-effective method of disposal, but until then it's best stored in the reservoir.

Q. And you extract from several facilities on the gigantiform's hand, right? How many Juna Explorations facilities are there on Ouron?

A. Eleven.

Q. Okay. Thank you. This is all very helpful information, so I appreciate you walking me through it.

Now, to get to more specific issues, you were managing director of Ouron during the events of the Distal Brook Flood, correct?

A. Yes.

Q. By the way, I should ask, since we may be getting to sensitive territory, did you personally know anyone who was in Distal Brook?

A. I did not.

My position as managing director is somewhat solitary.

I rarely leave my post in the wrist facility, so I haven't had the opportunity to visit many of the settlements.

Q. Understood. Well, my condolences nonetheless. These were your people, after all, so the loss must not have been easy.

A. Thank you.

Q. So after the Distal Brook Flood occurred, Juna conducted an internal investigation as to the cause, correct?

A. Yes.

Q. And if you look at the investigative report previously marked as Exhibit 78 in your stack of documents there. There's a section that's signed by you, Ms. De Leon, right?

A. Yes.

Q. And it says, "To the best of my knowledge, the results of the foregoing report are a complete and accurate record of the events concerning the Distal Brook township." Do you see that?

A. Yes.

Q. So you reviewed this and signed off on it, fair to say?

A. I did.

Q. And above that there's a summary by the investigatory body in that last paragraph, do you see that? If so, can you read that into the record, please?

A. It says: "Based on our interviews with relevant personnel and a review of available sensory data, we conclude that the Purlicue Dam spillage was most likely caused by an unanticipated seismic event (U.S.E.), which resulted in an overflow of the Purlicue Dam. Though we recommend construction of additional bulwarks, we believe Juna Explorations took all reasonable and foreseeable measures it could have undertaken to safeguard the hazardous material."

Q. And what might cause a seismic event of the kind referred to in that report?

A. There are many possible causes. Shift of tectonic plates under the planet surface. Unexpected rupture of a cronesium deposit in the gigantiform's veins. Gas pockets uncovered while drilling.

Q. Okay. The report doesn't specify, so I'll ask you. Of those reasons you just listed, what was the cause of the U.S.E. that triggered the flooding of Distal Brook?

MR. SRIN: Objection. Calls for speculation.

A. Sorry. What?

Q. What was the cause of the U.S.E. that triggered the flooding of Distal Brook?

A. I'm... Well I wasn't involved in the investigation, so I'm not sure I could speak to that.

Q. Okay. But you agreed with this report. So I guess my question is, how did you come to the conclusion that the Distal Brook Flood was caused by a U.S.E.?

A. Well, I had no reason to doubt the investigative body.

Q. But, to be clear, you reviewed no underlying data to support that finding, did you?

A. I did not.

Q. Okay. Let's change gears a little bit. Could you look at the photograph in the investigative report, the visual evidence of wreckage in Distal Brook—two pages earlier.

What do you see in the background of that landscape?

A. It's... I believe it's the Purlicue Dam...

Q. Anything about that look strange to you?

MR. SRIN: Objection. Vague.

A. I'm not sure what you mean.

Q. Do you see any damage to the dam in that picture? Cracks, fissures, anything of that nature?

A. It's difficult to know for sure from one photograph. But based on this... I... I mean... No. It doesn't seem to be damaged from what I can see.

Q. Now, if the dam had cracked, it'd be a large undertaking to repair it, I assume. You'd have to call in construction teams, halt extraction at nearby facilities, if not do more?

A. I... Yes. That's right.

Q. And as managing director of Ouron, you'd *know* if something as major as reconstruction of portions of the dam occurred?

A. Yes.

Q. So to your knowledge, was the dam repaired in that fashion?

A. No... not to my knowledge. I believe... the Juna Explorations teams analyzed the damage and told us no further work was necessary.

Q. And that didn't seem odd to you?

MR. SRIN: Objection. Vague.

A. I guess... at the time, there was a lot going on, and I trusted the process.

Q. Earlier you were talking about your responsibilities as a managing director. Is safeguarding the health and safety of the colonists one of those responsibilities?

A. I'm... yes.

Q. And you mentioned that you chose to work on Ouron because you wanted to help humankind, essentially, right?

MR. SRIN: Objection. Misstates prior testimony.

A. Yes.

Q. So if you had the opportunity to protect your fellow man on that colony, you absolutely would have done that, right?

A. Yes.

Q. But when Juna's off-planet team told you Purlicue Dam didn't need repairs, and didn't identify any specific cause for the flood, you didn't find that strange. Didn't bat an eye, right?

To put it simply, you didn't actually do *anything* to try to figure out what killed all of those people, did you?

MR. SRIN: Objection. Kim, this is out of line.

Q. Mr. Srin. A question is pending, and Ms. De Leon is in the middle of the answer.

Madame court reporter, read that back, please.

COURT REPORTER: To put it simply, you didn't actually do *anything* to try to figure out what killed all of those people, did you?

A. I did... I did what I could.

MR. SRIN: We're going off the record, right now. Kim. Outside.

Q. Thank you, Ms. De Leon. Let's take a short break.

COURT REPORTER: And we're off the record.

Excerpt from the Deposition of Charles Bailer – Standard Date 110650

Q. Mr. Bailer, did you get any daily reports about activities on Ouron?

MR. SRIN: Objection. Vague.

A. That *is* vague, isn't it? I don't know if I understand that. Ask it again.

Q. Mr. Bailer, did you get any reports about activities on Ouron?

A. Well, as CEO, I get a lot of reports. Juna Explorations has over two hundred colonies. Over three thousand research facilities. Over ten million colonist-citizens. So I'm sure I got reports, but it's hard to know what you mean without looking at a specific document.

Q. Okay. And do you know what a "U.S.E." is?

A. Again, I can't be sure without reviewing documentation. Unanticipated Seismic Event, or something like that.

Q. Let's move on to something else. Is the gigantiform dead?

MR. SRIN: Objection. Vague. Calls for legal conclusion and/or expert testimony.

A. Uh. What?

Q. Simple question. Is the gigantiform on Ouron dead? Yes or no.

MR. SRIN: Same objections.

A. It's an organism that doesn't meet any of the established USS criteria for life. It doesn't metabolize, grow, adapt to its environment, respond to stimuli, or reproduce, as far as we can observe.

Q. Is it dead?

MR. SRIN: Same objections. And asked and answered.

A. Look, it meets no specific criterion for life.

Q. Interesting choice of words. Let's take a look at the following, previously marked as Exhibit 49. This is a public document. Take a minute to read it.

A. I don't have to. I know it. My father had a copy of this framed in our house.

Q. What is the document, Mr. Bailer?

A. It's a press statement from Juna's Chief Science Officer, Dr. Malcolm Oswald, from when they announced the discovery of the gigantiform.

Q. And Dr. Oswald was also the previous managing director of Ouron, correct?

A. That's right.

Q. And he established the first extraction facilities and their protocols on Ouron thirty years ago, correct?

A. Yeah. You got it. I like this guy. He's very prepared.

Q. Thank you, Mr. Bailer. I appreciate your confidence. Now please look at the bottom of the first paragraph. Could you read that into the record, please?

A. "This is a remarkable step forward for Juna Explorations and humanity as a whole. Already, this organism has revealed great wonders we have yet to fully understand. Our estimates, judging from the limbs that remain visible on the surface, indicate that its span may be almost 3,000 kilometers, which is larger than most countries and nearly a quarter of the diameter of Ouron itself.

"Based on our silicon dating, we believe the organism is millions of years old, and its positioning and depth in Ouron's crust suggest it may have collided with the planet's surface, quite violently, some time ago, after traveling for some time in the vacuum of space."

Q. The rest of that page too, please.

A. "The organism appears humanoid, with appendages and an anatomy that suggests it may have, at one point, held itself upright. Though it, interestingly, has no oral cavity or identifiable ocular organs that we've been able to observe.

"Ultimately, however, based on our initial testing, the organism currently meets none of the established USS criteria for active life. It seemingly does not metabolize, grow, adapt to its environment, respond to stimuli, or reproduce. Perhaps the organism did, long ago, function in some way, but either because of its exposure in space or its impact on Ouron, that no longer seems to be the case."

Q. What would be different, if the gigantiform were classified as life?

MR. SRIN: Same objections.

A. We have a whole legal department to figure that out. I'm the wrong person to ask.

Q. You might not be allowed, legally, to extract cronesium from the organism at all?

MR. SRIN: Same objections.

A. Look. I said I don't know. What does this even have to do with this case? Did someone put you up to this? The TC?

Q. When you say "TC", are you referring to the Titan Church?

A. Who else would I be referring to? Yes. The nutjobs.

MR. SRIN: Maybe we should take a break?

A. No. It's fine. I just don't like this religious activism invading scientific industry. It isn't right. And you know they're lobbying the Xenobiological Association too. So I can smell them a mile away.

You asking for them or what?

Q. Mr. Bailer. I assure you that the only people I represent are the victims of Distal Brook and their families, but let's change topics.

I'm going to mark the following as Exhibit 161. Please take a moment to review.

What is this, Mr. Bailer, if you know?

A. It appears to be an annual seismometer output aggregation report for Ouron.

Q. And you see that first line, where it says: "Standard Date 112146"? And then next to that it says "U.S.E. registered", right?

A. Sure.

Q. And, next to that, there's a reference to "B.E. engaged".

What is B.E. a reference to?

A. I—I wouldn't know exactly. You'd have to ask the managing director, Ms. De Leon.

Q. Okay. As you can see the document goes on with similar dates and U.S.E.s for Standard Year 46, the year prior to the Distal Brook Flood, and by my count there are about one hundred thirty-five U.S.E.s registered, or an average of ten or more, a month.

My question to you is, if these "events" occur with that kind of regularity, how could they possibly be "unanticipated"?

MR. SRIN: Objection. Calls for a legal conclusion and/or expert testimony.

A. You'd have to ask the seismometer technicians. That's just how we classify them.

Q. I'm asking *you*, Mr. Bailer. If there are this many seismic events, at this frequency, your position is that Juna Explorations *doesn't* anticipate them?

MR. SRIN: Same objections. And asked and answered. *And* harassing the witness.

A. I'm saying, I don't know.

Q. But, to your knowledge, no employee of Juna Explorations takes the position that these seismic events can be predicted, right?

A. I... I can't speak for every single employee. I don't want to misstate anything.

Q. Mr. Bailer. Please stop looking at your attorney. I know Mr. Srin is about to explode in a minute, but he knows full well that you have to answer this question.

I'd also remind you again that you're testifying under penalty of perjury.

Has any Juna Explorations employee, to your knowledge, *ever* asserted that these seismic events can be predicted?

MR. SRIN: This is outrageous. I'm dialing the judge's chambers *this second*. Mr. Bailer, please step outside. Counsel, we're going off the record.

COURT REPORTER: And we're off the record.

—

COURT REPORTER: And we're back on the record.

Q. Now that we've stretched our legs and Mr. Srin has gotten that out of his system, let's try this again. Has any Juna employee, to your knowledge, *ever* asserted that these seismic events can be predicted?

A. It's possible someone may have.

Q. Who?

A. Dr. Malcolm Oswald.

MR. SRIN: Per our discussion, we're going to designate this portion of the testimony highly confidential pursuant to the stipulated protective order.

[Remainder of testimony redacted.]

Excerpt from the Deposition of Teresa De Leon Vol. 2 – Standard Date 062652

Q. Ms. De Leon. Welcome back. It's been some time. Almost a year and a half.

A. Yes.

Q. I apologize for the delay. It took the attorneys a while to work out a second day of deposition. Nonetheless, we're glad we were able to proceed, as I'm sure you are.

A. Yes. I'd just—I'd like this to be done.

Q. Before we start, I want to go back to some of your statements in your prior deposition, and we can refer to the transcript if you need it at any point, just let me know. Okay?

A. Okay.

Q. The last time we spoke, you briefly mentioned the previous managing director on Ouron, Dr. Malcolm Oswald.

How well did you know Dr. Oswald, if at all?

A. Reasonably well. He stayed on for a year after I arrived to help with the transition. He taught me everything he knew about the gigantiform, the colony, and his work on Ouron before he returned to Earth.

Q. And did you ever keep in contact with him after that?

A. Unfortunately, no. He passed away, and we didn't get a chance to connect in the intervening years.

Q. Are you aware that after his tenure on Ouron, he began writing publicly about the gigantiform?

A. I don't think I heard that... exactly.

I've been told he'd declined a bit in his old age and became a bit troubled, but I'm not aware of the specifics beyond that.

Q. Were you aware that, later in life, he disavowed his work as managing director for Juna Explorations and believed that the company had engaged in unethical, abusive practices?

A. I... was not. No.

Q. Were you aware that his writing gained traction with a number of individuals on Earth, and, after his death, they started an organization dedicated to some of the tenets of his work—an organization known as the Titan Church?

A. I've... heard of them. But I'm not sure what this has to do with—

Q. Don't worry. We'll discuss that in a moment.

Now, during your last deposition I asked you if you knew anyone in Distal Brook, and you said you did not. Do you recall that discussion?

A. Yes.

Q. I'd like to introduce the following as Exhibit 284.

What is this, Ms. De Leon?

A. It... appears to be a request for leave that I signed for an employee to attend a family event. It's standard for me to do so for certain supervisory positions.

"Child's birthday", it says.

Request came from a... Dr. Mark Granger.

Q. Who is Mark Granger?

A. He is—I mean he was—a researcher who worked at the wrist facility.

Q. Were you close?

A. I wouldn't say close, but we knew each other, yes. He was part of a team that tested cronesium applications, so I'd interact with him regularly as part of my duties as managing director.

Q. Ever meet his family?

A. I... I might have. Maybe a few times for certain special tours. I'd sometimes greet the company families on those occasions. I think I spoke to his wife.

Q. How about his kids? Meet his kids?

MR. SRIN: Objection. Harassing the witness.

A. Two boys, maybe. I'm not sure.

Q. And what happened to Dr. Granger, if you know?

A. He—excuse me.

He was in Distal Brook at the time of the flood.

Q. Meaning he died, correct?

A. He—yes.

Q. His family too, correct?

MR. SRIN: Objection. Harassing the witness!

A. Yes.

Q. In fact, his older son died on his tenth birthday, the day of the Distal Brook Flood, correct?

MR. SRIN: Same objections. What the hell is this, Kim? Are you seriously going to try and—

Q. Counsel.

I'm making it clear that we're going to be thorough in correcting the record. I also want to remind Ms. De Leon of her responsibilities as managing director of Ouron before we revisit her other answers.

Now, I've tolerated your interruptions in the past, but I ask that you please refrain from this extensive commentary, which, you know as well as I do, is impermissible during your client's testimony.

MR. SRIN: You—

Q. I mean it, counsel. Anything beyond simple objections, and I'll be forced to file another motion for sanctions. And you know the judge will be open to granting it again.

Okay.

Now, with that out of the way, please answer the question regarding Dr. Granger's son, Ms. De Leon.

A. To my knowledge... Yes. Dr. Granger's son was one of the victims of the flood. His school was... The Distal Brook elementary school was one of the buildings that flooded. A number of colonists, teachers, students were... from what I know... they didn't make it out of the township.

After the last time, the deposition. What you said to me about taking care of the colonists and my responsibilities as a managing director, I—I didn't take that lightly. Really. I took some time to go through the records of people who were in Distal Brook, to get a better sense of who was there. Fathers, mothers, kids, community members. There were... they were all... it was a lot that was lost.

I understand that better now.

And I didn't mean to overlook any of that the last time. Really. I didn't.

Sorry, I don't know what I'm trying to say. And I didn't mean to be overly... emotional about this.

Q. Thank you, Ms. De Leon. For what it's worth, I think you're being appropriately emotional, and I appreciate that clarification.

Please set that aside.

Now, the last time you were here, I also asked you how many Juna Explorations facilities were on Ouron. You told me eleven. I assume you were just under stress and overlooked this as well.

I'm going to allow you to correct that statement, right now, if you'd like. I strongly suggest you do.

How many Juna Explorations facilities are on Ouron?

A. I...

Q. Go ahead, Ms. De Leon.

A. Twelve.

Q. Thank you. There are eleven extraction facilities on the gigantiform's hand, and then an additional "temple facility" near what we believe to be the organism's skull, correct?

A. How do—yes.

Q. Thank you.

Now, I told you we'd discuss the Titan Church and its connection to this matter, so let's go back to that.

It turns out, the Church followed Dr. Oswald very closely, and they maintain quite a comprehensive collection of Oswald's personal papers. It makes it convenient to subpoena them, in cases like this, where the opposing party is not always so forthcoming with documentation, and I'd like to share some of that documentation with you now.

Let's enter in the following as Exhibit 300.

What is this diagram, Ms. De Leon?

A. It's... it's... Okay. Okay. A moment please.

Q. Are you ready to continue?

I'll ask it again.

What is the diagram in Exhibit 300?

MR. SRIN: Objection. Document speaks for itself. Calls for specula—

A. It's... well—

MR. SRIN: —tion.

A. It's a draft schematic, showing the designs for a device developed by Juna Exploration for use on Ouron.

We called it the Bitemporal Electrode.

Q. And what is the "Bitemporal Electrode"?

Ms. De Leon?

What is the "Bitemporal Electrode"?

A. It is a two-part mechanism, drilled and implanted on either side of the gigantiform's skull.

Q. And what was the purpose of the Bitemporal Electrode?

MR. SRIN: Objection. Vague.

A. The device was designed to generate a large amount of energy between the electrodes, which in turn disrupted nearby electrical activity.

Q. Meaning, electrical activity in the gigantiform's skull?

MR. SRIN: Objection. Misstates prior testimony.

A. Yes.

Q. If you look at the report previously marked as Exhibit 161, next to indications of U.S.E. events there are concurrent denotations for "B.E. engaged".

Are these recording incidents where the "Bitemporal Electrode" was engaged by Juna personnel?

MR. SRIN: Objection. Document speaks for itself—

A. Yes.

Q. Why did Juna engage the Bitemporal Electrode in these instances?

MR. SRIN: Objection. Calls for speculation.

A. Whenever we detected the beginnings of a seismic event, usually with an alarm system associated with the seismometers in the wrist facility, we would engage the electrode as a precautionary measure.

Q. Why?

A. By disrupting electrical activity in the gigantiform, we found that we could often mitigate the seismic activity and lessen the time of the U.S.E.s or halt them altogether.

Q. In other words, you'd detect an incoming U.S.E., activate the electrode, and the U.S.E.s would lessen or stop, correct?

A. Yes. That's often how it would go.

Q. Okay.

In your previous deposition you stated that there were several causes for a seismic event, including tectonic plates shifting, unexpected pockets while drilling, and so on.

Given what you've just told me about the connection between the B.E., the activity in the gigantiform, and the U.S.E.s, is it possible that the gigantiform's body itself is a possible cause for these seismic events?

MR. SRIN: Objection. Calls for speculat—

A. Possibly. Yes.

Q. Could you repeat that?

A. Yes. Movement in the gigantiform's body could theoretically be the cause of a U.S.E., though we'd never observed it directly before.

Q. Before Distal Brook, you mean?

Strike that. Withdrawn.

Give me a moment.

Do you remember, in your prior deposition, our discussion of photographs of the Purlicue Dam? In particular, the fact that the dam had not been visibly damaged?

A. Yes.

Q. That's because the dam breaking didn't cause the flooding of Distal Brook, did it?

MR. SRIN: Objection. Calls for speculation.

A. I... Based on what I know, that does not seem likely. No.

Q. Before I get to this next question, I want to remind you of everything we discussed so far and in your prior deposition—the reason you joined Juna, your duties as managing director of the colony, and your relationship with its citizens, including your colleague, Dr. Granger.

With all that in mind, Ms. De Leon, what, based on what you know, could have caused the flooding of Distal Brook?

MR. SRIN: Mr. Kim, could we—

A. Wait, Mr. Srin. I think I should... I think I do want to answer this.

MR. SRIN: Ms. De Leon, I'd really prefer that we discuss this off the—

A. Based on the concurrent U.S.E. and the volume of water that cascaded outside the containment area, it's... possible... again I don't know... it's possible that the waste water could have been displaced.

The gigantiform's finger could have shifted, even just slightly, and that would have been enough to trigger the flooding that we observed.

MR. SRIN: Objection.

Q. What is your objection, Mr. Srin? There's no question pending. Are you objecting to her answer?

MR. SRIN: I—withdrawn.

Q. Is that what you think happened, the gigantiform's finger shifted?

A. I don't... I don't have any direct evidence to confirm that for certain, and, after my last deposition, I spent some time... trying to find records that might give a clearer picture of what occurred.

There is only, to my knowledge, a single flight report from the day of the flood, which references a fault line forming near the gigantiform's index finger. A shuttlecraft pilot radioed for permission to investigate when he was en route to the wrist facility, but the results are heavily redacted except mentions of wreckage in the area—fallen timber that needed to be hauled and service roads to be repaired. I haven't been able to find any more information than that.

Nevertheless, based solely on what I do know about the gigantiform's physiology as well as our facilities and history with the organism... I... I do believe that it's at least... capable of moving as a general matter.

Yes.

Q. So, just to be clear, the day the flood occurred, you, as managing director, were at least aware of the *possibility* that the gigantiform could move, correct?

A. Again, only theoretically.

But yes. That's correct.

Q. And were any of the colonist-citizens of Ouron aware of this theoretical possibility too?

A. Not to my knowledge. No.

Q. Was your colleague, Dr. Granger, or any of his family, aware of this theoretical possibility?

A. I'm— Sorry— Give me a second.

Not to my knowledge... No.

Q. And did you, or anyone else in Juna Explorations, take steps to inform anyone on Ouron of the theoretical possibility that the gigantiform could, in fact, move?

A. No. We did not.

Q. So all of those colonist-citizens who died when that hazardous material overflowed into Distal Brook, they had no idea they were risking their lives, creating a settlement so close to the organism, did they?

A. No.

I'm sorry.

Q. Why didn't Juna just tell them, any of this? Any of what you're telling me now?

A. I... I don't know.

Juna had been mining for decades without incident, and we believed we had an effective mechanism for minimizing any such risk. If... I mean... knowing what I know now, if I could warn them, if I could have foreseen all of this, then I would have.

I just didn't know—

Excuse me.

Q. Take your time.

Okay.

Now, whether or not Juna had minimized risk from the gigantiform with the B.E., the organism's movement could potentially indicate that it's still alive, couldn't it?

A. It could.

Q. And that classification by the USS could complicate Juna Explorations's extraction operations, couldn't it, Ms. De Leon?

A. Yes. It could.

Q. That could prevent the USS from extracting cronesium, a resource it relies on to produce its fuel rods and that is key to expanding its colonies?

A. It... could have that outcome, yes.

Q. So it's in Juna's interest to withhold any information that would lead to that outcome, isn't it?

A. It would cause problems for Juna if that information were known to others. Yes.

Q. Okay.

Okay, Ms. De Leon.

Thank you.

This is... this is a lot of new information we've covered just now, so I'm going to want to go through this again in more detail. It also looks like Mr. Srin is signaling to me that he needs to contact his client, and he and I may have a few more things to discuss as well. But before we go off the record momentarily, I have to ask.

If Juna is suppressing the gigantiform's movement, is it at all possible that the organism is aware of what's happening?

A. Aware of what's happening? I don't...

Q. That it knows what's going on on Ouron—what Juna is doing to its body, I mean?

A. I don't think... I mean there's no way to really know if... I don't know.

Q. Never mind.

A. Sorry—

Q. Forget it.

Withdrawn.

I think that's enough for now.

Let's go off the record please.

COURT REPORTER: The time is 11:32 AM, and we are going off the record.

Afterword – JUNA EXPLORATIONS PRESS RELEASE – Standard Date 081652

NEW DISTAL BROOK, Ouron, and NEW YORK CITY, New York—Juna Explorations has reached a $20 billion-dollar, global settlement with the colonists affected by the Distal Brook Flood. The settlement includes dismissal of all current suits concerning or related to the flooding of the Distal Brook township. All other terms of the settlement are confidential.

"Juna Explorations stands behind the brave men and women who comprise our colonies, and we hope that, with this settlement, they, and we, can look toward a safe and secure future among the stars," said Charles Bailer, CEO of Juna Explorations.

"My clients are relieved that they can finally move on with their lives," said lead Plaintiffs' counsel, Arthur Kim. "They believe, and hope, that this tragedy will instruct Juna Explorations operations going forward, so that no one else has to suffer the losses that they have suffered, and no one else will have to endure what they've endured."

Second Afterword- Letter from A. Kim to X.A. Chairman Campos- Standard Date 011254

Dear Chairman Campos,

I'm writing in response to the Xenobiological Association's request for a comment on the "historic victory" achieved by the victims of Distal Brook, as it was phrased in the letter directed to my office. I understand you would like to potentially use any such response as a postscript to a compilation you are preparing concerning the events of the flood. While I cannot discuss the substance of the settlement beyond what is publicly known, I am writing primarily to correct your characterization of the resolution of this case.

As you, and all of the USS, probably know well by now, my clients lost far more than Juna Explorations could compensate them for, and I suspect those who've survived will not know a semblance of peace or normalcy for many years to come. Though the dollar amount presented by Juna Explorations is impressive at a glance, it results in very little for the individual victims once costs are deducted and the settlement is divided by the tens of thousands of plaintiffs, many of whom aren't alive to see that award anyway. The simple truth is that we only accepted the settlement because my clients could not afford, financially or emotionally, to fight the mega-colonies of Juna Explorations in court for another five years. It was for that reason that my firm abstained from collecting its full fees, as did a number of other firms involved in this case.

Meanwhile, mining operations continue on Ouron unchanged. To date, there has been no public analysis or even recognition of the "seismic" risks associated with extraction from the gigantiform. Nor are there any public investigations by the USS that I'm aware of into the classification of the gigantiform as a non-living entity.

The organization known as the Titan Church has filed for various injunctions, but those suits have yet to go anywhere as of the writing of this letter. So, for all intents and purposes, everything on the colony remains the same as it did six years ago, barring the absence of one small town and everything it once contained.

You asked for a response to include in your compilation regarding our victory, but the only response I have for you is this:

"What victory?"

Sincerely,

Arthur Kim

See Thomas Ha's story "A Compilation of Accounts Concerning the Distal Brook Flood" online at Metaphorosis.
If you liked it, leave a comment. Authors love that!
Remember to subscribe to our e-mail updates so you'll know when new stories are posted.

About the story

I was a lawyer in another life, and I always found it funny in legal dramas when some major revelation resolved a case decisively and tidily. While I wouldn't claim the legal mechanics of this particular story are realistic, I wanted to write something that captured more of the anti-climactic reality of most cases (albeit in a grander, sci-fi setting), which is that, even if cases do uncover something substantial, they usually just settle, often to the benefit of the more powerful party and without much disturbance to the status quo. As for the ecological disaster described in the story itself, it's loosely based on coal slurry floods, which are unfortunately a real byproduct of the mining industry and have catastrophic effects on communities and surrounding environments.

A question for the author

Q: What kind of pieces are the most fun to write?
A: I tend to enjoy writing slower, contemplative pieces. I like faster-paced action too; I just don't think I've ever been able to write it believably.

About the author

Thomas Ha is a former attorney turned stay-at-home father who enjoys writing speculative fiction during the rare moments when both of his kids are napping at the same time. Thomas grew up in Honolulu and, after a decade plus of living in the northeast, now resides in Los Angeles.
www.thomashawrites.com, @ThomasHaWrites

May

Vertical Flight

Laura Duerr

Welcome to Quantum Ridge Vineyards! We'll be tasting six wines today, all red varietals from the 2068 vintage sourced from Quantum Ridge vineyards across multiple universes.

To answer a couple of the most common questions: yes, there is almost certainly a tasting going on in this exact spot in another dimension further downstream; and no, most likely you aren't at that tasting due to inherent variations in the dimensions we visit. This is particularly true in the more distant universes like Alpha-Nine, and especially the Beta universes, where anything from who's president to which butterfly species exist could be different. Any other questions about our vineyards or interdimensional shipping can be directed to Doctor Fischer, our founder and resident physicist.

It's a warm April Saturday and the valley is full of weekenders going wine tasting. Quantum Ridge is packed, but I'm the only one available to serve customers. A bachelorette party of seven has just departed, leaving wine glasses scattered across the bar. Three couples, all standing around the bistro tables as far from the bar as they can get, have just enough time to breathe a sigh of relief and enjoy a sip of wine in silence before another bachelorette party arrives in a limo. This time, there are ten of them, and the bride is wearing a white lace minidress, a sequined sash, and a tiara that looks like a pageant crown.

I conceal my own sigh. It's a typical Saturday at the Quantum Ridge in Alpha-Two, and I'm ready to move on.

My request for a promotion has just been denied for the second time. Derek, my manager, thinks I'm thriving where I am, and he trusts me to run everything when he has meetings or seminars—which he has whenever he's sick, hung over, or just doesn't want to come in that day. There are two other hosts, but Richard is on vacation and Jill called out sick, leaving me alone on a warm spring weekend with wedding season ramping up.

I smile mechanically and welcome the latest group.

After the first pour, I glance at the clock. It's 11:22—eight minutes until the shipment from Alpha-One arrives.

Our first offering—our own Alpha-Prime's red blend—comes from the Zinfandel, Grenache, and Tempranillo grapes harvested from the vineyard just beyond that window. Since this universe is where the technology allowing us to access other dimensions was invented, our universe is named Alpha-Prime. In the nose you'll notice some blackberry and plum, and your first sip will be fairly fruit-forward, tapering into a lingering spice finish.

11:32. The shipment has arrived, but Bachelorette Party 2, already at least two wineries deep, is giggling over their third pour. One of the couples leaves without buying anything. I load glasses in the dishwasher and resist looking at the clock too frequently.

Now we're going to sample the same red blend harvested from the Quantum Ridge vineyard in the nearest alternate universe, designated Alpha-One. Similar nose, but you'll notice distinctly more spice and even slight tobacco notes when you taste. Alpha-One experienced a slightly hotter and drier summer than we did, which concentrated the flavor of the grape just before harvest. If you hold it up to the light, you'll notice a darker ruby color, too.

The bridal party leaves at 11:42. I feel sorry for their driver: one of those bridesmaids is definitely about to vomit in his limo.

The other two couples are lingering. They each have only one pour left and don't seem to be in a hurry to get it.

I slip out of the tasting room and hurry down the concrete hallways to the warehouse.

The shipping gate is still open, the four prisms stretched apart by their own force field lines to form the corners of a shimmering, translucent rectangle. Through it I can make out Alpha-One's warehouse, identical to Alpha-Two's except Alpha-One's industry barrels are taller and skinnier. My heart beats faster just seeing them. Just one dimension lies between me and the headquarters of Quantum Ridge on Alpha-Prime, the dimension below which all the others are stacked, and the source of all my heartache.

The Alpha-Two Doctor Fischer, the one I work with, is going over the gate data with the Alpha-One Doctor Fischer. Alpha-Prime's Doctor Fischer invented the dimensional gate technology, and once her US government hammered out regulation with the other dimensions' US governments, she spread the winery business—the industry her parents had worked in—down the stream of accessible dimensions, bringing her other selves on board as she went. Given all the possibilities her technology offered the government, they were only too happy to allow Fischer to apply it to wine production. I'm not sure exactly how wealthy it's made the original Doctor Fischer, but the answer lies in the vicinity of "extremely".

Two warehouse managers—Eduardo, one from here and one from Alpha-One—are studying the data as well. In pairs, Eduardo and Doctor Fischer jointly operate the quantum gate, evaluate dimensional integrity, and exchange data. Most of the Quantum Ridge warehouse managers are an Eduardo, just like most of their tasting rooms include a Cate—or a Kate, depending on how we spell it. At the moment, I spell it with a 'C', though that's changed more than once.

Both Eduardos wave at me as I enter the warehouse, but both doctors remain focused on their tablets. All of the Doctors Fischer are obsessed with gate safety. The technology is safe enough, having been continually studied and improved over the last seven years, but the Doctors are still vigilant. No one wants the PR nightmare of losing a shipment—or an employee.

The two warehouse crews are nearly done. Cases of wine from Alpha-One and Alpha-Prime are being unloaded here, while product from Alpha-Two and the lower Alpha and Beta dimensions is sent through the gate for distribution upstream. Only two pallets are left on our side.

The visiting Doctor Fischer nods to me and exits through the gate. Glowing ripples cascade in sparkling fractals across the gate's surface when she passes through. I can still see her on the other side, distorted, as if she's standing behind a ripping sheet of water.

Alpha-Two's Doctor Fischer also nods. I back away casually, fading among the barrel racks to wait for her.

The rest of the pallets pass through the gate and Doctor Fischer confirms clearance. With a wave to her double, she initiates gate closure. The prisms begin to slide back together, collapsing the blurry window into the other dimension and exposing the rest of our own warehouse like a veil lifting. My eyes water. I've worked around Quantum Ridge gates for five years and there's still something about the dimensions opening and shutting that my mind refuses to process. What it sees registers as a rush of nausea, a refocusing of my eyes, and a moment of inexplicable dread before the worlds right themselves.

There's a flash of light as the prisms close in on each other, forming an ordinary-looking cube perched atop a post. It stays there, always, as a sort of locus, a point that exists across all the known Quantum Ridge dimensions.

Doctor Fischer joins me among the towering barrels.

"Cate," she greets me.

"Doctor."

"Kate got the promotion."

I feel the words like a door slammed in my face. Kate, the version of me in Alpha-One, had the good fortune to have worked for a Derek who got himself fired by headquarters earlier this month. Now she's been picked to replace him as manager—something I'd been striving for here, but with Derek still in my path, my chances for advancement are slim. I needed her where she was, in order to switch with her, get the promotion myself, and come one step closer to headquarters.

Doctor Fischer isn't done: "And you're on the verge of getting fired. Derek's been asking the others if they think you're pulling your weight in the tasting room."

Defeat immediately flares into defiance. "I am."

"We know. Everyone knows he's grasping at straws." She doesn't bother to keep her voice down; who would fire her? Quantum Ridge would cease to exist without her. "But we have a filing cabinet full of résumés for a job like yours. Derek won't keep a troublesome employee when he could simply get a new one."

I have been far from troublesome, but that argument is moot. "I still want to talk to her about switching. You and your doubles still want to write about me, don't you?"

"Cate, you've come all the way from the Betas. Is one more dimension really going to make a difference—to either of us?"

"Two more." I meet her gaze steadily. "I didn't just come from the Betas—I came from Beta-Three. After the fire. I'm going all the way to Prime."

Doctor Fisher is not easily fazed. Her surprise registers only as a single raised eyebrow. "Why Prime?"

I can't tell her exactly or she'll refuse to help me. "You know what headquarters did to the Beta dimensions. If I don't get to Alpha-Prime, they could do it again." Hopefully she'll think I'm progressing towards Prime in order to lodge a complaint or confront the managers at headquarters; if she knew my intention was to dig up enough dirt on her winery's broken promises to ruin it across every known dimension, she'd probably report me. "What if it's Alpha-Two next time?"

Doctor Fischer checks our surroundings with a sigh. The fact that she doesn't dispute me only confirms what I always suspected: with the gate technology allowing access to potentially infinite universes and infinite resources, any one of those universes could be expendable.

"Visit Kate during the next shipment," she says finally. "See if switching is even feasible. Then we can talk."

Yes, the year Alpha-Three was inaccessible temporarily put a serious hitch in our inventory! Gravitational fluctuations of that magnitude are rare, but they do cause quite the bottleneck given that shipments have to move sequentially up and down the dimensional ladder. Unfortunately, even with shipping restored, we won't have any wines from Alpha-Four for quite some time given the global impact of severe drought conditions there. If you have an Alpha-Four vintage in your cellar, save it for a special occasion.

Our final blend comes from Alpha-Five. You may notice a note of melon that isn't normally associated with reds, but there's something special about Alpha-Five's viticultural area that brings out unexpected flavors in the grapes. Before Quantum Ridge, wine standards dictated that those flavors didn't belong in a red wine, but now they're viewed as unique glimpses into the viticulture these other universes offer.

I get my break around one. The bridal parties are off tormenting the local eateries, and Derek has gotten out of his "seminar" and come to help for the afternoon.

I check my social media feeds while I eat my sandwich in the break room. Everyone else's dreams seem to be coming true on my screen: Shanté was elected to the state legislature, Dani just announced her first pregnancy, Stacie is making props for a sci-fi blockbuster, and Alice just quit her job to remodel a vintage Airstream and travel-write.

I stick my phone back in my pocket.

I don't even really want the managerial role. All I want is to dismantle Quantum Ridge brick by brick, then find a different job with a company that doesn't use up and cast aside whole universes —but to get there, I first need better standing within *this* company, and that means managing a tasting room.

If I can't get the job here, I could get it in Alpha-One—in fact, I already have. It doesn't surprise me that the other Cate—she spells it Kate—is advancing faster than me. Everyone I know seems to be doing better than I am; it makes sense that I'd be doing better than myself, too.

My phone pings. It's a text from someone the previous Cate labeled Matt From Café Pia.

Hey. :) I know it's been a while but I wanted to check in. Interested in getting lunch sometime? Let me know.

I don't know Matt From Café Pia. Does he work there? Did they go on a date there?

"Cate!" Derek hammers on the break room door and I jump. "Gotcha!"

"What do you need, Derek?" I force my voice into a pleasant, Stepford-esque tone.

"Need you up front. Another big group."

I still have ten minutes on my break. Derek probably knows, and he's probably expecting me to argue. Every Derek so far has gotten his kicks from trying to get a rise out of me; I'm well practiced at not giving him the satisfaction.

I put the remaining quarter of my sandwich back in its container and stand, smoothing my skirt and smiling.

"Be right out."

I need to last until the next Alpha-One shipment. If I'm fired before then, I'll have come all this way for nothing.

It's now time for our Cabernets, all products of the Beta dimensions, which produce our finest Cabernet grapes. The Beta dimensions are distinguished by some pretty significant variations that most Betas share but aren't found in the Alphas, like sociopolitical changes and

divergent plant and animal species. You'd be surprised how much the terroir is affected when a particular pollinating butterfly never evolved there!

If you've visited us before, you might remember that Beta-Two and Beta-Three experienced massive wildfires four years ago that we were afraid might cripple the industry there. We're pleased to say that those vineyards have bounced back, thanks to some rapid-growing strains of grapevines developed in collaboration with viticulturists here on Alpha-Prime. Now every Quantum Ridge location once again carries wines from Beta-Two's reopened Quantum Ridge.

Notice the slight smokiness in this wine, along with classic blackcurrant and vanilla flavors. Notice also a distinct lack of oakiness: since oak trees are almost extinct in that dimension, most Beta-Two wines are aged in steel.

I hate the Beta-Two wines. They're not bad wines; it's more what they represent. The drought experienced by the more distant Alpha universes was a minor inconvenience compared to what hit the Betas. The wildfires in Beta-Three burned for seventy-eight days. My home burned on the fourth day; the vineyards were ash by the end of the second week.

Quantum Ridge contacted us from their headquarters on Alpha-Prime pledging to help us recover. They were the only ones in a real position to help, anyway; it was the fifth year of increasingly cataclysmic fires on Beta-Three's Earth and no organization or government had any resources to spare, certainly nothing approaching the resources controlled by a wealthy transdimensional corporation. While we waited, we got back to work, salvaging from a sea of green glass shards and ash. Even Doctor Fischer helped, though she, like the rest of us, watched the undamaged shipping gate locus constantly, waiting for the distortion that would signal help arriving from Alpha-Prime.

Then the message came through: Beta-Three wasn't going to get aid. Beta-Two had also burned, and headquarters had evaluated the damage and determined Beta-Two stood a better chance of recovery. Rather than divide up their resources to help both, they made a choice. We were on our own.

We were always aware that Alpha-Prime held all the cards, but that was the first time we'd witnessed how they were dealt. Any unique resource, any surplus, any profit in any dimension, all went up the ladder for Prime to decide how to allocate. Tales came down the line of Alpha-Prime's fabulous wealth: their state-of-the-art winery, cutting-edge viticulture, a destination tasting room that functioned more as a showroom for the gate technology than a means to sell wine. Stories reached us, too, of Alpha-Prime's political and environmental stability. It sounded like a utopian paradise from fourteen universes away—but with the wealth of all those universes converged at such a distance, we never knew exactly how much had accumulated. Enough to fund an experimental fast-growing grapevine for Beta-Two, apparently, yet somehow not enough to send even a cleanup crew to Beta-Three.

I don't begrudge them their political stability. I've traveled through enough universes to know that should never be taken for granted. I don't even begrudge them their wealth: they started a hugely successful company and deserve the rewards of their success. What I want to hold them accountable for are their broken promises and their mindset of helping only a few when they're more than capable of helping all. It's neither a new nor a unique mindset, but after what it did to Beta-Three, I vowed not to let them inflict their particular version on anyone else.

Doctor Fischer agreed to my plan before I'd even finished explaining it. To her, Alpha-Prime's betrayal was personal: their Doctor Fischer would have had to agree to their decision, meaning she'd broken a promise to her own self. I don't think anyone ever expected the company to do what it did, least of all her, and she didn't want to see it happen again.

Technically Beta-Three is still part of Quantum Ridge, but only as a distribution center, a stepping-stone to keep product moving between dimensions. Aside from the breezy tasting room script mention, no one really talks about Beta-Three anymore. Two years later, they did the same thing to Alpha-Four, promising to send aid and instead reducing them to a glorified warehouse staffed by workers wrapped up in hazmat gear and NDAs.

Every night before I go to sleep, I take time to remember: we had different pollinators there, lime-green bees and black butterflies that shimmered like airborne shadows. In the spring, the daffodils bloomed scarlet and orange. In summer, the poppies gilded the hillsides in pink.

When I lie in bed remembering home, I feel like Dorothy, peering through her ransacked cabin door into an alien world where even the light was different—only in the end, Dorothy gets to go home, to her comfortable, familiar colors. I just keep clicking my heels, and instead of *there's no place like home*, I'm praying *almost there. Almost there.*

The Alpha dimensions have oak trees, at least. White oaks in Beta-Three were endangered; by the time I turned twelve, they'd been obliterated by unrelenting fire and drought. I didn't see another oak until I exited the shipping gate on Alpha-Nine and witnessed the forest of silver-mossed behemoths climbing the sides of the valley. They seemed almost sentient: indescribably ancient monoliths, beings that had been eradicated from my home dimension but had guarded that valley since the dawn of time. It felt like they would outlast us all.

Our final tasting of the day comes from Beta-Seven. Because these universes are farther away in spacetime, they're also more challenging for our inventory managers to reach. Beta-Seven was the most divergent universe we were capable of reaching this season. You'll notice right away that this wine pours a distinct dark purple, almost indigo blue—this is in fact our famous Blue Cabernet, which is the result of some unique varietals of the Cabernet grape that only grow in Beta-Seven. Flavor-wise, this is a strongly tannic wine, with exotic spice notes—and I do mean exotic: about three percent of the herbs and spices on Beta-Seven's Earth don't exist here!

The best I can say for this dimension's Derek is that he isn't as bad as the Alpha-Four Derek. The week crawls by. On Thursday, I'm four minutes late thanks to road work, and I drive up the gravel lane to find Derek out front, arms folded, tapping his foot.

"You're late."

"They were filling potholes on Dunraven."

"This is becoming unacceptable, Cate."

I'm consistently punctual, and we don't open the tasting room for another hour anyway. There's nothing to find unacceptable, but Derek says it so he can feel important.

Maybe someone told him that the other me got his job. I hope the news gives him indigestion.

That night, at home, I organize. I make lists of my passwords, bank information, favorite coffee shops, and where my relationships stand with coworkers and locals—everything the other Cate gave me to take over her life, and everything Kate would need to take over mine. The switch could happen on very short notice. I have to be ready, both for my sake and for Kate's.

If she even agrees to switch. I try to tell myself nothing is certain, but I've come this far—it's so easy to take momentum for granted.

On Friday, we host an event for a local alumni organization. It makes for a long day, and a lot to keep both me and Derek busy. I don't mind it. Being busy keeps my mind off the waiting, and Derek being busy keeps his mind off my employment.

Saturday arrives. I check my phone all morning, monitoring traffic, and even though the roads look clear, I leave for work fifteen minutes early. Halfway there, I grow paranoid that Derek will read something into my being early, so I stop at a roadside espresso stand for a coffee. I'm already nervy, but it doesn't occur to me to order decaf until after I've left. By the time I turn up the drive to Quantum Ridge, my hands are trembling on the steering wheel.

It's a standard Saturday morning: setting out glasses, restocking the antihistamines for the inevitable allergic reactions to the Blue Cabernet, reviewing sales figures. We're all so worn out from the previous night's event that we don't talk to each other much, which is fine with me. I'm too afraid that I'll say something to betray myself.

At 11:20, I bring a random file, ostensibly something for Doctor Fischer, to the warehouse. She's preparing the gate, and she's not surprised to see me.

She sets the file aside without looking at it. "Their barrels are tall enough to hide behind, but you'll have to move fast."

"I know."

"Be back over here by the time they complete the shipment."

I stand behind the gate locus and wait. At 11:30, the gate activates, the other dimension yawning open. Alpha-One's warehouse comes into view like it's emerging from a tunnel, its barrels taller, the sunlight streaming through its windows brighter. I can't see anyone. They are all standing with the shipment, right where I'm standing. I shiver. Someone is occupying the same space as me, one dimension-folding away.

The Alpha-One Doctor Fischer steps forward into view, followed by Eduardo and the pallets. I step forward, too, into the new universe.

I hear the next set of pallets rolling towards the gate, so I run and duck behind the nearest assortment of barrels and make my way at a crouch out of the warehouse.

I wait at the edge of the tasting room, out of sight of the customers. Kate is running tastings with both Richard and Jill.

She does a double-take when she notices me. To her credit, she doesn't scream.

She doesn't ask who I am (obvious) or where I came from (also obvious). However, she's not gentle as she shoves me into the office supply closet.

"What are you doing here?"

"I know you're busy, and I have to get back before they complete shipping, so I'll be quick," I say. "How would you feel about switching?"

She blinks and releases me. She has purplish shadows under her eyes that concealer can't fully disguise, and there's more gray in her chestnut hair than in mine. "Why?"

"I still work for Derek. He hates me. I'm about to get fired."

"Doesn't sound like I'd want to be you, then."

"But you're *better* than me. You could run that place, easily, like you do here."

She hesitates. "But I hate it."

"What?"

"I hate managing. It's exhausting. I just feel like I can't cope with anything, not since Matt...you know."

"Matt," I recall, "from Café Pia?"

She looks like I just asked her what color the sky is. "Which other Matt could I mean?"

I can't think of what to say. Matt clearly meant a lot to Kate, but I'm missing some important pieces of her story, and I don't want to fill them in with wrong assumptions.

She puts the pieces together faster than I can. "You two—you weren't—" She looks horrified. Only now is she realizing the extent to which I am not her, and however Matt makes us different, it hurts her deeply.

"I got a text from him," I say carefully.

Her lips compress. It's what we do when we're trying not to cry. "He's alive there?"

"Yes."

She almost smiles. "We were engaged," she says. "It was a long engagement—doesn't matter. He died in a car crash coming home late from work. He fell asleep, swerved..."

"I'm sorry."

"You've never even met him?"

"No. Not yet, anyway."

"But he texted you."

"He texted...Cate." I haven't had to explain myself in a while. "I'm originally from Alpha-Four." A lie, but everyone here remembers what happened to Beta-Three and it just creates more questions. By the time Alpha-Four was abandoned, it was no longer a shock. "I've been moving around a bit. The original Cate must have known him."

"That's illegal." Her expression has closed off. She looks wary. She should look stunned.

This, I think, I can interpret. "How did you get Doctor Fischer to let you switch?"

She sighs. Her shoulders droop. "I figured she'd want to do research on someone who left to live in a different dimension. I offered to be a test subject. You?"

"Pretty much the same, only I'm going more for quantity over quality."

"Every Doctor Fischer agreed to help you?" She looks impressed.

"Well, they're pretty much all on the verge of being mad scientists."

She chuckles. Good—she's loosening up.

"So when you were engaged to Matt," I ask carefully, "was that here or in Alpha-Prime?"

She sighs. "I call it a long engagement because it was actually two engagements, to two different Matts. The first was in Alpha-Prime."

"What happened to him?"

"Drunk driver."

"So you came here to find him again."

"And I did." Her smile is empty, joyless. "For a year and two months. Then I lost that one, too."

"It's not *your* Matt in Alpha-Two," I say gently. "Not really." Other Kates and Cates had to have this discussion with me, early on, when I was still looking for familiar faces—for familiarity in general. The Alice in my social media feeds is always doing some ambitious DIY project; Shanté is either an activist or a politician; Dani is a mother or nearly one. None of them are the friends I left in Beta-Three. After the first couple of switches, I found it easier to just keep them all at arm's distance.

But this Kate has already switched once, and suffered loss twice. While I kept myself closed off, she pursued love, even when it broke her. The only question is whether she's willing to endure that again.

"I know." She nods rapidly—another gesture we intend to distract from the fact that we're crying. We may be moving for different reasons, but the core of our longing is the same: *almost there.* "If you didn't know him, though…do you know *anyone* out here?"

"Not really."

"Then why? Is the management job really worth it?"

"The job is a means to an end." I pause, all my aching words bottled up; I have maybe three minutes before the shipping window closes. "I'm going to Alpha-Prime. This company is built on the bones of discarded universes and I'm not going to let it continue. Alpha-Four deserved better, and they're not the only ones."

She blinks, aghast, her sorrow gone. "I'm sorry—you want my job just so you can sabotage my employer?"

"I want your job so I can..." My stopped-up words evaporate. It had never occurred to me that I'm planning exactly that, or that other people, even other versions of me, are still happy working at Quantum Ridge. My flaring anger falters.

Kate frowns. "I understand wanting revenge—honestly, I do. But if you destroy Quantum Ridge, which I don't even know how you'd accomplish, think of the damage. How many employees does Quantum Ridge have, three hundred? Five hundred? You'd ruin all those jobs, all those families, to avenge a dimension that will never know the difference?"

"They've ruined ten times that by abandoning those dimensions," I retort.

She shakes her head, undaunted, as stubborn as me and then some. "What they did was awful, but if all you're going to do is wreck my livelihood and everyone else's, I'm not leaving Alpha-One. Not even for Matt."

"But what if—"

"The gate is closing." Her eyes have hardened. I've never seen such anger on my face, not even in the mirror. "You should go."

I pass the rest of the day in a daze, mechanically going through the tasting script and pouring glass after glass of blood-red wine. No one's ever said no to switching. Everyone else has been as desperate as I am to see if they can make a better life in another dimension.

I should never have told her the truth.

During lunch, Matt texts again. I never responded and he's afraid he had the wrong number. I still don't answer—what would I say? I'm not jealous of Kate and what she might have with Matt, but I keep thinking about her devotion: how different, and yet how similar, her reason for switching is compared to mine.

We're both being selfish. The difference is that her moving dimensions makes Matt's life better, not just her own, while my move might actually make others' lives worse. My self-centeredness eats at my insides. Whose lives have I worried about, besides mine? Whose pain have I acknowledged beyond my own?

What other option do I have?

Around four, Eduardo catches my eye from the hallway to the warehouse.

"Derek left early," he hisses. "And he didn't sign off on the sales reports for the month. I've been reminding him for days."

"Really?" Missing month-end reports is unacceptable. If we don't send them to Alpha-Prime, they'll restrict our inventory selection, costing us customers and prestige. It would have been exactly the kind of opportunity I'd take advantage of if I hadn't already met Kate. Alpha-Prime would eventually relent, but if— when—Derek made another mistake, there'd be no further forgiveness, and then one less Quantum Ridge to bring down. I wouldn't even have to go all the way to Prime.

Instead, I hear myself offer help. "I know where they are," I tell Eduardo. "I'll sign for him and send them through."

He looks amused. "You're going to forge Derek's signature?"

"You've seen it—it's not like it's hard."

"I don't know what we'd do without you, Cate." He pats my shoulder before heading back down the hallway to the warehouse.

I stay there, frozen, for another breath. For the first time in four years, I don't know what to do next. I always wanted Quantum Ridge to make the harder choice: to help rather than abandon. Now I realize I've been doing the same thing, abandoning Quantum Ridge when there's a chance—however small—that I could help them instead. I have no idea how, but Kate would want me to try.

I catch Doctor Fischer at closing the following Friday. "I need you to get a message to Kate in tomorrow's shipment."

"I thought you said your meeting didn't go well."

"It didn't, but I think I know how to fix it." I hand her a plain envelope. Inside are five pages I typed up over the last week: what happened on Beta-Three, where I went after, how I did it, and why. I've laid myself bare in those pages, admitting to my self-centeredness and my anger and how I let them fuel me for so long. The last page, however, is different: on that page, I dare to dream.

"Please make sure Kate reads this."

She shrugs. "No guarantees."

I have to wait an agonizing week until the next shipment. It turns out Alpha-Prime was so impressed with our numbers from the form I salvaged that they allocated us additional cases of Blue Cabernet, along with extra Cabernet from both Beta-One and Beta-Two, two of Quantum Ridge's highest-rated wines. The best part is that Derek knows I'm responsible; his attitude turns deliciously ingratiating. The transformation is the only thing sustaining me through the week while I await Kate's response—if she sends one at all.

I slip out of the tasting room at 11:49 on Saturday and linger in the break room, where I can see the shipping gate closing. The flash of light throws shadows of the barrel racks over the hallway floor. Doctor Fischer's clicking heels follow close behind.

I can't stand it any longer; I wait in the doorway, watching her approach, not even pretending to be doing anything else. She's as expressionless as ever, and she doesn't pause as she passes me.

"She'll do it. Be ready in two weeks."

Thank you all for joining us today, and we do hope you enjoyed this interdimensional tasting flight. Your tasting fee is waived if you join our wine club, but please note that we can't guarantee the availability of wines from any particular dimension due to gravitational and Heisenbergian fluctuations. That said, quantum forecasting for the more distant dimensions looks promising—Eight, Nine, and possibly even Ten in Beta all show good odds of being safely accessible this season! Come back and visit Quantum Ridge soon!

I leave my nametag—now spelled with a 'K', and 'manager'—on my desk. One dimension away, Kate—now Cate—is doing the same thing. Hers might not say "manager," but she's resolute and clever; I have no difficulty believing she'll have Derek's job by the end of the month, and with Matt back in her life, she'll be glad to have it. If her plans worked out, she's meeting him tonight at Café Pia.

It's a beautiful Thursday evening. Jill and Richard went home at six while I stayed behind to do some paperwork and get things in order for the weekend. The additional tablet Eduardo requested for inventorying has arrived, so I set it up with the necessary software and leave it on his desk for him. I double-check that the bathrooms are stocked and ready for the next day, then stop by my office to collect my things and turn off the lights. The pile of tax paperwork I've spent my first week tackling is still daunting—it's easy to see Kate hated that part of the job—but I've made good progress, and it's amazing how different the place feels without a Derek lurking over my shoulder.

I lock up and walk through the sunset-shadowed gardens to my car. I've survived drought and totalitarianism, wildfire and workplace abuse. Everyone I've ever loved is a dozen dimensions behind me. I've fought my way here fueled by bitterness, but now, one dimension away from my destination, the bitterness is draining. Something that could be described as hope replaces it.

Maybe Kate was right that I didn't know exactly how I was going to avenge Beta-Three, but I believe she was wrong to say they would never know the difference. I don't know exactly how I'm going to fix Quantum Ridge yet, either, but I'm learning. I have access to Quantum Ridge's inner workings now, plus a trail of Doctor Fischers who know the journey I've taken, and who will support whatever changes I manage to implement because they know their dimensions are at stake, too. With the influence I've gained, the respect I've accumulated, and the knowledge I'm gathering, I'll not only ensure no one in any Quantum Ridge universe loses their home again, I'll restore the ones that did. I can keep my vow and still make myself—and all my other selves— proud.

Just one dimension to go.

See Laura Duerr's story "Vertical Flight" online at Metaphorosis.
If you liked it, leave a comment. Authors love that!
Remember to subscribe to our e-mail updates so you'll know when
new stories are posted.

About the story

I come from a family that loves wine, and I married into a family that also loves wine. My sister-in-law even worked at a winery for several years, which gave us all some insight into the industry as well as allowed us to try some wines we otherwise might never have even seen. It's through her that I learned about 'vertical flights', a tasting format that samples one specific wine produced over a number of years to see how the end result changes over time. My nerd brain wondered how wines might be different not just across time, but across parallel dimensions.

That led to this story's earliest iteration as flash fiction. It consisted entirely of the tasting room script, a tongue-in-cheek sendup of the more pretentious tendencies of wine-tasting that also hinted at something dark going on in the background that the tasting room host wouldn't — or couldn't — address. At the time the title was "Tasting Notes from the 2038 Interdimensional Flight, Quantum Ridge Vineyards".

After submitting that flash piece a few times (and after reading Sarah Pinsker's amazing "And Then There Were (N-One)" and thinking about other selves living other lives in other dimensions), I realized there was more story lurking in the background of that flash piece, specifically the story of a winery employee who lived through some of the hinted-at darkness. I kept the tasting room script for world-building purposes, but the speaker is never identified: the story now belongs to all the Cates and Kates trying to make their worlds better. So a new title became necessary, and thinking of those wine-tasting outings gave me the perfect one. "Vertical Flight" describes both the tasting session and Cate's progress up through the universes, away from her difficult past, adapting and changing along the way.

A question for the author

Q: Do you prefer your SFF as books or movies?

A: While I have experienced phenomenal examples of both, I have to go with books, and not just because I'm working on one. I love being able to visualize the world and characters in my own way. I also think themes and messages can be conveyed more subtly, but also more powerfully, through writing. Honestly, though, I might pick a third answer: comic books, where gorgeous writing and stunning visuals give the reader the best of both worlds.

About the author

Laura Duerr is a speculative fiction writer from Washougal, WA, where she lives with her husband, a rescue dog, and two cats. When she isn't conjuring words, she can be found hiking, reading, playing video games, or baking. This is her second appearance in Metaphorosis and her other stories can be found in Cast of Wonders, Escape Pod, and Shoreline of Infinity.

lauraduerr.wordpress.com, @laura__duerr

The Song of the Moohee

Emmett Swan

The vast Ossinian sea, empty and calm, spread out before me in all directions. The cloudless sky was brilliant blue. And alone I rode, on the back of a creature the size of a small house.

But this amazing animal was no mere brute. It was a professional transport, capable of communication. In fact, I had spoken to it, though I was certain my words had offended it. And now it swam stubbornly onward, ignoring my frequent hails.

My original destination had been an island called Lath. But my transport was now taking me elsewhere, though I did not know where, or even why. I was certain, however, that the change of plans was connected to my offending comments.

I should have known better than to speak my mind.

The leaders of the planet of Ossine had applied for membership into the Planetary Commerce Sphere. But there was little published information available, so I had been assigned by my employer to research the planet's native culture, and assess its prospects for setting up a mining operation. A professional assessment required that I remained objective and emotionally detached. That I keep my personal opinions to myself.

My lapse in professionalism had been compelled by this creature's subservience. The creature not only accepted the mastery of the Ossinians, the planet's dominant race, but served them enthusiastically. It was the enthusiasm I found disturbing.

I looked at the creature's huge head, partially submerged as he plowed through the sea, and called. But as before, I was ignored.

I had no choice but to wait, look out over the featureless ocean, and think back over the sequence of events that led me here.

A few days earlier, I had taken a surface shuttle down to Ossine's only spaceport, joined by an engineer and a surveyor, who were working for separate companies. After disembarking and passing through customs, we exited the barrier dome surrounding the facility and I got my first look at the surface of Ossine. The spaceport was considered a technology enclave. Advanced technology, available to all civilizations that belonged to the Planetary Commerce Sphere, was allowed inside the dome, while the rest of the planet was forbidden access. But the port's bland, familiar features were much less interesting than the Ossine landscape, which I now surveyed with pleasure. Mounds of reddish soil, glowing in the late sun, dotted the plain that surrounded the dome. Scattered between the mounds were gray-colored plants that sent sword-like shafts towering into the air. A hard-packed dirt road wound among the mounds and into the distance. Austere but beautiful.

"Now, how are we supposed to ride this thing?" asked the engineer. We stood on a simple wooden platform, awaiting our transport to the capital.

"You'll see," replied the surveyor, a veteran of four previous trips. "There's a place on the back of the creature where we can all sit. Plenty of room for our bags."

It surprised me that the Ossinians relied on animal transport. It was true that their culture was relatively primitive, yet they possessed a basic electrical grid and even state-sponsored research facilities. Why not mechanical modes of transport?

I was listening to the surveyor describe the wiggly creatures that inhabited the red mounds, when a loud snort cut him off mid-sentence. We turned toward the dirt road and watched a bulbous, lumbering, four-legged beast approach the platform. It was nearly ten meters long, with a massive head angled slightly upward, and alert, expressive eyes. Powerful muscles were visible beneath its skin, which was covered with a fine gray fur.

It positioned itself so that its body was parallel to the platform, and shifted its bulk laterally toward the platform's edge. No one was guiding the creature.

The surveyor propped a movable metal staircase against the brute's side and climbed up. We followed him and stepped down into a recessed cavity located in the middle of the animal's broad back. The curve of its spine protruded below our feet, and a wooden bench was attached along the side of the cavity, large enough to seat all three of us. I looked over the edge of the recess and watched the creature ease away from the platform and, keeping its back remarkably level, amble away at surprising speed. I could feel the creature's muscles working as I leaned back against the interior wall of the recess.

After half an hour, during which time the beast kept up its pace without pause, we passed a cluster of buildings and I got my first glimpse of the native Ossinians. They were humanoid beings with large heads and shoulders, and short necks. Their rough-looking yellowish skin was laced with a spider web of black cracks. Tufts of coarse jet-black hair formed extravagant eyebrows above their eyes and goatees under their chins, but their crowns were bald. They gaped at our group as we came galloping by, but offered no gestures of greeting.

The buildings were constructed of a reddish wattle, apparently made from the same soil that comprised the abundant red mounds. The structures were narrow and tall, many of them three stories high.

I waved at another group of locals walking beside the road, but again received no acknowledgment.

"These Ossinians don't seem to be very friendly," I said to the surveyor.

"They don't like outsiders," he said. "Personally, I think they're a bunch of assholes. They tolerate our presence only because they have to. That's my take, anyway."

"I see."

I looked up to see another great brute like the one we were riding go galloping by in the opposite direction. It was pulling a wagon loaded with red adobe bricks. I saw no back cavity. Instead, it had huge muscular shoulders around which the wagon's harness was attached. The creature had no driver.

I shook my head in wonder. "It amazes me that no one needs to guide these animals."

"Their whole relationship with the Ossinians is fascinating," replied the surveyor. "They are used for brute labor, to plow fields, even to rotate electric generators."

We watched another great beast speed by.

"They are called Moohee," continued the surveyor. "The Ossinian breeders have been able to modify their form. Some have hollowed out areas like this one, others have huge muscles for pulling carts."

"Is this relationship unique?" I asked. "Or have the Ossinians domesticated other species?"

"A few, for livestock. But their relationship with those animals is nothing like what they have with the Moohee. They're indispensable to the Ossinians."

"What about higher races on the planet? I mean, besides the Ossinians."

"Higher? You mean higher intelligence? The ability to reason?"

"That's right. I read there was a history of warfare with beings of another culture. Was this other race destroyed?"

The surveyor leaned back and patted the creature's fur. "No, Mr. Lader. They weren't destroyed. In fact, you're riding one!"

I looked down at the creature in amazement. "This brute is intelligent?"

The surveyor nodded.

I realized I'd been listening to a melodious sound for some time, barely discernible over the rushing wind. But now I gave it my full attention. It was a beautiful and haunting song, full of sadness. I watched the head of the creature and could see its mouth moving. My transport was singing! The words were in a tongue I didn't know, but the music moved me.

I was fascinated by this revelation, but uncertain what to think about it. Were these Moohee simply a service race, employed by the Ossinians? Or were they enslaved, subjugated by the Ossinians as a result of war and forced to do the Ossinians' bidding? That was something I would have to find out.

The capital was clean and orderly, with dense clusters of the narrow reddish buildings. The streets and alleys were wide, presumably to allow room for the large Moohee creatures, which I saw everywhere carrying Ossinians or pulling loaded wagons.

My companions and I were taken to the residence compound provided by the Ossinian authorities, where we went to our separate living quarters. I found them spartan but comfortable. As I was eager to get started, I dumped my belongings and took the short walk to the Ossinian administrative complex to introduce myself to the commercial liaison.

"I'm the envoy from the Cygna Mining Corporation," I told the individual attending the front desk of the commercial ministry. He nodded and motioned toward a nearby waiting area.

I took a seat and looked around. Seated near me were off-worlders, no doubt working with the other companies setting up shop for Ossine's assessment period, during which Ossine's application to the Planetary Commerce Sphere would be evaluated. I was more interested in the Ossinians themselves as they shuffled in and out of the lobby area. They walked with stiff, upright postures and their eyes were dark and expressionless, giving their visages a reptilian character. The genders were similar in appearance, each sporting bald pates and distinctive black and bushy eyebrows and goatees, but the female Ossinians were smaller, with large breasts pushing against their tunics.

After what seemed an excessive wait, a female Ossinian approached. She was dressed in the typical coarsely woven tunic, but the neckline and shoulders of her garment were decorated with small colorful stones. Her awkward smile bunched up the black lines that reticulated her yellow face. Her dark eyes did not reflect her smile.

"Mr. Lader? I am Murlemi. I've been assigned to your company as official liaison."

She led me to a nearby nook which offered a bit of privacy. There, we exchanged a few pleasantries and then she asked about my duties.

"In order for my company to set up shop on your planet, we will need to thoroughly research your world," I replied. "It's my task to familiarize myself with all aspects of your culture. Therefore, I request permission to travel throughout the planet. I am interested in meeting with labor leaders, managers of production facilities and the common workers in your factories. I want to know what they think about the Planetary Commerce Sphere, and about off-planet companies like Cygna."

"I see. You want to determine if we are...acceptable." The words were uttered slowly, her lips pursed. I sensed my mission displeased her.

I nodded. "You could say that. At least suitable for our business interests."

"You will have free access," said Murlemi. "I'll assign you a competent guide who will arrange all the..."

"If it's allowed," I interjected, "I'd prefer to travel alone. Approaching workers with a government official at my side may influence their responses."

"It's allowed," replied Murlemi. "But it'll be more difficult to arrange your transportation. Is this really necessary?"

"I would prefer it. I apologize for the added inconvenience." Surely she realized my concern was valid.

"It will be as you ask."

"Thanks for your cooperation. I'm sure that Ossine and the Cygna Mining Corporation can work together in a seamless and mutually profitable manner."

At this remark, Murlemi scowled, as if she had eaten something unpleasant. "Your company, and others like them, will exploit the resources of our planet, while we receive a mere nine percent of the profits. I make this clear to you up front. We do this for one reason and one reason only—arrangements of this kind are required for membership in the Planetary Commerce Sphere. We believe the technology ban is audacious and a violation of our autonomy. We don't understand why we Ossinians, who are the unquestioned masters of this planet, are forbidden access to technology commonly available to hundreds of other cultures. The sooner we go through these motions and—how else can I say it—pay for our improved status, the better."

Although there was some merit to her view, my company didn't make the rules. I politely nodded. "I appreciate your transparency. It is unfortunate that your people must follow these tedious guidelines. But at least this phase of the assessment period lasts only two years."

"Treatment of this kind, no matter how short in duration, is an insult to our culture."

"And a quite remarkable culture it is, I must say," I said, hoping to steer the conversation down a more positive track. "This city and surrounding areas seem exceptionally clean and well-maintained."

"Thank you. We keep all production sites and their unhealthy emissions far from our living areas. Workers commute to offshore facilities."

"A thoughtful setup. And I reviewed the cultural items your leadership submitted with their application for membership. I was especially impressed by the art and poetry. Absolutely beautiful."

Murlemi bowed her head.

"And the relationship your people have with those Moohee creatures is fascinating. I am told they are intelligent beings, and I see them everywhere in the service of your people."

"Without access to technology allowed to other cultures, the Moohee must be used for menial labor. Our one-time enemies recognize their place and have dedicated themselves to the Ossinian race."

"They are not forced into their servitude?"

"Not at all."

"It seems unprecedented."

"I suppose what seems natural to us may be viewed differently by outsiders," said Murlemi. "It may interest you to know that our two races waged a series of wars lasting over a century. It's all ancient history now. Our race ascended to our proper station and the Moohee, to their credit, chose to cooperate with their superiors rather than face extinction."

I tapped my chin with my finger. "Please help me understand. Why are you considered their superiors?"

Murlemi shrugged, an awkward gesture given her short neck. "Did we not conquer them?"

I decided to begin my investigation at offshore production facilities. I was interested in seeing how the Ossinian managers employed the Moohee in their mines and factories. With the technology quarantine in effect during the assessment period, my company would have to use those same creatures to set up shop.

I had Murlemi arrange the details and went to the passenger docks early the next morning to await the arrival of a seafaring Moohee. As I stood waiting at the passenger wharf, I watched other Moohee transports as they swam up to the loading docks, where Ossinian workers unloaded freight from the cavities on their backs. These sea-based creatures were larger than their land-based brethren, with huge, rotund bodies that floated high in the water. And judging from the substantial amounts of cargo I saw stacked by the loading ramps, their recessed compartments were quite commodious. I marveled once again at how highly adapted the Moohee were to the needs of Ossinian society.

A rather short Ossinian holding a clipboard approached me. "Mr. Lader, I presume."

I nodded.

"Your transport should arrive shortly. And have no concerns about crossing the ocean. They are nearly always calm. And the Moohee are excellent swimmers. He will transport you to your first destination, an island called Lath, a few hundred miles from the coast."

At that moment, the harbor official pointed to the entrance of the sheltered harbor, and I spotted a smaller Moohee enter and head in our direction. As before, no one was guiding it.

I turned toward the harbor official. "I am amazed these Moohee are so cooperative. Do they ever disobey?"

"The Moohee know their place," he replied, his reptilian eyes reflecting no emotion.

"Yes, but why are they so willing to serve? Do you pay them well?"

The official glanced back over toward the loading ramps and motioned for two workers to come over with the wave of his hand. He looked back at me. "We allow them to live. And we give them what they need."

"It seems puzzling."

"I suspect it is because it gives them a higher purpose—to serve their betters."

I turned to hide my frown and watched the newly arrived Moohee position itself adjacent to the wharf where I was standing.

"This Moohee will take you to Lath," said the harbor official. He directed the two workers to prop a mobile staircase next to the creature and carry up my luggage and supplies. Then he motioned for me to go up the ladder. "The trip to Lath takes just one day. You should have everything you need."

I waved farewell to the official, who made no return gesture, and climbed down into the Moohee's passenger area and took a look around. Toward the back of the recess was a covered area containing supplies and some simple furniture, including a wooden table and a cot. It was a cozy little spot to spend a day traveling.

I felt movement, and watched attentively as the Moohee glided away from the loading dock and began moving its muscular limbs in a rotating motion. Though the creature worked up to a brisk pace, the passenger area remained steady.

A light sea spray made its way into the cavity, but the sun was warm and the mist refreshing. I sat down and leaned back against the creature's thin fur. It felt warm and gave off a slight and not unpleasant odor. I took in the blue sky and the Ossine harbor shrinking in the distance and pondered the plight of my transport. I wondered what sort of being would so willingly give up on their freedom. In the beginning, just after they were conquered, I could see it. But now? Was it still fear that drove their cooperation? Or was it just the weight of history? Their fathers and fathers' fathers had served willingly, so perhaps it didn't even occur to them to plot their own path in life.

After an uneventful hour, I dug into the supply containers and was helping myself to breakfast when a melodious tune reached my ears. I climbed up on the edge of the passenger recess and looked down at the head of the Moohee, which it kept mostly out of the water as its buoyant body swam along. As I had expected, it was the Moohee singing the song. The words were, on the whole, unfamiliar, but I caught a fragment of a phrase commonly used in Engliss, an ancient language I had studied at the Academy.

I knew these beings were intelligent, but wondered whether it would communicate.

"Hello. Can you speak?" I asked in the ancient language.

The creature stopped swimming and angled its massive head in my direction, scanning me with one eye. "If I could speak, what would you have me say?" asked the Moohee, the words coming slowly.

For a moment I just stared, lost for words.

"You do talk!" I managed. "You speak Engliss."

"It's not our natural tongue, but that of old Earth poets. One must understand the mother tongue before one can understand the mind."

"Amazing."

"I agree," said the Moohee. "I've never spoken with an off-worlder. My name is Loomso."

"I'm honored to meet you, Loomso. It's not often one gets to converse with their means of transport. I'm Mark Lader, a researcher for the Cygna Mining Corporation."

"Ah, a man of intellect. I, too, am honored."

"Thank you. So tell me, how do you come to be a transport craft?"

"I was born into the role," the creature said. "Just like my parents, and their parents."

"To serve the Ossinians?"

"All Moohee serve the Ossinians. It is our place."

"Do you get compensated in some way?"

"The essentials. And we are allowed to live. What more could a being require?"

I frowned. "What about your own interests? And those of other members of your race? Or your family? Do you have families?"

"I have fathered three, though families are lost to the past. Our Ossinian masters take care of such matters."

It seemed a one-sided arrangement. "You give yourself over to the Ossinians to a great extent. My Ossinian liaison gave me the impression that your race is not forced to serve the Ossinians. That you do so willingly."

"We accept our destiny. We are Moohee. We create art. We sing songs. And we serve the Ossinians. That is what we are."

As before, I struggled to make sense of the arrangement. Many dominant races had forced their subjugated enemies into servitude. That was slavery and it was something I could understand. But this, it was different. There was no compulsion, no threat of harm. I found it distasteful.

"To willingly serve your conquerors without reservation... it seems undignified."

As soon as the words left my mouth, I regretted uttering them. No matter how disturbing I found Loomso's unquestioning acceptance of his subservience, he seemed a noble and kind being, and I was certain my words were offensive. And there was the matter of my professional mission on Ossine. I was to objectively observe and report, not to judge or interfere.

Loomso didn't reply but faced straight ahead and recommenced swimming. I sat down on my chair and kicked myself for opening my big fat mouth.

Eventually I finished off what remained of my breakfast. I resumed my seat at the edge of the passenger compartment and waited quietly.

Loomso resumed his plaintive song, but after a few minutes he stopped swimming. The creature again angled his head back to look at me.

"Your words sting my heart."

"I'm sorry, Loomso. Please forgive my rudeness. I know nothing of your plight."

"That is true. Would you like to learn?"

It was likely that my company would need to employ the Moohee in its mining operations, so an understanding of the history of the Moohee could be of value. "Sure," I said.

"Long ago, the Moohee and the Ossinians battled one another. Our masters love war and revel in victory. We Moohee prefer peace. One by one, our mother islands were lost until, after our defeat at the Battle of Gildenmor, we became utterly subjugated.

"We decided to become as useful to the Ossinians as possible. Today, due to Ossinian modifications, few of my brethren resemble our ancestors. I, for example, am several times larger. Others have been given muscles with which to pull large loads."

"I understand," I said, trying to be agreeable. "You had to cooperate. Or you would've been destroyed."

Loomso didn't respond at first. His large eye looked me over carefully.

"In the beginning, we were less...cooperative. We rebelled after our subjugation. Many Moohee were lost, including our greatest poet, Dilino Ust, along with many of his works. We keep what remains alive through our songs. The one you just heard was based on his poem about the unbroken spirit of the Moohee."

"It's a beautiful tune."

"But do you, my dear passenger, believe that the Moohee spirit is unbroken?"

I looked down at the placid sea. It occurred to me the Ossinians might have bred the Moohee to be docile and cooperative. "It's not my place to judge. I'm not a Moohee."

"You are not of our race. But I would know how others, not of this world, think."

"All right. What I think is that all intelligent races are valuable in their own right, and should have autonomy. The Moohee are not enslaved, I know that. But you have right to plot your own course in life, independently of the needs of the Ossinians."

"A noble thought," said Loomso.

"I can't help but believe that the Moohee see themselves through the lens of the Ossinian-dominated society, and so they see themselves as inferior."

"An interesting conjecture."

"Yes, but to shrug off these long-entrenched constraints would require fundamental social change, a difficult road." I rubbed my chin and looked off toward the distant horizon. "However..."

"My passenger has a thought?" asked Loomso.

"It could be that your situation will improve in the near future. Once Ossine's application for membership into the Planetary Commerce Sphere is accepted, commonly available off-world technologies would be introduced. The Ossinians would be able to construct a multitude of mechanical contrivances and would no longer need to exploit the Moohee. Over time, these changes should free the Moohee from social bondage. You could acquire a more respectable place within Ossinian culture."

Loomso's eye narrowed. "How do you know this?"

"What? About the new technology? Like I said, I'm an employee of the Cygna Mining Corporation. We are here to set up mining facilities as part of the evaluation period. If Ossine is successful, and I would be surprised if it weren't, this planet will undergo a technological revolution in a short amount of time."

"Once this...evaluation period is complete, the Ossinians would no longer require us?"

"It could mean the social liberation of the Moohee. But of course, cultural change can take a long time. There will likely be decades of discrimination while the Moohee slowly..."

"I am disturbed," interrupted Loomso. The creature closed its eyes and did not speak for several minutes. Finally, he looked at me again. "I am sorry, dear passenger. I cannot take you to Lath, but must head north."

"North? What do you mean? I have to go to Lath."

Loomso didn't answer, but lowered his head and began swimming once again, this time with greater exertion. I heard him sing no more.

So I became a captive on the peaceful Ossinian Sea. Loomso continued to ignore my hails, but swam on relentlessly. Eventually, the sun set behind the sharp horizon and the cool of night sent me to the cot, where I wrapped myself up in a blanket. I was anxious and uncertain, but the swaying of Loomso's steady strokes and the sound of his even breaths eventually lulled me to sleep.

The next morning, my rest was broken by a biting chill. I wrapped my blanket tightly around me and climbed up on the edge of the passenger recess just as day broke over the quiet sea. My breath cast out billows of condensation into the frigid morning air. Here and there, small pieces of ice floated on the slight crest of the sea. I had no idea where I was going or why. Loomso swam tirelessly onward, ignoring my efforts to communicate. Guilt continued to haunt my thoughts.

After a few hours of scanning the empty horizon, I spotted a dark speck dead ahead and it became clear that we were heading toward an island. Soon, I was able to make out the nature of its coast—craggy cliffs broken with inlets and small bays. As we approached, we passed through a large crack in the cliffs and entered a wide, enclosed harbor.

"This is Slingafol," said Loomso, catching me off guard. "According to our mothers, it is the home of the Moohee. Few of us live here now."

"Loomso!" I cried. "I demand that you take me to Lath immediately."

"There is no reason. But do not fear. You will not be harmed."

"What the hell is this? Aren't you my transport?"

"Sorry, dear passenger. Soon you will understand."

Inside the harbor, the expanse of water was perfectly still, broken by boulders and pinnacles of various shapes, all of which were encrusted with ice. The quiet beauty, sparkling in the morning sun, moved me. I felt lighter, less fearful.

Loomso wove among the rock obstacles as he swam toward the opposite side of the harbor. We passed between two distinctive pinnacles and through the entrance of a large sea cave set into a sheer rock headland that abutted the shore. It took a few minutes for my eyes to adjust to the relative darkness, but enough light filtered in from above to illuminate the expansive interior of the cave—a wonderland of cobalt-green water, stalagmites, and sparkling icicles. Among the larger boulders and the patches of sand that circled the perimeter of the cave were intricate creations of carved stone. There were hundreds of them, each one about the size of a man. The forms of most of these sculptures were abstract, but I saw several that seemed to represent beings of some kind, beings that had a passing resemblance to the Moohee.

The style of the art was familiar to me and I suddenly remembered where I had seen others like them.

"These sculptures, they resemble the ones the Ossinians sent as part of their application to the Planetary Commerce Sphere."

"The Ossinians do not sculpt."

"And the wonderful poetry they sent?"

"The Ossinians do not write poetry."

"But..."

"The Moohee serve the Ossinians in many ways," said Loomso. "We are their brute muscle, but we are also their creative spirit. They use our culture to elevate their own."

It seemed wrong that the Ossinians would not only subjugate the Moohee race and alter their physical form, but that they would also take credit for their artistic achievements. I was beginning to take a dim view of the Ossinians.

Movement on a small beach on the far side of the cave caught my eye, and I made out several gray figures. Loomso swam toward them. As I got closer, I could see that they resembled Loomso, but they were not nearly as large and had no cavities in their backs, though they had the same thick, pudgy bodies. One was sitting on its back haunches and was in the process of using its agile front limbs, resembling flippers, in a most humanoid fashion. I realized the creature was creating a sculpture similar to those that populated the cave, its paws easily grasping its tools. Two other Moohee were leisurely reclining along the water's edge, their bodies partially submerged in the icy water.

Loomso spoke to the sculptor in an unfamiliar tongue. After a brief exchange, their conversation became animated and continued for several minutes. Then both were abruptly quiet. Loomso looked back at me. "This is Iglum, the Father Elder of the Moohee race. He welcomes you to Slingafol and apologizes that you were forced to come."

I nodded at Iglum and he returned my gesture. He then turned to the two Moohee lying at the water's edge and spoke to them. They submerged into the blue-green water and swam away.

"These others are part of his family—the only ones that have escaped the Ossinian breeders," added Loomso. "At one time, every Moohee looked as they do."

I heard splashes from several directions and saw a number of other Moohee, previously camouflaged by the shadows and stone, launch into the water.

"There are seventeen in Iglum's family," said Loomso. "They will alert the others. In the meantime, please be our guest."

"Alert the others for what?" I asked. "What is going on?"

Loomso didn't respond to my questions, but exchanged a few more quick sentences with Iglum, who then returned to his work on the sculpture, voicing another song characteristic of the others I had heard the Moohee sing—haunting and plaintive, with swaying melodies in minor keys. I still had no idea what was in store for me, yet I was not afraid. The serene visages of these creatures eased any concerns I had about my welfare. Loomso swam toward another area of the sea cave.

"There is a dry nook ahead. There you will wait. If you wish, you may climb up to the island's surface. Take your ease, and soon I will convey you to wherever you would like."

"I want to go to Lath."

"If you wish. But there is no point."

"But why not? Tell me what's happening."

Loomso's large body positioned itself next to a flat shelf of rock that extended out over the water. I could see a dry area behind the shelf.

"The news you bought us is concerning to all Moohee. Iglum's family, strong swimmers all, have been sent out to all corners. Many Moohee will quickly assemble here. We must decide our future, and whether to end the Ossinian mastery over the Moohee."

"What are you going to do? Surely not a rebellion, not now? Just when social change is on the horizon. And you said yourself, the Ossinians are warlike and revel in victory. Has any of that changed? You would be slaughtered."

I began unloading my supplies onto the sand, stepping from Loomso's back directly onto the edge of the rock shelf. "Loomso, please listen," I said, working as I spoke. "I have a tendency to speak my mind, even when I shouldn't. Please ignore my stupid remarks."

"You are concerned?"

"Concerned? Yes. The Ossinians control all the resources of Ossine society. And the Moohee are...well, I hate to say this, but a race of conveyances. No disrespect. It's hard to see how a rebellion could succeed."

"I am touched," replied Loomso. "But do not trouble your heart. You and I will speak on this further. But now I must leave you. There is much to do." Loomso immediately pushed away from the ledge and submerged out of sight.

I sat with my furniture and supplies in the sandy enclave and waited several hours at the water's edge, using the blanket against the chill of the cave's interior. But as I saw no sign of any Moohee, I decided to climb up a rock fall toward the back of the enclave and check out the island proper. On the surface I found a jumble of boulders and reddish hills, with a few of the Moohee's distinctive sculptures scattered around. I did find patches of sparse trees and other vegetation along a freshwater stream that tumbled down from on high, but it was clear that no one lived on the surface of the island. As darkness approached, the temperatures dropped significantly, so I returned to the relative warmth of the interior of the cave.

I lay on my cot and thought about the Moohee. It didn't seem probable that an offensive comment from a single offworlder could cause a rebellion. Yet, something was clearly afoot, something related to my words. I didn't relish the idea that I had somehow triggered the events taking place.

I could certainly understand the desire to rebel, to cast off the shackles of servitude. But there seemed such small prospect for success. Could the Moohee have trained an army, or concealed caches of weapons during their years of servitude? Given how their Ossinian overseers controlled everything, even down to their families, it did not seem possible.

The demise of the Moohee seemed inevitable.

The next morning was quiet, although I spotted a few gray bodies swimming at the opposite end of the sea cave. They didn't respond to my hails. I had food left, and retrieved fresh water from the stream above, but as the day wore on, I became increasingly anxious.

As I sat glumly on the sandy ledge, a large form emerged from the blue water. Loomso tilted his back, dumping out water from the cavity, and edged up to the ledge.

"Come," he said. "The Father Elder wishes to speak to you."

"What's going on?" I asked.

"Come, and you will see."

I climbed onto his back, and Loomso swam through the sea cave and out into the boulder-strewn harbor. There, in the bright sunlight, I saw an incredible vision. All around the harbor, sitting on boulders, pinnacles, and the edges of the harbor, were thousands of Moohee. I was amazed at their variety of forms. Vehicles of every sort were there, ranging from big brutes to smaller, sleek Moohee, all designed, no doubt, to be useful to the Ossinians in their various ways.

And then, in perfect unison, they began to sing one of their distinctive songs. The cumulative effect of this amplification was overwhelming. At that moment, I could feel the deep pain of the Moohee subjugation, and was overwhelmed with sympathy for the plight of their nation.

The death of a race was tragic. Yet it occurred to me at that moment that perhaps life under the weight of ignominy was worse. When the Ossinians conquered the Moohee centuries ago, they hadn't destroyed them, but neither had they stopped at mere enslavement. The Moohee were not dumb brutes, but intelligent beings with artistic impulses. Yet their breeders had manipulated the genetic make-up of these beings. They had taken the identity of the Moohee and transformed them into a race of artifacts—mere tools for use of the Ossinians.

If the distortion of one's identity was indeed worse than annihilation, should I begrudge them the opportunity to try to shake off the shackles of domination? Even at such a risk? Perhaps the Moohee viewed their doomed effort as a great catharsis? The sadness was exquisite.

Loomso glided his huge mass next to one of the exposed boulders, where I recognized the seated form of Iglum. I climbed onto the boulder as Iglum began speaking to Loomso.

"Iglum says he is glad you are here to witness this. It is an important moment for the Moohee."

"I'm amazed," I said, looking around the harbor. "There are so many of you. How did they arrive so quickly?"

"The sea is our natural home. Despite Ossinian breeders, we remain strong swimmers."

"I see. I take it this gathering was for deciding a course of action."

"Yes. We discussed the information you brought us and the time is ripe. We end centuries of humiliation. We move against our masters."

"No, no, Loomso, please don't do this! Tell Iglum that a rebellion is ill-timed. As I said before, once Ossine is admitted into the Planetary Commerce Sphere, new technologies will catch on like wildfire. The Moohee will no longer be needed for manual labor. It will be your chance to break free of your subservient role."

"Ah, dear passenger, but that is why we must act." Loomso looked around the bay and expelled a long sigh. "During the war, our leaders gathered here, on Slingafol, as our island homes became lost. This island is too far north to be comfortable for the Ossinian race. Here in this very harbor, our fathers and mothers created a new strategy. We would submit to our cruel enemy. Only by serving the interests of the Ossinians could our plan succeed."

"Your plan?"

"Yes. And as the lives of Moohee came and went, the plan was passed down from old to young. Our strategy, dear passenger, was to become so useful to the Ossinians that they would come to rely on our kind and to trust our intentions. Now is the time for our sacrifice to bear fruit. We have to act now. Once the Ossinians have new technologies, their reliance upon us will be lost. Our opportunity will be out of reach."

Iglum spoke to Loomso in their native tongue, and then Loomso turned once again to me.

"Iglum believes peace is always preferable to war and death, and asks if it is my opinion that once the Ossinians acquire new technologies, they would welcome the Moohee into their society as equals."

I thought about what I knew about the Ossinians and their attitudes toward the Moohee.

"Probably not," I conceded. "At least not for a long time."

"Then there must be war. Will the members of the Planetary Commerce Sphere intervene?"

"No, not a chance," I said. "The culture on Ossine is still designated as nascent. While that designation is in place, Ossine will be left alone to sort out its differences without outside influence."

"Then we have won," said Loomso.

"I don't see it," I said. "How can a swarm of, well, how else can I say this, tuneful vehicles do battle with the Ossinians and win?"

"We are artists, Mr. Lader. And art can be found in surprising places, including as part of a war strategy. The Moohee do all the menial work for the Ossinian people. We transport their goods and workers. We generate their electricity with our muscle-power. Production facilities have been relocated to off-continent areas so that their living conditions remain pristine. This we have done for centuries. More recently, massive storage silos have been placed on offshore islands. From them, we willingly transport food and manufactured products across the sea, and then haul the loads to Ossinian cities.

"Their reliance upon the Moohee is complete. Without us, they have no access to food. And before the Ossinians can grow more, they will starve."

"But if the storage facilities are just off shore, couldn't they gain access to them?"

"They will try," said Loomso. "This swarm of tuneful vehicles, as you call us, will soon be on its way to the shores of the Ossinian cities, and to alert thousands of other Moohee who could not make it here today to do the same. When the Ossinians build and launch hastily constructed vessels to reach the food supplies, we must sink them."

What had seemed impossible to me just minutes before began to make sense.

"Winter soon approaches," continued Loomso. "It will be terrible for the Ossinian population. They will become weak and vulnerable. Many will become sick. Many more will starve to death. It is a cost that must be paid. For though we value the right of the Ossinians to live, we also value our right to equality. Perhaps, by taking this path, all will be put back into proper balance."

Iglum walked up to me and extended one of his front paws and shook my hand. "Thank you for alerting us, Mr. Lader," he said, in heavily accented Engliss.

He turned and began speaking loudly in his native language to the assembled mass of Moohee. They began splashing into the water and leaving the harbor.

I pondered the implications of this rebellion. Of course, the application for membership into the Planetary Commerce Sphere was kaput, not to mention my company's new business venture. And if my involvement in the Moohee rebellion were discovered, it could mean the end of my career as a commercial attaché, although, in my defense, all I had done was to reveal to the Moohee the pending influx of new technologies, something they would have eventually discovered on their own. Yet, as I thought about the history of Ossinian culture and the willingness of the Ossinian race to degrade the Moohee, I couldn't help but warm to the Moohee cause. It was true that the suffering of the Ossinian race would be great. And that those Ossinians alive today had not set up the current arrangement with the Moohee. Yet, they willingly perpetuated it. The prospect of the Moohee emerging from centuries of ignoble servitude seemed just, even at a great cost.

Loomso angled his head toward me. "I must swim my assigned area. But first, I will take you where you like. The shuttle port, perhaps?"

"Yes. If you please."

"Will you tell your leaders about the war? And let them know the Ossinians are no longer our masters?"

"It is my duty as an objective observer to convey the facts," I replied. "I'll report these developments to the governing board of the Planetary Commerce Sphere. I should mention that a rebellion, successful or not, implies instability. It will be a long time before the board considers another application for membership."

"I understand."

I climbed back into Loomso's passenger recess, and soon we were back on the placid sea, now dotted here and there with the figures of the other Moohee swimming toward their respective assignments.

I sat at my familiar place on the edge of the recess and took it all in. It seemed incredible that a race of beings, as part of a strategy to overcome their conquerors, would endure centuries of total subjugation. Yet the Moohee had done just that. And now that I understood, I had little doubt they would succeed. Without the Moohee to assist them, the Ossinians were extremely limited in their means of fighting back.

I wondered what role the surviving Ossinians would play in the new world order. For centuries they had humiliated the Moohee without hesitation, merely to serve their own ends. So perhaps it was just that they, in return, would be treated in similar fashion by the Moohee. Yet I did not think that would happen. From my interaction with Loomso and his kind, I was inclined to believe that they would carefully craft a new society, one in which all beings would be valued. I wasn't sure exactly what I based that belief on. More a feeling than anything else, but the feeling was strong.

Loomso began to sing another beautiful melody. But this time, there was none of the plaintive sadness of the other tunes. As I listened to the song, I felt the rushing wind blowing through my hair and the brisk spray upon my face, and smiled. Despite the pain and suffering that was to come, I felt certain the planet was in good hands.

Abruptly, the sun dipped below a bank of low ranging clouds and cast a golden hue upon the world of Ossine.

*See Emmett Swan's story "The Song of the Moohee" online at
Metaphorosis.
If you liked it, leave a comment. Authors love that!
Remember to subscribe to our e-mail updates so you'll know when
new stories are posted.*

About the story

Most of the stories I write, and this one is no exception, are driven by conceptual explorations. For "The Song of the Moohee", the concept I was interested in was social identity. If we look at the historical record, social identities, such as cultural or racial identities, are often treated with neglect or even downright disrespect.

An extreme example is when a social identity is virtually obliterated through conquest. Think of Rome's treatment of Carthage after the Second Punic War, or American politicians forcing free-ranging Native Americans into reservations.

Enslavement is another example. African slaves were captured from different tribes, each with their own cultures. Though in most cases their cultures persevered on their home turf, relatively little was retained by the communities of slaves at their new locations.

More common and banal examples are driven by economic or political dominance, especially for small-sized social entities living within a non-sympathetic majority.

Perhaps the loss of social identity is inevitable, much like the extinction of species is inevitable, though the loss of a culture, with its language, its religion, its cuisine, its way of seeing the world, seems especially sad. In the story, the Moohee were not only defeated, but their genetic code, which is the core biological identity of any race of beings, was altered, and altered only for the convenience of their masters. It seemed to me the most repugnant variant of social loss imaginable.

I imagined the Moohee to be a noble race of beings who greatly valued their social identity, and were strong enough to endure this ultimate degradation and without giving up their dream of reacquiring it. To succeed in getting it back, the Moohee nation would have to practice patience and sacrifice for generations. Will they succeed? Well, you gotta read the story to find out.

A question for the author

Q: Aliens. Are they out there?

A: We all want there to be, right? And we have all heard the argument based on the large numbers of possibilities in the universe. So many stars, many of which have planets, means tons of opportunities for intelligent life to develop. The odds are favorable, I believe, that there are aliens out there. But now comes the bad news. Space is big. I know that you know it's big, but it is hard to fathom just how big. This may put it in perspective: The Voyager probe, travelling at 35,000 miles per hour, reached Pluto in ten years. How long would it take to reach the nearest solar system? 835 centuries! For comparison, scholars place the dawn of civilization at 50 centuries ago. But, you say, surely we can build a faster ship. How much faster? Ten times? One hundred times? Even at one thousand times faster, it would still take nearly a century to get to the closest solar system.

And if there are aliens out there, it is not likely they are in the next solar system over, or even the one past that. Heck, they may be hanging out in the next galaxy over. Even traveling at the speed of light, it would take millions of years to reach the nearest large galaxy.

Yeah, there are aliens out there. But it's just the dismal reality that we will never get to meet them. Ever. Almost makes it worse than them not being there at all.

About the author

Emmett Swan lives in Louisville, Kentucky, where he savors the world's finest bourbon while sitting on his front porch, waving at the neighbors that walk by. His odd sequence of occupations includes beach lifeguard, college professor, magazine publisher, photographer, and building contractor. Nowadays, he combines all of these skills into wacky flights of fancy, which he has the audacity to write down on paper.

www.emmettswan.com

Leiprenese 101

Jason A. Bartles

I scrambled to find the arm hole in my gown as I ran toward Zorah's office apartment. Synthetic fabric should not get this twisted, but the wind tested my best efforts to arrive precisely on time. Zorah lived in the central Administration Building that towered over Mount Leipren University. They occupied the second-highest floor, but unlike the Chancellor right above them, Zorah invited their students and coworkers inside. I untangled the gown and situated the cap, trying to catch my breath. Then I checked my watch. A minute to spare. As I waited for the elevator, I reviewed my mental checklist for the final interview that stood between me and tenure.

My blood pressure rose with each passing floor. An MLU professorship was not a job for the lazy, the purposeless, or even the decently competent. Imposters and flakes were weeded out. It was tenure or bust, admission into the inner circles of academia or irrevocable banishment from this campus and this career. I could not fail now.

The elevator chimed, and at exactly six o'clock the doors opened to reveal—*you've got to be kidding me*—not Zorah, but Rafa.

"Good morning, Charlie!" Rafa practically burst with self-satisfaction. They had been waiting in front of the elevator to gloat. I could have sworn I had reserved the earliest office hour. I wanted to set the bar high, to become the standard against which others were compared, but Rafa had outmaneuvered me. "Good luck," they said insincerely and squeezed past me to take the elevator down.

I shot them a fake smile and stepped into Zorah's foyer.

"Come in," Zorah called, and a door opened at their command. I shook my wrists and took a deep breath before proceeding to their study.

"Good morning, Zorah. Thank you for meeting with me so early," I said. I had planned that greeting, but after Rafa's surprise attack, my words took on a double meaning.

"Never mind about Rafa," Zorah began. They had anticipated my reaction. "Everyone assumes going first gives you a leg up, but the truth is," they leaned forward and gestured for me to sit, "the patterns of the recent past are no guarantee of the present."

Zorah was dressed in the finest regalia. They sat behind a grey marble desk. On either side, bookshelves lined the walls. They were crammed with old lesson plans, monographs overflowing with sticky tabs, and personnel files. Somewhere in there, I thought, must be Zorah's field notes for the first English-Leiprenese dictionary and countless other treasures. Behind them, floor-to-ceiling windows opened onto the Appalachian ridges that wrapped around the campus.

The view from this elevation, and Zorah's reassurances, washed away the disappointment and most of my nerves. They had a way of making the world feel right again.

"Let's get down to business," said Zorah. I took a seat, while they opened my file. Zorah skimmed the summary of my publications, peer evaluation scores, and the data collected about my work-life balance. They mmhmmed and appeared to be quite pleased with my performance over the past decade. Then they tapped the page with their finger and looked at me over the rim of their glasses. "This says you have a new essay forthcoming. A report on the influences of Leiprenese on Earthling languages?"

"Yes. It will be published next month."

Zorah gestured for me to explain the work. This was an interview, after all.

"Right. Leiprenese is a pidgin language developed by the Renner to facilitate the colonization of Earth. At first, the Renner envoys used it to communicate with Earthling leadership about commercial matters. For the Renner, Leiprenese was an undignified but necessary mode of speech."

"Some of your peers would disagree with that statement," Zorah interjected.

"Well, they would be mistaken. There is a somewhat popular, but unfounded, notion that the Renner cherish Leiprenese for its simplicity. However, such scholars fail to distinguish the moral value the Renner assign to efficiency from their own yearning to be respected by the Renner. It's pure solipsism."

"Let's assume that's true. How, then, do you explain the Earthling desire to borrow from a language of such low esteem?"

"Earthlings are banned from learning any of the Renner's native languages while on Earth. The Renner have always insisted on maintaining a certain distance from their colonial subjects," I explained, and Zorah finally nodded in agreement with something I had said. "On Earth, Leiprenese was, and still is, the only possible means of communicating directly with the Renner. Speaking the language provides a way to improve one's station in life. For those born around the time of Earth's discovery and who came of age just as the Renner reconstructed the economy to ease its entry into the galactic marketplace, Leiprenese became associated with the progress and prestige of the Renner and their Homeworld."

"You're speaking of my generation."

"Precisely. In fact, I analyzed many of your early speeches."

"Is that so?"

"Yes, as if overnight, you stopped using gendered language."

"That was intentional. The Renner practically demanded it. Are you arguing that all of the changes were conscious?"

"Of course not. Most occurred over time as the result of code-switching, of constantly living between the two languages. Over a span of ten years, you adopted new vocabulary and even smoothed out some of the harsher consonants not used by the Renner. The *th*, for example, became an aspirated *h*."

"And?" Zorah prodded.

"And the hard *k* softened into sibilants."

"When I think back to how I used to speak, these changes seem drastic," said Zorah. They traded the steely gaze of peer review for a more wistful expression. "But I suppose those born into this world never knew anything else."

"Now you're speaking of my generation," I replied with a wink.

"And speaking of your generation, I have to say I'm quite impressed. With two of you anyway. You and Rafa can count on my endorsement."

"Thank you, Zorah, that means a lot." I could have melted in relief.

"You've earned it," they added.

"What about you? Is there any news about your ascension to the Homeworld?"

"You never know about these things," Zorah said cryptically. Without a doubt, they were the most qualified candidate. Every year, the Renner chose one professor from each planet in the empire to retire among them. Zorah had been favored for last year's opening, but at the eleventh hour, the Chancellor received word that the Renner had suspended all ascensions due to unforeseen circumstances. Something about the collapse of the housing market on a distant planet. Zorah stood and turned toward the windows. "But I try to remain optimistic," they said and invited me to join them.

"I'm sure this will be your year," I said as I approached the wall of glass. "I can't wait to be where you are. I lie awake most nights and dream of escaping this backwater planet."

"I take it you've watched the latest video of the Homeworld?" Zorah's gaze rose toward Renner Hall as they spoke, and mine followed. Perched on the highest peak, the site where the Renner had made first contact almost fifty years ago, its gold-plated facade reflected the sunrise over the entire valley. Originally, the building had been reserved for Renner envoys, until they stopped visiting the planet in person. Ever since, the hall had taken on a ceremonial role, housing the person chosen to ascend for their last night on Earth. The rest of the year, it looked down on the campus as a comforting reminder of the Renner's promise: Paradise awaited those who worked with passion and perseverance.

"Who hasn't? Rethinking your plans now?"

"Absolutely. I had always wanted to stay in the capital. I love living in the mountains, but I thought for my retirement I'd try something new. The sprawling city with its glass towers and plastic-lined boulevards. The personalized pods to carry you to the Anthropological Museum of the Galactic South and then to the beauty spa for a quick chemical peel. I'd watch the sunset in one of those open-air wine bars in a heated pool near the coast. But that train, is that what you would call it?"

"I suppose. There weren't any tracks, or at least none I could see."

"It made me rethink everything. Having your own private car while touring the planet," Zorah's voice soared with their imagination. "The quartz canyons, the cloud forests, the petrol rivers."

"I had no idea those even existed."

"No one did. And being granted permission to study the local languages as you pass through each region."

"It's a dream come true for language nerds! Any favorites?" I asked.

"I'm partial to Milonian. I find the short, shocking phonemes to be an irresistible challenge for my palate."

"Hacher would be my choice."

"The language of austerity," they added. "It all sounds marvelous."

"I wish they'd allow for more opportunities to visit the Homeworld. You'd think if people got a taste of that lifestyle, they'd be more motivated to develop their own planets."

"I'm sure they have their reasons," cautioned Zorah.

"Of course," I agreed and shifted the topic. "It's exciting to think I could get tenure the same year the Renner choose you to join them."

"That would be nice." They spoke in hushed tones, as if another line of thought were running under the surface. "You're following closely in my footsteps."

"I've had a fantastic mentor in you," I said, at risk of crossing that line between gratitude and groveling.

"But best not to get ahead of oneself. There's still plenty of work to do here."

I watched as Zorah traced a finger over a hairline fracture in the window. The gesture was unassuming, as if out of habit, but it left me uneasy. I couldn't help but imagine the entire pane shattering into a million shards and pelting the ground below. I took a step back from the edge and returned to the other side of the desk.

"Look at the time," Zorah said as they turned toward me. Their voice helped shake the irrational vision from my mind. "I have eight more interviews to complete, and you have a class to teach."

"Thank you again." I bowed in deference and left Zorah's study. For a moment, it felt as if everything were lining up just as I had planned.

The students in my Leiprenese 101 class were arranged in their mobile desks like ten little bowling pins. It was my job to knock them down in order to build them back up. Now that I had secured Zorah's endorsement, I could focus on defending the record I had set years ago as a student in this very classroom. Today's unannounced oral exam was designed to do just that.

"My value is my work," declared Student 1, leading the repetition of the weekly motto. Rankings were all that mattered at the introductory level. Scores were tied to biometrics, and only the top twenty percent would survive the first year. Only then would I bother with their names.

"My value is my work," said the other students in unison.

Student 1 had been Student 1 for almost a month, which gave me until the end of the week to depose them. They knew I would be relentless to them in defending my title, while lobbing easy questions at their competitors. There were no friends in that classroom. Only ten adversaries. And I had all the power.

"Today, I will assess your understanding of pronouns," I said. "Student 1, are you ready?" I had switched to Leiprenese, and they knew resorting to English would move them immediately to the back of the class.

"Ready," they responded.

"Student 1, fill in the blank: The employee is late. *Blank* lose ten percent of their wages."

"*They* lose ten percent of their wages," they affirmed with annoyingly accurate pronunciation.

"Correct. You earn one point." I pursed my lips.

"Student 2," I said, slowly and in English, freeing them to respond more easily. "True or False: *I* is the first-person singular pronoun."

"Umm."

"Student 2, you have three seconds."

"False?" Their voice cracked with uncertainty.

"Such a maynard," mumbled Student 1. "Pathetic."

"Wrong," I said in disbelief. "Did nothing trickle down from my recorded lectures? Minus four points."

At my command, the scoreboard in the front of the room docked four points from Student 2, who became Student 4, though they deserved to be in the back of the class. As always, I had been too generous. The desks rearranged themselves, moving Student 2 back a row and sliding Students 3 and 4, who became 2 and 3, into higher-ranked positions.

Just then I noticed Rafa lingering in the hallway, checking to see if Student 1 had outperformed me yet. Time to strike.

"Student 1," I said, returning to Leiprenese, "Fill in the blank with the proper first-person plural pronoun: *I* am the foreman. *They* are the Manager. *Blank* always reward efficiency."

"*They*, wait—" the student's eyes popped as they began to self-correct. I had my opening.

"Sorry, Student 1. The correct answer is: *I and they*. Minus—" I turned to look at the scoreboard. Student 1 was now in the lead by twenty-four points. "Minus twenty-five points."

The star student became outraged at their failure to best me. While the chairs for Students 1 and 2 swapped places, I walked toward Rafa, winked, and shut the door in their face. I would count this as payback for the little trick at Zorah's office.

"You'll just have to try harder, Student 2," I said as I turned. It was better they learned how the world worked under my guidance than on the job. This was for their own good.

The day of the Promotion Ceremony had finally arrived. I and Rafa and the other eight candidates for tenure waited behind the auditorium with luggage in hand. Anyone not tenured would be escorted from campus immediately. A lucky student had been assigned to usher me and the others through the loading door and into the wings. In the audience, the tenured faculty were arranged by rank in the shape of an inverted pyramid that pointed toward the stage. At stage left, the Chancellor teetered behind a podium, while Zorah oversaw a folding table draped with purple fabric. It bore the MLU sigil of a black bear under a maple tree. I counted two golden sashes and two flower crowns.

I and the other candidates drew lots to decide the seating arrangement on stage. I drew a front-row seat, and Rafa, poor thing, would have to sit behind me. As they settled in, their shoe kicked my chair. It was not an accident. I was used to the spats, the little digs at every turn, the subtle, but not unnoticed, affronts. It would be a long road beside them, but then again, every Arguedas needed their Cortázar. Rafa's disparagement drove me to new heights, to push harder than I ever imagined as I worked to outshine them.

The Chancellor tapped the mic. They praised the faculty for their increased output and commitment to student success, but then they deviated from the perennial format of their speech. "This year, I'm proud to report a special honor bestowed upon the campus." The auditorium brimmed with anticipation. This must be Zorah's moment, I thought. Zorah took a step toward the podium, and a hush fell over the crowd. "Mount Leipren University," the Chancellor continued, leaning toward the mic, "finally pushed into the number one spot for most accumulated unused vacation days on the entire planet."

The faculty cheered as a wave of ceyah washed over the room. Such a frugal loan word from the Leiprenese. It named a feeling that had become prominent under Renner tutelage. Ceyah is similar to pride, but without the enduring sense of satisfaction, because no record is ever unbreakable, no limit impossible to surpass. Ceyah is that brief moment you celebrate before going back to work.

"Now, on to the final event," they said.

The faculty were caught up in their own success, but I kept my eyes on Zorah. They would not ascend yet again this year. They appeared sullen, as if something had broken, as if they had known it would slip from their hands but picked it up regardless, only to watch helplessly when it crashed to the floor. As the lights dimmed, they stepped back to the table and tried to put on a brave face.

Suddenly, my chair began to move. I and Rafa and the others swirled and rotated around one another at center stage. The big reveal had begun. My chair pulled me upstage, and my pulse pounded in the side of my neck. This was the wrong direction. I felt the blood drain from my cheeks, and Rafa rolled beside me. The others enjoyed the view from downstage. I stared at Rafa, and they at me. An uncharacteristic nervous sweat had beaded around their brow. At least if I were being banished as a failed professor, I thought, so were they. But to my relief, the bigger group was then split in half and dragged toward the wings. I and Rafa were pushed through the open space between them, and in a reversal of fortune, the undeserving eight were swept from the stage entirely. I dared not turn around for a final look at my former colleagues.

The spotlights landed on me and Rafa. I stood to receive a handshake from the Chancellor and my sash and crown from Zorah. Rafa received the same in reverse order. This was the moment I had been working toward my entire life. On paper, it was my greatest achievement. I was happy, or I would be, I told myself, once the reality sank in.

Still, there was no denying this competition had taken its toll, and it was far from over. Earning tenure had been a simple sprint. Now, I would need to adopt a new regimen if I wanted to beat Rafa —and if I hoped to avoid Zorah's fate—in this marathon toward the Homeworld.

I unclenched my toes and let my head drop onto the pillow. Rafa rolled off my bed and rebuttoned their shirt.

"That was productive," they said, hopping as they pulled their too-tight and too-short pants up to their waist. "What are you going to work on tonight?"

I usually experienced a renewed clarity as soon as I and Rafa finished, sometimes even a hurried need to start drafting a new lesson plan before they were out the door. But my mind felt mushy.

This rivalry paused twice a week. Wednesdays I visited them, and Saturdays they visited me. The calendar was marked for a strict twenty minutes. I and they toasted to recent accomplishments, in this case tenure, and allowed for a quick release.

"Afraid I'll steal your next great plan?" Rafa prodded.

"Please, you couldn't scoop any idea of mine."

"Then tell me." Rafa almost knocked over a stack of journal articles piled on the nightstand as they bent over to pull on their socks.

I didn't know what to say. For the first time in my career, a blight had spread over the vines where my upcoming ideas usually ripened and waited to be plucked. "Didn't you—" my voice trailed off as an impossible idea skulked around the corners of my consciousness.

"What?"

"Expect the Chancellor to announce Zorah's ascendance last week?"

"The thought did cross my mind."

"They should have ascended last year. To be passed over twice is incomprehensible. If Zorah can't make it, who can?"

"I can," declared Rafa. They never missed the chance for self-promotion.

"Seriously, the Renner have to realize Zorah is unsurpassed in their generation. No one at those old-world Ivies even comes close."

"That entire generation began to slack the minute they got promoted. I and you both produced more plans and better research than Zorah last year. The way I see it, none of them have earned the right to get to know the Renner in person. They were just lucky enough to not have serious competition."

"Still, I wonder—" I sat up and pulled on my undershirt. There was a tear in the seam under the arm. I would have to get this mended.

"Out with it, Charlie. The clock is ticking."

"Maybe ascendance isn't worth it."

I watched their mouth droop a bit. The thought had never crossed Rafa's mind, and it ought not to have crossed mine either. The mere doubt in my voice approached the treasonous.

"That's absurd," Rafa scowled.

"I just mean—" I tried to backtrack. "I thought this would be Zorah's year."

"Yeah, well, it wasn't."

My proposition had been outlandish, mindless, even violent. If I were Rafa, I would have been over the moon, plotting the best strategy to reveal my great mistake.

"It was a dumb thought. Don't pay me any attention."

"Sure thing," said Rafa as they opened the door. They chose not to confront me in private. Their energy would be better spent on a whisper campaign that would slowly erode the high hill on which I currently stood. For now, they shook their head and slipped out the door.

I should have been panicked, or angry, or rushing to preempt Rafa's next move. Right then, for a reason I could not explain, it just didn't seem to matter. The calendar alarm sounded, but instead of getting back to work, I sat on the edge of the bed and stared blankly at the reflective poster of the Homeworld hanging over my desk.

A sea of purple caps and gowns with golden doctoral stripes packed the roof-top deck of the Administration Building. I stood with my back to the party, sipping champagne, and stared out at the campus. The valley shone under flood lights on this chilly evening. Going into the New Fiscal Year, I had to reclaim my sense of purpose.

Looking for inspiration, I turned toward Renner Hall, but the campus lights had imprinted on my vision. I lowered my eyes, blinking away the glare, and noticed a crack in one of the deck boards. It appeared to be quite deep, like a fault line on the verge of fracturing. I traced it as it zig-zagged beneath my colleagues' shuffling feet, but I couldn't see where it led.

I was taking another sip when a hand landed on my shoulder. I recoiled, and champagne dribbled down my gown.

"Charlie, hi, sorry, didn't mean to startle you," said Zorah. They reached for a cocktail napkin and dabbed at the wet spots.

"No worries," I said. "It won't stain."

Still, they folded the napkin and patted at the spot once more. "Why are you standing over here all alone?"

"I'm just in my head tonight."

"I know that feeling."

They noticed the doubt in my silence.

"Seriously," they said, getting quieter as they rested their lower back on the bannister and crossed their arms.

"Did something happen?" I asked cautiously.

"The Chancellor informed me the moratorium on ascensions has been extended indefinitely."

"Let me guess, another unprecedented crisis on the other side of the galaxy means Earthlings have to tighten their belts?"

"Pretty much."

"And by indefinitely, they don't just mean a year or two, do they?" I turned to look back at Renner Hall as I asked. Zorah should have been spending their last night on Earth over there, waiting for the shuttle to pick them up first thing in the morning.

"It could be five, ten years. Maybe never. Who even knows?"

Zorah turned around with me. As their words echoed in my thoughts, the future I had imagined, the one the Renner had promised, slipped from my fingers like a balloon from a child's hand.

I felt dizzy and braced myself on the bannister. "This champagne is strong."

"I don't think it's the champagne," replied Zorah. "A little birdie told me you're also having some doubts."

My face burned, and my shoulders went stiff with the thought of Rafa's version of the events. I tried to strategize a counterattack, still unsure of Zorah's motives. Before I could muster the energy, they reached out and rested their hand on my upper back. Their touch, friendly, released some of the tension and quieted the growing sense of abandonment.

"Rafa, blissfully unaware, approached me the day after your accidental revelation," Zorah said, laughing a bit.

They stood beside me and waited, patiently, as I debated what to say next. Even if this was a trap, I thought, even if confirming Rafa's accusations meant some sort of punishment, I decided to risk it. I couldn't hold back any longer.

"I can't explain it, but this—" I looked around.

"Doesn't seem worth it?"

I almost dropped the glass, so I set it on the bannister. "How did you know?"

"Because, Charlie," they sighed and paused. Exhaustion settled in the crow's feet around their eyes. Meanwhile, Rafa kept to the opposite side of the deck. The busybodies kept buzzing around them, perpetually reconfiguring the dynamics of the swarm. "It's not worth it. Only a handful ever made it to the Homeworld. And the rest, what did they get? What did I get? What will you get? I'll tell you what. Nothing."

Zorah's words confirmed a fear I had so far kept from surfacing.

"The Homeworld is a lie," I mumbled, still concerned I might be overheard. Worse, I realized, is that I would never get the chance to prove to the refined and upstanding citizens of the Homeworld that I was an elevated example, if not an exception, to the human race.

"The Renner withdrew long ago," said Zorah. "Yet, they control every dimension of this little planet from a distance."

"So they don't have to get their hands dirty?"

"Yes, and also to avoid being blamed for the world they built. Today, Earthlings discipline and drive other Earthlings. As professors, I and you play a key role in churning out the managerial class that keeps this system humming along. One of the strategies the Renner developed was to prohibit the use of Earthling languages in the workplace. They believed they could prevent, or at least slow, any nascent sense of solidarity by alienating the workers from one another. Of course, the crushing debt they acquire just to make ends meet and the lack of alternatives keep most people from stepping out of their assigned role. Not to mention the threat of being sent to the mines. Meanwhile, the Homeworld keeps those who are better off shut into the system, running in circles to achieve a vague promise of another world, another life."

"Not just running, but constantly trying to outpace everyone else," I added.

"Right. The Renner never force you to run faster, technically speaking. They don't crank some knob. The faculty here do it to themselves. All in pursuit of a dream that was imagined by another. Meanwhile, the Renner sit back and feast on the fruits of Earthling labor. And every time the Renner move the goalposts, everyone accepts this as a greater challenge. Look at Rafa."

"Between my blunder and your failure, Rafa couldn't be more motivated."

"You can't blame them. I've been in their shoes and acted no differently. Everyone is playing the same game here. But I think, Charlie, like me, you're growing tired," Zorah offered.

"I am."

"You know, you and I really are quite similar."

"Do you think—" I started to say. "Wait." The word order was wrong. "What did you say?"

"You heard correctly, Charlie." Zorah smiled and took my hands in theirs as the unnoticed anagram unscrambled itself. "You and I," they repeated.

Zorah's words sprouted before my feet. Their syntax went against everything I had believed, everything I had been taught. Yet somehow it perfectly described one of the many sensations that had been surfacing since the Promotion Ceremony. I let my toes inch their way toward that new growth. It was soft and squishy, like a bed of moss. Zorah, quite literally, had put me first. Not their work, not their own interests or ambitions, but someone else. I felt light as air and stood tall.

"Yeah, you and I," I repeated slowly. "You and I." I had to untrain my mouth to break the deeply ingrained grammar, but with practice, the words would take shape, and one day I might be able to return that generosity or pay it forward.

Zorah squeezed my hands once more and then, as the final seconds of that year wound down, left me to make a decision for myself.

"In the year 2035," I recited in slowly enunciated Leiprenese, "the Great Navigator discovered a primitive culture with the potential to be molded." I paused. The students, arranged before me in two opposing lines, furiously transcribed my every word. They were competing to reproduce the most accurate text in the least amount of time.

In the interim, Zorah's "you and I" kept rattling around my brain.

I read the next sentence. "Upon contact, the Renner demonstrated the benefits of cultivating a highly intensive culture of achievement."

Such a clunky phrase, "you and I". A more succinct way to express that idea, that connection, had to exist. It was on the tip of my tongue.

"The Great Spaceship dropped through the atmosphere to the wonder of all Earthlings, who freely offered—" I stopped the dictation mid-sentence and looked out at the obedient students. I had to stop repeating the Renner's lessons. This could not go on.

One by one, each raised their head wondering why I had paused for so long.

"Professor, you may continue," the student currently in first place informed me.

I would not go on. There were no words, in Leiprenese or any other language, that could reach across the void and explain to the students I had trained so well what I was about to do. Out of habit, I gathered my notes from the podium, tucked them into my briefcase, and walked silently out the door.

I could hear the disbelief in my wake. A few sat frozen. Others buzzed with gossip, and one suggested they follow me outside.

Renner Ridge surrounded me. Even from my relative elevation at Leiprenese Hall, it was impossible to look off into the distance. There was no horizon here, only a barricade sealed by Renner Hall. If someone happened to let their gaze wander beyond themselves, their work, and their rank, the building's shiny walls would grab their attention and redirect it toward thoughts of the Homeworld.

That was where I needed to go.

The Hall could only be accessed by a narrow staircase. I hopped the gate. Before my little stunt, no one had imagined a need for greater security. The minds of each member of this campus blocked access better than any physical barrier.

My gown whipped in the wind as I plodded along. I clutched my cap reflexively, but then I ripped it from my head and tossed it over the railing. It soared above the campus for quite some distance before landing in a thicket. A student, still playing by the rules, rushed over to retrieve it.

Higher and higher, I climbed until I finally reached the launch pad next to Renner Hall. For a second, I saw myself from the outside. I laughed at the absurdity of it all. Here I was trespassing on consecrated grounds during a workday for no apparent reason.

Up close, Renner Hall did not look the same. The façade was scratched, and the shiny surface only coated the walls that were visible from below. The others, made of concrete, were covered with mold and old growth. I had an urge to smash the windows, but I changed my mind when I noticed they were made of plexiglass.

For the first time, I saw Renner Hall for what it was. A vacant tower. A few crumbling walls coated in fool's gold. A monument to deception and exploitation. A cardboard box left out in the rain.

I walked back to the stairs, peered over the railing, and saw bodies pouring out of every building. They gathered around a central figure—Rafa—who steered the swarm's bewilderment. They directed outraged hands and fingers to point in my direction.

A corrupting influence on such impressionable minds!

A defender of society hiding in plain sight!

Meanwhile, the briefcase tugged with the weight of the world below. *Why was I still holding on to this?* The lesson plans and ungraded essays begged for their release, so I popped the clasps and dumped out the contents. Pages and pages burst from their folders and fell out of rank. As the papers hung over each stunned student and staff member, time itself lurched to a halt.

An irreversible first strike, for those below. From here, a moment to contemplate the slow beauty of my disruption.

The sheets fluttered in the wind. Some drooped toward the crowd and caught in treetops, while others glided into the distance. I dropped the empty briefcase and stripped off the gown as I walked to the other side of the launch pad. There, I climbed on the railing and sat with my feet dangling over the far edge. My idleness occupied a forbidden space and time. But it also revealed a horizon that had been missing from my life.

A hand touched my shoulder, and I steeled myself to be cuffed and dragged back down the mountainside.

"Charlie," said Zorah.

"Don't try to talk me out of this," I shouted, but they shook their head.

"I had no such intention." They climbed on the bannister, took a seat beside me, and removed their cap. They had not come to stop me. They had been waiting for me to join them. "You and I sure are going to give them something to talk about today."

"*You and I.* My mind resists that phrase at every syllable, and yet it feels somehow right to foreground you instead of me."

"*I and you* wasn't always the grammatical order," Zorah explained. "It was imposed by the Renner in the early days, and I thought, just maybe, you'd have noticed in that last article you wrote."

"Oh really? No, there are no oddities in the use of pronouns in your recorded speeches."

"In the ones that still exist. Many documents from the first years were purged, and by the time you were born, those changes had already taken hold. They were taught to you in school and in every interaction. They even reflected the hierarchies and values built into the environment all around you. But language cannot be controlled completely from above."

"It was so disorienting, and yet freeing, when you said 'you and I'. You named this thing I couldn't quite put into words, this thought I didn't know how to express. I sensed there had to be more than this competition, this life of working without rest. There had to be more than my little academic achievements."

"See, you get it."

"You're the one who invited me to hop off the treadmill. There was no going back after that."

"Indeed."

Zorah took a deep, renewing breath.

I did the same.

It was quiet here, calming. There was an ease to it all.

Mountains stretched before Zorah and me. I could have stared at those blue ridges for days. No roads or trails pointed the way. No rope guided my descent. Only a steep drop, and beyond that, the open woods. Not long ago, the thought would have terrified me.

"What now?" I asked. The timeless questions had resurfaced. "How do we undo all of this? How do we build something better?"

"*We*, Charlie. You do know that word after all."

"We!" I shouted in surprise at myself. The ancient pronoun had crept up from the back of my mind. Not *I and you*. More than *you and I*, even—Zorah and I became *we*. The word echoed in the distance. So elegant and unassuming. It joined, not through isolating chains of conjunctions that mark order, but by allowing individuals to come together in a collective syllable.

We sat here together. We were exhausted and burned out. We let ourselves, *ourselves!* We let ourselves rest, shoulder to shoulder, and for a moment, we chose not to do anything at all.

Our collective inaction sent a shudder through the campus behind us. We had opened a hairline fracture in the foundations of this place. We had cracked open a door. There would be no guarantees, of course. It would take more than two to change the world, for we could easily be discredited, cast out, and replaced.

Yet, for us, being tired together formed the strongest bond we had ever known. This was our first real lesson, one we were writing together. Ours was a small offering, intended as only one of many more to come. For now, though, we would wait here on the cusp of something unforeseen as long as we could. We would invite others to take a seat beside us. To rest and linger here for a while. To contemplate a new sense of time, one that did not consume, but endured.

And after that, we just might have the strength and the stillness of breath to speak with one another and imagine where we go from here.

See Jason A. Bartles's story "Leiprenese 101" online at Metaphorosis.
If you liked it, leave a comment. Authors love that!
Remember to subscribe to our e-mail updates so you'll know when new stories are posted.

About the story

Burnout. Achievement culture. The trivial matters that become blood feuds among academics. Administrators who rebrand the defunding of public education as a meritocracy. These are just some of the things that had been weighing on my mind going into 2020. If there's a very small silver lining to be found amidst the ineptitude and indifference toward human suffering that has been on full display, the pandemic brought some modicum of clarity to a number of issues for me. In many ways, "Leiprenese 101" is the result of a lot of processing that took place in quarantine.

There's this thing called "the post-tenure blues". When I describe it, it sounds like the epitome of privilege, especially in the context of the orchestrated crisis in academia. In the wake of the 2007-08 economic collapse, neoliberal administrations across the country took advantage of the situation to gut higher education. It's a very complex scheme, but the gist is that universities have been taking on massive amounts of debt to replace public funding, and they pass those costs on to students in the guise of tuition. Meanwhile, doctoral programs that rely on student and adjunct labor to teach most of their undergraduate curriculum for cheap continue to churn out highly qualified teachers and scholars for a job market in which, in a good year, not even half will have a chance at a tenure-track job. As one of the lucky few to get a tenure-line job (and it really was luck), the reality today is that if you don't get tenured, you will be unlikely to find another tenure-track job. That pressure only exacerbates the performative nature of academic culture in which people send e-mails in the middle of the night as if to prove how much harder they are working than everyone else.

Tenure should feel like a celebration. It's an incredibly privileged position, and for a gay kid from West Virginia, even more so. But the post-tenure blues are real. Once you get to the other side, the burnout mixes with the realization you don't know what else you want out of life. Then you hear how whiny it sounds to complain about this situation. It's an exhausting negative feedback loop.

Most of these ideas were present in some form in the earliest drafts, and anyone who has studied neoliberalism or read Byung-Chul Han's *The Burnout Society*—which I highly recommend—will recognize the ideas that structure the world in my story. However, the original spark was something like the desire to tell the story of a language teacher who comes to regret working for the aliens that colonized Earth.

A question for the author

Q: What is your favorite fairy tale and why?

A: Rub-a-dub-dub, three men in a tub! What's not to like about that? Okay, I suppose that's cheating. It's a nursery rhyme, not a fairy tale, technically speaking, but since this answer doesn't have to go through peer review, I'm sticking with it. Though the lyrics have changed over the centuries, I can't help but hear it as a quintessential queer image hiding in plain sight, and it always makes me wonder: Who are these gents? Why are they floating out to sea? Just how big is that tub? And importantly, is there room for one more?

About the author

Jason A. Bartles, originally from West Virginia, now calls Philadelphia home. He lives with his husband and two dogs, a blue-eyed husky and a pit-mix who will lick your face off. He teaches Latin American literature and Spanish at a regional university, but he promises his stories are entirely fictional.

jasonabartles.wordpress.com, @jabartles

The Nocturnals

Mariah Montoya

Part 1

Damien had discovered the marsh after their last Move.

A portion of his school's portable fence had been damaged during the long trek from west to east: during recess, he and his friends could now wiggle between crooked wires and flump onto the soil beyond the playground turf. Mrs. Zemukil never noticed them sneak away. She was usually yelling at Timby Jenkins for some shenanigan or the other. Right now, Timby was near the shiny new playset, selling cups of his own color-dyed piss to classmates.

Mrs. Zemukil's shrieks faded as Damien and his friends crept through the weeds around the school's storage shed, giggling. The great marsh glimmered behind it, oozing with promise: it was here they always found all sorts of new bugs and spiders squirming beneath the mud.

"Okay, we've only got half an arcsec!" Damien told his friends when they reached the edge. They thudded to their hands and knees. Mud spattered their pants, but that was okay; last time Mrs. Zemukil had asked where all the filth came from, Timby Jenkins had asked her where all *her* filth came from, and Mrs. Zemukil had been quiet about the mud ever since. Damien didn't like Timby Jenkins and his pranks much, but bless that boy's heart for saving him and his friends from recess ban. "Whoever finds the biggest one gets to have everyone else's cookie at lunch!" he added, because when sweets were the motivation, they usually found a monster.

The boys all got to work, punching fists through the mud in their search for alien critters. Damien glanced at the sun lodged low in the eastern sky. It was, the clocks read, about twelve degrees from the horizon. Mom said they'd have to Move again soon, when the sun sank two degrees lower and the bells started clanging, but he would be sad to leave the marsh behind. They'd been learning about the planet's rotation in school; if only the Aro spun the other way—if only the sun rose in the east and set in the west like it did for other planets—the days and nights wouldn't last so long. They might be able to survive the night, to Stay, and he'd be able to play at the marsh's edge forever.

But as it was, the night was endlessly dangerous. The night would kill them.

He slid his fingers beneath a thick carpet of moss, trying to locate anything other than slimy sludge. Nothing. The marsh smelled like spoiled eggs, and the same old gnats hovered above its surface. The clattering sound of his classmates playing and screaming wafted over the storage shed, and the sun's lingering warmth bathed his back. The boy kept digging, found a few familiar flopping worms. Then, after a quarter arcsec had passed, he felt a sharp pinch on his fingertip. He withdrew a hand dripping with muck and blood.

"Hey, check it out!" he hollered.

His friends came sloshing over. He showed them his finger, and soon they were all tunneling with sticks and rocks until they excavated the beast: a caterpillar-like beetle with pincers lining its back and a single, bulging yellow eye. As they passed it from palm to muddy palm, the beetle's pincers clamped furiously. Its eyeball began oozing a sour green pus.

"Cool!"

"It looks like a deformed penis."

"Let *me* hold it!"

Damien opened his mouth to announce what he was going to name his discovery, but his mouth stayed hinged open. No sound came out. The creature fell between his fingertips and squirmed back into the mud.

His skin tingled. Goosebumps frosted his neck.

I'm having a reaction to the bite, Damien managed to think, staring wide-eyed at his friends. In the distance, the school chimes clamored. Half an arcsec had passed, but he couldn't move. The tingles scuttled up his body.

"Damien, we've got to go," he heard dimly. Slimed hands clamped around his wrists, tugging him away from the marsh. But the tingles were telling him something now, planting words into his head—not like a voice, but like thoughts, like he was talking to himself.

Go west, where the sun rises every sixty years. We need you in the west, Damien. It will not be scary. You will only be going back the way you and your community came.

His friends were shouting now, shaking his shoulders, but the boy merely repeated it to himself, tasting truth in the words:

I'll go west, where the sun rises every sixty years. They need me in the west. It will not be scary. I'll only be going back to where I came from. The tingles cocooned him, swaddling him in armor made of goosebumps and strange, brilliant new ideas.

I'll go west, where the sun rises. They need me. Not scary. I'll be going back.

Ignoring his friends, the boy shook off their grips and drifted toward the marsh. Going west would be easy. He wouldn't have to squint at the sun. He was headed toward the purple part of sky, where darkness crouched and would welcome him with twilight arms. And *they* were there, the creatures who wanted to tell him something.

Something important.

"Damien!" his friends wailed behind him.

He felt himself trudge toward the bank, his shoes squelching and sinking deep into mud. He threw himself into the marsh, where he treaded thick water, leech-like plants clinging to his skin. There were many things beneath the mottled green surface, bugs he and his friends hadn't dared to discover. He felt them bite his legs and fasten onto his arms, but the pinpricks were only an echo of pain, as if they were happening to someone else, not him.

When Damien finally kicked and clawed his way to the other end of the marsh and crawled up the bank, his body was covered in sucker slugs that had attached themselves to his neck and blood fish that dangled from his elbows.

West. Sun rises. Need me. Scary. Going back.

His friends' shouts were distant now. The school chimes had stopped. Damien left the marsh and his classmates behind, stumbling toward the foothills beyond the community limits, where swaying grass rose high above his head. He barreled into the grasses, away from the sun, toward the darkness that whispered his name.

"Damien Fertheli. Ten years old."

Joah Cadshaw read his notes as he weaved between vendors and whisked down an unnamed dirt street between trailer houses. "Mother: Lupita Fertheli. Father: N/A. Trailer Three-Five-One in the Dirt Slums. Three-Five-One, c'mon, where are you?"

Joah hated the goddamned road developers. They never assigned street names for the smallest trailers at the end of a Move. No, the poor could just clump together in one big marked territory and bicker about which pot to piss in. Joah had been summoned to break up a fight more often than the ice moon rose and fell in the sky.

The trailer numbers weren't in order, either. Joah passed numbers five, four-fifteen, sixty-three... People sat on their portable wood steps watching him through the holes in their sunhats. A few children raced down the rows, hitting an old aluminum can with crooked sticks. One of the kids was naked. A nasty rash had turned his left butt cheek into a bloodberry patch.

"You need something, Mister?" a voice rasped.

Joah looked up, but didn't locate the source of the noise until an old woman banged a saucepan against her wood window-frame. The woman's wrinkled face poked between two flaps of blanket nailed to the outside of her trailer.

"Yes, actually." The sun was half-concealed behind her house, but even at twelve degrees, it still made him squint. When they'd finally stopped Moving to set up camp here a little more than a year ago, it had been at a twenty-two degree angle in the sky: fierce and hot and blinding. Joah had always shuddered to imagine ninety degrees, when the sun would blaze directly overhead. "Do you know where Lupita Fertheli lives?" he asked the woman. "Her son, Damien, went missing about seven moon cycles ago."

"Ah, yes, Lupita." The woman jabbed a thumb to her left. "Just keep walking till you get to the trailer surrounded by rocks— Jarold Hansen likes to mark his shithole with pebbles, it seems— and then make a right. Lupita's is the one with all the mud holes in front." She paused. Scratched her crinkled forehead. "Damien liked to dig."

"Thank you."

Joah strode on, trying not to catch all the eyes staring at him. When he found the mobile home surrounded by holes, he paused. Damien Fertheli had apparently liked to dig until the ground resembled cavitied cheese. Besides the demolished land, though, Lupita's house was nothing remarkable: shabby, stained white trailer, its wheels sunk in mud, sheets for curtains.

The door opened. A woman flew down the steps, her hair in frazzled knots.

"Oh, thank God you're here! Why'd it take them so long to send someone? You're Detective Cadshaw, right? Come in, come in, please."

The woman took him by the hand and tugged him up the steps, into the dim interior of her home. Joah wiped his hands on his pants when she released him—her fingers had been gloved with cold sweat—but Lupita Fertheli didn't notice; she was too busy fussing over the fire stove, trying to pour him a cup of tea with shaky hands.

"Mrs. Fertheli, it's okay. I'm not thirsty. Please just sit down."

"Okay. Yeah, okay."

They sat at the cramped table, facing each other. Joah brushed aside some crumbs and slapped down his notes, but before he could start, Lupita spoke through a plugged nose.

"Y-you look familiar, Detective. Have I seen you before?"

"No," Joah said automatically, but he felt a chill despite the stuffiness of the trailer. This woman probably *had* seen him before. In the newspaper headlines. Or maybe she had been in the crowd lining the High Road during the incident itself. But that had been years ago, before the last Move, too long ago for strangers to remember the details.

When Lupita nodded absentmindedly, Joah cleared his throat, whipped out his pen, and looked down at his notes.

"Okay, I have here that your son, Damien, never came inside from recess seven cycles ago. He was playing with friends off school grounds. All his friends returned to the school saying that he'd wandered off without them."

"Yes, yes." Lupita tugged at a hangnail with her teeth. Her eyes were puffy, like half-moons hiding behind swollen pink clouds. "That's what Rayna Zemukil said, anyway. I never got to talk to Damien's friends. Apparently, they were all upset and wanted to go home. But look, I know Damien wouldn't just... wander off. I—I think maybe the N—"

"Do you remember what Damien was wearing, Mrs. Fertheli?" Joah said, cutting her off.

He knew what she had been about to say. At the word *Nocturnal*, his blood always seemed to freeze beneath his skin. Parents *always* wanted to blame their runaways on the Nocturnals, but the Nocturnals only chose one victim a year, and it was never a child.

Lupita didn't respond. She stared at him wide-eyed, and Joah saw his hunched silhouette reflected in her glassy pupils. Fresh tears shined them.

"What was Damien wearing, Mrs. Fertheli?" Joah repeated gently.

"I think it was—yes, it was his green shirt with the cat on it. He always wanted a cat. He loves how wild they are, but I—I always told him no. I shouldn't have told him no."

"It's okay," Joah said. He paused. "Can you give me the names of Damien's friends?"

"Y-yes, sure. There's Pedar Montrone. Cale Lyle. Sampson—I don't remember his last name. I'm not sure Damien ever said. And then he always talked about Timby Jenkins. I don't think they were actually friends, but maybe you could interview Timby too?"

"Timby Jenkins," Joah repeated, jotting the name down in his notes. "Thank you, Mrs. Fertheli. Now, tell me—what's Damien's behavior been like lately? Has he been acting out—throwing tantrums or avoiding you? Showing any other signs of distress?"

"No." Lupita blinked up at him. She grabbed the swaying tail of the sheet hanging from her window, pressed the cloth to her nostrils, and blew.

"Can you tell me about Damien's father?" Joah said, trying to avoid looking at the crusted red bulge of her nose.

"No, I can't." Tears leaked from the swollen humps of Lupita's eyes. "I can't tell you about Damien's father because this has nothing to *do* with his father. Damien wasn't acting out. He was a happy boy. He'd never leave his friends or his school or *me*."

"Lupita," Joah started.

"*No*. Detective, I know you want to uncover some shit reason why my son ran away, but he didn't run away. I'm telling you—just like I told Rayna Zemukil—I think the... I think *they* got him." She lowered her voice to a nasal whisper. "The *Nocturnals*."

"Listen, Lupita." Goosebumps tickled Joah's neck, but it was no longer an iciness that flooded the pit of his stomach; it was heat. An old anger. "The Nocturnals have never infected anybody younger than twenty. They wouldn't have taken a child."

"Says who?" Lupita whimpered. "I'm sorry, Detective, but what if they wanted to change their... their *taste* in victims? My baby might be stumbling around in the darkness as we—"

"Your baby is not," Joah said through a carefully clenched jaw, "stumbling around in the darkness. We can *crawl* faster than the sun moves across the sky."

"Exactly. My boy could have walked to the Eternal Night by now."

"He can't have walked to the Eternal Night," Joah said, his voice rising, "because first, the Eternal Night doesn't exist—a night lasts the same as a day, thirty years. It's not eternal. Second, there's twelve degrees between us and the first signs of darkness, which means your boy would have to walk more than a thousand kilometers just to reach *sunset*. I don't know if you've ever been at zero degrees, Mrs. Fertheli, when the sun is sitting on the horizon —"

"Of course I haven't," whispered Lupita, pressing a palm against her heart.

"Imagine all those times the sun's hidden behind a tree or a hill or something, then. Even when it's sunset, there's still light outside. Sure, pink and purple light, maybe strange light, but *light*. Which means even if the Nocturnals had infected your boy, he *wouldn't have reached the darkness* by now, okay? He can't have —"

But this time, it was not Lupita Fertheli who cut Joah off. This time, the sound that crashed over them was more piercing and terrible than a grieving mother's pealing wail.

Both Joah and Mrs. Fertheli clapped hands over their ears. No, it couldn't be. Joah checked his wristwatch. The hand hovered steadily at twelve degrees. He yelled at Lupita over the swelling noise of the bells.

"What's your clock say?"

Lupita fumbled for a timepiece behind her and thunked it onto the table.

"Twelve degrees!" she screamed.

It was too early—two degrees too early—for the Moving bells to ring. The bells were only supposed to clang across the city when the sun had reached a ten-degree angle in the sky, when the first faint signs of pink laced the clouds; they still had about ninety moon cycles until that happened. *Why* the bells were ringing now...

"Excuse me, Mrs. Fertheli."

Joah jumped up, bounded out the door, and raced down the nameless streets, pushing past streaking kids and shouting adults who had fled their trailers.

Three Moves ago, when they had set up base near an oil reserve, the warners had thrashed their bells through the open windows of moving vehicles. Now, however, the warners stampeded throughout the community on horseback, weaving between alleys with their brass bells held high above their heads.

"Pack your things!" one bellowed now, his voice hardly distinguishable over the clanging. He kicked his mare, who came trotting down the slum streets. Joah and the other onlookers stumbled back to avoid being trampled. "Check your wheels!" the warner called. "Time to Move! General Deckler's orders! Pack your things!"

When the warner, his horse, and the cacophonous bell had rounded a corner, Joah hurtled his way out of the maze-like Dirt Slums and onto the edge of the black-tarred High Road.

He could think of only one man to go to for answers, a man he hadn't spoken to since his own name had glowered on the front page of newspapers:

The leader of the community. Joah's ex-boss.

General Aoif Deckler.

"Excuse me, sir, we're not taking visitors at the moment."

Joah stopped mid-stride to look at the secretary behind the office's marble front desk—or, at least, the desk looked like marble, though it was speckled with gold. The miners must have found a new type of rock since they had settled here almost a year and a half ago. The secretary herself looked fairly new too.

"Look." Joah turned back and leaned against the marble. The secretary's cup of pens rattled as the bells continued wailing outside and footsteps stomped on the floor above their heads. "You can't have been here long. I'm Joah Cadshaw. I used to work here. For General Deckler. I was a retriever."

"I'm sorry, sir," the secretary said, with a brave quiver of her chin, "but there's only been one retriever who got relieved of duty in the last five years, and he's not allowed here."

"Yeah, I am," Joah grunted.

He turned away from the secretary's stutters, took the stairs two at a time—why Deckler insisted on *stairs* was beyond Joah; it had always made Moving a hell of a battle—and rounded the corner, to Deckler's office.

Without pausing to knock, he hurled open the door and saw Aoif Deckler, with his white sideburns and boxy build, bent over a table, talking rapidly to a female assistant. They both turned to stare at him. The assistant's eyes widened as she took in Joah's panting figure.

"Joah," Deckler said. His salt-white eyebrows raised for the tiniest second of surprise. Then, in typical Deckler style, he recovered from the shock and boomed, "Get over here, Joah, we need you! Thank God you're here. I was *trying* to find someone to go with Crane."

"Why the *hell* are the bells ringing, Deckler?"

Joah hurried to the table, which was strewn with various maps and documents. Deckler's office was a mess. His desk had been rammed against the table to increase surface space, papers littered the carpet, and all the awards and certificates usually pinned to his wall had been crudely taken down, so that empty nails spotted the plaster. Only one poster still hung above a filing cabinet, but Joah didn't want to look at the hunched, many-eyed drawing of a Nocturnal.

"What is it, Deckler?" Joah asked, moving closer.

"Look." Deckler thrust a thick finger at the map that he and his assistant had been poring over. "The scouts came back just an arcsec ago. Brought bad fucking news. The High Road has been destroyed. Must've been a quake. There's a deep fissure in Aro's ground, about seven meters wide and two kilometers deep. Cracked the High Road in two. Maybe the retrievers' crew could cross it with the right equipment, but our whole *community*? Forget it."

Joah peered at the map, where new red ink marked the fissure the scouts had found.

The High Road, which Joah's community had been taking for decades, and which his ancestors had used the last time they had set foot on this continent, was dotted by fading black, showing the endless trek from west to east. They had been about to reach the Green Sea, a vast body of water Joah had only heard stories about, but the red ink sliced across the familiar dotted line, blocking their path.

Joah traced the fissure with his finger.

"Looks like it runs, what, five thousand kilometers north?" he asked.

Peculiarly, he didn't feel the panic that Aoif Deckler seemed to feel. An iron sense of calm had sunk deep into his stomach. Ever since he had been relieved of his retrieving duties, he'd hated how the world kept its sickly slow spin and the people around him kept their plastered smiles, as if everything were okay, despite what had happened to him.

Now here at last was proof that something was wrong.

That the world was breaking apart.

"Yes, five thousand kilometers north," Deckler said. "That's how far the scouts went, anyway, but they said the fissure kept going. And it runs about a thousand kilometers south. Then the fissure tilts southeast and finally—right here—eastward." He pointed at the curve of the red ink, which was like the graceful arc of a bowl.

Elegant, for a quake's doing, Joah thought.

Deckler massaged the bridge of his crooked nose.

"At the rate we travel as a group—twelve measly kilometers a moon cycle—we won't make it to the sea in time. We're running out of working vehicles, not to mention fuel. The horses aren't breeding fast enough. Even if we head south right now—which we're going to, that's why the bells are ringing—the sun'll go down before we make it to the end of the fissure."

Joah said nothing. *Maybe Lupita Fertheli will get to experience sunset after all*, he thought.

"We won't have time to backtrack and continue taking the High Road," Deckler continued. "We'll have to keep going east into uncharted territory. At least, we'll have to if we don't want to get swallowed by the Eternal Fucking Night."

Joah suppressed an urge to give his ex-boss the same lecture he had given Lupita.

"And then when we reach the sea," Deckler sighed, "who's to say we'll have enough time to build ships? The Nocturnals might just find themselves a *feast*. C'mon, Joah. Why aren't you saying anything? Say something or I'll lose my goddamn mind."

"Look," Joah said obediently, "we'll pick up the speed. Some people may need to abandon their things to lighten the load for the horses, or else we'll travel in waves. The first wave can go on ahead, and the horses can come back for the second wave. Sunset won't kill us. It's a few cycles *after* sunset... that's where... where *they* live. Trust me, I'd know," he added.

"I *know* you know, Joah," Deckler said. "Which is why I need you now. You working on any assignments for the law enforcement office?"

"Yeah, I'm searching for a missing kid. Never came in from recess. Why?"

"Forget the kid," Deckler said.

"What?"

Deckler glanced at his assistant, who Joah looked at properly for the first time. She was round-faced and pink with excitement. A silver pin gleamed on her uniform over her chest.

Ah, she was a recent graduate of the Retrieving Institute. Not an assistant.

"Look, Joah," Deckler said, "I'll tell your command that it's an emergency and I need you. They'll understand. Don't argue," he growled as Joah opened his mouth. "The kid'll be found during the Move, mark my words. If he's hiding in some alley, he'll come to light when the buildings around him start rolling. If somebody's got him, they won't have him for long. You can't keep a secret when you're constantly Moving. Secrets only stay secret if they're stagnant, and God knows our people can't stay stagnant. He'll be found."

"I—what do you want me to do, then?" Joah asked stiffly. Behind Deckler's blocky shoulder, the graduate was wide-eyed, leeching onto every word.

"You were the best retriever I had, Joah. Until the incident. You could find anyone within a thousand kilometers: miners who'd strayed too far, hunters trapped in a ravine, the Infected. Well, now we have *hundreds* of miners and hunters and gatherers who don't know the bells are ringing early. I've sent out all my retrievers, every single one, to go find and warn them, but I don't have enough. That's why I'm sending her—" He jerked a thumb at the graduate "— but I need someone to go with her. Someone experienced. She doesn't have a partner yet, see."

"You want me to go retrieve people again," Joah said, his stomach clenching.

"Yes. Joah, this is Misla Crane." The graduate smiled at him again, bouncing on the balls of her feet. "Misla, you're going to do everything he says, understand? I'm sending you two west. To track down the grahsm miners and oil scavengers. You remember that cylindrical tower we passed on the High Road? The one every damn man, woman, and child wanted to gawk at?"

"Yes, General," Misla Crane said eagerly.

"Good. Should be some scavengers around there searching for oil in an old reserve nearby. They left on horseback, but I'm sending *you* two in one of our last iron steeds so you can get to them within a few cycles. Should be about seven degrees where they're at, but they won't be planning to leave till five degrees." He surveyed them both with gray-eyed sharpness. "It's your two's job to tell those scavengers and miners they need to Move *right now*. You'll stick together, and you'll head back in ten cycles. Am I clear?"

Misla Crane nodded. When Deckler glared at him, Joah hesitated, grunted, and bowed his head, all too aware that he was leaving the case of Damien Fertheli behind.

"Perfect. Now get the hell out of my office," Aoif Deckler said.

The noise of the early bells dimmed as Joah and Misla Crane drove away from the city in a boxy steed, its hooded back filled with duffels of clothes, canned food, blankets, weapons, and canteens of water. They took the High Road snaking through the foothills, where bugs buzzed and the grass occasionally rustled with some kind of scurrying animal.

Nobody knew how the High Road had originated, only that it had always been there, stretching from coast to coast, constantly repaired by those who used it: Joah's people, who called themselves the Sunsetters, and the Sunrisers who migrated on the opposite side of the world and sometimes left words carved on stones to mark their passing. Occasionally, whenever they found a place to settle, they'd find squashed and crinkled cans littering the ground like community shit that wouldn't disintegrate, and they'd know the Sunrisers had found this a good spot to Stay for a couple years too.

But there were rumors of others besides them and the Sunrisers. Others besides the Nocturnals, even. Growing up, Joah had heard stories of the Leather Skins, a people who could endure the scorch of ninety degrees, who roamed freely throughout the day as they pleased, their tough skin protecting them from the sun's death rays.

Must be nice, Joah had thought as a boy, *to live in midday. You wouldn't have to Move as often.* He'd wondered why his community of Sunsetters couldn't just catch up with the Leather Skins, keep away from the dangers of night.

Joah's granddad, a retired retriever, had answered this question by dropping a purple squash in their stove and allowing it to crisp. When he'd speared the burnt squash with a poker and offered it to Joah, he had said, "You got leather skin, boy? Or would you blister?"

Joah's dreams about taking the High Road to midday had disintegrated. And now it seemed a portion of the High Road itself had disintegrated, severed by some unknown force.

"I wonder if the Nocturnals use this road," Misla Crane said now, jolting Joah from his reveries. Somewhere in the dim caverns of his mind, he realized she'd been chatting the whole time. "I wonder if they have, like, a Road Repair Crew." She laughed. "Or Traffic Control."

"Mmmm," Joah grunted.

There it was again, that word—*Nocturnals*. Better to focus on driving than let the word bind him to his old anger and the terror that simmered beneath it.

The iron steed bounced as its wheels cruised over rocks strewn across the road. It had been years since Joah had operated a vehicle, but his movements were mechanical. He was *made* for this kind of constant forward movement. If only the miners could find more fuel for the tanks, more steel and latex for vehicle repairs...

Misla Crane, shattering his thoughts again, made a second stab at conversation.

"I know I look old for a graduate. I'm twenty-six. But I used to live with someone who didn't want me to be a retriever, so I had a late start."

She smiled at him. Joah kept his eyes on the High Road, fingers curled tight around the steering wheel. The sound of the bells had been swallowed by chirps, buzzing, and the swishing of grasses in the wind. It didn't help that Misla had rolled down her window, so that warm air channeled inside, thrashing their hair and stinging their eyes.

"Are you going to ask why I decided to become a retriever anyway?" Misla said after a stretch of silence. The sleeves of her uniform flapped in the wind and whipped her in the face.

"No," Joah said.

"And why not?"

"I already know how the story'll go." Joah had made up his mind that it would be best to quiet her. He had no interest in entertaining strangers with polite chattering, especially if that snaking whisper of a *word* was going to be tossed into the conversation as casually as sugar cubes in tea. "You realized your 'true worth' or 'full potential' or something fantastically uplifting like that. Frankly, I don't really care."

This, apparently, wasn't enough to quiet Misla Crane. As the High Road crested a hill and they rattled downward between patches of tall, swaying shrubs, she snorted with giggles.

"That was a good one, Detective Cadshaw. I get it. You want to play asshole."

Joah tightened his grip on the steering wheel. He didn't answer.

"Look," she said, "Your cranky mask doesn't frighten me, okay? I know you're unhappy about doing this mission, because last time you came back from retrieving, your wife—"

"Stop," Joah said.

"And I really *am* sorry about your wife." Misla's hair flapped backward as the wind gushed through her open window. "It was horrible, what happened to her. I was there when it happened, you know. In the crowd. I—"

"Stop it," Joah said. His old anger flashed beneath his ribcage.

"But I bet you missed getting away, seeing the parts of the world we pass so quickly through," Misla continued rapidly. "It's part of the reason I—"

Joah roared. He rammed a foot on the brakes, and Misla Crane was finally quiet.

They had turned around a bend. A sea of white, like a blinding cloud, blocked the High Road before them, cutting across their path just like that vicious red slash on Deckler's map. In the midst of the white, thousands of curled slices of orange glowered at them.

"Are those...?"

"Birds," Joah grunted.

It was a horde of them, perched on the High Road and in the grasses surrounding them: skeletal, leathery, and blinding, it was as if their skin had been slapped by the moon. Their beaks were sharp and pale, but their eyes were like curved slits of sunset-orange.

"Well, there's your Traffic Control, Crane," Joah muttered.

"I've... I've *seen* these birds before," Misla said, hushed. "Among the cotton trees at the edge of the forest. Right before we passed that tower General Deckler was talking about. They were picking at the cotton. For nests, I think."

As they stared, one of the birds gave a crowing warble. Joah squinted at it. He *hadn't* seen these creatures before, but he knew at once what they were doing in the grasslands: their homes, the cotton trees, had been drowned out by the thirty-year night.

The birds were Moving.

"Misla," Joah said quietly, "roll up your window."

"What?" She turned to look at him. He saw himself reflected in her pupils, and was momentarily distracted. But then his peripheral vision caught movement among the birds.

"Roll up your fucking wind—"

As if this were a signal, the birds on the High Road burst toward the vehicle like a white sea. More exploded from the shrubs, their leathery wings flapping like boat sails. Before Joah could so much as twitch, one had stuck its neck through Misla's open window and begun tugging at her shirt with that pale, curved beak. Its wings thumped against the side of her door.

Joah punched his pedal to the steed's floor and ripped through them. There was a dull series of *thuds* as the ones before them were pummeled, but then Misla was screaming. The bird clinging to her hadn't let go; its wings flapped frantically as it tugged at her uniform, and now more birds were poking their necks through the window, screeching.

They wanted cotton.

"Your shirt. Just give them your shirt!" Joah said.

Misla shrieked as the bird ripped a strip of cloth from her body. One-handedly, Joah ripped off his own tunic and flung it into the abyss of snapping beaks, hoping it would satisfy them, but they only continued pecking at her, and now he was almost veering off the High Road.

He jerked the wheel back. Left and right, those curved beaks rammed into the glass, causing pebble-sized chips in the windows. A sudden violent *crack* in the windshield obscured Joah's vision, and he swerved to narrowly avoid a crooked tree bowing over the High Road. Misla panted, practically playing tug-of-war with her shirt now. One of the birds had ripped it until it resembled a frayed blanket, but she hugged a sleeve to her bare chest.

"Let *go*," Joah hissed. "Let go, dammit."

"No, no, no," she said, gritting her teeth.

Cursing, Joah reached across her lap and helped jerk her arm back inside. He twisted her window crank until the glass slid to a close. The birds were dispersing now, many having been bashed by the steed's steel mouth, others flapping out of harm's way, unable to keep up.

Misla sat back, panting. All that remained of her shirt was a tattered slip of fabric draped around her left shoulder. Her neck and arms had been pierced in various places, the bleeding cuts like oozing half-smiles, but Joah's gaze was inadvertently drawn to her chest: right beneath the underwire of her torn bra, a burn scar as big as a dinner plate marred her skin. It was a raw, flaring pink, bumpy and textured with lines like veins.

"Go ahead, keep staring," Misla muttered, crossing her arms over her breasts and looking out the window as the last of the birds gave a final squawk and fell behind. "You're the first one to see it. I hope you feel honored."

Joah forced himself to focus on the twisting road before him as they bounced over rocks, his cheeks warm with the guilt of looking at something she had so obviously tried to hide. He wanted to tell her to put some antiseptic on the fresh cuts, but his words got tangled on the way out of his mouth.

"What happened?" he asked quietly, fully expecting her not to answer.

She surprised him, wiping her tears with her remaining slice of sleeve.

"When I left my partner a few years ago, he—he didn't want me to leave."

"Didn't want you to..."

"Leave, yes. He threw a lantern at me. It shattered and... well, you can see what it did."

Lantern. The word was vaguely familiar. Joah imagined orange, sparkling glass.

Misla smiled weakly.

"It's what the miners invented to see underground, where the sunlight can't reach. He—my ex's dad had been one. A mineworker. My ex, he liked to remember his dad by nailing these thick black blankets over all his windows to keep the house dark. Like a cave. He lit candles and oil lamps for light. He taught me how to make fire out of friction and a whisper. But then I decided to leave, and—well, he decided to use his light against me."

Joah felt his jaw pop. He was suddenly glad, for the first time since joining, that he worked for the law enforcement office instead of the retrieving unit now.

"What's his name?" he said immediately. "I can turn him in when we get back. Unless—did you already tell someone? Is he in jail? If not, Crane, I can put him there."

But Misla just smiled. As they bounced over a rut, she covered her chest with her hands, smearing blood on the top of her chest. "I think it's a little too late for that. But thank you."

Joah swallowed thickly. He had the rest of this mission to convince Misla to report her abuser. For now, she needed bandages to stop the bleeding.

"There's a red case in the back," he said, eyes flickering toward the cuts on her arms and hands. "You'll find some tape and antiseptic cream in there. And take a couple of those green capsules while you're at it. It'll relieve the pain."

"I don't need—" Misla began.

"*Now*, Crane," Joah growled. "Deckler told you to do everything I say. Find a couple of new shirts for both of us while you're at it too. I packed some in my duffel."

She relented and turned, rummaging in the back. As the ravine to their right sunk lower, however, and the hills to their left became steeper, a flash of green caught Joah's eye. It was brighter than the deadening grass around them, a color he recognized as the exact shade of green the community seamstresses had collected from hillside plants and made into dye in the last year.

He slowed. Parked the steed. There were no signs of the cotton birds. Still, he peered in all his mirrors, ignoring Misla's inquisitive, flushed face, before hopping out and crunching over to what lay like an alien lizard in the dirt, the air stale and brittle against his bare back.

It was part of a ripped shirt, ripped like Misla's had been. It showcased the left side of a cat's slender yellow face. The spray of loose yellow threads was like drooping whiskers.

A green shirt with a cat on it.

His chest hammering, Joah bent and rubbed the fabric between his fingers. He looked around, but there was no sign of the boy who had once worn it—no sign of the boy who must have wandered this far west, who must have been ambushed by the same cotton birds they had. The last remnants of grass patches surrounding them were still.

Joah stood, clutching the shirt. The ice moon was mounting Aro's sky, reflecting UV rays with such intensity that the back of his head pounded. They would have to stop and sleep for a dozen arcsecs until the moon fell again, but as he returned to the steed and told Misla to prepare the beds, Joah had never felt less tired.

Lupita had been right. The Nocturnals had, for the first time ever, infected a child.

Numb, he let Misla take the half-shirt from him to examine it. Despite her earlier chatter, she didn't ask him why he had stopped to pick up a strip of kidnapped cotton. She only turned the fabric over and over. Her fingernails traced the cat's canines etched with white thread.

The Nocturnals have infected a child. The Nocturnals have infected a damned child.

Which meant Joah wasn't leaving the case of Damien Fertheli behind at all. He and Misla Crane were following the boy toward what everyone called the Eternal Night.

And they would, Joah promised himself, find him.

See Part I of Mariah Montoya's story "The Nocturnals" online at Metaphorosis.
If you liked it, leave a comment. Authors love that!
Remember to subscribe to our e-mail updates so you'll know when new stories are posted.

About the story

I first thought of the idea of an "Eternal Night" and the creatures who might live in it during a hike through the woods with my mom and sisters. We had done that thing you should never do, where you look at the next hill or bend and go, "Let's just see what's on the other side of that___, and then we'll turn around," a bunch of times, until you've gone further than you should have. It was only when shadows started checkering the barely-existent trail that we finally did turn around. On the way back, I thought, what if we can't find camp before dark? And then: what if the dark lasts forever?

I overthink things, as you may have guessed. We made it back to our tents before sunset, and no one at the camp had even missed us.

A question for the author

Q: If someone wanted to make an animated series out of your work, based on the title or recurring themes, what would it look like?

A: When I hear the term 'animated series', I tend to think of bright colors and loud noises (Why does Cocomelon come to mind? Help). I'm not a huge fan of that kind of eye-watering intensity, so I'd hope that an animated series based on "The Nocturnals" would depict darker, more subdued colors and sounds—like if the style of Game of Thrones and the tone of The Queen's Gambit had a baby, only in animation form.

About the author

Mariah Montoya is a writer and new mother from Idaho. She loves watching movies and losing at chess games on cold, blustery days. On sunny ones, you can find her running with her husband and a stroller along the Boise river. You can't convince her to use Twitter, but she's sometimes on Instagram @mariah_author.

June

The Secret Keeper

Pauline Yates

Keeping a secret is dangerous. Secrets mess with emotions and can cause illness from depression, anxiety, and stress. The darker the secret, the heavier the burden; it can shorten your life by years. Even Demigods, like Mother and me, need to be cautious when keeping a secret. We're gifted with powers to balance emotions, but if we reveal a secret, we'll suffer its burden. It's crucial we stay strong, because we help battle the gods who draw their power from misery and suffering.

Like Hades. He doesn't mind if a person troubled by a secret dies young. He draws his power from the souls of the dead. And in his realm, the bearer suffers their burden three times worse. But we have Harpocrates, the god of silence, on our side. He uses hope to encourage a bearer to reveal their secret and clear their conscience. To deliver hope, he needs a Secret Keeper, and now I'm sixteen, that's what I'm about to become.

"Repeat after me," Mother says. "Listen without—"

"—judgment and heal the harm," I say, not needing her help. I've committed these vows to heart. "Bind the secret with a Keeper's charm. If by fault I break the faith, suffer the burden the thorns keep safe."

Mother slips a charming binding ring onto my finger. The gold band, engraved with a pattern of linked roses, is the token of a Secret Keeper.

"How much hope do you give?" she asks.

"Only enough to ease their pain; too much hope is a secret's gain." Giving too much hope can make the bearer believe that keeping their secret won't cause them harm.

"And how much burden do you take?" Mother says, her voice low like a brewing storm.

I sigh, wishing Mother weren't so melodramatic. I know what to do. But she expects an answer. "Only enough that hope shines through. Though it harms, they need the burden, too." Removing all the burden takes away the incentive to reveal the secret. That defeats our purpose.

Mother smiles. "Balancing emotions is tricky, but your charm will help."

I raise my hand to the rising sun and admire the ring. The charm curls from the band and weaves around my fingers like a glittering ribbon of light. Feeling its power makes me giddy with excitement.

Now I can heal using a true god's power. Until now, I've only ever had demigod powers to work with. That power allows me to grow herbs from nothing to make the remedies we sell to the local townsfolk. We're the talk around town because of their potency, but we hide our true identity. Mother 'has a green thumb'. I'm 'the homeschooled girl'. Receiving the charm makes me feel like I've graduated.

Lowering my hand, I touch the charm with my finger. It shapes into a glittering rose, Harpocrates' symbol. He created the charm, but I fuel its strength by imagining where I find hope. All Secret Keepers have their preference. For me, hope is in a sunrise, in a rainbow, in seedlings bursting through the soil. Hope is also in my desire to be the best Keeper Harpocrates has ever had.

"The ability to heal the harm caused by a secret is a rare and wondrous gift," Mother says. "However, Harpocrates does not give this charm freely. You are now his servant, as I am, and my mother before me. Harpocrates uses his power to keep hope alive in the world and expects you to do the same. Without hope, the world would fall under the influence of those gods who favor darkness and despair."

She opens her hand, revealing her ring. Years of use make it appear fluid, like a circle of lava. Her charm curls from the band and takes the shape of a burnished gold rose, similar to mine. Mother blows on it. The rose dissolves into a spray of mist that fills the air with a mixture of sweet and pungent perfume.

Turning her hand, the bitter perfume overpowers the sweet. "Polemos draws his power from conflict," she says. "Oizys, misery. Dolos, pain." She tilts her hand again and the sweet perfume overpowers the bitter. "Hestia, compassion, Eros, love, and of course, Harpocrates, hope. There cannot be light without dark, but, tipped out of balance, chaos will ensue." With a flick of her hand, the scents collide. They splatter on the ground like splashes of water.

"Do you think we make a difference?" I ask, tilting my hand so my charm dances on my finger. "We're only demigods. What good is our strength in a battle for power between the gods?"

"You're stronger than you think. The strength of all Secret Keepers runs in your blood. Collectively, we are Harpocrates' most powerful allies. Just be mindful of your vows and replace the burden you remove with hope. You don't want to leave a person feeling as dark and empty as the day Hades stole Persephone from this world."

"Does a burdened soul give Hades extra power?"

"No, but he benefits by receiving a soul quicker. A burden left unattended leads to premature death," Mother says. "Otherwise, he has no interest in warring for power. It's why he lets Persephone return for half the year. But don't dismiss him. Now that you channel Harpocrates' power, Hades will watch to see if you stay true to your vows. He's never broken an oath, and values the laws of morality over everything."

It's a value I share. Secret Keepers heal, they don't harm. Breaking my vow would also desecrate the moral law of our kind.

I glance across the gardens at the many roses that grow between the herbs. All were grown by Mother to keep the secrets she heard. Each sprouts thorns glistening with the secret's burden —guilt, sorrow, remorse. In all our history, no Secret Keeper has ever broken her vows. Suffering any of those emotions would be a deserved punishment. Revealing a secret breaks trust. Breaking trust would destroy hope, and we're tasked with keeping hope alive.

But I needn't worry. Even without history on my side, I'll enjoy showing Hades how committed to my vows I can be.

With the commitment ceremony complete, I revert to my daily chores. Weeding the garden. Growing more herbs to replace those we've used. We're out of dried lavender, so I fetch my gardening clippers. As I snip the stems, my charm grows brighter. It draws hope from my thoughts about lavender's healing qualities.

Customers arrive throughout the day. Some seek a herbal remedy. Others request a pot of living herbs to grow in their gardens. All wander through the gardens while Mother prepares their purchase. All ask the same question on their return.

"Are the roses for sale?"

I've lost count of the number of times I say no because of Mother's fondness for the flowers. I smooth over their disappointment by revealing it's why I share the flower's name. I don't mind the interruptions. Before I became a Secret Keeper, I'd try to guess if a customer had a secret, to no avail. Now that I have Harpocrates' charm, it changes everything.

"Should we hear all secrets?" I ask, after selling a girl my age a jar of comfrey for her mother's arthritis. I'm worried I missed the chance to hear my first secret. The charm grew warm in my hand and my mind filled with an image of the girl kissing a boy.

"Only if you want to," Mother says as she ties a string around the lavender stems to hang them in the kitchen. "Happy secrets can still cause worry, spoiling a surprise, for example. But those secrets get revealed in due course, so we rarely bother. It's the dark secrets that need our help the most." She glances out the front door. "Your chance to learn the difference has arrived."

A woman in her early twenties approaches the house. Her face is pale and the dark circles beneath her eyes suggest something is amiss. My charm curls into my hand, but no images suggesting a secret fill my mind.

"How do you know she has a dark secret?" I ask, wondering how Mother can detect what I can't.

"A lifetime of practice," she says. "Now, always try to coax out their secret first. Offering them someone to confide in works as well as the charm."

"Yes, Mother."

"If they won't tell, which many don't, use the charm. But remember, dark secrets are not pleasant."

"Yes, Mother."

I hurry from the house. Her warning fills my stomach with fluttering butterflies. Mustering my bravest smile, I approach the woman. "Hello. I'm Rose. Can I help you?"

"Hi. I'm Miranda. But everyone calls me Mim." She fidgets with the cuff of her sleeve and looks toward the gardens. "Your roses are beautiful. I admired them from the road." She hesitates, then turns her attention to the herbs. "Would you have a herbal remedy to help with forgetfulness? It's for my mother," she adds. "She has Alzheimer's."

"I'm sorry to hear that. How bad is she?"

Mim sighs. "Stage seven. She's in a nursing home and not expected to live much longer. We're trying to keep her comfortable."

"That must be difficult." I motion her to a table and chairs set up on the porch.

"I have to remind my mother who I am every day," Mim admits, walking with me to the porch. "It's hard."

The butterflies in my stomach close their wings and settle. It appears Mim is just exhausted from caring for a dying parent.

"Gingko will help your mother," I say, pulling out a chair and encouraging Mim to sit. "It's wonderful for helping with memory problems. And chamomile for you, to help you cope. Would you like to try some chamomile tea while I prepare a remedy for your mother?"

"That would be lovely," Mim says, sinking into the chair.

I hurry inside to boil the kettle, but Mother stands with a steaming pot of tea, already made.

"An infusion of chamomile," she whispers, handing me the pot. "I couldn't help overhearing. I'll prepare the gingko. You heal Mim."

"She doesn't have a secret," I whisper. "She's exhausted from caring for her mother."

Mother raises an eyebrow. "Are you sure? What does your charm tell you?"

I glance at my ring. The charm dances along the band, making the ring glow like fire. Frowning at my ineptitude, I grab a cup from the kitchen bench and return to Mim.

"Mother will prepare the gingko, but what about you?" I ask, pouring the tea and sitting in the chair opposite her. "You said 'we', before. Do you have other family members that can help?"

"Only my brother," Mim says, taking the cup of chamomile. "He's not around at the moment. He works away." She gulps her tea, her face turning bright red.

I don't need the charm to know she is lying. I wonder if Mim's secret involves her brother. Though itching to use my charm, I follow Mother's advice and offer Mim someone she can confide in.

Looking toward the roses, I sigh. "I love our roses, too. Do you know the story about Aphrodite's son? He gave Harpocrates a rose in return for keeping his mother's indiscretions secret." I pause. "I learned that in my Greek Mythology lessons."

"I didn't know that," Mim says, lowering her cup.

"It's only a myth, of course. But Aphrodite's son was lucky he found a confidant in Harpocrates. Imagine going through life having to keep something to yourself. It would place so much burden on your conscience."

Mim's cheeks flush redder. "It would be horrible, I suppose."

"Worse than horrible. If you don't clear your conscience in life, you'll suffer the burden three times worse in death."

"You do?" Mim asks, shifting uncomfortably.

"Yes." I sigh again, then clasp my hands and rest them on the table. "But a conscience is easy to clear. Confiding in another person will lift the burden." I pause because Mim looks mortified. "I suppose revealing a secret can be difficult."

"Impossibly difficult," Mim mutters, clenching her hands around her cup.

I reach across the table and place my hand over hers. "If you need to, you can confide in me. I'm a healer, which is the same as a doctor, so anything you say is confidential."

Mim's mouth parts as though she's about to accept my offer and spill her secret. But then she shakes her head. "Nothing's wrong," she says. "I appreciate the help, but I'm just worried about my mother."

"Of course you are," I say. "Keep in mind what I said, though. There's more truth in myth than we realize."

I'm not disappointed I couldn't coax out her secret. That's why Harpocrates gave us the charm. Mim keeps her secret buried for a reason. But she's so overwhelmed by dark emotions, she can't see the damage keeping a secret does to her. What she needs now is hope, to help her see that she doesn't have to suffer alone and in silence.

"It must be difficult caring for your mother on your own," I say, squeezing her hand. As though sensing it's time to go to work, the charm jumps from the ring. It shapes into a ribbon of light and winds around our hands, binding us together as one. Mim can't see the charm; it's invisible to her. But it exudes hope's calm confidence, and the subtle effect helps Mim relax.

"It's hard," Mim says, squeezing my hand in return. "I show her photos to help jog her memory. Sometimes they work. I also play her favorite music..."

While Mim talks about her mother, the charm fades through her skin to go in search of her secret. In what feels like an eyeblink, an image filters into my mind; Mim and a man who could be her twin. The charm has found the secret, but as Mother warned, it's not pleasant—

Mim's brother died two weeks ago, but Mim keeps his death secret. Her mother asks about him every day, and every day Mim says he'll see her tomorrow. Mim thinks it would be better if her mother died hoping to see her son than grieving his death. She hasn't even told the nursing home staff. She doesn't want anyone telling her mother the truth. But pretending her brother is still alive prevents her from mourning. And guilt about the lie to her mother tears her apart.

It takes all my strength not to react to the secret and keep listening to Mim talk about her mother. I wasn't prepared to hear a secret so sad. Squeezing back tears, I trust the charm to know how much burden to remove and how much hope to give. In my distressed state, I'd mess it up.

The charm skims across Mim's conscience. It removes a layer of grief and guilt then replaces them with the hope I conjured when picking the lavender. It gives just enough hope to balance Mim's emotions, and already Mim's tense grip on my hand relaxes. Then the charm carries the burden it removed to me, and curls back into the ring.

It didn't look like a lot, but the grief and guilt hit my heart with a heavy thud. Easing my hand from Mim's, I clasp my hands, drawing comfort from the warmth in the ring. Mim stops talking and heaves a sigh. Then she picks up her cup and finishes her tea.

"This is lovely," she says. "What did you say it was?"

"Chamomile," I say, forcing a smile.

I'm pleased with her lightened mood. Hope shines in her eyes and her troubled expression fades. She doesn't know that I heard her secret, or that the charm removed some of her burdens. But the hope she received should help her consider whether it's worth keeping her secret. What she decides to do is up to her, but at least now she's not blind to her choices.

The layer of dark emotions throbs through my veins. Needing to trap it in thorns, I stand to fetch the gingko so I can send Mim on her way. Mother steps onto the porch holding two paper packets.

"Chamomile tea for you, and gingko for your mother," she says, handing Mim the packets. "The instructions are in the bags. I'm sorry to hear about your mother. The gingko will help make her last days more pleasurable. Be sure to look after yourself, too."

"I will," Mim says, standing and taking the packets. "Thank you, Rose. The tea has made me feel better already." She hesitates. "I liked your story about the roses. It's given me a lot to think about." Then she hurries from the porch, clutching the packets to her chest.

I'm relieved the hope is working, but I'm more grateful for her swift departure. Clutching at the ache in my heart, I hurry to the garden.

Finding space in a garden where none of Mother's roses grow, I crouch and sow Mim's secret into the soil. The ground around my fingers glows the same golden color as the charm. The emotions I took from Mim leach out, leaving me dizzy with relief. Pulling my hands from the soil, I roll back onto my heels and watch the secret grow.

A stem pushes through the soil. Tall and slender, it sprouts long thorns, green with guilt. Grief glistens like dewdrops on the tips. Standing, I cup my hands around the rose that blooms at the top. Red petals release a heavy scent that makes me think of funerals and death.

Stepping back, I study the rose. I'm elated that my first time hearing a secret proceeded exactly as expected, but I'm also uneasy.

Mim's secret was not pleasant, and I may hear darker secrets than hers. Though I trapped Mim's emotions in thorns, I underestimated the impact those emotions had on me. I hope I haven't also underestimated the strength needed to stay true to my vows.

Later in the day, I kneel beside Mother and help harvest evening primrose before the light fades. I drop more seed pods than I collect because I'm distracted by an image of Hades laughing at me for thinking it's easy to keep a secret.

"Mother? Have you ever heard a secret that is so bad, you don't have the strength to keep it?"

"Find the strength," Mother says. "Otherwise you'll destroy the hope you gave and suffer the secret's burden."

I glance around the garden. In the dying light, the thorns on Mim's rose appear to weep. But a rose growing behind hers draws my attention. It's grown in that spot longer than I've been alive. The red petals reek with an intoxicating perfume. The stem is thick and covered in large mottled-red thorns that speak of something nasty. I shudder to think what burden they trap and wonder where Mother finds the strength to keep the secret.

I'm about to ask when the rose wilts and the petals turn gray.

"Mother," I gasp, my heart leaping into my throat. "That rose died."

Mother stands and walks over to the rose. "Hope shines a light on choice, but sometimes that's still not enough to stop a secret going to the grave."

Scrambling to my feet, I follow. I've seen roses die before, but it hits harder now that I'm a Secret Keeper. Death doesn't release us from our vows. We're still bound to keep the secret. And we can still suffer the burden.

A milky-white mist rises from the ground in front of me. Mother grabs my arm and pulls me away. The mist takes the shape of a translucent figure; the ghost of an old man. My charm must enhance my sight. I've seen ghosts before, too, but never with such clarity. I didn't realize the depth of three-fold suffering.

The man's eyes sink into his skull and his mouth hangs open as though dragged down by weights. He reaches for the rose, but the thorns stab holes in his fingers. His face contorts as though feeling actual pain. Turning to Mother, he stretches his arms toward her.

"I've heard your secret," Mother says. "Hope showed you choices and you made yours. Accept your fate and go. I will not help you in death." She waves the ghost away. The mist disperses, but leaves a chill in the air.

"They're drawn here by the scent of their rose," Mother says. Pulling out the entire rose plant, she tosses it onto the mulch pile. "They forget that the cause of their misery in death is that they didn't clear their conscience in life. But don't let a ghost's suffering tempt you to hear their secret again. Emotions in a soul can't be balanced like in a conscience. If you try to remove some burden, you'll end up taking the lot and have to fill the soul with hope. That would allow the soul to be reborn, and Hades would lose his servant. He would demand the Keeper's soul to compensate, and Harpocrates would oblige. He values our servitude, but would strip your power to conjure hope to avoid a war with Hades.

Mother's words are as chilling as the cold left by the ghost. I thought Harpocrates would protect his servants, since we pledged our loyalty to him. To learn he'd strip my powers in favor of keeping good relations with Hades leaves a sour taste in my mouth. I wonder if we're nothing more than pawns in a power game between the gods.

I fall asleep resenting my commitment to a god who will not protect my allegiance and wake to pouring rain. My resentful thoughts must anger Harpocrates; the rain doesn't ease for three days. If he is showing me what a world without hope looks like, he paints the picture well. I stare in dismay at our wrecked gardens. Then I see the woman.

Fighting the wind to hold an umbrella over her head, she sloshes through the puddles at our front gate. Hurrying outside, I welcome her onto the porch. It's Mrs. Peterson, the elegant yet tight-lipped town mayor's wife. When she steps onto the porch, she sniffs back a sneeze.

Mother appears in the doorway behind me. "Good gracious," she says, taking the umbrella from Mrs. Peterson and shaking it dry. "It's no time to be out in this weather, Mrs. Peterson. Rose, boil the kettle. A pot of tea is in order."

Hurrying inside, I light the burner and set the kettle to boil. Mother and Mrs. Peterson sit at the kitchen table.

"My daughter, Rose," Mother says, introducing me.

"Rose, like the flowers," Mrs. Peterson says, placing her purse on the table and extending her hand. "And just as beautiful."

Blushing at the compliment, I shake her hand. My charm dances around my fingers, alerting me to what I should have guessed from her sniffles. Mrs. Peterson has a secret.

"How is your husband?" Mother asks. "Worn out from running the town, I imagine?"

"His work is his life, and he'll not hear otherwise," Mrs. Peterson says. "But the reason for my intrusion..." Her nose wrinkles, then she sneezes into her hands.

I fetch a box of tissues from the cupboard and slide it across the table. Mrs. Peterson plucks out a tissue and blows her nose. "Thank you, dear," she says. "Such dismal weather. As I was saying, my intrusion—"

"It's no intrusion," Mother says. "Rose? The tea?"

I fetch the kettle and make a pot of herbal tea. When I return to the table, my charm jumps into my hand. It weaves around my fingers as though trying to get my attention. Mrs. Peterson's secret must be bad for my charm to react with such intensity.

"I was driving past and saw your roses," Mrs. Peterson says. "I'd like to buy a bunch. My husband likes a well-presented office. Our usual supplier's flowers are lackluster by comparison."

"The roses aren't for sale," I say, giving my usual response.

Mrs. Peterson purses her lips. "If it's a question of money, my husband will pay well."

I glance at Mother, wondering if she detects the tinge of desperation in Mrs. Peterson's tone like I do. Mother keeps her eyes on Mrs. Peterson, but deep grooves form on her brow.

"I can spare a bunch," Mother says. "But I'll accept no payment. There's as much grace in giving as there is in receiving. Rose, would you go to the garden, please? There's a rosebush among the chamomile that could do with a prune."

Frowning, I glance out the kitchen window. There aren't any rosebushes among the chamomile. Maybe Mother wants me to use my demigod power to grow a bunch of roses. I never have, but it would be the same as growing herbs. I leave the kitchen, but stop at the front door, realizing why Mother asks me to go outside.

She's going to hear Mrs. Peterson's secret. If I've angered Harpocrates, *I* should hear the secret and prove I'm committed to his cause. I don't want to live in a world without hope. I was angry earlier because I don't want to be disposable.

"Mother," I say, turning around. "Could you point out the rosebush? I'm not sure which one you mean."

When Mother joins me in the doorway, I lower my voice to a whisper. "Let me hear her secret."

Mother frowns. "I'd rather you didn't. I don't like the feeling I get from Mrs. Peterson."

"Please, Mother. I know she might have a terrible secret, but I can help her, I know I can."

Mother sighs. "Very well." She looks back at Mrs. Peterson. "I'll return in a moment. Rose will keep you company while you wait."

When Mother goes outside, I hurry back to the kitchen and sit at the table. Mrs. Peterson smiles with indifference and gazes about our kitchen. I wonder how I'll engage her in conversation, when it's clear she has no interest in talking to a teenager.

"I love the color of your dress-suit," I say. "The blue is the same shade as a periwinkle flower." I don't know why I thought of that flower when there are so many others to choose from. The periwinkle is also called the 'flower of death'. The vines were used in wreaths for dead children.

"It's my favorite," Mrs. Peterson says, "but its wool-blend is a poor choice of wardrobe in our current weather."

The umbrella didn't stop the rain soaking her clothes. Her dress-suit gives off a damp animal smell. The rain ruined her makeup, too. It's splotchy in places, especially around her left cheek. Wondering why she applied so much makeup during wet weather, I stand and fetch a towel so she can pat herself dry.

"Appearances must be important to your husband if he sends you out for flowers in dismal weather," I say, handing her the towel.

Mrs. Peterson flinches. "When you live in the public eye, appearance is a necessity, not a luxury." She pats her neck dry, then sips her tea. "The tea is delicious. Peppermint?"

"Yes. Infused with ginger. For your sniffles. I'm sorry to sound rude. I sense something troubles you. It helps to talk, did you know?"

She lowers the cup to the table. "You'll find out, young Rose, that even if you had someone to talk to, some things can't be helped."

"I imagine it would be difficult to find someone to trust when you live in the public eye," I say, sliding into my seat. "But you can talk to me. I can keep a secret."

"Can you now?" she says. "What on earth makes you think I have a secret?"

"I sense it. I also feel it troubles you."

She gives me a tired smile. "You're a strange, sweet child, and I appreciate the sentiment. If you must know, it's a demanding job meeting my husband's expectations. I'll say no more on the matter, but I trust you'll never repeat this conversation."

"You can trust me," I say. "But if you don't confide in somebody, the burden your secret causes you now will haunt you three times worse in death."

"There's more to fear in life than in death, young Rose," she says, ruefully. "If being haunted is the price I'll pay for holding my tongue, then so be it."

She returns to gazing about the kitchen, dismissing me completely. I wonder if I've wrecked the opportunity to cast my charm by being too forward. I need to hold her hand, but doubt she'll welcome the consoling gesture. But her manicured fingernails gives me an idea.

"I've never applied nail polish," I say, "but if I did, what color would you recommend?"

Extending my arm across the table, I offer my hand. Mrs. Peterson looks down her nose at my fingers, but then takes my hand in hers and studies my nails.

"Nothing too bold," she says, tilting my hand from side to side. "I prefer pale pinks or pearl, or there's a lovely shade of ivory I've used..."

She prattles on about the best color for teenage girls, remarks on my ring, picks at my nails and advises how best to shape them. While she talks, my charm wraps around our hands, binding us as one. Then it goes in search of her secret. It feels like forever, but in less than a second, images fill my mind. The charm has found the secret, but it's so shocking, I nearly jerk my hand away—

She's not the happily married wife of the hardworking town mayor. She's the victim of a cruel and calculating narcissist. Her self-esteem has suffered because of his controlling and abusive behavior, and years of verbal and physical abuse have left her a broken woman. With her sense of self-worth corrupted, she's lost view of a life away from her husband. She believes that what she endures behind closed doors is her lot in life.

To learn she's a victim of marital abuse staggers me. It explains the other images that fill my mind. She applies extra makeup to cover a bruise on her cheek. She cowers before her enraged husband because the color of her dress didn't match his tie. Her desperate need to find roses is born from a need to keep her husband happy; protection against his abuse.

I fuel the charm with hope drawn from an image of a blue sky after a clearing storm. The charm whips around Mrs. Peterson's conscience. It removes a thick layer of hopelessness and replaces it with hope. Then it carries the hopelessness back to me.

"If you need more advice," Mrs. Peterson says, releasing my hand, "my nail technician has a shop near to the town hall. Mention that I sent you." She picks up her cup, pauses, then drinks the rest of her tea. When she lowers her cup, her sniffles have dried and her eyes shine with hope.

"Such an extraordinary taste," she says, smacking her lips with pleasure. "It's left me wonderfully clear-headed. I must take some with me."

"Of course." Going to the kitchen bench, I fill a paper packet with a mixture of dried ginger and peppermint leaves. Mrs. Peterson's hopelessness affects my usual care when preparing herbal tea, and I spill leaves on the bench.

Clenching my fingers, I take a deep breath and draw on my charm's power to help keep my emotions balanced. I don't know how Mrs. Peterson managed for so long, living without hope. Praying I gave her enough, I fold the packet and return to the table.

Mother arrives, holding a bunch of red and white roses that fill the kitchen with a heavenly scent. Feeling the hopelessness creep over me again, I catch Mother's eye and signal my desperate need to leave.

"Your roses," Mother says, her tone clipped.

Mrs. Peterson picks up her purse and stands. "Wonderful. And the tea?"

I hand her the packet. "A gift," I say when she opens her purse to pay.

Mrs. Peterson closes her purse and takes the packet. She looks me in the eye, as though reminding me never to repeat our conversation, then turns toward the door.

Mother escorts her out. "The rain has eased," she says, "but mind your speed while driving. The road into town is slippery when wet."

As soon as Mrs. Peterson leaves, I push past Mother and run to the garden. Dropping to my knees, I sow Mrs. Peterson's secret into the mud. The flooded soil reflects the charm's golden glow. When all Mrs. Peterson's hopelessness has drained out of me, I roll back on my heels and watch the secret grow.

A stem pushes through the ground, tall and thick with long thorns that droop as though they've lost the will to live. The rosebud that blooms at the top unfurls blood-red petals, with perfume so heavy it gets caught in my throat.

Standing, I stare at the rose. I'm supposed to listen without judgment, but I can't ignore what I heard. Mrs. Peterson faces more harm if she doesn't reveal her secret. The hope helped clear her mind, but will it be enough to encourage her to seek help?

I toss and turn all night, unable to get Mrs. Peterson off my mind. Thinking about her bruised cheek makes me lie awake with worry. Even if I broke my vows and revealed the secret for her, it wouldn't help. I'd destroy the hope I gave her, and she needs all the hope she can get.

Needing a slap of cold night air to clear my gloomy thoughts, I slip out of bed and go outside. The rain has stopped and the heavy clouds part, letting moonlight stream over the gardens. Taking a deep breath, I search the night shadows for Mrs. Peterson's rose. It's bathed a milky-white glow from the moon, but the light shifts as though moved by the wind. Wondering what causes that effect, I walk toward the rose. When I get closer, my heart stops.

It's not moving moonlight. It's the ghost of Mrs. Peterson. She hovers next to her wilted rose that's gray from death. Gone is the elegant woman who sat at our kitchen table. An unnatural force squishes her features, making her look like a lump of melted wax.

I stare at her, frozen in fright. How could I miss the signs that foretold her death? I compared the color of her dress-suit to the 'flower of death'. Mother warned her about the slippery roads. Did she have a car accident while driving home? Whatever happened, despite the hope I gave her, she didn't reveal her secret. She can't have, because she suffers her burden in death.

Three-fold hopelessness pours like black ink from her hollow eye sockets. Her mouth yawns wide, expelling the choking scent of her rose. Nothing I envisioned comes close to what stands before me. But what if I'm to blame? What if, in my haste to cast the charm, I didn't give her enough hope?

"I'm sorry," I whisper, creeping toward her. "I don't know what happened, but you don't deserve to suffer in death when you suffered so much in life. I can help you. I can fix this."

Her soul now belongs to Hades, but I can still hear her secret and fill her soul with hope. It means Hades may lose his servant. And he'll demand my soul to compensate. But if I'm responsible for Mrs. Peterson's death, that's a consequence I'm willing to accept.

I think about all the things that give me hope and fuel the charm with so much power it shines like two suns. Then I reach for Mrs. Peterson's hands. Her fingers find mine, icy tendrils that numb my skin. A strange blue light flows into my charm, turning its golden light a frosty turquoise. With increased power, the charm whips around our hands, binding us as one.

Mrs. Peterson tilts my hand and pokes at my fingernails. Though distracted by the icy pricks on my fingers, I urge the charm to find her secret again. Powered by the blue light, it works faster than usual. In a split second, the secret I heard when sitting in the kitchen with Mrs. Peterson fills my mind again.

This time, the images are so lifelike they make me think I'm experiencing them. When her husband strikes her cheek, I flinch as though struck. But then a different image appears, a new secret —

Still alive but soaked from the rain, Mrs. Peterson walks up a spiral staircase. She clutches Mother's roses to her chest like a shield. Mr. Peterson stands on the top step, his face a furious shade of red. When she shows him the roses, he knocks them from her hands. Then he shouts that a wife who appears in public looking like a drowned rat will embarrass him.

Encouraged by the hope, Mrs. Peterson scoffs at his expectations. She says if he wishes to remain married, she'll decide if her appearance is appropriate.

Mr. Peterson strikes her face with a backhand that knocks her down the stairs. Her head hits the bottom step with a crack—

The flow of images ends as quick as her life did. Numb with shock, I try to fathom what I saw. Instead, I see Mr. Peterson again, but his features are fuzzy, like I'm looking through a transparent veil. I can see enough to know he's talking on the telephone. Hear enough to know what he said. *Slipped on the steps. A tragic accident.* Then the image fades.

The blood drains from my face, making me feel as cold as Mrs. Peterson. I can't see her eyes, but I can sense her somber stare. The truth about her death burns through the charm, and screeches of "*liar*" and "*murderer*" ring in my ears. It's Mrs. Peterson screaming, though her mouth is shut. Again she's been silenced, this time forever. But her husband can't silence me.

Determined to end her suffering, I urge my charm to remove all the burden. It's like scraping away layers of sludge, but, powered by the blue light, the charm collects it all. Then it delivers hope so pure, the brightness hurts my eyes. But I'm not prepared when my charm returns with the burden.

Triple the amount of hopelessness drags me to the pits of despair, draining my will to live. But my determination to see her husband punished for her murder anchors me to life. Pulling my hands from Mrs. Peterson, I stumble backward to escape the lure of death.

Filled with hope, Mrs. Peterson's grotesque features melt away. She appears as she did when she sat at our table, elegant, spirits lifted, and taking pleasure in sipping our tea. Then she fades, like mist dispersing in a breeze.

"Rose?"

Mother's voice drives the deadness from my limbs. Dropping to my knees, I dig into the mud and bury both of Mrs. Peterson's secrets. The ground around my fingers glows turquoise, my charm's new color. Two stems burst through the soil. They weave around each other like climbing vines, sprouting long black thorns that droop with three-fold hopelessness. Above my head, a rose blooms at the top of each stem. The petals on each are an unearthly frosty blue.

"Rose? What happened?"

The shock in Mother's voice sends tears streaming down my cheeks. "She's dead. Mrs. Peterson is dead."

Mother crouches beside me, her hand flying to her throat. "When? How?"

I claw my fingers into the mud, wanting to scream Mrs. Peterson's secrets into the night. Instead, I imagine Hades again, his expression smug, as though expecting me to break my vows. But if I do, I'll break Mrs. Peterson's trust and destroy the hope I gave her. That would be like killing her again.

Mother's words about finding the strength whisper through my mind, and I realize where my strength lies. Wiping my eyes, I clamber to my feet. "Mrs. Peterson didn't deserve to suffer in death. I heard her secret again, removed her burden and filled her soul with hope."

"And condemned yours." Standing, Mother grabs my elbow and pulls me away from the two roses. "What were you thinking, child? If Mrs. Peterson chooses rebirth, Hades will demand your soul to compensate. I warned you of this. Harpocrates will strip your ability to conjure hope to avoid a war with Hades."

Without hope, I'll lose my will to live and hand my soul to Hades by taking my own life. Even revealing Mrs. Peterson's secret wouldn't help. I'd destroy her hope and prevent her from being reborn, but Hades would still get my soul. I'd suffer the three-fold hopelessness I trapped in the thorns and I wouldn't survive that. But I can save my soul another way. There's something Hades and I have in common.

"Hades won't come for me," I say. "He values upholding vows above everything. And Mrs. Peterson can't be reborn because we are bound as one. While I live in this world, she'll stay in the underworld." In Elysium, where pure souls get sent.

I fiddle with my ring. The blue light that changed the charm's color has also turned the gold band a deep shade of turquoise. I've guessed the source of the blue light's power, but I don't think either god expected this. "Harpocrates could strip my powers so I can't conjure hope, but while I keep Mrs. Peterson's secret, I'll always have hope. Look." I hold out my hand and tease my charm from the ring. It jumps into my hand, a flickering bluish-gold flame.

"It's drawing hope from Mrs. Peterson," I say, "but that hope contains Hades' power, which is why it's so strong. Harpocrates would be a fool to abandon me now. With hope this powerful, we could win every battle against darkness and despair."

Mother doesn't look happy, but I've never been more certain. Like all the Secret Keepers before me, Mother included, my strength lies in the commitment to my vows. It means Mr. Peterson will escape punishment in this world, but he won't escape Hades.

I have to listen without judgment, but in the underworld, Hades' judges don't. When they judge Mr. Peterson' soul with the secret he keeps, they'll send him straight to Tartarus. I can't imagine a better punishment for a man who killed his wife.

See Pauline Yates's story "The Secret Keeper" online at Metaphorosis.
If you liked it, leave a comment. Authors love that!
Remember to subscribe to our e-mail updates so you'll know when new stories are posted.

About the story

"The Secret Keeper" developed from an idea I had for another anthology call back in 2019. The theme for that anthology was based around the Zodiac signs. Being a Taurus, I wanted to write a story that focused on Taurus strengths, with loyalty and trust at the top of my list. I penned the original version, but put it aside to work on other projects because I needed more time to think about how best to show the traits I wanted to portray. The driving question behind the development of this story was this: What would the world look like if there was no one you could trust?

A year passed by the time I got back to it, and when I read over what I had, I thought it would be sad to waste the idea, so, with nothing else in the pipeline, I had another crack at it. As I've written for *Metaphorosis* before, I felt this story would be a good fit for what they like to publish. I submitted the first version of "The Secret Keeper" in October, 2020, but it was far different to the final published version. Despite much disarray in the world-building, the concept must have caught the publisher's eye because I was offered a rewrite opportunity.

Little did I know, it would take nine more versions, an extremely patient publisher, hours of research about Greek Mythology, and discussions with a church minister about the importance of vows, to pull together the finished version. My biggest issue was how to make demigod powers fit into the real world, because I was mixing the two. I've never written fantasy before, so this was more a challenge than I realized, but I am a fan of Percy Jackson and knowing how that world worked helped.

Ironically, every time I struck a hurdle, I'd find the answer. It was as though this story was begging to be told, and it was giving me all the clues. I just had to put them all together.

If you've read "The Secret Keeper", I hope you've taken from it the importance of staying true to your word. If you haven't read it, please consider doing so, especially if you keep a secret.

A question for the author

Q: Are you a Luddite? Or do you have the latest and greatest technology?

A: I don't like change. It's in my nature to immediately oppose any update to anything. It's not that I'm not open to improvement, rather I'm an 'if it's not broken, don't fix it' person. For example, while everyone spent the last ten years updating their phones to smart phones, iPhones, Androids, I stuck with my Samsung flip phone. All I could do was make a phone call and send a text, but that's all I needed. I always managed to find a way around the need for carrying a 'computer in a purse'. I had to buy an android phone last year, but only because I couldn't find another flip phone, when my old one finally died. And yes, I love it now that I'm used to it, but it got yelled at a few times in the learning process. It's the same with my laptop. It took me two years to convince myself to buy a laptop for my writing, and it's still the only one I've ever owned. It's twelve years old, had three hard-drive replacements, and I'm still running the 2007 version of Word. Will I update? Not until my laptop breathes its last breath. Do I feel behind the times? Nope. Until my situation changes and I need something flashier, I'm happy to keep things as they are. If the worst happens, there's always pen and paper, of which I have plenty.

About the author

From Queensland, Australia, Pauline Yates likes to explore the 'improbable' through her writing. When she's not burning the midnight candle researching her ideas, she loves watching movies that pit humans against nature, debates with anyone who'll listen about how dystopian societies start, and argues with her ancient cat about his demand to be fed at 3am. She also enjoys taking photos of the sunrise, if she wakes up in time.

paulineyates.com, @midnightmuser1

Satyajit Ray's Beard or the Lack Thereof

Abhijato Sensarma

"And why would there be multiple Earths in the same universe?" the counsellor asks me. She's not *my* counsellor—and this isn't my world. But she still has the same pair of spectacles resting on the bridge of her nose, and she peers through them to look at me. She must have been confused at the start of today's discourse. Usually, we talk about my marriage being in the wrong place, not my body being on the wrong planet.

I slip forward on the sofa. The woman sitting beside me looks at me with concern—but now that she's out of my line of sight, I can think better. It took me some time to accept the fact that she's my wife in this world. She has a shaved head here, but what truly took me by surprise was the fact that we were sleeping in the same bed when we woke up. And when I told her I shouldn't be there, she looked at me with an expression of love for me which I did not know she still allowed herself to reveal.

When I first came here, I did not know what to expect—in many ways, I still don't. But my professional life's turned out to be the same as it's always been. I'm still a quantum engineering professor. I'm still working on teleportation. And I still *feel* like myself—I'm a resident of my own mind, at the very least. But there're two big differences in this world that set it apart from mine.

"If the shape of the universe is flat enough, as evidence seems to suggest, then it's constantly expanding." My hands spread outwards in front of me as I start my monologue. It's a habit I have. "And if molecules are allowed to arrange themselves in every way they can over infinite space, they'll eventually run out of unique combinations. Patterns will start repeating—and the same worlds will arise in different parts of the universe."

The counsellor nods again. She steals the slightest of glances at my wife between looking up from her notebook and looking at me—"Have you considered the possibility … that this may be a reaction to your wife having cancer?"

I bend my head sideways, confused. Couples therapy has never been my favourite part of the weekend, but neither has the counsellor ever been this wrong. She thinks I'm going crazy.

My wife's bald head steals my attention more than her eyes. But oh, her eyes do read of pity. I don't want any.

"*My* wife isn't dying from cancer." I say it with an emphasis on my baritone. It sounds harsh, almost dismissive. *You're in denial*, the counsellor seems to think. But once again, she doesn't say anything. She simply brings up her arms to the handrest on her seat and leans on it, thinking of how to approach this case.

Just then, the alarm clock in her room goes off. She snaps her fingers and mutters "*Turn est.*" A switch moves by itself, and the alarm stops ringing. "Time's up, so that will be all for today. I think we're making real progress here so far. Same time, next week?"

She smiles at me, but I retain my nonchalance. I stare at the portrait of Satyajit Ray in the background—he's the most revered filmmaker in Bengali cinema. But here, he has a beard akin to a Tagore, whereas Ray was famously clean-shaven in my own world. This isn't my home. And this isn't the Ray whose films I've grown up watching.

The portrait shouldn't even be there—in my world, the counsellor hung her framed diploma on this wall, so that it would be facing us during the session. But in the strange new place I find myself in, the diploma's on the other side of the wall, where Ray's portrait should have been. It's a reversal which doesn't say much, except that this isn't my world to inhabit.

I look at the woman who claims to be my wife. As a way of compensation for my harshness, she says to the counsellor, "Thank you, Doctor." Then, she mutters something under her breath. I don't catch the spell this time around. She's intentionally using the tone she always does when she's cross with me. And before I can do anything about it, a white beam of energy envelops her. By the time the energy dissipates, so does she. I'll find her at home again.

"Umm," I say, looking around the room. I run my fingers over the leather on the sofa with my left hand, and run the other hand across my hair. "I guess … I'll just walk back home."

I nod awkwardly at the counsellor and pat my thighs before getting up. She looks at me with concern that brims over to amusement. She doesn't say anything, of course—but she's only human.

The counsellor's the least of my concerns as I walk down the stairs and make my way onto the road. The *autorickshaws* and taxis converge in the middle of the four-way intersection, pausing for a moment when the signal opens for the other side. Soon, their turn comes as well. I stand and stare at them for a while, until all the vehicles I tried to keep track of have disappeared out of sight. There isn't too much of a difference between the public transportation of the Kolkata I know and the one I'm in right now, except for the fact that all vehicles hover above the ground here. They have no wheels, but they do have drivers and an automated gear shift technique that does not require the assistance of hands.

I've learned about it on the Internet, which is no less fascinating or abusive than the one I know from my own planet. I'm a product from before the World Wide Web's time, but the evolution of science seems to have followed a less stringent path on this world, where magical spells do a lot of what science and maths account for in mine. I don't like this place.

It's been less than twenty-four hours since I found myself in this world, but in that time, I've come to understand that the most commonly used spell is the one which helps in transportation. People don't use it all the time, and prefer using public vehicles when they can—it's akin to not taking a helicopter every time you want to cross the street, I guess. But the spells used here are strange, as spells have always been. They're spelled in Latin, as well. What *is* the one for transportation, though?

I try saying it out loud. "Trans—transvec—*transvectio*—"

And just as I pronounce the spell—it's the correct one, it seems—I find myself disintegrating. It's a strange sensation, and I would think about it more if not for the fact that my mental facilities seem to be incapacitated. When I feel complete again, with my senses and my cognitive abilities returning, the first thought I have is—"What on Earth?"

It's an ironic choice of words considering my situation. I find myself looking straight at Satyajit Ray's bearded portrait again. According to the *Basic Dictionary of Magic*—whose online website I accessed yesterday—one's always transported to the place they're thinking about at the time of saying the spell. Using this spell effectively is an acquired habit.

I look down, and there is the counsellor again, peering over her spectacles and straining her neck with curiosity no longer censored by the hours she's being paid for. I see a notepad on her lap. She's probably filing away the minutes of today's session with us before the next client arrives.

"Hello … What may I do for you?" She tries to wear a smile on her face, but her lips twitch back to a more neutral position.

I chuck my head to the right and smile, embarrassed at this intrusion of mine. "I've just transported myself to the wrong place when I intended to go back home. You see, I was thinking about your place instead of mine, and I'm new to this magic business, so I didn't realise what would happen if I said *transvectio*—"

And just then, I can't feel my toes again. I realise what's going to happen next—*I've spoken the spell, haven't I?* But before I can think too much about the nuances of transporting for the second time in as many minutes, I'm no longer able to feel my thoughts either. It's serene, almost meditative, to not carry the worries of these worlds on my shoulders.

But when my feet touch the ground again, I throw up. It's on a familiar rug—the one I brought back home after spending a year in Switzerland working on the effects of extreme altitudes on my teleportation machine. The machine never worked. And in this world, it doesn't need to.

"Hey," I hear the familiar voice say. It's my wife's, even if it's mellowed down now. Probably because of the cancer. And also, because her husband seems to have gone crazy.

I look up at her. She's in her robes, getting ready for a bath. But before I can tell her anything—or apologise as a way of coming to terms with the place that is going to be my home for the rest of my life—I feel my eyes closing. I didn't even say a spell this time. *Where am I going now?*

But before I can take in my new surroundings, my face hits the floor. The first—and last—thought I have here is that my nose is going to hurt like hell when I wake up again.

On opening my eyes, I see the roof above my head. I can still hear the public vehicles making their way past our home on this main road of the city. I never liked this place, even though the apartment itself is fine. Furnished at the time of purchase too. It's just that the commotion of the bazaar and the cars have never been to my liking. On the other hand, my wife thought the familiar sirens and rhythmic honks which compose this room's overtones would give me comfort when I came back home after the uncertainty of conducting experiments at my laboratory. I didn't think it would help, but over time, the sounds of the street have indeed turned meditative for me.

I find a reflection of my life in the taxis which pick up their passengers below at inflated rates. You can bargain, you can curse, and you can go anywhere you want—but at the end of the day, the taxi always drops you off at home. You've seen the sights of the city, yet there's the same old bed you need to sleep on. Beside a woman you loved once, but now can't bear to touch.

She realises I'm awake, though, and moves into my field of vision. I still don't want to touch her, because she isn't mine to have, and she isn't mine to love. But even if she were, would I want to? I feel uncomfortable about the realisation that she's a mortal—in both this world, and the one I've come from.

Before I can grasp at the finer ends of this chain of thought, I'm brought back to reality by a sudden pang of physical discomfort. My eyes look down, and I can see the bridge of my nose —it's certainly not where it should be. It's bent way too much towards my right. It's on the verge of being numb, but isn't, which makes the pain intolerable now that my senses are fully returning.

This wife moves her fingers and says a spell which does not penetrate the ringing sound in my ears. But the sound eventually dissipates, and as it does so, I feel my nose align itself properly. It almost twitches—no, it *jumps* back into its place.

I want to move away from her, for no fault of her own. She reminds me of my own wife too much—the one with whom disagreements have turned into silent nights. But even now, when she seems as foreign to me as she's ever been, I cannot stop admiring her. She always was the more tenacious of us. During separation or a bout with cancer, how does she remain the pleasant one?

She looks at me now with a love in her eyes I did not know I'd been missing. A love which is unconditional and comes out in moments of solidarity that have not yet turned into gestures born out of obligation.

But I cannot allow myself to reciprocate the feeling, even if I feel a tinge of heartache. For, as much as I want to reach out now, and brush my hands against her hardened cheeks, she still isn't mine to love. So, I push my arms against the surface I'm lying on, attempting to get back up.

"No, you must rest. Have you forgotten about that time we went to Darjeeling and you transported twice in a minute?" The voice lets out a laugh, but she doesn't see it through. I've seen her do this before, but I realise now why she does it. We've hurt each other too much, you see, and expressing ourselves has become a luxury. A laugh about the good old times has long been replaced by a few more moments of silence in my world.

"What happened to me? Am I a serial fainter in this world?" The weather's always been oppressive in this part of the country during the summers.

"You've got the Paralysis Syndrome, or have you forgotten that as well?" she asks. I shoot her a look. *I never knew*, I would like to tell her, but it wouldn't help.

Her head bows down as a way of resignation. "Your heredity means you can't teleport yourself like the rest of us can. You can only do it twice a day. You get quite tired otherwise. You pass out, like you did today."

I try to nod, but my head doesn't seem to be able to lift itself from the pillow for now. However, I do seem to recollect a stray line from the *Dictionary of Magic*'s entry about the subject. Something about people being born with a rare variation of the 24th pair of chromosomes, the ones that grant humans their ability to interact with magic. A pair which—in my world—is considered to lead to deformities and death rather than magical abilities.

"I ... I really might not be who you think I am."

She places a hand on her temple and looks away. "The mosquitoes are going to start entering the room again—let me shut the windows. *Prope.*" And on cue, the windows move inwards, as if they're intoxicated by a breeze blowing out of the room. The illusion of normalcy is shattered when the latches attached to the bottoms of the windows pick themselves up and lock them into their positions on the windowsills. Estranged or not, my wife remains cool across realms.

And right then, the first lines of Rabindra Sangeet burst through our closed windows, drowning out the noise of the receding vehicles as the last strains of sunlight drain away and the artificial lights take over. *"Ami chini go chini tomake, ogo bideshini." I know you, oh, I do, foreigner.*

Ah yes, I do. She's going to be my life now—there's no escape from it, and somewhere deep inside, I don't want there to be any. It will take time to learn this world's spells, perhaps, and it will take time to convince the counsellor that I was truly having a nervous breakdown about my wife's cancer today. But things aren't as bad with my wife here as they are back home. Our time together will be curtailed, but maybe I can learn to love her again all the same.

"Did I ever stop loving you?" I ask her, as a way of enquiring about the work I would need to put in to have a better relationship with her.

She shoots me another look. But I've always been this way, asking questions about love and existence while lying on the bed with a broken nose, if only figuratively. So, she answers, "No. As a matter of fact, ever since my diagnosis, you've loved me more than you ever have."

I try to nod, but it ends up looking like an awkward twitch of the head. She understands, though, and she laughs. For the first time in months, I'm able to smile with her. Oh, how I've missed that feeling of having someone there for me. The baggage of death takes precedence over marital discontent, I realise.

"Why does my nose ... feel normal?"

"I fixed it. It's the first spell you ever taught me. Transportation helped us get away from either of our parents if they saw us when they weren't supposed to. You always landed on your nose whenever you fell unconscious. And I was always there for you. To fix your nose. Or just fix your hair."

So, in this world, I did find a way of escaping her parents. A less painful way than jumping out of her window from the first floor and breaking a bone in my leg that one time, for sure.

"Does this help you remember anything?" she asks.

"It does," I reply, remembering the exuberance of her youth—and mine—with a fondness I didn't think my marriage would still entail. "But then ... it doesn't." She sighs.

I've never believed in karma. Neither did I ever believe in magic before I saw it with my eyes. Perhaps this mystical experience of love I don't deserve is karma repaying itself for things I've done in lives I cannot remember. I would like to confess my sins to her, tell her how I've mistreated her.

But before I can, my wife rests her hands on my forehead. "You've become very tired because of this ordeal. Sleep now, and I'll sleep alongside you. Hopefully, you'll be in your senses when we wake up tomorrow. *Somnus*."

And I feel myself drifting away again. I slip into oblivion, akin to how I've felt while teleporting before. But this time, I'm not reappearing to a different part of the world. My mind merely guides me to a world of my own. I feel a comfort I haven't felt for a long time now—the comfort of falling asleep next to someone you love.

"So, you believe you're from another dimension?" the doctor asks. I nod and look around the room. I see laminated certificates hanging where Satyajit Ray's portrait should be hanging. The portrait occupies the space on the wall right behind me. If I didn't know

better, I would have thought the counsellor had just exchanged our seats as a way of giving the two of us a 'new perspective'.

But when I turn around to look at the portrait, Mr. Ray's likeness hangs up there without a beard on the man's face, as if it's a joke. His beard's the most iconic part of his appearance—and this world doesn't even have that. Alongside the fact that it believes magic exists only in escapist novels and ancient scriptures.

"Umm, yes, I do." I don't put in too much effort into my assertion, because I'm truly not interested in this session. This counsellor isn't the one I've been intimate with about my Paralysis Syndrome. And this wife isn't the one I've grown so close to because of her terminal cancer. She looks much younger sitting beside me now, untouched by fate or fear.

She loves me in this world as well. But she doesn't have terminal cancer—yet—and this makes her more placid, less lively, than my wife. The man who's actually married to her was the one who filed for divorce. On the other hand, my affection for her has turned platonic with the changing of worlds. I would like to embrace her, and apologise for the sins of another man, but I love her only as my confidant from a different life. It wouldn't be fair to love her any more than that.

She brought me in for an emergency counselling session today. She checked my temperature and cooked me a good meal first, even though I've become the one to do that in my own marriage back home. She cares for me, yes, she does—yet, as much as I care for this woman too, I can't seem to love her.

"Have you considered that this could be related to the fact that the two of you want a divorce?"

"Ah," I say. "It's the farthest thing from what I want, though."

My wife shoots me a look. "You're the one who wanted it the most."

I get up from my place, and throw out my hands—it's a sign of desperation in this world too, I hope. "I'm sorry, but this is all too much for me. Transvectio." I stand in my place, but nothing happens.

I'd forgotten. I don't have the chromosomes I need to perform magic in this world.

The counsellor bends her eyebrow at me. "I've been learning a bit of Latin to cope with all this stress," I inform her. It's a trick I picked up at school, whenever anyone caught me practicing spells in an empty classroom or in a corner of the playground—I've never been good at magic. The excuse usually failed to protect me from the ridicule of my classmates when I was younger, but now, it helps me slip out of my unsuccessful attempt at teleportation.

I look around this familiar room set up in an alien manner for what I hope is the last time. "I think I need a break. I'm unable to cope with the pressure, and I'd appreciate some space rather than being dragged down for therapy to this office. My apologies, I'll have to get going now." I do my best impression of storming out of the room and down the stairs of the large hospital. Theatrics, it turns out, will always convince others to leave an upset man alone, whether it has something to do with magical civilisations or not.

Some use the elevator, of course, but it's a relief to see most others walking beside me on the stairs. In my world, the presence of magic means people teleport themselves to the other end of a long journey in a matter of minutes. Everyone except for people like me, that is. On the other hand, everyone here needs to sit down and let a good old engine—and a decent driver—do the work instead.

As jarring as this reality has been to me so far, including the experiences with my very own wife, the biggest incentive for staying in this world has been the respect engineers are given here. In the society I've grown up in, engineering as a career has always been treated akin to a punchline. The electricity plants that power most of the world, the equipment that makes surgeries easier for Medical Wizards, and of course, the transportation that helps the less biologically gifted ones among us—they're only possible with the help of scientists like us. But it's the Wizards who are at the helm of affairs. They're the most influential politicians and academics. They get to decide what others are known as. Many books have called the people of my profession an 'afterthought', replaceable tools only there to help the Wizards accomplish their goals. But society wouldn't be able to hold itself together if our kind disappeared overnight.

This world, on the other hand, designs its fervour around supernatural elements of a different kind. I see the people praying in makeshift temples and on the rickshaws that carry models of their deities wherever they go. Not being treated as a dispensable labourer comforts me in a way I've never felt about my professional identity before. I wouldn't mind staying here—but I can't.

I've fought for a semblance of respect towards my profession for the longest time. It's the reason I started experimenting with manufacturing a teleportation device using scientific apparatus rather than relying on the genetic predispositions of the population. I've found what I've sought for all my life—but this isn't earned.

So, I make my way to the most familiar place I know after my home—the University I work at. The only difference being that here, the campus isn't guarded by magical sharks floating in the air.

Rather, the University's guarded solely by the same people I've become good acquaintances with back in my realm. It is closed off to students at this time of the evening, but when I flash my ID at one of the guards—a card which surprisingly does not morph itself into a miniature replica of its holder in this world—he lets me in. "Welcome, Professor," the man says, and steps aside.

I make my way up to the second floor. Room 616. *Here it is. I stand in front of the door for a moment, then another, and then another. It's on the last beat that I have to remind myself once more of the nature of human existence here. You've got to turn your own door handles in this world.*

I enter the room and switch on the lights. Here lies the machine. It looks the same. It's cylindrical, with a hollow, secured chamber in the middle of it large enough to fit a human—the place where the person must enter if they're to teleport. This machine remains in its prototype stage, just like mine.

The most essential discovery I've made exists here too, in the form of a neutrino battery on top of the machine, powered by an alloy of platinum and plutonium. A 'radiation cover' ensures the battery is shielded and the machine can be dealt with in normal clothing. As a matter of abundant precaution, I slip on the gloves lying on the counter.

I proceed to open the chamber and look at the controls when I realise these gloves are not infused with any magical spells. This means that they aren't really protecting me from any radiation-related accidents. But I carry on. A preliminary inspection should not take long.

The machine looks the same on the exterior as mine. The keypad has an extensive entry system which allows for transportation to different parts of the Universe, even though this is an ambitious addition to the machine's infrastructure. It's purely theoretical, because it cannot function. Mine didn't, at least.

I pick up a screwdriver and unshackle the interior of the machine. Another cursory glance reveals what I've been suspecting ever since I entered this lab. The prototype, it turns out, is indeed a bit different looking here—on the inside! *I shift my focus away from the similarities and study the differences between my device and the one this Earth's version of me has created.*

I put on my protection kit and start with my work. I note down observations in my favourite notebook—this world's version of it, anyway. Blueprints lie all around my corner of the lab, and my suspicions are confirmed.

He's created one half of the machine, with his work delivering solutions to the long-drawn questions I've asked myself over the years during its construction. His configurations reveal things like how the neutrino battery should be wired to the quantum transportation engine, and whether I should add a circuit breaker before or after the feed from the electronic transmitted attached to the keypad is integrated into the CPU (before, of course, but only with a special modification to the industry model to make it compatible with my work). His notebook combines with my knowledge to show me the full picture, and thus, I can now complete this Teleporter to make it a functional one.

The switch must have happened yesterday, under the improbable conditions across both ends of the Universe where similar worlds created two polar opposites of machines which also had perfect compatibility with each other. The alignment of similar cellular structures did the rest, and the ambiguity in the positions of supercharged, hyperactive atoms altered the probabilities of their positions. This simultaneously attempted operation of compatible halves led to some sort of superimposition of the machine and its contents before the eventual separation. During this time, our consciousnesses must have switched—because while my body feels the same, it's lost the power to perform magic here—so it's likely his body. My counterpart probably has my former abilities, under this hypothesis.

But again, it's just that—a hypothesis. I can't remember for the life of me how I ended up tucked in bed on this world. I was a mess when I woke up in the morning. Maybe it's just the machine that does it. All I know is that the rest of my life seems perfectly stored in my mental faculties.

Such a freak accident probably won't occur again—neither the transportation, nor the memory loss—but it doesn't need to. I now know how to configure this machine, and make it work from a single location. If I do manage to work things out soon, I can go home again, and help my other self out too.

Let's see how I go about rescuing both versions of myself now —and inventing intra-dimensional teleportation along the way.

When I open my eyes, I expect to feel her palm on my forehead again, ready to put me to sleep if I haven't come around to what she thinks are my regular senses. Sunlight is peering in through the windows, which are open again, and carrying in the familiar hum of the vehicles during office hour.

I slide up in my bed and feel the sour taste in my mouth. I'll need to brush my teeth. What was the spell for doing that, again?

"Puriter lavit dentes." Have clean teeth. It's the wordiest phrase I learned yesterday, but also the most convenient one of them all. I would also love to learn the spell which lets me floss, even though I've never done that as a regular human being before.

The brush should've been floating towards me with the perfect amount of paste on it, a proportion which no human hands could ever conjure. But it doesn't. I say the words louder. *"Puriter lavit dentes."*

"Have you really been taking your Latin classes so seriously?" my wife asks. She'd been asleep, beside me. "I didn't realise you were taking any at all."

I turn towards her. Yes, I'm seeing *my* wife, because she has her long hair again. She's also got the beautiful smile and that radiance which comes from being optimistic about what life plans for you next.

And then, the memories come back to me in bits and pieces. I recollect the strange feeling with which I was greeted when I met another part of myself in a world which seems too distant to exist now.

He told me the theory he'd postulated, and introduced me to his machine—it was incomplete, yet revealed all I needed to know to get home. We worked on completing it overnight, and now, here I am, before the break of dawn. I can't recollect all the details, but I remember enough. He said he's noted down all that I would need in my notebook to construct another machine. I want to rush down to the University's laboratory to check if the memories I've retained aren't betraying me. And if there already is a fully functional Teleporter in my lab.

I remember his parting words as well. *Love your wife as much as you can, for as long as you can. Some of us don't have her for much longer—but then, neither will you, if you stop loving her.*

She still wears a look of confusion on her face, though, as she should. This is the first time in months that we've shared the same bed—I must have slipped in while she was asleep. She would have no way of knowing I've changed overnight, once again.

"Are you … wearing a wig?" I ask.

Now, she shoots me the familiar look which indicates her confusion has been superseded by amusement. "I'm going to call the counsellor again. You could do with some medication—I didn't realise our divorce would get to you so much …"

"You don't need to do that," I say.

Questions of science can wait—it's the ones of my heart that need to be answered first. In this world, *my* world, I realise that the two of us still have time. My wife's concerned. She's been concerned for the longest time, hasn't she? There's a tinge of sorrow which hides beneath her façade as well, but it's not of the inevitable kind. We can make things better between us.

"I've got another question," I say.

"What's it this time?"

"Did Satyajit Ray ever have a beard?"

"No, he was an indie filmmaker—not a crazy loon."

I break out into a smile. "I've been feeling like one myself up until now."

She tilts her head to the left.

I reach forward to caress her hair, and then I hug her for the first time in months—I didn't want to before, but now that I can, I wouldn't be having this any other way. She tries to move away at first, but then, she embraces me too.

We need to work on our relationship—a lot. But I'm in my own world again, in the arms of my own wife, and with an enriched Latin vocabulary. It isn't going to be easy. But the time to try isn't a luxury everyone has, unlike us.

I break away from our embrace for a moment. "I want things to be better. I want us to be happy again. And I don't want to leave you," I say.

"Neither do I."

"We can try again, can't we?"

She nods. Amidst the moments of silence yet to retreat from our relationship, I reach forward and embrace her once more. She's never stopped loving me, and now, I realise that neither have I.

See Abhijato Sensarma's story "Satyajit Ray's Beard or the Lack Thereof" online at Metaphorosis.
If you liked it, leave a comment. Authors love that!
Remember to subscribe to our e-mail updates so you'll know when new stories are posted.

About the story

I've always wondered—is it our circumstances that define us, or is it us who define our circumstances? There's no definite answer, but writing fiction has always been my way of debating the merits of different philosophies.

In this story, I wanted to explore how a fundamentally same person—across both worlds— lives vastly different lives. One's marriage is on the precipice of collapse; the other's wife is dying from cancer. One's career is well-reputed; the other's is much-maligned. A different social standing in life, then, might just be the result of circumstances beyond one's control. It calls for the lending of empathy, which we could all do with, especially during times like these.

In my home country of India, there remains a perception that science-related subjects are the most profitable as careers—and thus, the most important as well. Even the most educated people subscribe to this ideology, which simultaneously contributes to the disrepute of both Humanities subjects, as well as a pursual of the arts for a career.

I wanted to see how things would be from a different perspective. So, I focused on how an engineer might feel in an India where it wasn't them, but the wizards and witches, who would be setting the narrative. The answer circled back to my intent with this piece—all of us deserve empathy, for sometimes, our circumstances might be beyond us even when our fates aren't.

A question for the author

Q: What kind of non-fiction do you like to read and how does it affect the fiction you write?
A: I've always believed that fiction reflects reality in between its lines. The recognition of fundamental truths is what connects the author and the reader beyond the scope of a story's immediate facts. My favourite kind of non-fiction is sports writing. I've always been a cricket fan, and it's another medium where human stories shine through amidst all its unnecessary grandeur. I've learnt a great deal from the likes of writers like Jarrod Kimber, Andrew Fidel Fernando, and Andrew Miller. The biggest lesson has been that telling a story is the primary job of all forms of writing, no matter what its purpose. This realisation has had quite an effect on me, and changed the way I deal with my craft.

About the author

Abhijato Sensarma is an 18-year-old student from Kolkata, India. He's on the verge of stepping into the real word, which does not prevent him from writing about fictional ones whenever he can. He's also been brought up on a steady diet of genre shows and books. So, even though he's expanded his horizons over the years, he still has an affinity for comforting stories. He dreams of becoming a professional writer hopefully one who'll also retain the belief that art is the key to answering the mysteries of life.

@ob_jato

The Stranding

Maud Woolf

There's a sparrow lying on the crust of the snow, beak open, one wing folded. George watches it from a wary distance, gritting his teeth to keep them from chattering, hands shoved tightly up under his armpits. There's something strangely perfect about it, no blood or scattered feathers. But nothing living could be that still. It looks like someone's glove, dropped and forgotten. It must have died recently, to be left bare like that.

The snow was still falling when George went to bed last night. He left the curtains open to watch. The snowflakes were made orange by streetlamp light, sliding past the glass in hypnotic, patterned flurries.

This morning the snow is no longer alive, but still, as still and dead as the bird. Unsettled, George looks away, up at the house. This is a curtain-twitching kind of street in a curtain-twitching kind of village, but the windows are dark and empty.

Come on, he thinks. *Come on. Open the door.*

His toes are starting to ache, and he shifts from side to side, trying to stamp away the cold. He should just leave. He will leave. He doesn't need Tom to come with him.

Even so, something in his chest unwinds when the front door finally opens. He's taking a breath to yell at Tom for leaving it so long, when he sees it's Julia standing there in the doorway. He stops stamping and tries to smile.

"Oh, hi. I'm just waiting for your brother." He looks past her to the hallway, hoping maybe Tom is hiding behind her in the dark.

"I know," Julia says and then steps outside, shutting the door behind her. George feels his smile become a little more fixed. Talking to Julia alone always unnerves him. It's not just that she's a year older than him at twelve, or even that she's a girl, though in

Tom's eyes at least that's enough to make her The Enemy. It's that George can remember a time before those things were important and it was just the three of them, having pretend adventures in the back garden. Julia had the best imagination out of any of them, telling them they were knights on a quest, superheroes, a wild pack of wolves. Nowadays, George can't look at her without remembering and feeling a squirmy kind of embarrassment.

"Is he coming out?" he asks. "Did he say?"

"Probably not," Julia says, kneeling on the step to lace up her hiking shoes. She's wearing a bright yellow puffer jacket that goes down to her knees, and when she stands up and zips it, she looks like a caterpillar. "He's still in his room."

"Well…" George says and lets out a huff of white cloud. "Can you tell him I'm here?"

"I did."

"Fucksake," George says but there's no heat in it. He knew really, even on his way over, that this was a pointless exercise. Tom hasn't answered his texts with anything more than single-word replies for a long time now. Still, George hoped that the message he sent Tom last night would have changed something. That knocking on Tom's door would have forced some kind of reaction.

"Sorry," Julia says, clearly not invested. She shoves her hands into her pockets and tilts her head to the side to look at him. It still reminds George of an owl, even if Julia's hair isn't short and tufty anymore. It's the same brown, but longer now and, George can't help but notice, greasy and unbrushed. There are purple shadows under her eyes and George wonders if she's only just gotten out of bed.

"It's fine," George says, scowling at his shoes. He wants to ask Julia to go inside and force Tom to come down, at least force Tom to *talk* to him, but that would be pathetic, so instead he just asks, "Where are you off to, then?"

He doesn't really care, but then Julia sniffs and juts out her chin. "With you. Thought I'd come and see what all the fuss is about."

"Tom told you where I'm going?" George asks. He tries to say it neutrally, but Julia must hear something in his voice because she scowls.

"Is it a secret?"

"No," George says, but then hesitates. "How much did he say?"

"He said you saw it fall." Julia says. "He said you're going to find it."

She says it bluntly, but that's nothing new for her. Julia doesn't act like the other girls he knows, who were always in groups, whispering and giggling behind their hands. When George saw Julia at school she was almost always alone.

Sometimes when Tom talked about Julia, his anger sounded wounded, as if she had betrayed them by growing up and becoming a girl. As if she had defected to the enemy side. George would never say it, but he finds this hard to believe. Julia doesn't seem to belong to any side at all.

George looks down and kicks at the snow a little with the toe of his boot. "He's talking, then?"

"Not a lot. I had to force it out of him," Julia says. Then she clears her throat and says, more brusquely, "It's not going to stay light for long. How far is it?"

"Er, not that far, but I'm not sure that..."

"Are we walking?"

George hesitates, aware that he's losing control of the situation. Tom was always the one to tell her to *Go away, no girls allowed*, but Tom isn't here and without him it's hard to remember why it's so important to stay away from Julia anyway. He imagined today with Tom there at his side, but now, when it comes to it, maybe anyone would be better than going alone.

He just shrugs, in the end.

"I was going to cycle some of the way. You could borrow Tom's bike, maybe?"

"I don't know how."

"Right," George says heavily. He looks over at his bike.

"I'm not riding on the back," Julia says quickly. "I'll fall off."

George sighs and resists the temptation to point out he hadn't offered. "Okay. I guess we're walking then. Can I lock this to the fence?"

He doesn't wait for the answer, pulling off his glove with his teeth to fumble numbly at the lock. His finger slips and he swears, muffled by a mouthful of wool. Last night, with his head stuck out of the window, snow falling in his hair while he waited for the sirens, this plan was exciting, almost perfect. Now, it's beginning to feel like a mistake.

With the bike secured, he walks back over to Julia, who is looking down at the sparrow with an unreadable expression.

"It must have flown into a window," he says, wondering if she might suggest they bury it or something. He doesn't remember her ever being very sentimental. The stories she had made up for them were always violent. When they were pirates, she had George walk the plank by bouncing off the trampoline. He misjudged the jump and as he lay winded on the grass, Julia had circled him, saying, *The sharks smell blood. Did you feel that one touch your leg?*

"They're not always dead," is all she says now. "Sometimes they're just stunned."

"It looks dead."

"Yeah," she says, frowning. "Yeah, I think it is."

George clears his throat. "So, should we, ah...?"

"We can go."

She doesn't say it like a command, but when they start walking, he makes sure to go in front. This is, after all, his expedition.

It doesn't take them more than ten minutes to reach the outskirts of the village and start cutting their way over the farm track that runs between the fields. George spends the time trying to think of something, anything, that they can talk about. Even back when they were little, it was always the three of them together. Without Tom, George doesn't know how to act around her. Julia makes no effort to fill the silence and George doesn't know if she feels the same way or if this is who she is now, this quiet, withdrawn person. In all his memories, she's talking.

The air feels muffled now that the wind has died down, and the clouds feel very close overhead, like big balls of cotton pressing down on them. It's quiet enough that the crunching noise of their footsteps feels startling. He can hear Julia struggle for breath as the track gets steeper and it makes him too aware of his own breathing, taking in air through his nose even though the cold of it hurts.

He can't help but keep checking over his shoulder in the hopes that Tom will pop up in the distance, a dark shape running to catch up.

The fourth time he does it, Julia makes a face. "No one's going to care that we're going."

"I know," George says, feeling defensive. "I'm not worried about that."

He is, though, just a little, but only out of habit. Technically, everyone is meant to stay in their houses for a full twenty-four hours after the sirens go off. A year ago, there might have been policemen about, even all the way out here in the countryside. There was a hotline you could call to report on your neighbors if you saw them out on the street.

No one cares much these days. Streets stay empty anyway. There are a few tattered posters left on lampposts, warning people of the dangers of contamination, but the policemen have all gone.

George doesn't know if this is because they're needed elsewhere or if there are just fewer and fewer of them.

Sometimes he thinks they've just stopped trying. Go outside or don't, it doesn't seem to matter. The same thing happens to everyone.

The sirens are the only constant, and George finds them almost comforting now. It means that someone, somewhere, is setting them off. Someone is still watching the sky and waiting with their finger on the button.

It's a relief when they finally reach the ragged treeline. When he looks back over his shoulder, the village has already shrunk down into the crook of the valley. It looks like a handful of toy buildings left out on a dirty white carpet. It looks like nothing at all from here.

"Which way now?" Julia asks, peering dubiously into the gloom. George hates to admit it, but she was right to worry about losing daylight. At this time of year, it is pitch black by teatime.

"West."

Julia snorts. "I'll get out my compass, shall I?"

"Up the hill," he says begrudgingly. "That way."

Julia doesn't step forward, frowning up at the trees, and George wonders suddenly when she last left her house. The village isn't large, and he thinks he knows all the people left. He's come across them from time to time, walking aimlessly like him. Sometimes they nod at each other or even stop to talk, but he's never seen Julia. Every time he passed Tom's house, the windows were dark and empty. Was she inside the whole time?

"Do you want to go back?" George asks her.

He tries to say it gently, but Julia sniffs, offended, and shakes her head. "No. But you're leading the way."

It's dark under the trees and they have to watch their step to avoid tripping on the roots. George is going first and when he pushes back a branch, he holds it to let Julia through.

The damp chill of the bark seeps through his gloves and he shudders, wrinkling his nose at the smell of rotting leaves. He's spent most of the last year going on long rambling walks with his headphones jammed in, but he's not an outdoors person by nature. Still, anything is better than watching television alone in the living room, pausing every time there's a creak from the floor above, imagining that maybe it's his mum and dad, that maybe they will come downstairs showered and dressed and smiling. *Enough lying about*, his dad might say, *I'm starving. Who wants breakfast?*

"Very chivalrous," Julia says drily as she pushes past.

You're welcome, George thinks darkly, but contents himself with scowling at the back of her bright yellow hood.

They walk in silence for a while and then out of nowhere she says, "He wanted to come along. Tom did, I mean."

"So why didn't he?" George asks, batting a leaf irritably out of his face.

"He's not...he doesn't leave his room much these days. Mum and dad too."

George is silent for a moment and then, because he can't stop himself, because he has to tell someone, he admits, "Mine don't either."

"For how long?" She doesn't sound surprised. She doesn't even look back, for which George feels strangely thankful.

"I don't know," he says. "Dad started getting quieter from the very start, the first fall. But mum was okay till last week."

"It comes on fast," Julia says. "I thought I would see it coming after mum and dad, but with Tom I thought he would be okay. I thought maybe it wouldn't happen to him. I thought..."

Her voice wobbles and she doesn't finish. George doesn't know what to say. For a moment it's too much, the frustration, the hopelessness of it all. He stops walking.

"Tom was fine," George says and to his horror the words come out thick and heavy. "Just a month ago. He was *fine*."

Julia stops then and looks back over her shoulder, and George thinks she's going to make fun of him, stamping his feet like a little kid, talking about how unfair it all is. Or worse, she might try to be kind. It would be wrong, George knows, for Julia to try and comfort him.

Tom is her brother after all, not his.

To his relief, she just nods, face tight and drawn.

"I just wish..." he starts and then, feeling stupid, he looks down at the mud on his shoes. "I just wish we could do something."

"We are, though," she says. "We're going to find the angel."

For a moment they look at each other in silence and then George nods.

"Yeah," he says. "Yeah, you're right."

"We should get on, then." Julia smiles at him. It's crooked and a little awkward, like she's not used to it, but George tries to return it as best he can.

"Yeah." He scrubs a hand over his nose, sniffs and sets off again, moving faster now. Soon he'll have to pull out the map and check the marking he made last night and the thought of that is comforting. This could still be what he wanted it to be last night. An adventure.

"You don't think they're aliens, then?" he asks when they're a little further on. He's speaking too loudly, he knows, but he's embarrassed to have almost been caught almost crying in front of her. Even when they were both kids that would have been shameful.

"Maybe they're aliens. Maybe aliens and angels are the same thing."

"You don't care?"

"I don't think it's important. If someone knows, then they won't tell us, but I don't think anyone does know."

"I think they know," George says quickly. "I think there's a reason they're not telling us."

"Oh yeah? Why's that?"

George can't see her face, but he can tell she's making fun of him. He doesn't care. He's spent too long staring at his computer scrolling through message boards and the itch to share his research wins out. It's not like anyone else is asking him.

"I think it's because they did it. It's their fault. The satellites sent out some kind of frequency that's poisonous to these things. Like whales."

"Whales?"

"The way our sonar messes with their echolocation and they beach themselves. That's why they're coming here. They're confused."

"Hmm. And who are *they*?"

George looks back over his shoulder, confused, and then nearly trips. "Huh?"

"They," Julia says. "With the capital T. The people doing this."

George sighs and tries to control his rising frustration. They talked about this on the message boards too, the way nobody seemed to care. George cares. Sometimes it feels like the questions are the only thing left in his head.

"The government," he says. "Companies."

"What companies?" Julia asks. "McDonalds? Facebook?"

There's no bite to it, but George doesn't want to play this game anymore.

"You asked," he says and then stops and makes a big show of taking out his map and compass so that she'll see he's not interested in continuing the conversation.

She looks over his shoulder at the map and, as if to make amends, she hums in a way that could be called impressed. "It's close. How did you work out where it fell?"

"I saw it. Last night."

She raises her eyebrows. "From your window? What did it look like?"

For some reason, George doesn't want to tell her. The memory feels private. His face was so close to the window that the skin of his nose went rubbery and cold from the glass. He was looking for it, but even so, the hair on the back of his neck stood up when it came into view. It only lasted a moment, but for some reason in George's memory it took a long time to fall. The storm must have been at its peak, but he remembers it being silent, so silent he could have sworn he heard his heart beating in his chest. Too fast. Like it wasn't his heart at all. Like a bird's heart.

"It looked like a star," he says. "A shooting star."

Julia hums. "I guess that makes sense. It was burning up in the atmosphere."

"Maybe," George says. The thought makes him strangely uncomfortable.

"I hope there's some left and it's not just a melted burnt-up lump." She must see the look on his face because she laughs. "Sorry, was that too gross?"

"Yes," George says shortly and sets off again at a brisk pace.

He's expecting, no, *hoping* for silence now, but if anything, Julia seems to have been cheered up by his increasingly bad mood.

"It isn't a bad theory," she says. "Your one. But how does it explain the fallout?"

"The fallout?"

"You know," she says. "The sadness."

"I don't know. I read something about it just being like shock. Of first contact." The article he read put it more scientifically than that, but George just skimmed it.

He doesn't care so much about that part. That part is too real. That part is his parents sleeping for twelve hours a day. Not talking for the rest.

"If I did think it was angels," Julia says, so quietly he almost misses it. "Then that would be evidence, I think."

"Why?"

"I don't know. It feels like a... I don't know... a spiritual sickness."

When George looks back, her cheeks are pink, and she won't meet his eyes.

"I guess," he says but it's dubious. His own parents aren't very religious, but he's seen the Bible in Tom's living room.

"Well what do you think it is? Radiation or contamination or whatever?"

"Well that's what they say," George says darkly.

Julia laughs. "Oh, *them*. At it again."

"Well it's a good excuse isn't it? For the sirens? For keeping us inside for twenty four hours, for not letting us get close?" He's riled up again, he can feel his face getting warm but for some reason it feels strangely good to be angry. "They just want to hide the evidence."

"Maybe you're right," Julia says slowly, like she's turning something over in her mind. "That would almost be nice, wouldn't it? If it were their fault. I think that would be easier."

They're both silent after that.

As the ground rises, the trees start to draw more tightly in around them. More than a few times they have to change direction in order to get around some tricky patch of undergrowth. This makes George increasingly nervous, and every ten minutes he makes them stop and check the map. It's only a little past midday, but already the light is changing, the trees losing detail, stiffening into stark silhouettes.

The edge of the forest comes without warning. There is no slow sparsening of trees. One moment they are picking their way carefully through the gloom and in the next they are stumbling out into bright emptiness.

Ahead of them, the ground veers sharply up to the bald head of the hill. The snow is thicker up here, and the wind snatches at their clothes, looking for gaps between glove and sleeve, scarf and collar. The skin of his face feels pinched.

"I didn't realize we were so high up," Julia says. Her voice sounds thinner out here, lost in the new space that has opened up around them. It felt better somehow, to only see the sky in gaps between branches.

"Let's get to the top," George says, teeth chattering. "I think we'll see it from there."

He doesn't step forward. They've come all this way. He could move if he wanted to. He should want to. He did want to.

We'll see it from the top of the hill. The thought feels sick, suddenly. Wrong.

George clears his throat. Maybe it would be okay to turn back now. Maybe they don't need to go any further. He wants somehow to convey this to Julia, but the words won't come.

"Julia," he says. "What if I was wrong? What if it *is* dangerous, to get too close to it?"

Hearing himself say it, he sounds childish and stupid. Maybe he should have stayed home, done as he was told. Maybe they were telling the truth, maybe there is no conspiracy after all, nothing hidden. Maybe it's no one's fault.

Julia looks over at him, her eyes pale above the red blotches on her cheeks. "It might be. But we're already here," Julia says. "And the worst that can happen is we end up like the others."

Something about the way she says it sounds almost wistful, and George has a sudden impulse to reach out and take the sleeve of her yellow coat, pull them both back under the trees.

"Do you want that?" he asks. "Why did you want to come here?"

"Same as you," she says. "I need to do something."

She opens her mouth and closes it and then, as if she can't help herself, she keeps going, the words coming out in a messy rush.

"It's too late for our parents and too late for Tom and maybe for you and me too. But I have to see it for myself. I have to *know*."

She looks at him like she wants him to understand and George thinks of her looking down at the bird, with that strange expression on her face. He didn't understand at the time what it meant. He thinks of her alone in that quiet house and he thinks of her listening, like him, hoping for the creaking floorboards.

"You can wait here," Julia says. "I'll look and come back."

She says it simply and without judgement, and George remembers all at once that the story didn't stop with the sharks biting at his toes. He remembered Julia looking up, widening her eyes and pointing, saying, *What's that on the horizon?*

Tom had been rolled over on a skateboard, reaching out his hand, with Julia calling out, *A raft, a raft, Tom's here to save you*, but even then George knew it wasn't Tom who rescued him, that it was Julia who took pity on him, Julia who saved him from drowning. He loved her for it then, and now he thinks that maybe it isn't embarrassment that makes his stomach twist when he sees her now, but guilt. Because Julia saved him and kept the sharks away and then he grew up and abandoned her for it.

"I'm going," George says. "I want to see it too."

It's suddenly very important that neither of them should be alone.

Julia looks at him for a moment, and whatever she sees in his face seems to bring her to a decision, because she nods and turns to go, head tilted upwards towards the ascent. George follows close behind, stumbling a little in the snow.

Walking is harder now, much harder, and with every step the snow drags at his feet. The climb gets steeper and steeper but somehow the hilltop seems to remain in the same place, always just out of reach. Twice he stumbles, and on the third time he falls forward onto his knees. Julia turns back, eyes too large in her head, but George waves her away, gets up. The fall was painless, but the wet seeps through his trousers and, even through the glove, his hand feels raw where he caught himself against the snow.

Everything is shades of white, the sky dirtied and yellowish, the ground like bone, and in the middle of it all is Julia in her yellow coat, always just a little ahead. George wants to rest, to hold back a moment, but he's scared that if he does, he'll be left alone. He wants to call out, wants to say, *Stop, wait*, wants to say, *Let's not look, this is enough, let's go back*, but he can barely breathe, let alone shout.

He gulps at the air and tries to stand upright against the slope, swaying, trying to keep his balance.

"Julia!"

It comes out as a raspy, broken thing, snatched away by the wind almost before it leaves his mouth, but it's enough.

She stops.

She is waiting for him, and George lets out a breath that is almost a sob, scrambling up faster to join her. Even as he closes the distance, he knows something is wrong. She is too still, her back too straight. She's not looking back at him. He reaches her and realizes why.

They've reached the top.

George isn't sure how long they stand together looking down into the valley. He only knows that it ends when Julia reaches over and takes his hand to pull him away. She does it very gently and he lets himself be led. He thinks he might fall without her. His limbs feel clumsy and mechanical. No one has held his hand like this, to guide his way, in a long time, not for years. She must have done this for Tom once, when they were both much younger.

When the ground levels out, just before the tree line, he lets go to wipe at his wet face. Julia turns her head away, giving him privacy.

For a moment he presses his hands into his face very tightly, counting breaths. When he closes his eyes, he can see it again, all tangled up in the telephone wires in that horrible scraped out wound in the earth, dripping out a dark stain. He keeps his eyes open, looks at the pink light between his fingers instead.

Julia says something, but it's lost in the wind and George takes his hands away from his eyes to look at her. The yellow hood has fallen down. A strand of hair is stuck to the corner of Julia's mouth, but she doesn't brush it away. She doesn't even seem to notice.

"What?" George asks. "What did you say?"

"It couldn't have survived," Julia says and the way she says it sounds like a question.

"It was dead," George says and when she looks at him, he says it again, to make sure she knows he means it. "It was dead."

They reach the trees and keep moving.

They walk side by side now, keeping close even though it makes the path more difficult to navigate. Julia holds back a branch to let him through and George glances at her face as he passes through the gap. He looks for some sign in her face, some lasting mark to reflect back at him the truth of what they've seen. She should look older, but she doesn't look any different than this morning. Her mouth is a thin, hard line, lips pressed so tightly together that it seems impossible that she could ever speak again.

Even so, George wants to ask her. He wants to ask her if she will be okay. He wants to ask her if it made a difference, coming out here today, if it was better to know, to see it for themselves.

"It's getting dark," he says.

"I know. But it's not far now."

He wants to ask, how could it be that big, how could it be possible for something like that to exist in the same world as his bike and their village? He wants to ask about the telephone wires and if she remembers the stories she used to make up or if he imagined that, if maybe he imagined a life before this, a life that was normal and safe and small.

He wants to ask her what happened after he walked the plank, after the sharks and the raft. He wants to ask her how it all ended.

Maybe she'll smile at him and laugh and say, *I remember. I remember that story. It never stopped. It just kept going.*

For now though, with the shadows gathering, they keep walking, as above them small snowflakes escape the net of dark branches and fall softly, soundlessly, to the ground.

See Maud Woolf's story "The Stranding" online at Metaphorosis.
If you liked it, leave a comment. Authors love that!
Remember to subscribe to our e-mail updates so you'll know when new stories are posted.

About the story

I grew up in a small Scottish coastal village, much like the one in "The Stranding". While it was a bustling tourist spot in summer, in winter the place became bleak and abandoned. The only bus to town came infrequently and my friends and I spent most of our time rambling around by the beach and in the fields nearby. Driven by boredom we went swimming in large rockpools and tried, mostly without success, to light small fires from the driftwood. Once, we crawled on our bellies through the large storm drain that ran under the town, but this experience was frightening and never repeated.

Living near the beach you see a lot of things washed up with the tide. Most of these things were already dead, but one September twenty-seven live pilot whales beached themselves on the rocky coast that ran between our village and the next. My friend and I took a bus to see them, talking so much we became breathless and bouncing in our seats in anticipation. We had never seen a live whale before, not even as distant lumps between the waves. We weren't the only ones excited; the bus was crowded and most of us got off at the same stop. Not much happened in the countryside and this felt like an event. I won't say too much about what we saw, only that of the twenty-seven whales stranded, only ten made it back to the water. The bus ride home was silent.

Although it affected me at the time, I filed this memory away and had almost forgotten about it completely until quite recently. During the first UK lockdown, I was living in Bristol and spent most of my time taking long, solitary walks. I remember thinking how strange it was to see nothing but empty streets but also how strangely familiar the experience was. An idea started creeping in, or, to be more accurate, an image. Two kids walking through a silent village in the snow. Setting out to find something.

Details like what it was they were hoping to find and why the streets were empty came later, but that initial image is still crystal clear in my head, even now. I couldn't write about the whales, and I didn't want to write about the pandemic. I wrote "The Stranding" instead and that, I think, was a pretty good alternative to both.

A question for the author

Q: What would your animal totem be?

A: I don't know if I would call them an animal totem, but I've always felt a strong affinity with magpies. I remember my grandmother teaching me to use them as omens (one for sorrow, two for joy) and even now, when I see them, I start counting. They may be known as thieves, but to me to me the act of writing often feels like thievery. Shiny objects are like good stories, to be looked out for and hoarded jealously.

About the author

Maud Woolf is Scottish writer with a particular interest in speculative fiction. Currently working towards an MLitt in Creative Writing at the University of Glasgow, most of her free time is spent either writing in the library or searching for a way into the city's abandoned network of underground tunnels.

@WoolfWolf

The Nocturnals II

Mariah Montoya

In a world where each day and night lasts thirty years, Joah Cadshaw is searching for a missing boy. Before he can find him, bells start ringing throughout the streets; it's time for his community to migrate east, toward the fading daylight, before the decades-long darkness and its night monsters overtake them all. Joah and his new partner, Misla Crane, embark on a quest out west to warn the people who don't know it's time to Move.

On their journey, Joah finds evidence that the missing boy may have been abducted by the Nocturnals—the feared humanoid creatures of the Eternal Night. Joah vows to bring him home.

Part 2

"Hey, Hicks, get up. Retrievers are here."

Hickory Glade groaned in his bundle of blankets, thumbing his pounding temples. His tent-mate had poked his head through the open flap to wake him, but the ice moon was still hovering above the northern skyline, sending a stripe of brilliant white through the canvas.

"Retrievers?" Hickory said, sitting up. "What the hell d'you mean, retrievers?"

Scowling, he checked the timepiece strapped to his wrist. Unlike the rest of the Sunsetters, who started Moving when the sun hung ten degrees above the horizon, the miners didn't have to pack up until five: at five degrees, the sun dangled low in the sky and nighttime prowled just around the corner.

But the hand of Hickory's watch still hovered over the spindly number seven. Not quite late enough to start chasing daylight like they had to do every two damn years. *Strange.* Retrievers usually only showed up when someone—some hunter or scavenger or miner—had gotten lost out in the woods and needed their asses saved from the Eternal Night.

"Yeah, retrievers," Sid said, pushing aside the flap so that smoke and murmurs filled the tent. "Apparently they've got something to tell us. General D's orders. C'mon."

Hickory groaned, stretched, and cracked his neck with a swift jerk of his head. Something felt off, as if warning bells were clanging in the back of his mind. Loud voices and crude jokes usually speared the morning air, but now he only heard gruff whispers and rumbles, quiet, anxious words masked by the roar of the distant river that ran along the edge of their campground.

"Alright, alright, I'm getting up. Wait for me, asshole."

He shook away his blankets and pushed through the dew-slick flap, following Sid to the wooded area outside their caverns. Here, a crowd of soot-faced miners elbowed each other and craned their necks to look at whoever stood in the center of the clearing.

Hickory wasted no time, shoving past his comrades until he had squeezed his way to the front of the pack. He jerked to a gut-wrenching stop when he saw who the two retrievers were.

No, it couldn't be.

Joah Cadshaw. *Joah Cadshaw* was poised in front of the conglomeration of tents and ashy, smoking firepit, his hands clasped neatly behind his back. Hickory rubbed his eyes, but when he opened them again, the horrible apparition was still there. Cadshaw was dressed in a tight, plain white shirt, very different from the crisp retriever uniform he'd used to wear. His hair was ruffled, his chin stubbled, his frame skinnier than the last time Hickory had seen him.

And he, Joah Fucking Cadshaw, was standing elbow to elbow with—

"*Misla*," Hickory spat, cutting through the low grumble of conversation.

When he said her name, the branches around them seemed to still, and the beetles scuttling up their trunks seemed to slow. The distant river, however, thundered with the spite thudding through Hickory's veins. Angry, white foam filled his chest.

"What the hell are you doing here? With *him*?"

The miners coughed themselves into awkward silence. Joah Cadshaw spotted him with the faintest spike of surprise, eyebrows lifting a fraction and narrowing again.

Misla Crane couldn't stifle *her* shock, though. Tilting her head, she said, "Hickory?" in that sickeningly sweet voice she had always used around him, the innocent one. It made him want to throw her onto a bed and pound that silly innocence out of her.

"You two know each other?" Cadshaw asked coldly.

"Yes, you Nocturnal-loving freak, Misla and I *know* each other." Hickory lurched forward, but rough hands cupped his shoulders, holding him back. "She was my girl. She was *mine*, and now you've taken her, just like you took everything else from me. Let me *go*."

But Sid's hold only tightened, and Hickory's worst memory swirled before him:

It was thirteen degrees. He stood in the middle of the High Road before the executioner's block, his ax glinting in the sun. People lined the road in thick rivers of hot bodies and excited whispers, watching as the retriever in the distance led his prisoner toward them. An Infected's execution was usually an exciting ordeal, but this time it was even more so: it was the retriever's own wife who had been infected, the retriever's own wife Hickory would kill.

He licked his lips, tasting the salt of his own sweet sweat. He'd never liked Joah Cadshaw. Ignorant, cocky prick. If he could pull the man's guts through his neck and dangle them around his own, he'd wear the necklace every damn arcsec. It served him right, in a way, that the Nocturnals had chosen to infect Blair Cadshaw. They picked one victim a year to lure to their shit-pit of never-ending darkness; Retriever Cadshaw had always tracked these victims down with ease, forcing them back to their deaths before they could sneak back on their own and wreak havoc on the community. Hickory himself had never hid his fascination with his ax, but Cadshaw had always pretended to be repulsed by the whole ordeal. A reluctant hero.

Until now.

Now Hickory could see, as Cadshaw and his chained wife drew nearer: the famous retriever was actually *repulsed. Pain twisted his face. When he finally reached the executioner's block, he addressed the man sitting behind Hickory's post, desperation in his voice.*

"I beg you to reconsider, General. I think she's trying to tell us something."

At his words, the woman opened her mouth and screamed, "WARN. WARN. WARN." Drool swung from her teeth. She looked as insane as all the other Infected scum Hickory had gotten rid of before, but behind him, General Deckler made a grunt of pity.

"I can postpone the execution if you have sufficient proof that she is not dangerous."

"What?" Hickory spat, spinning around.

The general had always loved Joah Cadshaw, true, but why was he falling for such a biased pile of shit? Even as Hickory watched, the Infected woman swiped a pale, clammy hand toward the onlookers, that drool soaking through her shirt.

No, she was still dangerous. Cadshaw would put them all at risk because he would never quit loving the monster his wife had become.

"I'll consider a life extension," General Deckler began, but Hickory marched forward. Before Cadshaw could blink, before the crowd could gasp, he raised his weapon. The blade sliced cleanly through the Infected woman's neck. Her head hit the ground with a thud.

A shivering silence.

Then Cadshaw was screaming. He threw himself forward and tried to wrestle the ax from Hickory's hand. His eyes bulged, and Hickory clung to his ax like a lifeline, and they threw each other to the High Road, rolling in Blair's blood, the blade narrowly missing Hickory's left ear...

General Deckler's men had jumped in to break them apart. Afterward, Hickory had been fired for misconduct, but Cadshaw himself had simply been transferred to another department for his own "mental wellbeing," or some soft-hearted, bullshit excuse like that. Hickory had watched in a drunken stupor as Misla, once an angelic little creature he'd wooed and won with all the right words, had packed her things and left him. He'd become like a headless pheasant, staggering around, making a wage by pounding grahsm from cave interiors like his father had once done. A regression in familial stance for sure.

"You lost me my job!" he said now, jerking against the arms wrapped around him. It wasn't fair that he, Hickory, was still out *here*, while Cadshaw had obviously wormed his way back into a retrieving position. Always General D's favorite, that was for bloody sure.

"Well, you killed my wife, so consider us even."

Cadshaw wasn't trembling, but his face had turned a blotchy, veiny purple that made Hickory feel triumphant. Oh, the mask was there, but it was slipping.

"Well, it looks like you paid me back, didn't you?" Hickory panted. "Looks like you've gone and stolen *my* woman. Is that why you left then, pretty girl? So you could be with *him*?"

He bit his lip. Tasted blood. His last encounter with Misla had not been pleasant, he had to admit, but she didn't look the worse for wear. She was wearing the same fitted white shirt Cadshaw was, but hers hugged her curves, and she had added a frayed scarf that bore a resemblance to the Retrieving Institute colors. She was plumper than he'd last seen her. Her hips were wider, her breasts lower, her cheeks rounder. A good weight gain. It added a flush to her face, a look of strength in her thighs.

But her eyes weren't flickering downward like they'd used to. They squinted at him with no trace of that soft, liquidy warmth he had come to associate with melting candle wax. These new eyes looked hard and gray and unyielding.

Before Hickory could say anything else, Misla cupped her hands around her mouth to address the crowd, as if his outburst had been nothing more than the irritating chirp of crickets.

"The Moving bells rang early because the High Road was severed."

At that word, *severed*, Hickory saw Blair Cadshaw's head at his shoes. The wisps of her hair brushing his ankles. Her blood soaking into the asphalt of the High Road.

"We have to stray from the road our ancestors have been using for centuries," Misla continued. "You all need to pack up immediately." She paused, glanced at Hickory, and cleared her throat, throwing a braid over her shoulder. "It's been easy to follow the sun our whole lives, because we can travel four times as fast. But this detour will slow us down. The Nocturnals won't be far behind."

"Any questions?" Cadshaw asked, his eyes trained on Hickory.

"Well, how come the High Road was severed?" someone called.

"We don't know," Misla said. "Possibly a quake. Some kind of natural disaster. Either way, it's going to take longer than expected to reach the Green Sea. So get Moving."

With that, *Hickory's* woman—yes, she was still Hickory's woman, he felt that deep within him—whipped around with her new bravado and strode back through the path of trees, that frayed scarf bouncing on her neck, Joah Cadshaw on her heel.

The arms holding him back loosened. Hickory turned to see Sid raise an eyebrow at him as the rest of the miners burst into movement, tearing down tents and lugging supplies to the pack horses in another clearing through the trees.

"Sorry, Hicks, had to do it," Sid said. "Couldn't let you kill the nut. Though I guess if you had, there's no General Deckler around to fire you."

"Good Old General D's *obsessed* with Joah." Hickory licked the last beads of blood from the cracks in his lips. "I knew it back then—if Joah wanted to delay his wife's execution, Deckler wouldn't just grant the wish. He'd blow kisses into Joah's asshole too, for good measure." Hickory mimed a kiss without humor. "If I killed him now, the general would track me down and staple my face to his office wall, right next to that shiny Nocturnal poster of his."

Apparently, Sid decided this was funny, because he belly-chuckled. The tension cracked inside Hickory, who laughed with him, eyes tracking the last patches of Misla's new, widened ass as she pushed through branches and disappeared in the thickness of the trees.

"So," Sid continued when they had quit laughing. He spit into the nearest fire. A coal sizzled. "You ready to Move, Hicks? The city's so slow, we'll catch up to those slugs in no time. Might as well bring the shiniest grahsm with us. Get some extra silvers for it."

"Oh, I'm ready to Move," Hickory said, still gazing at the place where Misla had melted into the woods. He could practically feel her shrill breath in his ears again, but that may have been the sudden breeze whistling between the trees. "I'm not Moving toward the sun, though."

Sid's eyebrows reached his shiny, slick hairline. Hickory laughed.

"I can't let him steal her again. I'm going to get my girl back." He paused, imagining Aoif Deckler. "I think my face getting stapled to a wall is a risk I'm willing to take."

Joah and Misla left seven degrees behind them like an old, fallen-off shoe.

When they reached six degrees a dozen arcsecs later, the sun cast dark purple shadows; its rays had shrunk until it resembled a neat orange ball hovering inches from the horizon behind them.

"Oil scavengers should've started Moving by now," Joah told Misla, forcing himself to sound as if he hadn't just exchanged words with his wife's killer. "We'll probably pass them on the High Road. We've just got to make it to that tower near the oil reserves, make sure no one got left behind. Then we can head back."

"Right," Misla said.

Five degrees. They continued in dense silence. The stretch of forest and caves where the miners had been residing morphed back into tall, naked cliffs, as if they were entering a dead zone between two forests. Beyond the tower, Joah knew, the woods would rejuvenate.

Four degrees. They'd be passing the scavengers any moment, but Joah hardly cared. His whole being quivered with suppressed rage. Oh, why hadn't he just charged at the man? Why hadn't he finally killed the monster haunting his dreams? And why hadn't Misla mentioned it—that she'd dated such a beast? That *he* was the one who had burned and abused her?

I was there when it happened, you know, she had told him. *In the crowd...*

Three degrees. Dark shadows leapt across the High Road. *Hares*, Joah thought numbly.

Then the steed's magnetic clock read two degrees, the bright blue of the sky glistened with dark streaks of orange, and he couldn't restrain his words anymore.

"It was him—" he began.

He glanced at her. His breath caught on his tongue. Under different circumstances, the new lighting might have made her beautiful. But dried tears striped her cheeks, and those smile-shaped scratches marked the hollows of her neck, which she had tried to hide by wrapping the tattered remains of her retrieving uniform around her throat like a scarf.

"It was Hickory Glade?" he grunted, before he could swallow himself into more silence. "You dated him? He's the one who gave you your scar?" *And mine*, he didn't add.

Misla sighed.

"He was charming, at first. He always told me the most fantastic *stories*. Some were about his father. The miner. He told me all about his dad's adventures, how his dad had discovered magic metals and secret caves, how he would come home with beautiful stones for their rock collection. Hickory still had those stones. He kept them in empty jars and placed them all around his house, and in the darkness lit by fire, it was all so...so *beautiful*."

Joah knew for a fact that Hickory Glade had loathed his status as a simple miner's son, had only told these stories to glorify the poverty-stricken childhood he had grown up in.

"But most," Misla continued, and her next words came as no surprise, "were about his grandfather. The general before Deckler. He told me about his grandfather's rise to leadership. How he developed the warning system. How he died. Hickory talked a lot about how he died."

Joah knew that Hickory's grandfather had been killed by Nocturnals about six decades ago. But he couldn't force himself to conjure any pity. He stared ahead as the High Road made a sharp bend around a crag. With the light dimming, branches and twigs that jutted from the cliffs looked more and more like long, crooked fingers. There were occasional muffled hoots and far-off yowls that sounded like glitches in the normal noise of life.

"Listen, Joah," Misla said earnestly. "I left Hickory after he murdered your wife."

Murdered.

Chills wormed up Joah's spine at that word. Not killed. Not executed. *Murdered.*

He stared without seeing at the bluffs before them. Everyone else had considered his wife's death a violation of procedure. Hickory Glade had been fired for misconduct, not *murder.*

Yet, finally, here was someone who believed otherwise like him.

"I always suspected Hickory enjoyed his little executions," Misla continued in a deadpan voice. "He always convinced me otherwise. He told me it was for the good of the Sunsetters. He was saving children's lives. The Nocturnals and everyone they infected were demons that would infest our community if left untreated. It wasn't until he swung that ax before General Deckler's say-so that I knew he'd been lying. He *liked* killing. I could see it on his face when—well…"

"Yeah," Joah managed to choke out.

The crests of the distant mountains glowed purple, like the treetops had caught a violet fire. Migrating birds freckled the sky. At the thought of birds, Joah became distinctly aware of the cushioning in his back pocket: the remains of young Damien Ferthcli's green cat shirt. Evidence that the Nocturnals had gotten into the head of a child.

Misla had asked about the shirt after they had scrambled into their sleeping bags three cycles ago, but he hadn't found the right words, had instead mumbled something about making sure she finish cleaning and wrapping her cuts. Now, though, after seeing the way she had addressed the miners so calmly in the face of her fanatic ex, he knew he had to tell her about the Infected boy.

He opened his mouth, but Misla spoke before he could.

"Anyway, I decided to become a retriever after I left Hickory. I've always hated how we behead the Infected as *soon* as we bring them back—"

"Not true," Joah retorted. The green shirt was pushed momentarily from his mind. "If we can drag them back before they reach… well, what you'd call the Eternal Night, we put them in a white room and wait to see if the madness subsides. Sometimes it does. More often it doesn't. But the public doesn't see that. The public only sees the Infected that managed to make physical contact with the Nocturnals, the ones who sneak back after a few years to ravage our community. Retrievers track down *those* ones before they can surprise-ambush us—"

"I know, Boss," Misla cut in. "I just graduated from the Retrieving Institute. I got top marks, you know. All that you just said was in our senior exam."

"Well, what's your *point*, Crane?"

"I want," said Misla, with a breath so deep it seemed to suck the air from Joah's own lungs, "to see if the Infected can talk to the Nocturnals and find out what they want."

Joah's heart thrashed against his ribs. All thoughts of telling Misla about the ripped green shirt in his pocket fluttered away, alongside the migrating birds overhead.

"Crane..." He tried to sound casual. "You don't think I tried talking to every single Infected person I brought back? You don't think I delayed missions to interrogate them?"

She looked at him. He kept his eyes pasted on the winding High Road. Fat rodents were pattering across their path now. He swerved to avoid running them over.

"You don't think I purposely ran out of fuel to give the Infected extra time to heal? You don't think I spent a whole *year* with my crazed wife out here in the wilderness trying to find a cure, only to fail, only for General Deckler to send more retrievers to force us back with a death penalty hanging over my head as well as hers?"

"I didn't—"

"Of course you didn't know." Snot clogged Joah's throat. "Everyone thinks retrievers are cold and cruel. But once the Nocturnals lodge their whispers into your head, they don't withdraw those whispers—but, of course, you'd already know that. Retrieving Institute, and all, right?"

"Look," Misla said, crossing her arms, "I know you're bitter. I know you're sad. But you don't need to treat me like—like—*scavengers*."

"Like scavengers?" Joah repeated.

"No. Look. Scavengers."

Misla pointed through their cracked windshield. During their conversation, the High Road had rounded a cliff and continued into a wide expanse of hardened, rocky aro. Now, perched on the opening beyond, the outline of a cylindrical tower bowed over the High Road.

But the High Road wasn't empty. Each strapped with bouncing silver canteens, sprinting toward them, were the oil scavengers who should have started Moving five degrees before.

They were hollering indistinguishably, their voices like blunt knives failing to slice the air.

Cursing, Joah sped toward them until they were close enough to hear each gasping word.

"Hey, hey, hey!"

"Did General Deckler send you?"

"Thank God you're here."

Joah punched the brakes as they met the scavengers, who were coughing and panting. Their mops of hair were gray with dust. Their hands were slimy with oil and blood.

"Hold up." Joah tugged on the parking stick and jumped out onto the dusted High Road to meet them. "It's almost sunset. Why the *hell* are you lot still here? I thought you might've taken a shortcut and that's why we didn't see you on the High Road, but I never thought—"

"Mack got killed," one scavenger piped up, breathless. "He's my friend, Mack is. *Was*, I mean. A night beast came braver than usual. Tiptoed into sunset. It got Mack—"

"And all our damn horses," another scavenger added.

"Aye, and all our horses," the first scavenger agreed, "it's like nothing I've never seen in my life. Like a cat, but bigger, and it's got scales."

"The night beast is some kind of reptile, you mean?" Misla asked.

All the men's eyes flashed over to her, as if they had permission now that she had spoken. They scanned her body for much too long, some with smirks.

"I guess," said the scavenger, his eyes on Misla's chest, "but a cat-like reptile."

"And how did this creature kill your friend?"

"It yowled at 'im. Horrible yowl, could've burst your eardrums. And Mack dropped to the ground, screaming and twitching. And then the cat drug him away into the forest by its claws. Same with the horses."

Joah and Misla exchanged glances. A grim understanding shot between them.

"You're sure it was a night beast?" Joah asked.

"Aye. Stayed in the shadows the whole time. Not that that's too hard, with the forest a little way back, and the tower. That tower makes a *long* shadow."

The group all turned to gaze at the strange construction, which looked, Joah thought, like a giant canine tooth, fat and round at the bottom, tapered and sharp on top. It was far larger and more permanent than anything the Sunsetters had ever created in living history. It had been quite the object of horror stories and conspiracy theories as they had passed it during the last Move, but General Deckler had been firm about Moving by, not staying to investigate. Only after they had settled had he sent some men back to collect the oil in a nearby reservoir.

"Can we ride back with you?" the first scavenger asked now. His canteen was dripping beads of that oil onto the dirt of the High Road. "We could cram in the back if we threw some stuff out." He peered through the window. "You don't need them tents if we head back now, and we'd only need 'bout half those cans if we ration. Should make it back in three cycles, yeah?"

Joah and Misla passed that knowing look again. Dimly, Joah felt warm surprise that they could already communicate the vague basics without speaking.

"You won't make it back before three moon cycles," Misla said firmly. "And Retriever Cadshaw and I aren't going back just yet, so no, you can't hitch a ride with us."

"Come again?" the scavenger asked.

"The Sunsetters already Moved." Briefly, Joah explained the fissure in the High Road. "Retriever Crane and I are going to investigate the creature that killed your friend. If the night beasts are starting to chance sunlight, General Deckler needs to know about it."

And we need to search for the boy, he didn't add.

"We'll give you some of our food," Misla said. "If you stick together and keep a steady pace, you should be fine. Just veer right after the grasslands. You might even catch up to the grahsm miners, they just left and there are a lot more of them, so they'll be slower than—"

Joah saw it coming a second before it happened.

The first scavenger tilted his head, his eyes flickering toward his mates, his pupils gleaming with that dog-like hunger for survival. His lip curled upward. His mates gave wisps of laughter, like schoolgirls giggling behind polite hands when a boy is doomed for detention.

"Crane, DOWN," Joah bellowed.

Misla didn't hesitate. She thudded to her knees; the scavenger's swinging fist missed her head by an inch, but another one, shiny with oil and dirt, met Joah's ear.

His skull exploded. His lungs seemed to jump out of his throat. Boots connected with his body from every direction. The High Road pounded his spine again and again, like a crazed, violent mother burping her baby. Dust heated his throat.

Far off, Joah thought Misla might be climbing the shafts of orange light in the sky like a stairwell, screaming his name. *Strange.* He couldn't remember who Misla was, exactly, but he thought perhaps she was his wife. Perhaps she was beautiful.

Then the scavengers gave his ribs a final kick, and the Eternal Night folded him in its calm, cold embrace.

Sleep cocooned him. No light disturbed his darkness and no sound punctuated his silence. It was as if he lay in a black pond, where the waves lapped over him seamlessly, lulling him into a cavern where light and sound didn't exist. And there was no light and there was no sound. No light or sound. Light or sound. Light. Sound.

A dull pounding sensation hammered the back of his head. It was not light *or* sound, but a *feeling*, like a beam of bright noise thumping itself into his skull.

"Stop it," Joah muttered, swiping his hand at the beam.

"Joah," the beam said back.

His eyelids betrayed him, opening him up to a bright, noisy world. A woman was leaning over him, chanting his name over and over, the left side of her face blotched and purple. The ice moon beamed beyond her shoulders.

"Keep waking up, Joah," the woman said, and her name came to him.

"Misla." He tried to sit up. The world tilted. The waves came back and spiraled around him. The woman pressed a palm to his chest and forced him to lie back down.

"Hey, hey, not so fast, take it slow, you'll be alright, just take it slow."

She said this all very fast, and her urgency cut through Joah's haze in a way the moon's ferocity couldn't. He blinked. He gazed at the bruise masking her left eye and cursed.

"They hit you," he mumbled. "The scavengers. Scum. Vultures. They hit you."

"They did a lot worse to you," Misla said. "I only wish I could've broken all their bones before they ran off. But I—there were too many of them. I think I knocked out a tooth, but..."

Her eyes darted left and right. For the first time, Joah became aware of how bright the moon was, stamped against the blackening purple sky. He tilted his head to find the sun, but it had shrunk to half a dome peeking between two cliffs behind them—a bloodred eye peering at them cruelly. Preparing to blink into nothingness.

"They took the steed, didn't they?" Joah spat, using his elbows to prop himself up.

Every inch of him ached. He did a quick self-evaluation and guessed he was concussed, with bruised ribs and a broken nose. Dried blood caked his upper lip. His jaw throbbed.

"Yes, they took the steed. Didn't leave us any food, either. They told me to kiss the sun's fiery red ass goodbye."

"How thoughtful," Joah growled.

"I know, right? Now, first things first, we need to get out of the open. If there really *are* night beasts lurking around, I'd rather not meet them for the first time with a damaged partner."

She paused, those eyes darting again. The noise of sunset swelled, but Joah couldn't tell where the creatures were, exactly; it sounded as if all the chirps and coos and cries were simply eddying around his head, ringing in his ears. As if the rocks were shrieking.

"I say we get to that tower," he grunted, nodding toward them. "I don't know if you got a good look when we passed by during the last Move. *I* didn't see any doors, but looks like it's made of metal. It'll retain the sun's heat long enough for us to form some kind of plan." He huffed as he tried to stand. "After the sun sets, it can get cold. Fast."

"Okay, tower it is. But don't crap yourself trying to get up so fast. Let me help."

Misla placed her hands in Joah's armpits and hoisted him up. He bit his lip to keep himself from crying out, then gasped anyway as his teeth pierced an already mangled lip.

"Don't worry, you can make as much noise as you'd like. I won't laugh."

"You're too kind."

Misla's lips twitched as they hobbled toward the outline of the tower before them, Joah's arm hooked around her neck, the moon glowing brighter above them. Sometimes he glanced sideways and mashed his teeth together at the sight of the bruise that had spread from her eyebrow to cheekbone. When—*if*—they caught up to the rest of the community, he'd have Deckler throw the scavengers in the smelliest portable prisons, *that* was for sure.

Greasy, slimy sons of Dirt Slum bitches, he thought. *Cowardly piles of shit...*

But as the tower rose, grating the gray mob of clouds that had accumulated in the sky, Joah's internal curses gave way to a dizziness. His fingertips tingled. Even as Aoif Deckler's best retriever, he had only ever ventured this far into the darkness once before...

He was standing in a meadow. Clouds fragmented the sky, casting a bloody light on the stretch of never-ending grasses and tufts of violet wildflowers. A figure was swaying in the distance, walking away from him, chanting something indiscernible as she staggered westward.

"Almost there," Misla muttered. "Come on, just a little further."

Joah stared at the figure, knowing it was her. Her, her, her. The one he'd been chasing for a year now, the one who, the night before she'd run away, had whispered against his neck that she wanted to try for a baby soon.

"Joah, I—I think there *is* a door. Or some kind of opening. Look."

He tried to look, but she had wanted to be a mother. Now she would never be a mother. She was a Nocturnal puppet, and Joah was almost too scared to call out her name. But he did *call out her name, and despite what they said about the Infected's inability to understand language after the Nocturnals had twined words around their brains, she turned.*

She turned.

She turned, and Joah saw the face of his wife wearing a mask of purest white. Bright purple veins crisscrossed her cheeks and forehead, like shattered eggshells.

No, it was not his wife's face, but the ice moon posing as his wife's face. He felt a newfound tickle, like a stroking finger, caress the back of his neck. A dim part of him realized that the moon was king. Maybe not king of the day, but king of the Eternal Night. And now it had plastered itself over his wife's eyes, and it was laughing at him.

Her manic smile spread her cheeks as she hobbled toward him, arms outstretched...

"Stay with me, Joah, don't fall asleep yet."

Hazily, Joah saw Misla push through a blanket of wool-like cobwebs and help him through a rounded hole in steel, into a cavern of deepest pitch-black. Their shoes crunched over brittle objects scattered on the floor. Misla was saying something else to him, but he couldn't hear. Tingles scuttled up his spine, as if his wife were *in his arms now. She was laughing up at him. Her eyes twitched in their sockets, like a rat was squirming beneath her eyelids, desperate to break free and nibble at Joah's skin.*

Blair, *he cried.* Blair, Blair, Blair.

But she just laughed and laughed and squeaked, "Warn you. Got to," *and then kept laughing, her tongue shooting in and out, her mouth so widely stretched he could see her uvula and each rotten tooth, and he knew then, although he would try to find her a cure later, that she was gone. Her body was here, but the Nocturnals had snatched her soul right out of his cradling arms. She was gone.*

"Gone," Joah croaked. "Gone. All gone."

"What are you talking about, Joah? I'm right here. Just lean back. One moment."

Misla's warmth disappeared. He was alone, his back pressed against a smooth, cold surface. His head throbbed. When he pressed his hands against the floor to steady himself, something sharp pierced his right palm. He sucked in a breath that made his chest ache.

"Come back, Misla," he murmured.

She didn't answer. He blinked, trying to rid himself of the memories infecting him so that he could assess his present situation.

He was slumped against the wall of what felt like a smooth cave. But the mouth, through which streamed a glum pool of bruised purple light, was perfectly square, and there had been no caves surrounding the High Road. He had told Misla to take him to the tower.

Somehow, then, she had lugged him *inside* the structure. As his eyes adjusted to the darkness, Joah saw that there was a hole in the floor, like a giant toilet bowl that might flush away anything wandering in its path. And surrounding the hole in a swirl...

Bones. Tiny skulls. Bird beaks. The skeletons of hares, rats, and other animals Joah knew no name for.

"Misla!" he called, louder, his eyes racing toward that inexplicable entrance.

She appeared at the door, illuminated by a ball of fire. He stared, dazed, as she hurried inside, bringing the fire with her. That flickering kind of light was usually only used for cooking, but Hickory Glade must have taught her how to make torches, because Misla had wrapped the remaining slice of her retriever's uniform around a dead branch.

"Glad to see you're awake," she said, closing the door behind her. The bruised purple light gave way to dancing flames as she skirted carefully around the hole leading underground.

"Yeah, glad to be awake," Joah mumbled.

They gazed around them, Misla's firelight illuminating their surroundings. Near the closed door, a stone staircase wrapped around the edge of the tower until it disappeared through the floor above. But Joah could not stop staring at the staircase that began at the edge of the hole in the ground and spiraled downward, into whatever abyss had been created beneath the tower.

"We'll—we'll be safe in here, I think." Misla started toward him, picking her way carefully so as to avoid stepping on skulls. "The night beasts can't get to us if—"

"But Misla, how did these *bones* get in here?" It took every ounce of determination to speak coherently. "I doubt all the sunset critters decided to have a death party inside a man-made building." Joah paused, his head spinning. "I...I just don't like this, Misla. Where'd that door *come* from? We—I—nobody saw any openings when we passed by during the Move."

"Maybe we all missed it." Misla bent down beside him. One hand still gripping the torch, she dug into her pocket and brought out a familiar green capsule. "Here, take this. It's the pain medication you wanted me to use after those birds attacked me."

"You didn't take—?"

"Oh, don't give me that look. It ended up working out. You need relief more than I did."

Joah grumbled, but swallowed the pill dry, realizing as he did so how his throat burned with a parched aridness. The scavengers hadn't even left them a water canteen, for God's sake. He opened his mouth to ask if Misla knew of any new curse words he could use, but she rammed a finger to her lips, nodding toward the ceiling.

A strange screeching noise, like grinding metal gears, echoed above them. Then came a *thump*, and a *clang*, as if something were banging two kitchen pans against each other.

Slowly, Misla bent and picked up a sharp, curved bone, holding it in a tight fist like a dagger. Her torch's fire danced and waved eagerly, its flames reaching toward the ceiling. Toward whatever night beast they had trapped themselves in this God-forsaken tower with.

Maybe it was the same reptilian beast that had hoarded all these skeletons, Joah thought with a barely suppressed moan. The same beast that had killed the scavenger Mack.

"Misla, what are you doing?" he hissed suddenly.

She had turned to creep toward the staircase by the door, torch in one hand, bone in the other. When Joah made to stand, she whispered, "I'm going to check it out. You stay there. You won't be able to help in your condition, so find yourself a sharp one and stay awake."

"Misla, *no*."

But she was already climbing those stairs, which were steeper than the portable ones leading up to Aoif Deckler's office. They had no side railings, and Misla kept her shoulder pressed against the tower wall as she stole upward, around and around, until she had ascended to the landing above. Her absence brought a horrible, mud-thick darkness.

"Shit. Shit. Shit." Joah pressed his shoulder blades against the wall to scoot himself up. His body ached, but the sharp, dizzying agony he had expected did not come. The capsules worked fast, then, or else his panic had overpowered the pain.

Please be a hare, or a possum, or any kind of small, harmless creature, Joah pleaded as he limped his way around the hole and toward the staircase, hands outstretched in the darkness. But even as he lugged his foot onto the first stone step, he heard a shrill, keening wail above him.

"I'm coming, Misla, I'm coming!"

Now he was bounding up the steps, ignoring his body's aching protests. The staircase rose until it met a rounded opening in the ceiling, and then Joah was panting in a perfectly circular room lit with Misla's torch like the one below. Except there were no skeletons infesting this one's floor. Instead, spirals of steel hung from the ceiling, and Misla was crouching before—not a night beast —but a boy.

"Damien," Joah whispered, awe-struck.

The boy was naked, but so muddy it looked as if he had developed a new, thick layer of armor. Even so, Joah recognized his face as the same one plastered on sketches in his office. He also recognized the Infected wildness that had crept into the boy's eyes, the look of shattered eggshells and popping purple veins and a moon-like glow shrouding his features.

"You know him?" Misla demanded.

She had dropped her weapon, which lay discarded at the boy's feet. Damien was shuffling and panting. He seemed unsure of where he was. There was no hint of that wry smile that Blair had given, only a delirious confusion, the cries of a small babe calling for his mother.

"I—he's—his name's Damien Fertheli. He's—" Dazed, Joah reached into his pocket and brought out the limp scrap of green shirt he had plucked from the High Road. He held it out to the boy, then shook his head. "What the hell am I doing? Here, Damien."

He pulled off his own shirt. Tentatively, trying to keep steady, he slipped it over the boy's head. Damien only jerked away half-heartedly. A good sign. Joah grabbed the boy's hands—which were cold as the dead of night—and forced them through the sleeves.

The bottom hem unraveled to Damien's knees, so that, in the firelight, it looked as if the Infected child had donned a translucent, moon-woven dress.

Misla inhaled, but she wasn't staring at the boy. She switched the torch to her other hand and squinted at Joah's midriff. Damien let out another wail.

Joah looked down. His body glowed blue and green with bruises. They covered his ribs and chest like ripples in a pool. And suddenly it seemed as if the three of them, standing together, formed an eerie, indoor sunset: Misla, with her dwindling blaze of orange like the dying sun; Damien, in his egg-white dress like the ice moon; and Joah, the bruises painted over his body like the looming darkness that came with the Eternal Night.

Then Misla retracted her firelight. The spell was broken.

"How," she asked in a wavering voice, "do you know this boy? *How is he here?*"

Joah's legs couldn't hold him anymore; the pain had crept back into his head and lungs and ribs. He lowered himself to the floor as Damien wailed again.

"Do you remember when we first met? How Deckler told me to 'forget the boy'?"

Misla nodded, frowning.

"Well, this is the boy. This is the boy I was assigned to find."

In whispers, Joah told her everything, including Lupita Fertheli's suspicions that the Nocturnals had infected her son. Misla's frown deepened. When he had finished speaking, Damien began turning in circles, his wails morphing into decipherable mumbles:

"West. West. Not scary. Scary. Going back. West. Need me."

"Honey," Misla said, taking Damien's hand. The boy flinched. "You can't go west. We're supposed to be going *east*, remember? We follow the sun. That's what we do."

"Sun," Damien said. *"No. Scary. Going back. West. Need me."*

Misla continued consoling him, but Joah stared. He had never witnessed an Infected person respond to conversation by repeating a word. *Sun,* Damien had told Misla, even though that had not been part of his original, mumbling vocabulary. Come to think of it, Damien was using a wider range of words than the Infected typically portrayed.

"Listen, Misla," Joah said urgently, "Damien's got a chance at returning to his old self. A better chance than most. But we need to figure out a way to get him home, and that's going to be pretty damn difficult without any kind of steed. We need to think of ways to—"

"The river," Misla cut in. She had coaxed Damien into a sitting position on the floor, where he rocked, mumbling his words, his hand still grasped tight by Misla's. "I've been thinking about it ever since the scavengers took off. It's the only way."

"That river by the grahsm miners?" Joah asked. "But we don't have time to build boats."

"What, are you afraid of getting a little wet?" Misla smirked. "We'll find some dead logs and float, of course. The river wasn't running parallel to the High Road, it was running—"

"Southeast," Joah said, excitement mounting within him. "The Sunsetters will still be heading south, so we'd run right into them! Yes. You're brilliant, Misla. If we start now, we might be able to reach the river before the sun's gone too far down." He hoisted himself up.

"Hold up. *You* need rest." Misla glared at him. "It's still moontime. We haven't slept in ages. And *he* needs washed." She nodded at Damien, who moaned.

Joah blinked at her. "How the hell do you expect to *wash* him without the river?"

Misla nodded at the twisted tubes of steel hanging from the ceiling like oddly misplaced rain gutters. "When I first came up here, I found Damien drinking. From those. Whoever built this place must have designed something on the tower roof to store rainwater for drinking purposes, because I think the water's clean."

"Well *that* would've been nice to know."

Joah hobbled to the nearest gutter, where a square metal container, almost like a mailbox, stuck out from the base of the tube. He lifted the hatch, threw his hands inside, and lapped the frigid water from his cupped palms.

Soon Misla couldn't seem to resist. She gently disengaged herself from Damien, who continued rocking on the floor, his arms hugging his mud-caked knees to his chest. Seconds later, Joah heard her gulping water from a neighboring gutter. He wiped his mouth on his wrist.

"Okay," he whispered. "How about this? We sleep for a few arcsecs. As soon as we wake up, we fill ourselves with water and head out. We'll have to keep a brisk pace, which might be..." He glanced at Damien uncertainly. Usually, the Infected struggled and fought against eastward travel. Sometimes they had to be lugged back in handcuffs or ropes. Damien, however, seemed momentarily uninterested in continuing his westward journey toward the Eternal Night.

Maybe because the darkness is already upon us. Maybe the Nocturnals are already here.

Shaking away this thought, Joah continued in a whisper, "He isn't showing any signs of trying to escape right now, but we'll need to watch him closely. And it might be hard to get him to cooperate in riding the river east."

"We'll manage," Misla said promptly. "C'mon, help me wash him."

Together, they brought Damien handfuls of water one cupped palm at a time, lathering it over his skin. The mud trickled away, revealing scratches and sores underneath. Joah tried not to cringe. The boy would need to be seen by a healer as soon as they reached the community.

When they had washed him as best they could, Joah caught Misla's eye and gave her a slow nod. She blew out her leftover fire, encasing them in a stony blackness. Joah heard the *clunk* of the torch as she set it down, and then they moved toward one another, feeling for Damien and each other's groping fingers. When they had found him, they settled onto the floor and eased the boy into a lying position, Joah pressing against his back and Misla hugging him from the front.

They grasped each other's hands so that the boy was swaddled in a tight cocoon. Now if he had the Infected urge to escape while they were sleeping, they would know.

"Who do you think built this place?" Misla whispered. She was so close, her breath puffed onto Joah's lips. Damien mumbled incoherently between them.

"I—I don't know. Whoever they were, they must have Stayed. You can't build something *this* big between Moves." Joah stared upward unseeingly, trying to imagine living thirty years in the constant light and thirty years in the Eternal Night. Who could endure *both*?

"Could've been the Sunrisers," Misla breathed. "These walls would protect them from night beasts, and the roof would protect them from the midday sun."

"Or it could've been the Leather Skins," Joah said, grunting as he moved his legs and renewed pain exploded in his ribs. The green capsule had worn off, then. "I'm sure there's enough insulation here to shield them from the cold of sunset and night."

"Or," whispered Misla, "it could've been the Nocturnals. We like to call them monsters, you know, but monsters don't have to be primitive. They could be really, really clever."

Of course, the Nocturnals who had been infecting Joah's people *couldn't* have built this particular tower: they'd been chasing the Sunsetters around the aro for the last six decades. But there were rumors of multiple communities of Leather Skins migrating at midday, so why couldn't there be a different community of Nocturnals who had built the tower instead?

Joah remembered the glossy poster in Deckler's office that he had tried not to look at: *that* hand-drawn imagining of a Nocturnal had been hunched, with many yellow eyes and pincers for hands and hunched shoulders, an insect-like beast incapable of creation.

But what if the insectile body straightened? What if the pincers shrunk into fingers and the eyes became two and the Nocturnal on the poster simply looked like his wife had, human, with a little cracked moon plastered over the skin of its face?

Damien was snoring between them now. Joah felt himself drifting. It had been a long time since he'd laid this close to other humans, since he'd felt this kind of warmth. Misla's hand was soft and small in his. In the darkness, it could have been Blair lying next to him, the child they had never conceived sandwiched between their bodies, safe and happy and alive.

"Dream well, Misla," Joah murmured before he let himself fall into this fantastic sleep.

"Damien? Where is he? *Where is he?*"

Misla's panicked voice snapped Joah from his grogginess. Fingernails pierced his bare chest, as if checking to see whether he was man or child. When Misla shifted away from him, crawling along the floor and screaming Damien's name, Joah sat up. His skull felt fit to burst.

"He's gone," Misla cried. "I don't know—how did we—? He was here! Right *here.*"

"Okay. It's okay. We'll find him. He—"

But Misla was already moving toward the staircase. Her knees clunked against the floor as she crawled in the darkness. Joah blinked rapidly, as if his brain were trying to process the impenetrable indifference between opened and closed eyes. *This.* This was like rotten death.

"Hold up," he muttered, crawling after her.

He tried to clear his spinning head. They had fallen asleep trapping Damien between them. The boy must have disengaged himself and tiptoed away without waking them. But Misla had closed that enigmatic door downstairs, and the Infected were hard-pressed to figure out things like knob-turning or door-opening. Surely, Damien was still inside the tower, wandering like a drunken Dirt Slummer on one of the levels above...

When his hands found the topmost step, however, the darkness seemed to thin. Joah blinked and squinted downward, through the gap in the floor where the staircase curled to the ground. A scabbed strip of light—perhaps not even light, but a lesser darkness—spilled from an opening near the base of the stairs.

"Oh my God," Misla said beside him. She clapped her hand to the wall and stood on shaking legs. Together they crept downstairs: Damien *had* managed to open the door, which stood ajar like a missing tooth. Outside, the world had morphed into graying shadow.

"He's gone," Joah said, dazed.

He had been imagining Lupita Fertheli's tear-shined face when she saw her son again. The furious look Aoif Deckler would give when they told him the Nocturnals were infecting children. The revival of the boy when the healers tended to him and he returned to his senses under the sun. Now he and Misla Crane would return to the community childless.

"We need to go," he muttered. He felt numb, like his fingertips had melted away. "I think it's past sunset. Negative degrees." He checked his watch blearily. It was stuck at zero.

"Yes, I agree. C'mon, can you walk?" Misla grabbed Joah's elbow and began marching him across the floor. He staggered after her, their shoes crunching over fragments of bones. "I'm sure Damien hasn't gone far. If we hurry, we might catch him before—"

"Hold up. Wait. We're not going after him. Damien's gone."

Misla stopped and stared at Joah. Her hand fell from his elbow.

"We're not going after him?" she repeated slowly.

"No." Defeat sunk to the pit of Joah's stomach. "It's too late. We need to get to the river. Damien—there's a chance he'll find his way back in a year or so. The Infected usually do."

"The Infected *adults* usually do," Misla said, and her eyes seemed to flash with the reflection of last night's fire. "Damien is a *child*. Plus, in a year's time, if all goes to plan, we'll be sailing the Green Sea. He will *die*."

"No. *We* will die, Misla." Joah watched the way her jaw jutted out and knew that their survival would depend on her cooperation. He clenched his fists, steeling himself to hold his ground. "Listen to me, Crane. General Deckler told you to obey my every order."

"General Deckler isn't here, *Detective*," Misla hissed, and the word was a stinging reminder that Joah was no longer a retriever. "If you don't want to go after him, fine by me. But *I* wouldn't be able to live knowing I let a little boy walk into the clutches of—"

"And you're going to fight off the night beasts?" Joah said, his voice rising. "Or are you going to have a civilized conversation with the Nocturnals? Tell them to leave our children the fuck alone? Say please and thank you when they just hand Damien back to you?"

"It's none of your business how I'm going to do it." Misla's raised voice echoed throughout the rounded tower. She bent and scooped up what looked like a discarded jawbone on the ground, clutching it tight in a determined fist.

"Misla, no." Joah grabbed her wrist, but she wrenched away.

"Don't touch me, Detective Cadshaw."

And with that, Misla Crane paraded outside with her jawbone, into the graying twilight. Joah withdrew Damien's remaining strip of shirt from his pocket and hobbled after her, goosebumps erupting on his arms as the brittleness of the night air found his skin. If he had to tie Misla's wrists together and haul her back like he'd hauled so many of the Infected, he would, dammit. He'd do it for her own safety—

But the outside world hit him like an executioner's blunt ax. Even Misla, already halfway to the High Road, stopped in her tracks.

The ice moon glared with yellowed ferocity from the darkened sky, no longer a simple time-stamp for their sleep cycles, but a bowl of concentrated light partially hidden behind the clouds. Joah and Misla must have slept for more than a few arcsecs, then. They must have slept for an entire *cycle*, too stuck in the pits of their dreams to notice Damien's escape...

And the sun. The sun was gone. In the east, a faint ribbon of purple clouded the cliffs, but the light no longer extended to Misla or Joah or the tower. The High Road had been reduced to a black strip. Its surrounding shrubs, ablaze with chirping and buzzing, were mere shadows under the cloud-shielded moon.

"Misla!" Joah cried.

She had resumed her march westward, chin raised, free fist swinging at her side. She didn't turn at her name. When the old anger flashed beneath Joah's bruised ribs, he took out the fragment of green shirt from his pocket and let it fall from his fingertips, onto the dirt.

Fine. *Fine.* If she wanted to leave him, if she was so determined to enter the darkness like Blair had, then all the wrist-tying in the world wouldn't stop her. She was not Infected. She was free to choose. She was free to ignore his warnings, his experience, his knowledge of the night.

Joah turned on his heel, cursing at the ache in his sides. He wanted to scream, rip out his hair, beg Misla to come back, but her newfound absence was already weaving a different kind of pain throughout his chest.

Trying not to think of her or Damien, he scowled at the potholes riddling the High Road.

Damn road developers, he thought. *Lazy, arrogant bastards. Well, it's their fault trailer wheels and horse hoofs got stuck in these holes during the last Move...*

Joah stopped.

No, it couldn't be. He had imagined the sound. He'd been thinking about hooves, but the scavengers had claimed all their horses were dead; there couldn't be one here.

Yet the sound of clip-clopping grew louder. And between cliffs in the distance, two blemishes appeared on the horizon, trotting westward at an easy pace. Male voices resonated across the valley, so brash that the chirping around Joah faltered as it hadn't for him.

For a moment, Joah wanted to wave his arms in the air, holler for his and Misla's saviors. Maybe the presence of other people would revive her sense. Maybe Joah could still save her.

But then he turned to squint for Misla, who was only a far-off, swaying smudge, and he remembered the scavengers swinging a fist at her. He felt their boots against his ribs and tasted the copper of blood filling his mouth. No, he should be cautious this time around.

Before the men on horseback could spot him, he dove behind a nearby shrub, swiping away a lazy horde of bugs hovering around it. He lowered himself to his exposed belly and watched between prickly branches as the men drew nearer.

There were two of them, and their booming laughter renewed the goosebumps on Joah's arms. They didn't sound frightened in the presence of the infamous Eternal Night. They sounded *casual,* as if this were merely a school picnic. As if the moon were a silly plate of cheese they might pluck from the clouds. And one of their voices rang horribly familiar in Joah's ears:

"Gotta tell you, Sid, I never cared much for the heat anyway. Wish Deckler would let us hang out in the sunset zone. So much easier on the eyes, you know."

"Sure, and then we'd be living up to our *name,*" snorted the other. "Why call ourselves the Sunsetters when we're so afraid of the sun actually setting?"

"Well," said Hickory Glade, "as soon as we find Misla and kill that bastard of a bitch she's been fucking around with, we'll go back and persuade everyone that nighttime is better."

Joah didn't dare exhale. He wished the insects would come back and swarm him again as Glade and the other miner passed his hiding place, their mares nickering when they were kicked onward. Dust ballooned in their wake.

Joah pressed a palm against his mouth to stop himself from coughing on the dust. The men were still close enough that he could hear their commentary on the tower, but his ears rang with Glade's previous words: *As soon as we find Misla and kill that bastard of a bitch she's been fucking around with...* Glade was going after Misla just as he'd gone after Blair. And maybe Misla could survive the Eternal Night for a few cycles until she realized her search for the boy was futile, but she wouldn't survive an angry man with an ax if he decided to use it.

An icy resignation sagged Joah's shoulders: he wouldn't be returning to the light of day.

He would *not* let Blair's murderer take another woman he had grown to care for.

The cough escaped him, but Glade was too far past to hear him now. He and his comrade were already smudges like Misla had been, and Misla herself had dissolved into the distance. Clouds now shrouded the moon completely, and Joah could barely make out the edge of the forest he knew lay on the lip of the west.

Hurry, Misla, hurry, he urged, scrambling upward. *Lose yourself in the cotton trees before they can find you.* And then, before he could reject the thought—*I'm coming for you.*

He cast a last look at the purple remnants of sunrays in the east, then turned his back to it and started down the High Road: toward Misla, toward Damien, toward Hickory Glade and the Nocturnals and whatever else lurked out of sight. The air frosted his bare skin.

Far off, in the forest, a night beast yowled.

July

Singot

E.C. Fuller

The first Sinmai I ever saw was watching my kindergarten class play from behind the fence. Round belly and stumpy legs, noodle arms, a short muzzle, and nubby teacup ears, lush with wheaten fur. Long fingers that threaded through the chain link like vines. I thought they were a baseball mascot. Yet, even from afar, they had an alertness, a flexibility to their face, not the vacant, manic expression of a mascot. They had the expression I saw on the children I taught and the expression I sought in adults. Curiosity.

They unwrapped their fingers from the fence and toddled down the sidewalk, still watching. The thirty-two kids pointed at them, waved, and called. I also waved, secretly wishing they would come over. My neighbor, who worked with the Sinmai, had told me a little about them, but that was no substitute for meeting them in person.

Then they rounded the fence and ventured towards us. I thought, *Oh no, I got my wish*, and called the class back. The other teacher on duty, Trevor, blew his whistle. Some children ran to his side. Some dawdled, disobeyed, and ran for the Sinmai.

"Stop!" I said in the teacher-voice I had been sharpening. The children halted, and so did the alien. "Back to class. Toby, Jeanne, now."

Toby and Jeanne whined, "But Miss Stacey..." but went. The Sinmai did not move, merely stared, friendly-looking. They were just a little shorter than me.

I approached them and spoke in the voice I used on frightened children. "Hi there. Can I help you?"

"Can... you?" Their voice was creaky and halting, as if needing to be oiled. "Where am I?"

"You are at Zeigler Elementary."

"What is Zeigler Elementary?"

"It is a school for young children."

"What is a school?"

"A school is a place where we learn."

Their ears wiggled. "I may stay?"

"I—no." Their ear twisted. I said clearly and gently, "I can't let a stranger into class without permission."

"Stranger?"

"Someone we don't know."

"Ahhh." They raised their hand, as if offering a solemn hi-five. The back of their hand was furred, and the fur was silky and dense. The palm was naked, pale brown, and rough, and the meaty parts of their palm and fingertips had raised pads like gold calluses or metallic blisters.

"*Singot*," they said emphatically. A frisson ran through my skin. Before I had ever known what the Sinmai were, I had wanted to singot. I just hadn't had a word for it. My attempts to connect with people had been like off-center, too-enthusiastic hi-fives: missing the mark, embarrassing, and stinging. I wanted the feeling of reaching for someone's hand when walking home together, and they not only let me hold their hand, but grasped mine tightly. The shared, unspoken knowing that we wanted each other, without risking mortification and only reaping the rewards of being aligned and connected. I'd felt out of alignment with the human race all my life.

And then I learned of singot, the supreme connection: wordless understanding of a person's entire life.

I pressed my hand to theirs. The pads were cooler than the rest of their hand.

"I am not a stranger," they said.

I had expected—I don't know. A flash of perfect understanding? Maybe our hands weren't properly aligned. While disappointment sunk in, three large men, led by my neighbor Anya, ran down the sidewalk, waving.

"Poche!" Anya jumped the fence and jogged over to us. I had last seen her sobbing on her apartment balcony after her girlfriend had broken up with her, her cheeks smeared with the icing of the cinnamon roll I had brought. Now she wore business casual with a badge clipped to her pocket and a stun gun clipped to her hip.

"Hi, Stacey. Sorry about this. Poche, it's time to return to the lab," she said, and held up her hand as if for a hi-five. They placed their hand over hers, and I realized the hi-five was a symbolic gesture.

"The one called Stacey says they learn here," they said. "I cannot stay?"

"Can't he?" Anya asked me.

I wished I could say yes. What did he want to learn? What was he like? Could he singot with us? "You should ask the school board first. I have to get back to class. I can give you their contact —"

Anya interrupted. "Time is of the essence. Poche, if you really want to go, we can go."

"Yes," they said immediately.

"What? No!" I retorted. I felt irritated that she wasn't listening to me, though I was curious to know why time was of the essence. Yet I couldn't in good conscience let him around the children until I knew it was safe. Poche's ear twisted again. "We have policies around letting strangers into the school. If something happened and somebody got hurt, we would never forgive ourselves."

Anya replied, "The federal government has agreed to allow Sinmai to go wherever they want in Golden to learn about us, so long as they abide by our rules."

"Then please abide by ours, and get permission. I'm not the one who can give it."

Anya said earnestly, "If he can visit just for today, it could mean we learn something that benefits both the Sinmai and humanity."

I wanted to let him in. I wanted to see what he could learn from us. I wanted to teach him, share with him what we did. In my more romantic moments, I thought of my job as teaching children how to be human. Pick up after yourself, wait your turn; if you see something wrong, say something; be kind to everyone... and it killed me that Poche's first lesson on how-to-be-human was to be cautious of strangers.

Reluctantly, I said. "I'm sorry, Anya. The children have to come first."

I returned to class on my own, kicking myself. An extraterrestrial wandering through the streets would be unusual anywhere else in America, but this was Golden, Oklahoma. The speed-bump-sized town made the national news for getting its first stop light in 2015. Ten years later, the Sinmai ship's landing rockets had flattened the stop light. The military moved in and the town had doubled and doubled and doubled. Yet, the first time I had heard of singot was when I met Anya. She had told me, through hiccups and tears on our apartment balcony, that she was the Director of Xenologic Studies at the Interplanetary Institute.

"Oh, wow!" I had said, "What's that like? Did you get to meet the Sinmai? Can they really read minds?"

"Yes and no. We're not sure what's going on. When they align the pads on their fingers and palms, they share information as pure experience. They call it *singot*. A moment where they share what it's like to be them. For example, if I wanted to singot—" she pressed her hands together "—what I did with you with my colleagues, I would pass on the sensory memory of your voice, the taste of the cinnamon roll, what I felt, what we said... We think it's a perfect transmission of information.

"But singot only works in person. Their technology can't support the volume of information needed to replicate singot or even substitute for it. Also, they must singot to stay healthy, and they need many Sinmai to singot with." Anya wiped her tears away with the heel of her hand. "Six is the smallest number of Sinmai who can singot for extensive periods of time without falling physically or mentally ill. They have a spoken language, but with a limited vocabulary. They think their language evolved so they can signal to each other that they want to singot. They want to learn language as an alternative to singot so they can explore the galaxy farther than they have before."

"I wish I could singot," I said fervently. "That would be amazing."

"That's why we're helping them. We're studying their behavior and anatomy to understand how they do it. In fact, they killed a crew member and gave us their body." My stomach lurched as she went on. "In this case, the one they killed had gone insane. They wouldn't singot with the rest of the crew," she answered my question before I asked it.

"That's..."

"They think of individuality differently than we do," she said, wiping her face. "Why do you want to singot?"

"Why wouldn't I?"

The question was both rhetorical and not. Sometimes I felt like I was hatched from a locker. Born to teach and nothing else. If I could compare my inner life to someone else's, I could understand why I felt different.

Questions pelted me when I slipped back into class.

"Where did the alien go? Is he here? Can we see him?"

Trevor jumped in. "Why don't we start our activity? Paint your favorite memory."

They groaned, but they pulled on their smocks and got busy smearing paint over their paper. If Sinmai were to study pictures drawn by children and took them to be an accurate picture of human life, they would be very, very wrong. Jeanne painted something that could be a dog or a cat or a cow—it had four legs and black and white spots and a bottle-brush tail. I wondered if Poche knew what those animals were.

Trevor gasped. Behind the window of the classroom door, Poche's big golden head loomed. Anya came in, followed by the men, Poche, and the superintendent. The kids gaped. Some ducked behind their canvas.

"We got permission," Anya told me, a little smugly.

The superintendent motioned me closer and said in an undertone, "I said he could watch and participate, but he can't touch the children or be alone with them. And one of the teachers has to be with him at all times."

I forced myself to take steadying breaths and to think deliberately. My eagerness to see what would happen warred with my conscience. How well did Poche understand human speech? Did he understand what we were asking of him?

I said to Poche, "Do you understand the rules?"

"Yes," he said. "Can't touch. Can't be alone."

"And?"

"And a teacher has to be with me."

Think of him as one of the students, I told myself. I took a breath. "Okay." I addressed the class. "Everyone? Poche will be joining us in class today. Let's give him a big welcome!"

"Hi, Poche!" they chorused. The enthusiasm made his fur flare.

"We are painting our favorite memory," I explained to him. "Do you want to try?"

"Yes."

I tied an apron around Poche's belly, handed him a paintbrush, and stood a blank easel with a big sheet of paper before him. "Jeanne, can you share your paint and water with Poche?"

"Yes." She scooted her easel over, shyly.

"Thank you, that's very nice of you. Could you show Poche how to paint?"

"Yes." Jeanne grabbed her brush, dipped it in water, and scrubbed it against the red paint. She poked her canvas a few times. "Like that."

Poche scrutinized the other paintings for a minute. At last, he swirled his brush in blue, and swept it in a circle over the canvas. Anya took notes while one of the men with her recorded Poche on his phone. Poche filled in the blue with patches of deeper blue, then green.

"Is that Earth?" asked Jeanne.

"Yes." More confidently, he loaded his brush with grey and drew a rectangle around Earth, then painted a yellow and brown figure at the bottom of the rectangle. He switched to red, and dabbed dots in a square outside the rectangle.

"Controls," he said.

"Spaceship!" said a little voice at my hip: Toby. The rest of the children abandoned their easels to ogle as Poche swept color across his canvas.

"Yes." He dabbed buttons in other colors and added squiggles —wires?—and added the ears and tails to the figures.

I asked, "Poche, would you share your memory with the class?"

"The memory is..." His fur slicked down and his eyes dilated, scanning blankly, as if searching the wrinkles of his brain. Other than his eyes, he was as still as a tree. At last, he said, "...not... enough... words."

"That's okay," I said. "That's what we learn in kindergarten. Words, and how we use them with others."

A few hours after he was led out of the school, the paperwork was signed, and the Institute rigged the classroom with cameras and microphones and sensors. Every interaction, every word, would be recorded and catalogued.

The next day, Anya hunched in a chair so small her knees practically hit her chin. Like the other kids, Poche had his own cushion, forest green corduroy to contrast with his flaxen fur. Anya looked around the room with a soft, wistful expression I often see on visiting adults without children.

The kids streamed in. When some saw Poche, they gasped and waved. Davy spotted him and dashed back to his mom, burying his head in her thigh. She unwrapped his arms from her leg.

Before we began class, we explained to the children what was going on and allowed them to pepper Poche with questions. Hands rocketed into the air.

"Why did you come to Earth?"

"What is your home planet called? What is it like?"

"Do you like it when we call you alien? Do you want to be called something else?"

Poche answered each question with an air of polite interest. I kept my hands in my lap, though I had a billion questions myself.

For our first exercise, Trevor and I asked the children about their weekend.

Janice's hand zipped into the air. "I wanna share!"

"Okay, Janice, go ahead," I said.

Janice recited, "I went to the recycling center with Mommy. We recycle everything. We got ice cream after. Daddy wasn't home and I sat in his chair. Angela licked my feet. The end."

"Who's Angela?" I asked.

"My cat."

"Excellent. Who's next?"

More hands. One was Poche's.

I called on him.

He said, "I woke when your side of the planet faced your central star, at the time you call 7:46:36 AM central time, in the mothership, in what humans call my 'bed', from a dreamless, 8.96-hour-long, oxygen-supplemented... thing we do at night?"

The children giggled.

"Funny?" he asked.

I explained, "You don't have to explain every little detail, Poche."

"But that was the weekend."

"We aren't trying to explain the whole weekend. We are sharing the most memorable things that happened during the weekend. What is the essence of the weekend?"

One of his ears twisted. "All of the weekend."

Anya wrote frantically, tearing the paper of her legal pad in her haste to flip to a new page.

"Homework for you," I said to Poche. The children tittered. "Five sentences. No longer than ten words each."

Both ears twisted and his fur frizzed.

"It's doable, I promise," I said. "You don't have to do it now."

He twisted one ear and replied, "Not enough words."

I pulled a beginner's dictionary from the bookshelf and handed it to him. "This is a dictionary," I said. "It will help you understand where words came from, how they are pronounced, and what they mean."

After that, he carried the dictionary around like a blanket. He only set it down at recess to watch the class shout and play. Anya explained games to him: Red Rover, tag, hide and seek, kickball. Mesmerized, he watched the children with the intense stare of a baby as they weaved, collided, argued, cooperated, and ran back and forth across the grass.

"How do they know how to...?" He trailed off. Then he riffled through the dictionary.

The kids pulled him into their games, but he could only stand, puzzled, as the kickball whanged off his belly. After the first brutal game, Kai ran up to him and hugged him.

"I'm sorry," he said. "I love you."

Poche merely said, "It's okay."

At the end of the day, Anya, Poche, and I stayed behind in the empty classroom to go over the day. I saw him turn to the page defining *love*. Anya had stepped out into the hall to have a phone call about confidential Institute stuff, and he and I were alone.

I said, "I don't think the dictionary will help you understand every word."

"Why not?" he asked.

"Sometimes things need to be experienced to be understood. But," I mused, "not everything can be experienced by everyone. Otherwise, there would be no need to communicate."

"Like *abai*?"

"What's abai?"

"Abai is..." His fur slicked down. After a long moment, he said haltingly, "Abai... is... when you don't singot. It makes one..." Poche flipped through the dictionary again, and he did not finish his sentence.

"Like loneliness," I suggested. "A fatal loneliness."

Poche flipped to both words. His ears wiggled. "Yes!" he said. "Some yes."

"Is there a cure for being abai?"

"Singot."

"Like loneliness," I repeated. "Our species are somewhat alike."

"What is the cure for loneliness?"

"Talking or writing to someone could help," I replied. "If the lonely person is honest. But sometimes they don't know what they need to hear. Or say." I hesitated. "I'm in that situation now."

"You need to singot," Poche said authoritatively.

"Agreed."

"Ergh." Poche drummed his fingers and his ears swirled. He looked like he was winding up for something serious. "You may die soon."

"No, I won't," I said, alarmed. "Humans can die from loneliness, but not that easily. Sometimes it can take years. Decades." *Oh God, decades?* said a little voice in the back of my mind.

Poche relaxed.

Anya returned. Her mouth was pulled tight as she set her phone down on the table to record. "Poche, tell us what you thought about today's events."

"What is love?"

I caught Anya's eye and hummed the famous bars from the song. Anya smirked.

She said, "Love is when you feel deep, tender affection for someone. Like how I loved my girlfriend. But it doesn't mean they will feel the same way."

"There're different kinds of love," I said hastily. "And none are less than others. Love for your partner, your parents, your friends, your children, your country—"

Anya cut in, "But the Sinmai don't have to worry about attraction getting in the way. They're all asexual. They don't experience sexual attraction, whatsoever."

I felt a strange internal fracturing, like an ice cube dropped in water.

Poche asked, "Then what is love for?"

I answered, quietly, "Love, I think, makes up the gap between language and understanding. People misunderstand quite often. Sometimes they don't listen. But, if they love each other, they can trust the other person and assume the best intentions from what is said." As I spoke, the fracturing traveled along my nerves and blood vessels. An odd sensation of horror—and relief. *Asexual.*

Poche flipped through his dictionary to 'misunderstand,' 'trust', and 'intentions.' He curled his hands into fists as he scanned the words.

Anya asked him, "What are you thinking?"

"I think I see now," he said. "Sinmai failed to use language correctly before. Yuche said they went abai on purpose. They said we had to... risk it. To test language." He turned the dictionary's pages to the word *risk*. "We did not believe them. And now there are six of us." He opened his hands. "I am thinking, what did Yuche think? They did not have the words that I have now."

Poche's hands clenched briefly, crumpling the page, and he smoothed the paper.

"If... language... can..." He put his hands together. "Singot. It can also..." He took his hands apart. "Stop abai."

"But you don't need to be abai to singot," Anya said.

"You need to be a little abai to singot," Poche replied. "Otherwise... why singot? That's why, I think, Yuche went abai. We... did not...." His mouth worked for a moment before he managed, "Trust."

My heart clenched for the Sinmai. Poche turned the dictionary to the first page of the 'A' section.

"I will need more words," he said. "I will test language, and go abai."

I passed a park, walking from my kindergarten to my apartment, and a couple relaxing on a picnic blanket under a tree. The woman leaned close to the man, laughing, and I could not ever remember being so radiant. *How are they doing it? What does it mean when she looks at his hands, what does it mean when he rolls up his sleeves, what is he doing to her that makes her beam like that? What does it feel like for both of them?*

Was this how Poche felt living with humanity? I thought, *Singot is better. Why articulate something to somebody else when you can just feel it together?* It made sense why the Sinmai would be asexual.

Yet that thought disturbed me. It couldn't be right.

I shut myself in my apartment and researched asexuality.

As I read articles, forums, papers, I felt myself draining into a deadly swallowing sea without bottom. My past felt empty, even as I questioned the emptiness, hoping something would answer back. I thought I had been in love before. A middle-school friend, a sleepover. The lights going out as if snatched away by the lightning storm that rolled in. As I groped for a light switch, I had found a hand. We screamed, then burst into laughter, grabbed again, and caught each other. We were as close as a pair of socks. I'd felt this time and again with others, believing that the urgent wanting (as I imagined sexual desire would feel) would come sometime for the right person. I wanted a light switch or a hand to hold. I tried to imagine sex, and couldn't.

The websites I found emphasized that asexuality didn't mean that you couldn't give or feel love. Asexuality had little to do with the lack of communication. At least, the kind of communication Poche sought. Yet, asexuality felt important to abai and singot, and I couldn't explain why.

I couldn't wait for humanity to invent something that would allow us to singot. Poche was right; language would have to suffice. But the dictionaries wouldn't be enough, because it wasn't just the lack of words—what words we didn't have could be invented. It was the lack of trust that someone else would understand you and be patient with you while you fumbled to explain yourself. But how could he learn patience when he didn't have the time? How long could a Sinmai be abai until they died?

The following day, when going over vocabulary with Poche, he said, "Yesterday, you reacted to Anya's words."

A pit deepened in my stomach. Anya was taking notes beside us. Her eyebrows quirked.

"Uh, yes." I had sworn that I would be honest with children when they asked me questions, and I counted Poche as one of them. "About love. She accidentally touched on something I had been thinking about for a long time."

"What is it?" he asked.

"I'm still thinking about what it means. How to say it." I asked, "Can I tell you later when I know more about how I feel?"

His lips lifted. His gums were black and set with chisel-like teeth beveled to sharp edges. I imagined the crew mate who had been sacrificed. "Abai, Stacey," he said. "That's abai."

He held up his hand suddenly, and I jumped, as if he had been about to slap me. "You will tell me?"

I put my hand to his. "I promise."

Poche flipped to the word 'promise.' He looked mollified, but still suspicious.

"Very good," Anya said, scrawling notes at light speed. "Very interesting stuff."

As class went on, I thought, *Maybe I should have just told them. Why didn't I want to?* Maybe it was because it seemed pretty hasty to tell people I was asexual so soon after discovering it myself. What if I was wrong? I wanted to be wrong. I was delaying for evidence to the contrary: a leaping heart at another person's appearance, an undeniable feeling between the legs. When I thought of a partner, I pictured myself standing next to a blot, like someone had put their thumb over a camera lens.

But it wasn't just that. I was like Tasha, who always could be found hovering outside play groups, waiting to be invited in. I always stepped in to help her. But now I wondered whether I needed an adult to do that for me with other adults. *But I'm an adult, damnit. I should be able to do it myself.*

We stayed behind after class to go over the day, as usual. Anya had brought a bag of clementines and the sweet lobes glowed in the sunlight. Her hand knocked against mine repeatedly as we reached for them. Each time it was like the tongue of a bell resonating through me. As I put a lobe in my mouth, I forced

493

myself to imagine it was her ear. The smooth, plump crescent, warm, tart, bursting.

And then I thought, *What am I doing?*

Anya caught my eye with her deep brown gaze.

Poche said gravely, "Stacey, you are red. Why?"

"Oh, hush." I was mortified, smiling awkwardly. I hadn't thought he would notice.

"You can't say that to him." Anya smiled with crinkling eyes.

"Noooo, I'm not going to say." I was laughing, even as she grabbed my hands. I was half-serious. She was getting the wrong idea. But the contrarian part of me said, "Yes, yes, yes." Where would this go? *Don't you want to know her more? Even if it starts with a misunderstanding?*

"You have to explain, or he won't know." She beamed like the sun. Nobody had ever looked at me like that before. I wanted to blind myself looking.

Both of his ears twisted.

He asked, "Why will you not tell me?"

"Well..." I couldn't answer. I didn't have an answer, at least, not one that I wanted to say out loud. Anya was listening. *Say it*, I thought. "I'm red because I'm sunburned," I said lamely. *Such a coward*, I thought. Breaking my pledge not to lie to children so I didn't have to confront difficult things. Anya raised an eyebrow.

Poche asked, "Why do you say that?"

Anya said icily, "Sometimes, Poche, people are uncomfortable with some sex flirting."

"I'm not uncomfortable!" I protested.

"Then why don't you explain?"

"Why don't you explain, Anya?" he asked. "Is this a power struggle?"

"No," Anya and I said together.

He asked, "Is there danger nearby? And redness is camouflage?" I chuckled. Anya blistered me with a look. "Is it a secret? Is it like how Sinmai treat *horkew'e* ceremonies, during which we send a young Sinmai into the *threwd* with *sled*, *vie*, and *wave*—"

"Poche," I said.

But he babbled, "—and we tell them, 'Go. Make yourself abai, see how plants go together, how water unmakes itself from clouds, and when you return, singot, and you will know Sinmai and know nothing and they will go out and grow abai with only two hands—"

Anya had pulled out her phone and dialed frantically. Was he going insane? Was this abai? I held up my hands. Fuck my feelings, I'd deal with the fallout with Anya later. But then his fingers wrapped twice around my hand and squeezed. It was like being caught in a machine—flesh bending too far in wrong ways.

I screamed, "I will tell you! Please, let go!"

He yanked his hands away as if he had touched a scorching stove. "I am sorry. Sorry. Sorry."

My heart raced in my throat. My joints cracked, and welts crossed my wrists.

Anya had pulled out her stun gun. When she saw my expression, she shoved it back in its holster.

"Let's end here," she muttered.

Poche's hands flexed and flexed, as did mine. Anya's clenched.

What would have happened if I had been honest? I had been... But I *didn't* know why I had blushed. I thought I was asexual. Right?

Idiot, I told myself. *Language only works if you use it.*

I didn't understand what had happened to me. I thought that if I could just explain what I felt to myself, I would understand. Then I would know what to say to Poche and Anya. I had to know perfectly. Otherwise, it would feel like I was lying to them.

But the contrarian inside me said, *You won't know perfectly. What are you afraid of?*

My answer was meager, pathetic. *I'm afraid they won't believe me.*

And then I felt angry with myself. *How will Poche learn how to trust if I'm not a good role model? I have to tell him soon*, I told myself. *Even if I'm not sure what it is, even if I stammer or stutter. He's trying. Meet him half-way. This I can do for him.*

A storm muscled into the following morning's blue sky. Trevor led the group in a lesson about the water cycle, how clouds form and rain falls. Poche watched the sky with a finger tapping his knee.

The lights flickered.

"It's okay, everyone," said Trevor. "We have our flashlights."

Then thunder shattered the air and the lights went out.

Children screamed. Trevor switched on his flashlight and called for order. The grey-blue disturbed light from the window was all we had, and the flashlights—and Poche, whose hands glowed. A pale blue light emitted from his calluses.

"Poche, how are you doing that?" Anya asked, and held out the recorder.

"The Sinmai evolved to singot," he said. His hands clenched, as if to crush the light. "The ship will be here soon."

The way he sat, the way he looked out the window, the tapping. Something else I couldn't understand.

"Poche?" I said uncertainly.

"Let's go out to the hall," Poche said suddenly, rising.

The hall was dark, except where the storm's light wavered through the windows. The gloom shied away from Poche's upheld hands.

"I have discovered something about the nature of abai," Poche said. In the dark, he looked misshapen, bestial. "Abai is not a disease. It is a stranger-maker, an evolutionary learning mechanism which—" He vibrated. "Which singot overrides." Suddenly, he said, "Do not let the others singot with me, Stacey. Explain to them. I promise I will tell them. I need to stay abai, just for a little while longer—it's the only way to test—"

His words jumbled together.

"Stacey, get away from him," Anya said. She reached for something on her belt, and there was an electric whine.

I said, "Tell me—what's wrong?" I raised my hand.

"Poche, walk in front of us to the lobby," said Anya.

"Anya, wait. I'll take full responsibility."

"For what?" she said tersely.

"Poche, I'll tell you—the thing I didn't want to talk about..." My heart clogged my throat. "The word that I reacted to—what Anya said—about asexuality. I have always felt a little... out of alignment, with people, all my life. When she said that, I realized I was... asexual. And my life made sense." Poche's fur stood on end. "But it scared me, because I didn't know what the rest of my life would look like."

Poche's expression was like none I had ever seen on Earth. He said in a garbled voice, "I don't understand."

I felt like he had reached inside my chest and crushed my heart.

The stormlight dimmed, and so did the slashing of the rain on the windows. Beyond the lobby, over the parking lot, was something that could only be the Sinmai ship. Like a black moon had descended from the sky and blocked the rain. Sirens keened, approaching.

Poche hurried out of the lobby into the rain. From the ship, five Sinmai descended on a platform. The way they glanced around themselves, their gestures, the way they stood—like five fingers on the same hand. Poche approached them and spoke rapidly in Sinmai before they could. He overpowered their attempts to cut in, repeating *abai* and *singot* amidst a torrent of English and Sinmai words. The five exchanged a complicated set of gestures like a secret handshake. Blue sparks danced between their palms like a cloudless summer day, when you can see infinity hinting beyond the sky. Poche shivered. But he stepped away, covered his eyes, and said something in a breaking voice.

The Sinmai lunged for him. They wrestled him down as military vehicles skidded round the corner. Their powerful lights caught the tussling aliens and obliterated individual features. Snarls juddered from Poche's chest. Claws extended from his feet and gouged earth from the lawn. One Sinmai had bit down on his arm with those teeth and another champed his leg, forcing him down.

Tears smeared my vision. I felt divided against myself. *Help him! Leap in, say something! Why don't you do anything? Something!* But what could I say that could replace singot? I had already failed.

The lead Sinmai pinned down Poche's arm, uncurled his clenched hand, and pressed their palm to his.

Light annihilated the schoolyard. When I recall that moment now, it is like a still in a movie, and a bomb has just gone off. It doesn't seem like it happened. I should have felt the blast like a ghostly wall. I know the soldiers who had been running to confront the Sinmai recoiled. I know the Sinmai pile fell apart. I saw one fall to the side, on the road, making an awful scream like an iceberg splitting.

And I saw that Poche lay still. Clearest of all was a black asterisk of soot on the asphalt where his hand should be, and his wrist cuffed with flames.

Next week, kindergarten resumed. I told the class that Poche might not come back. We all cried for a while. I put his painting on the wall so parents and children could see it with the rest of the class. We didn't know if he would come back, but we had to keep going like he would. We set out his floor cushion and put it away at the end of each day. I felt like an extra chamber had been carved out of my heart and my blood had leaked away, and I was only still moving because I was too numb to realize I had died. If only I had had better words and put them in a better order. If only I had told him sooner, he would be alive.

But then he returned.

Certainly, it was a Sinmai, toddling down the sidewalk on the other side of the fence, the stub of an arm bandaged. Children screamed and ran towards him, and Trevor and I ran to call them back. Trevor called, at least—I just ran. Poche waded into the children and they glommed onto him. Anya and the guards who followed him stepped away. Anya looked tense, expectant.

"Good morning," Poche said to me. "I'm sorry."

"We're all just glad you're okay," I said through a tight throat.

"No," he said emphatically. "*I'm* sorry. Poche has died. This body is now Oche."

The children quieted. *Poche has died. This body is now Oche.* These words did not go together with what I saw. They stood straighter. Their speech was clearer. They had Poche's body. Yet, I was looking at a stranger.

To me, Oche held up his hand. With trepidation, I placed mine over it.

"When we singot," he said carefully. "We pour ourselves together and redistribute equally among our bodies. We five Sinmai on Earth are all now Oche. Poche is within us all."

They had killed Poche, as easily as wiping words off a whiteboard. I couldn't believe I had wanted to singot. If perfect understanding with others meant self-destruction, I didn't want it.

Oche's ears were twisted as he watched me. This, I realized, was what Poche realized about singot.

"Humans don't die when they share themselves with others," I said. "We become people through other people, just like you. Only, we do it a little at a time."

He asked. "Then why wouldn't you tell me? What were you scared about?"

"I felt like I had become a stranger to myself. And to other people. I thought that nobody would understand who I was, and I wouldn't understand others either. And then I would be abai forever."

His ears wiggled. "Yes!"

The Sinmai had to leave soon. They had realized that there were too few Sinmai to stay safely on Earth. Before they left, I begged the school to give them the dictionaries, and helped the children write their names in the flyleaves. Anya invited me to watch them leave. One by one they put their hands to mine and disappeared into their ship. Gouts of fire billowed beneath it as it launched, punched through the clouds, and joined the moon in the sky.

I still miss Poche, the instance of individuality that wove into Oche. By now his name must have changed again. Does the whole planet share one name? Was there ever a difference between one of him and all of them? There must have been. And there must be now. Nobody can travel to another world and return unchanged. When the crew returns home, they will greet their citizens as strangers. There will be so much for them to know about Earth. I hope their hands won't explode.

The human body limits us. We can't understand everything all at the same time. We barely understand ourselves, let alone others. But the cool thing about language is that if communication fails, you can try again. I've been talking to Anya. I told her how I thought I was asexual. And she got it! I feel embarrassed for thinking she wouldn't. Things have softened between us, started to flow onward. We're not together, not really. But we're looking in the same direction. Towards the Sinmai home world.

I've started a new career at the Institute. Being a certified friend of Sinmai helped my application jump to the top of the pile. I'll be studying Oche's language now, so I can tell him, "I know why you painted the moment you saw Earth. You were curious to know whether you were alone in the universe. And then you discovered you weren't." The Sinmai trusted that humanity was worth discovering. To live, I must too. And I can't imagine a better life than spending it with people I'll never really know, who will forever surprise me with new aspects to love, unfolding forever together.

See E.C. Fuller's story "Singot" online at Metaphorosis.
If you liked it, leave a comment. Authors love that!
Remember to subscribe to our e-mail updates so you'll know when
new stories are posted.

About the story

"Singot" was inspired by two things: a screenshot of a Tumblr post about how kindergarten teachers are perfect for teaching people how to be human and an NPR podcast about anthropologists believing they had discovered a new emotion. The idea that you could discover a new emotion gripped me. I had recently realized I was asexual, and I didn't like it at all. I wanted to feel something for another person; I felt messed up, but ached to share, and wanted not just to be seen, but found and spoken to. And most importantly, to be understood. Hence, singot: the wordless understanding of a person's entire life.

But if given the chance to singot, I'm not sure I would take it. When thinking back over my life I wonder, God, how I did I miss that I was asexual? I usually answer, because I was happy as I was. I love learning about the world and the people who walk on it. Why introspect when there's a zillion things to learn? And if we understand immediately, perfectly, does that mean we lose learning? I wanted to explore what we lose by understanding perfectly or imperfectly, using a strong chain of causal and emotional logic, and find an answer I could live by.

A question for the author

Q: Are titles easy or hard for you? Do you start with the title or the story?]

A: Story first, always. Usually when I begin to write a story, the title is just a descriptive tag to separate the story from all the other drafts. Titles are usually the last part I revise because they're the first thing readers read and they color the rest of the story. For example, "Singot", was nearly titled "Abai" instead. While singot appeared to be a useful solution to the character's goals, the frightening but necessary abai powers the story forward. What's more important? The push or the pull? I ultimately chose "Singot" because I felt it was the more positive title, though the end may shake that impression. Even now, I'm still not sure whether I chose the right title.

About the author

E. C. Fuller lives and works in Tulsa, OK.
ecfullersbooks.com, @birdshapedhat

Souls Like Sea Glass

Josie Smith

My entire life, I'd known three people: Pa; Ma, before she'd died giving birth to a still baby when I was four; and the ferryman who brought us our supplies and rations each month. The world I was raised in would have been an empty one for anyone else, but, for me, it was full to bursting. Our island was populated by cliffs the wind loved to beat against, a savage sea, and the stretches of sand where the wild ponies dozed. And at the edge of the island was the lighthouse built from white stone. It had risen above me from my first memory, and its light acted as a stern warning to those that sailed past our desolate part of the world.

Each evening, Pa would walk with me along our island's rocky coast, a lantern held in one hand and my fist secured in his other. He never told me what exactly we were looking for, but I found plenty to carry home in my pockets, anyway. Even at ten, I was collecting whatever I found: smooth pebbles, sea glass in countless colors, sometimes even a whole sand dollar. For me, it was full pockets, full heart. Whenever I found the rare conch shell, Pa would press it first to his ear, then to mine.

"Listen, Cora," he said. "There's no sweeter music in all the world. Even when I'm away from the sea, I can hear that tune in my dreams."

I laughed at the thought of Pa anywhere but at our lighthouse or on Hestur Island. All the time I'd know him, I'd never once seen him leave. Why would anyone want to? The island had always felt like home, like magic, to me. This place was built of it, woven from magic like a tapestry. Nothing else could explain all the wildflowers bursting from the hillsides each spring or the soft sand I'd learned to walk upon or the light always keeping watch over us.

Pa held a hand to his heart at my laughter, doing his best to act solemn despite the hidden smile twitching at his lips. "I swear it. The mainland's more than just a word. I've been to it. Even made memories there."

I wrinkled my nose. "Any that mattered?"

Pa scooped up a piece of red sea glass I'd missed, wincing at his bent back. "Nope. All the important memories are right here."

I took the sea glass from him and held it up to the sinking sun. With the last rays of light shining through it, the smooth glass burned ruby red in my hand, like a dying star. Once the sun had faded further, I tucked the glass into my pocket with everything else I'd collected.

I turned back to the lighthouse, its beam gaining brilliance against the darkening sky. "It's nearly night. Aren't we going to go back?"

Pa stepped over a large piece of driftwood and continued past me, further down the beach. "No, let's keep walking. There's something I need to show you."

I frowned and watched him go. Pa wasn't one for many rules. He had the simple ones, of course. No leaving dirty dishes, no wasting kerosene, no swimming too far out at sea. But the most important one had always been to stay inside after sunset. The island was too dangerous in the dark, Pa had insisted. Even if his own rule didn't keep him from disappearing out into the shadows every night himself.

I skipped to catch up to Pa, scattering sand as I went. "Are you finally going to let me help with the lighthouse?" I'd been begging him for years to let me do more, more, more. That it was a family role was the one thing I'd gleaned from his stories told beside the fireplace or over the dinner table. Years before I'd learned to traipse across the island's shore, Pa had taken over the lighthouse from his own pa. And from the first I'd learned of it, I'd yearned to do the same. "I can do it, you know. Everything."

Pa laughed and I crossed my arms at his amusement. "I already let you help."

"I want to do more. And I don't want to let you be alone in the dark."

"I'm never alone." He gestured back at the lighthouse. "There's always the light. But I will welcome more of your help."

We kept walking as the sky grew as black as a razorbill's wings. It was thrilling, walking along the shore after dark. My first time breaking the rule and there was a whole new facet of the island to see at night. I took it all in as I danced alongside Pa on raised toes. My hand stayed in his until he paused.

"Here." Pa handed me the lantern. I lifted it high as he coughed into his closed fist. "I did want to wait until you were older to heap so much responsibility upon you." The corner of Pa's mouth twitched, his best attempt at a smile. "But fate's done what it does best and forced my hand."

Pa might have been hesitant to hand over more responsibilities, but I didn't share his regrets. Instead, I held the lantern steady and waited beside him for whatever he wanted from me next. I would be a keeper, like him, like his pa. And I would protect this island and keep all who passed by it safe.

I smiled to myself. Maybe it was a good thing I was Pa's only living child. Someone had to be keeper after him and a short, bony daughter wouldn't likely have been anyone's first choice. But then maybe Pa would have chosen me first, anyway. He'd always said I was born of this island, built of wild winds and seagulls' cries and brine, rather than mere human flesh.

Pa was a poet, whether he was ever willing to admit it or not. The lighthouse, not me, was the usual recipient of his rhymes and uttered verses. Some days, it was 'the guide for souls lost at sea'. Others, it was 'the night's burning beacon'. I just called it the lighthouse.

Pa was less eloquent that night as he wordlessly pointed me forward. I raised an eyebrow, but didn't question him. I was too focused on the anticipation rising in me like the tide. Instead, I left Pa behind as I picked my way around a pair of tide pools and the brown boulders scattered across the higher parts of the beach. Pa's lantern lit the way forward, and I hadn't followed its light far before I paused.

There was a stranger on our island.

A pale sailor lay motionless on the sand, illuminated by the light I carried. His feet were bare and his faded blue uniform hung loosely on his bedraggled frame. The sea seemed to have spit him out onto the shore, but not before tossing him about a good bit in the waves.

Footsteps crunched in the sand behind me, and Pa's steady hand found my shoulder. I was shaking, but told myself it was because of the night's cold. Not because I'd never seen a stranger before.

Pa wasn't as bothered by the interloper on our shore. Instead, he motioned me forward. "Don't be afraid. This is what I wanted to show you tonight. Go on. Ask him his name."

I took small steps forward in the sand, tracking through the hoofprints the island's herd of wild ponies had left streaked across the beach. When I reached the unmoving sailor, I took a deep breath, swallowing all the courage I could. Eventually, I stretched out a hand and grazed his shoulder with the tips of my fingers. The sailor stirred at my slight touch, but it took another nudge from me before he lifted his head. He looked my way with eyes as empty as the night.

I bit my lip and glanced back at Pa. *Fortune follows fortitude*, he repeated often enough to be a prayer. Whether he was telling himself or me, I was never quite sure. But his words were enough to convince me then.

I stuck out my free hand toward the sailor. "Who are you? What's your name?"

"Irving." The sailor slowly rose to sit on the sand and shook my hand as his eyes lifted up, up, up to the light shining above us. "Oh. It's a lighthouse."

I held onto the lantern as Pa joined us and helped lift the sailor to his feet. "Irving, welcome to Hestur Island," he said. "The lighthouse I keep is what you saw, what brought you here. Now, if you'll follow me, I'll help you continue."

Irving pursed his lips. "That's it? Drown and move on?"

I looked between the two, curiosity singing loud to me as Pa stepped closer to the sailor. "I'm sorry. Some days the sea's kind, some days it's cruel. But you're safe here now and there's not far to go."

"My line came loose in a storm. Figured I was dead as soon as I hit the water. Never learned to swim, ya know? At least I'm not still stuck there." Irving lowered his head. "I had family back in Brighton. A wife. Two sons. There's no way to say goodbye?"

Pa tugged at the graying strands of his beard. "Afraid not. There's only going forward."

Irving let the sea wash over his feet one last time before he stepped away from it and toward Pa.

Pa clapped his shoulder and murmured, "Good man. Come, follow me and it'll all be done soon."

Pa started forward, away from the shore and inland, to where a peak rose at the island's center. I kept close to him, the way I often was, while Irving trudged along through the sand after us, his gaze focused on the ground.

"Who is that?" I whispered. "What does he mean 'drown and move on'?"

Pa took the lantern from me and held it aloft to better light the path in front of us. "This is our job, too. The light warns ships about the rocks and shallow depths. But it's also something for lost, drowned souls to anchor onto. Anyone who dies in the sea, they stay there disoriented and adrift. At least, until they find something to swim for, like moths drawn to a light."

The shore. And the light. I glanced at them both as we walked. I'd liked to imagine for years that the island was strung though with thin strands of magic. Perhaps I hadn't been so far from the truth. I had seen Irving myself. Touched him. He had been solid enough, but not entirely human. More like an echo of a person, standing there on the sand. And I'd never known Pa to lie to me before.

Pa lowered his voice. "How much time a drowned soul spends in the sea differs for each of them. And after they wash ashore here, I help guide them on to whatever comes next."

"And what does come next?" The oldest human question that even a small child knew how to wonder about.

"No more questions, Cora." Pa took great, heaving steps as the ground sloped. "Just watch."

I trampled through overgrown meadow grass, doing my best to keep up with Pa. He led Irving and me until we were almost to the island's center and the sea was a sounding afterthought. Here, the ground rose high enough that there was always mist, even on the days the sky was clear and bright, a seabird's paradise.

At the mist's edge, Pa shook Irving's hand so firmly it looked final. "Sorry you're going young. Sorry about your family. But there oughtn't be any hardship beyond, so go on and enjoy it."

Irving looked to the lighthouse, then to the mist again. He shoved his shoulders back, the same way I did whenever I was trying to be brave for Pa. Then, he eased his way into his mist on slow steps. Its silver, reaching tendrils shifted to cocoon the sailor, blocking him from sight. I bounced on the balls of my feet and waited for him to come back out. When he didn't, I finally reached up and tapped Pa.

"Where's he going?" I said.

Pa turned from the mist and used the lantern to guide us back to the lighthouse. "Where I guide all the others to. Someplace waits for them beyond the mist, but it's not our business. We're only here to make sure the drowned souls make it." Pa frowned down at me, his thick eyebrows shoved together. "Don't waste too much time wondering about what comes after. We're still living, so it's no use asking questions meant for the dead."

"Is it just our island? How many souls?"

"Patience, Cora. A man can only answer so many questions in a night. I'm keeper on this island. Not others. I can't speak for them. And ours is an ordinary place in every aspect but one."

I jutted out my chin. Our island was not ordinary. Pa had been raised here too, so he should have known better. But he continued answering my questions, so I didn't interrupt to tell him so.

"The souls are a secret we keep so they can have peace and not be hounded by mainlanders seeking them out. And there's one to guide to the mist every week or two, but we must always be looking for them. That's the way my pa did it, too. Found the souls here, figured out what to do, taught me the same. Now, I'm teaching you."

"And the Lighthouse Board keeps the secret over on the mainland?"

Pa grunted and shook his head. "They're good for paying us and sending rations. That's about it. Think, Cora. We tell them, they decide we're not in the right state of mind to stay here, and then there's no proper keeper for the souls or the lighthouse."

I pursed my lips. Pa rarely spoke kindly of the 'meddlesome' Lighthouse Board. The lantern flickered and Pa muttered something about the oil running low.

"Keepers don't get much sleep, do they?" I said.

He chuckled and ruffled my hair. "It's a hard life, but a good one."

I made my decision then, with Pa at my side and the lighthouse gleaming ahead. Souls, island, all of it. I'd never been born for anything else.

I was fourteen the last time I remember getting a full night's sleep and sixteen the first time I escorted a soul to the mist by myself. She had been an older woman with red hair and faint wrinkles around her eyes. Women's souls were a rare find on the shore. I had taken this one away from the lighthouse, past the moor where the ponies grazed, and right to where the mist gathered so thickly I couldn't see past it.

"Just through there," I said as I gestured the woman forward. "I don't know what happens after you step in, but good luck."

She let out a light laugh. The sound surprised me, as it didn't match the way she'd been walking earlier. Then, she had been like Atlas with the world, carrying sadness heavily on her shoulders. After thanking me for my help, the woman smiled and stepped into the mist. Then it was like she'd never been there at all, except for some slight stirring of the reaching, silver haze.

Most souls went easily, like she had. A few tried to stay, tried to fight against fate. But souls couldn't stay on the island once they had finally washed ashore. They weakened on land until they either entered the mist or faded away, losing themselves entirely. Pa had been at my side the first time a soul had argued against entering the mist right away. But from then on, I had been able to handle the more unruly souls on my own. All it usually took was a good dose of convincing, or simply sitting and talking away their fears of the unknown.

A year after I started guiding souls on my own, a particularly bad bout of pneumonia took Pa. It had been the worst winter I could remember, only made more frigid and lifeless by his passing. Since Pa hadn't drowned out among the waves, I buried him without a chance to see his soul and say a last goodbye. The dirt, the earth beneath our feet. This was home and familiar and what our souls knew. It was only those who were lost out at sea, in an unfamiliar world, that needed help and guidance.

It was Pa's death that brought me a grief as vast as the sea but also the full realization of the life I'd striven for. I became the keeper of Hestur Island, its lighthouse, and its souls. Each night, I would light Pa's old lantern and go wandering up and down the coast, collecting souls like sea glass and humming along to the tune of the crashing waves.

In my small corner of the world, I was alone. But, most of the time, I kept busy enough that the loneliness knocking on my windows couldn't find a way inside. Some nights the wind did echo too loudly and the cottage next to the lighthouse was suffocating with its emptiness. Then, I would listen to the melodies sung by my ever-growing collections of shells and mutter to myself that, even without Pa, I was not alone here on the island.

There was the herd of wild ponies that I'd tried and failed to ride as a child. They would gather on the beach at dawn each morning and both they and the sun would greet me. I always kept my distance, like Pa had taught. We were to be observers of the island's inhabitants and let nature choose its course without interfering, he said. But they were still my constant companions, along with the rough waves of the sea and the light I ensured never went out. I always had the light, and I told myself that would have to be enough.

The month after I turned twenty, I was standing on the island's one small dock when the ferryman arrived with his usual rations and supplies. He had rowed in on a dinghy from his sloop anchored out in deeper waters. On the bench beside him was a lanky, blond man. An apprentice of the ferryman's, I assumed. He was getting old, just as Pa had, and was likely to have retirement forced upon him soon.

The ferryman handed off a few crates to me, which I stacked beside my own dinghy moored to the other side of the dock. Besides the crates of supplies, the ferryman also passed over an unwanted parcel. I pursed my lips as the blond man climbed out of the boat. With unsteady legs more used to the sea than land, he clambered onto the dock. Onto my dock. Onto my island.

He stood with a hand shielding his eyes from the sun as he took in the island and the cliffs rising beyond us. The man gave a satisfied nod at the sight of it all. I ground my teeth, wanting nothing more than to chase him off the dock and out of sight. Or at the very least, shove him into the sea.

I tugged on a mask of cool politeness to help mask my sparking rage.

"Can I help you?" I said.

The man spread his feet and steadied himself as the waves swayed the dock. "I'm here to replace Douglas Timmons as the lighthouse keeper."

My eyes narrowed as I readjusted my grip on a wooden crate of rations. "Hestur Island already has a keeper. Me."

The ferryman never left his dinghy, but lifted a hand to get my attention. "The Lighthouse Board will keep on paying you, but felt more comfortable sending someone else out to help you with the upkeep of the light."

Of course, the Lighthouse Board was being meddlesome again. They and my family both considered the lighthouse to be ours, which is where the disagreements had first begun.

My face twisted. "I was raised here. I doubt some naïve recruit will be any help." I waved to the ferryman. "Take him back to the mainland, would you? I don't need another keeper, so tell the Lighthouse Board to shove that idea up—"

"Please," the man said. "The pay they offered me was more generous than any other job I could find and I have parents to support back on the mainland."

My eyes met the man's bright ones. They were the same color as the sea and I cursed myself for noticing. The ferryman said nothing, but offered me an encouraging smile. As much as I hated this, it would be a pain to fight the Lighthouse Board. Pa had never had any success with that while he'd been alive. It was difficult to argue against the orders of those that paid me and sent my rations. Coexist, it was.

My sigh was perhaps more dramatic than necessary. "Just promise me you won't be a hindrance."

The young man straightened the old, weathered cap he wore and stretched out a hand. Never mind that I didn't exactly have a free one to offer him. "I promise I'm only here to make your job easier, ma'am. I'm Morgan Fisk."

I repositioned the crate to rest on my hip and begrudgingly shook his hand. After that, I stepped aside and let him off the dock. Morgan grabbed a crate of his own to carry before stepping onto my island.

Back at the lighthouse, once the ferryman had sailed off, I hoisted a can of kerosene into Morgan's arms. He grunted at its heft and gripped its handle in a tight fist.

"Run that up to the top," I said. "I'll unpack the rest of these crates."

Morgan turned and entered through the lighthouse door, staggering under the kerosene's weight. So far, the lone tolerable thing about him had been his saving me time by helping to carry crates from the dock. Or the way I could make him climb all the stairs with the kerosene instead of doing it myself. If Morgan was going to remain here, he might as well do the less pleasurable parts of the job.

Dinner that night was near silent. I alternated between glaring at my tablemate and swallowing under-seasoned stew. Despite all my requests, the ferryman never arrived with nearly as many spices as I preferred to cook with.

Morgan chuckled as he scraped his bowl clean with a tarnished spoon. He'd left his nervous politeness behind on the dock. "I'm the only other person for miles. If you insist on hating me, it's going to be a very lonely life."

"I've done lonely. It doesn't bother me." I stared at the chair Morgan occupied. Not long ago, Pa had sat there filling the room with light and life. Some part of me had wanted the chair in use again, but not by somebody else.

Morgan tapped his fingers against the wooden table. "I didn't say you would be the only lonely one."

Not willing to have this conversation, I rose and hurried my used dishes over to the sink. Years of following Pa's rules hadn't been forgotten, and so I washed my bowl and spoon while standing with my back to Morgan.

The silence I'd come to know suddenly felt strange with someone else in the room. I didn't face Morgan again until I'd wiped my dishes dry and placed them in the cupboard above.

"I don't hate you," I said. "I just wish you weren't here."

His brows furrowed. "And there's supposed to be a whole lot of difference in that?"

"Make yourself useful on the island. Then maybe I'll change my mind."

I shrugged on a long woolen coat and grabbed Pa's old lantern. Morgan placed his own dishes in the sink before joining me at the door.

I shook my head. "Stay here and make sure the light keeps shining."

"Where are you going, then?"

"I'm going to look for…" The souls were certainly not Morgan's secret to learn so soon. The Lord alone knew whether he would be a danger to them or could even properly keep a secret. "The lighthouse keeps ships clear of the rocky waters here, but the far side of the island can sometimes be a magnet for wrecks. I walk that part each night to make sure there's no trouble."

Morgan nodded, fully accepting the way I'd masked the truth of this place. "Stay safe," he said. "I'll keep everything here in working order."

"Don't wait up." I opened the cottage door and stepped through it. "I might be gone a while."

The night was cold, and I found no souls on the shore. When I was done wandering the coast, I yanked my coat tighter around myself and let the lighthouse's beam pull me back home. I trudged back up to the cottage, already thinking about the fire I'd light. But when I was nearly at the door, a candle flickering in the window made me pause. Morgan must have put it there while I was gone.

I entered the cottage and yanked the door shut behind me, sealing out the frigid wind that had battered me the whole time I'd been gone. Morgan sat in an armchair, half-asleep and trying to read by a single lamp.

I hung my coat on a peg by the door. "Why the candle? We don't need one in the window and we can't waste light like that."

"I thought it might be a good signal." Morgan closed his book and set it on a side table. "If you're going to be out walking after dark often, then I'll keep it lit if I'm here and awake. That way you'll know whether to be quiet or not. Or if you need to look for me."

I laughed. "Are you a light sleeper?"

Morgan nodded.

"You won't stay that way."

But his candle in the window did end up becoming a habit of ours. A silent message saying, *I'm here, I'm home, I'm waiting.* And while I'd first let him do it because it wasn't worth the fight, I eventually grew to look forward to seeing it. I'd come home from the shore each night and there it was; a little lighthouse of our own gleaming against the windowpane. Meanwhile, the rare dark window meant I was alone for the night. I learned to despise the sight of it.

After so many days of silence, it took me time to adjust to the sudden influx of sound and song the new keeper had brought with him. There was someone else on the island and it wasn't Pa. But Morgan took to island life like a bird to flight, never complaining of the long hours nor the lighthouse's many chores. The constant roar of the sea in the distance was now often punctuated by Morgan's voice. He liked to talk and enjoyed singing even more. Old folk songs, ballads, shanties. He would utter them all while he worked.

I'd be at the lighthouse's peak, sweeping the dust and sand from the floor or clearing the grime from the windows when Morgan would hunt me down. Years spent nigh on alone had made me comfortable with my own company, but the mainlander abhorred the silence and repeated every thought that passed through his head.

While we worked on repainting the cottage a bright, pure white, Morgan recounted all his summers spent painting fences and buildings on the farm where he'd been raised.

"No wonder your paintwork looks so good," I said once he'd finished. My half of the cottage was functionally white, but Morgan's was all broad, smooth strokes and no streaks. His height made the difference, I told myself.

"Years of practice." Morgan gestured upward. "Like you with that towering lighthouse."

I dropped my paintbrush and wiped paint from my fingers. "Good, I'll let you finish painting the entire cottage then."

At his protests, I laughed and picked up the brush again. Morgan's hands weren't so steady and sure the following days as I showed him how to trim wicks and refill the lamp's oil and all the other daily tasks. He'd been here long enough and been enough of a help that I didn't mind teaching him more. Or answering his countless questions about the lighthouse and myself.

"And you've lived here your whole life?"

"Yep."

"Don't you want to visit the mainland? At least once?"

"Nope."

"What's your favorite part of the island?"

I paused, for the first time having to think about how to answer one of Morgan's questions. My attention left his hands, the ones I'd been guiding through trimming the wick. Instead, I met his eyes.

The souls. The words nearly flew from my lips, but I pressed them together to shut in any sound.

"The wild ponies," I said instead.

It was those same wild ponies that stole Morgan away from me weeks later. I roused right as dawn was breaking over the shore, ready to dampen the lighthouse's beam. But the cottage was empty, and when I called for Morgan to help, there was no answer.

Finding him again didn't take much time. I checked the lighthouse for Morgan as soon as I stepped from the cottage and sealed the door shut behind me. But it was on the shore that I found him, the echo of his voice carried my way by the wind.

The herd of wild ponies was there on the stretch of sand like they were every morning. Morgan knelt among them, right next to a mare lying on her side. My silent steps hurried along as I made my way through the sand. I reached Morgan and knelt beside him on the ground the lowering tide had left damp.

Wheeling birds called overhead, their cries nearly as shrill as the whinny the mare released. Morgan spoke to her, calm and quiet, slower than I'd ever heard him before. I remained still beside him, there if he needed the help but otherwise a motionless observer.

It was second nature observing, like Pa had taught. But for the first time, I went against it. Morgan was already fighting for this foal to live. I found myself desiring the same for his sake. Together, we urged the mare on as I knelt beside him.

Many days, with the souls, death was all I saw. I grew tired of witnessing it sometimes. Now, I sat back on my heels and tucked away a loose strand of hair. Nature could choose its own course, its decided deaths, another day. Today, I wanted this foal to live.

I scuttled backward a few minutes later as Morgan lunged for the foal who'd finally emerged from the panting mare. With hands that refused to shake, he eased the foal's head free and cleared its nostrils. The mare heaved to her feet and nickered at her baby. And as she licked him clean, the foal took his first breath of sea air.

I gasped with joy and tugged at Morgan's arm. "He's breathing. Will he be alright?"

He leaned back on his heels and nodded. "Should be. But I want to stay awhile to make sure mare and foal are both steady."

I stared at Morgan while he watched the ponies keenly. He knelt in the sand with dirty hands and not a single care other than the ponies', the island's, wellbeing. And it felt good to see something breathe and live, not be guided to the mist and sent away. There was more life on the island now, with Morgan's help. Perhaps it hadn't been such a cruel fate the day he had stepped onto my dock. Perhaps he would be good for the island. Every part of it.

"How did you know what to do?" I said. "Or even to come down to the herd at all?"

Morgan stepped a few paces away to wash his hands off in the saltwater. His mouth quirked and he smiled back at me. "Grew up on a farm, remember? I've delivered countless foals. I heard the mare's whinnies when I woke this morning and rushed down to help." He knelt beside me again. "Want to name the foal?"

I shook my head. "They're the island's. Not ours."

Morgan leaned over and kissed my cheek, nearly making me jump. "Good point. Thank you for your help."

I'd expected to hate his touch. But I hadn't. Not at all.

Inching closer together, we watched at the edge of the herd in silence as the foal took his first steps on long, uncertain legs. He learned to walk on that shore, just as I had years ago. From his smile and straight back, I could see that Morgan took pride in watching the foal walk; the foal he had acted to save and protect.

At that moment, I decided. Finally, I would trust him with the island's most precious secret, its shipwrecked souls. That night, I took Morgan with me from the cottage and used the lantern to light our way. Down at the beach, I stayed back and ushered him on ahead toward the one soul we found. Better to show him, rather than try to explain first. Morgan was cautious, curious, as he stepped closer to the soul. I recognized those tentative steps. They were the same ones I'd taken as a child when Pa had first shown me a soul.

We walked the man from the shore to the mist, both the lighthouse and my lantern illuminating the final steps he took. Morgan stood behind me as I directed the soul into the mist. He was silent the whole way back to the cottage, an irregularity for Morgan. He didn't speak again, and only to ask a few questions, until we were seated at the kitchen table, each with a tin cup of coffee. Bitter stuff, but a necessity for ever-tired lighthouse keepers.

Morgan's voice was unsteady, quizzical, and he kept looking down at his coffee rather than meet my eyes. Perhaps it had all been easier for a young girl to accept. So, I showed him this side of the island slowly, steadily, again and again. Morgan would walk the shore each night with me and, in the three weeks that followed, we guided four more souls to the mist. With each one, Morgan spoke more, touched their hands, and lost the hesitant look in his eyes. And eventually, it must have seemed less like a strange dream and more like the reality we shared. Funny how sometimes the two collided.

After the fourth soul, we sat in the kitchen with coffee again, something that had become habit by then.

"The souls, they really do come, don't they?" Morgan muttered, more to himself than me.

I crossed my legs and rested my hands on the table. I'd give him time for all this. As much as he needed. As many souls as it took.

Finally, Morgan looked up at me. "I hope that man can find peace," he said. His mind, like mine, must still have been focused on the soul we'd said goodbye to. It had been more hesitant than usual to leave this place.

"They do in the mist," I said. "I think." I swallowed some of my coffee. Pa and the souls themselves had never given me a reason to believe otherwise.

Morgan nodded and, while we sat there, I placed my hand on top of his so they both rested atop the worn table. The nearby candle in the window didn't give off much light, but it was enough to see by. Smiling, Morgan curled his calloused fingers around mine and we stayed that way until long after our coffee was finished. After that night, it was like he'd finally decided his role for himself, as he didn't hesitate with the souls any longer.

We spent our days and nights working at the lighthouse and guiding souls. Occasionally hand-in-hand, but always together. Daylight hours were for climbing up and down countless stairs and doing the necessary chores. After stars were threaded into the sky's dark tapestry each night, we walked the beach, sharing a lantern between us. The lighthouse's bright, burning beam never flickered or went out, nor did our candle in the window. And somewhere in between all that, we found time to splash each other in the surf and learned to share kisses that tasted of salt and sea air.

Our world was a steady one of light and life and long, working days. The lighthouse kept me strong and Morgan kept my heart light. We found we were good at forming our own small family.

Each for the other, we were solid ground and familiar, comforting sea breeze and a shining light in the dark.

One night, like always, Morgan and I were walking along the shore, searching for souls. We had found none so far and were debating returning to the cottage when cries for help caught my attention. I lifted my head and tugged on Morgan's arm. At my pointing, we both fixed our gaze on the ship foundering out on the rocks. Even with the light's warning, it had strayed too close to the shore. The rough waves and sharp rocks had met their prey wholeheartedly, leaving the ship in poor, wrecked shape.

After we sighted the ship, Morgan and I both hurried to our lone dinghy moored to the dock. Each of us with an oar in hand, we rowed out past breaking waves to the ship. I spent so much time guiding drowned souls that sometimes it felt like I overlooked the other part of my job: keeping living souls from drowning in the first place. I tightened my grip on the oar and leaned forward to row a little faster.

When we reached the ship, it had become stuck between two large rocks jutting out from the sea. The ship's surviving occupants had all gathered on the highest, least water-logged point. With both oars, Morgan and I kept the dinghy steady enough to maneuver around rocks and reach the soaking men.

"We're from the lighthouse," I called to them, hoping they could hear me above the wind. "We're here to take you back to shore."

Morgan surveyed the terrified faces of the men. "It's going to be tight, but I think one trip will make it."

I nodded. I turned away from Morgan as we tried to get the dinghy as close to the men as we could. Rather than risk our own dinghy being beaten against the ship by the waves, we kept it a few paces away. The men who were able to swim made it over and we hauled them aboard.

"Keep the dinghy nearby," I told Morgan before diving into the water.

I swam for the rest of the men, dragging each back to the dinghy and keeping their heads above the waves. The sea was cold and rough, but I'd grown up swimming in it. Eventually, I made it to the dinghy with the last of the ship's survivors. We left the wreck behind as I took my oar back and began paddling again.

The dinghy was heavier and more difficult to maneuver, but we made progress as Morgan and I continued to take strokes through the seawater. I groaned from the effort rowing took as we made it to the first of the breaking waves. Rather than aim for the dock, we headed for the expanse of shore, just trying to get everyone back to land.

One of the men crammed to the side was thrown over the dinghy's edge as a particularly rough wave knocked the boat. I cursed as I watched him go. Just when I'd been starting to dry off.

Before I could dive in after the man, Morgan had pulled off his own jacket and jumped into the sea. "You've already had your turn," he called to me. "Just get those men back to shore. I'll get this one."

I smiled my thanks. I was already shivering, so it was a blessing not having to dive back into the water.

"Take that oar and help me," I said, gesturing to one of the less pale-looking men.

Another round of hard rowing brought the dinghy close to shore. As it ground against the sandy bottom, I jumped out. Others followed and we pulled the dinghy fully onto dry land where it would be safe from the rising tide.

I shoved back a strand of dripping hair and turned to the sea, expecting to see Morgan swimming back right behind me. But even with no lantern, I couldn't see any man adrift in the sea. I ran to the edge of the waves and scanned the dark sea through narrowed eyes. Even calling Morgan's name brought no answer.

With no sign of him, I ran back into the sea itself. I swam out to where I'd seen him last and dove down, searching for him countless times. I looked for him among the waves until I had no breath left. Both Morgan and the man he had gone to rescue were gone, stolen away by the sea.

I returned to the shore once I was gasping for breath and my arms were refusing to take another stroke. Wordlessly, I led the rescued sailors back to the cottage. They sat gathered in front of the fireplace and wrapped in every blanket and towel I could find. We made the food and water stretch, and after another five days, the ferryman arrived for the month. When he left, he took the sailors with him and I was alone again with only the candle burning in the window.

I lit it again, night after night, while the cruel sea sang its song outside my dark, empty home. My work stayed the same, night and day, but this time there was no hand in mine and no light in my life. Summer eventually left and took the last of its blazing warmth with it.

Day after day passed, each filled with pacing and waiting and walking the shore for hours. Many nights, I debated aloud with myself in my empty cottage. My drowned love would return to me, to my shore. And it had quickly occurred to me that though I would guide him into the mist, there was nothing keeping me from following him in. Except that I had a duty here, a role to fulfill. There was no leaving this island so easily.

But there would be peace in the mist, with Morgan, and I wouldn't be keeping the souls and the lighthouse alone anymore. *This island doesn't need to remain your charge*, a voice would sometimes repeat in my head. But that voice was not me, no matter how many times I tried to convince myself that it was.

It took time, too much time, but eventually, the night I'd been waiting for arrived. I had been walking barefoot through the sand with my lantern held aloft while the wind whipped my hair about. Then there he was, lying on his side in front of me with ocean foam stuck in his hair. Like an apology from the sea, saying, *Here, look, I gave him back to you.*

I set my lantern down and ran to him. Tears dripped from my face and mixed with the saltwater at my feet.

"Morgan." I wiped away tears with the back of my rough hand. "You came home."

He stood, appearing as solid as the other souls had and sharing their lost, empty eyes too. But as his gaze focused on me, Morgan's lost look faded in a way that had never happened with the others. His footsteps were silent as he closed the last bit of distance between us.

He, his soul, pressed his lips to mine and while there was no longer any warmth there, he still tasted of salt and summer.

Morgan was home, for a moment, for as long as I could have him. He'd either enter the mist and be lost to me then, or he would stay and fade away until there wasn't a whisper of him left on the island. This was all that we had. A quick, final goodbye. It was more than I'd had with Pa, though, and I was grateful for it.

Morgan and I walked silently back to the cottage together. My lantern's light kept many of the shadows away, but some forced their way between us anyway. We strode slowly together, Morgan's hand gripping mine so tightly it seemed he wouldn't ever let go again.

He smiled when he first glimpsed the candle shining in the window. "You kept the light on for me."

I squeezed his hand and leaned my head against his shoulder. "Always." Another stray tear fell. "Morgan, what happened?"

He kissed the top of my head. "The man who fell out of the dinghy. He was too scared and wouldn't stop fighting against me. And the waves were strong. Eventually, we both grew too exhausted, I suppose. I'm just glad you're alright."

I turned to face him. Not without him, I wasn't. Not fully. For a moment, I thought again about walking into the mist with Morgan. I wouldn't be facing the dark and the loneliness anymore that way. But that idea left me as I cast my gaze out over the savage, singing sea and the moor where the wild ponies grazed and the lighthouse shining above it all. This island, these souls, needed me. I'd taken it all on years ago, chose it again every day, and I couldn't abandon it all now. Not even for Morgan. But I couldn't let him go into the mist thinking I wouldn't be alright.

I surveyed Morgan as the sea breeze whipped around my loose strands of hair. "Thank you for the time you gave me. But don't worry about me now. I'll be fine. I promise."

I'd done lonely before. Surely, I could do lonely again.

Morgan's eyes shone as bright as the light overhead. "I don't know if I can wait... there. The mist. But I'll try. If I can."

We exchanged no more words, only held onto each other tightly as we crossed the dark, windswept island. Our pace was slow but still we reached the end of us. In the distance, the sea serenaded us as we approached where the mist rested up upon the hillside.

"I'll keep the candle in the window," I said. "Stay safe wherever you go."

"I'd stay right here if I could choose."

I nodded right before Morgan leaned down to kiss me. He murmured his final goodbye so quietly I almost missed it. Morgan walked into the mist with his head lifted. He strode alone while I stood back, wiping tears from my face. And when he was gone, I stared after him into the mist, seeing nothing more than silver and light.

Though he'd gone, Morgan stayed with me in ways I hadn't expected. I was reminded of him each time I saw the black foal he'd helped deliver. The foal splashed through the surf on the shore each morning, growing ever stronger and taller. Soon he wouldn't need his mama anymore and would be mating himself. And every day, I made two cups of coffee, one for Morgan and one for me. It was a habit that wouldn't die. One I couldn't bring myself to let fade away.

The island refused to go back to its original silence. While I worked, I hummed to myself all the old folk songs Morgan had brought over from the mainland. He'd taught me many while he'd been here. Some nights by the sea, I swore I could still hear his voice on the wind.

His leaving had shattered me, but I slowly stitched the scraps of myself back together. I'd said my goodbye, decided to stay, and took each day as it came, one breath at a time. Eventually, the breathing got easier. And a few weeks later, just when I was getting used to the empty cottage, I discovered Morgan had left one last piece of himself on the island. One last gift from the dead to the living, set to arrive when the island became spring's canvas and wildflowers covered the hills again.

It was a girl I gave birth to one morning, right when the sun was dawning on the horizon. I'd never felt so grateful, knowing I was past the woes of pregnancy. I'd climbed a lot of stairs and managed as best I could with the lighthouse. For several weeks, I'd debated having another keeper sent out to help. But Morgan had been a stroke of fortune. I might not be that lucky again. No, I trusted only myself with the souls.

I smiled down at the small girl I held in my arms. Well, perhaps there was one more here I would trust with the souls and the island. But for now, she rested, her hands curled into fists and her eyes closed. From her first cry, she had chased away all the shadows left behind after Morgan's death. My own small sun. My light.

I clutched my daughter tighter as the slope I walked on steepened and meandered further uphill. She was wrapped in the gray blanket I'd knitted for her, and dozed as I crossed the island. It wasn't a far walk, but with the baby, I traveled slowly and kept stopping to pick wildflowers. White, yellow, blue. I added them all to the bouquets I gathered as I wove my way along the island's sloping side.

Further inland, I reached the place where I'd buried Pa. A wooden cross I'd made with my own hands from driftwood marked the place. A second was now rooted in the dirt beside the first, wind-battered one.

I set down the twin wildflower bouquets, each placed against a driftwood cross. With my daughter secured in my arms, I stood between the crosses with the mist at my back and the sea humming its wild song ahead.

"Ellen," I murmured, at last finding a name as my gaze came to rest on the lighthouse. Morgan's daughter with my mother's name. It was one way I could think to further merge our families, to make a place for both of us on the island.

"Ellen, this is all in your blood." I closed my eyes and let the sun kiss my face. "I hope one day you'll be a fine keeper."

Ellen grew like I had, raised under the sun and the stars and the lighthouse's shining beam. She had Morgan's eyes, a blue as pure as the sea. And it was the sea's shore she ran along so often, chasing seagulls and echoing their cries.

"Show me your pockets," was what I repeated nearly every day as I stood with a hand against the door, refusing to let Ellen go out until she obeyed. And often I caught the bread or rolls she'd been sneaking out to feed the birds on the beach.

"Please," she'd plead. "They're hungry."

"They already have food to eat. We need the bread."

Occasionally, I'd let Ellen feed the birds what she snuck from the dinner table. But with supplies and rations lasting us just until the ferryman next came, I couldn't allow it to become a daily habit.

Ellen's crooked smile was near-constant. I thought I'd been raised half-feral, but it was a fight to get the girl inside at all. She refused to wear shoes most of the time and insisted on keeping her hair shorn so it wouldn't get in the way. Every spring, she'd weave dozens of wildflower crowns and try to get the wild ponies to wear them. Lord knows the child would have been happier if I'd locked her out of the cottage and sent her to live with the herd.

Like Morgan, she adored music and songs. She collected them, like I had done with whatever I'd found on the beach when I was young. I taught Ellen all the songs I knew and the ones I'd learned from Morgan. The ferryman gave her others and the rest she stole from the island's songbirds or made up on her own.

The first soul she met, she chose to sing to. When I first brought her to the beach after dark, Ellen was younger than I'd been. But I wanted her to have the chance to grow with the souls, to know them before she was ever tasked with their care and guidance.

Ever fearless, she'd gone right up to the drowned woman. With her head cocked and one hand on her hip, Ellen had said, "What's your name?"

"Lillian."

"I'm Ellen." She jabbed a finger toward where I stood holding a lantern. "That's Ma. This is Hestur Island."

After gently explaining to the two how the soul had come to be here and what came next, I led Lillian to the mist. Ellen had been humming while we walked, and after a few minutes, Lillian turned to her.

"Will you sing louder?" She stepped around long blades of grass fluttering in the wind. "Music's always been a comfort to me."

Ellen smiled her consent and raised her voice. After that, the lilt of her song often cut through the dark. I tried to insist on Ellen staying at the cottage to sleep, but once she knew about the souls, there was no fighting her. She'd join me and bring her song with her, more often than not. The souls loved it. They loved her.

A thousand sunsets came and went. My daughter took to carrying kerosene herself. Her eyes grew bright, her legs grew strong, and her hands grew steady and sure. Morgan's child, my child, and I loved her more each time the sun rose. We guided souls together, she and I, side by side, until the night I stumbled.

I'd slipped on a stone slick from rain. It went clattering down the hill and I scraped my knees, landing on them rather than my hands. My best attempt at keeping the lantern's glass from shattering.

"Ma!" Ellen was at my side the moment the stone had gone clattering. She was stronger than me by then, taller too, and it was no trouble for her to pull me back up. The soul we'd been guiding stood nearby, watching everything without a word.

"Sorry," I said, coughing into my fist. After that, it took me a minute to get my breath back.

Ellen furrowed her brows as she looked me over. "Why don't you wait here? I'll finish the walk to the mist while you rest and then I'll be back."

I wouldn't have accepted her offer if my legs hadn't been hurting from the fall. Ellen left with the lantern and the soul. I found a boulder and crossed my legs to rest atop it. My daughter's first time escorting a soul to the mist and I hadn't even planned for it.

"I'm sorry," I repeated to her as we traveled back to the cottage later. "I should still be able to shoulder the task."

"Ma, there's no need to be Atlas. I've wanted this for years."

I turned away so she wouldn't see the tears that fell. I'd repeated the same thing to Pa many times.

"I'm afraid it's the bloodline," I said. "Pa had weak lungs and a bad back. It seems I might be afflicted too."

"Maybe it's duty, not illness, that's inherited." Ellen twisted her head and shot me that crooked grin. "Lighthouse keeper isn't an easy life. Fifty years of that, anyone would be the same."

Her words and the realization they'd brought silenced me until we made it back to the lighthouse.

"I don't regret it, you know," I said.

Ellen helped me out of my coat before pulling me close. "I never thought you did. Don't think I will either."

"You could go to the mainland. Live there awhile. The Lighthouse Board can send another keeper."

Ellen stepped back and shook her head. "No, it's our island. Our lighthouse. And we're the ones to guide the souls."

I started brewing coffee for two, the way I had for years. "I don't want to leave you here alone."

"I won't be alone. Not on this island." Ellen took the tin cup I offered her. "Besides, I had you for years longer than my pa did." She took a long sip. "I hope he's waiting, like he said he would."

I gave her a thin smile. "Me too."

We sat finishing our coffee as a candle flickered in the window, keeping the dark at bay.

I stayed with Ellen until the first snow of that year. Life had caught up to me quicker than I'd ever expected. I was nearly as pale as the snow itself and had trouble making it to the top of the lighthouse anymore. In the end, it had been Ellen's urging that convinced me. Go to the mist while I could still walk there and decide my fate for myself. After a lifetime of walking to the mist's edge, it almost felt right to walk in myself rather than being lowered down into the dirt.

My island and its souls were being left to the best possible hands. I'd seen to it myself. And maybe, just maybe, my old love would be on the other side of it all.

I left Ellen my lantern, my coat, and my love. She guided me like she would have any old soul, somehow not shedding a tear once.

"I love you, Ma," she said simply, like it was the clearest of facts.

I put my arms around her and didn't let go for a long, long time. My daughter, my girl, with eyes like the sea and a voice to rival its own tune.

"You are my light." I kissed the top of her head. "And you will be an excellent keeper. This island, these souls, are blessed to have you here."

It was Ellen who broke away first. She led me the last few steps, the same way we'd done for so many other souls. And then I entered the mist. It was peace and it was light and it was a joy fluttering in my heart like a seabird. It was a joy to rival what I'd known and found all those years on the island. A joy that embalmed me until I forgot all else.

ᴶ

Each morning, dawn rises on Hestur Island, painting over the stars with its fragile, pastel shades as the sea sings on below. In the place where the souls wash ashore at night, a herd of wild ponies gathers to watch as a new day is born. On the herd's edge, two bays with coats wet from sea spray stand and nuzzle each other.

The woman who guides the souls and keeps the lighthouse knows the herd well. She was raised with them, among them, nearly a wild pony herself in her youth. She doesn't recognize the two newcomers and notices them the first morning they appear. It's as if the sea sent the pair of bays itself, the way they appeared out of nowhere, out of the night.

The woman smiles to herself and goes back to her work. Soon, the two ponies become as much a part of the island as the mist and the shore and the cliffs. Like they were there from its very formation when it rose up out of the sea. Day after day, the island persists and so do they.

On the shore each morning, the two ponies stand, pressed close together as light appears on the horizon, right in the place where the sky meets the sea.

See Josie Smith's story "Souls Like Sea Glass" online at Metaphorosis.
If you liked it, leave a comment. Authors love that!
Remember to subscribe to our e-mail updates so you'll know when new stories are posted.

About the story

I'm a shameless Pinterest addict and keep an entire folder full of distinctive images that inspire me for one reason or another. One night while scrolling through the app, I came across an image of a woman holding a lantern aloft while standing on a windswept shore. Something in my mind whispered that she was searching for souls and I latched onto the idea.

I'd been taking a creative writing class for fun that semester and needed to turn in a short story. I love writing but tend to stick to poetry and novels so short stories were a new challenge for me. This idea worked perfectly for the length I needed to turn in and I had so much fun writing it. Not caring about making a first draft perfect, I had thrown in everything I love and always try to include in my writing: a wild, inspiring natural setting, tenacious girls, and hints of history and folklore woven throughout.

I'd never intended to take the story any further than my class, but after turning in my final, polished draft for the semester, I decided to submit it to a few places and just see what would happen. Then, with some more polish and rewriting, it found a home! I'm so excited to see my story in print and hope you enjoy reading it nearly as much as I enjoyed writing it.

A question for the author

Q: What is your favourite short story?

A: "Mother Carey's Table" by J. Anderson Coats. From the first paragraph, the voice wowed me, and the mix of fables, folklore, and history captured my attention. That blend is right where I try to place my own stories, so it was so fun to read. I loved the story, and the rest of the anthology, so much that I bought my own copy as soon as I finished reading the library's edition.

About the author

When not traveling, Josie Smith splits her time between Ohio and Alabama, where she is currently earning a dual degree in English and Spanish. She loves seeing new places, experiencing new things, and taking pictures of both the former. When not trying to catch up on homework, she interns for a literary agent and writes stories set in the place where magic and history intersect.

@_josiesmith

Free Hugs

Jennifer Shelby

Beware: Hugbot ahead, warned a scrawl of white paint across a brick wall. Cyndl paused in her journey through the dead city and stared at the words while a complicated blend of grief and hope blossomed inside of her.

She defied the graffiti and kept moving until the alley opened into a treed square. The Hugbot gleamed in the center, caught in a halo of sunlight and memory. Its body was vaguely humanoid: a metal torso with arms, a short vertical indentation to suggest legs, and tracks instead of feet. Its head was a silver egg with eyes and a mouth. Cyndl had heard that the original prototypes had been sleek, sophisticated, and more human-like, only to be scrapped when people used them for something more than innocent hugging.

The foam latex along the bot's inner arms, chest, and neck, once offering a pillowed embrace, now hung in ragged ribbons. Its pressure sensors would still be in good shape; the engineers had taken special care with those to prevent crushed customers and their associated lawsuits.

A thick chain around its left track tethered the robot to a link hammered into the concrete. A ring around this anchor had been grooved into the cement by the bot's desperate, hopeless circling. Cyndl curled her lip in disgust. "That kind of cruelty is never necessary," she muttered to herself.

The bot's ocular receptors were dark, and a dusty cobweb drifted lazily over the mesh speaker that was its mouth. Cyndl wiped it away, her hand lingering on the familiar oval of the metal face. A whisper of tears prickled at her eyes.

Someone had tied a filthy sheet around the neck of the bot, covering the solar panel. This had likely been meant as a kindness; a temporary means to keep the bot powered down. The rotten fabric fell apart under Cyndl's fingers as she untied it, and the sheet whooshed to the ground in a plume of disintegrated fibres.

The solar matrix beneath the sheet appeared to be in good condition. 'No wonder these things survived the Climate Wars,' Cyndl thought.

She knelt to detach the chain from the Hugbot's foot track. The links were strong, but she had a hacksaw in the patched pack that never left her side. She pushed dirty strands of silvered hair behind her sunburnt, peeling ear, set her jaw, and began to work.

Sweat soaked through her shirt by the time she'd finished and kicked the chain away. The bot had yet to wake up. It usually took a few hours for the solar batteries to charge.

Six-year-old Cyndl forced herself to walk. Her cheeks burned with the salt of dried tears. The wind whipping over the city stung her face, but if she turned away, she'd see the tower, and she did not want to see the tower.

Cyndl wasn't supposed to be alone in the ravaged world. She was supposed to be in the digital realm with the Technicians who'd built the tower, but they had flopped and soiled themselves as the electricity uploaded them to the realms. Her fear had overpowered her faith and she'd pulled out her upload cable.

Cyndl collapsed into a puddle, taking long drinks that tasted of earth and filled her mouth with silt. A glint of metal shifted in the space between her and the edges of the city, a reflected light that drew closer until a machine materialized.

The robot's shadow fell over her and it lifted her with gentle arms, cradling her body as it carried her away from the tower. She slipped in and out of consciousness. Each time she awoke anew, the bot's lights blinked. "Would you like a hug?" it asked her.

Cyndl shook her head to ground herself in the present. The Hugbot would be charged soon. She pulled a crab apple from an overgrown ornamental and sat on the ledge of a dry fountain, taking a bite and watching the city for movement. The crab apple tasted tart, but it was wet and fresh, and she relished the treat.

Wild animals had claimed the rotting city, birds flying from broken windows and raccoons skulking through open doorways. The old Tech Cults had been the last hangers-on to sedentary lifestyles, but people still marked their travels by these ruined cities. A Technician tower loomed at the edge of the western skyline. There was a tower for every dead city, but Cyndl didn't like to acknowledge them.

The first lights flickered on the bot's control panel. It opened its eyes and turned its head to her. "Would you like a hug?"

Cyndl closed her eyes for a moment, overcome by the emotional weight of the familiar, tinny voice. "Hey, Hugbot."

"I am Unit 2201. I was created to provide safe physical contact." The bot projected a hologram of a nondescript individual in a suit into the air between them. Cyndl had dubbed this person Hugbob when she was little. "Here at Lovelace Robotics, we know how hard it is to refrain from hugging your loved ones as we do our duty to defeat the virus. That is why Lovelace Robotics created the Safe Family Avatar. Now you can send Grandma what she really wants for her birthday: a hug from her grandchildren."

In the grainy hologram, an elderly woman wept into the robot's neck as it embraced her. "The Safe Family Avatar's upper body is made of soft, padded latex for the feel of a real hug. Using our patent-pending, non-invasive technology, our Safe Family Avatars scan the levels of oxytocin, the human happiness hormone, in your hug recipient's bloodstream. This enables us to ensure the optimal hormone levels for best mental health benefits have been achieved. Following each embrace, the Safe Family Avatar engages Disinfect Protocol, designed to destroy any germs that may have been transferred during physical contact."

The hologram shut down. "Free hugs," said the bot.

Tears tracked down Cyndl's cheeks, but a small smile waited on her lips. "The Hugbot who raised me played that hologram for me whenever I had nightmares." She cocked her head. "They found me after I escaped from the Tech Cults and they taught me how to survive. And, of course, I hugged them whenever their programming told them they needed one."

The Hugbot didn't say anything and Cyndl giggled nervously. "Sorry if I'm talking too much. It's been a while since I've had a Hugbot to talk to." She gave an awkward shrug. "I'm on my own a lot. I've tried to join traveling groups, but I never last long. The nightmares come back." She considered the crab apple core in her hand. Its pink flesh had oxidized to a rusty brown.

"Travelers do not like hugs," said the Hugbot.

"No." She tossed the core onto the ground.

"People are afraid of Unit 2201," said the Hugbot.

"That's not your fault." Cyndl gestured in the direction of the tower. "After the Tech Cults, people got superstitious of machines. You bots are the black cats of the modern world."

"Safe Family Avatars are not cats," said the Hugbot.

"It means they think crossing your path brings bad luck." Cyndl eyed the bot to gauge its reaction, but the robot did nothing. "It's not your fault that your programming tortures you when you have no one to hug, either. Your programmers just wanted you to work hard; they didn't expect this." She held up an end of the chain she'd cut away from its track.

"Would you like a hug?" asked the Hugbot.

"How long has it been since someone hugged you?" asked Cyndl.

"Thirty-two years, eight months, seven days."

Cyndl winced. "That's a long time, Hugbot. When your Disinfectant Protocol goes off after that long without use, it's probably going to kill you. I've seen it happen a few times with other Hugbots. But if it doesn't..." Cyndl tried to push down a surge of hope with a gulping breath. "We could travel together. I lost my Hugbot a long time ago."

A sob burst out of Cyndl as she lunged the wagon forward, stepping into the shadow of a Technician tower for the first time since she'd failed to upload. The Hugbot in the wagon listed severely to the right, its bottom half and track assembly melted into a blob of silvery metals. "FREE HUGS FREE HUGS FREE HUGS!"

Tiny lights inside the tower winked red and green; it still had power. An upload cable waited inside. Cyndl swallowed hard, her hand unwilling to reach out and grab the thing. The robot's voice burst through the memory that threatened to surface. "HUGS FREE FREE." And then the cord was in her hand and she was wrapping the Hugbot's metal fingers around it.

"Once I turn the power on, the current will fry your circuits. It'll be just like the Hugbot we saw that got hit by lightning. You'll be dead."

"FREE FREE FREE."

Cyndl nodded, swiped at her tears, and dashed into the tower. The breaker panel swung open beneath her fingertips and someone had written UPLOAD in red marker with an arrow pointing to a black plastic switch. The Hugbot still screamed, but a softness fell over the world. Her thumb and forefinger pulled the breaker to the opposite side with a heavy click. The blinking lights inside the tower pulsed, dimmed, and the Hugbot outside fell silent. For a moment, there was peace. Until the grief came.

The Hugbot in the square rocked on its tracks as if it were deliberating. A dried leaf wedged beneath its tracks pulled free and a breeze sent it tumbling across the square, then out of sight. "Free hugs," the bot said at last. "Would you like a hug?"

Cyndl got to her feet. "I would love one."

The robot's arms were rough as they wrapped around her slowly, double-checking their safety sensors to avoid crushing her. It had been too long since Cyndl had felt the gentle crush of a robotic hug. She let her longing for the old companionship expand and her tears slip free.

The Hugbot beeped to signal optimal hormone levels had been reached and released Cyndl from its embrace. "You're a good bot." Cyndl told them.

"Thank you," said the Hugbot. "Please stand back while I engage Disinfectant Protocol."

Cyndl walked away, giving the robot space. Protocol required the Hugbot to heat their surfaces to a minimum of five hundred degrees Celsius to kill off any germs. She waited for the pop before she turned to watch the contained explosion as the protocol malfunctioned. Smoke poured from the Hugbot's seams. "Free hugs," it slurred as its light dimmed for the last time.

Cyndl watched black smoke billow from the Hugbot until it faded to a noxious wisp. Only then did she pull a hand-drawn canvas map from her pocket, marked with Hugbot locations she'd gleaned from travelers eager to avoid the machines. With a sorrowful glance at the ruined bot, she crossed out an H.

The nearest city plotted to the east displayed multiple H's and Cyndl had heard rumors that it housed an old Hugbot factory. Maybe this would be her last journey alone. Her heart fluttered with hope as she put her things away, shouldered her pack, and headed east.

See Jennifer Shelby's story "Free Hugs" online at Metaphorosis.
If you liked it, leave a comment. Authors love that!
Remember to subscribe to our e-mail updates so you'll know when new stories are posted.

About the story

I caught the first threads of "Free Hugs" after seeing a heartbreaking status update from an older relative who didn't know how she was going to make it through the first pandemic lockdown in Atlantic Canada without hugging her grandchildren. I immediately picked up my notebook and wrote a story about an engineer creating a robot people could send to hug their aunties and grandmothers. After I let the story rest, I realized I was more interested in what might happen to those robots after they weren't needed anymore.

As someone who was raised in, and escaped from, a cult, I've always been interested in the cross over between cult programming and a robot's programming. It took a bachelor's degree in anthropology to understand my own programming. This past year, staying home, consuming far too much social media, it was hard to ignore the cult behavior that became unnervingly commonplace. While I'd never written about cult survivors before this year, they started populating my fiction. More than ever, I wonder who I'd be now if I hadn't stumbled into that first Intro to Anthropology class and recognized what it could do for me. Cyndl became a way to explore those might-have-beens. Once I knew who she was and understood the doctrine of the technology cult she'd escaped from, the trick became determining how she would survive in a post-apocalyptic world where she wouldn't have any access to deprogramming.

Pairing Cyndl with the Hugbots seemed a natural union, but of course story lives are never that simple, so I had to make it difficult for all of them. I hope readers look past Cyndl's brokenness to see how much hope she holds in her heart.

A question for the author

Q: What's your favorite story?

A: My current favorite story has to be the "overcoming the monster" story. I'm writing this a few days after my first shot of the coronavirus vaccine and it feels very much like the first step to overcoming the pandemic monster. This isn't humanity's—or my—first monster, and as much as I'd like it to be, it won't be the last. Having a supply of these stories in my memory and on my bookshelf keeps me inspired, grounded, and hopeful.

About the author

Jennifer Shelby hunts for stories in the beetled undergrowth of fairy-infested forests. She fishes for them in the dark space between the stars. As part of her ongoing catch-and-release program, this is Jennifer's second story in *Metaphorosis*. You can also find her stories in *Cricket, Kaleidotrope*, and many fine anthologies. Her first novella, *Slipstreamers: Plague of the Dreamless* is now available from Engen Books.

jennifershelby.blog, @jenniferdshelby

The Art of Unpicking Stitches

Jennifer Hudak

Technically, all I'd done was come up with the idea for doing a spell; Kimber and Cassie took care of the rest. As my father used to say, they cut their own pattern. I merely threaded the needle. That's what I told myself, anyway.

For Kimber and Cassie, this was an adventure, and way more interesting than just hanging out in a cafe on our last day together. It would be a ritual celebrating our friendship before we all went our separate ways. Really, before *they* went their separate ways—Cassie to state college, and Kimber to the Coast Guard Academy—and left me here. We knew we wouldn't see each other for a long time, and that even when we did reunite, things wouldn't be the same. I told them that rituals like this one created a space out of time, and that this one would sanctify our friendship and give us luck for the future. But it was just a game to them. Neither of them actually believed the spell would work.

I was the only one who knew it would.

Cassie, eager to help, hit the library and pored through books about herbal magic. Kimber thought it was more important to use intuition. She spread a creased, old-school map out on Cassie's bedroom floor. None of us were used to reading a paper map; nor were we used to doing this much research without online help. But that was part of the spell, Cassie insisted—no electronics, nothing but paper—and she and Kimber were so excited by the novelty of it all that I didn't have the heart to tell them they could have used their phones and it wouldn't have made a difference.

"We'll need a stream, for water," said Kimber, pointing at a blue line on the map. "We'll have to hike in, but I don't think it'll be too far."

Cassie groaned. "Can't we just bring water bottles?"

"Oh my god, Cassie. Where's the fun in that?"

"Fine, but you're going to have to carry me out if I hurt myself."

Kimber flung her arms dramatically over Cassie's shoulders. "I'll save you, my delicate flower!"

I'd miss this so much. Just this: Kimber's rough jostling, Cassie's wide-mouthed laugh, the typical formation of the three of us on Cassie's floor. We hung out here most often because Cassie's place was midway between mine and Kimber's, and I'd memorized every scratch on the hardwood, every sticky tape-remnant on her wall.

"Mish," Cassie asked me, "have you finished making the dolls?"

The poppets were the one contribution I'd made to the sprawling spell they'd cobbled together. They were also the only thing that really mattered. I'd started making them over a year ago, way before I'd floated the idea of a spell to either of them. Back when Cassie was helping Kimber study for the SATs, and both of them started getting excited about futures that took them far away from me—from *us*. I'd labored over the poppets in secret while the two of them applied to colleges; while they waited, in desperate limbo, to hear back; while they celebrated their acceptances and taped banners up on their walls and bought sweatshirts in their future school colors. The stitchwork on each doll took months to plan and execute, and I wanted all three of them to be perfect. Now, in the waning days of summer, the poppets were nearly done. This was the first spell I'd ever made from start to finish by myself, and it killed me that I couldn't share that achievement with Cassie and Kimber. But in the end, it would all be worth it.

"Just about," I answered. "They'll definitely be ready by tomorrow."

Kimber rolled onto her back and stretched her legs out over my lap. "Lucky us, to have a seamstress to do our bidding!"

"A tailor," I murmured.

"I don't know. I hear the word 'tailor' and I just think of your dad. You need a different title." I squirmed, and Cassie shot Kimber a look. "Sorry," Kimber said. "I mean, it's great you're going to take over the shop. I just meant—"

"It's fine," I interrupted. "Really."

Cassie changed the subject, thankfully. Neither of them understood why I hadn't applied to college. I think they suspected I was staying home just to make my father happy. Then again, they thought that all my father did was take in dresses and let out seams. They didn't know what he really was. What *I* really was. No one knew that, outside of my dad and me.

That was the first lesson he'd drummed into me back when I'd first picked up a needle and a scrap of fabric: *You can never tell anyone.* Back then, my stitches were halting and uneven, some so loose I'd catch my fingers in them, while other pulled so taut they puckered the fabric. My spells looked nothing like my father's elaborate designs, and I had felt certain they never would.

"Pull it out and try it again," he had said. And I did, but the fabric was no longer pristine. Thread always leaves a mark when you pull it out, the tiny holes a reminder that messy stitchwork can never be undone. Not entirely.

"It's just so *ugly*," I wailed.

"It doesn't have to be beautiful to work," my father reminded me. "It's what's *behind* the stitches that's important. Your intention."

I didn't believe him. How could he understand? His stitchwork was beautiful, and still he hid it inside the linings of coats, or folded into the seams of dresses and the cuffs of pants. Even the people who wore his garments weren't aware of the spells tucked inside.

I used to watch the customers come into the shop. When the door jingled, my father would take my fabric away; back then, I wasn't allowed even to practice without his direct supervision. Instead, I'd hide behind the table and watch. Once, my first-grade teacher had come in to try on a coat my father had altered for her. Even from across the room, I'd seen the flush of confidence that bloomed on her cheeks, confidence that she thought came from wearing a well-fitting garment, and not because of the threads of magic that spread outward along her sleeves and around her collar.

"You're a miracle worker," she'd said to my father. And she'd paid him and left the shop without a clue of the miracle he'd actually performed.

"Why do you even bother doing the spells?" I'd asked him. "When no one sees them?"

"Helping people is its own reward," he answered, and then laughed when I made a face. "Think of it this way: when people wear a dress or a suit that's been tailored to fit them perfectly, they feel good about themselves, right? And when they feel good about themselves, they spread that goodness around. They smile more; they're more likely to reach out to other people. That's what a tailor does, Michelle. It's not just about the clothes, it's about the community. The spells just add a little something extra."

"Plus, people will come back and get more clothes tailored."

He laughed again. "That, too."

"Still, if I could make spells that good, I'd want people to know."

"No one can *ever* know," he told me firmly. "You can never tell anyone."

"Not even friends?"

"Especially not friends. Not if you want to keep them."

Maybe it would have been better if I'd never made friends at all, but now that I had, I did want to keep them, more than anything. And yet, after years of following my father's rules, I was going to lose Kimber and Cassie all the same.

Unless I did something about it.

Cassie shut her notebook. "Okay! I think we're ready. Tomorrow?"

"Tomorrow!" said Kimber. "I can't wait!"

I squeezed her ankle. I couldn't wait, either. Tomorrow I was going to stop following rules. Tomorrow, I was going to take matters—and magic—into my own hands.

The next morning I put the finishing touches on the poppets—one for each of us, sewn together from scraps of old clothes we'd worn. I'd been working on them in secret, way past midnight, for most of the summer, before heading to work each morning at my dad's shop. But the last details had to be completed the morning of the ritual for the dolls to retain their potency. It was risky to use the workroom after dawn, even on my dad's day off, but I had no choice.

He walked in, fully dressed, just as I was clipping off a lock of my hair to braid together with the red and brown strands I'd collected from Kimber and Cassie.

"Do they know?"

Of course, that was his first question. I finished braiding the hair. "No."

His voice tightened. "Michelle..."

"I'm not stupid. I didn't tell them the truth. They think I'm just making dolls."

"That doesn't make this better." He looked at one of the poppets—the one that looked like Cassie—and shook his head. "You are not equipped to make a spell like this on your own. I can't believe you even attempted this." My dad sounded shocked. No: he sounded disappointed. And that pierced me in a way I wasn't willing to admit.

"I'm eighteen," I snapped. "I'm sick of you watching over every stitch I make."

"I don't care if you're sick of it! Those are the rules of this house."

I gathered up all three of the dolls and gripped them tightly to stop my hands from shaking. "I followed your rules my whole life. Now everyone thinks I'm just a boring kid who's too stupid to go to college. Are you happy?"

"No, I'm not happy. Not at all." He stooped over and put his hands on the table, bringing himself to eye level. "Magic is selfless. It *has* to be. Even if your spell doesn't go sideways..."

I bristled. "It's not going to go sideways."

"Even if," he persisted, "it's not going to go the way you think it will. It will be *wrong.*"

Lines ringed my dad's eyes, and I wondered how long they'd been there. He was changing, too. Everything was. I turned away from him and shoved the dolls into my bag.

"The spell isn't just for me," I told him. "It's for all three of us. You wouldn't understand."

"Michelle. You're stronger than you know. And you're right, this is your spell. You created it, you executed it. You own it. If it goes wrong, I won't be able to fix it."

His words chilled me. Every stitch I'd ever made, every thread I'd cut, I'd done so knowing my father could alter it if he needed to. Sometimes I chafed under that knowledge, but mostly, it was a comfort. It was *safe.* Now, my first time doing a spell on my own, it felt like my father was ripping off my only coat.

But I was going to have to learn how to sew my own coat eventually. Today was as good a day as any.

I shouldered my bag. "I don't need you to fix anything," I said, and at the time I believed it.

We'd planned to hike to the creek early in the day, before it got too hot, but it was sweltering in the woods anyway. When we got to the stream, Kimber crouched down with the crucible she'd brought in her backpack, trying to get more water than sludge.

"It doesn't matter if the dirt's in there," Cassie said. "Dirt's good. It'll help anchor the spell."

I busied myself with my bag to hide my nervousness. Cassie was right—the dirt didn't matter. But neither did the water, or the ritual itself. The only real spell was in the dolls I'd made, in their stitches and seams and in the precise clipping of loose threads.

Cassie pried a patch of moss from the forest floor and ground it up in a mortar along with some chamomile flowers, a sprig of sage and a sprig of rosemary, and a spoonful of grounds from the pot of coffee we'd shared that morning. The coffee had been awful, bitter and burnt—none of us were used to brewing our own—but we drank it anyway. Now, it sloshed uncomfortably in my stomach, sending waves of acid up my esophagus.

Kimber added the creek water to the mortar and Cassie mashed it all into a thick paste. "Okay, Mish," said Cassie. "You're up."

I took the poppets out of my bag. We each took a scoop of paste from the mortar and stuffed it inside the dolls. Then I threaded a needle and sewed up the seams, sealing the paste inside. The paste had been Cassie's idea, and it wouldn't hurt anything; all of the stitchwork my dad had taught me was strong enough to resist dirt and damp. Plus, I loved the idea that the poppets would always contain a bit of the ritual. It wasn't magical, but it would remind me of this moment: the bitter coffee I could still taste, the trickling water of the stream, the smell of the herbs, the moss beneath our feet.

When I was done, I struck a match and sterilized the needle.

"Are you guys going to poke your dominant or non-dominant hand?" asked Kimber.

"I don't think it makes a difference," Cassie answered.

"Non-dominant," I said. When they looked at me, I shrugged. "I mean, might as well, if it doesn't matter."

What I didn't say was that it was always the non-dominant hand. Had to be. You held the needle with your dominant hand. It was the other hand, supporting the fabric from underneath, that got punctured—accidentally or on purpose.

I remembered the first time I'd pricked my finger and looked aghast at the tiny bead of blood that blossomed from the nearly invisible wound. My father had gently grasped my hand and pressed my finger to the fabric, staining it with a small but shocking dot of red. "All spells need power," he'd told me. "Sometimes the stitchwork is enough, but some spells need more. Some spells need a sacrifice."

Remembering this, I almost lost my nerve. A sacrifice was no small thing. If we did this—if we spilled our blood to feed the spell —I'd have no choice but to see it through. But then I looked at my friends. Cassie, with her sharp eyes and her sharper mind; Kimber, the strongest and most daring of us, whose hair turned to fire in the sunlight. When we were together, our auras merged into a prism that scattered rainbows all over town, and neither of them knew it. And now they were leaving, and I'd never get a chance to tell them.

You can't tell them, my father had said. *They can't know who you really are.*

What if it would make them stay? I wanted to whisper back.

I pricked my finger. After Cassie and Kimber had done the same, we pressed our fingers together, and dabbed a bit of blood onto our dolls, right where the heart would be. I tucked the needle into a tiny envelope I kept in my pocket, and then we stood around the mortar, like three vertices of a triangle.

"For protection," said Cassie.

"For luck," said Kimber.

"For friendship," I finished.

Their eyes were closed, so only I saw the strands of light curling outward from the dolls like thread, wrapping us from hand to hand, braiding us together as tightly as the hair on the top of the dolls' heads. The magic pulled taut, like a too-tight elastic band worn around our wrists, but neither Cassie nor Kimber noticed a thing. You only feel what you expect to feel, and both of them still thought this was just a game.

The spell would work. The spell *wanted* to work. All those hours I'd spent sewing the dolls was worth it; the spell was strong —so strong, it looked like someone else's hand embroidering our circle, drawing stitches in the air to manifest itself.

This is how it will go, whispered the spell in thread and blood and magic. And I saw it. Our futures.

We'd open our eyes feeling shaky, as if we'd just had a shared dream. We'd laugh and joke, and say our goodbyes, but before tomorrow, both of them would cancel their plans to go to college. They wouldn't even know why; they'd just have a feeling that if they left, something terrible would happen. And they'd stay.

The magic continued to weave itself around our circle, sewing Kimber and Cassie's feet to the ground, anchoring itself with locking stitches, pulling tight, so tight that the fabric that made our friendship puckered and strained. I chanced a look at Kimber and Cassie; they both still had their eyes closed, oblivious to the magic working to tie them in place. Unaware that they'd been ensnared.

Magic is selfless, my father had said. *It has to be.*

The threads continued to pull and tighten. To strangle. Cassie wouldn't go to college. Kimber wouldn't go to the Coast Guard Academy. They'd stay in this town that they'd both been so desperate to get out of, abandoning the futures they'd planned. And I'd watch as everything I loved about them—their curiosity, their brightness, their drive—withered here. I'd watch them become something other than themselves.

Wait, I thought, and I tried to loosen the threads that bound us. *Not like this.* But the spell continued to rise. It had moved beyond me now, picking up strands of many possibilities and knotting together the sturdiest, the easiest to manifest. The stitches overlapped and reinforced each other, and I knew that I'd never be able to pull them out now without leaving tiny holes behind: the echoes of the spell marring our future.

In that moment, I wished—oh, how I wished—that my father were here. But he'd made it clear that this was my spell and mine alone. I had done this. And now there was no undoing it. I dropped my head.

Then, I saw a different kind of thread: a loose one, the exact orange of my t-shirt, emerging from the v-neck. I squinted. A delicate embroidery looped along the edge of the shirt: perfect stitches, so tiny they were nearly invisible. I imagined my father peering through his bifocals, imagined his fingers pulling the needle through. I imagined how much time he'd taken to craft the spell, and wondered how he'd known I'd wear this particular shirt today.

Or maybe he hadn't known. Maybe he'd added this layer of protection to all my clothes, and I'd never looked closely enough to realize it. My father's magic was always subtle, only used to enhance, never to overwhelm. Never to compel.

I heard his voice in my mind, as clearly as if he were standing in the circle with us. Holding my hand.

You're stronger than you know.

Guiding my needle. Showing me that even pulled-out stitches, even damaged fabric, could be powerful.

It's what's behind the stitches that's important. Your intention.

I took a breath and closed my eyes. What I wanted—what I really wanted—was to wrap my friends in a coat of magic, with all of my love tucked into its pockets and woven into the seams. I wanted the threads that bound us to stretch across continents and over waters—to stretch, not to bind.

But some spells need a sacrifice.

I held up my doll and looked at the stitchwork hiding in the embroidery. Then I pulled the needle out of my pocket, slid it under a stitch, and snapped the thread.

The spell didn't break all of a sudden. Our stitchwork is too strong for that, mine and my dad's. But as I unpicked the stitches, one by one, the tendrils of magic loosened, releasing Kimber and Cassie's feet and wrists. I pulled thread after thread, gathering it up into a small bundle, and the magic continued to retreat, until at last the spell dissolved with a sigh.

I examined the doll when I was done. It was still intact; only I would notice the tiny holes marring the fabric where the spell had once been.

I grabbed my friends' hands, our dolls sandwiched between our palms. Kimber and Cassie reached for each other as well, closing the circle. Even without looking at them, I knew that Kimber's polish was chipped and that Cassie had been chewing her nails again; that was how well I knew them both. I squeezed Kimber's hand once and, a moment later, an answering squeeze came from Cassie. Just a quick pulse that said, *I'm here. I see you. I know you.* I closed my eyes and imagined my needle picking up the loose threads of this moment: the scrape on Kimber's knee, Cassie's ragged cuticles, the callus on my third finger from holding fabric scissors. The late summer sunlight glancing through the trees. The pinpricks of blood on each of our fingers, our hands holding tight. Nothing was binding us together now—nothing but what we brought into the woods with us. And that would be enough. It had to be.

A squirrel skittered up a tree. The creek trickled inexorably from past to future. We opened our eyes.

"Do you think it worked?" Kimber asked.

"I don't know," said Cassie. "I think so? It felt like something happened."

I looked at them both, each of them on a cusp of a brand new adventure, and felt so full of love and hope I could have burst with it.

"I guess we'll just have to wait and see." I squeezed their hands once, and then I let them go.

See Jennifer Hudak's story "The Art of Unpicking Stitches" online at Metaphorosis.
If you liked it, leave a comment. Authors love that!
Remember to subscribe to our e-mail updates so you'll know when new stories are posted.

About the story

I wrote the first draft of this story the summer before my own daughter went to college. She was excited for the future but also desperately worried about her old friendships changing and perhaps even withering away. Her conflict really mirrored my own internal struggle to keep her safe and protected while also letting her take her first independent steps as an adult. Like Mish and her father, my daughter and I have a lot of the same interests and professional goals, which makes it even trickier for her to establish her own identity, and for me to let her forge her own path. Writing this story helped me work through my own feelings as a parent, but also reminded me what it was like to be on the cusp of adulthood, feeling like your life is about to change abruptly, and perhaps clinging a bit too tightly to the past.

The sewing came out of my desire to portray magic that's associated with domestic arts. In addition to being a knitter, I'm a baker and a gardener, and I think there's something incredibly powerful about creating something with your own hands that can go on to nourish or delight someone else. When I was Mish's age, I thought that I could change the world in a big, dramatic fashion. Now I think that the biggest impact I have on the world is in the relationships I develop with individual people—my kids, my friends, my neighbors, my community. Those relationships are built on small, quiet moments of caring and nurturing, but they're no less powerful for being subtle.

A question for the author

Q: What would your characters say about you?

A: I'd like to think that Mish would talk about me the same way she talks about her father: with a mix of love, embarrassment, admiration, and exasperation. She seems like a thoughtful enough kid that she wouldn't care that I'm desperately uncool. Mish's father and I would have long conversations about the difficulties of parenting through the teen years, and I'm pretty sure I would serve as both a model and a cautionary tale for him. Both Mish and her father would have a thing or two to say about the quality of my knitting, which is more enthusiastic than technically perfect.

About the author

Jennifer Hudak is a speculative fiction writer fueled mostly by tea. She's a graduate of the Viable Paradise writers workshop and a member of the Codex writers group. Formerly from Boston, she now lives with her family in upstate New York where, in addition to writing, she teaches yoga, knits tiny pocket-sized animals, and misses the ocean.

www.jenniferhudakwrites.com, @writerunyoga

The Nocturnals III

Mariah Montoya

In a world where each day and night lasts thirty years, Joah Cadshaw and Misla Crane have been sent out west to warn the miners of an impending roadblock that may prevent them from following the sun. Among the miners, they find an unexpected mutual enemy: Hickory Glade, Misla's ex-abuser and the man who murdered Joah's wife.

As the threat of Hickory's presence follows them deeper into darkness, they find Damien, a missing boy, on the brink of twilight. Incoherent and crazed, Damien has been infected by the humanoid creatures of darkness—the Nocturnals… and he is desperate to reach them.

Before Joah and Misla can bring him home, Damien escapes, Misla chases after him, and Joah overhears Hickory's plot to hunt them all. The light of day slips away. The Eternal Night is here.

Part 3

Wisps of cotton still hung from the trees like ghost tears.

It was these, more than the ice moon wrapped in clouds, that lit Misla's way into the forest, which seemed to swallow the High Road like a dark, greedy mouth might swallow a foreign tongue. The cotton glowed, almost as if the trees had absorbed and hoarded the last sunrays before the Eternal Night covered the world in its inky black cloak.

"Damien," Misla whispered.

When only rustling and chirping and hooting answered her, she veered off the High Road, into the cotton trees where she wouldn't feel as exposed. Or as *watched*.

Just keep the High Road in sight, she told herself. *It's your path home.*

She kept her fingers on the bark of trunks as she passed through them, her left hand clutched firmly around a jagged, curved bone. Her heart thumped in her mouth. She had to find the boy. Just *had* to. For three long years, she had trained to rescue the people the Nocturnals hypnotized and lured into the Eternal Night. She had known she might fail—General Deckler had warned his pupils of this grim possibility—but she had not expected to fail a *child*.

"Damien... Damien, are you there?"

The branches around her thickened as the cotton trees gave way to pines. Needles scratched her skin and the blossoming underbrush clawed at her ankles. She plunged onward, whispering the boy's name, not daring to shout in case her cry attracted a night beast.

And then something swooped overhead, sending prickles down her neck. Wings flapped against branches. The yellow pinpricks of eyes glowered at her from a tangled mass of trees, and there came a high-pitched, rasping yowl from somewhere to her left.

"Misla! Misla, where are you? Misla!"

The voice came from behind her. Misla, momentarily frozen in panic, uprooted herself and stumbled away from the howling, toward the High Road and Joah's calls.

She had not wanted to think of Joah Cadshaw, to even mention his name inside her head after he'd refused to retrieve the boy with her. But now her mind was racing with images of her partner's bruised and broken face. Her heart crashed against her chest.

He came for me. He didn't leave me. He's here. He came back for Damien. He—

The snorts of horses jolted her in her tracks. Horses? The scavengers had said their horses were *dead*, but there was no denying that steady *clop clop clop* of hoof against cobble. Misla stared through the cracks in the trees as what seemed like the carcasses of two mares rose from the rubble of the High Road. They burst through the branches, stampeding toward her with flaring nostrils and gleaming white eyes and flattened ears.

"Joah!" Misla cried. The bone slipped with sweat in her hand.

"I'm here, pretty girl."

There was a blaze of fire, and he appeared, his face shining with glee behind a cylinder of flickering glass. But it wasn't Joah. It was *him*, her ex-lover, the one she'd tried so hard to escape: Hickory Glade, straddling a mare, holding a lantern that looked horribly like the same one he had once swung toward her stomach, shattering its glass against her ribcage and watching with beady, unforgiving eyes as the flames devoured her shirt, as the oil melted her skin, as she screamed herself into oblivion. Now, in the lantern's twitching shadow of light, Hickory's warped features looked exactly like the night beast Misla had been imagining.

"Hickory," she choked out. "What—what are you *doing* here?"

She glanced behind him, at a second horse and the man astride it. He looked vaguely familiar. Misla guessed he had been in the clearing when she and Joah had delivered the news about the early bells. The miner's forehead shined with lines of grease. He licked his lips at the sight of her, as if in lieu of waving.

"I should ask you the same thing," Hickory laughed. "I didn't know Good Old General D sent you to the buttcrack of night. I mean, *look* at you, Misla, stumbling 'round in this darkness. That's one good thing about mining, huh, Sid?" He beamed at his companion. The lantern swung in his hand. "We know our tunnels and caves. We know how to live in the dark."

Misla swallowed thickly, fingers tight around the slick surface of the bone. Yes, Hickory had known how to live in the dark even *before* he had become a miner. She remembered the first time he had brought her over: his house had been dim and sweet-smelling, like moss rotting in a cavern. He had made her dinner in the candlelight, and, after a few drinks, told her of his dad's explorations in the various caves across the aro and his grandfather's adventures as the leader of their community before his untimely death. He'd even let a few tears slip down the hook of his nose. It had all lulled Misla into Hickory's personal cavity of darkness.

And now he was here, in front of her, trying to reel her in again five years later.

"I told you to Move, Hickory," she said, her throat dry, as if she'd swallowed the cotton she'd left behind. "General *Deckler* told you to Move. You disobeyed."

She tried glaring him down, but the hypocrisy of her own words made her lips tremble. Chuckling, Hickory slid off his horse with an easy grace. He tossed the lantern to Sid, who caught it by its rusted handle. Then he groped in his saddle pack and withdrew a glinting ax.

"Hickory, what are you—?"

"Where is he, Misla? Where's your shiny new retriever buddy? Thought I'd say hi, see."

Hickory stepped toward her, part of his face leaping with the light of flame, the other melting into the darkness. Misla's back hit the thorny fingers of a pine. She could smell the cloud of alcohol wafting from his open mouth: a bad sign at sunset, an even worse sign at night.

"H-he's taking a piss. Joah is," she said. "He'll be back soon, though, and then..."

She squinted over her shoulder as if she could spot Joah through the trees. Her heartbeat rose in her throat like vomit. The smell of Hickory's breath engulfed her. Before she could flinch away, he was inches from her face, grinning down at her with that ax in his fist.

The ax that had killed Joah's wife.

Misla didn't hesitate. She swung her bone toward the soft hollow of his neck. Hickory jerked away. The bone slashed his shoulder instead, and blood peppered Misla's lips.

"You *bitch.*"

Hickory flung his ax to the ground and grabbed Misla's hands with bone-crushing force. She dropped her weapon with a yelp. Pain exploded up her wrist. She heard *cracks* as her fingers snapped inside his fists, but Hickory laughed. Sweat oozed from the stubble on his upper lip.

"Why don't we speed up his return a little, huh?"

Hickory wanted, she realized with a sickening pinch in her stomach, to hear her scream for Joah as he tore her clothes from her body. His upper lip always gleamed with sweat when he wanted to get violent, when he wanted Misla to make noise. But Joah was nowhere nearby, and Misla would not give him the satisfaction of screaming—not anymore.

He flung her to the tangled forest floor. She caught a lopsided view of his companion; the man was still holding his glass container of fire, watching them with a greasy smirk.

"You're just going to *let* him, are you?" Misla cried at him. Hickory had found the buttons on her pants and was popping them off their threads.

"Ah, Sid likes stuff like this, don't you, Sid?" Hickory panted. "In fact, Sid, you can have this treasonous little bitch before I do. C'mon, then, it's not like she's new and clean anymore. I pounded that innocence out of her a long time ago."

This is what real darkness is, Misla thought as Sid blinked stupidly; his lips spread in a smile. He clambered off his mare to swagger toward them with his wobbling fire. Hickory's fingers were nailing her wrists to the ground. He had pinned her lower body with the crushing force of his thighs. *Fight them, hurt them, kill them,* Misla begged herself.

But when Sid approached, the two men swapped fire for Misla with ease. A dank, buzzing numbness had sprouted from her broken fingertips to her brain. She could not remember how to thrash or scream or do anything but lie there, letting them.

Sid was ripping her pants. He was touching her. Hickory was laughing in his drunken gurgle. The ax glinted a few steps away. The discarded bone glowed white just beyond it. Above them, the dotted orbs of birdlike eyes watched the proceedings with yellow apathy...

And Joah's voice was screaming her name in a distant world. Damien's muddied face swam above her. There were shouts. A *ping*. The pressure inside her released, but the full weight of Sid's body slumped against hers with a muffled *thump* that knocked the air from her lungs.

Misla gulped for breath. A slender steel dart stuck from the side of Sid's skull. His eyes stared vacantly at her chest. Hot blood pebbled her forehead. Men were shouting, but their mingled voices ceased to matter when Misla craned her neck and saw *him* standing over her:

Damien. The boy she'd come to find.

And he wasn't alone. Surrounding him, dressed in what could only be snowflakes or stars, willowy figures held what looked like wands, their dark silhouettes somehow sharp against the nighttime forest, their eyes stamps of furious, glowing violet in the night.

Damien, Misla knew even as that darkness pummeled her to sleep, had found them.

He'd found the Nocturnals.

The mares screeched and fled when Joah burst between their flanks.

His old anger returned with the swiftness of a hot knife when he saw the two men. They were bearing down upon Misla's limp figure buried halfway in scrub.

Without thinking, he lunged forward and scooped up the ax glinting in the brush. He held it high over his head and stumbled toward Hickory, who was mid-turn, the ghost of a laugh still wrinkling his face in the lantern's leaping light.

For a trembling moment, their eyes met. Joah imagined doing what he should have done three years ago. Swinging that blade down on his wife's killer. Ending his rotten life.

But the man thrusting himself into Misla had not turned, had not seen, had not stopped, and Misla was deathly silent, and Joah turned to bring the blade through *his* neck instead.

Goosebumps. A *ping.*

The man slumped onto Misla, dead, before he could bring the ax down.

A tornado of crisscrossing light whirled around them. Joah whipped around, disorientated by the sudden flare in glowing lines. He felt the ax wrenched from his grip. Hickory roared. A cold pinch of metal snaked around Joah's wrists. Icy sharp fingers—like talons—closed around his arms, locking him into place.

"No. *No.* Misla!" he screamed.

Something—a piece of the swirling puzzle of light—had broken apart from the others and was now hauling Misla upward by her armpits. When she stirred, the whirlwind of activity slowed around them, and Joah could see that figures circled them, illuminated by their own glow.

Everything, even Misla, was smeared from his mind when the eddying stopped and his eyes became accustomed to this terrifying new light.

Each figure's skin was a rich, blackish-blue that seemed made of the fabric of dusk, but glowing spirals, swoops, and lines etched their bodies like luminous tattoos. The effect was blinding, dizzying. It made them blend together, so that Joah had to squint to make out their individual faces. They had beaked noses, elongated arms that looked vaguely like wings, and tiny purplish feathers sprouting from where eyebrows would be.

No, it couldn't be.

They looked nothing like the buggy humanoids imprinted on General Deckler's poster in his office. Joah felt faint with unease; for a moment, he tried to tell himself that these people poised before him could *not* be the Nocturnals who had infected his wife and so many others in his community, not with the intelligence shining beneath the feathered frames of their faces.

Then one of them stepped forward—*male*, Joah somehow knew. Like the rest of them, he only had two eyes, and each one was a striking violet. He was clutching Hickory's lantern with those curved, talon-like fingers, while his free hand rested on the bony little shoulder of—

"Damien," Joah choked, twitching forward. The icy grip on his arms tightened. The truth lodged itself in Joah's throat like he'd tried to swallow a broken wristwatch. No other night beast besides a Nocturnal could have lured the Infected boy to their circle.

Damien was still wearing Joah's t-shirt like a skull-white dress. He wasn't shaking or rocking anymore. He gazed calmly and curiously into Joah's face. Then he looked at Misla, who was straightening in her captor's grip, and Hickory, who was still thrashing and cursing against the Nocturnal who held him.

Finally, Damien Fertheli glanced at the dead man lying curled at their feet, the slender dart jutting from the man's head like a single antler. He pointed at the corpse.

"*He*'s the only one who never worked for General Deckler."

If Damien hadn't opened his mouth, Joah would never have believed that these coherent words had flowed from his lips. Even Hickory fell silent to gape at the Infected boy, who had paused, gazing upward at the Nocturnal still gripping his shoulder.

"Yes, I know," Damien said eventually. He turned back to Misla and added, as if in explanation, "They don't tolerate what that man did to you here. Someone will take care of you when we get back to the others. But Prince Kal still wants me to—yes, okay."

Joah's mind reeled, trying to absorb the new information. All the other light-tattooed figures seemed to be looking at the lantern-holding Nocturnal as if he were their leader. Prince Kal. *Prince*. An insane chortle almost escaped his tongue. Oh, how General Deckler would have pissed himself laughing if he'd known the Nocturnals practiced a monarchy.

His strange mania died when Damien stalked toward Misla and peered down at her.

"This one here works for Aoif Deckler now," the boy told the prince Nocturnal, who cocked his head like a hawk examining a mouse. "She wanted to drag me back when she found me in the fuel tower back at sunset. She wanted to stop me from reaching you."

Misla whimpered. Damien moved toward Joah.

"This one *used* to work for him. He was the one who kidnapped so many of the bilinguals. He'd force them back to the community. To their deaths. My friends and I used to watch him lead the bilinguals back in handcuffs before our last Move."

Joah's throat had never been so painstakingly dry. Before he could attempt to speak, Damien moved to Hickory, who scowled at him. The boy's voice took on a frosty, forbidding quality that kissed Joah's neck with fresh goosebumps.

"*This* one beheaded the bilinguals. My mom didn't know, but I would sneak into the crowd and watch each time he did it. He would've killed me if he still worked for Deckler and I'd been forced back. He'd kill me right now, if he could. He brought his ax."

A flock of creatures swooped over their heads before Hickory could respond. Branches jostled around them. The pinholes of eyes blinked at them between trees, little half-moons that reminded Joah, inexplicably, of Lupita Fertheli.

"Damien," he said, ignoring the tightening around his wrists. "Damien, I've spoken to your mother. She's worried sick about you. Think about your mother, kid. She doesn't know where you've gone off to. She doesn't know that you—that you chose this. To come here."

He was determined to tread carefully around this newly revived Damien, but the boy only stared at him and said, his face blank, "My mother would've been the first to die if I hadn't come to the Nocturnals. They told me something, you see. Something important."

"What did they tell you, Damien?"

"Oh, the kid's ears are filled with Infected shit," Hickory hissed. "I knew you were a cockhead, Cadshaw. Didn't realize you were gullible too. These monsters don't even *speak*." He twisted his neck and spat on the Nocturnal locking him in place. The figure didn't flinch, but the others in the circle shifted. Hickory laughed. "I forgot, though. You don't give a piss about whether they speak or not. You always *loved* them Nocturnals, didn't you, Cadshaw?"

I always loved a good shut-the-fuck-up, Joah thought furiously.

He locked eyes with Damien again.

"Listen, kid, can you communicate with them?" When the boy nodded, Joah said, "Okay. I believe you. Can you tell him—Prince Kal—that we don't mean any harm? He can keep the ax. We just want to bring you home. We're not built to live in the night," he added, glancing at Misla, who was sagging in her captor's incandescent arms.

"They can't let you go unless you promise to help," Damien whispered. The lantern's firelight was fading, but the prince Nocturnal's strange tattoos irradiated the boy's face. "They told *me*, but I can't do much about it. They only called my name because they were getting desperate and thought a kid might listen better than a grown-up. They thought I might convince you. *You* could stop it from happening. You could save my mother. And the rest of them too."

Joah paused for a heartbeat.

"Yes, okay," he said before Hickory could intervene. "What is it, then? What do they want to tell us?" In his mind, he heard his wife's Infected voice squeaking, *"Warn you. Got to. Warn, warn, warn,"* and his heart clogged with renewed fear.

Damien glanced up at Prince Kal. The Nocturnal didn't nod, but something unspoken seemed to pass between beast and boy's locked gaze.

"They'll tell you if you can prove your innocence," Damien said. "In a trial."

"Prove our—?"

"Innocence, yes. Your loyalty."

"And how the *fuck*," Hickory spat without warning, writhing in place again, "do you expect us to prove our goddamn *loyalty* to animals who can't *talk*? They're even uglier than the pictures back home. *Vultures* is what they are. Great big buzzards without wings."

Damien stared at him in silence. Joah decided not to break it. He had lost track of time, of how many cycles it had been since he'd first set out with Misla to warn the miners and scavengers about the early bells; daytime seemed like a distant, decaying memory now.

He was surprised, therefore, when the sky above seemed to shift with moving wisps of clouds and a sliver of the ice moon grinned down upon them. *The moon is king of the Eternal Night,* Joah thought weakly. He glanced at Misla again, and his stomach twisted.

He needed her to be okay.

"You said she'd be helped, Damien," Joah said desperately. The prince Nocturnal turned his violet eyes upon him with fierce curiosity. "Get Misla some help, and we'll do whatever we need to do. Tell us how to prove our loyalty."

An exhale passed through the ring of Nocturnals. Moonlight glinted off something in their hands, and for the first time in his bewildered state, Joah noticed they were all clutching identical, foot-long rods. Somehow, he knew the rods contained darts like the one that had killed Hickory's comrade: darts that might imbed themselves in his or Misla's skulls too.

Damien smiled.

"You'll have to learn their language first," he said.

"Learn their—?"

"Language, yes."

Joah had never believed in the Eternal Night before now. Nighttime lasted thirty years. Same as the day. It had always been so. Yet the darkness spreading through him when he understood what Damien was saying—*that* seemed eternal, like endless ribbons of curling black.

The Nocturnals wanted to Infect them. And Joah was supposed to let them.

They were forced down the High Road, their footsteps loud as they crunched and crackled over dead pine needles and twigs.

The Nocturnals, on the other hand, trod soundlessly. Their tattoos blazed like some absurd, glowing maze of rivulets. Joah stared at them as they ducked beneath overhanging branches. General Deckler had always described Nocturnal skin as dark and dense, all the better to blend in with the Eternal Night and sneak up on prey. But this conglomeration of patterns would scare prey *away*. It would also confuse—maybe even blind—nighttime predators.

Were the Nocturnals hunted by something worse than themselves?

He shook away this absurd curiosity and craned his neck for Misla. She was staggering along behind him, unbound but prodded in the spine whenever she faltered. Joah bit his tongue until he tasted the copper of his blood. He'd have to play his part perfectly, refrain from raising his voice at these voiceless creatures if he wanted to save Misla and escape.

Hickory, however, didn't seem to care about offending the Nocturnals. Up ahead, he was bellowing names at them, spitting at their bony backs, and laughing.

The Nocturnal clasping his elbow didn't react, but Damien turned widened eyes upon him every so often, and the prince kept shooting glances over his shoulder with narrowed violet slits. Again, something besides terror clogged Joah's throat— *embarrassment*. For some unshakeable reason, he didn't want these night monsters thinking humans were inferior. Yet one of them had already been caught mid-assault, and another was roaring songs like a madman.

Focus on Misla, Joah bade himself. *Just get Misla the hell out of here, then re-evaluate your idea of the Nocturnals. You can tell Deckler everything when you find sunlight again.*

Ahead, the High Road snaked its way into a cave. Joah blinked, swooning, on the verge of collapse. He was shell-shocked, he knew, maybe even hallucinating. The branches of pines had shot braided arms across the road, clasping hands with their counterparts on the other side. It formed a kind of knitted roof overhead. Like an upside-down nest.

Even Hickory quieted when the party prodded into its depths.

The Nocturnals, it seemed, had used this forest to build their temporary home—not by chopping the trees down, but by lacing them together using a glistening, rope-like material Joah had never seen before. The shining spirals of more Nocturnals lingered beyond the edge of the trees. Glowing dots peppered the ceiling, moving in lazy waves.

"Sunflies," Damien told him. "They carry little lights in their butts."

Joah jumped. He hadn't noticed the boy fall in step beside him. Most of the Nocturnals were drifting off into the forest to join the subtle movement of a hundred other bodies, but Damien and Prince Kal led Joah, Misla, Hickory, and their captors onward. The dwindling party stopped at a hulking contraption blocking the High Road like a giant metal toad. Beyond it, a tangle of material, like the extension of branches, formed a wall. The back of the cave.

"In here," Damien said.

They turned left before the contraption, into the spaces between trees. The braided ceiling continued overhead, blocking them from the moon's glaring grin. More violet eyes watched them pass, pausing mid-work. Some were chiseling stones that formed unfinished, indiscernible statues. Others were tending to pens of what looked horribly like hand-sized spiders: Joah watched a Nocturnal gathering strings of silk from a nest of webs before his captor jabbed him onward. Everywhere around them, those strange glistening ropes wrapped around groups of trunks, forming miniature caves or nests or...

Houses, Joah admitted, shivering. The monsters he had always feared didn't have a dozen eyes. They killed rapists with slender darts and made statues and lived in little woven houses.

Prince Kal led them to a trio of cage-like structures surrounded by even more watching Nocturnals. They were all roughly the same height, Joah noticed, and their heads glimmered in the light of the sunflies, inky from those sprouts of feathers. They didn't wear clothes, but their tattoos were *like* clothes, and Joah suddenly felt naked without designs imprinting his own skin.

"You'll stay here until you can hear them like I can," Damien said. "They'll bring you food and water and medicine, but you can't leave until you prove—"

"Our *innocence*. Yeah, yeah," Hickory spat. "Just call me roadkill already."

They were ushered into the cages. The metal around Joah's wrists snapped open with a small *click*. He buckled to his knees. The walls surrounding him were porous. He could see flakes of Misla as she collapsed too, and Hickory as he rammed a shoulder into his closed door.

The next few arcsecs blurred together.

Buckets of water met Joah's lips. Wooden bowls were shoved into his arms. Hot liquid was squirted up his nostrils. Joah's body relaxed as the pain floated off his shoulders. His ribs quit aching. His throat quit burning. He nearly inhaled an offering of chewy, rain-sized seeds, not knowing or caring where the Nocturnals had found them.

Eventually, the violet eyes dispersed. Damien and Prince Kal disappeared. Refusing to sleep just yet, Joah watched Misla through the holes in his wall. She had regained a flush of color, and somehow, the Nocturnals had repaired her clothes.

"Misla," he croaked.

She turned her head, but Hickory snorted before she could speak.

"Okay, Cadshaw, keep trying to woo my girl, why don't you? I know how this'll go. You've got some magic connection with the Nocturnals. Not that I think these crows *are* the Nocturnals—they don't look like the things that killed my grandpa when he was general—but *you* think they are. I can see it in your eyes. You'll find a way to woo them too, get on their good side, and then Misla will choose you over me. Yeah, I get it."

"I am *not* your girl, Hickory."

Misla hadn't uttered a single word since the appearance of the Nocturnals. Since her attacker had slumped dead upon her body. Now her voice dripped with smooth venom.

"Don't *ever* call me your girl again."

"Oh, c'mon, Misla. You know I love you. I'd do anything to—"

"You don't love me, Hickory. You hurt me."

A sunfly wandered into Joah's cage, carrying its own little speck of sunlight. Joah wrenched his eyes away from the mesmerizing light in time to see the pain contorting Misla's face. Hickory's next laugh shook with forced humor.

"I'd never hurt you, pretty girl. It's Cadshaw—it's *him* who'll hurt you."

"You wouldn't hurt me?" Misla whispered. "You wouldn't *hurt* me? Four years ago, you squeezed my ass in front of your friends and told them you'd like it a bit thicker."

"Well, you did thicken up, and now you look better than ever, so I was right, wasn't I?"

"You called me a whore," Misla said, that deadly voice raising an octave, "even though you were the one sleeping with other women. *Pretty girl. Whore. Pretty girl.* You used those little nicknames interchangeably."

"As if you didn't dream of sleeping with other men. I saw the way you looked at some of them. The way you looked at *Cadshaw* whenever he led the Infected back."

Joah wished he could rip Hickory's tongue from his throat. Stop the beast from mangling Misla more. But Misla was rising, curling her fingers through the holes in her cage.

"You talked me out of becoming a retriever again and again, and when I'd argue with you, you'd yell and grab my arms and shake me until I couldn't breathe."

"Retrievers don't do *shit*, Misla. They let the Nocturnals kill my grandfather. They're scams, every one of them. You wouldn't have taken me seriously without a little yelling or—"

"You killed a woman before General Deckler gave you permission."

"She was *Infected*. A lunatic! A danger to the community."

"You were going to rape me after you watched your friend do it first."

Hickory's mouth jutted open, but Joah cut through the inhale.

"Don't you dare try to make some pathetic, half-assed excuse for this one," he said, his old anger roiling inside him.

Misla sunk back into a crouch, hugging her knees to her chest. A chorus of buzzing had swelled around them, but her last, lethal whisper cut through this new noise like a blade.

"You have never refrained from hurting me before, Hickory. So why start now?"

The sunflies outside their prisons scattered at her words. Despite that roof plaited somewhere between forest floor and treetops, Joah felt the moon's descent, a release of pressure in the back of his skull. One cycle down in the Eternal Night. How many more to go?

"You know, Glade, you're right," he said. Through the gaps in his wall, he caught a flicker of movement as Hickory's head snapped up. "I *will* woo the Nocturnals. Misla and I *will* escape. And if you don't rot in this cage, if I ever see your free face again, I'll bury one of those sleek darts in your head. Just like what happened to your little friend."

He had hoped this last threat would crumble Hickory's façade, but his wife's killer just grinned, and Joah understood with a jolt: night monsters didn't have any friends to weep over.

Can you hear me, Joah?

Over the last countless cycles, Joah's eyes had become more and more adjusted to the darkness, until his surroundings looked slathered in gray film rather than an ink-black cloak. By the time the whiskers on his chin had grown into a nest of facial hair, he could make out the other animals haunting this enclosed forest space. There were swooping, flapping creatures Damien called *bats*. Coons slunk from tree to tree, and owls hooted from the crooks of their branches. Reptiles with smooth, flexible bodies and centipede-like legs scuttled through the grass. Massive spiders caught hordes of sunflies in their sweeping webs.

Damien had been visiting their cages regularly to deliver more of those raindrop-sized seeds, along with heaps of nuts, roots, mushrooms, and cooked nettles. He'd tried teaching them the Nocturnal language by staring silently into their cells for arcsecs at a time.

"The brain's a mirror," he would say when Hickory only cussed and Misla and Joah stared blankly back. "Look into my eyes and find your own intentions reflected inside them. Only then will you be able to see beyond the mirror. That's what Prince Kal says, anyway."

They'd cough and stare. Damien would cluck his tongue, his bare feet, Joah noticed, digging into the dirt outside their doors, muddied toes burrowing deep.

"C'mon," the boy said once, "we're *close*. It's easier the closer you are. When you're far apart, it's like... it's like somebody's calling your name through the far end of a tunnel. Everything's dark and damp and squirming with bugs, and you've got no choice but to follow the echo to get to the light. But now we're at the end of the tunnel together. Look into my eyes."

Prince Kal always stood in the background, his willowy figure leaning into the crooks of trees, watching Damien teach. As nighttime deepened, tree trunks were shedding their bark like scabs, revealing fresh naked wood that oozed with interweaving streams of sap. Joah supposed it was a trick of his new night eyes, but those streams seemed to glisten, blending in with the coiling designs on the prince Nocturnal's inquisitive face.

After countless attempts to let the boy violate his brain, Joah had decided he simply wasn't capable of infection like his wife had been. He was immune.

Until now.

Can you hear me, Joah?

It was moontime. The forest buzzed and chirped and squawked and growled, as alive for the moon as daytime critters were awake for the sun. Joah had been lying sprawled on the ground. When Misla's voice whispered in his ear, he jumped, thinking she must have escaped and unlocked his prison door and slunk into his cage. But no. She was lying in *her* prison cell, her eyes peering through a hole in the twining wall separating them. Her lips weren't moving.

Joah. Can you hear me?

Those familiar goosebumps crawled up his neck. He wasn't sure how to respond.

I think I understand, Misla said.

Joah clapped a hand to his ear as if a sunfly had crawled inside, but her whispers were *inside* him, kneaded into his own thoughts.

The Nocturnals build these—oh, I don't know, these walls— whatever they're made of—to protect them from night beasts. But a long time ago, they must have been more exposed. And when you're exposed in the Eternal Night, making any kind of sound puts you on a pedestal. A dinner plate.

She blinked, and Joah saw the flicker of a memory that wasn't his: Misla clawing her way through the cotton trees, calling for Damien in terrified whispers.

Telepathy is safer during the Eternal Night, she said. *Invisible brain signals. Words without sound. Kind of like how flocks of migrating birds tell each other when to turn. Only more advanced.*

He stared into her eyes, let himself melt into their depths.

You've infected me, Misla, he thought. *God, this can't be real.*

It's not infection. It's connection. It's what we've been missing all along. Damien and your wife and all the others—they must've gone crazy because they were at the end of the long tunnel. But here, in the Eternal Night, we're closer to them. It's easier to hear and listen.

She paused.

I can hear you, Joah.

He had not meant to reveal his thoughts as he lost himself in the glow of her eyes, which had taken on a purple sheen. She was such a pure woman, no matter what had happened to her. She had a sharp mind, a soft heart. He thought back to her furious determination to save Damien in the conical tower, the way their bodies had cushioned the boy between them.

A tear pricked his inner eye.

I can hear you too, Misla.

For a long while, as Hickory snored in the cage beyond, they swapped their suspicions and plans voicelessly. They wouldn't try to fight. They would win the prince's approval, agree with whatever prompted the Nocturnals to lure their people into darkness.

And when the Nocturnals soften, Joah said, *we steal Damien and run.*

Misla nodded. Despite her insistence that it was telepathy, a tunnel-like connection forging their minds together, he kept thinking, *Infection isn't so bad, actually.* He thought of Blair, and his chin trembled with a smile: she hadn't died raging with fever, after all; she had died *bilingual.* His old anger seemed to sink below an exhausted horizon within him.

You're ready, then?

This was Damien. As the pressure of the moon descended, he had appeared noiselessly outside their cages. The Nocturnal prince lurked behind him. Joah blinked. The sap trickling down the deadened trees matched the bright purple veins intersecting Damien's Infected face. Both looked eerily similar to the designs clothing the prince's body, and Joah thought, *My God, is the Eternal Night just a maze of light?*

In a way, Damien replied, his eyes twinkling. *Come on, you two. As soon as Queen Usai heard the hum of your conversation, she had them set up the trial.*

Queen Usai. Another figurehead to contend with. Joah's mind burned as he focused on withholding his treacherous thoughts about escape. Prince Kal stepped forward and pressed a twisted stick of steel against the outside of their doors, which creaked open without prompting. Hickory stirred inside his cage, but by the time the ex-executioner had roused himself enough to shout insults through the cracks in his wall, Joah and Misla were already treading after Damien and Prince Kal, boundless, weaving between bleeding trees.

"You Infected TRAITORS!" Hickory bellowed behind them.

Joah wondered if newfound veins were protruding from his *own* face, just as they had on Blair's and Damien's. He peeked at Misla, but though her cheeks were bright and flushed, her skin hadn't yet split like shattered eggshells.

Damien, Joah said, struggling to keep up with the prince's long strides and the boy's quick pit-pattering. Despite the medicine, his ribs still vaguely ached. *Where are we going?*

To the mountaintop. Damien brushed aside a brittle branch, which snapped and tumbled to the forest floor. Misla stumbled over it, and Joah caught her by the elbow.

The forest is dying, Misla said, her thoughts fringed with fear.

Not dying.

This newer, deeper voice spiked Joah's body with chills. Prince Kal did not turn from leading them through the enclosed forest, which was conspicuously empty of both Nocturnals and other night creatures.

Shedding, the prince said. *You see, the trees cannot Move like you or me. They are not nomads. They are not anchored to a segment of daytime like your people. They simply have two skins. One for your sun, and one for my moon.*

Joah knew the vegetation couldn't possibly survive lack of sunlight for much longer, but he didn't want to cross with this foreboding creature picking his way through the woods ahead of them. He fought the urge to grab Damien's arm and run right then and there. It would do no good, he knew. His full strength had not yet returned, and they were still trapped inside this strange, nest-like cave.

In a haste to muffle his thoughts, Joah barked in their normal tongue, "Hey kid. Do you think—if Misla and I win this trial—you could have them give us some toilets? We've been having to shit in those empty water buckets, and I'm gagging myself to sleep every cycle."

Damien giggled.

"They thought the stench might motivate you to find your inner tongue more quickly. We don't have much time, you know. The clock's ticking."

Joah glanced at his own broken wristwatch as the forest floor began sloping upward. They panted as they climbed. The ground became jumbled with rock, and the ceiling above their heads began to fray, revealing pores like in their prison walls.

Eventually, when they had scrambled kilometers upward, the trees thinned and a light layer of snow dappled the ground. Roped ends of the Nocturnal-made walls had been staked to the dirt. The opening yawned like the mouth of a cave.

Or the end of a tunnel, Misla told him.

Cold air blasted their faces. At the same time, Joah's eyes seared with a sudden light. For a moment, he thought the Nocturnals had mounted the moon, but then his mouth fell open.

They were on a flat expanse of snow-laden rock, where a hundred Nocturnals sat in a circle on portable rounded chairs. Their designs glistened, and the snow gleamed, but neither were a match for the sky: despite the ice moon's absence, thousands—no, *millions*—of burning dots speckled the air above them, like a horde of sunflies too far to reach.

They are suns, Prince Kal said, finally turning to face them. The rest of the Nocturnals remained breathlessly silent, but they had all twisted their heads to watch Joah and Misla's entrance: two hundred violet eyes piercing their faces.

Suns? Misla gasped.

Faraway suns, Prince Kal said, giving the faintest nod. *We call them stars.*

He led them toward the circle of Nocturnals and four vacant chairs half-submerged in mounds of snow. An insistent buzzing rose as they drew nearer. Joah craned his neck for signs of new bugs or animals, but Damien nudged him and whispered, "It's the hum of conversation. Like the rumble of voices during recess or an execution."

Prince Kal nodded at the chairs, which were draped with sheeny cloaks that looked as if they were made of spider silk. Damien grabbed his and wrapped it around himself. Joah and Misla donned theirs too, then sank into spongy seats, shivering and looking around.

All eyes flickered toward the Nocturnal sitting at the head of the circle. Strings of teeth-like objects dangled from the sides of her head, where ears would have been if she'd had ears. Her designs, unlike the smoke-like spirals on Prince Kal, resembled a tangled mess of aged flowers—wrinkled circles ringing bigger circles. Wispy feathers stuck from her head like hair.

Queen Usai, Misla told Joah with a brief widening of her eyes.

Welcome to your trial, Joah Cadshaw and Misla Crane, the queen said, her thoughts booming over all the others. The buzzing quieted. *I was sad to hear of the other one's refusal to learn our ways. It was the only way this trial could commence. You see, our tongues are not made for verbal speech. Your people, however, possess the ability to receive our signals. When you are close to us, you can transmit those signals too.*

As she spoke, a few Nocturnals stalked away from the ring, crouching low over the mounds of snow surrounding them. They fiddled with something buried in the cold. After a series of *pops*, flames burst into being, encircling them in a loop of fire and heat. Joah squinted at the bonfire roots. He couldn't see wood or coal. It was as if the flames were feeding on snow.

Our light scares most monsters away, Queen Usai said as the fire-starters swept back to their seats. *But we still need extra protection from the Old Aro Calic. Our hunter. And in addition to the fire, you mustn't speak out loud. The Calic has excellent hearing.*

Joah felt that tingle of curiosity again, a zip of fear mingled with it. He was sitting among his own enemies, yet it seemed as though an even greater danger prowled the night.

Indeed, Queen Usai mused. *Now, I am going to ask the two of you some questions. It is much harder to suppress your thoughts in open spaces such as these, so being truthful shouldn't be too hard of a feat. I have been trying for nearly sixty years, you see, to contact your people, to warn you of the dangers ahead. But I do not know whom to trust.*

We are yours to ask, Your Highness, Misla sent, bowing her head. A grumble of voiceless laughter rippled around the ring. Queen Usai pulled back her lipless mouth in a smile.

Very well. We'll start with you, Misla Crane. Our young friend here tells me that you report to a certain Aoif Deckler. Is this true?

It is, said Misla, glancing at Joah uncertainly. He gave her a nod, his heart pounding.

And why would you want to work for such a man? It seems he orders you to abduct what your people call "the Infected". He teaches you how to kill us, in the case that we ever—

Joah couldn't help himself. It was much easier to chew his tongue than to withhold the roar of thoughts in his chest, especially, for some reason, under the vast spread of stars.

It's not abduction to bring back the abducted. Your Highness, he added. *It's rescue.*

Queen Usai's earrings tinkled in the silence. The fire swaying behind her made Joah's eyes ache. He looked up at the strew of stars overhead instead.

The people we make contact with have always chosen *to come to us,* Prince Kal growled when the queen remained silent.

Is that right? Joah asked, a heated panic rising within him. Sweat tickled his forehead. *So you think my wife—one night she wants a baby, and the next she'd rather leave me and her own home and the goddamned sun to hang out with a bunch of night monsters?*

Misla shot him an alarmed glare. Queen Usai stroked her chin.

If I am not much mistaken, she said, *your wife was Blair Cadshaw. Our people do not own two names, but I can see the practicality of joining a second one when you find a mate.*

Joah shook in his chair. Misla's hand slipped into his and squeezed his fingers.

Yes, your wife was Blair, the queen continued. *I can taste your grief over her loss, so I will excuse your outburst. Grief can strangle us for so many years. But may I remind you that it was not we who killed her. In fact, we never met her. Right before she reached us, she was snatched away.* The queen peered into Joah's eyes, the violet of her own reeling his gaze away from the stars. *Your wife chose to come to us, just as Damien here chose to come to us. We have made contact with others in your community, you see, who refused to come, who shook it off as a bad dream. More refused than accepted. We always respected their decision to stay.*

Joah shook his head. If this was true, Blair would have chosen to stay too.

Blair thought she could make Aoif Deckler listen, Prince Kal said. *Because she was mated with you. One of the general's best retrievers. She chose to find us, to get closer so that she could hear the full extent of our message. The closer she got, the more she understood. She knew the gist of it by the time you found her, but the further you hauled her away, the less she could communicate her findings. It's hard for your kind to access our language from a distance.*

Joah could taste the accusation in Prince Kal's tone. He gripped Misla's fingers, their palms slipping with sweat. The irony of this situation seared him: *he* was being accused of kidnapping his own wife. He almost laughed.

You are not being accused of anything just yet, Queen Usai said. The thoughts of the other Nocturnals buzzed around them for a flickering moment. *I want to know* why *both of you chose to work for Aoif Deckler. It is not your actions that matter here. It is your intentions.*

To Joah's left, Damien nodded pointedly at Misla, his warning like a faint breeze. Misla cleared her throat. The Nocturnals around her recoiled from the sound.

I can't speak for my partner here, she said, *but I wanted to talk to the Infected—the bilingual, if you will—to find out what made them leave their homes. I've always been horrified that we behead the Infected when we bring them back. I wanted to change things.*

The truth of her words shivered around the ring. The fire flared. Joah's mind bounced back to their conversation right before they had met the scavengers. He hoped the Nocturnals could access this memory to verify Misla's authenticity. Maybe *she* could escape with Damien, even if they threw Joah back into the twisted prison cells next to Hickory.

And what of you, Joah Cadshaw? Queen Usai asked after a crackling moment of silence. *Why did you become a retriever?*

Joah glanced at Misla, who nodded encouragingly. He swallowed.

Well, my granddad was a retriever. Even as he thought it, he knew this was not enough. He closed his eyes, allowed himself to sink into a cavernous honesty that he had never voiced aloud. *It's easy to believe in a day and night, okay? A darkness and a light. After I was fired—after my wife was killed—they put me in a community position. I had to catch the beasts living among us. It was much harder, because they all wore the same faces. But when you're a retriever, it feels good to pinpoint the monsters so easily. I was saving people from darkness.*

He paused.

I didn't know the Eternal Night could contain so much light. I didn't know you glowed.

The firelight was dropping, but those far-off suns winked above them.

I see, Queen Usai said eventually. *Ignorance, then. Not malevolence. What do you think, Damien?*

Damien twisted in his seat to tilt his head at Joah and Misla.

"Will you save my mom if they tell you?" His voice trembled.

"Of course, kid," Joah said automatically. "Of course we'll save your mom."

Damien turned back to the queen and nodded. Queen Usai made a peculiar twirling motion with her fingers, and a deep buzzing drowned out the sounds of popping fire. It became a roar of sound, like blood was thundering through Joah's ears.

Queen Usai dropped her hands. The roar smothered itself into silence.

Very well. I will tell you. I can see now that you didn't know... couldn't possibly have foreseen. Of course you'd think of us as monsters. But you have to abandon that notion now. You must promise to save your people from the darkness, not behind them, but ahead of them.

Yes, Joah and Misla said together, still holding slippery hands.

Good, Queen Usai said. *Here it is, then, what I have been trying to tell your people for nearly sixty years: there is no fissure ahead of you. The High Road remains unbroken.*

No, Joah said. Warning bells clanged in his memory. He saw Aoif's boxy figure bending over the map, his finger touching that vicious red slash. *General Deckler said the scouts—*

Did you talk to the scouts yourselves? Prince Kal asked. *Did you see the fissure with your own eyes? Or did your people jolt into emergency status at the word of one man?*

Joah flinched, but the Nocturnal queen plunged on before he could answer.

I knew Aoif Deckler sixty years ago, when he was a gangly teenager. I know him better than you do. She paused, her earrings rattling ominously. *I know the man still. So trust me when I tell you: the imposter has been planning this since he helped murder your previous general. He is not leading your community to safety. He is leading you straight into a trap.*

And Joah could sense the queen's genuine terror, and he felt Damien tremble beside him, and Misla's fingernails pierced the back of his hands as the dying fire spit feeble sparks into that everlasting night air, and he knew the Nocturnals were right.

Warn you. Got to, Blair's ghost sang in his head.

General Deckler was sending the Sunsetters to their graves.

Read the next installment of "The Nocturnals" next month in Metaphorosis.

See Mariah Montoya's "The Nocturnals III" online at Metaphorosis.
If you liked it, leave a comment. Authors love that!
Remember to subscribe to our e-mail updates so you'll know when new stories are posted.

August

A Wizard Comes to Shorehaven

L.J. Wetherby

Many years had gone by since a wizard last dwelled in the small seaside town of Shorehaven. It had been so long, in fact, since the town had enjoyed the presence of a wizard, that the people of Shorehaven had begun to forget why a wizard was such a desirable thing for a town to possess.

Children would finish their bedtime prayers with the words, "and please send Shorehaven a wizard before too much longer", but the words meant almost nothing to them, and little more to many of their parents. Wizards, as far as the younger generation of Shorehaveners was concerned, were a fantasy; something nice to dream of, but never seriously expected to come to pass.

The townspeople were surprised, then, when a wizard arrived one day. She was of middling height, with long twisting hair that was brown, grey, and white in different places, and wearing long robes the same colours as her hair. She looked very, very tired.

The only question on the town's lips was whether the wizard had come to stay or she was merely passing through. She spent her first night in a boarding-house, where (to the tremendous disappointment of the proprietor and the other patrons alike) she requested a private room and took all of her meals within it, never venturing out into the common areas. There were many in the boarding house that night who hoped for a chance to converse with the wizard, or at the very least to catch a glimpse of her, and there were many in the boarding house that night who went to bed disappointed.

The following morning, the wizard walked past Marsh's Stores in town, examining the glass-fronted noticeboard outside the shop and taking down notes in a small leather-bound book that she kept in the pocket of her robe. Then she walked out of town along the north road, towards the coast.

A few Shorehaveners were sufficiently intrigued by the wizard's arrival that they attempted to follow her out of town, but ill luck befell all who tried. Gordon Harris the baker's son stepped into a bog and ruined his socks and shoes. Amelia Connor the seamstress got her skirts so badly caught up in a patch of brambles that it took her almost an hour to free herself, and she came home scratched and bleeding. And Ghislaine Willis, who fancied herself something of a hedge-witch, became so lost while trying to follow the wizard that she found herself walking back into town along the south road, miles away from the north road that she'd taken out towards the coast in the first place.

A single cottage sat at the very edge of the cliffs, past the point where the north road ceased to be a road and turned into a path. It had lain empty for many years, almost as many as the town had been without a wizard. The notice announcing that this cottage was for rent was one of the oldest advertisements on the board outside Marsh's Stores, with its print almost completely faded and its edges yellowed and curled.

The wizard decided almost immediately after viewing it that she would take the cottage. She made one last trip into town, to put down a year's rent and to purchase some provisions from the store.

By this time, many of the townspeople were curious about the wizard, but everyone who attempted to walk out as far as her cliffside cottage to get a better look at her ran into the same kind of trouble as those who'd followed her out of town the day after her arrival — minor injuries and misfortunes, the sudden loss of their ability to navigate familiar roads, and in some cases a profound urge to turn around and check that they hadn't left the front door unlocked or a pan boiling dry on the stove. Eventually people started to complain about the situation, lamenting that after so many years of waiting, they should suffer the misfortune of only a very unsociable wizard arriving in Shorehaven.

The Mayor was a popular person to complain to, because he was ostensibly the most powerful man in town. In his private moments the Mayor would laugh to himself about this assumption, knowing as he did that being the Mayor gave him no power whatsoever — it merely made him responsible for dealing with all the problems that other people couldn't or wouldn't deal with themselves.

For the first week, the Mayor listened to the town's concerns about the new wizard with a solemn expression. He told each of them that he understood why they were worried — that he, too, was interested to learn more about the wizard — but that since it had been such a long time since the town had had any sort of wizard at all, everyone must be very patient. The wizard would reveal herself in her own good time; he was certain of it.

After three weeks had passed and there had been neither sign nor word of the wizard, however, and no further orders placed at Marsh's Stores, even the Mayor began to lose his patience. He decided that the townsfolk had been respectful enough of the wizard's privacy: he would force the issue. A wizard could hardly refuse an official visit from the Mayor, after all. And it would have been deeply undignified for the Mayor to have returned from attempting to visit the wizard with his legs scratched to pieces by thorns, his memory strangely absent, his socks and shoes ruined, or his sense of direction temporarily suspended, so he took Leonie with him as insurance.

Leonie was his only child, a quiet and unassuming person of around twenty-four years of age, who possessed a certain subtlety when it came to magic — it was said that Leonie's mother, who by this time had been dead for almost as long as she'd been alive in the first place, had been a distant relative of the town's previous wizard. The prestige of this connection had been one of the many reasons the Mayor had married her, and the fact that their only child showed the faintest hint of this familial skill had always been a source of particular pride for him.

Over the years, his child's ability had manifested on only a few occasions. Once, when the town had been suffering a drought, Leonie had managed to sense a raincloud nearby, tugging it by some unseen means towards the wheat fields that lay beyond the town. And there had been the time when a very young Leonie had managed to calm a rabid dog that was blocking the road to the schoolhouse simply by speaking soothingly to it, in a voice that sounded strangely ethereal, and nothing at all like Leonie's ordinary speaking voice.

Leonie did not enjoy being the Mayor's daughter, in spite of the Mayor's pride. For as long as Leonie could remember, people had watched constantly to see what the Mayor's daughter might do, and to ensure she comported herself with the same dignity and respect that the Mayor himself assumed. Something deep within Leonie writhed and squirmed away from this attention, seeking out a more dark and private place where it could merely exist, unobserved. The demands of the position sat very uneasily with the Mayor's daughter, who felt as an adult only very slightly mayoral, and not at all daughterly.

Leonie and the Mayor took their time walking along the north road, for Leonie had been born with one ordinary leg and another that tapered into nothingness halfway down the thigh. Leonie had hardly noticed this difference until the Mayor had made it clear that it was something to be managed carefully; as an adult, Leonie wore a prosthesis so artfully constructed that it was indistinguishable from a full-grown leg in every way, except for the fact that it caused Leonie to walk a little more slowly and carefully than other people. The small amount of magic that Leonie possessed had been very fortunate on the day when the rabid dog had wandered into town, given that running away at any speed had been out of the question.

Leonie could feel the wizard's presence all along the north road, even before they made it past the edge of the town. The charms and glamours that had prevented curious individuals from trespassing upon the wizard's hospitality until now were obvious to Leonie, glimmers faintly perceptible to the corner of the eye and easy enough to work around. They arrived at the wizard's cottage just after midday, picking their way through the nettles and weeds that had grown over the path to the cottage door, which was closed.

The Mayor knocked, with an amount of force and ceremony befitting his status in the town. There was no answer. He knocked again, but still no answer. After his third knock was similarly ignored, he motioned to Leonie. Leonie's knock was soft, gentle, and hesitating. After it had sounded, the wizard called out.

"It's open. You might as well come in."

The Mayor was old enough to remember a time when this cottage had not stood empty. It had been a pretty place then, full of light, with a lush garden surrounding the house on all sides. Now, even though the new wizard had been in residence for almost a month, it seemed a drear and dingy little hole. The floor had not been swept, half the shelves were bare and lined with a thick layer of dust, and the curtains, old and frayed and stained as they were, did a very thorough job of preventing any light from entering the house.

There were three rooms downstairs, the right-hand side of the cottage divided into a kitchen at the front and a sitting room at the rear, looking out over the sea. On the left side was one long room that the original owners had used for dining and entertaining. There were two bedrooms upstairs, but the Mayor assumed them to be out of use, given that the stairs had rotted and fallen in and no one had repaired them.

The wizard's voice had come from the room on the left, but when Leonie and the Mayor went in, there was no sign of anyone there. Just as they were about to check the kitchen and the sitting room, they heard a groaning sound from the corner of the room.

There they found the wizard half buried in a makeshift bed, beneath a bundle of blankets on top of a broken old sofa.

"I ought to get up and greet you properly, I suppose, except I don't want to," said the wizard, an unseen hand pulling at the pile of blankets to reveal her mouth.

There were a few chairs scattered here and there around the room, and Leonie and the Mayor selected two of the least dirty and broken ones and pulled them over toward the sofa where the wizard lay.

"I am the Mayor of Shorehaven," the Mayor began, in his most mayoral tone. "I would like to formally extend our warmest welcome to you on behalf of the town. It's been a very long time since we've had a wizard dwelling near Shorehaven."

"Oh dear," said the wizard. "I was afraid this might happen."

"Afraid what might happen?" asked the Mayor.

"That you'd all assume I've come here to be your new wizard," said the wizard.

"Well, what have you come here for, if not that?" asked the Mayor, trying to hide his disappointment.

The wizard took a deep breath beneath her pile of blankets.

"I have come here to die," she said mournfully.

The Mayor stared at Leonie, hoping the wizard could not see his expression.

"Oh," he said, after too long a moment had passed. "Well, I'm very sorry to hear that."

"Not as sorry as I am," said the wizard. "My only wish is to die here in peace, but the people of Shorehaven keep bothering me."

"We meant no disrespect," said the Mayor.

"Ah, but respect is poor currency for a dying wizard to hoard," said the wizard. "I neither relish nor require your respect; I merely ask to be left alone."

The Mayor did not know what else to say. He had rehearsed a number of talking points that he imagined might make suitable conversation in the company of a wizard, though he'd been but a small boy himself when the old wizard had died. Now, with the new wizard apparently nearly as dead as the old one, the thought of attempting to make polite conversation suddenly seemed ghastly.

"Anything you need, anything that the town can provide for you," he said instead. "You need only ask."

In truth, the Mayor was not feeling particularly generous — he'd expected a healthy wizard with many long years of wizarding ahead of them, and he'd already overexcited himself at the thought of the benefits that such a wizard might bring to the town. Now, with those hopes dashed, there was a part of him that wanted nothing more than to leave the cottage and pretend that the dying wizard had never come to Shorehaven. But he feared for the town's reputation; if word got out that a dying wizard had been treated with such disrespect, Shorehaven might never again attract a healthy one.

"Thank you," the wizard groaned, "but I require nothing except privacy."

The idea of staying when they were so clearly unwelcome made the Mayor feel awkward and uncomfortable, sensations that his position in the town normally insulated him from rather effectively. He cleared his throat, stood up, and motioned to Leonie to do the same. They left the wizard in a pile on the broken old sofa and went home.

Dinner that night at the Mayor's residence was a dour affair, and not even Leonie could brighten the Mayor's spirits. They both went to bed gloomy, and the next morning at breakfast it was clear that a good night's sleep had only compounded the Mayor's concerns about the wizard.

"It doesn't seem right," he said, applying a thin layer of marmalade to his crustless toast. "That she should come all the way here just to die alone in that cottage up on the cliffs."

Leonie nodded and murmured and made all of the noises the Mayor expected from his only child.

"If only there were something we could do," the Mayor continued. "Some way we could help."

The Mayor looked up from his toast just as a ray of morning light struck the window of his breakfast room. Framed by this sunbeam, Leonie seemed gently radiant, and an idea formed.

"What if you were to go and assist her?" the Mayor asked.

"Me?" asked Leonie.

"Precisely," said the Mayor. "You're a great help to me here, of course, but I'm still comfortably within my prime. I could do without you for a few months; certainly long enough that the wizard might pass peacefully."

"I thought she made it very clear that she didn't want to be troubled by anyone from town," said Leonie.

"Even so," said the Mayor. "Think how it might look if people found out that we had a dying wizard staying just outside Shorehaven and we did nothing to help her."

Leonie knew the Mayor well; well enough to know that when he said things like 'think about how it might look', he was thinking not only of the reputation of the town, but also the reputation of its

Mayor. Although Leonie's father had been Mayor long enough that many of the townsfolk had never known any other Mayor, he was constantly anxious about his position. He did not want to end up out of a job and forced to cut the crusts off his own toast, rather than having them cut off by someone else and served to him on a silver toast-rack.

Leonie did not want to go and help the wizard. Not because wizards were uninteresting, but because this particular wizard had made it abundantly clear that she wished to be left alone. The last time the Mayor had asked Leonie to do something unpalatable and potentially embarrassing, his only child had made the private decision that it would be the last time, and that next time, "no, that won't be possible" would be the only answer given. But the Mayor was very persuasive, and his only child had little experience of disappointing him; the middle of the morning found Leonie walking up the north road again, this time with a letter in hand.

It was easy enough for Leonie to avoid the additional charms and hexes that the wizard had put up since the Mayor's visit the day before, though the work was impressive for a wizard running up against the end of her stamina — once again they glinted, slightly listlessly, in a way that only the corner of Leonie's eye could perceive. It was a sense that Leonie was well aware that most people in Shorehaven did not possess or even understand; one of the many strange feelings and sensations that Leonie had grown used to never talking about with other people, lest they distract from the importance of adequately performing the role of Mayor's daughter in public.

When Leonie arrived, the door to the cottage was still unlocked, and the wizard lay in the exact spot where they'd left her the day before.

"I thought I told you to leave me alone," said the wizard from beneath the pile of blankets.

"That would have been my preference too," said Leonie, placing the Mayor's letter on the end of the sofa nearest to the wizard's head.

A skinny hand crept out from beneath the nest of blankets and snatched at the envelope.

" 'Please allow me to lend you my girl to ensure your comfort at this sad time, yours sincerely, the Mayor of Shorehaven'," she read aloud.

Then the skinny hand crumpled up the piece of paper, which had been embossed with the Mayor's name, title, address, and official seal, and tossed it into the fireplace.

"Fool," she said, as Leonie continued to stand around, unsure whether to say or do anything. "To call you his girl. As though you were a girl. As though he owned you."

Leonie felt very odd at that moment, as though the wizard had stumbled upon an unexpectedly pertinent truth.

"What do you mean?"

"You're old enough to be a woman, for starters," said the wizard. "Except you're not a woman, are you? Or a man, either?"

"I'm not," said Leonie, a strange feeling bubbling within that might have been anxiety or relief. "Is that what's always felt wrong about being the Mayor's daughter? Everyone has always assumed..."

"To hell with their assumptions!" cried the wizard, with more vigour than Leonie had realised her capable of. "You are what you are. Doesn't matter what people think you are, or what they expect you to be. Now, tell me how you managed to get up here today. You weren't deterred by my trickery yesterday morning, but the hexes I put down in the afternoon to stop anyone else approaching were sound."

"I don't know," said Leonie, still reeling from the wizard's previous observation. "I suppose I've always been able to perceive magic better than most people in Shorehaven."

"Well, if someone has to come up here, I suppose I don't mind as much if it's you. It was everyone else that I was trying to keep away."

"It seems a lonely thing, to die up here on your own," said Leonie wistfully. "I'd be happy to keep you company."

"Company is the last thing I need," said the wizard. "If I needed company, I'd seek it out. But since you're already here..."

Leonie took the hint. The cottage was in such a state of disarray that it was easy to find a place to start, because everything needed doing. First, Leonie swept the dust from the empty shelves and the corners of the room. Then they checked the wizard's pantry, making a note of anything that might be needed from Marsh's Stores in town. They boiled up a great quantity of hot water, reserving some of it for mopping, some for wiping down the windows, some for laundry, and the last of it for making tea, which the wizard accepted gratefully.

While the wizard drank the tea, Leonie carried on dusting, wiping, sweeping, and washing. By the late afternoon, the cottage was already looking significantly more presentable, even though there was still plenty more work to be done. The wizard didn't have much food in the house, but Leonie did what they could, making a big pan of porridge and leaving a bowl of it near the wizard's nest, covered with honey and nuts.

"I'm going to go back to town now," they said in the late afternoon. "I'll order some more things from Marsh's Stores and bring them up, and I'll speak to the carpenter about repairing the stairs. I'll be back tomorrow morning."

"Suit yourself," said the wizard from beneath the pile of blankets where she still lay, unmoving.

Back at the Mayor's residence, the Mayor was delighted to hear of Leonie's progress and he encouraged his only child to go back to the wizard's cottage first thing in the morning. And so Leonie did, carrying the supplies from Marsh's Stores slowly up the north road. They found the wizard exactly where they'd left her the night before, but the bowl of porridge had been consumed entirely and licked clean.

Leonie spent the morning clearing out the kitchen and arranging the groceries in the pantry. With fresh provisions laid in, they were able to make a much more interesting lunch for the wizard than mere porridge: fresh mushroom stew with wild rice and a green salad. Again, they left a bowl and a plate near the wizard and went off to do other things, and again, when they returned, the bowl and plate were clean. Whatever fatal concern was troubling the wizard, Leonie mused, her appetite was certainly remarkable.

On the third day, Leonie walked up from town with the carpenter's apprentice to make sure he found his way past the wizard's enchantments. They spent much of the day weeding, raking, and digging in the garden that surrounded the wizard's house on all sides while the carpenter's apprentice sawed, hammered, and sanded.

The wizard did not make herself visible when Leonie brought in her lunch — soup made from the remains of the mushroom stew with fresh-baked bread — but when they brought her a cup of tea at the end of the day, after the carpenter's apprentice had finished the job and gone home, the wizard's head emerged from the nest of blankets, and she motioned to Leonie to sit down in the chair nearest the sofa.

"I'm glad all of that hammering and banging is finished," said the wizard.

These were the first words she'd offered that weren't in response to a direct question. Leonie nodded.

"Why don't you sleep here at night, to save you dragging that leg up and down the road to town twice a day?" the wizard continued.

Leonie was startled. They'd mentioned nothing of their leg to the wizard, and indeed they'd been using the prosthesis for so many years that it now formed a well-integrated part of their gait; they were surprised that the wizard had been able to tell.

"It doesn't trouble me," they said.

"Of course it does," said the wizard. "The ache in your hip. The tender part that sits in the socket all day, that you cover in socks and bandages so that it doesn't ever get rubbed completely raw."

Leonie looked at the wizard again, no less startled.

"How could you possibly know that?" they asked.

One of the wizard's particular skills, and a focus for her magic, was seeing people exactly as they really were — something she'd hinted at the first day Leonie came up to the cottage on their own, when she'd debunked the myth of the Mayor's daughter. She was adept at looking past the layers that everyone dressed themselves in, the faces and façades they wore for the rest of the world, in order perceive their deepest essences. That was how she'd known that Leonie wasn't really a girl, even if they kept pretending they were for the benefit of the Mayor and the town. And the outline she'd perceived of Leonie with her magic, rather than with her eyes, included a leg that ended where nature had ended it, far short of the ground.

The wizard was loathe to explain how her magic worked, however, so she merely shrugged.

"The offer's there if you'd rather not keep making the journey," she said instead. "And if you want to take that leg off for an hour or two to give yourself a break, go ahead. It doesn't trouble me."

The idea of removing their leg in front of the wizard was on a par with the idea of removing all of their clothes and underwear, as far as Leonie was concerned; something they had never considered doing in front of any living person before. Their father loved to see Leonie walking proud and upright without any hint of pain or fatigue, and they had mastered the art of this performance so thoroughly that the idea that they might choose to stop performing it seemed entirely out of the question.

Their father hated to be reminded of his only child's disability, and in the years since the first in a series of legs had initially been crafted for Leonie, they had never once taken any of them off in his presence. They knew, somehow, that to do so would be to violate a holy and entirely unspoken expectation that stood between them.

It was also one of the many reasons they had never seriously considered forming a romantic attachment with another person. No one, as far as Leonie was concerned, wanted to see their body as it truly was, and they had taken on the idea that it was their own profound responsibility to manage their body in such a way that it might not possibly offend anyone. This had grown to the status of another holy and unspoken duty, one to be performed privately and in silence, the pain and effort of it never to be hinted at in front of anyone else.

"It doesn't trouble me," they said again, more quietly this time.

The wizard did not believe them, but neither did she press the issue.

Leonie kept returning to the wizard's cottage every morning, where they continued to put the place in order, and dreamt up meals to tempt even a dying wizard's appetite. And every evening, when they returned to the Mayor's residence, the Mayor asked them how the wizard was getting along, and whether they thought there was any chance of the wizard doing a spot of wizarding on behalf of the town at some point in the near future.

"She's dying, Father," Leonie would say every time the Mayor asked, which stunned him enough to prevent him from asking again the same evening, but not so much that he would not ask again the following evening.

And every afternoon, when the bulk of the day's work was done, Leonie would sit with the wizard and drink tea. The wizard gradually became more communicative as the weeks went on, and she began to sit up properly in order to drink her tea, rather than sipping at it from the side of her mouth as she lay on the sofa. Indeed, as the wizard's surroundings began to brighten up, so did the wizard.

And just as the wizard responded to the improvements that Leonie had made to the cottage, Leonie began to respond to small signs of improvement from the wizard. She mentioned one day, in passing, how much she might enjoy a scone with her afternoon tea. From that day on, during the quiet hour after lunch when the wizard took her nap, Leonie would stand in the kitchen conjuring up sweet things. It turned out that the wizard enjoyed cakes, biscuits, and brownies as much as she enjoyed scones, and Leonie enjoyed making them for her, and sitting with her in the late afternoon looking out over the ocean as they ate something fresh and small and sweet and drank their tea.

"Do you mind me asking what's wrong with you?" they inquired one afternoon, no longer able to suppress their curiosity about what possible condition could be killing the perfectly healthy-looking wizard in front of them.

"It is a long, sad story," said the wizard.

"I'd like to hear it, if you're willing to tell it," said Leonie.

The wizard sighed, and took a deep breath.

"Many years ago now, when I was a much younger wizard," she began, "I wandered all around this world until I came to a forest. For as long as I could remember, my head had been full of spells and noises, wonders, and curiosities. But when I sat for a while beneath a great ancient tree in that forest, for the first time in my life I felt at peace."

The wizard sighed again, more tenderly this time, before she continued.

"Given how thoroughly that sense of peace had eluded me until then, I began to imagine crafting a life for myself in those woods. I slept out beneath the forest canopy that summer, building myself a small hut day by day. There was a brook nearby, and in the evenings I would sit with my feet in the water, resting my body and allowing my mind to wander.

"One evening, I felt the presence of another with me on the bank of the stream. Every time I thought I was about to catch a glimpse of her, she slipped away from me. But I kept returning to the brook every evening, and eventually she took form one night, and sat beside me.

"She was a spirit of the forest, as curious about people and their wizards as I was about forest spirits and their magic. We danced around one another for months — metaphorically speaking, of course — before she finally kissed me. My hut was complete by then, and she agreed to live with me there for a time, to learn on an intimate level how human wizards conduct their private lives.

"We were very happy there together, for many years; I should have known that it would not last forever. No one has ever managed to keep a forest spirit captive for very long, not that I wanted to imprison her. I suppose it is a miracle that she stayed as long as she did. For what felt like an age, we lazed in the grassy glades together, splashed one another as we swam in the brook, slept beside one another each night. And then, one day, she was gone.

"I could not stay. The hut seemed empty without her. The whole forest seemed empty without her, even though I knew she lived on somewhere within it. The days of her sharing my life with me were over, and I was utterly bereft.

"It is said among my people that when a wizard tires of life, death must surely follow, and swiftly. After she left, I was more than tired of life. I felt nothing but emptiness. I ate little, slept either too much or too little, and as my strength waned, so did my magic. That is why I came here to Shorehaven to die, for there are few trees along the clifftops. I wondered if it might be easier to forget her in a place like this. To live out the final days of my diminution here."

Leonie listened to the wizard's story with interest, and they sat silent for a long time after the wizard had finished speaking.

"I'm sorry you lost her," they said at last.

"So am I," said the wizard mournfully.

"Is it not possible, though," said Leonie, "that you might have been mistaken about the nature of your illness? I understand why you felt as though you were tired of living after she left you, but I've seen a great improvement in you since you came to Shorehaven."

The wizard took offense at this, and made a huffing noise.

"I have been a wizard all my life," she said. "Surely I ought to know whether or not I am dying."

Leonie said nothing, nor did they give the wizard the pointed look that they strongly wished to. From their perspective, the wizard had only grown in strength and vigour as the weeks passed. She seemed less gaunt now, and her hair was shinier and less tangled, and she had even begun standing up from the sofa from time to time and walking out as far as the end of the garden behind the house to look out over the sea.

After this conversation, the wizard kept firmly to the sofa for several days, reverting to her previous position beneath a tangle of blankets, as if to prove to Leonie that she was indeed dying. Leonie considered asking the wizard whether she'd ever experienced a spell of low spirits before, if it might be possible that she'd mistaken the despair of such an episode for the fatal certainty of her own impending demise, but again they held their tongue.

Instead, Leonie set about clearing out the rooms on the upper floor of the house, which were now accessible thanks to the work of the carpenter's apprentice. The bedsteads that had been left up there by the cottage's previous inhabitants were still perfectly serviceable, so Leonie ordered new mattresses, linen, and curtains when they were in town, and asked to have them sent up. The wizard grudgingly agreed to temporarily remove some of the protective charms and spells along the road to the cottage so that the delivery people could bring up the mattresses.

"There's no way I can manage those mattresses myself," said Leonie sheepishly.

"There's no need for you to walk up and down the road to town every day," the wizard replied sharply. "Especially now that there's a bedroom for you upstairs if you want it."

Leonie said nothing, although they'd considered taking up the wizard's previous offer. It *would* save them a lot of walking every day, and their father the Mayor had only become more insistent as time had gone by that the wizard ought to begin to do at least some wizarding for the town, regardless of the state of her health.

And they were tired of the Mayor referring to them as his 'darling daughter'; ever since the wizard had confessed her perception of their true self to Leonie, they'd found it increasingly difficult to carry on the pretence of being the person that Shorehaven expected them to be. Life was slow and gentle up here on the cliff edge, and for the first time in their life they felt entirely unobserved.

"I'll think about it," they said this time, instead of ignoring the question altogether.

When they arrived at the cottage the next day, Leonie was surprised to see the wizard standing up near the window, wearing more than just a nightgown and looking out over the sea.

"Do you have much work planned for today?" she asked.

Leonie shrugged.

"Dusting, decorating the bedrooms, making an apple cake," they replied.

"Anything you can't put off until tomorrow?" the wizard asked. "Apart from the apple cake, which I'd very much like to eat later. Can you put together a picnic lunch while you're at it?"

Leonie agreed to postpone the dusting and bedroom-decorating, and set about preparing the requested victuals, curious about the wizard's intentions. When the apple cake was cooling on the kitchen windowsill and the picnic lunch had been packed up in a basket, the wizard nodded her satisfaction and strode out into the rear garden towards the edge of the cliff, which she stopped to look down over.

"Is there a path to the beach?" she asked.

Leonie shook their head.

"We'll see about that," said the wizard.

She knelt down at the far edge of the cliff and planted her hands firmly in the thin layer of grass and soil, massaging it gently. At first there was a faint vibration that grew more rumbling and distinct as the wizard continued her work; Leonie felt it radiating up through the bones of their right leg, and buzzing furiously where the prosthesis met the terminus of their left leg.

Slowly the edge of the cliff began to change shape, the rock rearranging itself beneath the command of the wizard's fingers until a new form emerged amidst the cliff face: a narrow staircase that looked as though it had always been there.

"Can you manage?" the wizard asked.

Leonie looked at the staircase, anxiety creeping over them as they considered just how many steps there were, and just how uneven most of them looked. The Mayor had drilled into them over and over again how important it was that his daughter appear normal in public. 'Normal', in the Mayor's eyes, meant things like never walking with a visible limp, and taking any number of stairs with equal amounts of agility and cheer. Leonie had internalised these lessons so deeply that most domestic staircases posed no challenge, but the stairs the wizard had just summoned into existence were an entirely different proposition.

They realised, however, that they were not exactly 'in public' out here with the wizard. Nor did they seriously feel compelled to maintain the pretence that they were the Mayor's daughter, especially not so far out of sight of the rest of the town.

"I'll be honest, I think it's going to be a struggle," they replied. "The leg is fine on shorter staircases, but this one might be beyond me."

"How would you approach it if the leg wasn't in the picture?" asked the wizard.

Leonie was instantly transported back to early childhood, a time they hadn't thought about for many years, when they'd accepted their body exactly as it had been, and they'd had no concept of legs or propriety or the role of a Mayor, or indeed the role of a dutiful daughter. They'd been more than happy back then to pull themselves up and down staircases in a seated fashion; it was the Mayor who'd insisted they learn to walk up and down the stairs like any other person.

They took a deep breath. Then they began to untie the leather straps that anchored the leg to the girdle they wore just below their left hip. Once the straps were loosened, they tugged at the socket of the leg until it popped off, and then slipped off the thin covering they wore over the tapered area where the end of their natural leg met the beginning of the prosthesis. Instead of placing the leg down carefully, as their father had always insisted they do, because of its great importance and the tremendous expense of its construction, they let it fall to the ground with a thud.

Standing before the wizard without their prosthesis, Leonie felt strangely exposed, but the wizard merely nodded and smiled.

"It's nice to see you as you are, for a change," she said.

Then the wizard began to clamber down the steep, narrow staircase towards the sea, hitching up the skirt of her robe and carrying the picnic basket while Leonie followed on their backside, their trousers rolled up as far as their right knee and the terminus of their left leg. By the time they reached the short pebble beach that lay between the base of the cliff and the sea, Leonie's arms burned from the exertion, but the effort left them feeling strangely exhilarated rather than worn out.

They followed the wizard down the beach, the sensation of the smooth pebbles beneath their right foot a delight as they hopped along. The Mayor had disapproved of hopping almost as much as he'd disapproved of taking staircases from a seated position; Leonie was surprised to find that they were easily strong and agile enough to hop the distance to the shoreline comfortably. The Mayor had been so insistent that they needed the leg in order to function that they'd never stopped to consider whether this was actually true.

The sea was fresh and salty and just a little too cold for comfort. After stripping off her clothes and leaving them just beyond the reach of the waves, the wizard began swimming, and Leonie joined her. They swam side by side for a while, pausing occasionally to tread water, and then they returned to the beach, where they lay in the sun until their bodies were mostly dry again.

The wizard rolled towards Leonie, stroking their arm, her lips parted and her eyes questioning. Leonie shrank away from her touch, not entirely understanding the expression on the wizard's face. They turned onto their left side, covering their thin, short left leg as much as they could with the sturdy bulk of their right. The wizard took Leonie's cue and did not pursue the matter; when they went back up to the cottage in the late afternoon, she strode on ahead as Leonie worked their way up backwards. At the top of the cliff, they sat on a rock and reattached the prosthesis, easing the end of their left leg into its socket and feeling the dull, familiar pain in their hip as they stood and began to bear weight on it again.

The wizard attempted no further advances that afternoon. Leonie finished up a few chores and left the wizard some supper. The wizard did not want to appear as though she was watching them, but she couldn't help noticing how they'd turned inward after she'd reached out to them: the pain and confusion visible on their face in moments when Leonie believed the wizard was not looking, the fact that their gait seemed clumsier somehow now that they'd reattached the leg. As they went to leave, the wizard caught their arm.

"Are you sure you wouldn't rather stay the night?" she asked.

Leonie pulled away again, their eyes flushing with hot tears even as they tried to blink them back. On the return journey to town, their mind swirled with memories and emotions, things they'd steadily and dutifully repressed in order to more deeply inhabit the role of the Mayor's daughter. A single, sweet kiss shared with a girl from school, never repeated for fear of what people might think if they found out. Their leg, and the extent to which they'd allowed themself to turn it into an excuse never to become intimate with anyone. But the wizard had seen them without it, and hadn't shied away; she had perceived their lower left leg's absence as a core component of Leonie, a radiant part of their truth rather than something to be obfuscated.

Dinner at the Mayor's residence that evening was subdued. The Mayor could tell that something was wrong with Leonie, but couldn't fathom what the problem might be. When he enquired as to whether the wizard was dying at long last, Leonie's response surprised him.

"No, father, it's not the wizard. She's doing well."

"Then what is it that troubles you, child?"

Leonie's next response surprised even Leonie.

"My hip aches terribly from all the walking I've been doing back and forth to the wizard's house, and I'm afraid that a sore patch is forming where my leg sits in the socket of the prosthesis."

The Mayor's eyes widened, and an expression as sad as the one Leonie had been wearing all evening crossed his face. But he said nothing more about the wizard or Leonie or their leg, just as Leonie had expected he wouldn't. And in that moment, they understood that a decision they hadn't even realised they'd been contemplating had just made itself.

The following morning, the wizard stood anxiously in the cottage doorway. Leonie was late, much later than usual, and the wizard was afraid she'd driven them away with a single wordless touch on the beach, and that they might never come back. As she watched, however, a figure emerged along the road from Shorehaven, moving slowly and springily. As the figure drew closer, the wizard saw that it was Leonie hopping along the road, the prosthetic leg and a pair of crutches that the Mayor would have preferred them not to own strapped to their back.

Leonie was annoyed at how long the journey had taken, even though they'd set out with plenty of time to spare. It was only a small annoyance, though; it paled in comparison to their delight in finding that they were easily fit and strong enough to make the journey from town without the assistance of the prosthesis.

Leaving town, they'd seen people they'd known their entire life staring at them and whispering. And although they couldn't hear any of those whispers, they could easily imagine what the people of Shorehaven were saying. *Goodness, there goes Leonie-the-Mayor's-daughter without her leg. Perhaps it's broken. Maybe that good-for-nothing wizard is going to fix it for her. Poor little dear. What a shame.*

But each hop they'd made past the town boundary had felt like a leap of triumph, the energy and propulsion of every successive step batting away the dreadful comments they imagined the townsfolk were whispering to one another. Every time their right leg landed on the road, it seemed to reinforce some deep, unadulterable part of themself: they were not the Mayor's daughter, there was nothing broken about the leg that nature had given them, nothing about them was a shame, and they were categorically not a poor little dear.

The wizard tried to appear nonchalant as Leonie approached the cottage, though her face was somewhat flushed. Leonie did not immediately comment on their journey or the leg, which they left propped in the hallway for the time being, but they did announce a change that made the wizard very happy.

"I've told the Mayor not to expect me back tonight," they said. "Assuming your offer of an overnight stay still stands?"

"It does," said the wizard, and when she slowly approached Leonie and placed her hand around their waist, they did not pull away this time.

As they kissed, Leonie realised that their anxiety at the thought of being intimate with another person had melted away entirely, only to be replaced with a different concern.

"I'm not sure I can measure up to a forest spirit," they said, blushing.

"If I wanted to be with a forest spirit, I'd go back to the forest," said the wizard. "I like you just the way you are."

The people of Shorehaven complained at length about the town's great misfortune during the many years that followed. To have been without a wizard for so long, only to have one arrive who showed no interest in using her magic to benefit the town or its people was a heavy burden for any town to bear. They felt tremendously ill-used, both by fate and by the wizard herself, and rather than teaching their children to pray for a wizard to come to Shorehaven, they now taught them to curse the wizard who *had* arrived, for her selfishness and lack of community spirit. Some even said that they wished the wizard would hurry up and die, as she'd said she was going to, for she had done absolutely nothing to help the town, nor any of its inhabitants.

That was not true, however; Leonie blossomed at the cottage on the cliffside. They managed to persuade the wizard to make an exception in her charms and hexes for their father, that he might come up and visit them occasionally, and the wizard agreed, so long as Leonie wasted no further energy pretending to be the Mayor's daughter.

The Mayor was made to understand that Leonie would no longer live with him, that they had tried a life of service in the town of Shorehaven and it had not suited them, and that they did not particularly enjoy being called "she" or "daughter" when those ideas were so foreign to the sense of self that the wizard's love and company had solidified within them.

The Mayor was also made to understand that the wizard would not live to serve the town of Shorehaven either, even though the wizard was indeed not dying, and no matter how much the town might desire her service. Much of the Mayor's professional life from that point on consisted of placating the townspeople on behalf of the wizard, and it was true that he did not enjoy his job quite so much once the town realised that the wizard was not inclined to help them in any meaningful way. He tried to point out to the townsfolk, as the wizard had pointed out to him, that they had managed perfectly well for many years without any wizard at all, but this was cold comfort as far as most Shorehaveners were concerned.

Finally, the Mayor was made to understand that any future wearing of the prosthetic leg would be done entirely on Leonie's terms. The first time he visited the cottage, they sat in a chair with the leg leaning against a bookcase in the living room, hopping into the kitchen as needed. It seemed to pain the Mayor to see this, but when he asked whether there was anything wrong with the leg, Leonie told him unceremoniously that they would no longer be wearing it purely for his comfort — only for their own, on the occasions when it was truly comfortable to do so.

And the Mayor had wrung his hands together, and said that he'd only ever wanted his only child to be happy and comfortable — and that surely the key to being happy and comfortable was to be as much like other people as possible, which was why he'd always insisted about the leg. But he was capable of understanding that he had been wrong, and of realising that the price of a relationship with his only child meant never mentioning his own preferences regarding their leg, or calling them "daughter".

And so Leonie remained in the cottage with the wizard, baking cakes to enjoy with her in the afternoon, swimming in the sea with her as often as they liked, working alongside her in the garden and talking about magic in a way that they both knew no other Shorehaveners would understand. Up on the cliffside, surrounded by the peace of the wind and the waves, they set aside all thoughts of how a Mayor's daughter ought to appear or behave, and allowed themself merely to be.

See L.J. Wetherby's story "A Wizard Comes to Shorehaven" online at Metaphorosis.
If you liked it, leave a comment. Authors love that!
Remember to subscribe to our e-mail updates so you'll know when new stories are posted.

About the story

The prime mover for this story was a dear friend of mine who has enjoyed a lifelong fascination with wizards. This friend organises regular storytelling events among our acquaintance, and since I began attending those events, I've always had it in the back of my mind that stories about wizards are likely to be especially welcome. This knowledge alone has offered plenty of stimulation for the imagination.

"A Wizard Comes to Shorehaven" was also partly inspired by The Mountain Goats' 2019 album *In League With Dragons*. I read an interview with band leader John Darnielle around the time the album was released where he mentioned that the record was originally a rock opera "about an ageing wizard whose seaside kingdom is under siege".[1] And I remembered my wizard-loving friend and thought that I could take a stab at a story closer to the original premise of *In League With Dragons*.

When I began writing the story, I didn't have a strong sense of where it was going to go, which is not at all uncommon in terms of my process. There seems to be a distinction between writers who prefer to plan, and those who begin in the hopes of seeing where the story might take them, and I definitely fall into the latter camp — I relish the surprise and delight of seeing what comes out during the process, and the end product is always much better than anything I could have crafted if I'd plotted it all neatly from the outset.

All I had in mind when I started was the central character of the wizard and the seaside location. I have a particularly strong inclination toward cosy settings, especially in fantasy, so it didn't take long for "seaside kingdom under siege" to transform into "small seaside town filled with the kinds of people who prefer things to continue as they have always done, only more favourably towards themselves as far as possible". The character of the Mayor as an embodiment of that attitude sprang up fairly quickly once the setting began to solidify.

Leonie was probably the biggest surprise of all the characters — they were not someone whom I'd intended to create from the beginning, but when they began to form as a character

---

1   https://wearetime.home.blog/2019/05/02/interview-the-mountain-goats-john-darnielle-on-his-toronto-star-studded-new-album

I soon saw the possibilities they offered in terms of giving the story purpose and focus, and shaping it towards its conclusion.

One of my incidental aims as a writer is to represent queerness, gender variance, and disability as facets among many that contribute to the makeup of complex individuals, rather than positioning those things as the sole markers or primary traits of the character. We still live in an era where these topics are often handled with an air of the after-school special, where someone's queerness or disability (or, rarely, both) drive the plot more as shortcomings to be defeated rather than natural variances that merely are. Leonie falls slightly short of my own mark here, given that their queerness, gender variance, and disability do drive the plot, but my hope is that this plays out in a way that is more liberating than constraining, and much more about Leonie's sense of who they want to be than about who they feel they ought to be in order to satisfy the expectations of those around them.

"A Wizard Comes to Shorehaven" was a story that I thoroughly enjoyed writing, and I'm delighted that it's found a home at *Metaphorosis*.

A question for the author

Q: What is your favourite part of writing?

A: To bend the question a little, there are two things I like most about writing. One is the sheer alchemy of creation, selecting and combining elements from the buffet that is the English language in order to craft something entirely new. I feel particularly fortunate that English is a language so rich with synonyms and with so much scope for style and authorial selection in terms of sentence order, for the sheer opportunity of innovation that this offers the writer.

My other favourite part of writing is the editing process. I'm a firm believer in the 'draft zero' approach, writing the first full-length version of a piece without editing at all during the process, then using subsequent revisions to shape and form the story. It feels as satisfying to carve, arrange and improve a piece of fiction during the editing process as I assume it must feel to sculpt — except with writing, I'm using a medium that I find myself far more fluent in than stone, metal, or clay.

About the author

LJ Wetherby (they/them) is a non-binary writer living in Cambridgeshire, UK, with a focus on speculative and historical fiction that centres queer characters.

ljwetherby.com, @ljwetherby

The Waves in Which We Drown

Rubella Dithers

June 8th, 2189

I'm afraid of space.

That's why you're up there and I'm down here, sitting on a dune with a broken nose and a split lip, stabbing a shuttle into my hand while I try to repair the net I dropped on a reef last week. We don't even have any spare rope; I have to scavenge what I can off of even worse nets. The fibers are all rotting and falling apart on me. It would be easier to get through this if you were here. Stupid of me to think 'friends forever' implied being together in some capacity.

It's easy to ignore the pain in my hand. I feel like giving up and just sewing the loose edges of this net together, but I know what your dad would say. *You half-assed it, as usual. This is your last chance. You should be grateful. What else do you have? You failed the first time, dropped out the second time. This is your only chance. Be grateful.*

The worst thing is you don't even write.

It's like you want to forget this place, like you want to forget us. Like when you swore that as soon as you left this town you'd never eat fish again, as if that amalgamated goop they pump into you isn't pasted together with carrageenan and anchovies and bonito.

I don't blame you. I want to leave too. It didn't work out as well for me, did it? Because now I'm stuck here with a bunch of old people and kids and everyone in between is dead or gone.

Can you believe your parents still buy into the line that we're doing something vital with our duct-taped trawlers and broken nets? Like we can't see the state's big commercial ships sitting on the horizon, picking up every fish that so much as waves a fin in their direction? Half the town works on them as it is. And our own catches keep getting smaller. Listening to your parents' cheering when another supply shuttle is launched makes my skin crawl.

While I'm on forced shore leave, I also get to watch over Nila. Did you forget about your real sister too? We don't have a shovel for her, so she's digging with her hands. We've been out here since before dawn and she's barely got half a bucket of clams. After this I'm supposed to tutor her, since the school server went down again.

I'm going to give up on fixing the net for today and help Nila with the clams. I don't have anything else to say, so I'll sign off. I miss you and I hate you and I really, really wish you'd get back to me.

June 10th, 2189

I'm at the bar reviewing Nila's curriculum, trying to understand why a 9-year-old needs to learn set theory. Instead of times tables, she's doing Cayley tables, because knowing $ab = ba$ is more important than knowing 7×6. Right.

A bar is the worst possible place for me to be studying, but it's the only building that's still on the power grid. If that goes down, they've got fish oil lamps, and everyone's too drunk to care about the smell. I miss studying together, it was easier to focus. For me, at least. I have no idea what you got out of it. I look at a proof and I'm like, sure, it makes sense, it's obvious to me. But I say that about anything, even if it's wrong. You were always so formal, so meticulous.

The only possible way this experience could be worse is if what's-his-face showed up. So of course he has. He's with some rich girl. I can tell she has money because she's wearing shoes, how fucked up is that? I have to scrub my feet with sand for half an hour to get all the dried wine and ash off. But that's how bad things have gotten since you left. It sounds like I'm connecting the two events, but I'm not. OK, maybe.

I never liked him. And no, it's not because dating him meant that you spent less time with me. It's because he's a creep. I mean, when you told him you were studying for the navigator exam, he dropped off. Then, when I failed and you didn't, he came up to me talking about how 'selfish' you were. As if I'd want to commiserate with him, of all people. I didn't just lose you, I lost the chance to leave.

Now he's got this new girl, like you never existed. This one looks like she's pregnant. I mean the dangerous, beyond the point of no return kind of pregnant. Why anyone would risk having kids now is beyond me, but people keep doing it. Do they think they'll get on a generation ship? Do they think there's still room? Who needs fishers in space?

I fixed the rope situation. Once I figured out what to do it was pretty easy. I sold some of your stuff. Nothing important, just your old computer. The one I bought parts for, when I worked between two ships all year and didn't see land once while you stayed in school.

I sold it to the scrap yard.

June 16th, 2189

The ping timed out for the last few messages I sent. Either the sat relay is down or you're still ignoring me. We both know which is more likely.

Your dad took the crew out and left me behind. Took the new net with him, though.

Since there is nothing else for me to do, I was thinking about taking the entrance exam again. I'm not past the cut-off age. Yet.

Nila wants to take it, after she finishes the standard curriculum in a few years. I think she'll do fine, she's a lot like you. The problem is, your parents can't afford the textbooks. I could try to teach her myself, but it's not like I'm doing a great job now. I don't even know if I'll be around long enough.

I could pirate the books if I hadn't scrapped your old computer for a net. And if we had internet access. I might turn into a real pirate if I can't figure out what to do with myself. I'd be robbing other poor people, though, so probably not.

If you pass by one of those nonresponsive satellites, do me a solid and hack it so we get free access in town.

June 30th, 2189

I got the bends.

I know we used to joke about it when we were diving, but this seriously sucks. I've been in bed for a week.

Nila is the one who spotted me. I don't remember being pulled out of the water. They think... Well, I'm sure you know what they think. If someone else went out alone on a banged-up fiberglass dinghy, without the sense to even tie a line to herself, I'd think the same thing.

I just wanted to try diving again. Remember how we used to freedive every day after school, jumping off that big sea stack in the cove? I haven't gone since you've left, and I pushed myself too far, that's all. And I'm paying for it. Everything hurts. There's this deep, frightening ache throughout my arms and legs. When I told the nurse about it, she just upped the oxygen intake.

Nila keeps checking on me. It's sweet, but kind of annoying. I hate that she saw me like that. Like this. I think she thinks it's her fault, that she should have been watching me closer. I'm supposed to be the one looking out for her. She treats me like your replacement. I'm not. I can't be the kind of big sister you were. I'm glad I'm an only child. What a shitty role model I would have been.

When I was down there, in the water, I could pretend I was with you. I could pretend that I wasn't afraid to drift through space just above Earth, from where you look down on the rest of us through the hazy veil of atmosphere. Falling weightless through that ambivalent medium, the vast and unknowable water that siphons heat and deadens sound, sustained the illusion. I felt terribly alone. My chest seized. I wanted to claw my way back to the surface, but I forced myself down. I needed to be deeper.

I didn't notice the regulator's pressure dropping until I was struggling to breathe. There was a leak in the line. I was fucked. I ditched the useless gear and struggled towards the surface, growing weaker with each stroke. I could feel the sun's warmth and I pushed through the current. The closer I got, the more blackness invaded the edges of my vision. I was tired, Sarah. I'm always fucking tired.

That's where my memory ends, as abruptly as a dream. It was beautiful, for a moment.

July 10th, 2189

I caught Nila going through a massive copy of Dummit and Foote. Kids these days. She's claiming it 'just showed up', but she probably stole it from the university library. At her age she shouldn't be skipping school to go all the way to the city for that, especially not alone. I would've done it if she asked me. Still, I don't think she's wrong for doing it, and we were worse at her age. She's mad I don't believe her, though, because when I asked if I could look at it she flipped me off. I didn't teach her that. Did you?

August 22nd, 2189

Your dad still won't let me on the boat. In fact, he's told everyone else in town not to give me work, period. I spent a few days walking up the coast to see if anyone would hire me. It was a bad idea.

At the first group of shacks I approached, an old auntie came out to shoo me away. Her hands were splotchy pink and shaking. I could see through the door she came out of. Inside there was another thin woman, holding a twisted child who screamed like a pig being slaughtered. Someone saw me looking and slammed the door shut, but I could still hear the kid. I walked down to the little cove they fished in. The waves were lethargic, lapping fetid red foam onto the shore.

The farther north I went, the worse it got.

I went home, thinking about clam digging. The problem is everyone's got their kids doing it these days. Even old folks are out there. They're pulling clams out of the sand faster than they can breed.

It took me a while to figure out, but I finally realized what I could do to make money. Salt. I'm a salt woman now. I can't say I came up with the idea on my own. I heard the packing house was having trouble getting shipments. It's only a matter of time before other people in town get the same idea. It's not exactly novel.

I borrowed a few sheets from your room. I hope you don't mind. I can't afford to keep a fire burning all day, so after I boil off most of the water I spread the salt over the sheets to dry the rest of the way.

Your mom talked to me about paying rent. Your dad must have asked her to; I don't think she cares. The original deal was I would work for your dad while staying there, which I did. For years. Of course he'd make me work, not pay me, and then charge me room and board. Honestly? I don't blame them.

Nila says she wants to accelerate her curriculum. I told her not to overwork herself and she rolled her eyes. I think she's sick of fish.

September 6th, 2189

I was at the bar again last night. It's kind of a regular thing now, a weekly ritual. Remember how much I used to hate drinking? The veil has been lifted.

I was sitting at the bar, nursing my watered-down seaweed wine. Normally I'd be studying at one of the tables, where the lighting is better and the surfaces less sticky, but the lights were out. That's been happening a lot more lately.

The counter is also farther from the pool table and its endless clacking. A few weeks ago the bartender dug this wind-up radio out of somewhere. I didn't know what it was at first, and now I'm obsessed with the thing. We take turns cranking it. It's the only way to get regular news. That's how I learned they're doing a mass launch next month.

The remaining cohort in orbit, your cohort, will start their flybys, siphoning gravitational force off planets and comets and whatever's convenient so they can be flung deeper into space. You'll break and scatter like billiard balls, each mapped trajectory a new path for humanity to follow towards some possibly viable world. Even if it takes us millennia, even if we never find a new planet to latch onto like a leech, at least you'll be out there, an eternal reminder of what we were.

Since trying to contact you directly isn't working, I'm relaying future messages. The navigation base enabled permissions for me to use their ground proxy, and confirmed your signal is extant. When are you going to respond?

When you finally get what you want, when you finally leave this place for good, how will I be able to reach you?

September 15th, 2189

This is a rude question. You're probably not in any shape to answer it.

What's it like to lose your autonomy? I know they say that isn't what happens, but that's not true. If something else, some executable set of instructions, controls your decision making you cannot be autonomous. By definition.

Is that why you aren't writing back? Am I sending this to an empty shell?

The idea of losing who I am. That is what I'm afraid of, more than being in space. What happens during that discontinuity? I think about it when I fall asleep. How easily I trust that I will wake up as the same person.

What happens in that space of time? Where do *you* go? Are you still the old *you*, or is this a new *you* that merely shares the same memories?

How would you even know?

October 24th, 2189

I have achieved a new low. Some people in town got together and set up a bigger salt operation. They've got an entire field for evaporating the water, huge piles of salt raked up. The packing house isn't buying from me anymore.

Since I can't pay him, your dad kicked me out of the house. I'm sleeping on the beach, living off of ice plants, kelp, and whatever else washes up. Like that dead sea nettle I've been eyeing all day.

I still carry a lighter, though you're not around to borrow it, and if you were there's no fuel for it anyway. I'm trying to start a fire with some driftwood but most of the pieces I find are still wet. I've spun the flint wheel so many times my thumb's starting to bleed.

I did, finally, get a couple of sticks to light up. It's not very warm, but at least the flames are pretty.

November 20th, 2189

Nila turned 10. When that was us, we thought it was a big deal. Double digits and all that. It was significant. Nila wasn't that excited.

The bar radio's been less reliable lately. Some of the usual bands we pick up are garbled. I took Nila with me for her birthday, figuring she'd enjoy the novelty of it. Not that a bar is the best place for a kid, but it's not like we've got anything else around here. We were able to hear a few pieces of news, nothing interesting to a child, but she seemed happy enough. Whenever the sound cut out, or was jumbled, I pretended it was an encrypted message from you. I told her that you said how much you miss her, how grown up she is now. It made her day.

December 15th, 2189

I always hated it when you called me negative. I think you were trying to turn it into a joke, or maybe you wanted it to be true so we could be opposite. Magnetic poles. Negative, positive. You know, the designations are completely arbitrary.

This morning your mom said something that reminded me of that. She lets me in the house when your dad's out. We were in the kitchen, threshing foxtails, bitching about how hard it was getting to find *weeds*, of all things. She told me to shut up, that I never have anything good to say. But I do. I'll prove it.

On the first of the month, that big factory purser went dark. Dead in the water. At the bar, people were talking about some satellites being knocked out of orbit. The reports we got over the radio just said 'systems malfunction'. I don't care what happened, I'm just glad it did. It took a week for tugboats to get out to the purser. Its crew had to abandon their net.

As soon as the purser limped out of sight, the town fishers moved in. I've never seen your dad move so fast in my life. Together, they got the abandoned net up. The town's still arguing about what to do with it, like anyone can actually use it.

Ever since, your dad has been able to go out farther than usual, and he got a big catch of quality herring, not the chewed-on stragglers he normally pulls up. The packing house needed extra workers and they hired me on the spot. So I've been gutting, filleting, pickling, and packing fish for the past three weeks. I know we said we would never work there, but what choice do I have?

It'd be better if they had enough gloves to go around.

December 16th, 2189

I forgot to mention that I watched the new cohort launch last month. Those improbably perfect orbs always creep me out. I know you're in one too. It's still weird. Plus, the speed, those maneuvers, aren't things a living person could withstand.

January 1st, 2190

Happy New Year. Can you tell I'm excited?

Nila got a tablet for her New Year's gift. She said I can use it when she's at school. I don't know where your parents got the money for it. Or high-speed sat access, for that matter. They seemed as surprised as I was when Nila opened the box. Maybe someone upstairs is looking out for us.

Through a combination of Nila whining and bribery, my 'gift' was your parents letting me stay in your room again. It's a bit infantilizing to have to follow their rules, but at least I have a bed. It beats fighting seagulls for half-eaten crabs any day.

More commercial ships showed up, effectively trapping us in the bay again. The fish rush is over, which means I got laid off from the factory. I'm back to harvesting salt, but I've got a new idea for it. I thought of it when I had to make lye water for the lutefisk. Who eats that stuff? Me, me eats it. Anyway, after my shifts I raided the dumpsters for the offal. I've been boiling it and skimming oil off the top to resell to the factory. I make less than I would if I were hired by them to do it. It's bullshit.

I put some aside for myself, and your family. Do you know how many kilos of fish guts it takes to make a bar of soap? I do. I have to render it a couple of times to get the fishiness out. I don't have anything to make it smell good, so the best I can do is make it smell like nothing.

In six months you'll be passing Jupiter in your space orb. At the rate I'm going, I'll be tanning fish skins in their own offal. Once I am clad entirely in fish leather, you will know I have accepted my lot in life.

February 13th, 2190

Every time I see a matrix, I think my brain dies a little. I'm on Jordan decomposition, it's a nightmare. There is no practical use for it; a computer can crunch linear equations faster than I could put them in normal form. A computer doesn't need to change the base first. Programming exists. Why should we have to learn something that a calculator can do? Whoever decides what material goes on the math exam is forever on my shit list.

I know what you'd say. You'd say it helps create convenient neural pathways to implement said programs, if one so chooses. A place where a memory can be stored. To exploit what we have that a computer lacks: consciousness, agency. Choice.

I don't care how many organic parts they replace, the human brain is not a computer. It shouldn't be treated like one. You're still a person. You're still in there, somewhere. Right?

I have money saved up for the exam. The way it ended for me last time was embarrassing. I freaked out during the first round of injections. I only got half the shots and felt like shit for weeks after, like I was going through withdrawal. Next time, they'll probably sedate me and keep going. If I get in.

I don't know. I mean, there aren't that many able-bodied adults anymore. I'm a bigger help than your parents want to admit. And what about Nila? It's not all about me.

I've been making the same excuse for years. We both know the truth.

I'm not as brave as you.

March 22nd, 2190

I saw him again at the bar. He actually came up to me, asking about you. I asked him about that pregnant woman. I haven't seen her for months. No baby, either. It was a shitty thing to do. I knew as soon as I saw the look on his face that she was dead.

If you had wanted kids, would you have stayed? Is it worth dying for?

April 21st, 2190

Your dad got it in his head that he wants to be a shrimper. I mean, if you've seen one eyeless cod with its scales slipping off and an oozing hole in its side, you've seen them all. No need to change careers over it. I'm pretty sure shrimp are bottom feeders and are at the top of the list for 'things in the ocean horribly deformed by pollution'.

His crew is very literally falling apart. Mercury poisoning is leaving more of the older folks too fucked-up to work. They're all shaky and confused. So, he's got me out on the boat again, picking crabs out of the traps and tossing them back in the water. They pinch me every time. You'd think they'd be happy for the chance to grow up before being killed. That's more than you can say for the rest of us.

The way these white shrimps' little legs flail around is too relatable. I'm close to throwing them all overboard. I mean, most of them are under the size limit. Not like anyone gives a shit about that.

Your dad has hinted, i.e., outright stated, that he wants me to take the shrimp up to the city's farmers' market this week with your mom and sister. He says he's already paid for a spot, assuming we can even get past the tent cities.

We'll have to borrow a truck to get there, and the toll fees, and I'll probably be up all night working the generator, charging the battery.

I think his usual clients aren't buying from him anymore. And if they aren't buying from him, they aren't buying from anyone else in town.

I don't know what to do. I suggested to your dad that we, as a town, could consolidate our resources, find a better distributor, and split the profits. You know, like a co-op.

He told me I'm the reason he has high blood pressure, but really, it's the mercury.

June 3rd, 2190

Well, Sarah, a funny thing happened. The commercial fishing ships went down again last month. Three at once. We were packing up for another drive to the market when it happened. Feds came through town a few days later, interrogating anyone who might have a motive. So, like, everyone. I'm surprised they didn't leave as soon as they took a look at how run down we all are.

Coincidentally, it was just in time for halibut season. There's a two-fish bag limit, so I'm out trolling on the boat again. We pulled up a six footer, took us nearly an hour. Imagine existing for that long just to end up on a hook. I prefer salmon. When we catch the run headed for the delta, at least I know they're going to die either way.

July 16th, 2190

I'm reviewing complex analysis, which is a relief. I found your copy of Ahlfors. I'm surprised your parents didn't sell it. The cover's faded to grey, and the pages are all soft along the edges. After this, it's all modular forms and L-functions.

I'm doing fine, I guess. At least with respect to the exam. Pretty confident. I got a copy of the official review material. The core content hasn't changed, so I'm not worried. About the exam, at least.

Your cohort's final flyby of Earth is coming up. Then you'll be swinging past Jupiter, Neptune, hurtling back to the Sun, glancing off it and getting the hell out of here. A human couldn't stand the acceleration. And you will reach a point when and where time stands still. You'll leave the galaxy in the time it takes to translate thought to action.

What I'm saying is, if you are planning to get back to me, do it soon. In a few months you'll be 20,000 years too late.

September 2nd, 2190

The exams are next week. I paid the fee in advance so I'll have some incentive to go through with it again. I hate finishing early, then reviewing my answers, then reviewing it again, then just sitting there doing nothing until time is out. I just want to get it over with.

Your sister's excited for me.

Does she know what happens to us? Not that 'ambassador to the universe, next stage of humanity' bullshit, but what they actually, physically, do to navigators?

Maybe she doesn't. She was only 6 when you left.

I don't know if I should tell her. People like us don't have many choices. That's how they reel us in. Give us the opportunity to become 'more than what we are'. If I tell her the truth, she might not go through with it. Maybe that's the best life for her. Maybe she will be too afraid of that choice, like me. And look at me, what kind of life is this? I have no dreams, no goals. My only friend isn't capable of verbal communication and is on the other side of the solar system. Is this the kind of future Nila would want for herself?

I keep sending these, hoping you'll actually say something. Instead I get these enticing little hints that I'm half convinced are just in my head. Just talk to me, please. I have no one else.

September 16th, 2190

I went swimming tonight. It's been hotter than usual, clinging to the upper 80s even this late into summer. They've been shutting down the power grid an hour after sundown. For the entire coast. We're all using fish-oil lamps. The beach is the only place I can get fresh air. The wind picks up in the evening, blowing away the lingering haze, exposing the stars cluttering the sky.

They say that when you get to space you'll be among the stars. But, really, you are surrounded by emptiness, caught in the vast distances between bright spots. That perfectly encapsulates how I feel about my life. Maybe I do belong up there.

So, I'm swimming. It isn't quite high tide, but it's getting there. I swim past the few summer algal blooms still clinging to what's left of the pilings. I'm out far enough that I won't get pushed back to shore right away. When the dunes blend into the murky sky, I stop. I float on my back, looking up at all those stars. Too many, if you ask me. The waves are gentle, as you might remember, and they pass under me. There are a few boats out, not many, too far away for me to care. I'm trying not to think about the exam tomorrow. This time it feels inevitable. Irrevocable.

Me. Ocean. Stars. Obsessive thinking. Have I set the scene yet? Good, because next thing I know, my pity party gets crashed. I hear something big slam the water, and it sends a huge wave over me. I flip over and swim under it, coming up to face the direction of the sound. I push wet hair out of my eyes, but I still can't see it. What I do see is a wave coming, and a shape bobbing on top of it. I swim for it fast, muscles burning, spitting out salt water. After a few minutes, when my arm comes down for another stroke, it hits something firm. I hit it again, and with a dull thud, it yields under my fist. It's enticingly warm. Somehow its surface is bending light, reflecting, refracting, I don't know, and I suddenly hope the physics portion doesn't include optics. I swim around the object and start pushing it towards shore. It is disturbingly light. I attribute this to the relative density of the salt water.

I get to shore and roll it through the sand, above the tide line. Since it rolls, I know it is spherical, and I feel a heavy sense of dread with that realization. I still can't see it that well, amid the confusion of sand and stars, but my hands tell me it's there. Two meters in diameter. I don't want to touch it again; it terrifies and disgusts me. But what if?

I keep my hands on it. I feel its warmth, the way the surface feels like skin, and nausea swells over me. I think about how humans are homeomorphic to the sphere. You would say a torus, to be pedantic. I'd counter with n-torus, to be worse. It depends on how many holes there are.

I think of more stupid, old arguments we had, trying to detach myself from the hands exploring this thing. I trigger something, or it reacts to me in some way, because light flashes across its surface like an asterisk, leaking some clear fluid, defining the shape. It abruptly splits along these lines with a wet, sucking sound, opening like a lotus, and the liquid oozes thickly over my bare feet. I squint against the light, but it only continues for a moment, then it dulls. Dies. My eyes start to readjust to starlight. I move in close, any caution I had erased.

I always thought it would smell bad inside these things, but there is no smell at all and that's worse.

Vision restored, I see long hair, a rounded face, lips slightly parted, an upturned nose, swaddled in dusk. And then I see all these things together and my heart cracks because it isn't you.

It's some other girl, naked and curled like a fetus in her womb, asleep. Her spine has been replaced with a bundle of impossibly thin strands of glass that shimmer with rainbows, even in this distant light. Her body is prosthetic. Mind and body are fundamentally the same; when they tried to entirely eliminate the latter, integration simply did not work. I know this much. And though human brains are not constructed to last forever, this silicone will last hundreds of years. You can synthesize it. These new parts of you can be replaced.

My next thought is to cover her. I believe there is no true her to mind, but if it were you, I would want you covered, against the cold wind coming off the water, against invasive eyes. Maybe it's a stupid thing to care about. My shirt is drenched with salt water, but it's the best I can do, so I peel it off. I step closer, between the petals of her ship, and lay my shirt across her. And then I go for help.

Within the hour, a team arrives, cordons off the entire beach. One of the helmeted workers in dark, rippling layers of complex polymers looks for a moment at the shirt I have left on her. They leave and return with a silvery safety blanket to replace it.

The questions they ask leave me unsettled, and they grow disturbed with my answers. If this were some simple error, an accident, they wouldn't need to ask anything at all. They ultimately decide I have nothing to do with this. I did the right thing by bringing her to shore. I climb up the dunes to go home, to your home. I take one last look as they guide the petals gently back into place. It's for her own good.

Now I'm home, failing to sleep. My thoughts keep jumping to her face, looking as if she were about to cry, forever locked in that expression. The exam is in a few short hours.

It was a violation. Touching that sphere, that ship. Touching her.

November 1st, 2190

I passed. Top ten. I'd be impressed if I weren't a decade older than everyone else.

Nila was thrilled. I acted like I was too, though I know she will follow me, like I'm following you. Your parents looked relieved. I leave in two months.

I wish I had something to make this headache go away.

December 31st, 2190

This is the last New Year I will celebrate. No gifts this time. Just food, the things we never have. Gritty bread, a few withered tangerines. Desalinated water without the aftertaste of iodine. Your mom managed to find chicken somewhere, or at least something that tastes enough like it for us.

There is nothing left for me here. There's no reason for me to feel so sad.

January 1st, 2191

I'm standing in front of the house. I didn't bother waking anyone up to say goodbye. The small pile of battered textbooks I've left for Nila says it all.

The power's still off, this early in the morning, so it's pitch black. I barely notice the white van pulling up. The headlights make it stand out, make it more obvious how the mist clings to everything. Someone comes out wearing a white hazard suit, white helmet, and an impenetrable silver visor. They don't dare breathe the same toxic air as us poors. I take a deep breath, testing the air. Brine, ammonia, decay. The ubiquitous, scentless, heavy metal particulate.

They open up the back, revealing a shadowed interior, then turn their mercurial expression on me. Inside there are two benches loaded with teenagers. I stand out as the only adult. I'm at least twice as old as the youngest. I look at these children and think *neuroplasticity*. I take the end of the bench closest to the driver, who is distorted by a thick pane of fluted plastic. The air has an odd, metallic tang to it.

The girl sitting across from me bounces minutely in her seat. She keeps leaning forward, stealing glances at everyone else in the faint light. The van starts, and we're all clutching the benches so we don't go flying.

After half an hour, I can't take the loaded silence, so I tap on the plastic. No one responds, so I knock it a little harder.

"Hey, is it okay if we talk back here?"

The kids look shocked that I have the balls to ask. Still, no one responds.

"I think it's fine. Go ahead, talk to each other."

As if they'd been waiting for my permission, they all start babbling. After a few hours, as the conversation rises and falls, things quiet as the van slows, stops, and lets on another kid. We bump along, increasingly nauseated. No one talks to me, though they keep looking at me. I cross my arms over my chest and pretend I'm comfortable.

Indeterminable hours later, the van slows, and we hear the rattle of a gate being pulled back. We rumble forward, tilting down, into a tunnel. The van brightens intermittently, the air becomes dry and stale. There is no talking now.

The van shudders to its final halt. The back opens to two more people in haz suits. Behind them the cement tunnel curves up into darkness. We are quickly escorted into an empty room bathed in a cold, clinical light. They take us into an adjacent room, one by one. No one returns. I go last.

January 15th, 2191

My stomach hurts. My upper arm is a knot of pain.

I don't remember this from last time. I don't trust my memories. Remembering is such a feeble thing, it seems strange to have tested us based on it. How can it compare to simultaneous access and near instant recall? I see the appeal. What I have now feels fragmented and lossy. Still, what is a person if not their memories?

It's hard to think when I feel this bad. I don't know how I managed it before. I think the injections are meant to break us down in more than one way.

February 2191

I don't mind the acrid taste of the nutritional fish paste anymore. Soon, I won't be able to taste it at all. Or need it.

My relationship with time has changed. As endless billions of neural proteins crystallize into invisible silicate lattices, new connections are forming in me and with the others. The others linger on the fringes, but they are there. We have formed a local network for our cohort. It's strange, to be present both with them and within myself, and yet remain undivided. This new unity helps us forget the people we've left behind.

They have access to all of this, these things we share with each other, that we keep to ourselves. We are not our own creatures. I know, now, that to respond to me would have been to reveal yourself. I comfort myself with this.

It is almost perverse to compose these missives. I feel closer to you, as if I could drift across this electromagnetic field that spans between us and find you floating behind the crest of an oncoming wave.

November 2191

We who are left are now fully encased in our sacs, our albumen, and I note with disinterest the titanium mesh beginning to coalesce about me. It creates a shimmering, fibrous network that will be my interface for external stimuli. A second skin, a third eyelid. It scrapes against the delicacy of my consciousness.

I look outside of myself, while I still can, at what remains of some other girl. She is curled and suspended in her own electrolyte bath. A sleeve has been fitted over her spinal bundle, and code streams across the surface of her tank. An external cue, a flicker of her otherwise vacant eyes, and I know *she* is still in there.

2192

I thought the question I asked you was one I'd be able to answer myself at some point. Are you the same? Am I? How much control over myself could I have, when all these pieces of me have been co-opted? The *me now* and the *me then* seem as different as the *me* at 29 and the *me* at 19. The changes were imperceptible. I feel like I'm the same person, but I suspect I'm not. I don't think I'll ever know. The Fleet of Theseus, one of the girls calls us. It's supposed to be funny, but none of us can laugh.

They've got us rolled out on the beach this morning, like some massive carton of filigree eggs. Boosters and fins abrade our shells. We don't have an audience, just our own silent and discrete company.

There is no preamble, no ceremony. The launch is abrupt. We huddle close as the ice-white flames propel us through the atmosphere, leaving cutouts in the clouds we pass through. I feel the temperature like a breath, a blush, a fever. Our flight accoutrements, depleted and useless as they are, melt and adsorb into our hulls. I feel the first wave of unabated radiation splash across me, converted into electricity that courses through me.

I expect the fear to come, choking me back down to Earth, but it doesn't.

They said I would feel starlight on my skin. All I feel is sick.

????

I measure time in tedious revolutions about Jupiter and Neptune.

They   have   me   on   a   course $\left(\cos(\frac{\pi}{24}), .17\sin(\frac{\pi}{6}), -.28\sin(\frac{\pi}{6}), 1.63\sin(\frac{\pi}{6})\right)$ rotated from your initial trajectory.

I adjusted it to   .

Asteroid 5772156 Aglaonoe will aid in correcting this to your vector in 13,268 lightyears.

I guess those fucking matrices were useful after all.

One more pass of Jupiter, then the Sun. I'll greedily store her gamma rays and x-rays. Then I'll be riding your wake, deeper into space.

I'll be there soon. I'm right behind you.

See Rubella Dithers's story "The Waves In Which We Drown" online at Metaphorosis.
If you liked it, leave a comment. Authors love that!
Remember to subscribe to our e-mail updates so you'll know when new stories are posted.

About the story

I had been writing a story about a poor kid obsessed with freediving for pearls. There was an ex-boyfriend and a sea god and angst. It wasn't working out.

A few summers ago, my friend and I were driving around the fairgrounds. We stopped to watch the sunset, and she told me she was scared of space. I didn't really get it. Like, why? It's just kind of there.

I was trying to figure out what I could salvage from the freediving story. There was a scene where the dude is watching his cousins running around the beach, so I started with that. Then I think I got annoyed? I don't know, but for some reason I remembered my friend's fear and I was like screw it, start with that. Make it epistolary. Who is this person, why is she here, where is she going? How has no one caught me writing at work? These questions demanded answers.

A question for the author

Q: What kind of pieces are the most fun to write?

A: I've been studying viola for three years. It's a very difficult instrument to play. Footwork, weight distribution, shoulder rests, chin rests, strings, bow hair tension, bow grip, elbow angle, bow direction, humidity, finger height, bow weight, finger angle, thumb position; so many things work in unison to produce a single note. To make that note sound good takes years of practice. When you see a piece performed with beauty and taste, decades of study produced that. There are no shortcuts. Brutal dedication to the craft is the only way to attain any semblance of competence.

What I'm saying is that I like animal antics and clown husbandry. I wrote a story about a clown park (like a dog park, but for clowns) and the clown bites a kid. My master's thesis has a fish drawing in it. People have cited that paper. It's not even about fish.

About the author

During a family trip to Coos Bay, a pair of pirates wandered up from the beach and asked Rubella if "the lass 'ad a bit o' seaweed in 'er 'air". Alas, the lass did not.

Rapunzel Dreams of Elephants

Rachel Delaney Craft

Rapunzel wakes like she does every morning, with the woman standing over her, smiling her motherly smile.

"Did you sleep well?" the woman asks.

Rapunzel shrugs. She is on her lumpy air mattress in the attic, her hair twisted around her like a mummy's wrap. She knows about mummies from the History Channel. "Not really."

The woman's smile twitches, then rights itself. "You haven't been dreaming, have you?" She says this like dreaming is an affliction, a symptom of some dread disease.

"No," Rapunzel says. She knows plenty about dreaming from TV shows, though she has never experienced it herself. "I can barely sleep, it's so stuffy in here." This summer has been hotter than usual, and the attic is painfully close to the sun.

The woman's smile broadens, and she lays a motherly hand on Rapunzel's shoulder. "I'll see what I can do about that, dear. Now, ready for a cut?" She holds up a hefty pair of scissors.

Rapunzel nods. The hair clings to her like a young animal, heavy and ever-growing, giving her a headache.

The woman cuts Rapunzel's hair at her ears and gathers it into a big cardboard box, then drops the box through the attic trapdoor. It lands on the living room floor with a smack. She and Rapunzel climb down the rope ladder to the small living room, with its couch and coffee table and gangly floor lamp.

And TV.

The woman keeps the TV on constantly, even when she's not watching it—any channel will do. It's just loud enough to be annoying, like a gnat buzzing in Rapunzel's ear.

This morning the channel is Discovery. While they sit on the couch eating breakfast—toaster waffles for Rapunzel, a cup of unnaturally pink fat-free yogurt for the woman—Rapunzel learns about tensile strength and Kevlar and spider silk, and how a head of human hair can carry the weight of two elephants without breaking. Rapunzel wishes she could tune it out, but the harder she tries, the more the noise seems to burrow into her brain, burying these useless facts in her memory.

The woman pushes her half-empty yogurt cup away, saying some nonsense about being too full. The woman is constantly on a diet.

When Rapunzel returns to the attic, carrying a bottle of water and a PB&J sandwich for lunch, the woman kisses her on the forehead and locks the trapdoor. It's for Rapunzel's own protection. There are bad people in the world, the woman always says, people who carry baseball bats and break down doors and steal TVs.

The woman descends the rope ladder and goes out to work like she does every day, with her oversized Coach purse and her box of hair. Rapunzel watches her through the attic window. She hears the woman's tall black boots click across the cement like anxious teeth, sees her pause to glance over her shoulder in Rapunzel's direction before disappearing around the corner toward the wig place. She makes the most marvelous wigs from Rapunzel's hair, or so the woman says—glamorous, expensive wigs, mostly purchased by actors and old people with too much money, and occasionally people with cancer.

Rapunzel has seen people with cancer on TV. She knows it's wrong, but she feels slightly jealous of them with their shiny, bald heads. She knows she can never get cancer, because whatever magic makes her hair grow fast seems to keep her from getting sick. She has never had a cold, or the flu, or so much as a plantar wart. If the woman were smarter, Rapunzel thinks, she would sell more than Rapunzel's hair. She would talk to the scientists, the universities, give them Rapunzel's cells to study in their glass dishes. Those cells might turn out to have a cure for something, something worth enough money for the woman to buy everything on the Home Shopping Network.

But the woman doesn't share her treasures.

The sound of the TV downstairs drifts up through the air ducts, some commercial about a vacuum cleaner (*Groundbreaking suction technology!*). Rapunzel massages her forehead. She can always hear it, a never-ending waterfall of sound, like there is a tiny TV plugged into the back of her skull.

Rapunzel kneels and rattles the trapdoor, just in case the woman has forgotten to lock it today. Of course not. Rapunzel does not even think of escaping the house, only of turning off that damned TV. The noise is a living thing. It weighs on her, heavier with each passing day; it surrounds her like smoke, working its way into her nose, her lungs, the small spaces in her brain. Closing around her memories.

The first thing she remembers is holding the woman's hand and being led down the sidewalk to this house. It is a tall, narrow structure, slightly crooked, and it tapers toward the top like a pointed hat. The woman rents out the first two floors and lives on the third. It's small: living room, galley kitchen, bathroom filled with creams and serums and glycolic peels—and the mysterious bedroom, which Rapunzel has never seen. The woman herself never goes in; she keeps the bedroom locked and sleeps on the couch every night. Then there is the attic, at the tip of the hat, where Rapunzel lives.

She had other memories when she first came here, Rapunzel is sure of it—memories of Before. But when she first set foot in this house and first heard that TV, her thoughts began to grow hazy. With each passing day, the memories faded. First went the names, then the faces. Now all she has is a sort of fuzzy shape resembling a mother in a place resembling a house. It could be this house, this woman. But she feels sure there was someone else, once...

When the woman returns in the evening, she brings with her a large, plastic, box-shaped thing. She hands it to Rapunzel magnanimously, then tells her to carry it up the rope ladder—not an easy task, because the thing is quite heavy. She shows Rapunzel how to put it in one of the attic windows, where it makes a loud, grumbly noise and begins pumping cold air into the room.

Rapunzel loves it.

After the woman tucks her into bed, Rapunzel sits up and stares at the shuddering A/C unit. She imagines a face in it—power switch and temperature dial eyes, cold-breathing grate mouth. The closest thing she has to a friend.

When she finally lies back down and closes her eyes, she realizes something is missing. No voices are drifting up from downstairs. No commercials, no soap operas, no reality shows. Miraculously, the A/C's humming is loud enough to drown out the TV. With a sigh of indescribable relief and contentment, Rapunzel falls back onto her air mattress and falls deeply asleep.

This is when she has her first dream.

She dreams she is in the attic. Everything appears the same —lumpy air mattress beneath her, clock ticking on the wall, A/C groaning in the window. Yet Rapunzel senses something different.

She tries the trapdoor. Here, in the dream world, it is not locked.

She moves slowly, cautiously, down the rope ladder. The living room is the same as usual—almost. The coffee table, scattered with emery boards and sugar-free candy wrappers and a half-drunk mug of metabolism-boosting green tea. The couch where the woman sleeps each night, complete with the indentation her body has made in the cushions over the years.

But the woman is nowhere to be seen. And the TV screen is black.

Rapunzel tiptoes up to the door of the bedroom. She doesn't know why it is never used—any time she asks, the woman irritably changes the subject—but she's always guessed it has something to do with a man. She curls her fingers around the knob and turns.

It is unlocked.

As she steps inside, Rapunzel nearly chokes on the dust. She doubles over, coughing.

"Shh!"

Rapunzel straightens up. Did she imagine the voice? It's too dark to see anything, so she fumbles around until she finds a light switch. A small table lamp flicks on, casting a puddle of weak light over the room.

It is a place frozen in time: the bed unmade, a half-drunk glass of water on the nightstand, a basket of laundry in the corner that never got folded. A pair of pink slippers lies askew on one side of the bed, kicked off in haste. On the other there is a duffel bag, open to reveal a pair of enormous sneakers and a pile of clothing: T-shirts, jeans, baseball cap.

"Down here!"

This time the voice is undeniable. Rapunzel crouches to peer under the bed. There, hidden behind the duffel bag, is a small cage. And inside is a little yellow finch.

Rapunzel lifts the cage out carefully, its gold bars glittering in the lamp's feeble light. The bird stares up at her with gleaming black eyes.

"Be quiet," he says, "or she'll hear you."

This may be the first bird Rapunzel has met, but she knows (from Animal Planet) that birds do not generally talk. She wonders if, on the inside, he is really a bird. But Rapunzel isn't picky. She hasn't had anyone to talk to, except of course the woman, in years —how many years? It's all so fuzzy. She must have had people to talk to before, a *real* mother or father perhaps, but she can't remember.

"Wh-who are you?" She is breathless with excitement, or maybe fear.

"A prisoner," says the bird, "like you."

Rapunzel sets the cage on the mattress, sending up a plume of dust. "Are you...real? Or are you just a figment of my imagination?"

The bird gives a scoffing chirrup. "We are not in your imagination. We are in *her* dream."

Her. Rapunzel swallows. For some reason, she does not think the woman would approve of what she is doing right now.

She glances at the duffel bag. "You tried to leave her. And she...locked you in here?"

"*Cheep!* She'll do it to you too, if she finds you here."

"I don't understand," Rapunzel says, frowning. "How am I in her dream and not my own?"

The bird tilts its head toward her hair, now knee-length. "You have some sort of magic. Magic can do strange things with dreams."

Rapunzel blinks as the meaning of this sinks in. "Does *she* have magic?"

"Of course." The bird's black eyes glitter. "You know what she is."

"She's...my mother." This comes out more like a question than a statement.

"You don't believe that," the bird says. "You've always known."

He is right, Rapunzel realizes. It's like this knowledge has always been in her, deep in the corners of her mind, but until now it has been clouded by thick fog.

"No," she says slowly. "She loves me."

The bird laughs, a high-pitched chirrup. "Love and cruelty are not mutually exclusive. I should know. She is more dangerous than you thi—" He pauses, tilting his head, listening. "Get out. Hurry!"

Leaving the cage on the mattress, Rapunzel runs for the bedroom door. She barely has time to shut it behind her before—

"Rapunzel?"

She wakes in a daze. She is not on her air mattress—not in the attic at all. She is on the floor of the living room, tangled in her hair, which is now past her ankles. Light is streaming through the kitchen window, and in front of it is a silhouette, tall and dark.

The woman looks down at her with alarm. "How did you get here?"

"I...I don't know. A...dream?"

At this, the woman looks even more alarmed. But Rapunzel is not paying attention. She is thinking about the bird in the cage behind the locked bedroom door. This thought sparks a rare memory: She met another bird, once. A normal, non-talking bird, at the zoo. It perched on her finger and ruffled its painted feathers, and she fed it little pieces of fruit, and there was someone with her —

"Here, sit down." The woman, still in her nightgown, takes Rapunzel by the arm and guides her to the sofa. A children's show is playing on the TV, showing a cartoon knight trying to fight off a dragon and rescue a princess. The woman clicks the volume up a few notches.

Rapunzel's head begins to throb. She leans forward and presses her fingers to her temples. She feels the TV's noise invading her skull, pushing her memories back into their corners.

"Headache?" the woman says brusquely, heading to the kitchen. "You'll feel better once you eat breakfast."

She brings out the waffles and yogurt, and they eat, as usual, in front of the TV. Rapunzel does not taste her waffle as she chews —she is too busy trying to dig up memories from the hard, dry earth inside her skull.

The children's show ends. Another episode starts.

Rapunzel furrows her brow at the woman. "Don't you have to be at work?"

"I'll call in sick."

"But you're not—"

"I just want to spend some time with you, dear." The woman smiles and puts her arm around Rapunzel.

Rapunzel has always believed the woman truly loves her, in her own strange way. But now she is beginning to wonder: Does the woman love her the way a mother loves a daughter? Or the way a dragon loves its treasure?

After another mindless episode, two cooking shows, and a murder mystery, the woman slathers gray mud on her face and paints her toenails with glitter. She says she's found a new weight-loss thing to try: hypnotherapy. She saw it on TV.

Rapunzel is not listening.

In the past, Rapunzel didn't mind sitting on the couch with the woman—it was cooler down here than in the attic. But something has changed. She feels like she is seeing her tiny world for the first time. The woman, filled with dark magic. The TV, enchanted to suffocate her memories and shut her out of dreams. The locked bedroom door, the bird-husband, the void he left behind.

She wonders if she was meant to fill that void.

Lifetime is showing a movie about a lady with cancer who wears a scarf around her bald head. Rapunzel looks down at her own hair, now dragging and coiling on the ground, a shining yellow chain.

The woman with cancer has a young daughter. They do things together, sweet and innocent things, walking through parks and playing board games and ice skating and, later, lying together in the woman's hospital bed. As Rapunzel watches, they dissolve into pixels and LEDs, their voices fading into meaningless syllables.

She had her own mother, once. She is sure of it. But her head is too foggy to remember what her real mother looked like, or how her voice sounded, or the way she laughed when they fed the birds together at the zoo.

This causes something to stir within Rapunzel. Deep beneath the hum of the TV and the shadows clouding her mind, something is beginning to smolder.

Rapunzel wants her memories back.

So when the woman goes to the bathroom to wash the mask off her face, Rapunzel unplugs the TV's power cable from the wall and stuffs it into her pocket. The room is suddenly silent, Rapunzel's head suddenly clear. As she climbs the rope ladder, she sees vividly the curves and edges of a woman's face—her true mother, years ago. She sees what she must do, laid out in front of her like the rungs of the ladder, one step after another.

She takes the padlock off the outside of the trapdoor and puts it on the inside. She locks herself in. In the glorious silence of the attic, she lies down on her air mattress and falls asleep.

This time, the dream world feels less foreign, less disorienting. Rapunzel goes straight for the trapdoor. She loops her hair over her shoulders and climbs down the rope ladder. The woman is gone, but still Rapunzel hesitates. She can sense the woman's presence, as if she has left the room but her shadow remains, watching, waiting.

Taking a deep breath, she creeps into the bedroom.

"I'm leaving," she tells the finch in a hushed voice. "I'm... running away." Again, it sounds too much like a question.

"Good," is all the finch says.

Rapunzel leans over his cage, running her fingers along the wires, searching for the latch.

"You can't," the finch chirrups. "It's—"

But there are no locks in the dream world, and Rapunzel pops the cage door open.

The bird goes still for a moment, as if unsure this is really happening. Then he hops along his perch toward the opening, slowly at first, then faster. He tests his wings and flutters out, his movements stiff and clunky. Rapunzel feels his sharp claws curl around her fingertip as he lands.

It brings back the memory of the parrot, the one she fed at the zoo. This time, she can see her mother's face as she hands Rapunzel a chunk of fruit to feed him.

"Hurry!" The finch stiffens on her finger. "I hear her."

Rapunzel leaps up. "Hide," she whispers as she runs across the bedroom, lifting her hand to her neck. The finch hops off and curls his claws in her thick hair. She hears footsteps as she hauls herself up the rope ladder, faster than she has ever climbed before, eyes wide, chest heaving. She lurches through the trapdoor and slams it shut—

"Rapunzel!"

She wakes violently at the sound of the woman's voice. It is sharper now, less like a mother's voice and more like the screech of a bird of prey. The trapdoor rattles as the woman pounds on it. The lock is still there. When Rapunzel runs her hands over her hair, the finch is still there too. It gives a frightened cheep in her ear.

"Yes?" Rapunzel asks, shrinking away from the door.

"You took the TV cable, didn't you?" the woman calls.

Rapunzel's lip trembles. "No."

"I know you did. I need it back, dear. It may seem like a small thing to a child like you, but it is very important to me."

Rapunzel does not like being called a child, especially by this woman. She straightens up, setting her jaw. "I don't know what you mean."

"You've been dreaming, haven't you?" There is an accusatory edge to the woman's voice.

"No."

"You know how important it is to tell the truth, dear." The woman says it in the irritating tone of an adult talking to a three-year-old. She says it as if she really is talking about the truth, just the truth, as if this whole thing is about *the truth*. Rapunzel finds this ironic, considering everything about the woman is a sham.

Rapunzel says nothing. After a long moment, she hears the creak of the rope ladder and the click of footsteps across the living room floor, and the woman calls, "You can't stay in there forever."

Rapunzel knows she is right. There is no food or water here in the attic. Perhaps more urgently, there are no scissors, and the ever-growing weight of her hair is pulling her down, making movement slow and difficult.

But she can hear the woman down below. She prowls the living room floor, pacing back and forth beneath the trapdoor, sniffing the air. This TV business has wakened something feral in her.

"Dream it," the finch whispers in her ear.

He's right, Rapunzel decides. The only thing to do is fall asleep. In her dream, she will open the trapdoor and climb down the rope ladder and tiptoe out of the house. She'll run as fast as she can, straight to the nearest laboratory to sell her cells, and then she'll have enough money to buy her own house—and all the locks she needs to keep the woman out.

But as Rapunzel climbs out of her dream bed and drags her hair across the dream attic, she sees that now, even in her dream, there is a heavy black padlock on the trapdoor. Somehow, the woman—the witch, for that is what she is, what Rapunzel has always known her to be—has magicked her way into Rapunzel's dream and locked her inside.

Rapunzel runs to the window and slams it open. The finch disentangles himself from her hair and flutters around her head, and together they look down, down, four stories to the sidewalk below. Even Rapunzel's magic cannot protect her from a jump like that. She looks around the attic, searching for something, anything that can help her. But she is alone, except for the finch and the shivering A/C unit and her endless hair.

She pauses, winding a glossy tress around her finger. "Elephants," she whispers.

Her hair is very long now, perhaps longer than the house is tall. Twisting it into a rope, she loops it through the wrought-iron loop of the padlock on the trapdoor. Then she climbs through the window and lowers herself down, the bird fluttering alongside her.

It is remarkably easy. Her biceps sting only a little as she drops to the ground and pulls her hair down into a golden puddle beside her. She walks tentatively across the front lawn, her hair unwinding behind her, feeling the dewy grass between her toes— infinitely softer than it looks on TV. She takes a few steps down the sidewalk. The sky is so much bigger than what she can see from her window; the buildings and streets seem to stretch on forever. The air smells of garbage bins and pizza grease and air pollution— it's intoxicating. It brings to mind memories Rapunzel never knew she had, memories of her other mother, her real mother.

"Rapunzel!"

She jolts but does not wake. The woman is here, in Rapunzel's dream. Her voice is the low growl of an animal that's been lurking in the shadows, awaiting its prey.

Rapunzel starts to run, but something jerks her scalp and she tumbles to the sidewalk. The creature at the other end of her hair starts pulling, hand over hand, dragging Rapunzel painfully over the cement. Her nightgown rips, her skin tears.

When the pulling stops, she is on the sidewalk at the foot of the front door. Her sham-mother is standing over her, clutching Rapunzel's rope of hair in clawlike fingers, her face pinched with anger. She looks older, as if shutting off the TV has deepened her wrinkles and set shadows over her eyes.

"You've given me no choice," she says through gritted teeth. "I'm going to have to put you in timeout."

In the early morning sunlight, the sidewalk is streaked orange with blood. Rapunzel's stomach and thighs and breasts sting, and her nightgown sticks to the wounds. She is silent as the woman pulls her, by the hair, into the house and up the stairwell. There is no one else, no tenants or neighbors in this dream world, no police. The woman drags her to the third floor and shoves her across the living room to the rope ladder. Rapunzel climbs slowly, fighting the weight of her hair with each step, her head aching. She collapses on the floor in the dream attic, amid a tangle of bloody, grass-stained hair. She hears the trapdoor slam shut and the padlock click outside.

When Rapunzel wakes, her scalp is stinging with pain and the woman is pounding on the trapdoor.

"Are you ready to tell the truth, Rapunzel?"

The woman's voice no longer holds any semblance of the sham-mother or the wigmaker. Her voice is witchy through and through. And Rapunzel knows she is not the good kind of witch, but the other kind, the kind who kidnap children and steal memories and turn husbands into birds. The finch was right, Rapunzel thinks: the witch is far more dangerous than she appears.

But so is Rapunzel.

The witch thumps on the trapdoor again. "You can't stay up there forever. You have to eat. Tell me the truth, Rapunzel."

Rapunzel looks down at her hair, so long now it almost fills the attic, a sea of gold waiting to drown her. Slowly, deliberately, she gathers it up and twists it into a rope. She makes a knot, a special kind of knot she saw once on the History Channel.

"If you don't tell me the truth now," the witch yells, "I'll have to punish you." Her voice curls on the last two words, as if she is thinking of all the cruel, witchy punishments at her disposal.

Rapunzel stands over the trapdoor and bends her knees, rooting herself to the spot. "I'm sorry," she calls. "I'm ready to tell the truth now."

A pause. A witch this powerful should be able to sense trickery, Rapunzel thinks—but perhaps she has been in control too long, she is too used to winning at her own games. Perhaps in the witch's mind, all people will cave eventually.

People are just people. Hair is just hair.

"There's a good girl," the witch says.

The key scrapes in the lock. The trapdoor creaks open. The woman's head emerges through the opening.

It is remarkably easy. All it takes is one quick motion for Rapunzel to loop her hair around the witch's neck, one swift tug to make her lose her balance. The witch scrabbles at the rope ladder, but it is swinging now, and Rapunzel's grip is strong. The rope of hair sways and twitches. Her biceps strain. All she has to do is wait. She waits, waits for the woman's witchy breath to dissipate and her magic to ebb away, before going downstairs.

The TV screen is black and dead. The front door is unlocked. When Rapunzel opens it, there is a man standing outside, brushing feathers from his hair and wincing in the sunlight. He takes a hopping step toward her, wobbling on his new legs.

"You changed," Rapunzel observes.

"Yes," he says in a whistling voice. "I forgot what it felt like. What the world looked like."

"So did I." But as Rapunzel peers out at the cars and the streets and the dandelions springing up through cracks in the asphalt, she feels memories pressing at the edges of her mind. Ghosts of an old life—or perhaps a new one.

She walks out the door to meet them.

See Rachel Delaney Craft's story "Rapunzel Dreams of Elephants"
online at Metaphorosis.
If you liked it, leave a comment. Authors love that!
Remember to subscribe to our e-mail updates so you'll know when
new stories are posted.

About the story

This story was inspired by a run-down house I rented one summer in college, where I lived in a tiny attic-turned-bedroom complete with trapdoor and rope ladder. The idea hit me one morning on my commute to work—why not write a fairy tale retelling with that stuffy attic room as Rapunzel's tower?

That was over five years ago, when I was fairly new to writing and even newer to short fiction. I ran the first few drafts by my critique group, then started submitting to publications —and getting rejection after rejection (and the occasional tidbit of feedback). But I always thought this story had potential, so I kept submitting, revising, and repeating until Rapunzel finally found a home at *Metaphorosis*. It just goes to show that if you believe in your work, persistence and hard work will eventually pay off!

A question for the author

Q: What's the story no one else thinks is as good as you do?

A: Howl's Moving Castle! Everyone seems to adore the movie, but the book is way better (in my opinion). Its quirky characters, magical worldbuilding, and swoon-worthy romance put it at the top of my list of desert-island books.

About the author

Rachel Delaney Craft is an engineer who dreams of writing full-time. She's dabbled in everything from poetry and blog writing to children's science articles, but her main focus is speculative fiction. Her latest project is a young adult sci-fi novel, and last year she edited her first anthology, WILD: Short Stories from Rocky Mountain Fiction Writers, which was a finalist for the Colorado Book Award. She lives in between Colorado's mountains and prairie, which often serve as inspiration for her work. When not writing, she enjoys baking, gardening, rock climbing, and exploring the outdoors with her goofy Bassett hound mix.

racheldelaneycraft.com, @RDCwrites

The Nocturnals IV

Mariah Montoya

In a world where each day and night lasts thirty years, Detective Joah Cadshaw and his new partner, Misla Crane, have been captured by the monsters who lurk in the Eternal Night—the Nocturnals. The only way to escape and return to daylight, Joah comes to realize, is to learn the Nocturnal language and pretend to be one of them.

After Joah and Misla master telepathy, Prince Kal leads them to a nearby mountaintop, where the Nocturnal queen interrogates the two about their past motives. Why, she asks, did they kidnap and kill those who wanted to join the Nocturnals? Why did they call those people "infected"?

What Joah and Misla learn will shape their futures forever. The Nocturnals have only been trying to warn them of a massacre lying ahead, a wicked deal made between a king and a crook. The Sunsetters are in danger, and their leader, General Aoif Deckler, has betrayed them all.

Part 4

Prince Kal closed his eyes to avoid watching the anguish crumple the alien's face.

He poured forth his memories instead, allowing the foreign guests to access his wordless thoughts, all the sights and sounds and smells of a cruel cycle sixty years ago, when he had just reached manhood. Back before they were forced to Move.

It was finally sunset. His people had been hiding from the scorching heat of daytime for thirty years, unable to step outside, forced to hunker in the shadows of their towers. Kal had never seen the moon; it was always washed out by sunlight, a faint white halo among the clouds. Oh, he had dreamed about it, though, that piercing disk pinned to its black curtain of night sky.

Now the beastly sun was actually sinking into a bloodred grave over the sea, and twilight would soon sweep over them, and he'd be able to bask in the moon's pool of light at last.

Kal.

It was his mother. He had been squinting through the window in a turret on the fourth floor, watching the rays of sunset stroke the dappled water; he jumped when she swept around the corner. The queen was swaddled in her usual silk cloak that would shield her if she were to accidentally stumble into sunlight. Kal had thought she'd scold him for exposing himself at the window, but her thoughts were harried, choked.

Kal, come with me. There is a commotion in the Grand Hall. It seems a Diurnal has snuck into the castle. I want you close to me, in case there are more.

Not a sunman. A Diurnal. One of those strange people who, despite their name, followed sunrise or sunset religiously, Moving every few years to avoid the heat of day and terrors of night.

Prince Kal wrapped his cloak tight around his body and raced after his mother, through the twisting halls where firelight flickered from steel brackets. They cut across the indoor courtyard, past the tinkling fountain, and eased open the doors of the Grand Hall together.

Nobody noticed them. Their cloaks blended into the shadows, but King Isce and his guardsmen had taken their own off; the glowing patterns on their skin highlighted the alien-looking creature screaming and writhing in their midst.

Reddish mops sprouted from the Diurnal's head, and strangely muted clothes hugged the curves of his body. His ears were large, ugly, and crimped, sticking out from the side of his face. Nothing about him glowed.

You have broken into our domain. Killed two of my sentries, Kal's father snarled. He was sprawled in his usual spiked stone chair, unflinching, though his patterns flared. *Why?*

I know what you do to my people, the Diurnal hissed, trying to wrench himself from the grips of the guards. *I know how you— how you... infect them! You lure them away.*

Beside Kal, Queen Usai's thoughts fluttered in alarm, but she didn't let them extend beyond their bubble hidden in shadows. Kal knew why she was afraid, though—the Diurnal knew their language, had unleashed his thoughts as if he were a native. They, on the other hand, had never been able to make those peculiar sounds of speech the Diurnals practiced.

Well, said the prisoner, *I followed some of them, followed them away from the High Road, all the way here. It took them twenty cycles just to reach your fortress. Clever, making your food prance to you instead of catching them yourself. You don't even have to leave your roost.*

Now Prince Kal and the queen passed confusion, though Kal sensed dread lacing his mother's thoughts. Food? What did the alien mean, food? The sunmen brought them carcasses to eat during the day, when they couldn't afford to step outside, and during the Eternal Night they scavenged for carrion themselves, but when had they ever lured—?

A screech from behind him. Kal ducked as a great horned owl swooped through the cracked doorway and landed with a *flump* on King Isce's patterned shoulder. The owl shook its body—feathers floated outward—and wretched: the corpse of a vole, slimed with mucus and blood, poured onto King Isce's naked lap.

Lowering his head, the king extended his spiked tongue, wrapped it around the vole, and reeled it into his mouth. When the owl took off again with another screech, King Isce extended his hands, as if to say, *See?*

That's not what I mean, pouted the alien. *You don't just lure owls.*

The king laughed before Kal could form any kind of half-baked conclusion. Air puffed in quick waves from his lips, and humor riddled his next words.

Fine. You've caught me, Diurnal. I have my ancestor's taste, I will admit. When your people wander past us so willingly, just within reach... when I can sense the abilities some possess, the abilities to understand us, to answer our calls... but why have you come here, Diurnal? Have you come to scold me for my choice in dessert?

Queen Usai gripped her son's elbow, her nails piercing his skin. She tried to pull him away, back through the doors and away from the truth, but he wrenched himself from her grip. He stared at his father. He had never loved the man, but... would he really prey upon *Diurnals*? *Living* Diurnals, nonetheless? Walking, *talking* Diurnals?

I have come, the alien panted, *to offer you a deal.*

The Grand Hall silenced. Kal and his mother stiffened in their efforts to close their minds, to not make a sound. King Isce leaned forward.

A deal? What could you possibly offer me that—?

A year ago, my mother got sick, said the Diurnal. *I met with our general, begged him to send scavengers to find some medicine. He's the one with the authority to make those decisions, you know. He met with me, alright. Told me he couldn't help me. Said he* needed to use the scouts and scavengers to find more ship *supplies,* or else we wouldn't have enough vessels to take everyone across the Green Sea when the Eternal Night comes. And my mother died.

King Isce stroked his jawline, where one of his glowing designs angled crookedly from a scar. *I don't understand what this has to do with me. What do I care if a nomad dies?*

He chose the Dirt Slummers over my mother, said the alien. *The Dirt Slummers! They squabble and fuck and overpopulate, and he chose* them. *Meanwhile, my mother was a prominent member of the community. An inventor. She created the magnetic watch strapped to General Glade's own damn wrist, but he let her die! No, he should've left the Slummers behind, abandoned them to the Eternal Night like he abandoned her.*

King Isce said nothing. Blood still smothered his lips. Kal tried to control his shuddering breaths. He thought of their castle cellar, piled high with the bones of rodents and sometimes even mammals. Were there *other* creatures trapped inside? Creatures with mops of hair and crimped ears and plain skin that his father had lured from the High Road over yonder?

Help me overcome General Glade, the alien said. *Help me take the general's place, and you can have all the piss-poor schmucks you want. No need to lure them. I'll give them to you. You can lock them in that cellar of yours, let them rot to the ripeness of your liking. Help me fight, and I promise—in sixty years, when the poorest, dirtiest of us have squabbled and fucked and overpopulated again, I'll give you them again. And again, and again, for as long as I live, for as long as my children lead in my place. Help me kill our general, and you've got yourself a feast.*

Now Queen Usai's nails sunk deep into her son's arms; blood oozed from the curved indents, like a trickling frown. This time, Kal let her tug him backward, but not before he heard his father ask, *What's your name, son?*

And the alien replied, *Aoif Deckler, Your Highness.*

How long had Joah known General Deckler? Since he was a boy, as young as Damien, and his school had hosted a career day where all the professionals—miners, healers, scouts, scavengers—had ringed their wheeled gymnasium, thrusting out fliers that said things like:

THANK YOUR LOCAL WARNER.

COME DE-STRESS WITH A SEAMSTRESS.

A NOMADIC PLUMBER'S GUIDE

When General Aoif Deckler himself had walked into the room, his hair already salted with white, the students had *oooh*'d and *ahhhh*'d, turning away from their current interests. Joah remembered straightening in his crisp school uniform, breathless as he watched the general march to the center of the gymnasium and hold out a neat stack of business cards. His classmates had streamed around the man, and by the time Joah got to him, there were no business cards left.

"Ahh, you're too late, sonny," General Deckler had said, chuckling. "Well, that's okay. I've got in *here*," he said, pulling another, smaller card from his inside pocket, "my *real* contact info. Can't have all you little tykes sending letters to my office, can I?"

"No, sir," Joah had said, taking this newer card with delicate, trembling fingers.

"No, indeed. Say, you've ever thought of being a retriever?"

"My granddad was one, sir. But he retired before he crossed the Green Sea."

"Your granddad! Tell me, what was his name? I must know..."

So it had begun: Joah's relationship with the man he had come to trust, the man he'd always admired even after he'd been fired. Yet he could not deny the sincerity of Prince Kal's memories. Nocturnals could withhold, but they could not, Joah had learned, so blatantly lie.

His chair seemed to sink deeper into the snow. The fire ringing them had dwindled to embers, and the cold of the mountaintop bit his body with frosted teeth. To his right, Misla was looking up at the stars, as if hoping to find an answer etched somewhere in the aro sky. To his left, Damien's fingers fidgeted on his lap, and now Joah knew what the boy had meant when he had said *"My mother would've been the first to die if I hadn't come to the Nocturnals."*

Damien's mother was a Dirt Slummer.

After witnessing what happened in the Grand Hall, Queen Usai said now, using her voiceless speech like thoughts sent along a cold gale, *my son and I snuck to the cellar. There, we found a handful of Diurnals... decomposing among the skeletons of other creatures.*

She seemed to sense the lingering question rising, smoke-like, from Joah and Misla's tilted heads: why let them decay? Of course, Joah thought he knew the answer, but it made him feel sick, and he wondered if he'd ever be able to stomach meat again. Maybe he'd eat those raindrop-sized seeds for the rest of his life.

We cannot digest fresh produce or flesh like you do. We eat what is abandoned by the sun. Although the land and its vegetation doesn't die during the Eternal Night, there are enough plants and animals that do. We clean it all up, so to speak.

Joah thought back to that mysterious tower at sunset. At the bone fragments crunching beneath his feet. Then he thought of the seeds again, seeds that had also been left behind by whatever squirrely creature had hoarded them. The Nocturnals were, in the truest sense of the word, scavengers. They were not predators. Yet King Isce had obviously accepted General Deckler's offer. He had agreed to hunt and capture and kill.

And now, sixty years later, he was about to do it again.

"You've been infecting us all this time," Joah said aloud, "to warn us of an upcoming massacre? A massacre like the one before?"

He realized his mistake when Misla inhaled sharply and the Nocturnals made a collective twitching motion, as if the sound from his lips had struck them with a spark of electricity: there was a reason the Nocturnals didn't make noise outside their protective netted cave. In the Eternal Night, when light and sight were scarce, sound exposed you to the monsters lurking in shadows.

They all waited, breathless, for something to happen, but there was only the creak of trees and snapping of branches in the distance as the wind broke into a howl.

I'm sorry, he said. *I forgot. I*—he was so shocked at what he had learned that his thoughts had turned into speech. The beasts they'd thought of as ever-evasive ghosts, always trailing them, always hypnotizing and luring their people into the darkness, had only been trying to stop them from the real darkness that waited for them at the Green Sea like an open jaw.

I never loved my husband, Queen Usai said, her sharp-angled shoulders relaxing slightly in the absence of a night beast. *It was an arranged partnership. When we saw what he had agreed to, I begged him to reconsider, but...*

A yowl cut through her words like a bloody ax.

The surrounding Nocturnals jumped from their seats, the feathers on their skulls bristling. Damien sprang to his feet too, and Joah saw the glint of a pole clasped in his small, muddied hand. The embers had died. Through the last torrents of steam rising from the snow, a curled set of horns bobbed over the mountain's edge.

The Calic, Queen Usai moaned.

A massive reptilian cat prowled into view. Scales covered its sleek body, and horns protruded from its jawline, curving upward like spiked ears. Its tail whipped behind it like a snake. Its eyes, each the size of Joah's palm, glared at the mountaintop party with slanted fury.

Queen Usai opened her lipless mouth and made a strange screeching noise. It was far more terrifying than if she had screamed instruction inside her own head: it was the rickety, rusty howl of a throat that never got used unless the enemy was already upon them.

The Nocturnals flew together, forming a tight knot within the circle of chairs. Joah grabbed Misla and Damien and pulled them into the tangle of limbs. The Nocturnals' glowing designs burned orange, and when they started swaying in unison, their mass of bodies waved like open flame. Joah was reminded, suddenly, of the mass of birds that had attacked him and Misla on the High Road on their way to retrieve those who had been left behind.

The night beast paused. Its lips curled backward, revealing a clutter of yellow, needle-like teeth. Mid-sway, the Nocturnals pulled out those identical poles, and the mountaintop roared and crashed with waves of that rising sound: a cacophony of grinding screeches from a hundred unused throats. They were trying to scare the beast away.

Damien slipped from Joah's grip and ducked under a Nocturnal's legs.

"Hey, kid!" Joah called, reaching out for him, but his hand was slapped away by an elbow, and Damien had already disappeared in the thickness of fiery bodies. "Come back!"

His voice was lost in the screeching discord. The boy had weaseled his way out of the fireball and now stood, exposed and alone, in the monster's warped shadow. His pole tumbled from his fingers into the snow. Compared to the crouching cat, Damien was nothing but a rodent. A single one of those curved claws would impale his chest like a sword.

What are you doing, child? Queen Usai cried.

Let me talk to him. I always wanted a cat, came Damien's voice, and the roar plummeted like an arrow arcing to the ground. The swaying stopped as everyone watched.

Joah saw himself, as if through a ghost's memory, picking up that green strip of fabric in the High Road's collection of dirt. Only now it was Damien Fertheli reaching a palm toward the cat, and Joah heard Lupita's sniveling voice as clearly as if she stood beside him now: *"He loves how wild they are, but I—I always told him no. I shouldn't have told him no,"* and Joah didn't have time to break from the Nocturnal huddle.

The cat leapt forward in a high arc, claws extended.

The Nocturnals moved in unison: left hands clutching the front of their poles, right hands gripping the back, they twisted each half in opposite directions as if unscrewing a lid.

Darts shot from their weapons like flaming arrows. Most *ping*'d against the cat's shelled skin, but two found its eyes, another its gaping mouth, and the beast shrieked in midair.

A flash of movement. Damien flew sideways as one of the Nocturnals, a slender one with dotted skin patterns, shoved him out of the way. The cat landed with a harrowing *THUMP* on top of the Nocturnal, right where Damien had been standing moments before.

Its serpentine tail kept thrashing for what felt like forever, its eyes blinking palm-sized beads of blood into the snow. Joah and Misla unglued themselves from the jumble of bodies and raced toward Damien, wrenching him backward. Frost had actually formed on the boy's eyelashes where tears would have clung. His lips had turned blue, and his fingers felt like icicles.

As the Nocturnals streamed around them to move the beast off their friend, Joah caught Misla's eye. Their breath fogged out in front of them, merging in midair above Damien's stiffened hair. Joah didn't need the Nocturnal language to understand the shine in Misla's eyes.

We need to go home, she was saying. *We need to save our people.*

Back within the humidity and warmth of the netted forest, they buried the Nocturnal who had saved Damien along with the parts of the Calic that had crushed him: a claw ripped from the paw, scales sawed from the chest, a strip of leathery skin from its chin. The rest of the beast had been picked apart to be eaten or used in other ways, to respect the beast itself, Queen Usai said, and in honor of the Nocturnal it had killed. The Nocturnal would live on in the blood they used for paint or the sinews that they would strip and use to make baskets, blankets, and bags.

His name was Gritz, Prince Kal told them as they watched Queen Usai herself push dirt into the grave, using one of the Calic's femurs like a shovel. They were only a few paces from the cages Joah and Misla had been living in, where the soil was loose and moist. Beyond Queen Usai's shoulder, Hickory Glade had crawled to the door of his own cage and pressed his face against the twining fibermud that contained him, watching her cover the grave.

Damien was standing rigid as a bone, staring at the patches of the Nocturnal's face still visible beneath the clods of dirt, at the dots on his skin that had faded like cold coals. Joah could hear the horrified whispers inside the boy's head—he had not meant to get anyone killed. He had only meant to tame the great cat, to ride the Calic to dawn so he could save his mother.

Because Damien's mother, along with the rest of the Dirt Slummers, was in danger.

"It was a good idea, kid," Joah whispered, clapping a hand on the boy's shoulder. "But we're going to have to find another way to reach the Green Sea in time. Maybe the river..."

Even as he said it, he knew the river wasn't fast or strong enough to carry them, even on a boat, to the point where the sun would still be winking on the horizon. How many moon cycles had they been stuck here? Twenty? Thirty? Joah had lost count, but he knew it might be too late.

Queen Usai straightened from her shoveling, her earrings clinking.

There is a way to get to your people in time. I am sure they have yet to reach the Green Sea, though they will soon, much too soon. If you can just get fuel for the Shooting Star...

"Shooting Star?" Joah asked. "What do you mean, Shooting Star?"

At his mother's nod, Prince Kal conjured an image of that strange contraption at the back of their netted cave, squatting in the middle of the High Road like a fat metal toad. A machine. The Nocturnal version of a silver steed. But instead of wheeling across the landscape, it...

Flies, Prince Kal confirmed with a nod. *We didn't make them. My father found them long ago, a dozen of them, half-buried in rocks near the Green Sea. He said they looked like fallen metal stars. He spent years trying to figure out what might power it, but nothing worked... until a sunman—what your kind call a Leather Skin—told him to try the very thing the sun people suck from the stems of perennial trees. The sunmen were our slaves, you see,* Prince Kal added, his forehead wrinkled with shame. *They brought us carrion during the daytime. And supplies.*

He paused.

They were the ones who killed so many of your people for my father and Aoif Deckler.

Joah jolted. Leather Skins had always seemed the opposite of a Nocturnal. They were like far-off sun gods, epitomes of light, fighters of night. To imagine them as slaves, forced to murder and drag bodies back to their master, was like trying to imagine the moon swallowing the sun.

Yes, the moon does occasionally swallow the sun, Prince Kal said with a wry twist of his lipless mouth. *There are other communities of Nocturnals and Leather Skins, you know. Some choose to Move every thirty years. Some choose to Stay and hide from the heat of the day or dangers of night. My father chose the latter. He built our fortress on the edge of the Green Sea where he'd found the starships. But every thirty years, when daytime kept us in our towers, the nomadic Leather Skins would come around. And he would enslave them.*

"How?" Misla asked. "How could he even *get* to them, let alone enslave—?"

Some could communicate with us just like you are communicating with us now. My father used our language to lure them, to overpower them, to cripple them and force them into servitude. And they—the slaves—gave us the secret to the Shooting Stars, the fuel we needed to ignite the machines and travel the aro faster than the moon can rise and fall. The fuel was too bright and hot for us to touch, but the Leather Skins could gather it for us...

And now Joah heard a new word flutter from Prince Kal's mind like a single moth. But it was a word that somehow snapped the pieces—the mystery of the Eternal Night—together.

Sunsap.

It's what the trees and other perennial vegetation of the aro hoard in order to survive the thirty-year night, Queen Usai said, pausing in her efforts to fold Gritz within the aro's eternal embrace. *They collect excess energy from the sun, convert it to sap, and store it in an underground vault where it flows like a river from one forest to the next.*

Joah imagined a horde of roots wiggling beneath the aro, reaching for a steaming liquid that ran like golden blood through the veins of the aro.

And this same sap can be used to fuel the Shooting Stars, Queen Usai said. *When he discovered this, my husband sent some Leather Skins to mine more of it a few hundred kilometers out west. This was about a decade before Aoif Deckler approached him with the deal of a lifetime.* Her thoughts oozed sarcasm, and Joah briefly wondered how long a Nocturnal lifetime really *was.* Longer than his, by God. *Ironically, the largest sunsap reserve runs alongside your High Road. A good latitude, I assume. I believe you're already familiar with the access point?*

Within the aged, streaked mirror of her mind, Joah saw that strange conical tower again. Only now he understood what it was for: an entrance to a tunnel that led to the very thing keeping the aro alive during the Eternal Night. The thing Leather Skins consumed. The thing that would have fueled King Isce's flight across the sky. Because if there were other communities of Nocturnals, of *course* a tyrant like Isce would have wanted to soar over the rest of them. To dominate the world. To ascend in a way his wingless body never could.

To reach the moon.

"We need to mine the sunsap, don't we?" Misla said after a lengthy stretch of silence, in which Queen Usai resumed shoveling dirt into the grave at her feet. "You have a Shooting Star, but you don't have fuel. We need to fill the tank, so to speak."

Queen Usai bowed her head so low, she looked in danger of toppling into the half-filled hole. She steadied herself by spearing the aro with the curved edge of the Calic bone.

*The starship we have with us now—Kal and I stole it and used it to fly after your general about a year after the Leather Skins dragged all those corpses to our cellar. This was long after the sun had gone down, when it was safe for us to do so. When we finally touched down on the other side, we'd caught up to sunset again, and our tank was near empty. We've been dragging the starship with us for the last sixty years, but I do believe it would still work. If you want to save your people from this—*Queen Usai brought the femur bone to her lips; her tongue shot out and spiraled around it like King Isce's had in Kal's memory—*you're going to have to gather sunsap, yes.*

"We're not Leather Skins, though," Misla said. "What if it burns us?"

Queen Usai smiled.

I have no doubt that bathing in the stuff might kill you, she said. *I would be careful not to touch it. But your bodies can withstand direct sunlight whereas ours can't, so I'm quite certain you'd be able to go near it, to collect it as carefully as you'd gather fire.*

There came a laugh from behind her, high-pitched, yet guttural. Hickory's eyes glimmered at them from within his cage, and Joah saw his grimy face splinter into a grin.

"You're not miners! This sunsap thing you mentioned, or whatever the hell it is... you think it's as easy as skipping down a tunnel and cuddling the stuff to your chest? No. You don't know a thing about caves." Hickory's eyes targeted Joah, and they glowered at each other with the pin-straight ferocity of shooting darts. "*You* didn't even know what a damn lantern was. You'll never make it without the light of the moon or these wretched flies buzzing around."

Joah glanced at Misla. For the first time in three cycles, he let himself remember Hickory standing over her again, berating her, laughing... he let himself remember the squishing slice of Hickory's ax through his wife's neck. His chest squeezed from the injustice of it all. How fitting, how perfectly goddamned ironic: they needed a miner to save their community in time.

But no, there had to be another way. He squinted at the pieces of Hickory he could see through the fibermud walls. "What's down there, then? What's in these caves you know so well? Tell us what to watch out for."

Hickory laughed again, his fingers curling around the ropes of his wall.

"Well, sometimes there's no good air to breathe. You'd never know until it's too late and you're choking on the gases of underground. Sometimes the walls come crashing down around you. It's never happened to me, because *I* know which signs of weakness to look for, but oh, it's happened plenty of times to others." His smile widened. "Sometimes there are creatures. Giant insects the size of a dog. Snakes and spiders and scorpions."

Damien's tiny chest rose and fell in awe struck breaths as Hickory continued describing the monsters that might or might not stop them from accessing the fuel they needed. Joah could feel the boy's thrill and eagerness, like a rapid heartbeat drumming up his neck, and he remembered the old Dirt Slummer's words from so long ago: *Damien liked to dig.* Yes, he did. And Damien would beg to come with them. In truth, Joah wasn't willing to separate from the boy until they returned to sunset and saw him safely in his mother's arms.

Was he willing, then, to lead the child into the unknown, without a guide to protect them from the beasts lurking underground? Beside him, Misla bit her lower lip and shook her head.

"I can help you," Hickory said now, the faintest crinkle of earnestness replacing those creases of his manic grin for the first time. "Let me out, and I'll help you find this... this sunsap. I just want to get out of his ruddy cage. I want to see the light again. Please."

Joah looked at Queen Usai, who shifted the last piles of dirt overtop Gritz's grave. Her blue-black feathers lay flat against her skull as if wilting. She set the femur bone at her feet.

To free your people, she said, *sometimes you need to free your monsters too.*

Prince Kal led them back toward the High Road, the glow of his figure swaying like a condensed sky of stars. Joah followed with tight unease, clutching a dart-loaded rod that Queen Usai had lent him. Misla marched beside him with Hickory's ax in one hand and his old lantern flickering in the other. Hickory glared at those hands as he slouched after them, his own locked behind his back with the snakish metal that had once handcuffed Joah too.

Damien—bless the kid—ignored their tension. He skipped around the peeling trees and hummed school tunes, inspiring a good number of Nocturnals to peek from their braided houses with hawkish eyes. Their thoughts of farewell rang in Joah's mind like Moving bells.

Yes, finally; they were Moving again.

"Hey, Prince," he said when the High Road finally appeared between trees. They weaved their way to the Shooting Star contraption squatting upon it near the back of the cave, and he asked his next question voicelessly, so that Hickory wouldn't hear. *Why do you call us aliens?*

Kal stared at the sunflies haloing the starship's metal head like a fiery crown.

You call us monsters, he said hesitantly, *but we have our own beliefs about your people. That you aren't native to the aro. That you came from the sky in a* hundred *starships centuries ago, and have since abandoned those starships. That you've forgotten where your people come from. I mean,* he added, *the Leather Skins can thrive in any time of day—all 180 degrees. We can flourish during all shades of night. But you—you're bound to a small, twelve-degree section of evening. Your bodies weren't built for such a fluctuation in light and heat. It's as if you weren't made for this planet. As if you really are aliens.*

The prince scrutinized them, ripping his gaze from the lifeless starship. They were all wearing silk cloaks to protect them from the bite of a cold night once they left the netted cave. Joah and Misla also shouldered supple, stretchy bags filled with dozens of ceramic jugs that they would fill with sunsap when they reached the vault beneath the conical tower.

"Why?" Joah asked suddenly, his thoughts forming a new question. *Why did you bother to warn us? Why were you so persistent all these years, if you think of us as aliens?*

Prince Kal flexed his fingers, staring at the swirls on the back of his hands.

It was more of an escape, at first. After the servants started serving us those Diurnals on a platter, my mother and I didn't want anything to do with our fortress anymore. We flew—just her and I— away from it all, to the other side of the sea. We should have brought some others with us. Aro knows there were hundreds of enslaved Leather Skins and subjugated Nocturnals who would have loved to escape his regime too.

This didn't make sense, though. Why the hell was there a whole *village* of Nocturnals if Prince Kal and his mother had flown off alone? For a moment, incest crossed Joah's mind, but no... not enough time had passed for the two to have reproduced so quickly. And two couldn't create *hundreds*.

"What's incest?" Damien asked aloud. Hickory gawked at him.

"Never you mind that," Misla said, glaring at Joah. "Go on, Prince."

My mother and I Moved with the night. We always loitered just behind the brink of sunset, never too far behind your new shiny general and his new shiny power. But we visited other communities of Nocturnals along the way. Some were whole cities to the south. Others were tribes to the north. No matter whether they Stayed or Moved every few decades, we kept hearing the same story over and over: a Nocturnal king from across the sea had sent stars flying over their heads, dropping acid on their people and land.

Joah imagined poison raining from the clouds and gave a low whistle. *That* was one way to piss off the whole world. It was also a fine way to keep all your subordinates from running off to other cities or tribes. Like an abuser killing off his victim's resources to the outside world.

When we told them what King Isce had done to the Diurnals, they were furious, Prince Kal continued. *They thought your kind strange and foreign too, but that perspective didn't make them feel better about your slaughter. We collected the most passionate ones along the way. Activists, artists, allies of all sorts. They wanted to come with us, to help stop it from happening again.* His internal voice cracked. *They've been helping us call out to your people for sixty years.*

So it was more than just guilt, the reason Queen Usai had been so intent on warning them. It was outrage. It was a fight for justice. It was an aro-wide attempt to halt evil in its tracks.

A lump bobbed in Joah's throat as they turned away from the metal star and began walking the High Road. A thick layer of moss now caked the pavement, muffling their footsteps.

It's as if we're already in the tunnel, huh? Misla said, smiling a little.

We've always been in a tunnel, in a way, Joah said. *Always heading in one direction, just following the High Road endlessly, blindly believing in General Deck—*

Again, Deckler's betrayal washed over him. Misla pursed her lips and nodded. Joah glanced sideways at her. His breath stuck inside his throat.

Her braids were knotted and frazzled. The ghost of a bruise still yellowed her eye. Dirt highlighted the smallest wrinkles in her forehead, and veins were starting to pop like tattoos in her temples. But she was somehow beautiful in her exhaustion, in her endless determination to keep marching forward, and Joah couldn't hide his urge to hold her again like they'd held each other in the conical tower. To touch her, to kiss her...

I'm sorry, he said, embarrassed, before his thoughts could expose more of this strange internal heat. Beside him, Damien stifled a snigger, and he sent a wordless warning at the boy.

I didn't hear anything, Misla said, passing him a wink.

A bluish glow the size of a coin highlighted their exit ahead. Joah let himself fall into musing silence as they approached it. He hadn't yearned for a woman since Blair. The desire felt awkward, clumsy, like he'd swallowed a lit cigar that was puffing out tendrils of guilt inside his stomach. He could just imagine it: his last night with Blair. She was whispering about babies, her lips cold against his earlobe, and her hands were creeping beneath his shirt, hardening him... but suddenly Misla's warm body flumped onto the quilt between them, and it was *her* fingers stroking his skin, and Blair dissolved in a wisp of moon-colored smoke.

Be prepared for anything, Prince Kal said, cutting through his visions.

Joah held up his rod. Misla gripped the ax with whitened knuckles. Hickory grumbled something about his tied hands, but nobody paid him attention as they ducked beneath stray fibermud tails hanging from the ceiling and entered the night.

Darkness had suffocated almost everything. Only the crooked remains of cotton trees rose toward the sky, which blazed with stars. As they crept down the High Road and passed these stumps, however, Joah saw tiny orange buds blossoming from the naked branches.

This phase of night is like grief, Prince Kal said. *It's as if the world has to grieve the loss of its sun before it can grow again. But after a few dozen moon cycles, the leaves come back. New grass grows. Animals you wouldn't dream of creep from their hideaways.*

Kal stroked his rod. *That's why we have to be on the lookout. The Calic is the only beast that dares attack us in high numbers, but other things can rise from the mud if we're alone.*

Damien, it seemed, couldn't control his excitement as the conical tower rose in the distance. The boy's breath fogged in front of him in quick bursts.

This was where I first heard you clearly, he told Kal. *You told me how to find the door.*

Yes, Prince Kal said. *I sensed the Calic prowling around the outskirts of our camp and wanted you to hide out somewhere safe until I could reach you. But that didn't go quite as planned, did it?* Here, Kal glanced at Joah and Misla. No, it hadn't gone to plan— because Joah and Misla had found the boy and frightened him into running away that very moon cycle.

As the tower loomed closer, Joah saw flicks of Damien's memories: he watched the boy stumble toward it and run his fingers along the outside wall, until he found a small notch and pressed his hand against the metal plate below it. Instantly, the walls slid apart with a rickety screech, revealing a gap like a popped-out tooth that now, cycles later, stared them in the face.

My father didn't want the Leather Skins getting in or out on their own, Prince Kal said, *so he made the door respond to cold fingerprints, not hot ones. In fact, the Leather Skins he sent to mine this sunsap never came back. He didn't want them spilling the secret of where the reserve was, see. There aren't many reserves as big as the one you're going to.*

"You mean the Leather Skins are still in there?" Misla asked, hushed, staring upward at the coned roof as if she could see watchful windows. "They could be in there right now? We didn't see any—"

Oh, my father wouldn't have let the Leather Skins live. After his guards obtained enough sunsap, he killed the ones who'd mined it before flying the starships back to our fortress by the sea. Prince Kal shrugged off his bag and tossed it to Damien, who caught it with quick fingers. *Go on in and see for yourself. I'm sure their skeletons are still there.*

"Hang on."

This was Hickory. He was whipping his head back and forth between Misla and Prince Kal, as if he could tell they'd been whispering to each other but didn't quite know what they were saying. "All this talk about something being in there. I need my hands free. What's the point of me coming along if I can't even punch a beast in the mouth, huh?"

"No," Joah said automatically, his jaw twitching with the effort to stop himself from punching *Hickory* in the mouth. "No way we're untying you."

Apparently there was a way, though. With a swift look at Prince Kal, Misla strode forward and stuffed the rusted handle of the old lantern into his mouth. Hickory tried to jerk away, but Kal held him in place until he bit down, eyes narrowed.

"I'll untie you," Misla said. She would have sounded sweet if her eyes hadn't been reflecting the glint of the ax now grasped with two hands. "But if that light falls, I won't hesitate to bury this blade into your heart. A blow for a blow, okay?" And she pointed at her chest, where her burn scar marred the soft place beneath the collar of her shirt. Hickory's doing.

Gagged by his own handle, he couldn't do anything but nod.

Joah wasn't going to make the mistake of undermining one of Misla's decisions again, but he couldn't quite look at her as he nodded goodbye to Prince Kal. It was enough to make his stomach writhe, the stench of Hickory's sweat and shit. For his wife's killer to walk beside them, free-handed? After the scene he'd come upon in the woods? Nauseating.

You can do it, Prince Kal said. *Just be wary, and not just of him. Remember, the Eternal Night may be... protective of the only thing keeping it alive for the next thirty years.*

Joah drew a deep breath, gripped his rod, and pressed forward into the tower. Misla, Damien, and Hickory followed.

Inside, bone fragments haloed that conical hole leading downward like a toilet bowl, but this time Joah focused on the bones he couldn't identify. As his eyes adjusted to the denser darkness, he squinted at a round one near his feet.

"Was this here the last time we were in here?"

They gathered around the object, which flickered in the light of Hickory's lantern. It was like a disk of shiny gray cartilage, umbrella-shaped and sprouting a stem of bone like a mushroom. Damien squatted to inspect it more closely.

"That's not a bone," he said solemnly. "It's a shell. Or *part* of a shell."

Gazing around, Joah saw dozens more littered around the room. He must have been too sick or worried to have noticed them the first time he had been here, but Damien was right—the objects were shells, and they had been abandoned here as surely as the skeletons of other creatures had.

The remains of Leather Skin slaves.

"I wouldn't—" Joah began, but Hickory had already bent to scoop up the shell at their feet. He held it by the stem and hugged it to his chest so that it looked like a shield.

His light didn't fall.

"Okay," Joah said, nodding to the edge of the hole in the ground. A narrow staircase wound down its rim into even more darkness. "You can go first, then."

Hickory grunted agreement and shuffled his way to the staircase. Joah wrapped his cloak tighter around himself as he followed suit. The hole seemed to exhale frost, and when he took his first step down, he felt like a man sinking through a frozen lake.

They moved carefully, pressed against the side of the winding wall, which roughened into dark, wet rock halfway down. The light from Hickory's lantern bobbed in front of them. Joah hadn't realized how much he had been depending on Prince Kal's skin until they reached the bottom, where murky water pooled on the ground. Here, the lantern only illuminated a few meters in front of them. A narrow channel, like a rocky throat, seemed to lead endlessly onward. Wiry white roots waved from the cracks in the rocks like hair in wind.

"Well, Glade?" Joah said. "See any booby traps? Are the walls going to collapse on us, or can we keep going?" He half-wanted to be told to stop, to turn around, to ascend.

Hickory struggled to talk through his rusted handle.

"There nothin' here. Keep going."

They splashed their way forward. The lantern flickered. The roots sprouting from the walls became thicker and longer, and they seemed to be swaying, wiggling like worms. Twice, Joah did a double take, thinking he'd seen a snake shoot from the mud as if to strike them. But no, it was just one of those tapered roots, and the lunge must have been a trick of the eye.

Hickory kept his Leather Skin shield in front of him. The air thickened the further they trekked, until puffs of hot air beat their faces. Hickory raised his shield. It blocked the worst of the heat, but the groundwater still wavered with steam that pricked their ankles.

There's something in here with us, Damien thought. His dark hair shined and curled with sweat. *I can tell by the—*

They turned a corner. Misla's sudden scream was gagged as something—thick and long and flexible—shot from the mud to wrap around her throat.

In that fractured moment when the spin of the aro slowed and Misla lurched backward toward the mud of the tunnel wall,

Joah understood perfectly. It wasn't snakes or spiders or scorpions that squirmed beneath the conical tower. It was only the roots of the Eternal Night.

And the Eternal Night would defend itself from thieves.

Joah rushed forward as more roots, some thick as tubers, others skinny as vines, wrapped themselves around Misla's body, pinning her to the mud. He yanked at the one choking her throat, but it only tightened, and Joah felt the sticky mucus coating its wood like a leech.

"Get off her!" he bellowed, wrenching and punching and kicking at the things that strangled her. The rosy flush in her cheeks was draining to her neck. The roots had pinned her arms above her head, and even the ax she had been holding disappeared in the squirming mess.

The light behind him dropped. A hand shoved him backward.

"Take *that*, you little fucker," Hickory snarled.

He pressed the shell of his Leather Skin shield against the root around her neck. It contracted like a branded worm, shrinking back into the mud.

Misla gasped. One by one, Hickory pressed his shield against the roots until they shriveled or wilted, releasing her from her rigid confinement. Joah could hear a sharp *tssss* as the shield made contact with each one. The shell was hot, had been absorbing the heat ahead of them like a beetle's back. That was probably why the Leather Skins had been able to mine the sunsap—not just because they could withstand the heat, but because their shelled armor grew as hot as the sunsap itself and allowed them to pass undetected.

Joah fished his rod from a steaming puddle. He didn't remember dropping it, but it wouldn't have been any use against the roots anyway... the dart could have missed and struck Misla instead. Now he pointed the rod at Hickory's back as Misla slumped to the ground and Damien scrambled forward to help her up.

Hickory withdrew, saw Joah pointing his rod, and gave a wheezing laugh.

"You're really gonna kill me for saving your new lover?"

"No," Joah said, "but I'm going to keep this right here until Misla picks up her ax."

Hickory's laugh was broken by a cough, a hack, and a flying wad of spit that landed near Joah's shoes. "I have a *shield*, Cadshaw. Better think twice before one of those darts bounces off and gets you in the eye. Or... no, don't think twice. Just do it. Let's see."

He tossed the Leather Skin shell from hand to hand as if preparing for a sports game, but Misla had already seized the ax. She stood there, panting and gripping the weapon with both hands. A red bruise noosed her neck. For a moment, she looked at the dead lantern lying half-submerged in a pool of water at her feet and seemed to consider following through with her promise to kill Hickory despite his reason for dropping it. Then her shoulders sagged.

"The sunsap's got to be close," she rasped. The tears in her eyes swam with light: an orange glow highlighted a widening in the tunnel ahead, where more tapered roots swayed from the ceiling like tentacles. "Hickory, you go first with your shield. I'll follow with —"

"Misla," Joah started. "Let me do it. I'll chop those things to pieces if I have to."

"No, I've got this. You just watch *him*." She jerked her head at Hickory. "Make sure he doesn't try anything funny." She threw a ragged braid over her shoulder. "Come on."

Joah didn't dare argue, not with that same fierce determination clenching her jaw like when she'd decided to go after Damien. They pressed on. The air shimmered with heat waves. Hickory held his shield out, but the shell could only block so much. Joah watched the back of Misla's cloak bloom with sweat as she swung at stray roots, and he couldn't help but gape in awe until beads of his own sweat rolled into his mouth—she'd been burned more than the rest of them, but still she plunged onward, wearing her newest burn like a goddamned necklace.

Don't make me blush, Misla sent back to him. *My face is hot enough as it is.*

Before long, the roots thickened into a squirming nest, crisscrossing and twisting and braiding together like the fibermud walls. Misla grunted as her movements quickened: raising the blade—*thwack*. Raising the blade—*thwack*. Whenever a stubborn one tried to twine itself around her arms or legs, Hickory pressed his shield against it and the thing would cringe away.

The tunnel curved again. Misla chopped through a final thicket. They rounded the corner.

"I'll be damned," Joah whispered, hushed.

They were on the edge of what looked like an underground river spreading from left to right, where the tunnel walls had split into a T. The liquid was thick, bubbly, and golden, radiating a furnace-fueled heat that reminded Joah of the fabled molten rock spewing from mountains in the north. More roots waved from the muddy ceiling, while others had sunk into the slow-moving stream to drink the sunlight they could no longer capture from their leaves.

Damien crouched and ran a finger through the sludge on the edge of the river. He winced as it no doubt blistered his skin.

"Strange," he said, staring at the surface of sunsap with eyes that reflected its fire. "I don't know of a single bug or slug that could survive this heat..."

"But?" Joah said, suddenly anxious at the awed gape of the boy's mouth.

"But we've been following a trail of mucus for the last few dozen meters or so. Whatever made it went straight into the river. And whatever it is, it's bigger than us."

Indeed, Joah could see the thin white film slathering the rocks and mud at their soggy feet now that Damien had pointed it out. He shivered for the first time since entering the tower.

"Okay, let's move fast, then." He dropped his bag and rummaged through the capsules within. A single liter would fuel a hundred kilometers, Queen Usai had told them, so they'd only have to fill five or six to fly themselves to the Green Sea, where the sun would still be winking on the horizon. "Damien, can you hand me the capsules while I fill them?"

They got to work. Joah positioned a capsule on the edge of the river until tails of sunsap rolled into its open ceramic mouth. When the container had filled to the brim, he screwed the lid back on and returned it to Damien, who passed him another empty one. Misla and Hickory stood guard on either side of them, poised to shield or hack if something were to lunge their way.

It happened three capsules down. The tip of Joah's thumb grazed a drip of sunsap. He cursed, popped his thumb in his mouth, and hissed when it burnt his tongue.

Misla jolted toward him, relaxing her hold on the ax, and Joah saw the quick, spinning arc of Hickory's Leather Skin shield: it flew through the air, plopped into the sunsap, sank into its depths, and disappeared. Hickory had chucked it aside to spring for Misla's ax.

For half a second, they wrestled with it. The blade swung dangerously close to Misla's nose. Hickory yanked. Misla released her hold, fell back, and howled as the roots behind her twined around her waist and began reeling her in again.

"*No,*" Joah said.

He made to stand, dizzy with panic—how foolish could Hickory have been, tossing aside the Leather Skin shell that had saved Misla last time? But when Hickory staggered around with the ax raised like a flag, a crazed smile ripped his face, and Joah knew the man neither knew nor cared that the woman he used to love was clawing and retching and dying once again.

In a flash, Joah scooped up his rod, pointed it at Hickory's throat, and twisted. A dart whizzed outward but stuck into a swaying root above his head instead.

Hickory charged, swinging his old weapon with a roar. Joah raised one of his capsules like a shield, but it was no Leather Skin shell. The ceramic shattered as the blade struck it. The sunsap from within poured onto his chest, and he fell in a writhing spasm to the riverbank. Heat waves curled around his neck, and his chest pulsed with scorching agony.

"*I'll bury one of those sleek darts in your head,*" Hickory jeered. "Remember telling me that, Cadshaw? Remember *threatening* me?" He pressed his boot against Joah's throat, pinning him to the hot, rocky ground, searing his skull. "Don't make promises you can't keep, bitch."

Hickory brought up the ax again, and Joah's vision turned white. He knew he was about to die, knew his neck would split like his wife's had. From what seemed like far away, Misla was still shrieking.

Then the river exploded in a flurry of tiny, burning droplets that peppered Joah's cheeks with new pokers of pain.

Hickory howled. Joah squinted in disbelief at what he was seeing: a hunched figure rising from the depths of the sunsap, one hand clawing its way toward the bank with long, blackened fingers, the other pushing against the sunsap with the Leather Skin shield that Hickory had thrown in. The figure hoisted itself upward, sunsap dripping off its shelled body, and fixed its beetle-like eyes upon the ax reflecting fire in Hickory's hands. It didn't have a dozen eyes, but the rounded marks on its shell of a face *looked* like a dozen eyes.

Leather Skin, Damien cried from across the cavern.

Joah knew the boy was right, but he couldn't see how it was possible. *My father wouldn't have let the Leather Skins live,* Prince Kal had told them.

Yet here one stood, apparently immune to the heat of the sunsap, its hands curved like pincers, mucus oozing from its face. It wasn't leathery by any means, but its skin was like a snail's armor, like the shell in its grip.

"You." Hickory's hand trembled with the effort to point a finger at the creature.

You, the Leather Skin said back, a single voiceless word that escaped its mind like steam through volcanic cracks in the aro. It raised the shield in its pincer. *Where did you get this?*

Hickory, of course, didn't hear. "You," he said again, staggering around. Ruddy blotches had sprouted all over his face. "*You're* a Nocturnal. A true one—"

Stop. The Leather Skin pointed at Hickory's ax with a hairy finger. *Drop the weapon. There shall be no more murders here. This place is sacred.*

Joah tried to stand, but collapsed in a panting heap. He had to get to Misla. Across the cavern, Damien was pouring sunsap from the capsules onto the roots that bound her, but he was only succeeding in pissing the things off, it seemed; they would retract and snarl forward again, wrapping around Misla's ankles and wrists as she thrashed in their grip.

Joah began crawling toward them, never mind the mud that blistered his palms and knees through his pants. But Hickory saw him and seemed to decide, with a vicious scowl, to finish Joah off before attending to the monstrous creature before them. He raised his ax again.

The Leather Skin hurled his shield. It struck Hickory's raised wrists, and the ax spun from his hands, landing with a *thwump* a breath from Joah's fingers.

Hickory screamed and dove toward the Leather Skin instead, closing his hands around its shelled throat. The creature's eyes popped in their sockets for a moment, bloodied with shock—then it twisted, and soon both monsters were writhing in each other's grips.

Joah wrenched his gaze away from the humanoid insect that had once stared at him from the poster on General Deckler's office wall. He crawled around the ax, grabbed the shield wobbling beside it, and dragged the thing toward Misla across the cavern. He shouldered Damien aside and pressed the shield against the roots coiled around her.

They retracted like worms touched by sunlight. Misla fell forward, coughing and gasping, onto her hands and knees.

"We need to fill the capsules," she panted, her voice hoarse, "and get the fuck out of here. This place is going to kill us." She made to stand, but crouched back down when the spinning mass of Hickory and the Leather Skin shot past them.

"You killed my grandfather," Hickory was panting. "They drew pictures of you." He rammed his fist into the other's ash-black jawline. "You're the Nocturnal I've been waiting for."

I'm not a Nocturnal, the Leather Skin spat, trying to close his pincers around Hickory's throat. *The Nocturnals killed everyone here but me.*

And Joah got flashes of the Leather Skin's memories: when King Isce's men had executed the others, this one had slipped away, had taken refuge in the sunsap and remained here for more than sixty years. But now the skeleton of one of its fellow slaves had sunk into its home, and the flicker of Hickory's blade had brought that violence back with blunt force.

So they spun in circles, a boulder-like man dancing with a humanoid creature on crooked scuttling spider legs. Hickory's fury had cracked his face into a million pieces, and the heat rash scaling his skin made him look less than human. He pummeled the other again and again, rooted in his belief that the creature in his grip was a Nocturnal, that it had killed his grandfather so long ago and sent Hickory's family cascading into poverty. Executing the Infected had never been enough for his revenge. Now he had the opportunity to kill the actual thing he thought he hated.

"Hickory," Joah choked out. "Hickory, open your mind."

Hickory didn't hear. He had knocked the Leather Skin to the ground and was thumping a fist into his face... a fist that bounced back; unfazed, the Leather Skin closed his pincers around Hickory's throat again and threw him sideways... They rolled closer to the sunsap.

"Hickory!" Joah was suddenly shouting. "*Listen* to him. He didn't kill your grandfather, it wasn't him! And the ones like him never wanted to! It's a whole lot more complicated, dammit! OPEN YOUR MIND AND LISTEN."

But Hickory either couldn't or wouldn't listen. He ripped himself from the Leather Skin's hold and plunged for his ax.

The Leather Skin barreled toward him and wrapped his arms around the man who would, if left unchecked, turn him into a headless corpse, as his fellows had been so long ago. The pair seemed to hover sideways in an embrace for a small eternity, the ax handle slipping from Glade's beefy fingers like a stubborn fish: going...going...gone.

Then Hickory and the Leather Skin toppled into the river as a single unit. The sunsap embraced them both in a slurping kiss, swallowing Hickory's scream whole.

Silence. Damien's eyes were round as moons. Misla was still panting. Holes riddled her clothes where the splatters of sunsap had burned her, adding to her collection of scars. Various parts of Joah's body flared with blistering heat. The chill of the Eternal Night sounded like bliss, yet he and the other two waited, breathless, for Hickory to emerge.

After a dozen heartbeats of silence, Joah knew he never would. The Leather Skin would be laying his body to rest beneath the blood of the Eternal Night.

He glanced at the remaining ceramic containers lying in the water at their feet. They needed to fill the things and get away from this underground gut of fire before it cooked them. They needed to ride the starship to daybreak and save the Sunsetters from being killed or collected like cattle. But Joah felt mesmerized by Hickory's death. At how it had happened.

If Hickory had let himself become Infected, he would have known the truth of things. He wouldn't have gone for a guiltless Leather Skin. He wouldn't have raised the ax on Joah. Hell, he wouldn't have swung down on Blair's neck all those years ago. He would have heard her thoughts as Joah had led her—God, *led* her —to her death. He would have understood that the real threat was a corrupt general and a king waiting for them on the edge of the Green Sea, not a crazed woman in shackles or a slave who had been hiding from violence for over sixty years.

But Hickory had not opened his mind. And now he was gone. Blair's killer was gone. Misla's abuser was gone. The man who would have executed Damien with a smirk on his face was gone. He was gone along with the ignorance Joah might still be harboring if he'd never ventured into the Eternal Night.

All that remained now were the capsules of sunsap, the three of them holding each other, and a suffocating tunnel of boiling grief. And Joah was ready to find his way out of it.

"C'mon," he told the others. "We have a sunset to catch."

See Mariah Montoya's story "The Nocturnals IV" online at Metaphorosis.
If you liked it, leave a comment. Authors love that!
And see the conclusion of "The Nocturnals" next month in Metaphorosis!
Remember to subscribe to our e-mail updates so you'll know when new stories are posted.

September

Tumbler

B. Morris Allen

A spider hung across from me, the barbed spikes of its legs dug deep into the walls of its prison. It was caged in a network of tunnels and tubules that wrapped around and through each other in an immense tangle. Trapped. Just like me.

I freed a leg and waved at it. They never waved back. Something drove me to keep trying, some visceral urge to communicate, to share more than just "Good fungus this way" or "Break in the tunnel ahead". I did a little dance, to show I wasn't just stretching. I lifted each leg in turn, sending a ripple of motion around my perimeter. It was a pointless risk, and yet it felt good, and I sent the ripple around again and again. *This is forever,* the ripple said. *Though it starts and stops, though it is incomplete, this is a cycle capable of endless repetition.*

The other fixed its eyestalks on me, but made no move. Perhaps metaphysics is too much to ask from a simple dance.

In the Out, white scudded across the blue. Soon, we would roll. I could feel it in the flexing of the tubes, in the shifts across the tangle. In its tubule, the other spider bobbed back and forth with the flex. Or I did. We came closer, tantalizingly close, the transparent walls of our tubules almost touching, our bodies almost belly to belly across the distance. Then the flex pulled us apart again, and we were rolling. As we parted, I saw the other raise one leg, then another, in a clumsy imitation of my dance. And then it lost its hold with the roll, and it wrapped its legs around it in a tough, chitinous ball that rattled away down the tubes toward the ever-shifting bottom.

I watched it go, until distance and tunnel walls obscured it from view. It had answered, or tried to. I was sure of it. Why else let go so close to a roll? *Because the fungus was exhausted,* common sense answered. *Because it was frightened of your strangeness*, said my own fear.

Because it understood, hope responded. *Because it too wants more than this endless maze. Wants purpose, wants togetherness.*

What togetherness consisted of, I wasn't sure. Someone I could talk with about the hazy, half-formed dreams that came to me while I digested, the drive that had led me to learn to dance, to turn jerky, unnatural motion into a smooth, gliding celebration of freedom.

I wanted to fold my legs in, to pull my head in and curl into a ball and let gravity take me where it would through the tunnels, to proclaim my happiness by letting nature have its way with me. I could feel my tip segments flexing with the desire to let go. But if I did, how would the other ever find me?

Instead, I clung like a mite to a spore body, too young to know the world, too soft to survive it. I clung, and I waited.

Our roll was a short one. The tangle fetched up against a boulder in the Out, and though wind pushed us to and fro, we were fixed in place once more, until the wind should shift.

My loop of the tangle had fetched up near the top, the curves of the tube slanting down to both sides. Above me, the blue was achingly clear, only accentuated by wisps of white floating away to the unknown. They moved slowly, like a spiderling just learning to crab its way across the walls and past the dense mycelium of the spore body. Were the white things tangles, I wondered? Distant relatives of our own, but unbound from the soil of the surface, and with spiders of their own living amongst the white?

I would never know. No one would. We were trapped here, all of us, in the endless labyrinth of clear walls and soft surfaces.

Eating always makes me feel better. I released my barbs and scuttled across to the mat of fungus that had brought me here in the first place. To my under-eyes, it was even juicier than it had first appeared, and I gathered it eagerly with my mandibles, ripping out hunks and passing them to my mouth for ingestion. Other spiders avoided these outer paths, but the warm light that made them feel strange invigorated me. It had made me larger than most, my outer shell tougher, more rigid. There were paths in the interior where I could no longer pass, like a spiderling barred forever from the spore bodies that had borne it, its hard body no longer welcome in the cushioning moss of the spore beds.

It didn't matter to me. Out here, the fungus was richer, the light brighter. And there was the Out — the fascinating reach of plains and gullies, of boulders and trees, those strange creatures with their straight trunks, and wild, tangle-like tops that swayed in the wind, but never rolled away.

'Watch for the Out!' was the cry that came down the passageways at times. 'Break ahead! Cling tight!' And we let those tunnels fill with fungus until they healed or closed entirely. Because to approach the Out was to be lost forever, to never feel the roll of wind again, to be left behind, exposed and alone.

You can be alone in the tangle, said my contrary mind. *You are alone*, said my heart.

I wasn't, though. Before a day had passed, that other spider was back. It was the same, I was sure. It had been a Seven, its strong, thick limbs a sharp contrast to my own more fragile nine. And the scarlet swirls across the upper carapace that had reminded me of a tree shedding its tangle were the same.

It settled itself on the wall of the tunnel opposite, clinging to the far side, so that its upper-eyes could stare across at me. I scuttled up to a similar position and waved.

It watched me. I imagined the climb it must have had, from wherever the roll had flung it. It would be tired. And uncertain whether what it had seen was a message, or just a spider in the throes of mold-sickness.

I did my circle dance again, once, twice, three times. Then I reversed course, and ran the circle the other way. Three times. No mold-sickness here.

I could see Red Tree cast an eye to the blue above. It was still, with thick sheets of white layered on each other like a fungus mat not touched for weeks. With a slow, tentative motion, Red Tree raised one leg, planted it deliberately. Lifted another leg, planted it. Then another. With each leg, it moved quicker, more surely, until at last its dance was a slow, stately, seductive ripple. Once, twice, thrice around.

I did a little dance of my own, a formless, bouncing swirl of jubilation. At last! After countless weeks of blank stares, I had a partner in my mania at last. I raised two legs to it in a salute. After a moment, it raised its own. The two of us, reaching out to each other across the gap, across the tubes. Pointless, unless we met.

And yet, how could we? The tangle was a maze of tubes that wove in and out, that crossed and knotted, and occasionally connected. But where? I had never given much thought to it, had never tried to map the tangle beyond In and Out, core and edge, up and down, and those latter changed with ever roll, every shift.

Here, we could see each other, could dance for each other and ourselves. It was more than I had ever really hoped for. And already it was not enough. Already, I longed to touch the other, to feel the hard gloss of Red Tree's shell beneath my barbs, to talk, to ask my questions that had no answers.

I looked through my tubule, across the gap. I could see where Red Tree's tube curved up to the left, to where it entered a dense knot of threads that promised narrow passages and tight spaces. Too tight for me, and perhaps even for Red Tree, with its smaller, stiffer Seven body.

To the right, Red Tree's tube spun down into a coil that wrapped around several others before diving briefly toward the core and then lifting back out — toward me! And my own right hand tunnel sank down in a similar direction.

I lifted one leg, then, two, then a daring three, and pointed them, waved them all to the right. *Go right,* I urged with all the power in me. *Meet me — there.*

Red Tree raised a leg. Not one of those on the right, however. Instead, it waved it up and down, in a languid motion, like a spiderling testing its balance. Then it scuttled forward, up the near side of its tube, until its underside faced me, and its under-eyes emerged to to give what was no doubt a blurry picture at such distance.

We marked walls from time to time, of course, scratches at the intersections, a few symbols that meant 'Break' or 'Fungus' or 'Danger! Water!'. But those were superficial, and lasted only a day or two before the walls healed. I'd never seen such deliberate damage, damage that would take weeks to regrow, or even months. A careless jab might even let water in, and with it the strand-sickness that could turn a spider's legs to useless, ductile sprigs of bristle.

Regardless of the danger, Red Tree raised another leg, plunged it in and ripped out another chunk of wall, over and over until a rough circle of divots surrounded it. I'd never seen anything like it.

When it was done at last, Red Tree gave a two-legged salute, then backed down to the floor of its tunnel, where it could see me with its upper-eyes.

It seemed to be waiting for something. Was this a dance of its own, I wondered? Its own celebration of life, of risk?

It seemed impatient. It raised its nearest leg, waved it in my direction, then raised it and slowly, pointedly, lowered it to the floor, barbs extended. I watched as it repeated the motion.

It had repeated my dance. It seemed only polite that I should do the same. I scuttled up to the tunnel wall closest to Red Tree. From my under-eyes, I could see no more than a vague shape, a blob of red and black across the way. I could see the wall of the tunnel much more clearly. It was bare here of fungus, which tended to grow on the inner, more protected surfaces. The wall was thick, its tough outer rind barely visible through a softer, more flexible inner surface the depth of my shortest legs. Mine was a tube in middle age, still growing, still well nourished from the core, with feeder hairs that picked up moisture when it was at the bottom, and blocked some of the harsher light when it was at the top like now.

It was a healthy tube, in other words, unlikely to crack open no matter what I did to it. I was safe from the Out, would be taking no chances. I raised a leg tentatively, and saw Red Tree bounce in satisfaction. I thrust the spike of my leg hard into the wall. It sank in smoothly to the first joint, and my barbs came out instinctively, anchoring me against unexpected turbulence. I withdrew the barbs and pulled the leg out.

I saw immediately that it wasn't having the desired effect, that the spike simply withdrew as smoothly as it had gone in, just as it was designed to do; as it had always done before. Across the way, Red Tree hunkered down in disappointment, as I read it.

I stopped, and pushed the leg back in. I had never reused a spike hole this way. It felt strange, the gel of the wall giving way before my spike, almost welcoming it. I extended my barbs again, and pulled. I pulled tentatively at first, uncertain. But the barbs held as they were meant to, and the material of the wall refused to give way. I pulled harder, and harder, until I began to feel a pain in my joint. It grew and grew, until it felt as if the leg would part, the way they sometimes do in really terrible storm rolls. It had only happened to me a few times, but it hurt — a lot — and took weeks to regrow.

Across from me, I could see Red Tree with my under-eyes, a blurry figure doing something with a near leg. I ignored it and went back to my pulling.

The strain was worse, and I felt as if I'd done something to the joint. It hurt worse now, and the barbs were moving less, if possible.

The barbs! Red Tree had partially retracted its barbs, I remembered. Of course it had. I laughed and bobbed as I realized. My joint hurt, but I gleefully raised another leg and plunged it into the wall. With a smooth motion, I retracted the barbs almost all the way and jerked it loose. It felt unnatural, this half-in, half-out position, but the barbs cooperated, and the leg ripped loose from the wall along with a satisfying crumble of wall material.

It made an unsightly, distinctive mark, and suddenly I understood. The mark was the point of it all. Red Tree had marked its tube so that it would know where our meeting point was, and now I had done the same with mine. The tubes would shift a little, with time, but now we knew where our initial meeting place had been. At least in this one place, we were close enough to see each other, to communicate in the limited way we had. I gave Red Tree a two-legged salute, then went back to my marking, working all around my perimeter, in a violent version of my circle dance, until I was surrounded by my own ring of divots. They would take weeks to heal. Where once that would have filled me with an unnamed dread, now I felt only warm satisfaction. No longer the telltale sign of a risk of the Out, this ring was my mark. Mine and Red Tree's.

I crabbed back down to the floor of the tunnel, where I could deploy my upper-eyes. Red Tree saluted with two precise legs, then pointed off to the right, to where our tubes might meet. I did the same, and with slow, excited purpose, we set off.

We lost sight of each other soon enough. My tunnel was unfrequented, and hazed with fungus across most of its breadth. Not thick, but enough to obscure my vision. When I paused to eat a space clear, I found the fungus tough and chewy, the result of infrequent harvesting that ate away the juicy upper layers and left the thick lower ones alone. When I'd cleared a fair portion, I crept away and looked through with my upper-eyes. I could see what I thought was Red Tree's tube, angling away now toward the core, while mine traveled perpendicular, along the middle surface.

It wasn't long before I reached an intersection, a place where tubules had grown close enough that their walls had merged, and the interior barriers atrophied to nothing. One of the ways led down toward the core, and I turned to follow it with joy.

I had gone only a few bodylengths when I turned back. Red Tree had taught me to mark my way, and I returned to the intersection. The new tube was younger, thinner, but more pliable. I settled for a shallower trio of marks, pointing back the way I'd come, like the spike of a thick leg pulling out of the wall.

Toward the wall, I told myself. *You come from the wall, go back toward the wall.* It should be enough. If I could remember to look. I crawled away down the new tunnel, mind tight with discipline, heart warm with adopted cleverness.

I wandered for a week before I came back to the surface. We had rolled this way and that, and I'd spent a whole day, once, clinging tight to a tunnel while a storm flung the tangle around, battering us against rocks and trees until tubules broke on every hand, and deadly water found its way into the tunnels. Spiders crawled frantically one way and another to avoid rivulets, rills, and even puddles until the walls could absorb it all. When the rain stopped at last, a gale rolled us on, and spider after spider fell through the gaps into the Out. I was tired and bruised by the time I found my way back to my ring of divots.

I had mapped extensively since I left, from the surface toward the core, from the loose, dangerous outer paths to the tight, constricting inner ones. Half my paths had broken open, it seemed, and it had taken me days to find alternate routes. In none of them had I seen any sign of Red Tree.

Yet here it was, waiting by its own ring of divots, in the tunnel across from me. The tubes were nearer each other now, and I could see it more clearly. The swirls of red looked less like a tree now, more random, and I thought Red Tree itself looked larger. Perhaps it had spent its time nearer the surface, while I had been forcing my way into the smaller inner tunnels.

I saluted it, and shrugged. *What now?*

It climbed over next to its mark, and made several more. They looked like a square with a point at the top, pointing toward the divots.

I understood it, this time. I climbed up and made my own triangle of marks, pointing toward my divots, then climbed back down. Our signatures. I had seen plenty of marks in my wandering, but none of Red Tree's. A shrug from across the way said it had not seen mine.

Was this all there was? Had we found each other, spent so much effort, only to have it come to nothing, to nothing more than vague philosophy across the distance? *This dance is forever*, my mind mocked bitterly.

Red Tree was dancing anyway. It was a complex sequence, full of stops and starts and circles and shifts, with sometimes one leg in motion, sometimes two or three or four, and I marveled at Red Tree's bravery. We were at rest, our tubes low on the side of the tangle, but a wind might roll us at any moment, and with only three legs holding, Red Tree would be forced to ball up and let fate have its way.

It took time, but eventually I thought I understood. Red Tree had found a distinctive intersection, where a total of five tubules crossed and merged in a complex pattern. It suggested we should try to meet there, or near there. With so many intersections, our odds of success should improve.

I had seen no such cluster, but the idea of a definite target gave me hope. And it was something I could ask about. I had tried, in my travels, to ask about Red Tree, but the other spiders seemed confused by the notion. 'Some spiders are red and black,' they had said. 'Some are green and black, like you.' We had gotten no further than that.

I bobbed up and down to signal assent, but Red Tree was not finished. I caught on quicker this time. With much awkward stretching and stroking of eyestalks, it indicated that it had only *seen* the intersection, but not yet reached it. Nonetheless, it seemed a good target.

Somewhere *that* way, it indicated, with a leg jabbed toward the interior and the upper left. Direction could be tricky in the tangle, I'd found. The tubules wrapped and twisted so much that no direction remained constant for long, but for coreward and surfaceward, and In and Out.

We spent the day resting and eating, and occasionally dancing. We communicated nothing but joy and partnership, and longing, but it was enough. I crept as close to the wall as I could, and watched Red Tree hungrily, forming the scarlet spirals on its shell into trees and clouds and fungus and desire. It watched me the same way, both of us reaching out for something more, something that would bring us beyond the pointless maze and give us meaning. When I changed my circle dance, so that instead of just lifting legs, my whole body swirled in a circle, it bobbed and saluted in a three-legged gesture of joy.

The next day, we set off again. I went to the left this time, down the path that seemed to lead away. But I had already learned that the tunnels seldom went where they seemed to. And off to the right, I'd seen no sign of the five tube crossing. This way was as good as any other.

I wandered for two weeks before I came cross a hint of it. I was down toward the core, wedged in as close as I could get, where the spiders were more plentiful, and even spiderlings hesitantly crawled the walls. They shied away from me, as small next to my bulk as our tangle was to a tree.

One spider, though, a mottled yellow Five, knew the intersection.

"Yes," it said, after we'd given up on any explanation of why it was important. "This tunnel. That way." It waved a leg. "Old tunnels, fragile." Answer given, it scuttled off in search of fresh fungus.

I followed the tunnel it indicated, waiting at every intersection until a spider passed by who knew the way. I found three way intersections, and a four way intersection, but not five, and I began to despair, thinking that perhaps one guide or another had simply miscounted. But to a spider, four is an unnatural number. It's hard to confuse with five. I still had hope.

Yet it was with surprise that one day I suddenly found myself in the intersection itself. I'd been wandering slowly, stopping to eat at every opportunity, for fungus was scarce here. The tunnel walls were old and brittle, in some places almost dead, with few of the xylem veins the fungus tapped into. The walls had opaqued with age, a sure sign of malnourishment, and in one perilous place, I had even found a leg-sized hole right through the wall to the Out. It had been a dry day, but I'd passed the place by as quickly as I could manage, ignoring the intriguing scents that flooded the tunnel nearby.

The memory of those scents had stayed with me — the tantalizing richness of the air, the fearful feel of moisture, the shuddery sense of Out coming In.

I had stopped at a three-way intersection to rest and mark my way. That done, I wandered into the new tunnel, searching for fungus, when I realized that the new tunnel intersected another, and that that one crossed yet another. Five tunnels! Five tubules intersecting! This was it, or at least its double, and I'd seen no other such intersection in all my wandering.

I had made it. It was a strange mix of excitement and disappointment. While I had searched, I had had a goal, a purpose. Now that I had reached that goal, I had nothing again. Red Tree was not here, and though I searched and searched, there was no sign that it had been here. The fungus was sparse and tough and hardly worth harvesting. The whole region was so rickety that it felt unsafe even to sit here with all nine legs dug into the wall. The walls themselves felt so thin they might be pierced by a careless spike, and they were so opaque that that I could barely see a body length outside them.

But I was here. Red Tree would come. It should be here already, in fact, for it had known of the intersection before. But only from a distance, I reminded myself. It had seen the intersection from outside. Which meant it had been in a newer, more transparent tubule.

I flung myself into the search again, looking now for fresh nearby tubules. Heedless of risk, I sought out the thin spots in old walls, where their scarred opacity was offset by attenuated frailty. There was barely enough to hold onto here, but I could see. Toward the end of the second day, I found it —— a clear, thin window of tubule from which I could see a familiar red and black shape, legs waving welcome.

I returned from another fruitless exploration to find Red Tree already waiting. Not only waiting, but marking, ripping out chunk after chunk of wall with a fervor that made me worry for its sanity. We were near the top of the tangle today, and I could see from the dark clouds above that a storm was on its way — a wild thing that could pick up our tangle and throw it bodily through the air. I would have to move away to find a safe spot to shelter, away from these friable walls and their risk of the Out. I had come by only for a few more moments close to Red Tree.

It continued its assault on the tunnel walls, well past a circle now. With every pull of barbed leg, a larger chunk of wall material ripped out, until it was clinging to a veritable pit, its body so deep in the wall that its head was flush with the surface. And still it kept digging.

Red Tree had already demonstrated that it was smarter than I was, or more intuitive. It wasn't until it plunged a spike all the way through the outer wall that I finally understood. It was cutting through. If we could not find our way to each other through the tunnels, it would come to me across the Out.

I could feel my flesh creep away from my shell inside me. To go to the Out, deliberately! Knowing the risk. Knowing it might never come back. And all because I had danced.

The moment seemed to stretch for days, but perhaps it was only moments before I too was attacking my wall. The old material chipped away easily, but in tiny flakes. Across the way, I could see Red Tree's scratched, battered spikes cutting through the wall of its tunnel, ripping away long shreds of glassy fiber.

Around us, the roar of the wind picked up as the storm reached us. Within moments, we were rolling, tumbling this way and that, and bouncing high into the air one moment, crashing down onto the plain the next. Through it all, we continued our assault — Red Tree tearing its hole wider and wider with its barbs, and I throwing myself bodily against the wall until I was covered with a dusting of powder and flakes.

The storm worsened, and I began to fear that the rain would come before we finished, before we made the crossing. I'd seen a spider with the thread-sickness once from stumbling into a storm leak, and it had been pitiful. Unable to grip the walls, unable to roll into a proper ball, it had been battered to pieces by the roll of the tangle. I didn't want that to happen to Red Tree, or to me.

The rain held off, but the wind began to howl, and the pressure through the holes we'd carved made it even harder to hold on. But we did, and at last the holes were big enough for Red Tree's smaller body. I forced my way as far into my hole as I could, stretching four legs across the gap, with four more inside, and one more braced on the outside of the tube. It was surprisingly rough and hard, not like the soft gel of the interior. But it gave a good grip, and that was all I cared about.

Across the way, Red Tree bobbed a few times, then gave a quick salute, and jumped. I think it jumped. I'd never seen a spider jump before, but Red Tree was a wild one; it had already proved that. Perhaps it was only the roll of the tangle, or the jolt of the wind, but I like to think it jumped.

In any case, before I knew it, it was on me, its shell hard next to mine, smooth and glossy as seven legs scrabbled for purchase. I threw my four outer legs around it, tangling awkwardly with its own, and extending my barbs in desperation as I felt it slip, slip away.

I felt Red Tree's own barbs extending, felt one catch in a knee joint, then another, forced my own spike through one of its legs as well, until we were locked together as tightly as a mite swathed in a spore body.

And then the storm ripped us loose. A gust of wind threw the tangle high in the air, and slammed it down hard on a boulder. I felt a leg tear loose at the joint, felt Red Tree fall away.

I didn't stop to think, to fear. I pushed with all my inside legs and felt a part of my shell crack as I forced it through the outer wall. The storm lifted the tangle, and we fell, away from it, into the Out.

We landed hard. I felt two more legs break, and the crack in my shell widened. When I put out an upper-eye, I could see all the way through my shell, into the soft flesh of my interior. It struck me how much I was like the tangle, in a way — supple on the inside, tough on the outside. And now my inside was out, and I was too.

"I liked your dance," said Red Tree, and I whirled my eye stalks toward it. It lay next to me, its beautiful red-black shell still whole, the abstract swirls more beautiful than ever before, even less like a tree than ever, but more like something else, something better, more pure. More Red Tree. All its legs were broken, two of them ripped out completely, and I could see the ichor leaking out of them. Treacherous rills of it wended their way toward the pool that I could see under me with my under-eyes. I watched as they merged into one sickly white puddle.

"You're beautiful," I said.

The rain came down and washed us clean. Already I could feel the thread sickness, and I could see the tendrils creeping out of Red Tree's broken joints. I stretched out three legs, and dragged my way over to it, ignoring the pain in my shell, and the odd, cool feel of the rain pouring into me. I stretched my long limbs over Red Tree's dark shell, ignoring the long hairs that stretched blindly toward the water and the soil below. They dug their way in, and I could feel myself tied down, anchored to the Out, where I would never move again.

"It feels right," Red Tree said, and I didn't have to ask what it meant. It felt right to be here, to be with each other at last, no matter the cost. And it felt right to have the thread-sickness, to feel it tie me closer to the earth. I could feel the water now, feel myself drinking it up through the root tendrils, feel it giving rise to new growth inside me.

Under me, Red Tree's shell began to soften, and I could feel the echo of my own pain inside it — the good pain of change and discovery. Already, a stem was rising from the soft muddle of Red Tree's innards, and I felt one rising in me as well. With a last clumsy thrust of my eye stalk, I pushed my stem to the side, and watched it wind around Red Tree's, in a tangle that might never come free.

See B. Morris Allen's story "Tumbler" online at Metaphorosis.
If you liked it, leave a comment. Authors love that!
Remember to subscribe to our e-mail updates so you'll know when
new stories are posted.

About the story

I don't remember the genesis of this story, only that I had the image of people living inside a giant, transparent tumbleweed, able to signal each other, but having to develop a kind of semaphore. It was only later that they turned into spiders, and later yet that I understood what they wanted and how the lifecycles of spider and tumbleweed intertwined.

Till All the Hundred Summers Pass

J.A. Legg

"*Spindle*, this is *Sky Castle*; come in, *Spindle*."

Aurora grabbed a handhold and pulled herself to the front of the command module as the voice came through her headset—the first signal from home the ship had received since travelling back through the wormhole. The first word from Earth in over a year.

Her pulse quickened as she pressed the button on her mic. "This is *Spindle*," she breathed. "Aurora King speaking; how soon until you can bring us home? Over."

She heard the cold slap of palms against rungs in the ladder shaft that led down to the spinning gravity wheel. It was Fairburn, come to relieve her at the end of her seven-hour shift. He thrust himself up the tunnel and grabbed a headset hanging near the entrance. He was a few minutes early, and she thought about clocking out, but Commander Grimm could be pretty rigid about time stamps. She pulled up the map on the monitor in front of her, trying not to look at him. Her muscles tightened.

Fairburn nodded. "Talking to someone?"

"*Sky Castle*," she nodded. "We're in home space. Just short of Neptune's orbit." The *Spindle*'s blue dot blipped toward a green light on the far end of the screen. *Blip. Blip.*

"Almost home," he breathed.

Home. It seemed strange to Aurora, after all she'd been through, to describe Earth that way. Especially since the one thing she had missed—the one thing she really wished she could come back to, the one person that really felt like home—wouldn't be there.

Phil.

The engagement ring he had given her still hung around her neck, and she'd clipped a photo of him to the glass on her ship's berth. They were good reminders—but just reminders. Shadows. Cheap copies of the real Phil. They weren't enough.

Especially because he was *supposed* to be here. On the ship. With her.

"Where's Grimm?" Fairburn asked.

"Dinner break," she answered flatly, careful not to turn her head. "He'll be back soon, I'm sure." She reached down to the communicator clipped to her belt and clicked the pager button. The commander would want to be here when the next word from *Sky Castle* came in.

Fairburn glided through the module's null gravity, then coasted to a stop beside her at the control interface. She fixed her attention forward, away from him.

"*Spindle*, we have a lock on your coordinates and we're sending you our information," came the voice in their headsets. "Can you confirm your trajectory?"

Fairburn scanned the information. "Confirm, *Sky Castle*." He took his hand off the button, then paused before speaking again.

"Will you tell?" he asked.

Tell what you did to him, Fairburn? she thought. *Tell how you took him from me?*

"No," she said at last. Even if she did, it wouldn't change anything. Phil would still be gone.

More silence.

"He's long dead now, you know," Fairburn said.

Aurora glared at him. Her fingers clenched into a fist. "Do you have to?" she rasped.

He turned back to study the interface.

"Look at me," she said, louder.

His finger traced the ship's trajectory across the monitor. He drummed against the edge of the control panel in time with the blue dot flashing on the screen. Her shift ended.

"*Look* at me."

Aurora wrenched his shoulder back so that he faced her, away from the starboard wall. He stared and let the uncomfortable silence hang in the air. She studied him closely, searching for a hint of remorse. Nothing.

Unbelievable.

Somewhere in the back of her mind it registered that Commander Grimm could come back at any moment, but she didn't care. She had had enough. She kicked off from the edge of the control panel and pushed him hard against the far wall, teeth clenched. Fairburn collided with the metal, his face still hard as her blow sent her back toward the module's other side.

"You got what you wanted. I'm here. You're here. And he's not. Isn't that enough?" There was a crack in her voice. *Damn it.*

"*Spindle*?" asked the headset. "Looks like you'll be crossing into our orbit in another twelve hours. We're adjusting course to meet with you then. You'll be home soon."

Fairburn kicked toward the interface. "Confirm, *Sky Castle*," he said. "See you then."

He looked out into the void. The sound of hands on rungs came up again through the tunnel. Grimm was back from dinner.

"I didn't get *every*thing I wanted, Aurora," he told her at last, levelly. "You know that."

Didn't get everything I wanted. She thought back to the offer he'd made her, back on the planet. It still made her stomach turn.

You didn't get me.

"Yeah," she said. "Yeah, well, neither did the rest of us."

The commander emerged into the module. Aurora ignored him and made for the exit. She pushed past Fairburn, past Grimm, swung her body toward the tunnel, then dropped feet-first toward the floor below.

"Not even close."

Aurora had been eleven when she'd first studied NASA's launch of the *Dove* and *Olive* probes through the wormhole nearly a century before. She'd been working on a school project with her dad; he was an amateur astronomer himself, and he knew how to talk about science so that everyone in earshot would love it like he did. Especially Aurora.

She listened in rapt attention as he explained the physics behind the wormhole using one of her mother's crochet needles and a Post-It note. "A wormhole," he said, poking the needle through one side of the paper, "bends space and time so we can travel vast distances and back again quicker than we would ever be able to do without it. Like this." He bent the note around the needle and poked it through the other side. "So fast," he added, "that time actually passes slower on the way through the wormhole than it does on Earth." She'd used the same illustration with her class the following day.

She was thirteen when the probes' data came in to the research base stationed on Triton. *Dove* and *Olive* had sent back a host of new discoveries—chief amongst them a new exoplanet, the fifth in orbit around the star NASA had dubbed Perrault. By the end of five years, the astronomers had reached a consensus:

Perrault V could support human life. Nearly every condition necessary for human colonization was in place, from temperature to gravity to distance from its star. The planet boasted an ample water supply and thriving plant ecosystem. While oxygen levels in its atmosphere were minimal, preliminary simulations had predicted successful terraforming over the course of only a few generations using comparatively simple breeding techniques. Discussions were already under way to send a crew to the planet that could bring back its native plant life, to splice the DNA the probes had found with that of native Terran vegetation. Aurora swore she would be a part of it.

For the next four years, she learned everything she could about space travel. At age fourteen she did a science fair report on the launch of the first moon colonies. At fifteen, she aced 12th-grade physics. At graduation she walked across the stage to shake hands with her beaming science teacher amid the applause of proud parents. Next stop: MIT.

Two months later came the car crash. Dad had been crushed under an overturned roof. Mom died in the ER eight hours later. She grieved them, then pushed her grief to the side and kept studying. She convinced herself it was what they would've wanted.

Aurora was just finishing the first year of her undergraduate degree when NASA announced plans to construct the first manned interstellar spacecraft. The project would be helmed by the esteemed astrophysicist Dr. Pyotr Chekovsky, who had named the ship the *Spindle*. It was shaped like a gigantic wheel, rotating on an axis to simulate gravity in its rim, and driven by a long propulsion shaft that stretched behind the central hub, like a *Spindle* without thread. The vessel would bring seven astronauts and a handful of robot aides through the wormhole to land and survey the exoplanet beyond. Once there, they would spend a full Earth year collecting plant samples and conducting a series of experiments on Perrault V's surface before returning home. If all went well, the *Spindle* would emerge from the wormhole to a fleet of cryoships, ready to carry whole colonies of frozen humans (and the first crop of plant hybrids) to the virgin world.

Soon after finishing her degree, Aurora came onto the project as an astroengineer. As a graduate student, she'd been commissioned to design an elbow mechanism for a robot intended for use in the ship's construction. Several months later, an email confirmed her place at NASA, engineering landing gear for the *Spindle*'s suborbital craft, *Odyssey*. The job was a dream come true —the moment she saw the subject header, she grabbed her roommate from in front of the TV and danced her around their apartment for joy. It wasn't just a job with NASA; it was an opportunity to help contribute to the most ambitious step in space exploration to date. One that would soon be looking for a field engineer.

From the beginning, she gave the project everything she had. Every second in the laboratory was well-spent, as she pored over readouts and tinkered with blueprints to optimize the lander's design. She spent hours of overtime testing new ideas and running the simulation programs like an addict with a drug.

Sometimes the lab would receive a visit from a group of clean-shaven men with gray suits and lapel badges, scribbling down notes about her team's progress. Sometimes those clean-shaven men would interview team members about their performance. The rumour spread that they were looking for candidates for the ship's maiden crew. Aurora's heart skipped every time she saw one of them gesture in her direction. For anyone else, the pressure would have been crippling. Not for her. She wouldn't *let* it be.

She was getting on that ship.

It was two weeks into her work on the *Odyssey* that Aurora first met Phil. It was late, and she was hard at work on one of the lander's main gear actuators. Something was wrong with the computer simulation, and she wasn't willing to let the glitch sit untouched for an entire weekend. After a quick caffeine boost, she figured she'd be able to get the program working by midnight.

She ducked out of her office, keys in hand. Her footsteps echoed through long, empty hallways, clicking a steady beat across the linoleum. Presently, though, she heard another sound between her steps: a loud, deep, expressive voice singing at the far end of the hall. She recognized it: he (yes, definitely a he) was singing Aerosmith's "I Don't Wanna Miss a Thing". Aurora followed the sound through the maze of corridors to another office door, cracked ajar. The name plate read: "Chekovsky: Astrophysicist".

She was curious. She'd heard Pyotr Chekovsky speak in briefings and lectures before, and knew the voice serenading the empty halls couldn't be his. The graying physicist's voice, though strong, was that of an old man—far from the young, vibrant voice that echoed Steve Tyler across the abandoned building.

Aurora pushed the door open on the sight of a young man about her age spinning in his office chair, his fingers picking across an air guitar. He swivelled to face her and broke off from the music, a startled look frozen on his face.

Their eyes locked. Brown eyes, she noticed. Handsome features. A shock of auburn hair.

He flashed her a grin; embarrassed, playful. "Hi," he said perkily.

Aurora smiled back and tucked her hair behind her ear. Her stomach fluttered. Without breaking eye contact, his hand slipped over to his computer keyboard to the volume button. The 1990s-era crooning grew quieter.

"Most people use headphones," she said.

"Sorry. I'll keep it down."

"No, it's... it's fine. You sound good." She pointed to his name plate. "Chekovsky?"

"Phil Chekovsky, yeah."

"Related to Pyotr?"

"His son. And you are?"

"Aurora King. I'm in the astroengineering department."

"King?" he asked. "I've read some of your work. Your preliminary designs for the *Odyssey* landing gear are really impressive."

"Thanks," she said. She felt a swell of pride, and at the same time, wished her hair looked a bit neater. "Working late tonight?" she asked.

"Yeah. You headed home?"

"Actually, I was gonna go for a coffee run before settling in for another couple of hours." She hesitated. "You wanna come?"

"Sure," he said, grabbing his jacket. They made for the exit.

"So Aerosmith, huh?" Aurora remarked. "Old song."

"I like old songs," Phil shrugged. "I'm impressed you recognize it." He held the door as they left the building, then led her across the parking lot to his silver Toyota.

"My dad read me a lot of old sci-fi when I was a kid," she told him. "With all the wormholes and exoplanets showing up in the news, he wanted me to understand what it meant that the mythology of the past was becoming real in our lifetime. Read to me every night before bed—Herbert, Clarke, Heinlein. We watched a lot of old movies too. I saw the one the song was written for."

"That why you joined NASA?" he asked. "Science fiction with dad?"

"Something like that," she answered. Phil opened his passenger door, and she thanked him and ducked inside. He gunned the car's engine.

"I get it. When I was a teenager, I saw my dad looking over some of the data the probes sent back. He was bent over the table, pages open, morning sun streaming through the windows with

Mom's pot roast still on the table. Cold from the night before. It was a big deal to him—how close we'd just gotten to actual interstellar expansion. It became a big deal to me too, I guess. All the more so now that we're about to launch the *Spindle*."

Aurora bit her lip. "I'm—I'm going to be on it."

"Really?" Phil pulled out of the parking lot. "Like, you've already been accepted for the crew? I thought that wasn't going to be finalized for another few years."

"No," Aurora corrected herself. "Not yet. But I'm determined. It's what I've been working toward ever since they announced the project."

"Isn't your dad gonna miss you?"

She hesitated. It wasn't something she liked talking about, especially with new people. She traced mental fingers over the throb of old grief.

"He died," she said at last. "Both my parents did. Car crash, years ago."

Phil braked to a halt at an oncoming stop sign. He looked across at her. "I'm sorry," he said. He was, too; she heard it in his voice, that sense of loss that so many people tried to fake when they heard her mention the crash. Not Phil. She could tell almost immediately—Phil wasn't fake.

"I know they're proud of me," she said. "My dad gave me this dream. My mom taught me I could reach it. I'm going to be on that ship."

"They sound like pretty great people," he said. "And honestly, you might make it. Like I said, I've read some of your work. Your parents have good reason to be proud." He checked the traffic and turned onto the street-lit road.

"Thanks," she said. "How about you? Would you join, if you had the chance?"

"Hey, if I apply, I won't need anyone else," Phil joked.

"Yeah?" Aurora raised a playful eyebrow. "You're going to pilot the ship through a wormhole, leave her in orbit, camp out alone on an alien planet for a year, run a series of complex atmospheric, botanical, and microbiological tests, adapting to any and all problems you find along the way, and then come back with the appropriate plant samples—by yourself?"

"Totally," he said.

Aurora chuckled.

"Honestly, I dunno yet if I want to ride the *Spindle*," he said, more serious now. "I probably could. I'd miss everyone back home, but my parents would be proud."

"But?"

Phil held his breath, deciding whether or not he should say any more. "I feel like a lot of people think I'm only here because my dad's in charge. I don't want to give them another reason to think that. Like I'm inheriting a kingdom or something."

"But you're not."

"I hope not. I wanna work for it. Just like anybody else."

"Okay," Aurora said. "So, you're not at NASA just because your dad got you a job. The project is clearly something you care about. If you were in my situation, you'd apply, right?"

He glanced across at her. "Definitely," he said. He checked his mirrors.

"So why?"

"Because it's the next big quest," he said. "The next leap forward in the human journey. Like we're looking for something, on orders from deep down in our collective gut. It's something... almost primal, I think. Like the first time somebody rubbed two stones together to make fire. Or the day you moved out of the house because it was time to grow up."

Aurora nodded.

"And this isn't just your leap, or mine, but everyone's. Once a few of us do it, all of us can do it. You know what I mean?"

"Yeah," Aurora whispered. "Yeah I do." She nudged his elbow with hers. "I think you should go."

"Yeah?"

"Yeah. I'd fly a starship with you. Who cares what anyone else thinks?"

"Sounds like you want me to care what you think."

She rolled her eyes, but couldn't hide her smile.

He nudged her back. "Hey. Maybe I will," he said.

Questions and answers bounced back and forth between them ("What's the first thing you would do once you touch down on the planet's surface?" "What do you think will change the most on Earth during the voyage?" "If you could take one famous dead scientist to Perrault V, who would it be?"). Phil was smart, she found. Smarter than most of the guys she'd met in college. Funny. Confident. Inventive and curious. Any silence between them during that evening didn't last long. Aurora was almost disappointed when they reached the drive-thru and put their conversation on hold while the speaker box took their order—and sighed, only half in frustration, when Phil insisted on paying for her coffee.

They returned to the research building, and a small, responsible part of Aurora thought that would be the end of it. She'd go back to her lab, he to his office, and both would have a productive evening. They reached her door, still talking, neither quite willing to part ways, until one or the other realized they'd been standing there for almost three hours. It was two-fourteen in the morning when Aurora drove home, her glitch still unsolved, remembering what Einstein had said to explain time dilation. "An hour sitting with a pretty girl on a park bench passes like a minute. That's relativity."

Phil asked her to dinner the following week.

By the end of that year, Phil had gotten his PhD, and both of them were candidates for the *Spindle*'s maiden crew. Aurora was ecstatic. The following September, the project coordinators shipped Phil, Aurora, and the rest of the relevant personnel up to the *Sky Castle* space station for further trials and training. The selection process would conclude in orbit.

Aurora could still remember the day she'd first seen *Spindle* in her *Sky Castle* dock—almost-built, glimmering white in the sunlight, drifting out from Earth's shadow in the launch station's slow, graceful ballet-orbit around the planet. Technicians and construction droids hovered in and out of her shadowy edges like dragonflies over a pond, edging the proud vessel nearer and nearer completion. She hung on Phil's shoulder as he pointed down the *Spindle*'s propulsion shaft, where her lander blueprints had begun to take form. He wrapped his arm around her waist and pulled her close.

"See that?" he whispered to her. "That's *yours*."

Aurora and Phil met Malcolm Fairburn the day after their arrival. He was one of thirteen other candidates for the mission—an astrophysicist, like Phil, who'd served as a critical consultant for military spacecraft. He had angled features, a patch of beard over his chin, and focused, iron-gray eyes that never missed an atom.

"Chekovsky?" he asked, on hearing Phil's name. "Like Pyotr?"

"He's my father."

No response.

Fairburn was smart. Solitary. He'd been working in space a few months longer than Aurora and Phil had, and his experience made him a prime candidate for the crew. But something about him irked her. His curt manner with the other contenders, maybe, or the way he studied her in the mess hall without a word.

Training on the *Sky Castle* was intensive. Space exploration had come a long way since the early years, but the candidates still needed to learn how to manoeuvre the craft. They logged hours together piloting space suits and operating maintenance equipment, running and repeating drills and tests for every situation they might encounter. The purpose was to give each of them a well-rounded practical fluency with all the ship's operations. Should anything happen to one of them, the others could still make it home.

Aurora noticed Fairburn's approach to the program early. He was competitive. Incisive. Any perceived mistake on the part of his fellow candidates, no matter how invisible to anyone else, and he'd slice into them like a scalpel—without anaesthetic. Actual *kindness* seemed out of his reach, like a skill he had never learned before.

Maybe no one's ever been around to teach him, Aurora thought.

Only she seemed exempt from Fairburn's snide remarks. Phil thought he knew why. "He's in love with you," he said, one night over dinner.

The words made Aurora cringe. While Fairburn's rage never settled on her as a target, there was something else in him that did; a silent, hungry attention that made her edge to Phil's other side every time she caught Fairburn staring at her in the dining hall.

Even Fairburn's attempts at friendliness, especially to Phil, were seasoned with a tone of subtle but unmistakable condescension. It was especially potent in the nickname he chose for him: "Prince." *So much for not inheriting a kingdom*, Aurora thought.

"He's projecting," another candidate, Dr. Basile, told Phil after a particularly tricky exercise.

"What do you mean?"

"He was working on a project for the military before this," Basile said. "Project Diablo. I heard his dad was the project director. I doubt he really *worked* his way up here."

Aurora wasn't sure. Fairburn might be an asshole, but he was also smart. And he wasn't the only other qualified candidate under consideration, either. Dr. Basile had applied as the crew's geologist. Dr. Kavita Tennyson was a veteran biologist who had been researching Perrault V fauna from the beginning. Dr. Percy Forrest had been a child prodigy, designing parts for the *Spindle* when he was seventeen years old. Aurora wasn't sure how she and Phil could compete. And if only one of them was destined to reach the new world, she knew that they couldn't remain a couple forever.

That was the problem with time dilation. Relativity. Time on the voyage would pass slower than time on Earth. The seven explorers who set out on the *Spindle* would have to leave everything behind—their homes, their families, their whole lives— with little remaining on their return. Aurora's only living family was an estranged aunt living in Alaska—but her attachment to Phil wouldn't so easily dissolve. If she boarded the *Spindle* without him, or vice versa, their relationship couldn't last.

She'd tried to talk to him about it already, on Earth. Four times she'd screwed up her courage to do it. Twice she'd let the opportunity slip. The third time she'd gotten distracted; he'd cooked them dinner, stubbed his toe on a corner at his house, and spilled spaghetti sauce all over the floor. She'd laughed. He'd started a meatball fight. By the end of it all, they'd given up and ordered Chinese.

And the fourth time—well, the fourth time she'd asked him. Out loud. He'd changed the subject.

But Aurora was resolved to talk about it before the final roster was revealed.

Phil took her to the observatory tower the night before Director Walter was scheduled to make the final announcement. He'd brought two ration packets for dinner, and together they hovered in front of the bright-strewn glass dome, gazing out at the glittering promise of faraway starlight. Deep purple gas threaded its way across the porthole. Phil reached for her hand and wove his fingers into hers.

Please God, let them send us both.

"Hey, Phil?" she said.

"Yeah?"

"What happens,"—he cocked his head, waiting for her to continue— "tomorrow, I mean,"—her pulse quickened, screaming at her not to ask the question— "what happens if they only take one of us?"

The words hung heavy in the weightlessness.

"I hadn't thought about that," he said at last, with a theatrical nod. "I figured they'd just—*give* us the mission and tell everyone else to stay home."

"I'm being serious, Phil."

"So am I," he said. "I don't need six crewmates to make it through a wormhole and back." His fingers stretched, then tapped against her knuckles. "Just you."

She paused.

"What if I can't go? What if they send you and not me?"

Phil let go of her hand and rotated himself around her, his back to the glass. She stared up at him, meeting his dark eyes against the backdrop of the stars. He took her hands in his, and she felt him pull her up towards her, like gravity, like the beginning of a dance. His hands were warm.

"You're the youngest person in the running," he whispered, "and the smartest person on this station. You'll be the first one on the roster. Trust me."

"But what if—"

He shook his head. "No. No what ifs. No backups. Whether we're on one side of the wormhole or the other, you're the only crewmate I really need."

She nodded and smiled. *Man.* Those brown eyes.

Please, God.

He rotated again to look up through the inky veil of gaseous whorls to the stars on the other side. "One more night," he said. "And then we leap."

Aurora woke the next morning to find Phil already out of bed, clicking through his messages.

She unclipped from her berth, slid open the glass partition, and scrambled forward, desperate with anticipation. She touched her hand against his back and ran it up under his arm, wrapping him in a close hug. She inhaled deeply, stretched herself upward and glanced toward the screen from over his shoulder.

He spun around to face her, blocking her view of the monitor. He rolled his bottom lip back against the edge of his top teeth— Phil's telltale sign of disappointment.

"Did we make it?" she whispered.

When he didn't respond, she raised her eyebrows. "Come on. Don't joke about this."

His eyes darted around the compartment. Other candidates, bleary-eyed and slow, began to unclip from their berths. Fairburn glared at him as he emerged from behind his glass. Phil said nothing. His eyes began to water.

"Phil!" Aurora said, as she tried to push him away from the monitor. "Did we make it!" He reached behind himself and grabbed the underside of the keyboard in an effort to steady against her push. She pushed harder.

"Answer me or get out of the way, Philip Chekovsky. Are we on the *Spindle*?"

He shook his head and bowed low. "I'm sorry, Aurora," he whispered. He pushed up toward her, his arms outstretched in a comforting hug. She heard a catch in his throat. She shoved him away from the keyboard to look at the screen.

She scanned the opening paragraph and down to the list of names. Her mind barely registered most of them. But there, in professional black font, in a column with five others, were the names "Chekovsky" and "King."

Phil sputtered a mischievous giggle and floated to his berth. Aurora checked the list again, praying she wasn't dreaming. Andersen. Basile. Chekovsky. Grimm. Forrest. Tennyson. King.

They were going. *Together.*

Aurora turned to Phil and grinned, then shot toward him and pressed him against the bunks. They locked eyes, and she grabbed his arms to pull herself close.

"Hey," he said, grinning. She felt him poke at her stomach and looked down.

There was a small felt box in his hand, open.

"Will you marry me?"

A white diamond sparkling against the black. Like starlight.

"I kinda want to say no now," she said, smirking through the tears.

"Would you say yes if I got down on one knee?" He grabbed a handhold and tried to edge himself lower, fumbling an attempt to remain kneeling. He stared up at her, weightless.

She savoured the tension as long as she could, but in the end, couldn't stop the laughter. "Yes," she said. "Yes, I'll marry you."

He pulled his fist back in triumph, then pushed upward.

Aurora shot a playful blow to his abdomen. His torso crunched forward, and he gave an exaggerated *oof.*

"Don't do that again," she lilted. Whatever shock Phil had felt from the hit had vanished, replaced with a wide smile. She grinned as he pushed himself forward, and pulled her close, his hand on her back.

Then she kissed him.

The clock read 4:23 am. Three hours before wake-up call. Four before departure. Aurora unlocked the glass partition and pushed out from the berth. She hadn't slept.

She slipped on her jumpsuit and floated to the observation deck. The Earth spun beneath her, cities radiant in the shadowy blue.

Another planet. She was going. The most important journey in human history, and she would be a part of it.

And the *Spindle* was only the beginning. Once they made it back through the wormhole, the colony arks would be close to finished. Research into cryonics technology had already begun; the hope was that this would make it easier for the colonists to board their ships *en masse*, as well as conserve supply storage space on board. On reaching orbit, the colonists would remain frozen, then be thawed in waves as the settlements grew in population capacity. With any luck, in only a few decades after their arrival, Perrault V would have a thriving human colony on a breathable new world. For Aurora, the morning's launch would mark a new beginning for the human species—the dawn of the interstellar age.

And she and Phil were going to be a part of it. *Together.*

She admired the ring against the starlight.

A few hours and a wash later, she made her way to the dining hall for breakfast. Basile and Forrest greeted her as she gulped down her rations. Phil wasn't up yet. By 7:42 she still hadn't seen him—under half an hour before launch.

She drifted into their quarters and found him lying still in his berth. She tapped her fist against the glass.

"Phil."

No response. He looked sick.

"Phil!"

His eyes, half-opened, were rimmed with fatigue, and the rest of his skin was an inflamed red. At first Aurora thought it was the light in the berth—but no, after a closer look she could see something was wrong. She pushed toward the exit and saw someone blur past.

"Dr. Tennyson?" she called into the corridor. "I think something's wrong with Phil!"

Dr. Tennyson grabbed a handhold, turned, and floated into the sleeping quarters. She peered at the body beneath the glass.

"How long has he been like this?" she asked.

"He was fine last night."

"Anything he could've eaten? Any change in his schedule that might have let an infection into his system?"

Aurora shook her head. Her stomach turned with every question. The station's crew had been under rigorous hygiene standards since their arrival—Earth's germs were a far more serious threat in orbit, to say nothing of whatever microbes they might find in the alien star system—but there was no mistaking it. Phil was sick.

"You need to get to the medical bay," Dr. Tennyson said, pushing Aurora into the corridor.

"But Phil—"

"We'll take a look at him once we've got everyone under quarantine. We're going to have to push the launch back a few days at least, no stopping that now—but Director Walter will still want to limit the delays as much as possible. If we can figure out how the disease got into his system, we can still salvage the mission."

Aurora knew she was right. A deep space voyage would weaken the immune system and strengthen diseases in ways that could prove fatal if the dangers weren't addressed as quickly as possible. They couldn't afford unnecessary risks. They notified Director Walter, and after a brief consultation with the medical crew, Aurora and the rest went into quarantine. Until they could be sure that no one else was contaminated, the *Spindle* project was on hold.

Aurora lay strapped against the infirmary bed, cringing under the medprobes and trying not to ask for news of the others. She knew the doctors were doing the best they could, but the suspense was growing unbearable. They'd come so close to beginning the journey, and now they faced a danger that could halt the whole project.

Phil. Where was Phil?

She tried to sleep, with little success. Another doctor came in to run more tests—blood scans, micro-x-rays, psych evals. She pressed him for updates, but got nothing. Finally he sent her to wait with the others. Silent stares haunted the room as they waited for the ordeal to end.

By morning they were free to move about the station. Phil's berth had been decontaminated, and he'd been transferred to a medical station for further diagnosis. The rest were given a clean bill of health. Director Walter met with them that evening to brief the remaining crew.

"Research into what happened is ongoing," the director told them grimly, "but we're confident the disease is contained." His attention bounced from one crew member to another. "What that means is that we're going ahead with the *Spindle* mission—but we're going to do it without Dr. Chekovsky."

Aurora's stomach knotted.

"We need an astrophysicist," Dr. Andersen pointed out. "We can't complete the mission without one."

"Dr. Malcolm Fairburn will serve as Dr. Chekovsky's replacement."

"There's no chance waiting for Phil to recover?" Aurora asked.

Walter shook his head. "It's still too early to know how long that would take," he said. "That's why we're sending Dr. Chekovsky Earthside to recover. But we can't afford to wait. If we do, the Earth's orbit will carry us away from the wormhole. It'll cost us precious time and resources."

Aurora wanted to hit something.

"I know you two were close," the director told her. "I'll give you until tomorrow."

"Phil?"

"Hey," he breathed. Even in her headset, he sounded different from the man who had proposed to her less than 48 hours ago. Weaker. Aurora's stomach turned.

From the communication tower, she could see the bright white of the medical station hovering over the tinted horizon, falling forward into the Earth's grim shadow. How had things gone from so right to so wrong in only two days?

"How are you feeling?" she asked.

"Pretty tired," he replied. "Doctor says my fever's at 103. Last few trips to the restroom have been kinda brutal. They're sending me home in a few hours."

Aurora nodded. "We're going ahead with the mission," she whispered.

The medical station began to fall past the sunset.

"I heard."

"We didn't decide what would happen. If one of us couldn't go."

"Didn't we?" Phil's voice cracked.

"You said you wanted me to be your crewmate," she whispered. "That whether we were on one side of a wormhole or the other, I was the only one you'd really need."

"Yeah," he said. "Yeah, I did." His voice gave way to silence—a burning, heavy silence, buffering the next painful word like the wall behind her buffered the fury of solar radiation.

"So now what?" she asked.

"Well," he said, "I think you get on that ship, and you bring us back some plants."

Aurora shook her head. "I can't."

"Can't what?"

"Can't leave a day after you asked me to marry you. I mean—I love you, Phil. I can't abandon you after that."

"You also can't pass up this opportunity."

The silence was uncomfortable.

"You need to get on board that ship, Aurora," he said. "I'll be here when you get back."

If only that were true, she thought. "I can't."

"Alright," Phil said. He took a deep breath. "Then, Dr. Aurora King,"—God, she loved how her name sounded on his tongue—"I'm breaking up with you."

She gave a bittersweet laugh.

"You're just no good for me," he continued. "You're smart, and beautiful, and *awesome*, and bound on a journey through a wormhole to an alien star system. And that's just not the kind of woman I can, in good conscience, tie down. So I'm leaving you."

"I'm leaving *you*," she said, wiping a tear from her smile.

"Hey, promise me this," Phil added. "Make sure you're the first to touch your foot to the new planet. And say something good."

"I love you, you know," she whispered. "I'll always love you. Make a girl really happy for me someday, okay?"

"I will," he said. "I love you too." The words sounded casual, like he was just leaving for a night and would see her again in the morning.

If only.

Aurora saw almost no one else until the pre-launch briefing nine hours later. She felt their eyes on her, heard the whispers when her back turned, and endured the silences that told her how little they felt they could say. She sat through the briefing, hardly listening to any of it, praying, instead, for one last chance that Phil might be well enough to go with them after all.

But the crew boarded the *Spindle*, and Aurora and the others watched from the observation deck as Commander Grimm unlocked the ship from her docking bay. The launch sequence blurred past in what seemed like minutes. She didn't try to savour it. All of the excitement she'd expected to feel as the *Spindle* broke away from *Sky Castle* seemed forced and insincere the moment they actually detached. How could any of it matter, without Phil on board beside her?

The crew slept in shifts. With no sun to distinguish between days, a preset twenty-four hour schedule served as its replacement. Aurora woke every cycle feeling sick, loss churning through her insides like machinery. Sometimes she wished it would end. Other times she dared not let it. It would feel like betrayal, letting her memory of Phil float out into the void. Like he hadn't really mattered to her. And no matter how much the loss of him hurt right now, she refused to admit that he had not mattered.

For most of the voyage, she cut herself off from the rest of the crew. Dr. Basile tried to keep them occupied as best he could—the man had an endless supply of games and anecdotes—but Aurora found it difficult to stay interested. She secluded herself for days in her quarters, combing through the selection of books and movies on the *Spindle*'s mainframe. Sometimes recorded a few video greetings to send home. No one ever replied. And in the silence between the stars, her grief howled.

The others worried. All of them had had some idea of what Phil had meant to her, and most had been there for the proposal. Dr. Tennyson noticed the ring around her neck, and tried talking to her about it once or twice. Aurora brushed it aside. As kind as the thought might be, Aurora was perfectly capable of doing her job without a breakup counselor. She could deal with loss, she insisted. She'd done it before.

Soon everyone's concerned looks gave way to indifference. She'd join them when she wanted to, they reasoned, but until then, pressing her was futile. Eventually most of them got used to her absence.

She wondered if Phil had gotten used to her absence.

It wasn't just grief that drove her further from contact with the others. It was Fairburn. The distance from Earth had increased his irritability. Whereas Aurora kept to herself as often as possible, Fairburn hovered right on the edge of nearly every activity, silent— until he saw the opportunity to mock someone. His insults grew sharper, crueller, followed by deafening silences as everyone realized that shooting back would waste oxygen.

Once, at dinner, she heard him mutter something about moving on. "It's not like they were evenly matched, after all," he said. "*She* made the roster on merit."

Aurora couldn't take it any longer.

"You talk as if Phil were some third-rate hack who just lucked his way into his candidacy," she rejoined. "Like you think mocking him will make us forget the truth. But it won't. We all know you were second choice."

Fairburn glowered, and she knew she had struck a nerve. *Good*, she thought. She kept on. "And if you really have a problem with nepotism, I think it's time you looked in the mirror. Everybody knows how you got to be on the *Spindle*."

"And how was that?" He raised an eyebrow.

"Wasn't your dad the director of some military project?" she asked. "Project Diablo? Pretty easy to get a position like this when your father's willing to pull strings for you, I bet."

He paused. It was the first time she'd ever seen him hesitate in responding to someone. Then he smiled, a harsh, self-satisfied smile.

"Project Diablo was a disaster," he said. "It was a waste of precious time and manpower, and the military cut the funding for it early, on my advice. Since the director of the project resigned in disgrace, I don't see much point in asking favours from him." Not *my dad. The director.*

His glare, unbroken, forced her to retreat back to her dinner. But she went to bed that night thinking on it, and realized that at last she had found a chink in his armour. A weakness—one she wouldn't soon forget.

It wasn't until the *Spindle* reached the entry to the wormhole that Aurora began to take a real interest in the mission again. The call went out across the ship; Commander Grimm's firm German voice woke the few sleepers, and everyone filed into the command module. Aurora crowded in with the others, strapping in and grabbing a handhold on the far wall.

The wormhole gaped before them on the other side of the glass. Distant stars and gases warped along its rim like shadows on the ripples in a pond. Aurora felt a lump in her throat as she thought about what they were seeing. They were already farther away from Earth than any human being had ever been. And now, there it was: that sphere-shaped gravitational anomaly tunnelling through spacetime and across the observable universe. The one she had been chasing since grade school, the one she'd left behind everyone and everything to find. The crew tethered themselves into place as the ship arced around the tunnel, orbiting toward it in a long, silent fall.

"Hold on, everyone," Grimm said. "Here comes the drop."

The spatial shimmer began to twist and elongate like a rubber band. Aurora felt her stomach turn inside her. Her teeth clenched. She heard something rattle at the back of the module, something that she hoped was tied down. Another rattle. She felt vomit burn the back of her throat and prayed the ship would hold together.

She looked back to her fellow crew members. Fairburn's head was tipped upward, wide-eyed in a silent expression of terror.

Basile held his head in his hands. Tennyson had gone unconscious. She wasn't sure how long this went on, but then, everything went still.

Aurora relaxed. Her stomach heaved, her head ached, but it was over.

"We made it," Grimm said.

Aurora breathed a sigh of relief as others whooped around her. She unstrapped herself and floated forward, hardly daring to believe it. They were through.

The *Spindle* entered orbit around Perrault V about two months later. The clouded white atmosphere veiled a world of virginal ocean blue, patched with continents of dark red deserts, snow-capped mountains, and blue-green forests stretching low and deep through waiting ravines.

Aurora made Grimm promise to put her on the first landing mission. If something went wrong with *Odyssey*, she argued, it would be good to have an expert aboard. Tennyson and Andersen went with her, while the other four remained in orbit.

Dr. Andersen winged the *Odyssey* lander toward a grassy clearing at the mouth of a river, near where the long-dead *Olive* probe had landed to conduct its atmospheric tests centuries before. The three women felt the landing gear unlock, then touch down gently on the alien turf. Aurora felt Tennyson's hand on her shoulder, and the biologist mouthed "Well done" under her helmet glass. The astroengineer smiled back. Then the boarding hatch opened with a slow *vvvvt*, and at last Aurora saw the alien world.

"This is for you, Phil," she whispered into her oxygen mask, though no one heard it on the official recording. It wasn't 'One small step for man,' of course, but she didn't care. There was a victory in that step, even if it felt bittersweet. A step violated for being taken in Phil's absence.

The ground was damp after heavy rain a few hours before, and glistening water droplets clung to the edges of tall blue-green grass. Her suit's readout confirmed the old probe's findings: the sliver of oxygen in the air was too sparse to breathe, but still detectable. *We'll change that*, Aurora thought. She inhaled deeply, and thought of what it would feel like to set foot outside on this planet without an oxygen tank on her back. *One day*.

The rest of the crew arrived several days later to set up camp. The planet was astonishingly well-suited to human life; its days were about eighteen hours long, its gravitational pull was comfortable, and there was a vast landscape to explore. Aurora and Basile spent the following weeks mapping the surrounding area, cataloguing plants and animals, taking soil samples, and testing the water supply. After a month, they traded the ship's rations for food native to the planet: large, egg-shaped fruits that tasted halfway between an apple and a peach. Dr. Tennyson took DNA samples from Perrault's vegetation, and spent days poring over the data in the lab. Fairburn spent the evenings in isolation.

Aurora was reading in her room one night, though, when his silhouette appeared in the doorway. She looked up from her book and swallowed.

"What do you need, Dr. Fairburn?"

He stepped inside. "Call me Malcolm."

"Why?"

"We don't have to go back with the plant samples," he said. His voice was hard. "The air filtration system in the habitat would provide enough oxygen for the two of us for a long time. After the others leave, we could wait here for the first cryoship." He walked further into the room and stood at the foot of the bed. "We—you and I, I mean—could give them something to find when they arrive."

A sense of unease crept into her at his words. "Something like what?"

"A colony."

Aurora was incredulous. "You're asking me to have your children?"

"With Chekovsky gone—"

"You took his place on the ship. That doesn't mean you have a right to take anything else."

"It wouldn't have worked out, you know. You and Phil. It never does."

"Get out, Fairburn."

Fairburn was silent, but didn't leave. Fine, then. If he wouldn't leave, she would make him. She knew by now what would make him uncomfortable.

"Is that why you boarded the *Spindle*?" she asked. "Something didn't work out? A breakup, maybe? Or a divorce. Or maybe you just realized that no one on Earth would miss you. And you don't know how to change that—so you tell other people that no one really cares about them either. For you, that's all there is left."

He bristled, but said nothing.

"Is that what your dad did to you?" she continued.

"My dad didn't do anything to me."

"Did he do anything *for* you?"

Fairburn glared.

"So he left," she guessed. "And you found him again. Or someone did, anyway. In charge of a flashy new experiment for the US military."

His silence told her it was true. For all his talk, Fairburn never denied the truth when someone else spoke it. Especially now. He couldn't.

"Beloved father and husband to a great big happy family," he finished.

"But not yours," she realized. There it was. Fairburn's wound. She eased up. "I'm sorry, Fairburn."

Fairburn didn't seem to notice her apology. "He was a decorated soldier who failed the only thing he was ever good at," he said. "Dismissed from his new post in weapons development because his own son tanked his idea. Because he was too proud to admit who I was. Even to his other family." There was contempt in those last two words.

"And now his own son's made history," Aurora finished. "In a way he never could. He can't claim credit for that without acknowledging who you are."

Fairburn nodded.

"I'm sorry he hurt you, Fairburn," she said at last. "But that doesn't change how I feel about Phil."

"Still?" Here, too, there was contempt. Bitterness.

"Still."

"Decades have passed on Earth. Even if he survived the typhoid, by now there's nothing left."

It was her turn, now, to feel the wound throb. Damn you, Fairburn. *Just when I start to feel sorry for you, you show me why I shouldn't.* "I thought I told you to get out," she said.

"Aurora—"

And then she realized.

"Who said it was typhoid?"

Fairburn looked like a deer in headlights. "The doctors—the medical personnel said—"

"No one said it was typhoid." Her feet slid off the bed and she stood, glaring. "We left before the final diagnosis."

Fairburn said nothing. She felt the old scar of Phil's absence bleeding anew, and the blood turned to venom in the silence. She stepped closer. "You bastard."

"We cured typhoid long ago, Aurora."

She cut him off with a cold slap.

Fairburn let out a trembling breath. "I didn't kill him."

"'Decades have passed'," Aurora spat. "'By now there's nothing left.' God, how did you even get the virus onto the station? You must've been planning it for ages, just in case you didn't get in."

"You won't tell," Fairburn said. "You can't prove anything—and our mission can't afford to lose a man if something goes wrong. You need me. They all do."

"Get out," she ordered, "and I won't tell anyone."

He glowered and obeyed.

Fairburn kept his distance in the weeks after she rejected his proposal. He had to. He knew, by now, how much she hated him; how nothing in the world would ever reverse what he had done. *Fine*, Aurora thought. *If that's what it takes.* Hatred was the language Fairburn understood best.

He tried to pretend it never happened. Avoid unnecessary contact. He knew she knew the truth, and that she would always know the truth. It was true that telling anyone right now would cause further division in the crew, and they might still need each other to return home safely, but once they did, she wouldn't need him anymore. If he wanted her to keep his secret once they arrived home, it was in his best interests to behave himself. Yes. That, at least, was a barrier Fairburn would respect.

But there was no healing in this. Knowing the truth, warding him off, didn't bring Phil back. She felt it all the more now, in fact. Phil was dead by now, probably; and if he wasn't, he would be before she got home. She thought of her parents all over again, the way she had wept at their funeral as they lowered the coffins into the ground. They'd been killed by a drunk driver. She'd seen a photo of him once online, and had felt sorrow for him, more than anger. He'd done a bad thing, but he probably hadn't woken up that morning with murder in his heart. But Fairburn had planned this. He'd *wanted* to take Phil from her.

She felt empty. Like the wormhole. After Phil's death at Fairburn's hand, that emptiness was the only thing left.

Little changed for Aurora in the final months on Perrault V. Dr. Basile kept taking soil samples. Dr. Tennyson continued her survey of the planet's greenery. By the end of their stay, they were confident the biology teams on Earth would be able to engineer a strain of Perraultian flora to terraform the planet's atmosphere. Their tenure on the planet ended, and at last, the seven explorers returned to the *Odyssey* lander, docked with the *Spindle*, and began the long trek home.

Aurora woke to a knock on the door of her quarters. It was Dr. Tennyson. Several hours had passed since contact with the *Sky Castle*, and she was here to announce their docking with the station. The ship had stopped spinning, and dozens of astronauts, scientists, and executives were waiting on the other side of the airlock, eager to hear the details of the voyage. Aurora dressed and followed her colleagues through the airlock, dizzied with new faces beaming smiles.

She was shipped to Earth with the rest of the crew and met with a triumphant welcome at NASA headquarters. The new director called a press conference, and ushered them down a hallway lined with photographs of directors past (Walter's and Pyotr Chekovsky's among them—Aurora noted the dates printed beneath each one with a twinge of grief) and into a room filled with shouting reporters, cameramen, and public sponsors, eager to learn all they could about Perrault V.

After the commotion had died away, one of Aurora's attendants tried to explain what had changed in her decades of absence. Private corporations had begun to expand their reach beyond the moon's orbit, and asteroid mining had made great strides in the construction of a colony fleet. The first ten colony arks were nearly ready, and they could expect to begin human migration in less than two years. Cryostasis had been successfully tested soon after her departure, and with the data the *Spindle* crew had gathered, everyone was enthusiastic that plant breeding could begin in the labs of the colony ships.

The *Spindle*'s crew spent weeks in a cycle of briefings, board meetings, and talk show appearances as people clamoured for insight on what was next. Aurora found it difficult to keep up. She found it difficult to even want to. Eventually she requested a year-long sabbatical. She needed distance from the busyness of the world. She would use her time off for research; to catch up on the various advances in astroengineering that had occurred since her departure. When the year was over, she could then resume her work preparing for mankind's next great leap.

Once the new director granted her request, Aurora bought a small home in Orlando and began her research. It was a welcome escape from all the media attention—and gave her something to do aside from thinking about Phil. After all, for all his cruelty, Fairburn had been right. Phil was long gone now.

One morning, though, Aurora heard a knock at her door.

"Dr. King?"

The woman was tall, with curly raven hair and mocha skin, dressed in a gray pantsuit and carrying a briefcase. There was something about her eyes that looked familiar—something Aurora at first couldn't quite identify.

"Yes?"

The woman offered her hand. "I'm Dr. Penelope Chekovsky," she said. "I'm a medical researcher at the University of Miami. It's an honour to meet you."

Aurora furrowed her brows. By now Phil, if he had still been alive, would be 108 years old. The middle-aged Penelope was too young to be a wife. "Like Philip Chek—"

"His niece," the researcher corrected her. "His younger brother Troy was my father."

"Oh," Aurora nodded. They shook hands. "Dr. Chekovsky, I don't know what they told you about me and Phil, but—"

"Everything," Penelope interrupted. "They told me everything. Your first date. Your work on board *Sky Castle*. The proposal. And the day after, when he got sick and you had to leave him behind." Her mouth curved upward in a kind smile. "You told him to make a girl really happy someday."

The memory of her own words stabbed.

"What I can do for you, Doctor?" Aurora said. Whatever else happened, she wasn't going to break down in front of a stranger at the front door.

"I'd actually like to do something for you, Dr. King," Penelope said. "There's something of Phil's that I'd like to show you." She nodded toward the ring, still hanging around her neck. "Is that the one he gave you?"

"With all due respect, ma'am, that was a long—"

"Please," Penelope insisted. "Do you still love him?"

Aurora didn't know what to say. It all flashed through her mind again: boarding the ship, crossing the wormhole, her first step onto the planet. The bitter night with Fairburn, and all the anger and confusion that had come after it. And then the return to dock with *Sky Castle*. It all felt so hollow. Marred by his absence. A full year of her life—the one she'd spent her life working for—and he hadn't been in it.

Did she still love him?

"Yes."

"Then come with me."

It was sunset when Penelope's SUV pulled in front of their destination a few miles out from Orlando: a wide gate in a high chain-linked fence with thorns of razor wire lining the top. The guard at the toll booth waved them through, and Penelope led Aurora into a lifeless gray building, with tinted windows and a handful of cars in the parking lot. Aurora followed, trying to understand what all of this had to do with Phil.

Penelope had refused to address her questions during the drive. "I'd rather show you than tell you, Dr. King," she'd answered.

They walked past the secretary and down a few labyrinthine hallways to an elevator waiting for their arrival. A black scanner stared from the wall, and Penelope pressed a key card to it.

The elevator began its descent. Penelope hummed a familiar tune under her breath, and Aurora strained to hear it. Gradually she recognized the melody. In a hundred years, she could never forget that song.

"Aerosmith?"

"I heard that was how you met."

Aurora nodded.

"You haven't asked about him," Penelope remarked. "Philip, I mean."

"Is that a question?"

"Yes."

"I meant what I said. I really did want him to move on. Continue his work. Fall in love." She paused. "I just didn't want to have to think about the man I loved—the man I *love*—wasting away over long years with someone else. I didn't want to think about him dying." She stared at her blurred reflection in the elevator door.

"We've cured typhoid, Dr. King."

"Can you cure time?"

"Maybe."

The elevator stopped and the doors slid open to a well-lit medical examination room. The place was set up with a heart rate monitor, defibrillator, hospital bed, refrigerator, and various other medical instruments. On the far side of the room lay a long box of padded gray, waist-height, topped with a long near-opaque white glass cover the length of a full-grown man. A circular light along the side glowed white, and along the floor a series of cables fed into the box's underside.

Aurora approached the box like a pilgrim approaching a shrine. The blurred outline of a face stared out at her from behind the glass. She drew her fingers over the surface. It was cold.

"Philip Chekovsky wasn't just an astrophysicist," Penelope said. "After his rejection from the *Spindle* mission, he went back to school. His work in cryonics is a big part of the reason the Perrault colonies are now possible."

Aurora looked to Penelope in awed disbelief. "You mean he's —"

Penelope nodded. "A little cold, maybe, but he's in there. He's been waiting for a long time." She pointed to a fingerprint scan beside the white light on the side of the cocoon. "It's coded to you. You want to wake him up?"

Aurora's heart quickened.

Alive.

Phil was alive. Dreaming. Right in front of her. A fingerprint scan away from waking up.

She pressed the scanner.

The bar of light rolled up and down the screen. There was a beep and then a click, and then the glass cover slid off the sarcophagus with a steamy hiss. She heard short gasps of breath spurting out from an ancient respiratory system.

Aurora peered inside.

Dark brown eyes looked up at her and blinked. Squint. Blink.

"Phil?"

She touched her palm to his frozen cheek. Breath steamed from his mouth, warm to her touch compared to the cold of his skin. A hand reached up and grabbed the edge of the coffin. Phil pulled himself upward, shivering, his face still caked with ice. He wiped his hand across his eyes and stared at her. Another blink.

"Aurora?"

The voice. His voice. The one she'd heard echoing Aerosmith lyrics through the halls of the research building so many years ago. God, she'd missed that voice, the one that should have filled all the silences she'd travelled since their call before the launch. Aurora grinned and wrapped his frigid hand in hers. For all the weakness his body had endured during cryosleep, she felt the strength in those fingers as they closed between her own.

"You're alive," she breathed.

The icy Phil nodded. "I promised you I'd make a girl really happy someday."

She kissed him, and it was as if all the years that had stood between them melted away in that kiss. He was here. Here, and alive, and young, and *hers*. Her lips remembered the taste of his, eager and lively even under the cracks that had formed in frozen years. She smiled between each caress of his mouth with a delight far greater than she had ever expected to feel again. His kiss woke something in her, and promised it would never again have to sleep.

"I love you," she gasped between kisses. "I'll always love you."

"Always," he replied.

Finally they pulled away. Phil staggered to his feet. Penelope found him a blanket, and together they checked his vitals. Fifteen minutes later he sat on the hospital bed, eating a ration packet.

"What was it like?" he said. "Perrault V, I mean."

"Do you want to see it?"

"Go there?" Phil asked. "With you?" He reached behind her hair to unclasp the ring from around her neck.

She nodded, moving her hair out of the way. "They're projecting only five years before the first colony ships launch," she told him. "You ready to make the leap with the rest of the human race?"

"Yeah," he said, smiling. He took her hand and slipped the ring back onto her finger. "I mean... I've got the only crewmate I'll ever need."

See J.A. Legg's story "Till All the Hundred Summers Pass" online at Metaphorosis.
If you liked it, leave a comment. Authors love that!
Remember to subscribe to our e-mail updates so you'll know when new stories are posted.

About the story

One of my favourite things about being a story audience is when a story comes to a crisis point that goes one or two ways, and realizing to myself, "This next part could go a number of different ways, and I don't know which one it's going to be, but I'm certain I'm going to enjoy it." Of course, every writer has to commit to a direction (or end the story and let you wonder for yourself what happened next), and that gives the rest of us the opportunity to imagine the alternate ending. That's how "Summers" began for me; I took a popular rendition of a classic fairy tale and privately wondered what would've happened if the tale had gone another way. The science-fiction setting came later, and with it, a resolution that brought the twist back to its roots.

A question for the author

Q: What inspires you?

A: Other people, mostly. I'd be a fool not to recognize how much I am indebted to the genius of those who came before me—from famous storytellers I may never meet to the family and friends that have helped me sharpen my skills along the way. Somebody once said all art is theft, and if I ever try to disagree with them, I'll be on pretty shaky ground.

About the author

Jordan Legg is originally from Oshawa, Ontario, and holds a degree in English and Creative Writing from the University of Windsor. He is an amateur cyclist and sketch artist, as well as an avid reader and writer of speculative fiction. He currently teaches literature and history to preteens and teenagers at a private school in South Asia, where he's lived for several years.

@TheJordanLegg

A Seedling in the Dark

Eleanor R. Wood

He pined for the sky first. It was a constant he had always taken for granted, even when stargazing on crisp winter nights with his dad. But he soon missed the ground more. The cool scent of earth, the lush green of grass and clover that concealed an entire world of wonders. He'd spent countless hours on his belly in the meadow, watching beetles and ants and grasshoppers going about their lives in their towering forest home. Spindly harvest spiders, ladybirds, and snails. He missed them all with a terrible yearning. The toads would be spawning in the pond about now, long threads of jellied beads left in the wake of their orgies, to be collected and grown into tadpoles on windowsill jars.

He wondered if he would ever see a tadpole again.

"When can I go outside?" he'd asked his mum on the third day.

She had taken his hand and looked into his eyes.

"Darling, we can't go outside. Not for a long, long time."

"But why? There haven't been any explosions for days!"

"We've been through this, Jeremy. The explosions have filled the air with germs. It will be too dangerous for years. We're safe down here. But we have to stay here until it's safe up there."

"But what about all the animals? Won't the germs make them poorly?"

"I don't know, love. But nature always finds a way, you know that."

She hadn't answered any more of his questions, and he'd sat on the sofa in the tiny living area thinking about them on his own while she warmed tinned pasta for dinner.

As the long days crawled past, he began to realise how caged bears felt at the zoo. All their pacing, with no trees to rub against or leaf mould to dig through for grubs. He wanted dead leaves under his feet, and trees to look for birds' nests in, and badger setts to wait outside until it got dark and they woke up and nosed their way into the world.

He'd tried to pretend he was a badger and the bunker was his sett, but it was no good. Setts had tunnels that led to fresh air and forest and sky. The bunker had a door that led to a metal ladder that led to another door, sealed and bolted and windowless. He wasn't even allowed outside the first door, never mind that one.

"Why don't you play a board game with Charlotte?" Dad interrupted his misery.

"I'm fed up with board games." It had been weeks. They'd played every game in the bunker half a dozen times.

"Don't be daft — you love them. Come on, I'll play too. What d'you fancy?"

"I don't care." He knew he was sulking, but he didn't care about that either.

"All right, we'll let Charlotte choose." He called her in from the bedroom Jeremy and Charlotte shared. It had barely enough room for two beds and David's cage.

Charlotte chose Hungry Hungry Hippos, which was stupid and noisy and nothing like real hippos. Jeremy played anyway, because there was nothing else to do and he kept imagining the toads trying to spawn but dying from the germs instead, and it made him feel like the whole world was ending and nothing would ever be alive and free again. He and his hippo gobbled up dozens of plastic marbles until Mum said it was time to get ready for bed.

He put fresh water in David's bowl and covered his cage with its night-time cloth. The cockatiel chirped at him and settled down. To David, the world was exactly the same as always, only with a different view. Jeremy envied him.

They did school around the dining table every day. Sometimes David was allowed to perch on Jeremy's shoulder. Charlotte was learning her numbers and letters. Jeremy was learning about volcanoes. There was a chapter on fossils coming up and he couldn't wait to get to that.

"If all the animals die, will they turn into fossils?" he asked Dad.

"I expect some of them will, but it takes an awfully long time."

"I know. Hundreds of thousands of years." But still, the idea of a paleontologist in the future finding fossilised mice and stoats and blackbirds made him feel a little better about their probable deaths. Maybe they'd draw impressions of blackbirds with scarlet plumage or mice with long fur.

It had been three months since they'd all been bundled down the metal stairs. Three months since Dad sealed the top door with a hiss. Three months since Jeremy had seen a beetle or a spider at the centre of her intricate web. But at least he'd seen a living bird every day. He'd had David to feed, and clean out, and draw in intricate coloured-pencil lines. And now even that was gone. Jeremy had found him on the bottom of his cage, cold and stiff. He'd been off his seed for a few days, but there was no vet down here in the ground and all they could do was keep him warm and hope he perked up.

But he didn't. He died. Jeremy had held his soft little body for hours, refusing Mum and Dad's attempts at gently prising him away. He had cried until his throat was dry, and touched every inch of David's soft grey feathers, the white ones on his folded wings, the bright yellow down on his head with its vivid orange cheek spots. He'd stroked David's delicate crest, forever flattened now, and his curved seed-eater's beak and tiny branch-gripping claws. He mourned his friend, his bird, and with him, all the other birds he would never see. He grieved for the last non-human in his life, and hated, with a ferocity he had never experienced, the people who had dropped the bombs.

When he finally relinquished David's body to his dad's care, he curled up on Mum's lap and sobbed anew.

"Oh love, I'm so sorry." She had tears in her voice too. "I know how much he meant to you."

"How will I ever be a naturalist now, Mum?" His breath snagged on a sob. "What if I never see another animal?"

"Of course you will. One day, we'll all climb out of here and greet the world, and you'll see animals and birds and insects again."

"But how?" His anger flared. "They're all dead! Everything is dead except us! What if David was the last bird in the whole world?"

She had tried to soothe him with more words, but he barely heard her over his weeping. The scope was too great. The sadness was too immense. He wanted to walk in the woods more desperately than he had ever wanted anything in his life.

They had art class with Dad once a week. Everything in the bunker was precious, but Dad had provided enough art supplies. They had to use both sides of the paper and all their pencil shavings went into the composter, but there were plenty of watercolours, and Jeremy was painting David from memory again.

"Beautiful shadowing, Jer!" Dad peered over Jeremy's shoulder.

"Thanks, Dad." Jeremy admired his painting. "Do you think I could make a model of him? A lifesized one?"

"What, like a sculpture?" Jeremy heard the approval in Dad's voice. "Now that'd be an excellent project for our next lesson."

Jeremy smiled. "Yeah. A sculpture."

"Fancy that, Charlotte?" Dad asked.

"Like playdough?"

"I'm sure we can get playdough in on the action." Dad winked at her.

They spent the next week finding sculpting materials. Recycling was the bunker's foremost rule, so anything discarded was fair game.

Jeremy's first David sculpture was a wire coathanger frame coated in papier-mâché. It wasn't very good; the frame was wonky and its head was out of proportion. But Jeremy curled its wire feet to the perch in David's cage even so, covering it over at night as if it were inhabited by David's chirpy soul.

Looking for new materials became Jeremy's obsession. He was allowed to experiment with heating old tins into malleable form. He cut a plastic tub into interlocking shapes like a balsa model. Mum got very cross when he unravelled one of his jumpers to wind around a new wire frame. He heard them talking about it in the kitchenette one evening.

"This can't carry on, Craig," Mum said. "Everything we brought down here is precious. We need to repurpose all of it if we're going to make it out of this."

"I know that," Dad said. "But just look at him, Heather. He hasn't been this content since we left home. I can't see anything more worthwhile than directing his energy."

"We need to survive for at least five years to be sure this thing's died out. We didn't bring sculpture materials into our calculations."

"We didn't bring our nature-obsessed son into our calculations either. You've seen how he's been. I'm afraid it's going to break his spirit, being stuck down here without so much as a blade of grass. Maybe... maybe it's time to show him."

There was silence. "You know how I feel about that," Mum said at last.

"We put it there for a reason." Dad's voice was soft.

"Yes. And that wasn't to give our son false hope."

Jeremy had no idea what they were talking about, and if he dared ask, they'd know he'd been listening. So he boxed up his curiosity and shelved it at the back of his mind. For now.

He was allowed to continue making sculptures, but only with materials he was given. He made models of David until he'd perfected a cockatiel. His aluminium body was almost the right shade of grey and his head was the perfect size, painted dandelion yellow with bright orange cheeks and a soft crest of brushed yarn. His talons could be bent around a perch, or flattened to stand on a table, or tucked into Jeremy's jumper so the bird could sit on his shoulder.

He'd been so proud.

"That is fantastic, Jer," Dad said. "From the corner of my eye, I'd think that was really David on your shoulder."

He wasn't really David, though. He didn't chirp, or turn his head on one side and whistle the way Jeremy had taught him. His body was cold metal instead of soft down, and if anything, he made Jeremy even sadder that David was gone.

He awoke one night from a dream he couldn't remember, a dream filled with loss and grief. He was sobbing before he was fully awake. His whole body ached with it. He curled on one side and wept, wanting Mum and Dad but unable to get up and go to them. His David sculpture perched on his bedside table, silent and pretend, and he just wanted to see a real bird again, just one, flying or nesting or singing in a treetop. His head throbbed, his pillow was sodden, his body was racked with it.

And then Dad was there, gathering Jeremy in his arms, holding him tight, Mum just behind, reaching a hand to his back.

"It's a dream, Jer, it's just a dream, mate. You're safe. You're all right." Dad rocked him in strong arms and soaked up Jeremy's tears with his nightshirt.

"I wish it... was... a dream," Jeremy hiccuped. "But it's not. We're really down here, and I can't go outside ever again."

Charlotte was awake now, and she was crying too. Mum went to her. She and Dad looked at each other across the cramped room.

"All right," Mum said. "You can show him."

"Show me... what?" Jeremy's breath hitched as he tried to stop the flow of tears.

"Come with me," Dad said, and took his hand.

He'd always thought it was just a cupboard, housing pipes and electrics and boring things not worth investigating. And it did have those things... but behind them, at the back, there was a ladder of metal rungs protruding from the wall.

"Up you go," Dad said, right behind him.

He climbed, still shaky from crying. At the top of the ladder was a square platform, just big enough for two people to sit side-by-side. The ceiling was only a few feet high, so Dad had to crouch low to squash into the space.

And set into the ceiling was a skylight.

"The sky..." Jeremy craned his neck to peer up at the blackness. It was cloudy, but there was a moon.

"There it is," Dad said, pulling Jeremy close so they could look together. The oblong of sky was small, but the spill of moonlight was enough to illuminate the space where they sat.

"Why is this here?" Jeremy asked. "Why didn't you tell me about it?"

Dad inhaled slowly. "Well, it was supposed to be at the centre of the bunker, so we'd have some natural light. But Mum worried it might make things harder for us, being able to see out to the world when we couldn't be in it. And I thought maybe she was right about that. So I changed the layout plan and built a cupboard around it, so it was still there without being a constant reminder of what we were missing. We didn't tell you because... we thought it might make you sadder than you already were. But I've never seen anyone as sad as you were tonight, so we realised maybe it could help you feel better."

The realisations were dawning on Jeremy. "I'll be able to see what the weather's like! And look at stars... and..." *What if a bird flies over,* was his thought, but he didn't voice it because there might not be any birds and he didn't want to feel sad again.

"Can I, Dad? Can I come up here sometimes?"

Dad kissed the top of his head. "Yeah. If it makes you feel better, of course you can."

At first, he went up every morning before breakfast, to check the weather and report to his family. Charlotte came up a few times, but she soon got bored with the view.

"You can't see anything," she complained. "Just the sky and nothing else!"

"Don't come up here, then," Jeremy said, defensive of his patch of sky.

He started going up the ladder whenever he missed the outdoors. Just looking at a piece of the outside world soothed him and made him feel connected to it again. One evening, he and Dad piled blankets and pillows on the platform and stargazed, watching pieces of constellations glide in and out of view until Jeremy fell asleep. He woke up there alone the next morning, sunlight on his face.

"You let me sleep up there," he said to Dad at breakfast.

Dad dolloped porridge for him. "I didn't have the heart to move you."

"Can I sleep there again tonight?"

Mum and Dad looked at each other. "I'm not sure that's sensible," Mum said.

"Please?"

"Yeah, can he, Mum?" Charlotte piped up. "I liked having my own room."

Dad laughed and gave Mum a helpless shrug. Mum sighed. "All right. But if it starts making you feel upset, you come back to your bedroom. Okay?"

"Yes!" It was half agreement, half joy. He hadn't felt upset at all since Dad had shown him the skylight.

The platform became his new bedroom. The skylight was his own private window. He would fall asleep looking at the stars and wake up amongst a shaft of sunlight or a patter of rain on the thick Perspex. He was still confined, but the outdoors was there, right there, and contentment began to nudge at the empty places in his soul.

It had been a year since they stumbled underground and closed the world off. A year of cramped space and brittle emotion. A year without the breeze on their faces or new grass between their toes. A year without a single insect or stream minnow or trill of birdsong.

Jeremy's hours of gazing through the skylight had shown him that Earth still turned on its axis, that the Moon still accompanied them on their journey through space, that the seasons still brought rain and sun and snow that hid the sky until a thaw. He'd watched grass grow at the edges of his view, reaching tall and turning to seed and then dying back again. He'd seen leaves scutter across the skylight and frost form branching patterns and clouds of all varieties.

But he'd seen no signs of animal life.

He hoped that his view's limited scope simply meant he was missing them as they bypassed the bunker. That he'd never been looking at the exact moment a bird flew over or an insect buzzed past. But as time went on, he had to acknowledge the germ-filled air must have harmed them. That they just weren't there anymore. It broke his heart, but he didn't dare share it in case his parents made him return to his bedroom.

He watched David Attenborough documentaries until he could recite the narration by heart. He learned about the nitrogen cycle and copied pictures of leaves from his tree guidebook. He fell asleep every night with his face turned to the skylight and imagined the world full of animals, happy and thriving with no people around.

And then, one morning, a snail was there.

His breath caught in his chest as he woke to find himself looking up at it sliding slowly across the skylight, oblivious to the racing heart and burgeoning joy its passage caused in the human four feet below. Its trail glistened in the morning light as its suctioned foot propelled it across Jeremy's window to the world. He stood and pressed his face as close as possible, palms flat against the skylight, drinking in the sight of a living creature, willing it to slow down so he wouldn't have to watch it leave. He moved with it, his nose separated by inches of Perspex. As it glided over the side of the skylight, back to dew-damp grass and whatever hollow it sought for its daily rest, Jeremy felt his heart simultaneously squeeze and lift. He hated to see it depart, but the wonder and beauty of it made him soar.

His first proof that things still lived outside the bunker. That all creatures hadn't been killed. He leapt down the ladder and yelled his newfound truth.

"A snail! Mum, Dad, I saw a snail! Everything isn't dead, it's not! There was a snail on the skylight!"

Mum looked up from laying the breakfast table. Dad stopped stirring the porridge.

"That's fantastic, love." Mum smiled at the grin on his face.

"If animals are alive, it must be safe now!"

"Not necessarily, mate." Dad's tone was cautious. "It's great news, but one snail doesn't make it safe for us."

"But... maybe it's the beginning of it being safe," Jeremy said. "If a snail's alive, other things must be too!"

"Jeremy..." Mum put a bowl of porridge in front of him. "I'm delighted you saw a snail, but it's not evidence that other animals are alive, or that we could be. You don't even know it was healthy. Now eat your breakfast."

Even the monotony of porridge couldn't dampen his spirits. "But it looked healthy! And there can't just be *one snail*. Ecosystems don't work like that. There have to be other things living out there."

"*Jeremy.*" Mum raised her voice. "Eat. Your. Breakfast."

He swallowed a lump in his throat. He thought they'd be as excited as he was.

"It's great, Jer," Dad said. "It is. But you mustn't let it get your hopes up."

Jeremy looked down and ate his porridge in silence.

"I wish *I* could see a snail," Charlotte said wistfully.

Dad was an engineer. Mum was a mathematician. What did *they* know about nature? Jeremy knew lifeforms couldn't exist on their own. He just needed more proof, and then they'd listen to him and maybe realise there was no need to stay stuck down here. It could be his first Great Discovery: that the poisoned world wasn't poison any more. He didn't tell them; he knew if Mum sensed this new fixation, she'd ban him from the skylight. He couldn't conceive of losing his only link to nature. He'd shrivel up and die like a seedling denied the sun.

So he lay under the skylight every spare moment, feigning tiredness or headaches or interest in a new book. He gave up television; why watch recordings of living things when there were real ones he might miss while his attention was on a dead screen? His snail didn't return. He watched clouds scudding past, stared at pattering rain, witnessed the pastel reflections of a dozen sunsets, but no sign of what he longed for.

Patience was something every naturalist had to cultivate. You could sit in a bog for hours waiting for a sighting of that rare frog, or train your binoculars on a single tree for days to witness chicks fledging, or stare at a skylight for weeks to catch a glimpse of proof that nature fought on despite the worst of humanity's follies.

When it finally came, he thought he'd imagined it. A flicker of movement, high and tiny at the periphery of his rectangle of sky. He blinked and stared. The light was fading and he'd been about to call it a day. His mind was playing tricks on him.

Again — that fluttering glimpse. And... another! Dipping back and forth, the erratic, flitting flight pattern that could never be mistaken for a bird. Jeremy felt the grin spread across his face even as tears pricked his eyes.

Bats. There were bats in the sky.

He gazed upwards and watched them dash back and forth across his foot-wide field of vision. He was laughing and crying at once, overwhelmed with joy at the sight of little mammals hunting for their supper.

As the light dissipated, he lost sight of them, but he lay there for a long time, high on relief and delight.

Hunting bats. That meant there were insects. He'd witnessed the top and bottom of the food chain. Predator and prey. An ecosystem supporting itself. Life went on outside the bunker. Animal life. Plant life. It all had to be there, thriving and well. Everything wasn't dead.

Everything was all right out there.

He climbed down the ladder on trembling legs and ran to his family, who were huddled together watching an old movie.

"Mum... Dad," he began, trying to curb his excitement so he could calmly present his discovery. They looked up at him.

"I just saw bats." It gushed out of him. "Bats! Above the skylight, hunting insects!"

Dad smiled. "Wow. That's fantastic!"

"Wonderful, love," Mum said.

"I mean... they were hunting. That means there're insects, which means there's all kinds of life. They didn't all die!"

His parents glanced at each other. "That's really excellent news," Dad said. "Maybe tomorrow we can all look out and see them."

"Yeah! But..." They weren't getting it. "It must be safe now. If they're all right, it must be safe for us too."

"Jeremy, we've been through this." He could sense Mum trying to remain calm. "Seeing creatures outside is wonderful, but it doesn't mean the air is safe. Biological agents last for a very long time."

"There's a whole ecosystem out there, Mum!" His own calm was fleeing and he was powerless to hold onto it. "I know there is! And if they're thriving, why wouldn't we?"

Dad stood up and put his arms around Jeremy.

Jeremy shrugged away. "You're not listening!"

"No, *you're* not listening," Mum said. "The only way we're going to get through this is if we all accept the facts. The bacteria might not harm animals, but they *will* harm us. We all want to get out of here, Jeremy. We all miss nature. But it is *not safe*. It won't be for a long time. And I think..." She closed her eyes and took a deep breath. "I think it's time to go back to your bedroom."

Dad made a pleading gesture.

"No, Craig. Enough is enough. This isn't doing any of us any good. No more skylight."

"No! No, no, you can't!" The lurch in Jeremy's chest propelled him forward. "Mum, please! I won't look for any more wildlife, I promise!"

"Enough, Jeremy! I've had enough. We all have." She went to the cupboard and up the ladder. Jeremy tried to follow, but Dad held him back with a firm but gentle arm around his chest.

"I'm sorry, mate. Mum's right. We need to be together to get through this. You can't keep living half out there, breaking your heart and ours."

"No, Dad..." he sobbed. "Please, I need it."

Dad just held him tightly while Mum dragged his bedding and notebooks and David sculpture out of the cupboard and into Charlotte's bedroom.

"Why does he have to come back in here?" his sister whined, following her mother.

"Because he does, Charlotte."

Dad bent his head to Jeremy's and hugged him. The tears drenched Jeremy's face.

He stayed in bed for the first two days. He didn't eat. He couldn't bear the thought of being shut back in this underground box with no windows. Especially now he knew there was wildlife out there. Charlotte sulked about having him back in 'her' room. Mum and Dad had hushed arguments, and Jeremy knew some of them were about the skylight. When he emerged, finally, with a touch of appetite, everyone tried to pretend nothing had happened.

"Macaroni cheese for dinner!" Dad said, mixing a packet of cheese sauce. Jeremy missed real cheese.

He glanced at the cupboard. He'd had half a plan to sneak up to the skylight after Mum and Dad had gone to bed, but he'd known they wouldn't make it that easy. The cupboard door was padlocked. He turned away and ate half a plate of macaroni before going back to bed.

Dad tried to interest him in art projects. Mum read aloud to him. Even Charlotte tried to cheer him up with board games and terrible knock-knock jokes.

But he didn't care about any of it. Nothing mattered any more.

Anger slowly replaced his sadness, and with it came a flash of rebellion he'd never imagined. He lay awake one night and hatched a foolish plan. He knew it was foolish and he didn't care. He just wanted to show them they couldn't keep him from nature. The cupboard door was locked, but Jeremy knew where Dad hid his keys. The secret nook was inside a kitchen cabinet, behind tins of beans.

He'd unlock the cupboard, barricade it from the other side, return to his skylight, and there'd be nothing they could do about it. He'd even sneak a stash of food from the pantry. He knew it was an unsustainable protest, but what could they do? They'd already taken away the only thing he cared about. There weren't any punishments worse than that.

He lay still and listened. The bunker was silent. Mum and Dad had gone to bed; Charlotte's soft breathing told him she was asleep. He tiptoed into the kitchenette. In the dim nightlight glow, he retrieved the keys from their hidden nook, grasping them so they wouldn't jangle. There were only a few on the keyring... there weren't many doors in the bunker.

The padlock key was the smallest. He was on the verge of sliding it into the lock when it dawned on him what he was holding.

One of these keys opened the main door. The door which led to the ladder which led to the outside door which led to the world. He wondered why the existence of this key had never occurred to him. He knew which one it was: it was bigger than the others.

He looked at the door, ten paces away beside the kitchenette. The door he'd only been through once.

You can't.

But he could. All he had to do was open it.

And then what?

Then he'd be able to climb up to the outside door. There was a lever to unseal it. He could go outside. Come back before anyone woke up. He could prove to them that they were wrong, that nothing would happen to them if they came out. Whatever they said, humans *were* animals. And animals were surviving out there. The bats and the snail were his proof. He would be theirs.

He'd made up his mind before he even realised it, before his conscience could protest again. He was at the main door, all thoughts of the skylight forgotten, and the big key slid in smoothly and turned with a soft click, as though the lock had been waiting all this time for him to open it.

He glanced over his shoulder, afraid someone had heard. But the bunker slept on. He opened the door.

The dusky light barely illuminated the short passage and steep steps. But he didn't dare leave the inner door open in case Mum or Dad got up. Later, he'd tell them he'd been outside, and they could all reunite with nature. But now was just for him. He was a few steps away from the outdoors, from fresh air and wild things, for the first time in a year and a half. He didn't fear it. He knew he wouldn't drop dead from bacteria. If they'd seen the bats, they'd know that too.

The cramped stairwell was pitch dark with the inner door shut. He found the railing and groped his way up. The only patch of light came from a keypad beside the top door. His heart sank. He couldn't just pull the lever and go out.

ENTER YOUR FOUR-DIGIT CODE, the display read.

What would Dad use as a code? He thought for a moment, then keyed in his own birth year.

It bleeped its acceptance and a mechanism clunked.

Jeremy grinned. *Too obvious, Dad.*

His heart rate increased as he pulled the lever downwards, releasing the door's seal with a soft hiss. He pushed it open and stepped outside.

His eyes closed in bliss at the cool night air against his skin, sweeter than anything he'd ever breathed. Tears squeezed under his eyelids and he laughed out loud as he lifted his head to the sky and spread his arms wide. *Outside, I'm outside!*

The relief overwhelmed him. He fell to his knees in the long grass, clutching the fronds and relishing their smooth stems against his skin and the rich scent of the soil beneath, and the ground, cool and firm and uneven and holding him up as it rooted him back to where he belonged.

When he lifted his head, it was later than he'd realised; dawn was glowing on the horizon. He stood and walked through the tall grass, leaving the bunker behind without a backward glance. The breeze caressed his skin, stirring the trees to whisper their greetings. He reached the steadfast boulder at the edge of the field. Its surface was rough and cool against his palm, and lichen tickled his fingertips. The landscape stretched away here, open and green, all the way to the distant city. He climbed the boulder and waited for the sun.

A blackbird began to sing. A thrill ran up his back at that sweet melody, the purest sound in nature. He drank in the song like a parched boy at a stream, and felt it restore him. *Birds. Birds are alive.* A robin joined in, and a song thrush, and the dawn chorus rose up around him like a devotion, welcoming the day, welcoming him back.

He watched the sky pale and turn to flame until the land was bathed in sun and at last he beheld what the bombs had done.

The once-ploughed fields were a sea of meadow grasses. His house, perched alongside, had been consumed by the Virginia creeper his mother had continually pruned. The lawn was a jungle, the fence was woven with ivy, and saplings grew in the driveway's cracks. The first bees of the day began their work amongst the wildflowers, and house martins dipped and dove in the air.

Bombs had sent people into hiding, and nature had rejoiced.

Far off on the horizon, where once spires had risen and sunlight glinted on glass, there was an indistinct mass of broken things and a ring of scorched earth. Yet even amongst the burnt wreckage, he could see hints of green at this epicentre of human disaster.

His parents had been wrong. Life was thriving stronger than ever out here. His heart exploded with it.

He had no notion of time passing as he revelled in creatures living and flowers opening. And then, from behind him, Dad's voice.

"Jeremy... what have you done?"

Disappointment, grief, despair... his father's tone reflected nothing of the joy in Jeremy's soul. He turned to see him walking through the grass, his pale face lined with hurt.

"Dad..." He smiled. "Look! It's safe out here! I told you it was."

"No, Jeremy, no, no, it's not." There were tears in Dad's eyes. "There are deadly germs out here. We told you that."

"But — look at the wildlife!"

Dad's arms dropped at his sides. "You don't understand, Jer. And it's our fault. We should have explained it to you properly. Wildlife is here, yes... and it's glorious. But humans can't be. No one knew if the biological agent would harm other species. It's wonderful that they don't appear to be affected. But for people, everything out here is contaminated."

Jeremy's protests died in his throat. He couldn't believe it. But Dad's face... he looked lost. Broken. Tendrils of fear crept around Jeremy's heart.

"Then... we have to go back inside?" he asked.

Dad clenched his jaw. "No. We can't go back inside. We're contaminated too now, you and me."

Jeremy noticed a pair of rucksacks on the ground outside the bunker.

"We can't go back in without putting Mum and Charlotte in danger. They mustn't be exposed."

"But... they can't stay down there on their own!"

"They have to. And the two of us... we have to get moving. Our best chance is to get as far from the biological radius as possible. If we're lucky, and if there are any doctors still alive who've figured out treatments, we might be okay."

The foundation of Jeremy's world buckled under him. "No, we can't leave them, Dad!"

Dad pressed thumb and forefinger to his eyes to push away tears. "We don't have a choice, mate."

Jeremy slid down off the boulder and ran towards the door he'd been so desperate to exit. Dad caught him with one arm and reeled him in tight.

"Let me go... I need to tell Mum I'm sorry!"

"You can't. You can't. They have to stay safe."

"Why did you come out, then? Why, if it's dangerous?" He twisted to face Dad.

"For you. I came out for you, Jer."

Jeremy felt the weight of his mistake like a mountain about to crush him.

"And now we need to go."

Dad went to the rucksacks and shouldered one. He handed the other to Jeremy. Poking out of the top was his David sculpture. Jeremy stared at it, numb and bewildered.

Dad stopped beside the skylight. Jeremy's window was just a strange hump in the grass from out here. Dad beckoned to him, seemingly unable to speak. Jeremy came reluctantly and looked down, into his haven... the tiny space that had instilled in him so much hope.

Mum and Charlotte's faces looked up at him, tears in both their eyes. Mum reached a hand to the Perspex and Jeremy knelt, sobs erupting from nowhere, and pressed his face to the skylight, still inches from theirs. *I love you,* Mum mouthed to both of them. Charlotte clung to her, weeping.

Dad inhaled a ragged breath and tugged Jeremy's shoulder. "Come on. We've got to move."

Jeremy peeled himself away, sick with regret. Dad was already on his way to the lane beside the house, wiping his face on one sleeve. Jeremy watched him for a moment, frozen, and then took David from his rucksack. He stroked the soft crest and then placed the memento of his beloved bird in the grass beside the bunker door. To stand guard? As grave marker for his first loss?

He didn't know. But this David was of the bunker, as Jeremy was of the outdoors, and their ways had parted.

"Dad... wait!" Jeremy called as he turned away from David. Everything was happening too fast. He didn't have time to make sense of the upheaval he'd caused.

Dad turned back to him. It hurt Jeremy to look at his face. "What? Jeremy, we need to leave. Right now."

Jeremy fought the tears that kept trying to flood out of him. "Can't we just... stay at the house? At least be near Mum and Charlotte?"

Dad closed his eyes and took a long, slow breath. "You know we can't do that. And you know why."

"But I've been out here for ages and I'm not ill!"

"We don't know that."

"But —"

"*No*. No more 'buts'. No more 'maybes'. We all heard the bombs, we know how close they were, we know they brought deadly disease. We have to find help, Jeremy, if there's any help out there to find."

"Are you cross with me?" He didn't mean it to come out in such a tiny, sad voice.

Dad sighed, wearier than Jeremy had ever seen him. "There wouldn't be any point in that, would there?" He reached out his arm.

Jeremy ran to him and clutched him hard.

"Come on." Dad's voice was softer now. He rubbed Jeremy's back. "The sooner we're away, the better our chances."

Jeremy wiped his eyes and held onto his dad's hand like a little boy.

They left the bunker. They left the house. They began their long walk, and Jeremy knew, as his dad knew, that it might not save them. The long-rotted bodies they passed, in cars, in front gardens, were proof of the danger Jeremy had exposed them to. He squeezed his eyes shut at these confirmations of death's brutal reign.

But despite his loss, his fear, their terrible uncertainty, Jeremy's heart was soothed. For the hedgerows they passed were wild and teeming with life, and birds sang their summer songs of fertility and survival.

See Eleanor R. Wood's story "A Seedling in the Dark" online at
Metaphorosis.
If you liked it, leave a comment. Authors love that!
Remember to subscribe to our e-mail updates so you'll know when
new stories are posted.

About the story

This story arose from several sources, but its overriding inspiration was British naturalist Chris Packham's astonishing autobiography, *Fingers in the Sparkle Jar*. In it, he describes his early passion for nature - not only his childhood obsession with the natural world, but the deep solace and sense of belonging he found there, particularly as a boy who didn't fit in anywhere else. Around the time I read this book, I'd been toying with the notion of writing a story set in a survivalist bunker, and suddenly I was struck with the concept of a child who was deeply connected to nature and then cut off from it entirely. What would that do to a kid like this? What would it have done to Chris Packham as a boy? What would it do to me...?

I've also loved and thrived on nature since childhood, and the idea of being completely severed from it terrifies me. Being amongst nature is being surrounded by life. Being amongst non-human lifeforms takes our gaze away from ourselves and reminds us that this planet is host to far more than just human beings. In the story, Jeremy's desperate need to have that affirmed overrides every other concern in his imprisoned life, and ultimately takes him to a place of both tremendous joy and bewildering sorrow.

A question for the author

Q: Where do you write?
A: I write at my desk, in a room full of books and plants, both of which I find infinitely inspiring. My writing room has two large windows, so it's full of natural light, and there's normally at least one dog relaxing nearby. The desk is usually cluttered with hand-scrawled notes, as I vastly prefer writing story notes by hand, and although it may look chaotic to the untrained eye, I always know exactly where everything is.

About the author

Eleanor R. Wood writes speculative fiction and eats liquorice from the south coast of England, where she lives with her husband, two marvellous dogs, and enough tropical fish tanks to charge an entry fee.
creativepanoply.wordpress.com, @erwrites

The Nocturnals V

Mariah Montoya

In a world where each day and night lasts thirty years, Joah, Misla, and Damien have traveled into the Eternal Night to make contact with the humanoid creatures who live there—the Nocturnals, a people they used to fear. Now that they know the Nocturnals' terrible secret, they must warn their nomadic community of a planned massacre lying ahead.

To get back to sunset in time, Joah and the others travel deep underground to find fuel for Queen Usai's ancient starship. Deadly traps, a prisoner's betrayal, and a mysterious Leather Skin lurking underground threaten to tear them apart, but through it all, the three must persevere.

It's time to return to daylight. It's time to tell the Sunsetters the truth about the Nocturnals. It's time to destroy the real darkness once and for all, before the sun leaves them behind forever.

Part 5

Someone was knocking on Aoif Deckler's door.

He ignored the noise, staring out his window at the mountainous shadows darkening the valley where he had forced his people to settle. He could smell the salt from here. Just beyond those cliffs, the sun was balancing on the edge of a great sea, a sea he had been yearning to taste again ever since his boots had crunched back on brittle sand fifty-eight years ago.

"General Deckler, sir," a voice called from behind the door. "Please."

He tried to ignore the wretched knocking, but his captain's voice whined through the wood incessantly. After a few more ticks from his wristwatch, Deckler withdrew his feet from his polished desk and slammed them to the frayed, thin carpet.

"Okay, fine, don't piss off," he boomed. "Why don't you come in, then, Lincoln? We can have ourselves a little tea party while we're at it. Act like princesses."

The door burst open. Captain Lincoln stood panting in his doorway, the hallway behind him strangely distorted—its walls had been dented during their most recent Move. A silver badge gleamed on his chest, his hair shined with gel, and his hands were naked of calluses.

"It's a woman from the Dirt Slums, General," Lincoln breathed. "She's going mad down in the office. Tearing her hair out, practically. Won't stop screaming that she wants to see you, and well…" Captain Lincoln massaged his lotioned hands together. "You sent most of our security ahead with the first wave. We don't have any jailhouses. Or handcuffs."

No, Deckler had not wanted the officers and retrievers to come running when the Nocturnals—or rather, the Nocturnal *slaves*—invaded the Dirt Slums. He had sent those individuals ahead to camp out with the scavengers and sailors on the edge of the Green Sea, where they'd be safe.

Captain Lincoln, on the other hand, would probably get snatched up in his haste to help the chosen victims. So would the Dirt Slummer apparently banging around his office downstairs.

"What's her name?" Deckler asked the captain, his eyes flicking open.

"Lupita Fertheli, General."

The name stirred something vaguely familiar in Deckler's chest. Ah, he needed a cigar. His fingers twitched toward his cabinet, where his last roll of tobacco lay tucked away—but no. When they sailed the sea and left this piece of the aro behind, he'd only get one smoke. Better to save it for something more disturbing, more frightening, than a piss-poor bitch of the slums.

Deckler grinned, opened his desk drawer, and popped a candy into his mouth. He rolled the thing from cheek to cheek until he felt his teeth turn blue.

"Send her up, Lincoln. Let's see what she has to say."

The captain bowed and scurried away, his footsteps clunking down the portable stairs past the bend in the hallway. Moments later, a door from below banged open. Lupita Fertheli's shrieks crashed into Deckler's office moments before the woman herself did.

"I can walk by *myself*, thank you very much."

Lupita yanked her elbow from Captain Lincoln's grasp, took one look at Deckler lounging in his office chair, and slammed the door behind her with a violent kick of her fraying sandal.

"Well, good evening," Deckler said, half-amused, half-irritated. "Or should I say good night?" He glanced out the window, where the cliffs cast pools of darkness. He imagined he could see the outlines of the ships Captain Lincoln's men had built on the shoreline.

"It *isn't* a good night," snarled Lupita Fertheli. Her hair stuck wildly in every direction, witch-like. The palms she slapped on Deckler's desk left grimy handprints on a stack of papers. Hatred and fury bandaged the grief lining her face. "My son is still missing."

"Is he, now?"

The gears clicked into place. *Yes.* This was the woman whose son Joah Cadshaw had been trying to find for the law enforcement office. Deckler himself had halted the investigation so he could send Cadshaw to do more important things, like getting the hell out of his way.

Judging by the repugnance pinching Lupita Fertheli's face, she already knew this.

"Where's Detective Cadshaw, General?" she asked now. Deckler felt a thrill of relief at the wobble infecting her voice. It wouldn't take long for the tears to flow, and when they did, she'd no longer seem to tower over him like a wiry-haired fortress.

"Cadshaw?" he asked, blinking up at her politely.

"Yes, *Cadshaw.* The one looking for my son. The one you sent away. I *know* he went to you after the Moving bells rang early. I *know* he left the community with another retriever. But I'm begging you—*begging* you..." And there it was: a glistening eye. "Tell me where Cadshaw is now," she said. "Has he found my Damien? Did h-he ever come b-back?"

"Listen, Lupita. It's Lupita, isn't it?" Deckler didn't wait for her to nod; he put a hand on the same wrinkled elbow she had yanked from Captain Lincoln. "I sent Joah out west to see if your son had... strayed. To see if he'd gone after the Nocturnals."

This was a lie, but when Lupita's shoulders sagged from their previous rigidity, he didn't regret it. He massaged her elbow, and she let him, sniffing up tears that wobbled on the edge of her nose. Such an *easy* lie. The truth hit harder, especially since he'd actually liked Cadshaw.

"But he didn't come back when I told him to, Lupita. Last I heard, he and Retriever Crane warned the grahsm miners about the early bells and continued west. The oil scavengers said they never saw them. As far as I know, Cadshaw's still searching for your son."

Or being hacked to pieces, he didn't add when Lupita split into sobs. He had his own suspicions about the fate of Joah Cadshaw: the man's enemy, the one who'd cut off his wife's head, hadn't returned from his western duties either. Just *poof.* Gone. Deckler had chuckled a little to think that the two would meet again when he'd sent Joah that direction, but now that neither had returned, it wasn't hard to imagine a bloody battle in the woods at sunset.

Ah, well. There were more important things. Like ships. Or the invasion that would tear through the valley within the next arcsec. Or the sobbing wench before him.

"Listen, Lupita, if you have an arcsec to spare, I could have my secretary make you some tea. Our herbalists found a new kind of mint on the way here, I'm sure it would help calm you."

He didn't know what made him say it. Why should he care for a grubby life like hers? The sooner she left his office, the sooner he could focus on his impending date with the Nocturnal king. But something in her wild, crazed face mirrored the smut of that horrible season after his mother's death and before he became general. When he had been poor and hungry and scared too.

Lupita Fertheli wrenched her elbow away from his stroking thumb, her eyebrows hardening. For a mad moment, she looked the same shade of sick Deckler's own mother had been so long ago. Flames pierced her eyes, and she thrust her chin in the air.

"I won't stay here if you don't have answers. I'm missing my *son,* dammit, and if you don't know what happened to Detective Cadshaw, I'll find someone who does."

She whipped around. Deckler's eyes followed her trembling figure to the door.

"Suit yourself," he said somberly, after one of those sandals had kicked it shut again.

He waited for the night to begin with tightly pressed fingertips. Nobody disturbed him again. He opened his drawer, popped more candy in his mouth, rolled it along his gums. The clock ticked. The shadows deepened. Eventually, Deckler hoisted himself up and approached the cabinet. He glanced at the glossy poster hanging above it, that many-eyed figure leering at him behind lamination. The image cheered him up. It was funny, really… he'd spent the last sixty years teaching his students at the Retrieving Institute that the creature painted on the poster was a Nocturnal: as far from the truth as day was to night.

With a whistle, he opened the cabinet door.

When the clock struck three degrees, smoke was already curling toward Deckler's ceiling. It was not quite nighttime, but the cliffs blocking the sun bathed them in a rich darkness. He strode to his window and thrust it open, inhaling that smell of salt and ocean breeze.

From the crevices in the distant cliffs, disfigured shadows scuttled into the valley. They wended their way between wheeled structures, into the slums that had Moved from *there* to *here*.

When the first screams rent the air, Deckler looked back at his pinned poster and winked at it, as if enjoying a silent joke with an old friend.

Joah watched the ground shrink through frosted windows.

As they rose above the netted treetops, the landscape became a mass of intersecting light. Patches of foliage were re-growing where their sun counterparts had died. Blades and leaves and trees glowed with the energy their roots had sucked from the ground. The plants were feeding off the reservoir of sunsap they had collected during the thirty-year day.

That same sunsap now fueled Joah's flight through the clouds.

As the clouds thickened, mist swathed his view of the aro below. He withdrew from the window and turned to find Prince Kal explaining various parts of the starship to a wide-eyed Damien Fertheli: there was the control system, slathered in buttons and knobs more complex than any vehicle Joah had ever seen; and over *there* were the storage bins, metal compartments filled with canned sugar water, spare spider silk cloaks, and weapons.

I can take you up to see the generator, if you'd like, Kal told the boy.

Even after spending a whole season with the Nocturnals, Joah still marveled at the words hissing, not from the prince's lips, but from his mind. Telepathy suited the circumstance, though. It was hard to hear voices over the rattling of the starship as they flew.

Oh, yes, please, Damien said, obviously trying not to appear too eager. His face remained nonchalant, but his thoughts quivered with excitement. *I mean, why not?*

This way, then.

Prince Kal pulled a lever dangling from the ceiling. A narrow ladder unfolded itself from the upper floor, and Kal mounted it, motioning for Damien to follow.

When he and the boy had disappeared into the crawlspace above, Joah turned to Misla, who was fingering the rough wooden edges of the table quivering in the middle of the room.

"Are you alright?" he asked, touching the other end of the table. His mind mimicked his tongue, so he knew she'd be able to hear him as clearly is if he were whispering into her ear.

She had bathed since they had retrieved the sunsap from underground. Her hair fell in tight waves below her breasts, and she wore a honied blue dress made from one of the queen Nocturnal's old cloaks. A bruise spiraled around her neck where the creatural roots had strangled her below the aro. Beneath her dress, she wore another scar, the remnants of an abuser now gone.

Joah moved closer. She gave a hesitant smile.

"I feel sick, to be honest."

"Couldn't have anything to do with the fact that we're zooming through the air faster than the sun moves across the sky, could it?" Joah asked.

Her lips twitched.

"Could be. Or maybe it's because I'm about to confront the general I swore an oath to and tell him his ass is fried if he doesn't step down. *That* would make anyone want to puke."

"Hey, you know that's not part of the plan."

No, Deckler would never step down. They all knew that, even Damien. Their plan was no longer to fly to the Sunsetters and dissuade their general from a deed he'd been planning for six decades. They were heading southeast, yes, but toward King Isce's fortress instead, where they would kill the Nocturnal king before he could give his orders. If they made it in time, that was. And if they *could* kill him.

"Don't," said Misla, clasping her stomach. "I really *might* puke."

Again, Joah felt that desire to hold her, or be held by her, or do more than stare at her with a table between them. But he swallowed his thoughts and said, "Why don't you go to bed, then? If Prince Kal is right about how fast this thing flies, we'll be there in a dozen arcsecs."

"Yeah, okay."

Swaying a little, she crossed the circular room and approached one of the rounded outlines by the control panel. She pressed her cold palm against it. The wall slid upward obediently, revealing one of the tiny sleeping compartments Prince Kal had shown them earlier.

She paused outside the door, jolting as the starship rocked violently.

Will you come with me, Detective Cadshaw?

Joah's heart raged inside him, louder and more fearsome than Moving bells could ever be. He clutched the table's edge, more to steady his mind than his body. Outside, rain began to thrash against the glass, and the mist flared with occasional bursts of light.

I mean, why not? he said in the same offhand tone that Damien had expressed.

She rolled her eyes and ducked her way into the compartment, which housed a pull-down cot beneath some overhanging shelves. She crawled onto the mattress, sinking into its spongy material. Joah followed. He could hear the faint drone of Prince Kal and Damien's thoughts in the crawlspace above, but when he lowered the compartment door behind him, the buzz of their conversation faded. The only sound in here, it seemed, was Misla breathing.

He sank onto the bed, reaching out to find her in the denseness of this new, rich darkness. His hand found her shoulder; his fingers traced her neck, hovered over the bruise, and worked their way up to her chin, her lips. Hot desire shuddered through him, as if he'd inhaled sunsap.

She grabbed the back of his neck and pulled him onto her, and then their lips brushed against each other, and her thighs were wrapping around his waist, drawing him closer.

I want you, they said together. Their thoughts were merging, twisting and twining like the glowing designs of the aro during the Eternal Night. And they were kissing—he was tasting her, and she smelled like sweetened sunshine. *Misla, Misla, Misla.* He pulled up her dress, and...

In the darkness, it might have been Blair, the corpse of his dead wife lying in his bed, running fingers through his hair, muttering that she wanted a baby...

And Misla's thoughts scampered with panic too. In the darkness, it might have been Hickory, the corpse of her ex-lover bowing over her with that greedy stench of rape wafting from his tongue, ready to sink rotting teeth into the burn scar he had inflicted upon her...

They broke apart, gasping for breath.

No! Joah cried.

No, no, no, Misla moaned.

Tears scorched Joah's cheeks as he rolled away. He had thought he was over his wife, that he'd come to accept her death. And God, he really *did* love Misla. But his body shook with tremors from that morbid vision, and he knew he had *not* healed, had not yet reached the light at the end of his vast and monstrous tunnel.

Neither have I, Misla said. She was crying too, her breath hiccupping as their mingled tears dampened the pillows. She still felt haunted by her own personal chasm of darkness too.

"What do we do?" Joah whispered out loud.

They found each other's hands as the walls gave a nasty jolt.

"We help each other find the light," Misla said.

He nodded, turned toward her, wrapped his arms around her waist and buried his face in her neck. Yes, they would help each other find the light. He closed his eyes.

They'd walk the tunnel together, even if it felt like that walk would never end.

When they finally shot from the clouds, sunset pierced them through the windows.

Joah, Misla, and Damien squinted, shielding their eyes with their hands. Prince Kal donned his hood and clipped the edges of his cloak together, skulking in the shadows.

I can't touch the control panel anymore, the Nocturnal said, nodding at the stream of thin, orange light running from the windowpane to the many knobs and buttons. *One of you will need to follow my instructions to land. We're almost there.*

"I'll do it," Damien said.

Joah and Misla glanced at each other, but the boy had pinched his eyebrows together in obvious determination. With a unified nod, they stationed themselves on either side of him, ready to pounce on the panel if he ever became overwhelmed.

Okay, see that gear shift in the upper left corner? Yes, that's the one. Put it in low.

Damien did as Prince Kal commanded, his forehead wrinkled with concentration. He pulled levers, pressed knobs, and tapped keys with nimble hands. Soon they were plunging into a maze of cliffs and valleys and winding rivulets.

"Look," Misla said with a half-laugh, pointing, "I think it's that river we were going to float. The one that ran by the grahsm cavern. See how it's heading southeast."

Sure enough, a widespread snake of water glittered between canyons, and it led to—

"Oh," Joah breathed.

The horizon expanded as they descended, winking with pink light. And the sun—that brilliant bowl of orange Joah had so missed—teetered on the edge of a sea he had only ever heard stories about. It was, he thought as he stared out the window, like an upside-down sky, filled with rippled green water and sprinkled with stars. The fabled Green Sea.

Hard left, Prince Kal said. *We don't want to land on my father's front lawn.*

Damien drove the starship into a gulch surrounded by walls of rock. With Prince Kal's thoughts puppeteering his bony arms, the boy landed the contraption beside a twisting stream, where bushes and scrubs throttled its pebbled bank.

Now go, Prince Kal said, sinking into a crouch against the wall. *I can't go too near the castle, or my father might sense me. This stream leads straight to his fortress. And remember...* They turned to look at him as they gathered their packs and rods. His eyes were mere violet slits within the darkness of his hood. *You may find it difficult to remember both languages without a Nocturnal by your side. Don't let yourself get disoriented. Find your tongue.*

A cold chill spread through Joah's abdomen at this newest thought. Of course. He had become so accustomed to using telepathy and his tongue, both with ease, that he had forgotten how Damien had described the Nocturnal language away from the Nocturnals: *"It's like somebody's calling your name through the far end of a tunnel."*

"Hopefully we'll find King Isce right away, then," Joah said grimly.

The star's double doors slid upward, steaming. Joah, Misla, and Damien clambered onto the rocks below, leaving the prince behind. The stream gurgled to their right, but they couldn't see past the tangled shrubbery congesting its bank.

"We'll follow the sound," Misla said, hitching her pack higher up her back. Joah adjusted his too and nodded. Inside their many hand-stitched pockets were packets of seeds, water cans, ropes of fibermud, and cloaks. But they clutched the most important tagalongs in their hands as they started down the narrow channel of pebbles between shrubbery and cliff: rods with darts coated in sunsap that they would shoot at King Isce when they encountered him.

The gulley twisted this way and that, narrowing and widening, sometimes speared with orange light, other times bathed in twilight shadows. As they trudged forward, the greenery thickened, and mud squelched beneath their shoes. They began ducking beneath gnarled branches, pushing through the thorny arms of bushes, clambering over moss-cloaked boulders in their path.

The foliage clotted like a shield. Spikes poked from stems, some the size of Joah's thumb, others needle-like and hairy, reminding him all too well of the Leather Skin living within the depths of the sunsap. Hickory's ax would have suited them well now, but they had left it lying in the water in the underground tunnel along with the broken shards of ceramic.

"C'mon, let's take the stream," Misla muttered.

They pushed their way to the bank and splashed into piercingly cold, glass-clear water, which rose up to Joah's knees. After a few arcsecs of following the current, their hands rigid around their rods, Damien whispered, "What's that smell?"

The stream had spread out like melting butter. The air tasted like salt and moss and something undeniably slimy. But it was fresh too, and Joah inhaled deeply.

"I think it's the Green Sea. We should be—"

They rounded a corner and stumbled to a stop, squinting at the sudden slap of naked sunset. The gulley had opened to a coastline spreading eternally in either direction. The stream itself joined an immense, lazy body of water up ahead, which met the sea with the tenderness of a long-lost lover's kiss. Soaring birds dotted the sky above the harbor.

And to their left, a vast, interconnected collection of turrets and towers lined the coast. This was King Isce's fortress, where the Nocturnal, his subjects, and his slaves Stayed.

"Okay, Kal said the cellar looks like a half-moon," Misla said, pointing.

One of the towers up ahead, separated from the rest, curved like a stone horseshoe. This was how Prince Kal had told them to enter the fortress. The cellar would lead to the kitchens, which would help them bypass any guards that might be standing by the front doors.

Joah nodded. They stooped low and trudged through the stream until it meandered right. Then they clambered onto the muddy grass and dashed toward that half-moon tower.

Joah's ears pounded with the impending crash of the sea. He didn't want to face King Isce. More than that, though, he didn't want to witness what lay inside that cellar. They had *planned* to gather any remaining human bones to bring back to the community. Proof of Deckler's treachery. Of their looming doom. But as they neared the cellar, Joah's heart sunk with a tingling suspicion that perhaps they were too late. Perhaps the invasion had already begun.

Okay, who wants to do the honors? he asked, his tongue too dry to speak aloud.

They had scurried into the cellar's shadows. Vines crawled up the stone, smothering the outline of those circular doors lining the curve of walls. One door stood naked, though, the vines around it snapped in pieces, as if someone—or something—had already pushed its brute way inside. Joah's head buzzed. He tried to expel his thoughts, but they resounded differently inside his ears. Weaker.

I'll do it, Damien said.

The boy was about to push his cold palm against the door when movement on either side of them made him flinch back. Two shapes emerged from the deepest thickness of vines: shelled bodies, hairy legs, imprints on their faces like many-eyed insects.

The Leather Skins stared at them. They didn't say anything, but Joah could hear the faint drone of their thoughts anyhow, like frantic voices behind closed doors.

The deed was done. It was too late. They, the Leather Skins, had been forced into the invasion, had hauled masses of bodies to this cellar. Their buggy eyes seemed to be bleeding a sour green pus, as if they had been hurt in the process.

Joah's head buzzed and buzzed, but he managed to say, *Get out of here, all of you. We're going to get rid of him. Head north. You'll find some ships. Steal one. Sail your way back to daytime.* He swallowed thickly, choking on tears. They could afford for the Leather Skins to steal a ship because the Dirt Slummers had already been taken. *We won't be far behind.*

For a moment, he thought they were going to close their pincers around his throat. But with a ticking, clicking sound, they withdrew hesitantly, then scuttled lopsidedly away.

Damien slapped the door in his haste to get inside, where his mother's body would no doubt be lying among bones. The door obeyed, grinding upward until a mouth-shaped hole opened in the stone before them.

Joah had a split second to process the heated, stifled darkness inside. Bodies stirred within the cellar's black abyss. There came the sound of grinding bones, clattering rocks, and clinking chains. Damien sucked in a breath, and Misla reached out an uncertain palm...

Then someone screamed.

Before Joah could back away, a hand emerged from the darkness within and jerked him inside. He hollered, twisting blindly. He felt his rod wrenched from his grip. Misla and Damien shouted beside him. The door behind them lowered with a resolute *thunk.*

"What are you *doing*? You can't let them see us," growled a horribly familiar voice. It was gravelly and gruff, and it belonged to the person now clutching Joah's shoulder, forcing him deeper into the belly of the cellar. "To the honest depths of hell, I can't believe it. Detective Cadshaw and Retriever Crane. I thought you two were dead. And this little boy must be—"

"Damien!" a woman shrieked.

The buzzing in Joah's head swelled. He clamped hands over his ears, and realized, too late, that his pack was gone. He felt, rather than saw, a woman tear from the mass of huddled bodies surrounding them. He heard Damien cry out and cling to his mother, reunited at last.

But his mind couldn't comprehend what was happening, and Misla's own confusion met his like a tentacle of thought groping for land, for something to cling to in this darkness.

Why was General Aoif Deckler in the cellar with the very people he had handed over?

Why were the people—the living, breathing people—here at all? Joah had been prepared for the stink of rotting bodies, not for the stench of sweat and piss.

What are you doing, Deckler? he tried to rasp, but he couldn't find his tongue.

His foot lurched forward, kicking something small and hard on the floor. At the same time, the people around him began murmuring, and Deckler boomed, "I appreciate you trying to save us, retrievers, but we have a plan. You could have been *seen*, sneaking in like that."

What are you talking about? Joah tried to ask, but once again, his lips couldn't move.

Deckler seemed to hear him, though, and it was this, more than anything else, that spread ribbons of fear throughout Joah's body. He was immobilized, caught between two languages, but *Deckler* knew how to execute both perfectly. *Deckler* was still playing his game.

"If they see us trying to escape, we have no chance," the general said, his voice carrying throughout the cellar. Lupita muffled her sobs against Damien's hair. "But when they come in *here* to butcher us, they'll be caught unawares. They don't know we've escaped our chains, see. They won't know what's coming. It's our only chance at getting the hell out of here."

So that was it. Joah wobbled on his feet, dizzy from the buzzing in his ears. Aoif Deckler was still playing hero. The disappearance of half his community would have looked suspicious to the rest—had perhaps been too suspicious *last* time—so he had developed a new plan with King Isce. One that involved his own acting skills. He had been kidnapped with the rest of his people, dragged to this cellar, and locked inside. He had freed his own prisoners from their chains and helped them develop a plan of escape.

But Deckler wasn't planning on winning. *He* would survive, along with a few witnesses, who would report back to the rest of the community that their dear, valiant general had done everything he could to rescue them from the nighttime monsters.

Joah wanted to scream. To curse. To charge at his ex-boss.

He couldn't move. Misla was a statue beside him, and Damien had frozen in his mother's arms. General Deckler's voice hissed inside his head, stabbing him with needles of pain.

It's no good, Joah. Your little plan. Forget it, and you can be one of the few that live.

Joah closed his eyes, though it made no difference in the darkness. He remembered Prince Kal's words: *Don't let yourself get disoriented. Find your tongue.*

Yes, if he were to save these people from pointless butchering —if he were to convince them that Deckler was lying, that their best chance at escape was to lift the door again and stream toward the cliffs—he'd have to find his tongue.

He opened and closed his mouth, ignoring the increased muttering of the crowded bodies. Shapes emerged beneath his closed lids: he was on the High Road, surrounded by swarms of eager onlookers, but he was not leading his wife to the executioner's block. He was leading *himself*, his own handcuffs cutting into his wrists, his footsteps slow, clunky, deliberate.

"Warn you," he choked out now, opening his eyes. "Got to."

The cellar hushed. Deckler withdrew his hand from Joah's shoulder.

"What is this?" the general whispered, a cruel coldness hidden beneath his façade of shock and suspicion. "You'd like to warn us? Of what?"

"Warn you," Joah spluttered again, lurching forward.

"Scary," Damien piped up from the crook of his mother's arms.

"D-don't listen," Misla said, breathing fast. "Don't listen. Don't listen. Don't listen."

And now the muttering in the cellar rose to match the pounding buzz in Joah's ears, and somebody cried out, "They sound Infected!" and Lupita gasped and wailed.

Find your tongue, find your tongue, find your tongue, Joah begged himself, but it was too dark to find his tongue, and the prisoners were reeling, shouting insults, throwing rocks at Joah's legs. Somewhere in the back, a child wailed, and a mother said *shhh*, but the insults rose to a roar.

"Grab them," Deckler commanded. "They *are* Infected."

Damien was wrenched from his mother. Joah's wrists were pinned behind his back. He was forced to his knees between the boy and Misla, where fragments of bones stabbed his ankles, as if shattered pieces of glass coated the cellar floor. Lupita screamed.

"They'll ruin our plans," Deckler said, his voice smooth with apathy.

The prisoners responded with screeches of desperation. Joah did not blame them. They had been kidnapped by strange, scuttling creatures and forced into a cellar like pigs to a slaughterhouse. In their eyes, the Infected were threats now more than ever.

"The Nocturnals will be here any minute," Deckler said. "These three will only help them kill us. We have to get rid of them before that happens."

"*No!*" Lupita wailed, plunging forward.

Deckler ignored her, raising something into the air. As Joah's eyes finally adjusted to this new darkness, he made out the outline of a handheld saw—the same tool Deckler must have used to break the chains—bearing down upon Damien's neck.

Lupita threw herself over her son. The saw's serrated edge lodged in her neck.

"NO!" Damien roared. "MOM. NO."

Before Joah could jolt or even process what had happened, several circles of light shot into the cellar like a dozen violent stars. The outlines of a hundred Nocturnal bodies flowed into the cellar, the glowing designs on their skin glinting off the cleavers in their hands. They were cloak-less, and their figures blended together in a whirl of chaotic light.

The prisoners shrieked, bumping into each other, trying to escape like caged chickens. They had expected their kidnappers, the enslaved Leather Skins, not these new vulture-like creatures whose arms rose and fell like wings. Some tried to stab their butchers with tapered bones, but the maze of light was dizzying, and cleavers cracked into skulls with the increased rapidity of popping corn.

Joah looked up, bleary. He saw General Deckler standing in the middle of the cellar, his hacksaw dripping with Lupita's blood. He was standing shoulder-to-shoulder with a Nocturnal whose designs twisted and flared like a lair of glowing baby serpents.

King Isce grinned as he surveyed the massacre.

Find your tongue, find your tongue, find your tongue, Joah cried within himself. But it was no longer his tongue that he needed. He put his forehead to the cellar floor and let his thoughts explode, so that even some of the Nocturnals paused, their cleavers quivering in midair.

PRINCE KAL, WE NEED YOU.

His silent cry rippled through the stone of the cellar, soared against the current of the stream, weaved between foliage. It re-traveled the length of the gulley, found the starship, and embraced the cloaked figure hunkered within it.

King Isce looked up. His violet eyes narrowed when he met Joah's gaze. He had heard. He knew his long-lost heir was somewhere nearby, knew that Joah had just contacted him.

The Nocturnal king swept toward him. Joah could hear Misla gasping beside him, and Damien weeping into his mother's body, which still lay draped over the boy like a shield of flesh. He, Joah, wanted to remember his light when he finally met the dark tendrils of death.

He spread his freed hands to try to touch the woman and boy he'd come to love—

The walls shook, and *BOOM.* The world blasted apart.

A great star burst through the cellar's eastern walls, crumbling the stone and roof in a blaze of fire, exposing them to the spears of sunset's light. Prince Kal drove his ship into the ground, and it exploded on impact, sprays of sunsap flying like shards of sky.

Joah grabbed Misla and Damien, pulled them closer. Around them, King Isce's butchers clawed at blisters blossoming on their skin. King Isce himself had halted; his skin was blackening, falling to the floor in scabbed flakes as the sunset pierced him.

The king half-turned, seeming to realize, too late, what his son had done.

Kill him, he murmured.

Then his body crumbled. It collapsed into a heap of ash on the floor. And all around him, his soldiers crumbled too, until all that remained were piles of ashes, the mangled bodies of prisoners, and a handful of survivors wailing through the smoke and dust.

General Deckler himself swayed on the spot. Joah groped for his fallen rod, which lay in a heap of cinders, and aimed it at him. He was going to twist and shoot. He was going to kill the general he had obeyed and admired his whole life with a dart smothered in sunsap.

Before he could force his hands to move, Deckler's hacksaw dropped from his fingers. It landed on a pile of ashes with a soft thud. Blood spiraled around Deckler's neck. He staggered forward, then collapsed as suddenly and violently as the starship had.

Joah lowered his rod. He saw what stuck from the back of his skull, and understood.

King Isce's last command had been *kill him*. One of his butchers had stuck his cleaver into the head of the man who had failed his king. There had never been any true alliance, only a kind of hunger and greed that couldn't endure even the weakest streams of light.

"Are you okay? Are you hurt?"

Both Misla and Damien were sobbing into his chest. His own body shook as he rocked them. Deckler and Lupita were dead. King Isce had disintegrated. Prince Kal had been blasted apart. They had only managed to save a few dozen prisoners from the carnage. If they didn't get to the rest of the community soon and start sailing, that precious sun would leave them behind once again.

"It'll be okay," Joah said. "We'll find our way out of here. It'll be okay."

And he realized, despite the smoking destruction around him, that he had found his voice.

The water roared around them as the ships plunged eastward.

Joah stood beneath the foremast, watching those little white stars jump along the distant horizon. The sun had become a darkened sliver, preparing to leave them behind forever. But they hadn't let it completely shrivel into darkness. As they sailed onward, it thickened and rose until the Green Sea became a twinkling pool of orange and pink and purple.

He sensed the collective gasp of those on board, the halting of progress to watch the sun's ascent. Eventually, a woman joined him, curling her fingers around the railing beside him.

"Quite the sunset, isn't it?" Misla sighed.

Her hair hung in loose waves over her shoulders. The sunbeams made her skin appear golden, her cheeks like two glowing coins. Joah put his arm around her waist, pulled her closer, and pressed his lips against her temple. A long journey still stretched before them, but he felt peace—maybe even a little excitement—that they would cross this sea together.

"Yes, it's quite the sunset," he agreed.

"It's not a sunset anymore." Damien had appeared on Misla's other side, tiptoeing to see over the handrail. He wore a newly stitched green shirt, which had been emblazoned with the face of a reptilian cat: not just an homage to the Calic they had killed in the Eternal Night, but a reminder that darkness teemed with good *and* bad, hopeful civility *and* wild desperation. "It's technically a sun*rise*," he said. "That's what you call it when things get brighter."

"Aren't you supposed to be in school?" Joah growled.

There were a few classrooms on the lower deck for the children on board: windowless, of course, so that the students wouldn't become distracted by the sea.

"I gave Mrs. Zemukil the slip," Damien said matter-of-factly. He was barefoot, Joah noticed, his toes somehow streaked with dirt. As usual. "I wanted to see it. The dawn."

"And how'd you manage to give your teacher the slip?" Misla asked, folding her arms.

"Oh, I just passed Timby Jenkins a note. No big deal." When Misla cocked a threatening eyebrow, he added, "It was a dare, that's all. I bet him he couldn't burp a hundred times within the next arcsec. Well, Mrs. Zemukil had to stop writing on the board after his seventh burp. By his twentieth, she was yelling too hard to notice me sneak away."

Joah tried not to chuckle, but his mouth twitched.

"Watch out, Misla," he warned as the breeze picked up, smacking his face with salt. "This kid's going to be general one day. Mark my words."

They hadn't elected a new general yet. After Joah and Misla had explained to the remaining prisoners in the cellar about Deckler's arrangement with King Isce, they had agreed that escaping the fortress and boarding these ships were more pressing matters. But one of the survivors, a certain Captain Lincoln, had assumed temporary command, and *he* was the one who had convinced the rest of the Sunsetters of the truth, even with the community in disarray: between the attack on the Dirt Slums, the disappearance of their general, and a horde of Leather Skins swarming one of their three ships and taking off with it, they had been in an uproar.

But Captain Lincoln had calmed them. He had told them the truth in a giant assembly by the *shoosh* of waves, organized the remaining ships' takeoffs, and arranged for the planting of their Nocturnal seeds onboard. There weren't any penned animals aboard—no, that would've reminded them all too much of their own recent captivity—but a garden arena on the main deck sprouted with various squashes and herbs, reminding Joah of Prince Kal and the other Nocturnals who had chased them around the aro to warn them of the darkness ahead.

"I hope Queen Usai gets our message," Misla murmured, as if she could read his thoughts. Maybe a small part of her still could, although all three of them had lost their sense of the soundless Nocturnal language, like water leaking through outspread hands.

"She will," Joah assured her.

While Captain Lincoln had been busy organizing the ships, Joah and Misla had snuck into the main, unguarded fortress, where they'd found a young cloaked Nocturnal hovering near a window. With their last remaining telepathic breath, they had told her to wait for her new Majesty, a queen by the name of Usai, who would soon come along to resume King Isce's place.

The Nocturnal had taken flight, cloak flapping behind her as she raced down the hall and disappeared around a corner. But Joah had sensed the delight squirming beneath her terror, the understanding that King Isce was gone and the aliens would be leaving soon.

"I just hate to think of Queen Usai finding the remains of that Shooting Star," Misla said.

They all fell silent, immersing themselves in the crash of water and wind. Behind them, activities were resuming: gardeners returned to the arena, Captain Lincoln continued shouting orders, and helmsmen raced to and fro. The deck creaked with movement and life.

Joah didn't wrench his eyes from the horizon, though. The three of them deserved to see it expand, he thought, to feel the sunshine warm their faces. Their tragedies had snatched away that warmth for so long, after all. They deserved to feel daylight's ripe embrace.

So with Misla and Damien beside him, with the Eternal Night behind him, he watched the distant dawn yawn itself to life until the moon rose into its new bright sky.

See Mariah Montoya's entire novella "The Nocturnals" online at Metaphorosis.
If you liked it, leave a comment. Authors love that!
Remember to subscribe to our e-mail updates so you'll know when new stories are posted.

October

Ennui Tea

Ivy Grimes

Estella, the seemingly ageless proprietor of Dour Power Café, hired me the day I slumped in. I ordered a small cup of Ennui Tea (which honestly tasted like vinegar), quietly thrilled to have a new goth cave to hide in. Nowhere else in town was safe from patriotism, town pride, and school spirit.

I didn't even ask for the job. She seemed to know I needed one.

The only question she asked in my job interview was: "Are you happy?"

"Only fools are happy," I said.

"Well...no, but that's a start," she said as she tossed me my apron.

She told me right away that she was an herbologist, a witch who made potions, and that she went from town to town helping people ditch their false performance of joy and embark on the rocky path to enlightenment.

"Like some nonconsensual Oprah?" I asked. Estella seemed more like a hippie than a witch, and I could tell she'd let me get away with some impertinence.

"They only drink if their spirit is willing. I give them what they're searching for, even if they don't know they're searching."

It sounded ridiculous.

"I *believe* you, though," I said. "Why do I believe you?"

"I'm very persuasive when you want to believe," she said.

Of course, she was right. For once I actually wanted to trust someone, though I hated to admit it. She was the strangest person I'd ever met, and I wanted to be just like her.

I started the job that very afternoon, expecting all the cheery, pastel-clad people I'd gone to high school with to walk in, wrinkle their noses at the stark interior, and walk right out again. Instead,

Estella's magic made the place as attractive to them as a Target Starbucks, and she made them fans of bitter drinks like Ennui Tea and Doldrums Coffee. Within a week, both the chatty churchgoing types and the arrogant preppy types were wearing tight black jeans and reading poetry.

Like any good goth, I'd always dreamed of being a witch myself. Estella kept telling me she saw something special in me—some spark of power in my honesty. She kept inviting me to attempt her spells, but I declined. She said failure was part of the process, but I didn't want to fail in front of the only person I'd ever met who seemed to think I was special.

Most days, I worked out front alone while she performed her magic rituals in her private office, but sometimes she'd come out and unsuccessfully try to sell people more advanced drinks, little nudges along the path to enlightenment. Estella had spent most of her long life in places like Berlin and Paris and New York, and ours was the first Midwestern town where she'd set up shop. She thought that in a small town, it would be easier to see the difference she was making. I tried to explain the Midwest to her, but she just didn't understand the crushing burden of forced niceness and optimism. Melancholy was such a relief for my fellow townspeople that they weren't willing to exchange it for more heavy-lifting. People had been telling them to smile their whole lives, and they were finally having a rest from insincerity. Stuff like self-actualization seemed way too taxing to them.

After a couple of months of fruitless salesmanship, Estella was discouraged. One rainy Monday, she stood beside me at the front counter and looked out at our bleak clientele and asked, "Why don't our customers *want* to become enlightened, Eris? Why do they only order Ennui Tea and Doldrums Coffee? Why won't they try the Self-Acceptance Cold Brew, or even a simple Epiphany Tea? I've sold my potions in dozens of different towns, and I've never encountered a group so stubborn and stagnant."

"Well..." I didn't want to remind her I hadn't tried her more advanced drinks yet either. "I keep telling you—I'm not sure they can handle any more. It's a miracle they've come this far."

"Melancholy is only the first stage of enlightenment, Eris. Despair at the awful plight of the world is supposed to inspire us to grow and help others grow. I know you're capable if you open your mind. But please do it quickly! I need your help to appeal to your fellow townspeople."

Her advice would have annoyed me even more if she hadn't already told me I was the most mature person in town. Although based on how she described the other people in town, it didn't seem like much of a competition.

"Are *you* enlightened?" I asked her with as much politeness as I could manage.

"I'm on my way. That's why I'm here, to help others along the path."

So even she wasn't entirely enlightened. At least she was honest with me.

"I don't understand why it has to be so serious," I said. "Why can't this just be a cool place to hang out?"

"Do you find this place cool?" she said, gesturing at the clientele.

I liked the way everyone had changed. No one was propping up the world like Atlas anymore—no more catchphrases, no more masks of joy, no more pretending. On the other hand, I could see why Estella might find her new customers dull. Now they all acted like they had the flu, and they could only talk about mortality.

"They need to find the satisfaction in sadness." I loved heartbreaking songs and movies where everyone died in the end, and I took pride in drifting around town like a shadow. Most people thought I was miserable, but it took talent to find the perverse joy I'd found in misery. Due to Estella's powerfully depressing concoctions (sold with panache by yours truly), I was finally on-trend.

Estella shook her head at me and smiled the way that people in their 30s (or in Estella's case, her 130s) smile at people in their early 20s. I hated it when she treated me like I was a child wearing a paper crown.

"Someday you'll taste a melancholy fruit so bitter, it will open your eyes. Then you'll want to help others through their suffering," she said. Or prophesied.

I didn't have to wait long for the prophecy to be fulfilled. The next day, I fell in love.

A guy walked in wearing grandpa slacks and a baggy button-down shirt and thick glasses and an addictive smirk. He was charming and sensitive, witty and intense. He said his name was Berlin, and he went to college a few towns over and had been looking everywhere for a cool place to hang out.

He teased me about my stereotypical goth look—heavy makeup and funereal garb. But he said it was cool I'd named myself Eris, after the Greek goddess of conflict and being pissed-off. I teased him about carrying a copy of Sartre's *No Exit* under his arm like a first-year philosophy major.

"I *am* a first-year philosophy major. I'll be a sophomore this fall," he said.

"I'm not going to college. It's a waste of time," I said.

He shrugged. "It's only a waste of time if you aren't becoming enlightened."

There was that word again. To me, enlightenment was a product sold on TV, like an acne medication that promised more than it could deliver. But it made people feel good, as if salvation were just around the corner.

"College is too expensive."

"It all depends on your perspective. But yes, I won't relish paying back my student loans with my philosopher's salary." He smirked again, and I rolled my eyes, but I was already obsessed with him.

He asked what I recommended from the menu, and I poured him a cup of Doldrums Coffee (pre-magicked by Estella), but it didn't seem to dampen his high spirits. He had the enthusiasm of a kid on Halloween, and we were running the haunted house.

Estella came out from her office and asked him what he thought about Sartre. He stared at her like she was a sculpture. He'd been able to talk to me so easily, but he couldn't string two words together for her. As I watched them, my stomach began to burn. I hated Estella.

She invited him to her office where he could calm down and communicate. While they were gone, I was even more unfriendly to the customers than usual. I had never seen her take such an interest in anyone but me.

When he returned with an apron, I wasn't surprised.

"She offered me a job! And I didn't even apply! She says she sees something in me. Something special."

"Congratulations," I said without looking at him.

"And can you believe?" He got close to my ear and whispered. "She's a witch? And she can teach us some of her spells?"

"Yeah," I said, trying to pretend his breath in my ear hadn't made me shiver. "I tried her potion, too. What can I say? She hooked me."

I found myself jealous both ways—of his regard for her and hers for him. What made him so special to her?

In spite of the awful turn of events, I still wanted to be with him, so I tried to steer the conversation to things he liked to do, to make it easy for him to invite me on a date. He kept changing the subject, asking me what I knew about magic. I tried to tell him that magic was probably painful and difficult, but he wasn't listening.

"I'm going to ask her for instructions every chance I get," he said, ignoring my cynicism. He seemed to lose interest in me for the rest of the day, which pained me more than anything. I wished we could have met somewhere else, without all the distractions. Then again, he might have looked right through me without the intrigue of my job.

It galled me when people ignored me. I'd been the town sourpuss for years before Estella arrived. People hadn't even treated me like I was weird. They'd treated me like I wasn't there. Even now that Estella had changed everything, no one credited me with being melancholy before it was cool.

For the rest of the afternoon, I listened to Berlin's charming banter as he worked the cash register. I kept my back to him, pouring drinks. The job was the best thing that had ever happened to me, but I was thinking about running away—leaving the shop and leaving town, even though realistically, I hadn't saved up enough money to move out of my parents' house.

That evening, when Estella came out to help us close, Berlin begged her for some magical secrets. He explained at length why he could be trusted, gesturing with urgency. His arms looked like the elegant tusks of some beautiful wild beast, and I wanted to know what it felt like to hold them in my hands.

"I like your enthusiasm, but you seem to think it's so simple," Estella said. She gave him the same look she always gave me—that 'what a cute kid' look. That, at least, was some relief. She clearly wasn't going to fall in love with him. He acted injured, but he said he'd ask again after work every day. And he said he was going on a thirst strike—he wasn't drinking another of her potions until she showed him how to make them. I would have fired him for insubordination, but Estella seemed to admire his intensity.

Her obvious lack of romantic interest in him made me less despairingly angry. I was able to come back to work the next day. And the day after. And the day after. All week, I worked with Berlin, and I observed not only his sex appeal, but his kindness. If I was the employee who provided the dour credibility, he was the one who cared.

By the end of the week, she finally agreed to teach him one spell—as long as I agreed to learn it with him. I wanted to resist, but one look into his eyes made me relent.

"I'll teach you how to brew Epiphany Tea," she said. She opened one of the cabinets under the counter and pulled out some of her creepy-looking materials—sticks and herbs and seeds and other dried, misshapen things.

"You don't lock this up?" Berlin asked her.

"The ingredients are inert without the magic. Magic is like enlightenment, you see," she said, giving me a serious look. "It comes upon you after hard experiences and reflection. I asked you both to work here because I can tell you've already put in some effort. You're nowhere close to enlightenment, of course, but you're on the path. After you've had a try, I'll make an Epiphany Tea for you so you can have the genuine experience."

Berlin bent his head near mine, and we stared at the instructions together.

Mix a spoonful of grated ginger with three whole cloves and a pinch of lemongrass. Boil water. As the tea steeps, think of your own past epiphanies and put your hands around the mug to imbue the drink with your energy. After five minutes, strain and serve.

"Cool, sounds easy," he said, which made Estella laugh a little. He seemed happy to have made her laugh, even though she was clearly laughing at his ignorance.

After we'd mixed up the brew, Berlin put his hands around the mug first, and without looking up at him, I put mine above his so that our hands were barely touching. It almost burned to graze his skin, but I tried to concentrate on things I'd learned in my short, pointless life. I started small, remembering when I realized I had to pedal faster to learn to ride a bike. I tried to think neutral thoughts, but of course, my mind took me to more hurtful realizations. I remembered being the only kid in the class not invited to any birthday parties in the fourth grade, realizing I was going to be alone for the rest of my life if I couldn't find a way out. I remembered the day in sixth grade when everyone partnered up to kick the soccer ball in PE, and I was left with "Stinky Sarah" again (a new girl who ate cabbage rolls for lunch and was even more unpopular than I was), and I got so mad that I hid in the bathroom for the rest of the class in protest. I'd blocked the memory. I'd forgotten that I was an asshole, too.

I looked up and saw a tear on Berlin's left cheek. What sad scenes had passed through his mind?

After several minutes, Estella told us we could stop. I stared into the pretty golden drink, and for once, I was thirsty for it. It looked so sweet, I hoped it would relieve some of the sadness I'd unearthed.

"Go ahead!" Estella said. "We can all drink. I doubt there's enough magic here to give us epiphanies, but we wouldn't want the tea to go to waste."

We each took a sip, and I waited for the earth to quake under my feet or the sky to fall to pieces overhead. Although nothing loud or sudden happened, it occurred to me that in spite of my morose attitude, I preferred to keep my life unexamined. The truth was, I'd been alone and overlooked for most of my childhood, and learning how to embrace a style of sadness had freed me. It had meant I didn't have to take things so seriously. I didn't want the fun to end by looking too closely at myself or my life.

Was that it? Was my epiphany that I'd been avoiding epiphanies?

I looked at Berlin and Estella to see if they'd learned anything. Berlin stared out the window at the waning evening light. I wanted to ask him if he was okay, but I didn't want to seem too mushy. Estella was always inscrutable to me, but even she seemed a bit shaken.

"I didn't think you'd be able to do it yet," she said. "You're both wiser than I realized. I didn't realize..."

Without elaborating, she left us. She practically ran from the front counter to her office and shut the door.

"That was weird," I said. As always, my instinct was to play it cool, but I was dying to know what Berlin's epiphany had been, so I asked him. "I don't want to be nosy, but I saw you were crying a little. What did you realize when you drank the tea?"

He looked utterly forlorn. "I'm embarrassed to admit it."

The result of my epiphany was that I wanted to try harder to be honest, even though I hated to look like I was trying too hard at anything. "Look, you can tell me. I'll tell you first if you want."

"Okay, you go first," he said, refusing to look at me.

"I realized that...I've been a poser. I've wanted to seem deep, but I thought most of my deep thoughts when I was thirteen and depressed and alone. Things have gotten better since then, especially since I got this job, and so I haven't wanted to think about anything difficult at all. For show, I named myself after the goddess of conflict, but the truth is, I avoid every kind of discomfort. That means I'm not so different from the people I've always looked down on. Like the people who are our customers now."

My voice sounded different than usual as I made this admission. It seemed higher and squeakier, like the voice of a child.

"God. I relate so much," Berlin said. He finally looked up, and I could see the florescent overhead lights shining in his brown velvet eyes. "After I took that sip, I realized that I'm full of shit. I pretend like I'm a philosopher, but I don't know anything." He reached under the counter to pick up the book he'd brought in with him. "*No Exit.* I've been walking around with this under my arm for months to impress everyone, and I haven't read a word of it." He slammed it down on the counter.

I tried to hide my smile. I wasn't surprised.

He shrank back. "And I'm so transparent! People aren't impressed by me. They just feel sorry for me."

"Actually..." I hesitated. I wanted to take the plunge and tell him the truth, though. If I didn't take risks, how would I gain anything? "To tell you the truth, Berlin...I'm impressed by you. I think you're smart and interesting and weird and funny and...I know I just met you, but I think I really like you."

I closed my eyes so I wouldn't have to see his reaction. In the silence that followed, I hid my face in my hands.

"Forget I said anything," I said. But I didn't want him to forget.

"Look Eris, I think you're great, but I don't feel—"

"I don't want to hear it. Since you're in love with our ancient boss, why don't you stay and lock up with her? And while you're at it, tell her I quit."

With those bitter words, I took off. I went home and ignored my parents' greetings (though they didn't find that unusual), and I turned off the lights in my bedroom and listened to the saddest unrequited love songs I knew. I'd never been able to relate to them before. I'd had crushes, but I'd never admitted to having one, so it had never seemed real before. The next morning, I woke up sadder but wiser. I'd been humiliated, but it hadn't killed me. And in the process, I'd used real magic. I felt an urge to tell Estella about my heartbreak. Not only was she my witch mentor, but she was kind of my best friend.

I went into work as usual that morning. The doors were unlocked, but no one was out front. I checked the back office and found Estella peering over her notecards.

"Maybe you can find a recipe for happiness or something," I said. "Epiphanies suck, just like I knew they would."

She gave me such a tragic, apologetic look that I felt a little guilty for complaining.

"Oh, Eris. I'm so sorry. I didn't realize how condescending I'd been to you. I hired you because I believed in you, but I kept thinking you needed to learn so much more from me before you could do anything. Like I was the key. I open certain people's eyes to magic, yes, but then I act as if I'm so much more important than they are. I rarely even bother tasting the potions my students make. But I learned something from you yesterday."

"I learned something, too. I ate a piece of melancholy fruit, just as you predicted. I fell in love-at-first-sight with Berlin and confessed it to him. And he rejected me."

"I'm sorry, Eris. Well, he quit."

"He quit?"

"He said he needed to do some soul-searching and didn't have time for a job yet. I told him to come back in a few months when he was ready."

"Did he tell you that I tried to quit?"

"No! I had no idea you were unhappy here."

"I'm not, I'm not. But I knew Berlin was in love with you and not me, and I got angry. I'm sorry I was so rash. I realized that getting my heart broken isn't the end of the world. It sucks, but it's an experience, right?"

Estella laughed. "Sure. It's happened to me seventy-three times. And I'm glad you're not quitting after all. I have more spells to teach you. But I do think Berlin will come back eventually. I have a feeling about him. Do you think it would be too hard to work with him again?"

"I'll be fine," I said, though I didn't know if that was true. I didn't know whether my feelings for Berlin were like heat lightning or a hurricane. Either way, I was curious.

"Maybe the clients need a little boost themselves," she said. "I haven't been as good at promoting Epiphany and other healing drinks as I have been at selling Ennui and Doldrums. It's my own fault. I must seem so strange to everyone since I'm not from around here. You're a much better salesperson."

"I can try talking to them. Who knows?" I said.

I went to the counter and opened Estella's secret stash and started brewing up golden cups of Epiphany Tea infused with my own fresh melancholy memories. When Kaitlyn, a former homecoming queen and recently-converted goth, walked in, I knew she was the influencer I needed. She was still the town trendsetter, and if I could convert her, I could convert them all. I told her I'd discovered the best new drink, Epiphany Tea, and I was surprised to find that she actually cared what I thought and ordered one. When she took her first sip, my heart ached for her as her face bloomed with painful recognition. I told her it was going to be all right—that everyone was full of shit, and sooner or later, we were all doomed to realize it.

That week, most of our customers starting trying Epiphany Tea after seeing Kaitlyn drink it, and ours became a more complicated café. They began showing off a range of insights and emotions, and I had to admit, I was proud of them. I stopped being rude by default when anyone walked in the door. I at least waited to see if they did anything warranting my rudeness. Making Epiphany Tea was taxing and painful at times, but when I saw how much it helped everyone, I felt like I could handle the unpleasantness.

When Berlin came back to work that December, his eyes were still velvet, but my crush had died. I was almost disappointed.

Before I showed him some of the new recipes I'd learned, I asked, "Did you ever read *No Exit?*"

"Yes," he said. "It's where that famous quote comes from— *Hell is other people*. But it turns out that he doesn't just mean that other people suck. He means it's hell to have to spend every moment impressing other people. I get it now."

I looked at him skeptically.

"Well, that is to say, I'm figuring it out."

"Me too," I said.

See Ivy Grimes's story "Ennui Tea" online at Metaphorosis.
If you liked it, leave a comment. Authors love that!
Remember to subscribe to our e-mail updates so you'll know when new stories are posted.

About the story

I must have been feeling ennui while drinking tea, because "ennui tea" came to my mind first, and the story of a young woman learning magic at a goth coffee shop followed. I imagined how great it would be to have a goth coffee shop nearby and to live in a town where everyone mopes and reads poetry all day. Yet I could see my character Estella's point that enlightenment/growth requires stronger stuff than mere disillusionment with materialism and mundanity. Growth requires confronting who you are, strengths and weaknesses alike. Acknowledging our strengths can be as mortifying as owning our weaknesses. My pessimistic protagonist Eris has to accept that sometimes she can be a shallow jerk, but she can also do magic. Her powers might not be enough to make her crush fall in love with her, but they might have more important uses.

A question for the author

Q: What other writers inspire you?

A: I'm probably most inspired by writers who cling really stubbornly to their own vision and let themselves be weird and free...like Haruki Murakami, David Lynch, Shirley Jackson, Toni Morrison, Leonora Carrington, Ralph Ellison, and so on. I also love the creepy, moving fairy tales of Helen Oyeyemi and the tragic mysteries of Tana French and the mundane humor of Barbara Pym. For "Ennui Tea", I might have been inspired by a favorite tale of retail life, Sayaka Murata's *Convenience Store Woman*, which is about a woman who loves her work at a convenience store and rejects a traditional career or family; whoever you are, you'll love it. I'm inspired by too many writers to list, though.

About the author

Ivy Grimes is originally from Alabama and now lives in Northern Virginia with her husband and beagle. She is a friendly neurotic person who writes speculative fiction and is looking for more writer friends. She feels nostalgic about her Birmingham writing group that sometimes met at an Applebees where attendees ordered the $1 house beer.

www.ivyivyivyivy.com, @IvyGri

The Tick of the Clock

J.C. Pillard

The prince followed the sound of ticking. It was not an exact science, and he'd lost his way many times as his ear tricked him with woodpeckers and creaking branches. But he always found his way again, because while the other sounds would die away, the ticking did not.

Tick, tick, tick.

He was more exhausted than he cared to admit, eyes stinging from the effort of keeping them open. His feet dragged, ploughing into the earth as though they meant to sow seeds. His clothes were dirty and sweat-soaked. The long green scarf his mother had made him snagged on every branch, and he had to wrench it loose. He thought, bitterly, that he could simply stop freeing it when it became tangled, but he couldn't bring himself to leave it.

The forest seemed to go on forever, trees growing into obscurity in every direction. The ticking drew him deeper beneath the branches, and before he knew it, the sky itself was blotted out by the tangled canopy.

Tick, tick, tick.

As the days and nights bled together, the prince realized what a foolish thing he'd done, and the dull fury which had driven him began melting to despair, the guilt he'd been keeping at bay creeping in by inches. His fingers tangled in the chain around his neck, the one holding his father's pocket watch against his breast. The voices of the palace advisors echoed in his head.

One foolish act cannot right another. You cannot undo your mother's curse with sheer force of will.

Because that's what this was, wasn't it? His mother's edict, not a law of preservation but a curse. A curse that had trapped the prince—and everyone else in his kingdom—in time for one hundred years.

Tick, tick, tick.

His food had run out two days ago. Or was it two weeks? He wasn't sure. He couldn't remember when he'd last seen a river to fill his canteen. There were many inviting places to lay his head as he trudged on: mossy patches beneath spreading trees that looked like feather beds. But he knew that if he stopped, he would not get up again.

He really did try to keep going. He *had* to keep going. Yet, his feet grew heavier and heavier until he was lifting the entire world with each step.

Step, tick. Step, tick. Step, tick. Fall.

The prince remembered the day his mother had written her edict. It had been a strange day in many ways. Only a week since his father had died, a week of black crepe wrapped over everything, of murmured apologies and condolences, of food gone half cold before he remembered to eat it. A week of his mother staring blankly forward, as though her soul had departed with her husband's.

That morning, when the prince had finally dragged himself out of bed and gone through the motions of preparing for the day, he went down to breakfast only to find his mother was not there. He thought of leaving her alone, wherever she was. God knew all he wanted was to be left in solitude to grieve in peace. But she had been so blank and empty in the past week that worry climbed up his throat and choked him, forcing him out of the dining room to search for her. He found her in what had been his father's study. She was bent over the broad oak desk, a parchment unrolled before her. The only sounds were the scratching of her quill and the ticking of the grandfather clock against the wall.

The prince cleared his throat. "Mother. Have you eaten already?"

She barely glanced at him. "I'll come down in a moment."

"What are you doing?"

She didn't answer. The prince skirted around the desk, studying the parchment beneath her fingers.

Let it here be decreed that whatsoever kills a member of the royal family shall be forever banished from the borders of this kingdom. Any harm that befalls the royal family—

The prince sighed and stepped away, letting his mother continue her writing. His father's death had been sudden—an illness that swept through and took him in less than a week. He mourned his father's gentleness and kindness, but as the days had run on, he'd started to see that he'd lost more than one parent in his father's death. As his mother's grief began to consume her, he wondered if perhaps he'd lost them both.

It won't bring him back. The words were on his tongue, but he bit down, swallowing them, and left her to her writing. At the time, it had seemed like the right thing to do, to leave her alone to carve her grief into paper. But much had happened—or, rather, had not happened—since then, and the prince had come to reflect that perhaps if he'd said something, things would have turned out differently.

Of course, now it was too late to know.

The ticking had stopped. Or, at least, it was much, much softer. That was the first thing the prince noticed upon waking.

He opened his eyes to a pine-wood ceiling whorled with age. He breathed in, evergreens and honey filling his nose. He lay in a feather bed beside an open window that looked out onto a woodland glen. Sunlight glowed through the branches of the trees outside, and he stared at those trees in disbelief. The dense, impossible forest was gone. Had he only dreamed it?

"You're awake."

Starting, the prince turned towards the creaking voice. An old woman sat beside the bed, a stretch of knitting falling on her lap. She did not look up from it as she spoke again, her needles clacking softly.

"I wasn't sure if you were going to live. But you just kept breathing steadily. You've got a strong heart."

"Where am I?" His voice cracked from disuse, and he coughed, sending pain rocketing through his body.

The woman waited for him to finish coughing and settle back against the pillows. "My house," she said, setting her knitting aside. She picked up a worn cup from the side table. "Here. Drink."

Gratefully, the prince took it from her gnarled hand. He nearly groaned as the water hit his tongue, fresh and cool. He'd been thirsty for so long he'd forgotten what water tasted like.

As he looked down at himself, the prince gasped, sloshing water over the white cotton sheets. He wore no shirt. His scarf and pack, too, were gone, as was the watch pendant. His heart began to pound, his hands to shake. No, no, it wasn't possible, it—

"Your things are in there," the old woman said, pointing to a large cedar chest across the room. "I didn't want you getting dirt on my sheets."

The prince sank back into the pillows, relief and confusion and exhaustion all pouring through him. He drew a shaky breath, letting the pine-scented air fill his lungs.

"You'll be weak for some time," the old woman continued, resuming her knitting. "Stay in bed today. Rest. Once you have your strength back, you can tell me where you've come from that would have you collapsing on my doorstep."

The prince did not hear this last part. He'd fallen asleep again, the cup still clutched in his hands.

Later, he was not sure how much time had passed while he slept. The prince slipped in and out of consciousness as easily as day slips into night. The old woman was always there when he woke, often with food and water, sometimes just with her knitting. He grew used to falling asleep to the gentle clack of her needles, the very slight rasp of the yarn being pulled through the stitches.

"I found you unconscious in my garden," the old woman told him upon one of his awakenings. "You were face down in my cabbages."

The prince did not remember a garden. He just recalled the endless forest, the feeling of his feet sliding over the ground.

"Your pardon," he said. "I became lost some time ago, and I thought I was alone in the forest. I—I didn't see your house."

"My house is well hidden, and the forest isn't friendly to outsiders. You should count yourself lucky that you managed to stumble into it. But where were you trying to get to?"

"I'm not sure. I've never been there before." He cleared his throat. "I must be going soon, though." His hand crept up unconsciously to the watch that hung again around his throat. He'd retrieved it from the cedar chest as soon as he'd had the strength to stand.

The old woman made a dismissive noise. "You can barely walk to the door."

It was true. Each time he woke, the prince would stand and walk as far as he could. It was not very far at all for the first few days, and though he chafed at the delay, he couldn't fathom beginning his journey again so soon. Besides, what was a few more days lost? Nothing, not where he came from.

Eventually, the prince was well enough to leave the small bedroom, though not to leave the house. He often sat with the old woman in her parlor. It was a cozy room. She would sit in the rocking chair beside her large hearth, a cloak that reminded the prince of the night sky hanging off the back of her seat. He sat across from her, beneath a cuckoo clock that hung above the crackling fire. He often watched that clock as its pendulum swung with each moment, the bird crying out the hour. He never saw the old woman wind it.

"You're going to wear a hole in my floor if you keep that up," the old woman chided one evening, as the prince's leg bounced impatiently, sending a thumping tempo through the room. He flushed and stilled, chagrined.

"Young people," the old woman grumbled. "You always need to be moving. Take it from me—sometimes it's good to sit still for a spell."

A laugh burst from the prince, and the old woman gave him a chiding look. "My apologies," he said. "It's just...it's an ironic thing to hear. I've been stuck in one place for so long, now that I'm free of it, I can't imagine staying still."

"That would account for you collapsing in my garden," the old woman said. She liked to bring that up at every opportunity, as though driving home a lesson.

The prince leaned back in his chair, staring out towards the growing dusk. "How did you come to live here?"

"Hmmm. It's a long story."

"I'd like to hear it."

She sighed. "Perhaps a small part. I had many homes once. Castles by the sea, townhouses in soaring cities. This was always my favorite retreat. It was forever here, waiting for me. So, when I lost most everything I had, I knew that this house would serve me. Take it from me, prince, you should always have a plan for when everything collapses around you."

"You sound like my mother," the prince said with a half-smile.

"She must be a clever woman."

The prince grimaced, glancing away. "A little too clever, I think. In the end."

"Ah." The old woman reached across the space between them and patted his hand. Her fingers were warm against his skin. "I'm sorry for your loss."

He nodded but said nothing.

A few more weeks saw the prince well enough to begin his journey again. On what was to be his last morning in the cottage, he woke to find a new set of clothes laid out for him. His old clothes had been beyond repair, and he thought with some regret of the long green scarf his mother had made for him. His pack, though, was still in good condition, and he pulled it from the trunk and checked to ensure everything was there. He slid his new clothes on, letting the watch rest against his breastbone. Then he went to the window, peering out over the green forest beyond, trying to fix the image in his mind. Fear and no small amount of guilt pressed on his shoulders, and though he'd gone to fix what his mother had broken, the prince now wished he could live in this moment forever. Eventually, though, his duty could be put off no more. He hefted his bag and went out into the parlor where the old woman sat. He took his usual chair and leaned forward intently.

"I have nothing with which to repay you," the prince began. "I spent my last coin some time ago."

"Hmph," the old woman grunted, her needles moving steadily. The knitting had grown long since the prince's arrival in her house. "Well, perhaps you can repay me another way."

"How?"

"I seldom venture into the outside world," the old woman said. "It has been a long time since I have heard any word of it. Tell me a story from your country, wherever that may be."

The prince glanced at the cuckoo clock above the fire, then back to the old woman's nimble hands as the needles clacked together. He took a deep breath.

"Very well," he said. "I think I have just the one.

"Once upon a time, there was a kingdom with a wise king and a clever queen. The two ruled fairly for many years until, one sad day, the king died of a sudden illness. The citizens of the kingdom mourned for months, none more so than the queen who had loved her husband as a flower loves the sun. But the kingdom had to continue, and so the queen bore the burden alone. Yet, as anyone will tell you, cleverness untempered by wisdom can be a dangerous thing.

"The queen, having felt the pain of her husband's death deeply, decreed that when she died, whatever killed her should be outlawed from the kingdom. Her decree was spread to every corner of the land, and then subsequently forgotten, as she ruled for many years more. When she was old, with decades behind her, the queen went to bed one night and did not wake."

The prince ceased speaking for a moment, his eyes fixed on the pine-board floor. The old woman glanced up from her work, examining him.

"Is that the end?"

He smiled. "Almost. For, you see, the queen's decree was heard, and it was obeyed. That which had killed her was exiled from the kingdom."

"Old age."

"No. Time."

The needles—the ticking—stopped. The old woman peered up at the prince, who studied her with keen eyes.

"Time left the kingdom and has not returned for a hundred years. The people of the realm did not at first realize the price they would pay for their queen's folly. But when it became clear that every day would be the same, they started to understand. Eventually, the queen's son decided he would leave and seek out Time for himself."

The old woman's eyes narrowed. She set her knitting down carefully. "How did you manage to leave without falling to dust?"

The prince who was a king took the watch from around his neck and clicked it open, revealing the broken glass and unmoving hands of the clock. Wordlessly, he gave it to her, and she turned it over in her gnarled hands.

"Clever as your mother," she muttered, handing it back. He returned it to its place around his neck. When he'd woken without it on his person, he'd thought he was only seconds from death. After all, he had lived a single day for nearly one hundred years. But as the days passed in the cottage and he did not crumble, he began to realize whose house he'd stumbled upon.

"Why are you here?" the old woman asked. There was no anger in her tone: just curiosity and perhaps a bit of sadness.

"I am here to plead for my people. My mother made a grave mistake."

"She accomplished her goal. No one else shall die as she did."

"But they linger on when many would rather go," the king returned. "There are those who have been ill for one hundred years. Every breath is agony, but without Time to take them, they cannot die. There are children who long to grow up, lovers who long to have children." The king closed his eyes, seeing once again the pain on his subjects' faces. He blinked them open to meet the old woman's unflinching gaze.

"Without you, we are all trapped. I have come here to ask you to return and help me right my mother's wrong. Please. My people suffer for the decision of someone long dead."

The old woman sat in silence for some time, the only sound the crackle of the flames in the hearth. The king knew to wait, because Time could not be rushed.

At length, she spoke again. "What of you?"

"What of me?"

"Would you dishonor your mother's memory by breaking her final law?"

The king was quiet for a moment. It was a question he had asked himself often over the past hundred years, and never more so than when he left the kingdom to undo her decree. His mother had done what she thought best at the time. But times change.

"I have thought of my mother every day for one hundred years," he said at last. "For the first ten I loved her, for the next ninety I loathed her."

"And now?"

The king heaved a sigh. "Now, I believe I understand her. I think that might be better than either."

The old woman nodded, looking at him sorrowfully. "I would help you, if I could. But there is a price."

"Whatever it is, I'll pay it."

"Listen before you agree, boy," she said harshly. "Within your kingdom are thousands of lives, trapped in time for a hundred years. If I were to return now, everyone would crumble. So much time rushing in so quickly would destroy everything." She paused, studying him. "All that unspent time needs a place to go."

The king sucked in a breath. "Ah."

"Indeed."

The cuckoo clock on the wall began ticking again, and the king let his gaze drift up to it. He had expected a price, of course. He just hadn't realized it would be quite so high. But there was no one else to pay it, and he could not return empty-handed.

He turned back to the old woman, who watched him carefully. "I will pay it. I will take their time."

The old woman's eyes softened. "You would give up all your days for them?"

"It is all I have to give. Besides, I've had time enough to mourn a life unlived."

The old woman nodded once more. With a flourish, she bound off the final stitch of her knitting and pulled it straight. It was a scarf, the king realized, black as night and with cables like constellations running its length. She handed it to him, and he wrapped it around his neck. The wool prickled against his skin.

"I will come with you," she said. "We will right this wrong together."

The prince swallowed and nodded. He stood, hefting his pack, but the old woman's hand wrapping around his wrist stilled him. She watched him with her ancient, ageless eyes, and he saw in them all that had been and all that would be and all that might be, one day, though not for him.

"Remember what I told you, boy: sometimes it's good to sit still for a spell. You needn't be so eager to sell your life. We will go together, but not today." She smiled, releasing him and gesturing to his chair.

"Let us have another day, you and I. We have time enough for that."

See J.C. Pillard's story "The Tick of the Clock" online at Metaphorosis.
If you liked it, leave a comment. Authors love that!
Remember to subscribe to our e-mail updates so you'll know when new stories are posted.

About the story

Like many of my stories, "The Tick of the Clock" started with an image: a young man speaking to an old woman, begging for her help. It was a compelling image, but I wasn't sure what he needed help with, which really put a wrench in my plans to turn it into a story.

The idea stewed in my brain until I rewatched the old Twilight Zone episode "Nothing in the Dark," which personifies the figure of Death as a young man and centers around a conversation between him and an elderly woman. I have always liked the idea of anthropomorphic personifications (thank you, Terry Pratchett), and this idea combined with the image in my head. The old woman was not a woman—she was something wearing the figure of a woman. After some more fiddling, I arrived at who she was. Not death, but that which brings it: Time.

Once I had her character figured out, I turned my attention to the young man and how he finds himself with Time. I love strange, liminal spaces, so began the story with the young man —who, it turns out, is a prince—travelling through an endless forest before arriving at Time's cottage.

It was the prince, of course, who was going to be changed by the story, and who was thus the more challenging of the two to write. Time exists on her own terms—she has nothing to learn in the tale. But the prince does. That was probably the hardest part of the story to write: letting the prince come to terms with the curse on his kingdom, and allowing him to make peace with what he must do to break it.

A question for the author

Q: Why do you write speculative rather than realistic fiction?

A: The honest answer is that the ideas I have for stories are nearly all fantastical in nature. I have tried, on occasion, to write realistic fiction, but a speculative element always manages to appear regardless of my intent. In fact, I joke with my friends that I don't write anything that doesn't have a dragon in it—whether real or metaphorical. I find speculative fiction a more liberating place to explore thoughts and ideas, often because I can make abstract concepts more concrete. Beyond that, I spend enough time living in reality as it is: I'm happy to imagine myself in distant lands populated by the beautiful and strange whenever I can.

About the author

J.C. Pillard's parents read her *The Hobbit* when she was six, and she was hooked on fantasy from that point on. When she's not reading or writing speculative fiction, J.C. spends time knitting and running far too many D&D games. She lives at the foot of the Colorado Rockies with her husband and their sweet dog.
www.jcpillard.com, @JCPillard

Genesis

Lisa Short

Anne awoke to a crawling itch behind her ear. It had been months since her subdural alarm had triggered, long enough that she'd almost forgotten what it felt like. *The boys?* Even as she struggled to unwind herself from the bedcovers, then from William's leg that had somehow gotten tangled up in both of hers, she was conscious of a stab of cold annoyance—*the boys aren't my concern any longer.* Still, the habit of years kept her in motion—she emerged victorious from the bed and staggered over to the console, fumbling for the panel switch.

But the message alert wasn't from the creche. She stared down at the text scrolling silently across the screen, eyes uncharacteristically wide.

"Anne?"

She started—she had almost forgotten that William was there. "I have to go," she said over her shoulder, and strode across the room to the untidy heap of her coveralls on the floor.

"What? Now? Why?" His voice had sharpened.

She spared him a glance as she yanked the coveralls up her legs. "Meteorite." She paused long enough to smile thinly at his quick intake of breath. "A skipodder spotted it coming down. It's pretty far out though, so—"

"Can't someone else go?"

She stared blankly at him. "Why should someone else go?" His eyes narrowed and his mouth compressed. *Oh.* "I'm sorry." She tried to inject some regret into it, but her voice sounded mechanical even to her own ears. Perhaps it was better to just be blunt. "I *want* to go, William." She finished fastening up her coveralls and headed for the door.

"Anne, wait—please." The last syllable made her stumble a little, then drag to a halt—William wasn't a man who usually said *please* to anybody. Her fingers actively tingled with her desire to grab the door latch, but she made herself turn around and face him instead.

He hesitated; his mouth had relaxed a little, but his stare was still sharply trained on her face. "Yes?" she said, as patiently as she could manage, though her jaw had begun to ache from the effort of keeping her teeth ungritted.

"I—" His mouth firmed back into a line and he sat up straighter. "You know—I haven't had my kid yet." Anne blinked at him. Had she known that? William was a good fifteen years her senior, one of the second generation of the ark ship *Genesis*'s colonists—the first generation to be born on the planet—as Anne herself was third generation. She might have just assumed he'd gotten that out of the way before she'd ever taken an interest in his personal life, or she might've just not cared enough to think of it at all. "And—I realized that it was well past time—I knew that already, of course. I just—the Outpost. My responsibilities—" Anne nodded, managing to dredge up a little genuine sympathy at last. *Responsibilities* had been the entire reason she'd borne her own child as soon as she'd been medically cleared to do so after puberty. And speaking of responsibilities—she cast a yearning look at the door, which judging from the sudden rigidity of his posture, William didn't miss. "I'd like to have it with you," he finished in a rush.

Anne realized after a second or two that her mouth was actually hanging open and snapped it shut. There was always a list of names posted at the creche, of men looking to fulfil their own responsibility to produce a child for the Outpost; Anne had borne a second child for one of them, as soon as her first had been weaned. She had imagined her proactivity in doing so would spare her ever being confronted with a scene like this.

But William was undeterred. "I know you've already had two, but you haven't opted for sterilization yet." She started to nod impatiently, then stiffened up herself. "And yes, I *did* look at your medical history—I have the clearance to do it." There was the William she knew, the Outpost Commander at his most autocratic —irritation had steadied his voice and squared his shoulders at last. "I had a good reason. The mother of my child—"

"—is *not* going to be me. Ever. My God, how could you think I'd go through all that again?"

"You had easy pregnancies—"

"Easy!" She stared at him. "I see you did read my medical records," she said after a pause, dryly. "And you're right." She had hated the pregnancies, every second of them, but they weren't the reason she'd been so relieved to be done with the whole business. "But I didn't opt *out* of sterilization. I just hadn't gotten round to it yet." There hadn't seemed any urgency—though obviously she'd been wrong about that. "I'll schedule it as soon as I get back from the salvage site."

Anything else he had to say was cut off by the door slamming shut behind her. Anne broke into a jog down the corridor outside her quarters, rounded the corner, then stopped in her tracks—she had gone the wrong way; the whole debacle with William had set her feet mindlessly down the corridor in the direction of the creche instead of the skipod hangar.

Creche-side, the Outpost was nearly close enough to touch one of the ramshackle rock formations that littered the surface outside. While the planetary weather system was mostly as bland and featureless as its terrain, the occasional dust storm had been destructive enough to make locating the creche in the most protected area of the Outpost the obvious choice. The hangar, filled with skipods requiring unimpeded access to the planetary surface, had needed to be built on the opposite side.

Anne reversed course, but didn't slow her pace; while it seemed unlikely that William would go so far as to suspend her access to the hangar, she hadn't thought he'd try to talk her out of going, either. But the hangar doors opened for her without protest. She squeezed between the rows of waiting skipods, their long cylindrical bodies gleaming black under the high bay lighting. The feel of the exterior hatch rungs in her hands was positively pleasurable—it had been a long time, *too* long—she scrambled easily up her own skipod's curved hull, balancing atop it just long enough to pop the top hatch and slide down into the skipod's interior.

Its cabin was fabricated to match the height of its operator, but was nearly three times as long, a dimly luminescent tube densely packed with control panels, display screens, and sensors. She spent the next twenty minutes running pre-start checks and making sure that her heated compression suit was properly stowed —if the meteorite had churned up the terrain beyond what the skipod's repulsors could handle, she'd have to go outside on foot— then settled herself in the cockpit. The skipod purred to life around her, the vibration almost imperceptible through her cushioned seat. She spun it around neatly and pinged the inner airlock doors, letting the skipod glide toward them on its own stored inertia.

As soon as the inner doors closed behind her, the airlock's lights flickered out, leaving only the display imbedded above the outer doors shining in the claustrophobic darkness. *Pressure 101.3* *kPa, Temperature 20.2 °C, Concentration 21% O_2.* The numbers began to drop, slowly at first, then in a whirling blur until they abruptly stilled—*44.7 kPa, -5.1 °C, 6% O_2*—and flickered out, shifting to red letters large enough to fill the display: *PLANETARY ATMOSPHERE.* With a tortured howl audible even through the skipod's muffling walls, the outer airlock doors began to open.

The sky beyond them was nearly unrelieved black, its few small stars twinkling coldly down on the slumped and frozen landscape stretching out to the horizon. Anne barely glanced at it—it never appreciably changed—before folding the cockpit seat away and pulling the exoskeleton up from its floor compartment. She locked her hands and feet into the exo's padded grips, took a deep breath, and broke into a long, loping stride.

The exo's display flared to life, showing her pulse rate and blood oxygen levels along with the power she was feeding the skipod's repulsors. Fully charged, the repulsors were good for eighty hours run time, but it was better to use the exo assist to extend their power reserves. The view from the cockpit swung smoothly northward as another display blinked on, showing the uneven terrain reduced to flat rectangular grids, with a deep orange avatar on the very edge of the screen. The skipod fired its triangulation laser, pulled the meteorite's estimated trajectory from the Outpost's central data core, then threw up its best guess at its distance beneath the meteorite's avatar.

600 km.

The strong, smooth motion of Anne's arms and legs in the exo faltered. Theoretically, the repulsors could manage a 1,200-kilometer round trip, though she didn't personally know of anyone ever actually testing that theory out—but she'd have to run the exo twelve hours a day at a minimum to make it. At the skipod's top speed, she might be able to reach the meteorite in three days. *Three days, twelve hours a day every day in the exo*—and then the whole trip to do all over again, just to get back to the Outpost.

But *not going* wasn't really an option either, no matter what William might have said. William himself had shown her the real numbers once, back when he'd been courting her. She grinned humorlessly down at the display. Well, he'd been right about the sort of conversation that would pique her interest, hadn't he? Without a significant increase in the influx of new organic material, the next Outpost generation—not four, three, or even two more down the road, but the *next*—might be the last.

Unbidden, an image of her sons rose behind her eyes. She pushed it away impatiently and turned the skipod further north until its nose was in perfect alignment with the tracking display's route markers, then set off.

Anne pushed the skipod all through the night and well into the following day, until *Current Completed Run Distance: 253 km* shone redly down at her from the meteorite's tracking display. She stripped her sweat-soaked coveralls off and chucked them into the skipod's tiny reclaimer unit, then pulled the folded cot out of its side compartment and rolled onto it, eyes already closing.

Anne dreamed of her sons. She tried to fight the dream off, even sleeping—they were alive and well, her waking mind knew; she'd have been informed if they were otherwise. There was no reason for her to dream of them now.

But her waking mind was not in control and the dream gradually swallowed her whole. Memories of that first childbirth, red with agony, followed by the cessation of pain so acute it was nearly ecstasy, morphing into the gray drudgery of the work assigned to nursing mothers, the dull ache in her neck and shoulders that never seemed to subside, and the grinding buzz of her subdural alarm pulling her back to the creche, every hour on the hour—*the baby is awake—the baby is hungry—*

The waking Anne had forgotten most of those details, had deliberately forgotten them; the waking Anne saw no reason to dwell on things that couldn't be helped, that were past and unchangeable. Like the way her sons had screamed after her as she'd left the creche for the very last time, her body oddly weightless as she stepped through its doors, empty of pregnancy, of milk, of children's hands clinging to hers—

The blare of the six-hour alert she'd set on the skipod's panel kicked her into sluggish consciousness. Moving stiffly, she dug a tube of organic concentrate out of the stores and washed it down with some water, then clambered back into the exo.

But by the time the sky had begun to lighten once more through the skipod's viewports, she had to stop again. She untangled herself from the exo and collapsed onto her knees, forcing herself to breathe slowly and deeply. Vomiting directly into the skipod's reclaimer unit was a dicey proposition at best, and a lifetime of conditioning to never waste organic matter of any description did fierce battle with the nausea of dehydrated overexertion. Conditioning won; she finally crawled back onto the cot, pausing only long enough to hook one of the skipod's hydration needles to her bare arm before collapsing into unconsciousness, thankfully dreamless this time.

When she awoke, the pallid sun was sinking below the bottom edge of the skipod's viewports. From her vantage point she could see the tracking display, shining in the gloom of the skipod's interior—*Current Completed Run Distance: 407 km: 125 km to target*. At least the skipod's laser had finally found something to bounce back from, more likely than not her meteorite. Her hands shook as she curled her fingers around the exo's grips; there were deep tremors in her legs, and the muscles in her arms and back screamed as she pushed off once more.

She had set the skipod to retarget the meteorite every fifteen minutes, pinging her subdural implant with each successful attempt. Her eyes mechanically shifted from console to displays to the skipod's viewports, then lingered on the last—the endless, monotonous sweep of lumpy, grayish-brown terrain under the skipod's floodlights was hypnotic.

The skipod jerked—it righted itself immediately, but Anne snapped out of her haze of fatigue and realized, with a surge of panic, that the skipod hadn't pinged her for far too long. She found the skipod's tracking display and stared at it in shock—the meteorite's avatar was *gone*.

Anne wrenched her hands out of the exo's grips and slammed them palms-down on the console, fingers moving so fast across the panels they blurred. *Lost signal*, the skipod insisted, and Anne's stomach lurched. Diagnostics menus flashed past beneath her frantic hands, then she sagged back in the exo's frame, lightheaded with relief. The signal *was* still there—it was just buried in the background noise of the terrain itself, which had somehow increased three orders of magnitude over what it had been at the journey's start.

It was *there*, that was all that truly mattered. She quickly reprogrammed the laser to take a full baseline reading of the terrain. After several minutes, the console beeped and her gaze darted back to the tracking screen. *New baseline established*, it informed her serenely. *New target acquired.*

"What?" Anne muttered, hunching over the console. "I don't want a new target, I want the *old* target—"

Existing target: 51 km. New target: 7 km. The now-familiar, irregularly shaped lump of the meteorite's avatar shimmered into existence on the rescaled display, quickly followed by another, larger shape, strangely symmetrical on two sides and only one grid square away from the skipod. Anne recalibrated the laser for analysis and once more fired a pulse out into the darkness.

Minutes later, the display threw up a barrage of text. *New target composition: ALUMINUM. TITANIUM. GRAPHITE. FULLERENE (C60). FULLERENE (C80)*—she stopped reading even as the letters continued to scroll past.

The fates of two of the ark ship *Genesis*'s four original Outpost automated base units were well known. The first one had soft-landed sixty years ago, right where it was now—*home*. The second had come down some forty kilometers southeast of that—*not* softly, and its organic remains had been the main reason their own Outpost had survived as long as it had. But no skipodder had ever found so much as a trace of the other two Outpost base units, and they had never been able to afford the high risk of permanent organic resource loss to the Outpost by going out blindly searching for them. Every time a skipodder failed to return from a salvage run, the Outpost's projected overall population survival trended a little further downward—and the farther out the trip and the less certain the target location, the more likely that was to occur.

Every skipodder had memorized what the analyses results from an Outpost's original, unadulterated hull might look like. Their own Outpost's outer hull no longer read like that, of course; they'd long ago stripped every atom of carbon out of it and fed them into the fabricators. But every skipodder knew what to look for, and that was what was scrolling past Anne's unbelieving eyes now.

Anne ran an integrity check over her heated compression suit and rebreather helmet one last time, then stepped out of the skipod's rear hatch onto the uneven, rocky ground. Fifty meters away was the raised lip of what the skipod thought was the leading edge of a ravine, with the new target buried behind it. She hurried over to it, as fast as she dared without risking a trip and fall that might damage her suit. Easing herself up the lip, she gripped its top edge and hauled herself the last meter or so to its top.

The sheer scale of the wreckage that met her eyes baffled her first attempt to even comprehend it. The uncrushed half of the tortuous metal behemoth embedded in the ravine below her was easily twice the size of the entire Outpost. Stretching out from that strange, sinuous metal body were two arching arms, reaching blindly for the ravine's wall. What might have once been matching arms on its other side were now nothing more than mangled debris littering the ravine floor.

But whatever it was, it wasn't an Outpost, living or dead—she didn't know which she'd hoped for more, but it hardly mattered now. Her nose and eyes stung sharply, her breath hitching hard in her chest—*stop it!* she snarled at herself. *It's still a* partly *organic thing, a* salvageable *thing; more of us can come back, with better tools*—the truth of that calmed her and she began to pick her way down the ravine wall. Whatever it was, it had crashed a long time ago—though obvious traces of the burning rage of its descent remained, the jagged, blackened chasm it had gouged in the planetary surface had long since refrozen into the dead stillness of the rest of the terrain.

Anne lost her footing halfway down the ravine—arms windmilling for balance, she barely managed to skid the rest of the way down on her feet rather than her rear end, and finally staggered to a halt directly under one of the wreck's massive, unbroken arms. The light from her headlamp reflected back a sharp white glare from its metal arch overhead—*what?* She stilled, and the headlamp's beam froze in place on the underside of the arch. She hadn't been imagining it—there *was* something etched into the battered hull, in letters so large she hadn't quite realized what they were at first. Anne craned her neck back as far as it would go in the compression suit.

G…E…N…E…S—

No, she thought stupidly.

She knew, *everyone* knew that the *Genesis* itself had never been intended to land. The Outpost's central data core had always been vague on what exactly had happened to the *Genesis* after the colonists had abandoned it, and it hadn't mattered anyway—the *Genesis* had been too decrepit to take them back home again, and that was all anyone had cared about. She'd said as much to William once, in the early days of their relationship, after overhearing an argument about its possible fates. But William, with his Command access to the restricted parts of the Outpost's central data core, had told her that it had mattered, because the first colonists had originally intended to use it as a *satellite*, a concept he'd then had to explain to her. It would have helped them out a great deal, he'd said, in tracking the precious meteorites that so infrequently struck the planetary surface, in communicating with scavenging skipodders—perhaps in even more ways they'd never had a chance to explore. But the *Genesis* had never responded to any attempts at contact with its automated onboard systems.

It must have crashed soon after the Outpost itself had landed —nobody would have noticed what must have been a visually spectacular descent, or cared even if they had, in those first, difficult years. An almost superstitious awe gripped her as she stared up at it. *This* was the *Genesis*—their progenitor, this dead monstrosity that had carried them all here and then spat them all out onto this sterile hellscape to die—

A flicker of movement on the very edge of her periphery, the faint reflected gleam of light at an angle her headlamp couldn't possibly have reached, alerted her too late. She started to turn around, but before she had time to do more than shift her weight from one foot to the other, something exploded with agonizing force against the back of her helmet and all the lights abruptly went out.

Anne's first conscious awareness was of pain—her head throbbed mercilessly and something had dried to a tacky, pulling unpleasantness on the back of her neck. She automatically reached back, then froze when her fingers encountered not the edge of her rebreather helmet, but her own matted hair.

She pried her eyes open, squinting in anticipation, but the light surrounding her was dim, strangely yellow, filtering down from somewhere far above. She tried to tilt her head back to look, but her stomach revolted at even that tentative movement; she stilled, breathing deeply through her nose, waiting for the nausea to subside.

"You're probably concussed," said a harsh, grating voice. "Sorry about that—but better concussed than et, eh?" Faint aspirating sounds followed that remark—*laughter*? Anne's eyes snapped fully open as she struggled upright. A wild look around revealed weirdly bent walls, stretching upward into the gloom, and scattered pieces of what might once have been machinery—and a man crouched down barely a meter away from her, completely naked, staring intently at her from small black eyes lost in a sea of wrinkles.

Anne fought for analytical detachment in the face of her hindbrain's bewildered terror. He was old, clearly, but more than that, something else was wrong with him, like nothing she'd seen before—the quantity of loose flesh hanging off his face and the one skinny arm he'd raised to point at her were grotesque. She hoped she didn't look as revolted as she felt; if he'd been the one that had hit her over the head, she should probably try to not do anything to make him want to hit her again.

He wheezed laughter again. "Stinks in here, don't it?" Apparently he had noticed her disgust, but hadn't successfully deduced its cause. "I know where you're from, girlie—we've had a few of you wander in here, over the years. Most of who's left is too stupid to ask questions first and et later—I gave up trying to convince 'em after the last one, I don't remember how many years ago it was. But you know, the others was all men—I seen you and I could tell you was a woman, and I—" His voice choked off abruptly. "Maybe they *wouldn't* just et you first, and I—*I didn't want to see it!*" He shrieked the last, then looked around in obvious terror—but the silence that fell around them after the echo of his shout faded remained unbroken, and his bony shoulders relaxed.

Anne hadn't known it was possible to understand every word someone else was saying, yet not have the faintest idea what they were talking about. Something about a *smell*, had been the first thing he'd said—she inhaled cautiously through her nose. It wasn't any worse than the interior of her skipod after a full day's run—but this wasn't a skipod, inhabited for only short bursts of time and unable to support the sort of hourly reclamation cleaning intended to capture and recycle every last molecule of organic waste for recycling. "Why does it smell so, ah..." She trailed off, still wary of offending him. "Is there something wrong with your reclaimers?"

The old man jerked, startling a flinch out of her. "Wha—ha! Reclaimers? This is a *spaceship*, girlie! We wasn't ever supposed to be awake long enough to need *reclaimers*." Suddenly his eyes flooded with tears. "Wasn't ever supposed to be—I been awake aboard for a long time all right, a long time—" His voice caught.

Anne was briefly swamped with unwanted pity, and something else—*not ever supposed to be awake long enough* —"Were you—" It seemed impossible, but the old man stiffened, his eyes nearly vanishing in his wrinkles. "Were you...part of the crew? The *original* crew?"

His face pinched and he drew back from her, though his stare didn't leave her face. "And what if I was?" His voice was like broken glass.

She finally understood the extremity of his appearance, though. He wasn't ill; he was simply *old*. Not old as she had always known it, in the Outpost's earlier generations—the thinner, stringier, but still vigorous activity of early- to mid-sixties, before productivity declined to the point where personal organic consumption was no longer justifiable, and the pressure to voluntarily enter the Outpost's reclaimers began—but *old*. Eighty years old? *Ninety?* She was finding it hard to comprehend him at all as a living, breathing human being—his impossible age, his filth, his hair a wild explosion cascading over his shoulders instead of trimmed short and fed into the reclaimers. Yet there he squatted before her, irrefutable.

But if there weren't any reclaimers on the *Genesis*—and *no reclaimers* probably meant *no fabricators* too—"Didn't you—did you have any supplies at all, when you first landed?"

"Some," he grunted, settling back on his heels. "From when we was *supposed* to be awake on board looking at all the different planets we was *supposed* to fly past, to see which ones was best suited for a colony. All the different planets, ha!" He spat out the last syllable. "When we all woke up three thousand years too late, out in the emptiness between the stars, no planets, *nothing*—"

Anne knew the story. The old records in the Outpost's central data core indicated that the Genesis's crew hadn't spent much time trying to figure out exactly how or why they had drifted so incredibly far off their planned course—they had been far more interested in *where*, and that answer had been terrible. Somehow the *Genesis*, instead of heading up the Milky Way's Orion-Cygnus spiral toward the galactic center, had cut straight across it and away instead, into the flat black void stretching thousands of light-years between its arms.

But that void hadn't been quite as empty as it had first appeared—a few stars had been there, hidden behind the light-absorbing dust clouds scattered throughout it. One of them, a mere light-year distant, had been a yellow dwarf with a single terrestrial planet, and the *Genesis*'s analyses had confirmed an Earth-standard average density and an atmosphere containing non-negligible amounts of oxygen and water vapor. Only one oddity had stood out—the *Genesis* had failed to find any trace of organic compounds in either its surface or atmosphere.

The old man had hunched in on himself, shivering. The air in whatever disused part of the wreckage he had dragged her to was noticeably chilly; Anne was glad of her heated compression suit. She cast a quick look around for her helmet and spotted it just a meter or so away, an ugly crack running down its crown. It would still be better than nothing, if she could just get back outside the ship—she inched toward it, keeping a wary eye on the old man. "So," she said, hoping to distract him, and because she found she couldn't help herself, "with no reclaimers—after the supplies ran out and what you said before about, ah, being *et*—I guess that's how you've managed to survive this lo—"

It was the wrong thing to say. He suddenly lunged toward her and she scrabbled sideways and back, ending up as close as she could manage to her precious helmet. "*Don't you judge me!*" he screamed, then clapped his hands over his mouth, casting a terrified look around. Anne took advantage of his distraction to fling herself the last half a meter over to the helmet, shoving it quickly behind her back. After several seconds, he relaxed a little, though he was still glaring at her with an enraged expression so exaggerated it was almost comical.

Anne raised her hands placatingly. "I wasn't—I really wasn't," she said rapidly. "If we didn't have the reclaimers and the fabricators, we'd have probably ended up doing the same thing. I mean, we *do* do the same thing, right? Just with a lot more steps in between the dying, and the..." She trailed off, because the old man was staring at her in unmitigated horror.

His lips flapped, but no words emerged at first. "You," he whispered finally. "You...put each other in the fabricators...to make *food?*"

"Well...yeah, that's what they're f—"

"*That's* not *what they're for!*" he screamed. "You were supposed to use them for the *soil*, to enrich the soil with proper *nutrients* so that *Earth plants* could grow here—you were supposed to make this world *green* like Earth, didn't you know that, why didn't you *do* that? Why—" His voice choked off into great whooping sobs that shook his emaciated frame.

Anne tried to shout over his hysteria, why the original colonists hadn't done that—because they couldn't; because those long-ago designers of the Outpost automated base units hadn't envisioned a world with no plate tectonics, no seismic activity, no moons, no asteroid belts, *nothing* to seed its static, frozen silicate surface, to contaminate the sterile purity of its atmosphere.

But he clearly wasn't listening. Broken words and phrases emerged from between the hands he'd buried his face in—*knew an Outpost was there and thriving, those boys looked healthy enough*—with another lurch of nausea she finally realized that she now knew the fate of at least a few of the Outpost's lost skipodders over the decades. *Thought someday they'd ALL come here and save the KIDS, the poor little KIDS!*—she really didn't want to know what that meant, and was just about to risk climbing back up to her feet when his head jerked up and he fixed her with a look of cunning so grotesque that she physically recoiled.

"You know why the others keep me alive, girlie?" His tone was suddenly, weirdly conversational. "Ain't nobody else left who knows how to run the ship's reactor—I was engineer's mate. No fancy education but they took me on 'cause my wife wanted to go too. So I done it, I kept the reactor in good shape even though—even though—" His chin shook as if palsied, then stiffened again. "Because if I *didn't*, I knew the reactor'd blow. I knew the Outpost was close enough for men to reach us—it *could* blow, and then maybe it'd wipe out *all* the life in the Outposts too, the *good* life, the *civilized* life, not just this HELLHOLE—" He shrieked the last up, into the shadowy dimness above them that Anne's eyes couldn't quite penetrate. His attention returned, abruptly and fanatically focused on Anne's face. "But now I *know*, girlie. You ain't any different from us at *all*. I should've just let the others put you to work on your BACK bearing the next generation of *DINNER!*"

A shout, a harsh bark of sound, echoed from somewhere outside their cavernous space—the old man's eyes, already wild, lost what little sanity they'd had left. With an agility Anne would never have thought him capable of, he whirled around and fled; Anne scrambled to her own feet, staggering as her numb legs tried to collapse under her, then froze as a long shadow fell across the floor where the old man had been seconds before. Instinctively she flung herself backwards, rapping her already sore head on a panel leaning drunkenly against the wall—she darted behind it, jamming as much of herself as would fit into the narrow space behind it.

Seconds later, someone shuffled into view, shaggy head swinging back and forth on a neck invisible beneath snarled layers of beard. He was as naked as the old man had been—she supposed all the clothing had worn out long ago—but far younger, maybe even younger than Anne herself, though it was impossible to tell for sure under all the hair and filth. *Not* someone she was likely to be able to fight her way free of—Anne hunched in as tightly as she could behind the panel.

After several excruciating minutes, he turned around and ambled back the way he'd come. As soon as he was out of immediate sight, Anne eased out from behind the panel and pressed herself back against the wall—she could still see him, making his way towards what a quick look around seemed to confirm was the only visible exit in this vast space. With a spasm of pure adrenaline terror, she remembered what the old man had said before he'd fled—was it possible he'd gone to destroy the ship's reactor? Who knew how insane he had already been even before he'd happened across her, and how much further he'd cracked now?

In spite of the chill air, she was sweating—her palms were so soaked with it that perspiration squeezed out of her compression gloves and trickled down the rebreather helmet now clutched tight in her hands. She forced herself to breathe slowly and evenly as she crept across the floor towards the doorway that the shambling hulk was just disappearing through. If he happened to look back over his shoulder—if he *saw* her—

But he didn't look back, and she trailed after him, as far behind as she could manage without losing sight of him entirely. The exit led into a narrow corridor choked with debris, blackened wires dangling at odd intervals from its torn plating. It was only irregularly lit, by long, yellowed tubes—she was glad of it; she would be at least a little harder to see, hugging the wall as she was. Then he suddenly vanished from sight—he must have turned a corner that she couldn't see yet.

She dared to step up her pace then. As she drew nearer to where he'd turned, she started to hear something, sounds—faint and muffled, but getting louder—*voices*? Anne had the uneasy, crawling certainty that she was heading the wrong way, deeper into the bowels of the *Genesis*, but she didn't know what else to do. If she backtracked to the room she'd awakened in and failed to find another exit, and ran into yet another wandering resident—

She finally reached the bend in the corridor. A lightning-quick peek around the corner confirmed that the corridor beyond it sloped in both directions. The muffled voices were coming from the downward slope; Anne leaned back against the very edge of the turn and angled her head as far back as she could to see the upslope. She couldn't make out more than a few meters of it; it might be nothing more than a dead end.

There was no reason to look the other direction, though—she could hardly go that way anyway, towards the voices and almost certainly where the shambling hulk had gone. *You don't have to look*—she found herself peering around the edge into the corridor's downslope. It opened up abruptly, just beyond the turn, into a room with an oddly familiar layout—*medical bay*? Just like the one in the Outpost—a hot wave of stench struck her in the face and she gagged soundlessly. *You don't have to look!* But she couldn't stop herself from leaning out just a little more, a little farther—*people!* Seven, eight, maybe more—it was hard to see in the gloom—were crouched in various corners or sprawled out on rotted piles of material.

Then a flicker of movement caught her eye. One of them was struggling to his—*her* feet, Anne realized sickly as she turned towards Anne's hidden vantage point, her belly a hard, rolling mound under tiny, flaplike breasts. She couldn't have been more than twelve or thirteen, at most—but Anne had known, of course, as soon as she'd seen how young the second man had been, that the *Genesis* had a breeding population. Or she should have known—

Put you to work on your BACK bearing the next generation of DINNER!

...just like you've *done for the Outpost already?*

Anne recoiled from that jeering mental voice, almost relieved when an abrupt, metallic rattle drew her attention back to the girl. Anne's gaze followed the sound down to a heavy metal chain wound around the girl's ankle. The other end of the chain was fastened to what appeared to be a...surgical table? Just like the ones in the Outpost, right down to the integrated blood supply unit flashing busily away at its head...so the *Genesis* did have fabricators after all, of a sort. Though the blood supply units were highly specialized fabricators, only able to force living blood cells into temporary, rapid replication, and they were just as restricted as any fabricator in their inability to produce an organic substance without an organic raw material—and more restricted than most, as the only organic source they were able to utilize was a living patient's own tissue. But the lower half of the table appeared to be empty—as her eyes adjusted to the noisome, flickering dimness, she was finally able to make out what it was that was strapped down at the table's head, nearly lost beneath countless quivering coils of intravenous tubing. Something far too small for its fragile, sticklike legs to reach even halfway down the table's length—

Anne bolted for the upsloping corridor, not even trying to muffle the impact of her suit's heavy boots on the floor plating. Deafened by the pounding, roaring thunder of her own pulse in her ears, she didn't know if anyone was coming after her—they had to have heard her by now—but all she could do was flee, blinded by the unstoppable tears that scorched her eyes like acid. The corridor steepened sharply, turning into the stuff of nightmares, each bounding leap wrenched back by gravity, as if she were running through a thick, invisible sludge.

She rounded the next turn at top speed and nearly slammed into a hard, unforgiving but unbelievably familiar sight—an inner airlock door, so like any of the dozens in the Outpost that for a long, crazy second she wondered if she was hallucinating it. But no, of course it looked the same—it *was* the same—the *Genesis* and the Outpost had been designed and built together. Skidding to a halt, she jammed the rebreather helmet down on her head, then clawed the airlock's manual override panel open.

There was a gap, a sizeable one, between the edge of the outer airlock door and the lip of the ravine. She backed up a few steps, then ran and blindly jumped and somehow found herself on her hands and knees on the other side. Her ankle throbbed brutally—she must have twisted it without realizing it, but she staggered back up onto her feet anyway and hopped-ran to the skipod, still sitting fifty meters away from the ravine's edge, serene and unmolested.

Her hands shook so badly that she couldn't get the rear hatch open—her back crawled, jittering, but she didn't dare pause working on the hatch to look behind her. Finally, the hatch hissed open and she flung herself inside. As it closed behind her, she wrenched off her helmet and compression gloves and scuttled across the interior on her knees to the front console. She slumped down into the cockpit's cushioned seat as the onboard systems swung the skipod back in precisely the same direction they'd come from. *Back, back, go, RUN*—the repulsors hummed and the skipod shot forward, away from the *Genesis*.

A bare moment later, a tremor rocked the skipod. Anne stiffened in her seat, gaze darting to the skipod's rear camera display. A flicker of movement against the sky above the ravine— she rubbed her eyes hard. She might have imagined it—it was colorless, faint, more like a puff of vapor than anything else. *A puff of vapor*—the first faint exhalation of a reactor core with all its safety systems stealthily taken offline...?

You ain't any different from us at all.

"We are different," she whispered, into the skipod's warm, dim silence. "We *are*—"

Her own voice, answering: *I mean, we* do *do the same thing, right? Just with a lot more steps in between—put you to work on your BACK bearing the next generation of DINNER!*

Duty, ever since she could remember—the duty to survive and reproduce, *just enough* so that there would be someone left for Earth to find and save someday, as everyone knew they would because they *had* to, because otherwise their entire existence was nothing but a slow and pointless death. And if not in time to save *them*, their *children* or their *children*'s children or—

She had never wanted to bear those children. She had fought a grim, years-long battle to care as little for them as possible. She had known other people felt differently about their own duty, their *own* children, and many of them had disliked her for it. And William in particular had misunderstood her entirely. Though she supposed she couldn't blame him—she hadn't understood herself, not really. Not until now.

Anne switched off the rear camera display and huddled in the cockpit seat. She couldn't just stay there, though; the skipod couldn't make it back to the Outpost without the exo assist. It was going to be a close-run thing even with it. Though maybe it didn't matter anyway. That puff of vapor—*and then they'd ALL come here and save the KIDS, the poor little KIDS!*

Anne forced herself to her feet, broke down the cockpit seat, and raised the exoskeleton in its place with hands that felt like they belonged to someone else. She had to at least try to get back to the Outpost. William would want to *save the kids*, and salvage the remains of the *Genesis*, too. With all that new organic influx, those ugly numbers, the Outpost's organic supply versus consumption curve, would level out once more...almost. For a while.

The tremor that shook the skipod that time was impossible to ignore. Anne closed her eyes, locked her hands and feet in the exo's implacable grasp, and pushed forward blindly into the night.

See Lisa Short's story "Genesis" online at Metaphorosis.
If you liked it, leave a comment. Authors love that!
Remember to subscribe to our e-mail updates so you'll know when
new stories are posted.

About the story

The crosstrainer (as opposed to the stationary bike or treadmill) has always been my cardio gym equipment of choice, and one day, as I was on it, I was thinking about cross-country skiing (which the crosstrainer somewhat mimics)—for whatever reason, I started imagining a woman, inside a vehicle that operated similarly to that, alone and traversing an icy plain at night. On an alien world? Definitely an alien world! But why? Because, I thought, there might be limits on the amount of charge such a vehicle could store, and it would need the operator to put in some effort because of that... if one had to travel long distances... but why the need to travel long distances? And why limitations on the fuel? Our current vehicles are primarily fueled by hydrocarbons...ah ha, I thought. No fossil fuels. A world that had never evolved life wouldn't have fossil fuels in the first place. No hydrocarbons... wait—what if there wasn't any carbon at all?

While I'm no kind of geologist, I do know that the primary sources of carbon on the Earth's surface are either from outside Earth (via asteroids, meteors, etc.) or from within the Earth (from seismic shifts, volcanic eruptions, etc.). What if you had a planet with no seismic activity, one essentially alone in the depths of space—no asteroid belts in its system, as far from a galactic arm or the galactic center as you can realistically get, with no carbon dioxide in its atmosphere either? You'd have a world with no carbon, and therefore no ability at all to be life-bearing, neither of its own accord nor even artificially induced by humanity, not sustainably. How would a community of people survive under those conditions? Well, they would still have access to one reproductive source of carbon... still unsustainably over the long term, of course. But they could survive. For a while. With extreme changes in their social structuring to accommodate an existence built entirely around cannibalism...

A question for the author

Q: What work of art has been the most inspiring for you?

A: No one particular work of art, but when I was eight years old, my mother and I moved in with the man who would become my stepfather a year or so later. His closets were a treasure trove of comic books and speculative fiction paperbacks (which was definitely a huge influence on me as a writer!) but the thing that first caught my eye about his house were the posters he had taped up all over the walls. Prints by Frazetta, Vallejo, and more were plastered over every square inch, depicting mighty warriors, monstrous beasts, spaceships with guns blazing... I was enchanted, and whenever I had trouble falling asleep right away at night, I would think of one of those prints and a story about it. Who were they? What were they fighting for? What alien or fantasy world had they sprung from? Many of the stories I still write today took their earliest inspiration from some of those prints.

About the author

Lisa Short is a Texas-born, Kansas-bred writer of fantasy, science fiction and horror. She has an honorable discharge from the United States Army, a degree in chemical engineering and twenty years' experience as a professional engineer. Lisa currently lives in Maryland with her husband, two youngest children, father-in-law, and cats. She is a member of the Horror Writers Association and a Futurescapes 2021 alumnus.

www.lisashortauthor.com, @Lisa_K_Short

Tell the Crows I'm Home

Laurel Beckley

There is a place where the lost go to be found.

It is a small farm tucked into a bend in Highway 38, between Scottsburg and Elkton—two towns barely on a map, and even less so after the earthquake shattered much of the West Coast. Once, this road was a bustling thoroughfare from the interior of the state to the coastal towns of Reedsport and Winchester Bay. Now it sits empty, giving more and more of itself to the hungry river it parallels.

The farm is nestled in a broad gap between the road and the river, hidden by swathes of shallow-rooted white oak, whose thick strands of sea-foam lichen and brown moss create their own ecosystems, creating space for the ferns and the birds and the insects, although there are fewer of all of those, now.

Nicole tends this farm, same as she has for the past forty years. She inherited it through a twist of fate and negligence after her parents passed, and then kept it with the stubbornness of a disowned queer child still tending old hurts. She replaced the hard memories with new ones, slowly rehabilitating the structures of her home and her soul.

The first few years were hard: relearning the lost skills of childhood, accepting the weird things found in her pockets and glove box and shoes, navigating the conservative mindsets of her neighbors—who knew the reasons for her leaving and still disagreed with her lifestyle upon her return. Life got a little easier as muscle memory took over and the collective current turned grudgingly towards acceptance.

What never changed was being viewed as an outsider. Ten years away transformed her into a stranger, despite being practically immortalized for a high school track record that remains unbroken nearly fifty years later.

The gym with her record etched onto the walls flooded in the quake of '22, erasing history but not memory. The football field and high school have been reclaimed since the flood, but the town dwindles with each passing year.

Those old enough to remember Nicole's parents have died off or moved on to nursing homes in Roseburg or Cottage Grove or Eugene. Most of Nicole's former classmates left when the nearest hills were stripped in the first gasping resuscitation of the after, when everyone scrambled to take what they could while they could, before the fires devoured everything or another quake hit or the Yellowstone caldera finally blew or another recession or, or, or. The reasoning was endless and short-sighted. Consideration of replanting and maintenance vanished, along with the northern spotted owls and the wineries and the frogs and the Roosevelt elk.

Nicole stayed, even as the years passed and friendships eroded and the pile of lost things grew. She stayed, though each winter the river takes a swallow of asphalt, another gulp of concrete and mud sluicing off the hillside into the brown water below, until the highway is barely passable by car, no matter what season. There are no funds to repair infrastructure, much less to fix a road leading only to graves and ruin.

It has been ten years since the last clear-cut, and life is slowly returning to the hills north of Highway 38, beyond Nicole's farm. Spindly Douglas fir compete with red-bark madrone and scrub. Hidden trilliums emerge in the spring-time deep in the groves of mixed forest old-growth, and sometimes she finds shooting stars in the middle of July. Their vibrant purple headdresses and black-tipped noses give her small bursts of joy, tiny pockets reminding her that while the air pollution is high and the temperature scorching, life continues. Life will continue, even after the end, because nothing truly ends. And that is a small comfort.

Despite her isolation—with the road conditions and few connections to the rest of the world, the five miles into town is a day-long excursion, never mind the hurdles she must jump to arrange transportation to the nearest grocery store in faraway Sutherlin—Nicole is not lonely. Nor alone.

Finders are never alone.

This is what she tells herself.

This is what she has told herself for so long she believes it.

There is a routine to the seasons, and to the things she finds, and she's fallen into the rhythm of her life without quite realizing the rut she's dug.

Each October, a new band of Canadian geese arrive dazed and confused and diverted, and depart happily fat in April. April is also kitten and cat season, when mamas have babies and humans abandon the fanged teenaged terrors they had assumed were cuddly fluffballs. Dog season is year-around; runaways fleeing the terrors of a thunderstorm or wanderers ditched by their masters, for whatever reasons people leave their furred family members.

Nicole finds them all, save for the crows, who do not appear to be bound to the rules of the farm, and come and go as they please. Like Nicole, a crow is never lost.

She used to have quite a few human visitors, back when the world was only half broken. And a variety. More than one flying craft has made an emergency landing in the narrow, flat field that used to provide hay but now lies untouched. After the sixth time a lost pilot insisted they were in a different region of the county, Nicole learned to keep a map handy in her tractor or a back pocket, just in case. Summer was for lost kayakers and inner tubers, back when folks floated for fun. They'd put in around the high school to catch the rapids and came ashore on the lower pasture's pebbled beach convinced they'd arrived at Umpqua Myrtle State Park.

Her wife, rest her soul, stumbled upon the farm by chance after taking a wrong turn in 2006 while searching for a bed and breakfast in Scottsburg. It was raining, and late winter, and the banks of the river were rising. Nicole invited this stranger inside, and Christine never left until the day she took her last breath, two years before the quake.

Even now, a traveler might get caught out late at night, far from where they are meant to be, and see Nicole's porch light through the trees—a trick of the eye or the vegetation, as her house is guarded by a stand of fir and oak and hedges. She always keeps the guest bedroom ready, and has grown to read the signs of a new arrival's approach. She knows, with bone-deep intuition, if the visitor will go, or if they might linger a while.

Some visitors, like Christine, stay longer than a night. Some find what they are looking for, but most don't. Eventually, they depart, and never return.

Nicole stays, and she waits for her next visitor, even as the years stretch on and on, and the ache of loneliness morphs into something else. She knows there is a world out there, but she has convinced herself the larger world is not her purpose. She stays so she may find the lost and missing, like a lighthouse along a dark stretch of shore, a stationary point for the lost to be found, to reorient themselves and move on, in whatever way moving on means. Christine used to tease her about being a witch, but that's not accurate. Lighthouses are not magic, and neither is she. They just are. Nicole is a finder and crow-friend and sometime farmer and old woman in the woods, and that is enough.

This is what she tells herself.

It is early fall in Douglas County. The first snap has hit, a wet cold that seeps through clothes and penetrates deep. Nicole's root cellar and pantry are well stocked for the winter, although her arthritis has turned screwing lids into an ordeal, and her hip aches when she sits or stands or sleeps or moves.

This morning she found a set of car keys from a Mercury Cougar in her left house-slipper, and there's a white-tailed deer in the barn, sleeping between two milking goats. It raises its weary head when she arrives, blinking in exhaustion and covered in soot and ash. The nearest fire is fifty miles away, and its smoke has traveled to the valley, layering everything with a hazy smog that brings brilliant sunsets and displaced wildlife.

Nicole admires the deer's antlers as she feeds her small flock. First the cats, because they demand to be first in everything. Then the crows, who really should be first but who understand the cats in ways no other animal should. Then the goats, who eat and are milked, as much as it pains Nicole's hands—a part of her wishes another runaway teen would arrive, not because she wants to put in the emotional energy of caring for a sullen and scared and bewildered child, but because she wouldn't mind someone else doing the milking or morning feeding—and lastly the dogs and whoever else has wandered in during the night and refuses to feed themselves.

She is about to head into the house when a crow swoops, wings brushing her cheek as it lands on her shoulder, clawed feet digging through her jacket. It nuzzles her gray hair and chirps the word for *stranger*.

With a sigh, Nicole trudges out to the front, rubbing the side of her hip, pushing aside a feeling of trepidation. The crow remains on its perch, although its fellows have gathered on the eaves to watch the newcomer.

A car is parked outside the house, which means someone has fixed the roads. The car's engine ticks in the cold, steam rises from the hood. A person huddles against the passenger door, arms wrapped about their stomach, tucking their tan jacket to their body. Their pale face is drawn and tense, as if they are preparing themself for a task. Their brown hair is cropped short, highlighting round cheekbones and thick eyebrows. Their head jerks, eyes widening as Nicole emerges from behind the house.

"Aunt Nicole?"

Nicole's chest tightens. She does not know this person. She's taken in a lot of strays, and only the human children refer to her as *aunt*—the easiest term to explain if anyone questions her foundlings. But none of the children ever return when they finally leave. No one returns. That's the rule, unspoken and unwanted, but there all the same.

The person shoves off the car, shuffling toward her. Their bare hands are still tucked into their armpits. They are in their early twenties, maybe, or they might be forty-five, or thirteen with a stolen car. Nicole is bad at determining ages. At this point, everyone seems impossibly young.

"Um, you don't know me," they say. Nicole's left eyebrow crooks, and their shoulders hunch, as if they are trying to make themself small, either to be non-threatening or to diminish themself before her. "But my mom talked about you. A lot. Jessica? Jessica, uh, her maiden name was Canby?"

Nicole waits. She doesn't remember a Jessica Canby, but she has known a lot of Jessicas. Most of her strays don't have last names, or they give false ones, and often, she recommends they tell her their destination dream, and that becomes their last name. She has known quite a few Austins and Portlands and Harvards.

The person fidgets. "She um, she said a lot of things about you, and I think she was here when she was a teenager? She'd run away from home and you, uh, you gave her a place to stay. I think it was in 2010 or something? I don't expect you to remember—it was a really long time ago." There had been two Jessicas in 2010: Cornell and Seattle. "Anyway, I um, I'm Aubrey, Jessica's daughter. My pronouns are she or they."

Nicole nods, smiles despite her uneasiness. Most times she knows what her visitors will need. A place to sleep, a hug, a cup of coffee to keep going, a map, a spare tire, a band-aid, a locked door, even a quiet morning alone on the porch, listening to the crows and robins talk to each other in the garden. Some just need to be seen and heard. But for the first time in a long while, Nicole doesn't know what this lost person needs, and it scares her. Still. The child is lost, and Nicole knows her purpose. "Come inside, Aubrey. Let's warm you up."

Aubrey fiddles with a peeling strip of paint on the kitchen table, not meeting Nicole's gaze. Aubrey seems fascinated by the table—one of Christine's first furniture renovations, where she transformed the source of so many of Nicole's shitty memories into pure pride—and her finger moves down the red stripe, then the orange, tapping each color of the rainbow. The table was painted before the intersectional flag, and lacks the now-ubiquitous brown, black, white, blue, and pink triangles.

"I'm not lost, you know." *Tap, tap, tap.* "That's what Mom said? That you find the lost."

Nicole's hands tighten around her mug of tea. "Did she, now." The crow, who's followed her inside and hopped from her shoulder to a perch on the sink's edge, clacks its beak. "How is your mom?"

Aubrey winces, and Nicole bows her head. Well.

"I'm sorry," Nicole says. The words are inadequate. They are always inadequate. Most times she finds the right words, but this time the well inside her chest grows, choking off platitudes, and she stays silent.

"She passed away in April. Cancer. It was—it was quick." Aubrey still doesn't meet her eyes. One fingernail continues to worry the red strip, the paint separating further from the laminate. "I tried to keep going. College, chin up, all that shit." Aubrey looks up, gaze fierce. "I'm *fine.*"

Nicole nods. Aubrey is very clearly not fine, but Nicole doesn't think she needs comfort.

"She said you were her only family."

"Many do, I imagine. Where did she end up?"

"Pittsburgh." Aubrey breaks a chip away, and bites her lip as the scrap flutters to the ground. "She wanted me to find you. Tell you she, um, she appreciated it."

"That's a long journey." Pittsburgh is a lifetime from here. Dark shadows line Aubrey's bloodshot brown eyes, and she reeks of greasy fast food and unwashed flesh and hard journey. Nicole's instincts tell her to get this child into a bath and then bed, but there is something off. No one has ever traveled here *intentionally.* Not even neighbors, back when she had those. "Did you get lost along the way?"

Aubrey's chin jerks up. Her lip curls. "No. I knew exactly where to go. I always do."

Nicole exhales, long and slow. "I see."

She does not see. She's accepted her place for so long that she's stopped questioning. Reopening that part of her mind is hard, as it involves grappling with concepts and ideas and implications she has buried for decades. She knows her purpose, has accepted her strange gift, and that is enough. She stands up. "You must be exhausted. Let's get you a bath and a nap. We can talk later."

Aubrey sleeps for two days, and when she awakes, she's like the river—pushing beyond her boundaries, slowly carving new places and insights, whittling away at Nicole's reserve and resolve, always hungry for more and more and more. Seemingly determined to shove her history into the past, she follows Nicole, learns how to run the farm, how to prepare for a wet winter or a drought, how to gather the last of the berries and the vegetables. She refuses to talk about returning to college or next steps, but seems content to stay.

She roots through the house, relentless, curious. Over the years, lost items have found their way into Nicole's home: inanimate objects she doesn't recall bringing back but which somehow squirrel into drawers or a back closet or her root cellar, and are then dumped into the guest bedroom and spare closets. Aubrey seeks it all, fascinated by everything from spare change to baby clothes to shipping manifests to credit cards to half-filled day planners to stuffed animals to thirty-day return receipts to cell phones, but it is the stuffed and mounted six-point buck's head that really catch her attention. Nicole has to explain how it showed up on the hood of her car in 2003—or what it 2004? Time is strange—and the explanation drifts into the whole debacle of her attempt to find the trophy's owner.

Aubrey brings order to the clutter, the bits and pieces that were once content to stay crammed into overflowing piles but now seemed to scream for attention, for organization. She even finds the plastic tub filled with old coins, invaluable gemstones, and an ancient dented goblet. "Is this what I think it is?" Aubrey asks, tilting it back and forth, staring at the etchings from an ancient language.

"Most likely," Nicole replies, and Aubrey replaces the goblet into the bin reverently, returns the tub back to its place. She seems to understand that some things are best hidden from prying eyes. Nicole likes that.

But Aubrey's incessant desire to seek grates, and Nicole's unease grows as Aubrey comes to life over the winter, blossoming as the world dies down and the rain-bearing clouds leech color, turning the countryside brown and grey and damp. Having organized the house and the barn and the toolshed—even cleaned out Nicole's rusting solar-converted car—Aubrey crosses the abandoned highway, moves through the woods with the enthusiasm of an explorer, and returns with truffles and mushrooms and late-season elderberries.

Then Aubrey begins venturing into town, navigating her car over impossible gaps and washouts, returning with pizza and canned peaches and secondhand stories of community as December sprawls into January.

"Come with me tonight." Aubrey's breath wisps before her, twining through her hair and cold-chapped cheeks. She has taken over milking duties and many of the more physical chores, completing them before vanishing on her next adventure. She's explored the remnants of Scottsburg, and is now fascinated by the folksy vibes of the townsfolk of Elkton. The apparent ease with which Aubrey moves through the world is irksome and brings up feels of inadequacy and loss, and yet each time she leaves, Nicole worries. Despite her mixed feelings, Nicole...enjoys this strange person. She likes the company.

"Come where?" Nicole asks, although she already has an idea. She finishes feeding the goats, and massages her stiff hands. Aubrey's back is toward her. Hunched over as the girl is and dressed in Christine's jacket, Nicole can pretend—for a moment— that she is talking to her wife. Then the moment is gone and she is in a barn with a young twenty-something, instead.

"There's a basketball game at the high school." Aubrey turns. Her nose is pink from the January cold, and her cheeks are two round red apples. "It should be fun. You haven't left the farm since I got here. It'll be good to get out."

"I haven't left because you get everything we need." And the thought of leaving scares her. She hasn't stepped foot off the farm or seen a human face that is not Aubrey's since July, and Aubrey's relentless pursuits underscore Nicole's commitment to not leaving her home, solidifying and entrenching her position and reluctance and sense of place. Nicole has told herself the same things for forty years, and will not fathom a paradigm shift, even as the fear of *something* ending burrows deep into her core. She doesn't want to know why Aubrey's presence bothers her so much, because looking means digging deep enough into herself, uprooting her stories and unearthing the passivity of her existence. What will her roots look like? She doesn't want to know.

And yet.

The fact no one from town has come to check on her gnaws on that small place she keeps buried. She's an old woman who's had a strange youngster come along. It should send up red flags among the townsfolk, but then, Nicole is known both for being reclusive and for her mysterious, extended family. Aubrey's words sink in, though. "A basketball game?"

"Yeah. The girls are playing some team from Oakland? They're undefeated. It should be fun?" When she's nervous, Aubrey's up-talk returns, twisting her sentences into uncertainty.

Nicole has no desire to see the people of Elkton or anyone else. "It'll be dark when we return." It's a paltry excuse, and they both know it. Still. She has no idea how Aubrey navigates the roads. Last month she crept to the end of the driveway, and discovered the large washout was still there. It was impossible to drive around, much less over.

Aubrey smiles. "Already covered. Andrea Gardner says we can stay with her."

Andrea Gardner is the granddaughter of Molly Springs, who spat on Nicole in sixth grade and then outed her their senior year. When Nicole returned, Molly welcomed her back into the community, all smiles and acceptance and bygones being bygones and no apologies ever given or faults acknowledged. Nicole did not attend Molly's funeral, claiming the roads were washed out, but really, she has not forgiven her bully. This offer is uncomfortable, but perhaps there is change between generations. And if she bends on this request, perhaps Aubrey will find what she has been seeking.

Nicole tilts her head, and Aubrey's face lights with joy.

Trepidation builds as the day draws on. Nicole tries to push down the feeling this is the last time she'll feed her goats or walk this path or pet a crow or find a wheat penny, that this is the end of something. The emotion she's been suppressing all fall and winter, tamping down alongside all her other fears, bubbles over, churning acid up into her throat. She wants to hold on to everything all at once, and the pain in her chest builds until there is a bowling ball on her sternum, slowly crushing her. It doesn't help that everything she finds is trash—a mummified, half-eaten Snickers bar in her left shoe, someone's Walmart receipt for oranges bought in 2004 crumpled under her hairbrush, a used condom. She gingerly places everything into the trash and spends the rest of the day locked in her bedroom, staring out the window at the crows huddled on the fencepost.

But Aubrey steers her into the car an hour before the game, and glares until Nicole buckles herself in with shaking hands. As her house slips away behind the oaks and the ferns, the fear she'll be unable to return increases. Aubrey taps her on the arm, and points ahead as they bump and jolt down the driveway. The crows are gathered along the branches of the trees, watching them turn onto the pothole-filled highway, wings flapping in farewell.

Nicole closes her eyes as they near the washout, unable to comprehend the how or why or what of Aubrey crossing an impassable gap in the road. She leans forward, pressing her fists against her closed eyes. Purple stars dance against the thin flesh of her eyelids, little shooting stars shouting in fear instead of joy. Each breath is a rasping sob, a half-groaned *I can't*. This cannot be her end. Not now. She is not lost—she is *never* lost—and her home is *for* the lost and those who are found can never return. What if she *can't* go home? She's not lost. She's not *lost*. She's *not*—

"Aunt Nicole, are you—" The car stops. "I'll turn around."

Nicole stays hunched over, trying to breathe through the fear and the pain, until she feels the switch from asphalt to dirt. She holds her breath, peeping between her fingers until she sees her farm, her house, her fields, and all that is familiar yet again. Aubrey taps the brake as the house comes into view, and Nicole launches for the door release. The seatbelt pulls at her midsection, refusing to free her, until Aubrey presses the button and Nicole shoots out of the car, gasping, free, and home.

She presses her hands to her chest, breathing in the familiar air. The crows squawk overhead, wings rustling, and Nicole stumbles forward to lean against an oak. The brown moss squishes and crinkles under her hand, the opposing sensations grounding her. She is *not* lost.

The driver side door opens and closes, and Aubrey edges forward. "I'm sorry."

"Don't be." Nicole can't face her. Can't let her see the fear that's been brewing since September. Fears long dormant, fears she's pushed aside, that have risen and flourished. "It's not your fault."

It *is* her fault. Endings always have beginnings, and this the beginning of an end.

Nicole is so comfortable here, in her home, where she knows everything and everyone, where she maintains the memories and keeps the lost, and she does not want to leave. She does not want to see people who don't need her or understand her or who keep her at a distance. She does not want to take the chance of leaving, because she might never return. She cannot squash the fear of being replaced by someone who can bridge the gaps she cannot.

Footsteps crunch behind her, and Aubrey's hand presses against her back, tentative and comforting. "You know, when I was little, I never understood how people could get lost. I kept running into people who couldn't find their way, or their keys or their purpose or whatever, and it was so weird. I always, always knew exactly where I was and where to go."

Nicole stays silent, unsure what Aubrey is saying. Unsure how this relates to anything. How this is supposed to soothe her fears.

Aubrey continues, "I didn't know what being lost meant. Then Mom died. I knew exactly where to go, except for the first time there were two paths instead of one. I tried the first and it didn't work because it was the path I'd been going on, and it wasn't mine anymore." She takes a deep breath, releases it. "So I took the second path and came here. And I met you."

Nicole laughs. "And you think I'm lost?" The thought is absurd. The lost come to her to be found. She knows where she is. She always has. She has told this story often enough that she believes it.

"I think there are different ways of being lost." Aubrey's toe scrapes a circle in the dirt. "And, maybe, different kinds of being found?" Another scrape. "I know you're nervous and you've kept yourself isolated here for so long, but I thought—"

"You thought a basketball game would help?" Nicole turns, faces Aubrey. This kid can't be serious.

Aubrey twists her hands together. "No, the basketball game was an excuse. I found your name on the gym wall. For athletic records?"

"The quake flood destroyed everything."

Aubrey crosses her arms over her chest, hugs herself. "Well, turns out there was this sophomore who went digging through the old internet archives. She found the records and convinced the principal to put them back up. And she saw your record and how long it's stood, and she's thinking about trying to beat it." Her eyes dart to the right. "She's a junior now, and going to play in the game tonight, and I thought it might be interesting for her to meet you. Put a face to ancient history."

"Before she erases it."

Aubrey rolls her eyes. "Before she beats a fifty-year-old record! That's huge—for both of you."

Nicole steps back, towards the trees. The fear is back, although now it's competing with irritation and another worry. First the world ended, but everything was fine because Nicole found lost things and made a place for them, or gave them the space to find themselves and move forward. Now Aubrey is here to replace her, and this new child is going to remove her from history completely, never mind that she is erased already. She is a myth, a rumor, the old woman who lives with the strays on an abandoned stretch of highway. She finds the lost and has become lost in return.

Nicole finally sees the trench she has dug for herself. Years upon years of self-soothing stories, of unthinking rhythm and routine, of refusing to look outward, have built a fortress of isolation wrapped in false purpose and a fear of her fiercely protected comfort vanishing in a return to past prejudices. But she also sees that the walls are not so high she could climb out, if she had help.

"Please?" Aubrey asks.

Nicole stares at the branches, at the crows. She rocks side to side, hyper-focused on the black wings, the clacking beaks. They are not agitated, as she had thought. They are reminding her that all things end, and the ending makes space for beginnings. They are telling her there are finders, and there are seekers. There is alone and there is loneliness. There is family and there is community. There is fear and there is courage. There is the past and this is the present. They are saying *happy hunting* instead of *goodbye forever*.

This is a new beginning. A new story she can tell herself, over and over, until she believes it. This time, she will have help in the telling.

Nicole takes a deep breath and gets back into the car.

See Laurel Beckley's story "Tell the Crows I'm Home" online at Metaphorosis.
If you liked it, leave a comment. Authors love that!
Remember to subscribe to our e-mail updates so you'll know when new stories are posted.

About the story

I wrote the first draft of "Tell the Crows I'm Home" in March 2021, when the waves of hopelessness were crashing into me. I'm a bit of a latecomer to all things, so the loneliness of the pandemic was only finally hitting—I had left a stressful, toxic workplace to take some time to write before we moved (again), and was in between projects and packing and in transition. Throughout this shifting, I just felt lost, and I wanted to go home, and home, to me, is Elkton, Oregon, a place I have not lived since I was thirteen. For the first time in a very long time, I sat down at my computer and started writing a mood piece to capture how I felt. I had no plan, I just wrote what I knew and tried to tie my melancholy to a place.

I had somewhat intended the story to be about a payphone that people picked up to listen to the ghosts of their loved ones after a disaster, but it morphed into something else. Nicole emerged from the space between the river and the highway, inspired by Amal El-Mohtar's "Pockets", the myth of the old woman in the woods, and the stories we tell ourselves to cope with loneliness. What I ended up with is (fingers crossed) an intrinsically queer story of acceptance and the breath-catching fear of change and new things, and, above all, hope.

The story takes place in the mid-2030s, in a dystopian world rocked by climate change and the aftermath of The Big One (that Oregon boogeyman that is coming...some day). I have a feeling a lot of people who know me will think this is autobiographical, but it's not (the two exceptions being semi-estranged from family and the spitting incident). Many of the locations mentioned exist in real life, although the farm and the people are all fictional, and the townsfolk of Elkton are much nicer and more welcoming than they are in Nicole's mind. There are several track records that were set in the late 1980s that have yet to be broken, however, which was a surprising discovery (calling all enterprising Elks looking to make history), Highway 38 does wash out quite a bit in very rainy winters, and the Umpqua River is a lot of fun to float (pro tip: be careful around the rapids by the high school).

All told, I wrote this hoping a part of myself that was lost would magically appear, when instead I should have been like Aubrey, actively seeking, connecting and driving over impossible gaps in the road. I can't say I'm there yet. But maybe I will be someday.

A question for the author

Q: What was your favorite children's book?

A: I was a very introverted, socially awkward child (this has not changed, although I am no longer a child), and I found my passion for reading very early. Since I read practically nonstop, this is both a tough and easy answer, but I have to say my favorite childhood book is *Matilda* by Roald Dahl.

The idea of a little girl sitting alone in a library surrounded by books and a bemused-but-rolling-with-it librarian appealed to me, along with the thought of that little girl being super incredibly smart and developing telepathic powers because of her unused brainpower. Of course, I am nothing like Matilda save for my love of books, and even there my tastes run towards genre fiction instead of the classics.

No book is entirely separate from the author, however, and I was heartbroken to realize Roald Dahl was a massive anti-Semite and all around deeply unpleasant person. That being said, *Matilda* holds a special place in my heart, while simultaneously the author can kick rocks...hopefully that is acceptable to say here.

About the author

Laurel Beckley is a writer, Marine Corps veteran, and librarian. She is from Eugene, Oregon, and currently lives in northern Virginia with her wife, fur creatures, and a collection of gently neglected houseplants.

thesuspectedbibliophile.home.blog, @laurelthereader

The Azurian Shield

Karl El-Koura

The day after he registered his daughter's birth, Bathar began conducting the inspections of the shield himself. Every morning, about an hour before dawn, he rode out through the villages that surrounded the castle, past the fields of farmland, through the forest, finally to the old woman's hut, to give her whatever he'd brought that morning. Then, riding his horse at the outer edge of the realm, he inspected the dome-shaped shield protecting them from the chaos without.

For seven months, that precaution proved unnecessary. The shield looked as it always had—a cloudy blue structure as solid as steel; it glowed brightly during the day and dimly at night. He could circumnavigate it in about an hour, making sure he detected none of the signs of deterioration that Ryon, the king's chief advisor and the last remaining mage in the realm, had taught him to look for. He saw nothing unusual, day after day of Alia's young life.

But, all of a sudden, that was no longer true. He'd ridden past a section on the northeast side, his glance dancing across the blue shield, when his mind registered something, and he pulled tight on the reins.

He dismounted and walked back, eyes fixed on the ground for now, willing what he'd seen—*thought he'd seen*—to be a trick of his mind.

Then he forced himself to look up.

A crack had begun to form on the shield. Like the shell of an egg that had been gently tapped, that still needed to be pulled apart.

Bathar stepped back. No one liked being this close to the shield; except for the tiny hut the exiled old woman had built for herself, the land at the edge of their realm was wild and uninhabited. The work of clearing out a perimeter around the shield, to ensure that no tree, shrub or weed obstructed the view of the guards charged with inspecting it, was reserved for the vilest criminals, and those hardened men and women would often have to be punished severely before they would carry out their task. Even the members of the royal guard—the best soldiers in the realm, his own command, whose duty it was to inspect the shield daily—had been visibly relieved when he'd announced he would henceforth conduct those inspections himself.

The shield had never bothered Bathar, though—just the opposite. As a young man, he'd *volunteered* to carry out the inspections. The shield kept them safe—why worry about anything beyond it? He felt comforted when he could see the cloudy blue steel and know that it continued to hold back the chaos.

But a cracking shield?

He took another step back, blinking furiously.

As he stared at the zigzag crack, starting at the bottom and reaching a few feet up the shield, all of the fears that kept others from traveling past the forest flooded into his mind. He imagined the crack growing, growing, bursting open with a wave of screeching monsters—hungry, frenzied creatures that had been deprived of human flesh for hundreds of generations. In his mind he saw a mass of fanged, upright bulls rush through the breach, their heavy footfalls shaking the ground, the shield collapsing around them in great chunks. The dark army rolled through him as if he weren't there, continued onto the realm he'd sworn to defend, killing the old woman, the farmers and the villagers, then those who lived within the castle walls. Cyna and Alia.

Alia.

In his fear, he'd forgotten—no, never that. For a moment he'd *neglected* to think what this meant for her...not the imagined army of his childhood nightmares, but the very real crack in the shield. By the oldest rules of the realm, as soon as a fissure was detected —the very morning—the youngest child would be brought to the site of the breach and sacrificed. That was the cost of the spell that would restore the shield. No child had yet been born since Alia.

He whistled for his horse, who came trotting over dutifully, blissfully unaware, even lifting her head and neighing in the direction of the crack, as if in disdain of the danger it hinted at.

The break in the shield hadn't expanded—not that Bathar had seen, anyway.

He grabbed the reins and swung himself on top of the horse, then urged her up the hill, back toward the castle. He had no definite plan as of yet, except that he didn't want any of his guard to know what he'd discovered until he was ready to tell them. And the king? Would he lie to the man he'd sworn to defend with his own life?

Yes—*his* life. Not Alia's; he'd never sworn that oath.

In his frantic race back, he almost rode through the old woman when she appeared in the middle of the worn path of trampled grass. She stood hunched over, her wispy hair like thin plumes of gray smoke in the dim early morning light, her short body covered in a patchwork of old clothes. He pulled up just in time to avoid trampling her over. She'd never moved.

He bit back the curse of frustration rising to his lips, then began to guide his horse around her.

"Wait," she said. Her voice, as usual, sounded like someone trying to speak while being choked.

Bathar ignored her, as he always did. Seventy years earlier, when the shield had last cracked, when the old woman was still young, and King Nebed newly installed on his throne, she had refused to perform the spell and sacrifice to seal the breach, insistent that no danger lay beyond. Her apprentice Ryon, a child himself at the time, had stepped forward and completed the ritual. The woman had been exiled to the shield as punishment, and a penalty of death placed on anyone who spoke to her.

In his childhood, Bathar's parents had told him stories of the Banished One, as a warning of what would happen to him if he didn't do as he was told. He'd always felt sorry for her, especially since she'd transgressed only because her mind had become sick. As a child, when he was beaten for his own small transgressions, he'd often wished that she would come to his aid. She had been the greatest mage the realm had seen for many generations, before her mind had turned against reality. Some rumors, then and now, whispered that the old woman retained her powers.

When he'd spotted her hut one morning while riding out of the forest, he'd resolved to do her a kindness in honor of his childhood sorrow at her plight—bring her something to eat, a few apples he'd gotten from the market the day before, or freshly baked bread he'd picked up that morning. He'd initially left them at the door of her hut, but in the last few months she'd been outside, waiting. Often she didn't even thank him with words, just bowed to him, her wrinkled face spreading into a faltering smile.

But she'd never before left her hut and come out as far as the makeshift road into the forest. Why on this morning, of all days?

He paused for a moment, to look her over and make sure she wasn't injured. It was hard to tell, with her. As soon as he'd met her, Bathar had understood why she'd never answered his

785

childhood prayers for help. Would a woman with incredible powers choose to live a life of isolation and poverty in a wooden hut? Besides, she could barely speak in complete, calm sentences—should he believe she could cast spells? She seemed no worse than usual, though. He cleared his throat and indicated with a toss of his head that she should move out of the way.

"Bathar, please," she said.

He swallowed—he hadn't realized she knew his name.

"The shield doesn't protect us," she said. "No, no! It imprisons us. Is the king dying? Speak to Dara. There is no danger! You see? It wasn't cast to keep out chaos. No, no! In the time of the First King, yes? It was cast *over* us..."

Bathar stopped listening. Some days the old woman thanked him for his little morning gift with her crumbling smile, and he left quickly. Other days, awful days, she tried to make him stay by pretending to whisper dark secrets. But he didn't have time for tall tales of mythical kings on a regular day, let alone this one.

He nudged his horse past her as she continued to speak in her rushed, barely coherent way, as if the jumbled thoughts in her addled mind were all rushing out of her mouth at the same time and tripping over one another.

On the ride back, he pummeled the question of what could be done, furiously attacking it from every angle. But he was no further ahead by the time he rode through the castle's gatehouse. He handed his horse to the groom at the stables, grunting in response to the young man's friendly greeting. Normally he went straight into the keep after the morning inspections, but—this decision was clear at least—Cyna needed to be warned. He walked quickly across the central courtyard to their cottage, keeping his head low.

When he pushed open the wooden door, his wife said immediately, "You saw something?" She sat by the fire, nursing Alia.

He closed the door before nodding.

"How much time?" Cyna seemed to grip Alia tighter, as if she expected him to leap to her and rip their child out of her arms.

"I don't know," he said. "The crack wasn't there yesterday."

"They can't have her," she said.

"I know."

They looked down at the sleeping, feeding baby, the little face poking out of the blanket, the tiny fingers wrapped around Cyna's breast, the dimples in her knuckles.

"What are we going to do?" Cyna said, raising her own hand to brush back a wisp of hair from Alia's forehead.

Bathar didn't respond. Decisions had always come easily to him before. As a young royal guard, he'd had faith in the shield, which had protected them all his life. In the same way, he'd had faith in King Nebed, who had ruled over the realm since before Bathar was born. So when the king had executed a popular mayor who had criticized the royal family for their so-called acts of oppression, sparking a rebellion that swept up half the royal guard, Bathar had led the charge to subdue it. He'd never hesitated, never stopped to think whether the mayor was right or wrong—he'd sworn to defend king and realm, and he'd responded accordingly.

But now, for the first time in his life, he had no clarity of thought. This was a problem without solution.

Cyna's gray eyes studied his face. "We run away," she said.

"What?"

"The realm is a big place." They both knew it wasn't. His guard could search it in two days. "We hide, we keep moving."

He shook his head.

"Your old woman can help," she said. "Maybe she still has her powers. It wouldn't take much to hide us, would it?"

He'd never told Cyna that the old woman had spoken to him, or that on those occasions she'd seemed desperate to convince him that no danger existed beyond the shield, to infect him with her own madness. How could they trust their lives to her? "Suppose she can hide us," he said. "What happens when the shield falls?"

"We fight the monsters," she said immediately. "And if we die, we die fighting."

He shook his head again.

Cyna looked back at their child. "Then you have no other choice. It's time to...settle accounts."

Bathar stared at her, but she refused to meet his eyes. He'd saved King Nebed's life during the siege of the castle, so by law the king owed Bathar a life debt. But Bathar had been fulfilling a sworn oath. How could a debt accrue from someone carrying out their duty?

"Settle them how, Cyna? By sacrificing another child, even though our laws say it must be the youngest? All right—whom should the king slay instead?"

Tears began to form in her eyes, but she fought to hold them back.

"I'm sorry," he said, dropping to his knees. "I can't bear the thought of losing Alia." He wiped his wife's eyes gently. "But I also can't allow the shield to fall. I'm—"

A loud *rat-tat-tat* knock sounded at the door.

Cyna's glance dropped to the dagger he wore strapped to his thigh. He nodded, and she removed it, held it against her own thigh opposite the door.

Hand on the hilt of his sword, Bathar approached their entrance. He opened the door slowly.

One of his own soldiers stood outside, her gaze on the ground, kicking her boot into the dirt while she waited. She looked up as the door creaked open and said, "Are you alright, Sir?"

Bathar nodded curtly.

"The king would like to see you."

"About what?"

"Ryon didn't say. He bade me fetch you, and told me I'd find you at home. I thought maybe…"

"Everyone's fine," Bathar said. "I'll be there in a moment."

He closed the door, then walked back to his wife and child and kissed each one on the forehead.

"Give me time to find a solution," he said, withdrawing his sword. "But if anyone else comes through that door…"

He left the rest of the thought unspoken, then exchanged the sword for his dagger, and left without allowing himself a look back.

At the door to the keep, he heard from the guards that the king had taken a turn for the worse the previous night. King Nebed hadn't been able to make it to the throne room to conduct the day's business. Bathar rushed to the king's bedchamber, where the guards admitted him immediately.

Inside the curtains were drawn and the room dark, dimly lit by several candles. The king lay in bed under heavy covers, the princess Dara sitting on the large chair on the other side. Ryon had been pacing the floor but stopped when he saw Bathar.

"He's here, your majesty," he said.

"Bathar," the king said, the breath wheezing out of him. "Come close."

Bathar looked to Princess Dara for a sign of hope. She shook her head.

He kneeled beside the bed. "At your command, Majesty."

The king's eyes fluttered open. Even in the candlelight, his skin looked ashen, drained of blood and strength. His breath came in quick, shallow bursts. "This isn't easy for you, my son. But the realm must be protected at any cost. Dara will rule it well."

"Yes, your Majesty." For the moment, faced with this sight of infirmity from a man who for all of his life had been the symbol of power, he forgot about the shield. "But may your days be long still."

The king had closed his lips, but they came open again. A small smile played on the bloodless mouth. "You can see my days are finished." His words escaped in faint whispers interspersed with long pauses where he seemed to be gathering his strength. "But I die knowing that the sacrifice you make will preserve the kingdom for my daughter."

Bathar stood and faced the mage. "You know?"

Ryon had been listening from the end of the bed. "We know."

"How?"

"I saw the crack in the shield."

"But—if you're able to...what's the point of the inspections?"

"I could only see because you saw, Bathar."

A spying spell? Bathar hadn't thought that kind of power possible.

Without conscious thought, propelled by rage at this invasion of his mind, Bathar collapsed the distance between them. He towered over the shorter man, bent with age. Ryon's upturned gaze never left Bathar's. The cross scar, the intersecting diagonal slices like trenches dug into his face, always seemed deeper and redder when Ryon was struggling to restrain himself; Bathar had never seen them more pronounced.

Dara had risen from her seat and walked over, perhaps eager to diffuse the tension between the powerful mage and the chief royal guard.

She only put her hand on Bathar's shoulder, though.

Her presence—and the realization that knowledge of the shield's failure was no longer his own secret...and the corollary that Bathar had run out of time to plan an alternative that would save Alia's life—deflated his rising anger.

"Your Highness," he said, turning to face her. "I'm sorry I didn't—"

"I have no interest in dwelling on that," Dara said. "But we must move forward—and quickly."

Slaughter my daughter quickly, you mean. But what else was there to do? And what did she—or the dying king—or Ryon—care about Alia? She meant the world to him and to Cyna, but to them she was a child like any other in the realm. Except that this child had been marked out for an early, unnatural death. Her blood to him was precious, but to them it was simply currency, a price to be paid. To them the realm was the world, not one tiny creature.

So what else was there to do?

An answer appeared in his mind. Blood—or death? or suffering?—was required for the spell, but Cyna was right: it didn't have to be his daughter's.

As he'd been wading through those thoughts, the door had come open and two soldiers had stepped inside—not of his royal guard, strangely, but of the ranks who helped keep the peace in the realm. Bathar registered their presence without processing it. Dara and Ryon regarded him warily.

"Bathar," the king said.

Something about the old man's voice—even beyond how faded it sounded, as if the shadow of death had started to creep into it already—sent a cold shiver through Bathar's body.

He approached and bent down again.

"No one expects you to witness the sacrifice," the king said. "I have arranged quarters for you and Cyna in the keep. You can return to your cottage tonight."

Feeling that his body was a spring that had been compressed beyond endurance, Bathar willed it to keep still. He looked up at Ryon and Dara. On their candlelit, wary faces he saw all the confirmation he needed. He'd been called here as a pretense, to get him out of the way so that soldiers could be sent to his home to take Cyna and Alia captive.

He looked over his shoulder at the brutish soldiers. Likely two others stood outside the door, replacing his own guard, and more at the end of the hallway.

He had the dagger he wore strapped to his thigh, but he'd given Cyna his sword and hadn't thought to replace it before coming to see the king. With just that small weapon, could he fight his way past two?—four?—six soldiers on his own? Not to mention a mage who had the power, so it seemed, to invade his mind without his permission or even his awareness.

And even if he were successful somehow?

Despite his advanced age, Ryon had not yet chosen an apprentice, as he was supposed to do, as the old woman had done with him when she was yet very young. If Bathar killed Ryon now, and the old woman refused or was unable to make the sacrifice and cast the spell to seal the shield, then no one else could do it. Bathar would have sentenced *everyone* in the realm to a gruesome death.

Well—more realistically, the moment he reached for his dagger he'd be struck dead by Ryon, who continued to stare at him without blinking, who was perhaps even now reading his thoughts. And he'd have lost any chance of saving Alia. He would be dead, Alia would be sacrificed, and Cyna—what would happen to Cyna?

He filled his lungs with a deep breath and held it for a moment, then let it out and forced himself to nod. "I understand, Highness."

A dark, heavy, oppressive spirit seemed to leave the room at his words. He felt that even the soldiers by the door relaxed their stances.

"The shield must not fall," he continued, "and spilled blood is required to restore it. Your Highness, I offer my life in place of my daughter's."

The king opened his eyes. Some of the old man's strength seemed to come back into his voice. "Do you think you're the first father in our history who's offered to trade places with their child?"

"I—"

"The law is clear," Ryon said.

"If blood must be—"

"The law is not arbitrary. It must be the child born closest to the time the shield begins to fall."

"Why?" That question had never mattered before. It had been sufficient for Bathar to know that there was a mechanism to restore the shield should it begin to fail in his lifetime, and he hadn't stopped to give the details a second thought—until it was his own child at stake. They'd happily brought Alia to Ryon to register her, as required by law, on the first day after her birth. They'd seen it as a fun tradition, until it was done and they'd walked out into the courtyard that morning. Then he'd realized that the certificate of registration Ryon had signed for Alia could become her death sentence. Bathar had resolved to carry out the inspections of the shield himself. He vowed to begin doing so the very next day and to not stop...well, he hadn't allowed the thought to be explicit even in his own mind, let alone when speaking to Cyna about his plan...to not stop until the registry showed a new baby in the realm. But now that his worst fears had been realized —the reasonable fear that the shield might crack, and the secret fear that it would happen before another child was born—the question seemed so important that he wondered he'd never asked it before. That no one had asked those questions: why did the spell of restoration need a sacrifice at all? Why did it have to be the youngest child?

He stood and approached the mage. "Please, help me understand."

Ryon lowered his voice so the others couldn't hear. "That banished creature you see every morning—yes, I know about that too. She wanted to understand. She wanted to see beyond the shield. When her powers proved unequal to the task, she was willing to sacrifice the realm to satisfy her curiosity."

For a moment Bathar couldn't find his voice to defend himself. Then he whispered back, "I haven't broken his commandment. I've never said a single word to her. She's just a crazed, lonely, old woman."

And yet...in his youth, before he'd understood that the shield could be restored whenever it began to fail, he'd had nightmares in which he stood alone facing a cracking shield. The crack spread upward, like a tent being opened from the inside. The previous stillness shattered as the air filled with the sounds of netherworld creatures.

Where had those images come from? Cobbled together from stories told to scare him as a child.

More questions rushed into his thoughts, as if the first question—why did his daughter have to be sacrificed, when he was prepared to give up his own life?—had unlocked a secret door in his mind. The door had been holding back doubts and misgivings that it seemed had always been there, unseen.

The last time the shield had begun to crack, almost three-quarters of a century before, Ryon had restored it, as had the mage before him, and the one before. For how many generations?

Because since the days when the shield had been erected by powerful magic, it had never fallen—always restored in time, or the realm itself would have been destroyed. How long ago had that been? Even the number of generations was lost to time. In all of their recorded history—even in the legendary stories of the First King—the shield surrounded the realm as always.

What if the old woman had glimpsed a truth, mad as she was? What if the monsters beyond had died out in all of those generations; the chaos subdued in time? What if his ancestors had shut themselves in to survive a tempest, but the storm had passed—and they had no way of knowing?

"Was it wrong for the Banished to wonder what lay beyond the shield?" he said.

"Chaos," Ryon responded immediately.

"Chaos once—but chaos now?"

"Chaos always."

Not good enough, Bathar thought, but didn't say. Not if it meant his child's life. He sensed more than saw the soldiers move closer to him.

He returned to the bed and knelt beside the prone king again, but spoke in normal tones rather than the reverential whisper he'd been using. "Highness—how do we know the danger persists? Let me report on what lies beyond. If I don't return within a set time, Ryon will be ready to seal the shield."

"And what comes through during your set time, Bathar?" the king said.

"My guard is ready to defend the realm." He'd promised Cyna he would think of something, and now he had. It would give them a chance. "At the first sign of trouble, you can—"

"No," Princess Dara said.

He turned to her sharply. "But—"

She raised an eyebrow.

"Highness?" he said to Nebed in frustrated desperation, then immediately recognized the mistake he'd made in appealing to the dying king over Dara.

"You are too valuable to the realm, Bathar," she said.

"Princess, I—"

"She has spoken, Bathar," the king said. "Do not test our patience further."

Frustration and desperation had pushed him into insulting the princess, and now a new wellspring of those feelings propelled him even further. "You are still the monarch," he said, standing and looking down at the king. "And you will grant me this request."

"Watch yourself—"

"I demand repayment."

The dark spirit that had departed only minutes before returned with renewed vigor, filling the air and making it heavy. The sudden invasion of that spirit also stole whatever response the king had been preparing to make. He shut his mouth, but his yellowed eyes filled with disgust.

After he'd saved his life, the king had demanded that Bathar ask him anything—up to half the realm's riches, he'd said. Bathar had refused reward for doing his duty. Now he understood why the king had been so adamant: he'd wanted the debt paid, at a price he'd set himself. The king had relented only reluctantly—perhaps, if it were true that Ryon could invade minds, after consulting with his advisor. Ryon might have reassured him that Bathar would never call in the debt.

Well, Ryon had been wrong. The thought comforted Bathar.

"My life is almost at an end," the king said, "and isn't worth what it once was. You, however, Bathar, are valuable. You will defend my daughter when she ascends to the throne, if she'll still have you. And you will help defend the realm at the shield's breach until we restore it."

Bathar didn't understand—the king seemed to be saying yes and no at the same time. He waited for the slow words to emerge.

"If you can convince her to accept, I will allow your wife to go through the breach. If she refuses, however, the debt is repaid."

The thin lips twisted into a sneer as the king watched the changes that must have been visible on Bathar's face. He didn't believe the stated reason—no one man was so valuable to the defense of the realm. No, this was the king's cruelty asserting itself —the cruelty that had sparked the rebellion that Bathar himself had helped quell. Even as he lay dying, Nebed had found a way to lash out at him.

"You're both young," the king said, interrupting his thoughts. "You can have another child."

How had he served such a mind of cold calculations? But he knew: it was easy to justify the king's severity as necessary when the decisions didn't directly affect him, easier to support the throne he'd sworn allegiance to than question the morality of its actions.

Bathar sighed deeply, then stood. "Can I see my family?" he said.

The two soldiers stepped forward at a sign from the king, and he gave the order. Bathar left without looking back. Two more soldiers stood outside the door as he'd guessed, and two more at either end of the hall. He was led across the staircase to the east wing of the castle, then down more hallways until they reached another door, similarly guarded by a pair of soldiers. They stepped aside to allow Bathar to enter.

Inside, Cyna paced the large room, while Alia slept curled up in the middle of the bed. Cyna turned a ferocious look on him when he opened the door, which resolved into joy. But the hopeful smile started decaying almost immediately.

"What happened?" she said as he said to her, "Are you all right?" Her right arm had been bandaged, and a pool of blood had leaked through to stain the white wrapping.

They sat on the edge of the bed and spoke in hushed tones out of a habit of not wanting to wake Alia. Cyna told him about fighting the soldiers who had come to their home, and how she'd eventually had to surrender to them. Bathar told her about his suspicion that the chaos beyond the shield might have resolved into order through the intervening generations, and how he had used his life debt to—

Cyna grabbed his leg. "You asked him to let you through the shield?"

"Yes."

She stared at him. He knew from the way her jaw clenched that she was imagining him dying a thousand ugly deaths.

"He won't let me go through, Cyna. He said he would allow *you* to. He's hoping that you won't."

She looked back at the tiny figure sleeping soundly in the large bed. "You were willing," she said softly.

"Willing, but terrified. We can figure out another way."

The door came open and Ryon strode in.

"Well?" he said, as they stood to face him. "Will she go?"

Bathar looked at Cyna.

"Yes," she said.

"Fine," Ryon said, then tossed a disdainful sneer at Bathar. "The king has allowed this concession as payment in full for a debt no subject should hold over his sovereign."

"I'd like some time to—" Bathar began.

"The crack has started to spread. We ride out immediately." He faced Cyna. "My assistants are already carrying out the stone of sacrifice. We'll overtake them, and you'll have until they reach the shield to leave our realm...if you can go through with it...and return...if you do return."

"How do you know it's started to spread?" But in asking the question, Bathar realized the most probable explanation—Ryon had not cast a spell that could invade the mind of an unwilling subject: he'd commissioned a spy to follow Bathar on his inspections. That spy had opened his mind to Ryon and allowed him to see the crack that morning; and he saw it now, spreading.

Ryon's disdainful sneer turned into an amused smile, and then a puff of air escaped his mouth, as if that were the only response Bathar deserved. Cyna had gone around the bed and picked up Alia, cradling her to keep from waking her.

"She rides with me," Ryon said, extending his arms.

Cyna and Bathar exchanged glances.

"That creature will save our kingdom," Ryon said. "No harm will come to her before we reach the shield, believe me."

After another moment of hesitation, Cyna placed Alia in Ryon's arms.

In the central courtyard a retinue of twenty-four regular soldiers waited on twenty-four horses. Attendants brought the princess and Ryon their own steeds.

"My guard can best defend against whatever comes through the shield," Bathar said, looking up at Ryon.

The old man shook his head. "They are needed here. We cannot delay—here come your horses, and swords for you and Cyna, in case a sword can even help her on the other side. You take the front."

They rode in silence. A line of a dozen soldiers separated Bathar and Cyna from their daughter; Ryon rode beside Princess Dara, and the remaining soldiers drew up the rear. After twenty minutes, they overtook the caravan transporting the sacrificial altar, a pair of mules pulling the wagon on which the concave table had been placed. It looked like an oversized creche with ornate golden legs.

Bathar resisted the temptation to stare at it as they rode past.

When they arrived within sight of the shield, Bathar drew in his breath. The zigzag crack had opened up at the bottom where it met the earth, so that a hole the size of a coin had appeared between their world and whatever lay beyond.

By the time he and Cyna had ridden down the grassy hill to stand a few feet from the shield, the hole had grown even more, now large enough to admit a small mouse. And yet—nothing came through. Or did it? He found it uncomfortable to keep his eyes fixed on that hole. As if a blinding power were seeping through already, burning the eyes of any who dared gaze upon it.

If simply *looking* at the light coming through could cause pain, what would happen to Cyna when she stepped into that world?

He turned his horse to face his wife, whose gaze was fixed on the shield. "Cyna—" he began, but she shook her head slightly.

A crowd started gathering on the hill, villagers and farmers tempted by the royal procession to follow and see what the commotion was about.

Perhaps righteously—or perhaps desperately seeking a distraction—Bathar felt anger rising up toward them. Would he allow their presence to turn his daughter's sacrifice into a performance? Did Cyna have to go through the shield with gawkers watching her every step? And what if her courage failed her?

He brought his horse around and approached Princess Dara, standing with Ryon at the foot of the hill, waiting for the caravan. The soldiers closed in against him.

The princess called out to let him through.

"I beg permission to disperse the crowd," he said to her. "I don't want spectators."

She shrugged, then nodded.

He turned and galloped his horse up the hill toward the largest part of the crowd, then suddenly pulled up on the reins. Covered in a patchwork of frayed and faded clothes, bent over, trying to hide behind others—his glance picked her out. The old woman.

He dismounted and followed her as she tried to disappear among the others.

"You shouldn't be here," he whispered, grabbing her and pulling her away from the pocket of people.

The hunched over head covered in a tattered shawl looked up at him as her smaller legs tried to keep up. "You...speak to me?"

He looked around to make sure no one was watching. "I'm sorry I never did before. You say there's no danger beyond the shield. Do you have any evidence?"

"Evidence?" She laughed, an ugly, croaking sound. "Destroyed! All destroyed!"

Bathar hissed to keep quieter. "What was destroyed?"

"Old—very old—*forbidden* texts. Buried, you see? I discovered them—I recovered them! Gone now...destroyed—guess by whom?—but I have them in my head." She tapped a finger against her skull. She spoke quickly now, eagerly, as if a bottle had been unstopped and all the words began spilling out like wine. "We did not cast the shield. Six other kingdoms cast it *over* us. To protect themselves from *us*, you understand? We caused great suffering in those days, and our cruel king vowed to never rest until he ruled all of the realms. So their greatest mages united to imprison us in the shield. It would fall once the king died and was replaced by a new monarch—as long as that one renounced cruelty." She began to cackle. "It didn't have the intended effect! When he saw his mages were powerless to destroy the shield, the king buried the truth. He insisted that the shield protected his realm, destroyed all of our previous records, and began to call himself the 'First King'!" She cackled again.

"Be quiet!" Bathar barked, keeping her moving. "How certain are you that those things are true?"

"My life." She spoke quietly now, deflated again. "I gave up my life."

Did he believe her? He wanted to, more than anything.

"Then sacrificing the youngest child is not required to seal the shield?" he said.

"No, and neither is the so-called spell. Any cruel act under the authority of the new ruler would suffice. You see? Our laws *are* arbitrary."

Bathar continued to stare at her. Her mind didn't seem as addled as he'd once thought. "You said you discovered old texts?"

"Protected scrolls. Buried in jars, secretly in the time of the First King, in the deepest part of the forest behind the castle. I sensed their magic—not a mage in a dozen could've found them. But I could. I did! Not a mage in a hundred could've opened the jars, you understand?"

Bathar nodded for her to go on. She seemed like a child desperately seeking approval.

"My mistake—I brought the truth to Nebed, prince of the realm then, because I believed he would be more reasonable than his mad father. Nebed destroyed the scrolls."

"Why?"

"Fear!" she yelled. "Generations of it, deep in our blood. He said the scrolls were a hoax by someone—he implied me!—who wanted to see the realm destroyed. Instead he had the *scrolls* destroyed, forbade me or anyone from speaking of them again. It didn't matter at first, but soon the mad king died and Nebed ascended to the throne, and the shield began to crack...and I begged for permission to allow us a glimpse—to prove the truth—"

"He refused, and he exiled you."

The old woman shook her head, smiled impishly. "He tried to have me killed. The scoundrel Ryon wasn't born with that double scar! I exiled myself, to watch over the shield. I've been waiting for this day ever since."

Bathar stopped looking around furtively and focused all of his attention on the old woman. He held her face in his hands, to stare into her eyes. "Then there is no danger beyond the shield? You're sure?"

She leaned her face against the warmth of his skin. He suddenly remembered that she hadn't felt human touch for seven decades. "No more than inside the shield," she said, her voice now soft and calm. "Less."

"Then why does it hurt to look at it?"

The gummy, toothless mouth opened in a smile. She looked past him at the shield. "I wanted to live long enough for a glimpse of that world." She stared at it for a while as he continued to study her face, still trying to decide if she was crazy or telling the truth, and if he could risk Cyna's life on his assessment. "It hurts your eyes, young man," she said, "because the light is brighter there. We have grown accustomed to darkness."

A murmur from those around him made him look over his shoulder, back down at the shield. The hole had grown significantly; if a mouse could've squeezed through before, now something the size of a large cat would have been able to dart into their world.

He told the old woman to stay hidden in the crowd, then whistled for his horse. Bathar rode down to Ryon; the soldiers seemed to accept now that he didn't intend harm and allowed him to approach.

Alia began to cry for him, and reflexively Bathar reached out for her, but Ryon shook his head.

"Why does nothing come through the hole?" Bathar said. "If chaos reigns beyond, why isn't it spilling into our world already?"

The satisfaction on Ryon's face made him realize how desperate he must have sounded. "You do not have to sacrifice your wife to the darkness."

"I just want to understand."

A horn sounded, announcing the arrival of the caravan and ordering the crowds to make way for it. As Bathar watched, the mules crested the hill.

"Once the stone is set up," Ryon said, "the ritual will be completed."

"No," Bathar said. "The king—"

Dara spoke up. "We can't risk the realm." She motioned toward the hole, which had grown even more, but still not enough to admit Cyna. "It is in the hands of the gods."

Bathar's horse turned one way and then the other, working out Bathar's own nervous energy. None of his royal guard had been allowed to accompany them, although his guard could best hold back whatever chaos spilled out. And to do what? Protect the dying king? No, Ryon and Dara had never intended to allow Cyna to leave.

Sensing trouble, the soldiers closed in around Ryon and the princess.

He took a deep breath and guided his horse back toward Cyna, who stood staring at the growing crack in the shield.

"They won't wait," he said. "Once the stone is in place, they're going to sacrifice Alia."

Cyna looked up at him. Something had changed in her. She'd been staring resolutely at the hole, the painful bright light Ryon called darkness, and in her unblinking eyes he saw none of the things he expected—no trepidation, no fear, no anxiety. Only resolution. Not a muscle moved on her face as she looked at him—looked *through* him, he felt.

Now that the caravan had arrived, the soldiers dismounted their horses and, with Princess Dara and Ryon at their center, began moving closer to the crack in the shield, to prepare for the sacrifice.

Cyna watched them pass by silently, then she leapt onto her horse and rode out toward the foothill, yelling: "By leave of our king, ruler of this realm, I have been granted permission to cross that threshold!"

Bathar followed, and soon he understood what she was doing. The crowd had begun to approach to hear the message Cyna was shouting as she rode back and forth. A panicked murmur went through them. They'd come out of curiosity, which had turned to fear as they saw the crack in the shield, but the soldiers had reassured them. Now they were waiting to see a once in a lifetime event, the sealing of the shield. But one of their own people *choosing* to cross over wasn't a lifetime event—it had never happened in the history of their realm. The anxious, pressing people slowed the descent of the caravan, so that the horn had to be blown repeatedly.

"Can't you see with your own eyes?" Cyna now yelled. "There is no danger!" She repeated the words like a mantra. Then, finally turning her horse around, she called out: "Come and see!"

The crowd was thrown into confusion. Some people—more than Bathar would have imagined—began to pull away from the others, to follow Cyna, approach the breach, see for themselves. Another group seemed to be chasing the first to pull them back. The better part of the crowd retreated a little further up the hill, perhaps afraid the approach of their fellows would finally cause whatever was waiting on the other side to come pouring through. Bathar looked for the old woman, found her being jostled by the waves of people as she tried to push forward. He rode toward her, then dismounted and helped her onto his horse, where she'd be safe from being trampled to death.

"She's going through the shield?" the old woman said, excitedly, reverentially.

The caravan was almost down the hill.

He swung himself back onto the horse, grabbing the reins around the old woman to keep her steady, and galloped forward, cutting through the smaller crowd.

A line of a dozen soldiers stood in front of the breach, masking it. But they faced inwards, their backs to the shield. Just in front of them the remaining guards formed a circle around Ryon, still holding Alia protectively, and Princess Dara.

Cyna was on her feet and trying to press through, but two soldiers had stepped forward to hold her back.

Bathar rode up beside her horse and handed the reins to the old woman as he dismounted. The smaller crowd was filling in the space behind them. The caravan's horn sounded again, more angrily; it was almost on top of them.

He approached the soldiers, two more stepping forward to meet him.

Behind him, more than thirty or forty of the villagers and farmers had gathered. They were young, strong, brave—but wary. They tried to look past the soldiers at the breach, as big as a large dog now, and murmured among themselves. He felt that curiosity and excitement had brought them this far—with two dozen armed men and women still between them and the shield—but that they were on the verge of retreating to join the others on the hill.

But if Cyna—and he!—proved that no danger existed? Would they follow?

In a loud voice, he yelled: "You will honor our king and his wishes! You will allow us to cross to the other side!"

Ryon turned his head to Dara and whispered in her ear. The princess touched the shoulder of the soldier in front of her, who moved out of the way. She stepped forward and said, just as loudly, "You dare speak of honor, you who have broken my father's law?" Her glance jumped to the bundle of rags gathered on his saddle, and a spasm of displeasure seized her features. Then, in a lower voice: "Your debt is repaid; you will not be killed for this disobedience, though you will live like her as a banished one."

"Highness—don't you want to know what lies beyond?"

Her glance now jumped to Cyna. "What will a mother not say to save her child? There is nothing beyond the shield but chaos. She would save one child and bring ruin to our kingdom."

The horn sounded right behind them, and Bathar turned desperately to see the smaller crowd parting to admit the mules carrying the stone table.

He grabbed Cyna by the arm and led her back to their horses. "They won't believe you even if you go," he said. "They'll say it's a trick, a lie. You were corrupted by the darkness. It won't matter."

She looked over her shoulder. "Then we fight."

We're outnumbered, he thought but didn't say. *They'll kill us.*

The heavy stone altar with its large curving legs had been placed on the ground. Ryon set Alia down in the middle of that cold, dead table. Over the neighing of the anxious horses and the rumbling nervousness of the crowd, Bathar could hear his daughter's unhappy cries.

Ryon lifted up a long golden dagger, then his voice bellowed out, deeper and stronger than Bathar had ever heard it, speaking the words of incantation, at the end of which he'd plunge the knife into the tiny body.

One moment Bathar had been despairing, certain they'd run out of options. The next, he knew only that his daughter wanted to be picked up, and that nothing more than a circle of soldiers and the possibility of death stood in his way.

He unsheathed his sword. Without a word, Cyna did the same.

They fought desperately, Bathar keeping one ear on Ryon's voice, unsure how long the incantation would last. Finally, they were almost at the stone table, and with a cry from deep within his belly, Bathar descended on the next soldier, the only one—for the moment—standing between him and Ryon. The soldier fell backward, his head cracking against one of the golden legs.

Ryon stopped speaking and his cold stare dropped to meet Bathar's. With one arm Bathar leveled his sword at him, while he reached out for Alia with the other, his gaze never leaving Ryon's.

The old mage smiled, then flicked his head to one side. As if obeying a wordless command, the sword flew out of Bathar's hand.

Before he could register what had happened, Bathar saw Ryon plunge the dagger through the air. Bathar leapt forward—or tried to—to stop or deflect or absorb the thrust. But his body didn't react. Ryon had immobilized him and now he would stand, helpless, and watch his daughter be killed.

Except, the dagger had stopped just above her bundled, wriggling, crying body, the sharp golden weapon shaking in Ryon's hands as if caught between two unseen but powerful and opposing forces.

Bathar felt the tightness in his body release. He stumbled forward and snatched his daughter from the table, held her close to his body. Then he allowed himself to look around.

Four panicked soldiers surrounded Princess Dara protectively, leading her back toward the shield—even toward the breach. The rest of her contingent was engaged in battle—because it wasn't only Cyna who fought them. Had those farmers and villagers joined the fight, he wondered, because they finally accepted that no danger lay beyond? Or, as he suspected most likely, because they saw this as an opportunity to defy, maybe even punish, the daughter of a cruel and oppressive king?

Out of the corner of his eye he became aware of a hunched-over pile of rags, a single arm sticking out from the sleeve, the fingers of its shaking hand outstretched. He turned his head as the old woman collapsed, then Bathar heard a loud clang as the dagger stabbed the stone table with all of Ryon's previously restrained force.

In the next moment, a mournful, drawn-out sound filled the skies, an amplified call from the magically enhanced longhorn set on the roof of the castle keep. The king had died.

Bathar leapt forward and grabbed the knife from the ground where it had tumbled, expecting a struggle with Ryon—but he couldn't see the mage anywhere. He spun on his heels and ran to help the old woman to her feet.

She pushed his hand away weakly. "Go," she said, her voice faint. "Go through the shield."

He moved his arm around hers and grabbed her, helped her to her feet. She felt as insubstantial as a bale of hay. "Come with us."

"Do you see?" she said, looking past him, her wrinkled face radiant. "I told you."

He followed her gaze. The hole had grown, as large as the giant door to the throne room, and seemed to be expanding even as he watched. Beyond it lay another world, a bright world, an expanse of green grass and large trees. Something was invading through the breach in the shield indeed, but it was light; like casting aside a thick curtain in a dark room. The world beyond was almost too bright to look at.

"Please come with us," he said.

Her hand dropped to touch the side of Alia's face, who giggled in response. She looked back at Bathar and—almost reluctantly—allowed herself to nod, relief making her face relax into a toothless smile. She'd been ostracized for so long, he understood, that even this small display of kindness seemed to touch her deeply.

Bathar whistled for his horse. But before the animal could reach them, he felt someone tugging at Alia, trying to rip her out of his arm. He turned quickly but no one was near him except the old woman.

"Go," she said, and seemed to gather up her remaining energy. The relief on her face had been replaced by exhaustion. But she raised her arm, and immediately Bathar felt the force release its grip on his daughter.

"Go," she said again, straining to speak. "I'll follow."

Bathar climbed atop the horse, holding Alia close.

The old woman's arm was shaking, but he couldn't see Ryon—not near the stone table on golden legs; not near the hole in the shield, where Cyna and her small upstart army of villagers and farmers had chased the princess and her remaining guards; and not on the hill, where the rest of the crowd watched and waited to see what would happen.

He galloped his horse forward, toward the fighting. "Stop!" he cried. "The shield is falling!"

Like an incantation of his own, the words seemed to wake them up to that reality, especially the princess—queen, now—and her soldiers, who had been so focused on defending themselves that they'd retreated toward the breach.

With a loud command from their queen, the soldiers took a step back, toward the shield. Cyna issued her own command and her fighters fell back too. Bathar led his horse in between the two forces.

"My queen," he said. "Look and see—there is nothing to fear. Lead your people!"

The queen pushed aside one of her soldiers and stepped forward. She looked past Bathar and addressed Cyna's small army: "Troops to outnumber you ten to one will be here shortly. They will crush you without mercy unless you lay down your arms."

"The shield will fall, Highness," Bathar said.

"As for you," she said, as if he hadn't spoken, "surrender now and I promise you and your wife a painless execution."

"Please—you can lead us to the other side."

From the set expression on her face, though, he knew she never would; because underneath that forced expression, he detected terror. What could convince her that the image beyond the breach wasn't an illusion? Would she believe even if someone crossed over and returned?

She looked past him again, and a smile stretched out her thin lips. The reinforcements had arrived—he knew it even as he turned his head to see the line of horses crest the hill.

Bathar looked at Cyna, then to the others. "There is nothing to fear!" he yelled.

The queen's soldiers had closed in around her and began to move her away from the shield. Bathar reached down for Cyna, pulled her onto the back of his horse, then galloped ahead and through the large, arch-like breach.

Squinting at the unnatural brightness, he took a deep breath; the air felt as fresh as any morning he'd ever experienced.

He turned his horse and waited to see if anyone else would cross. But already a few were coming through—slowly, hesitantly, then turning and calling and waving to others to follow.

"I have to help the old woman," Bathar said to his wife.

Cyna nodded, dismounted, eagerly accepted Alia from him.

"Be careful," she said. Then her expression softened and she put her free hand on his knee. "Bathar," she said, with a new voice, "we're outside the shield."

Bringing up an arm to protect his eyes, he allowed himself a look around at the verdant field stretching out endlessly before him, forests of tall, majestic trees to each side. Another blue shield surrounded them, rising up from the horizon, a giant and distant sky, like the reality on which their pale imitation had been based.

He looked back at his wife and returned her beaming smile.

Through the breach in the shield, which had grown as large as the castle gatehouse, he saw that the queen had retreated to the foothill, her tiny regiment reunited with the reinforcements. Incredibly, they were organizing themselves into defensive lines.

Queen Dara still expected monstrous hordes to come pouring through.

A small group of soldiers, led by Ryon, were marching toward him. One of them carried the old woman over his shoulder like a bag of flour.

For a brief moment, Bathar's confused gaze met Ryon's. Ryon lifted an arm and the golden dagger, which Bathar had shoved into his tunic, began to shake.

"No!" he yelled, and tried to grab it. The blade sliced across his palm as it flew through the air, then the hilt landed in Ryon's waiting hand.

Now Bathar understood: they weren't marching toward the breach, but to the stone table. They were bringing the woman there to sacrifice her; despite what was written in the law, Ryon had convinced the queen that the death of the old woman would suffice to seal the breach.

Desperately, Bathar tried to nudge his horse forward, but his arms and legs didn't respond. He'd been immobilized again. To watch the old woman die and do nothing?

It's not Ryon holding you back.

The voice inside his head reminded him of the old woman's, but full of strength and vigor.

He ignored it and willed his body to respond.

Ryon does not have the power to speak directly into anyone's mind. I will release you if you promise to stay where you are.

They dropped her on top of the stone table. Ryon stood over her, the golden dagger lifted high, his mouth moving with the words of incantation.

I can help you! Bathar screamed at her in his mind, then realized what he was saying. *If you have this kind of power, can't you stop them?*

To what end? My mind is strong, but my body is spent. I prayed to live long enough to see beyond the shield. I never imagined that I'd see any of our people cross to the other side. Or that I'd be able to send a piece of myself with you. Now, enough about that. Isn't this something? Ryon, petulant child that he was, claimed he didn't believe a word of what I said about the shield or our laws. But you see? Some part of him believes.

You don't have to— Bathar began, but the thought died out as Ryon brought down his arm, plunging the dagger into the old woman. A blink, and then Bathar saw nothing but cloudy blue steel.

Bathar dropped from his horse, then fell to his knees, staring at the shield.

After a few moments, he felt a hand on his back. Cyna, holding their baby.

"Look," she said, laughing.

Alia seemed to be playing a game, lifting her mother's necklace and letting it drop—except that her hands never moved, only her eyes.

"She said that a piece of her would come with us." Bathar ran his fingers against the side of the tiny, soft face. "Hello, little mage. Maybe one day you can help us show the truth to everyone trapped inside."

In response Alia giggled, her brown eyes shining.

Bathar kissed her forehead, then hugged them both tightly. After a while, he said, "We're falling behind."

Riding together on Bathar's horse, they followed the small crowd of freed people to discover the world that lay beyond.

See Karl El-Koura's story "The Azurian Shield" online at Metaphorosis.
If you liked it, leave a comment. Authors love that!
Remember to subscribe to our e-mail updates so you'll know when new stories are posted.

About the story

Some time ago, an image popped into my head of a soldier on a horse in a field, facing a cracking dome from the inside. I was so excited by the idea that I started writing the story almost right away (often, though not always, a mistake). I wrote about a thousand words of the soldier trying to hold the line while monstrous creatures poured through. I had this notion that the magic of the shield could only protect them while a righteous king or queen sat on the throne, but after about a thousand words the idea ran out of steam.

From time to time, I thought about that poor soldier facing the cracking shield, but I didn't have a strong sense of where to take the story.

Then one day it occurred to me: what if the shield isn't there to keep chaos out? What if they only thought it did? And what if the price to keep the shield whole is a terrible one?

I began to see the outline of this new version of the story: my soldier, named Bathar now, and head of the elite guard sworn to defend the realm, would have a deep need to ensure that the shield didn't fall (which would lead, as he supposed, to the destruction of the kingdom). But he'd also be unable to pay the terrible price required to restore a failing shield. An impossible position--except for the possibility of recovering a forgotten truth about their situation. That line of thinking seemed to unlock the story for me. Now when I started writing, I didn't stop until I had a fair-sized novelette.

A question for the author

Q: What five words describe you?

A: I can't distill the essence of my being into five words! I'd need six, maybe even seven.

That aside, one of the interesting things I've noticed is how much more joy I get from making a little bit of money from selling one of my stories compared with making much more money doing anything else. I sold my first story in 1997 for $15, and I carried the check (yes, paper check in those days) and danced around the house.

I'm less demonstrative these days, but the joy at selling something I've written remains in many ways undiminished. Why, when the reward is so minuscule, especially compared to the effort involved? I think it's the idea that you're being recognized—materially, tangibly—for something you love doing, and that you'd carry on doing even if no one paid any attention. But it is nice when someone pays attention, when an editor looks at something you've written and says, "That's pretty good. I'll pay to publish that."

So the five words I'm choosing to describe myself: "Writes; writes for money, happily."

About the author

Karl El-Koura lives with his family in Canada's capital city. He holds a second-degree black belt in Okinawan Goju Ryu karate, is an avid commuter-cyclist (on a stationary bike, lately), and works for the Canadian Federal Public Service.

www.ootersplace.com, @KarlElKoura

November

Treedom

AJ Cunder

We were playing in the park when Garold first took root. We stopped kicking our ball and stared when Jack pointed to the man standing motionless in the middle of the grassy field.

"Isn't that the homeless guy who sleeps by the shrubbery?" Thomas asked in a whisper. "How long has he been like that?"

Like a tree that had just been planted, the homeless man's legs remained frozen, and we inched closer almost without realizing it, edging along the stream cutting through the park. He placed his arms at varying angles, adjusting the bend in his elbows, shifting—never lifting his feet—as though trying to find a natural position.

No one else in the small park spared him a second glance. Dogs preoccupied owners, joggers ran along trails that wound into the encroaching forest, parents collected kids from an old playground with wooden structures on the verge of collapse. A rusty merry-go-round squealed as loud as the children. Only the three of us, on the cusp of adolescence ourselves, paid the strange man any mind.

"Should we go up to him?" Jack's lips curled in a telltale grin. Always the adventurous one, he often inspired our quests—exploring the schoolhouse after dark, or pushing Thomas up his chimney to search for treasure. He took us to a lake once, describing jewels and gems hidden beneath the waters, but blushed when I stripped to my underwear. "Girls can't do that in front of boys," he insisted, but I ignored him and dove in.

"And do what?" Thomas asked, shoving hands in his pockets, glancing around as though planning an escape.

"Mr. Morton says in science class we need to be good observers of the world if we're going to learn anything." Jack rubbed his hands as though trying to start a fire. "What if the man's turned to stone? A living statue? What if Medusa is loose in the park?"

Thomas swallowed, and Jack said, "Come on, let's find out." He started walking with his determined stride, hopping from stone to stone across the stream.

Three meters from the man, we huddled together. His gray hair coiled like vines to his waist, and silver tags flashed from his neck. I gave a tentative wave, but the man's eyes never moved. His face was rough and leathery, almost like bark, the embroidered name on his jacket—G. AROLD—sprouting threads as time picked out the stitches.

"*Garold*," Jack said with a chuckle. Somehow, the word had a nice feel to it, the way it started in the back of the throat and rolled off the tongue.

Thomas whispered, "My mom tells me never to talk to strangers." He probably remembered his mother's scream when she had found him with his head up the chimney, covered in soot, and the corporal punishment that followed.

"We're not talking. We're watching," Jack said. "Mr. Morton —"

"I don't think he meant this." Thomas pushed his hands deeper into his jeans, as though trying to bury his forearms.

I slid my own hands along the pocketless fabric of my dress, searching for a place to slip my fingers. Not finding one, I fiddled with a strand of long hair my father rarely let me cut, fidgeting in the clothes he insisted I wear. "He looks harmless enough." I fished a granola bar from my backpack stash, often used to feed the squirrels and woodland creatures we encountered, and held it out to the man, who slowly extended his arm. Inching closer, I dropped the bar in his palm, searching his face for...something familiar, perhaps, a kindred spirit, even if I didn't quite recognize it at the time.

A bell tower tolled, and Thomas jumped. "Come on, let's go," he said. "Or I'll be late for dinner."

With a last look at the man standing in Grove Park, we crossed the rickety wooden bridge and split for home along the cobblestone roads.

When a week elapsed and Garold remained rooted like a scarecrow, the tiny Welsh town of Gwernogle took notice. Some tried to approach him, but he never said a word, always staring out to his own horizon. Thomas's mother wondered if it was safe to let her son play where an odd man might prey on children, but Thomas argued that Jack would be there to protect him. Jack's father gave him a Swiss Army knife and made sure he knew how to flip out the blade. My own father, the town's pastor, went to see the scene for himself. "How long has he been there, Ash?" he asked me.

"Almost a week, I think."

"The police should check on him. He could be ill," he reasoned.

A cruiser came, and an officer tried talking with Garold, asking if he needed an ambulance or a ride somewhere—but Garold only said, "I belong here," his voice like leaves rustling. He broke no laws by standing in a public park, so the officer scratched his head, scribbled some notes, and shrugged when my father asked what the police could do.

Our parents all but forbade us to play there, but of course we didn't listen. Garold's mystery became our mission, our chance to play detective, investigating the strange creature who claimed this space. Jack imagined finding fame and fortune, the prodigy child who had discovered the first living statue. Thomas pretended to be a scientist, proposing hypotheses and theories, examining the soil around Garold's feet, taking samples and extracting conjectures— what kept him there? How did he survive? When would he leave? And I was a philosopher, wondering what it meant for Garold to stand there each day, unmoving, rooted to the ground, a singularity, a blip in the otherwise uniform grass that had grown for countless years undisturbed. The town groundskeeper grumbled at first, his routine altered. But finally he began mowing around Garold, who never shifted even as the ancient, roaring machine approached. Soon, the grass grew around his feet, swallowing his boots with their holes near the toe.

A week later, we were still no closer to solving Garold's mystery. I offered him another granola bar as we gathered around him, the only souls besides Garold in the heart of the park. Most of the other children, after spying Garold frozen in his eternal vigil, would abandon the swings and playground to the ravens keeping watch among the metal bars and plastic towers.

We never saw Garold ingest what I gave him, and no wrappers littered the ground.

"What do you think he eats?" I wondered. "Or drinks?"

"Maybe other people bring him food? And water?" Thomas wondered, sitting in the grass. He held up a hand to shield his eyes from the sun even as thunderclouds approached. "Should've brought glasses," he said as Garold slowly moved an arm. We froze, watching him, until he stopped, his hand between Thomas and the sun, a thin shadow falling across Thomas's eyes.

When Garold stilled, Jack continued notching a stick with his knife. "Maybe he absorbs nutrients from the ground, like a tree."

At this, Garold slowly turned his head. He smiled a deliberate, crooked smile, his few remaining teeth jutting from chapped lips. "You understand," he said, dry as kindling.

Jack jumped at the sound, eyebrows raised, and Thomas scuttled behind him. "Understand what?" Jack asked, smoothing his blonde-streaked hair, shrugging off his moment of skittishness.

Garold nodded. "Like a tree." We glanced at each other, and he shuddered, holding his silver army tags to his nose and squinting. He pulled on the chain until it was taut, in danger of snapping, but then he exhaled and slumped, the tags falling against his chest.

The first drops of a coming storm splashed our foreheads. "Come on," Thomas said. "We're gonna get soaked if we don't leave." He tugged on Jack's sleeve, who looked for a moment like he'd pull away.

"What about him?" I asked, a sudden spark tingling in my gut, an itch spreading through thoughts that had long swirled inside me. *Like a tree*, he had said. *Like a tree*. I pulled at a strap of my dress, resisting the urge to slip it off, to emerge from the wrappings that defined me, marked me as *girl*.

"If he doesn't want to get drenched, he'll move too," Jack said.

A thunderclap shook us to the bone like a bomb detonating, and Garold's face twisted as he shuddered. He raised his arms over his head as an unkindness of ravens croaked nearby.

We ran—but Thomas turned back and draped his poncho over Garold, quickly, as though afraid to stay in contact with him for too long.

"Come on!" Jack yelled. "I'm not waiting for you."

We didn't stay to see if Garold took shelter when the rain came, but the next day he stood, same as the days before, Thomas's poncho still slung over his shoulders.

When complaints came to city hall, the town council made their own inquiries with the Gwernogle police. The chief offered her apologies, but despite all biological laws, Garold didn't exhibit any physical distress. He only ever said, "I belong here," when officers approached, and even if parents feared for their children's safety, the police had no probable cause to forcibly remove him.

So the council of seven hosted a town hall which, despite our parents' reservations, we attended.

"It's just not normal," the townspeople said, fifty of Gwernogle's three-hundred residents crammed into the old stone inn that had for centuries served as the gathering place for official business. Gas lamps flickered along the walls—while most of the town had reasonably reliable electricity, the inn was so old that any renovations would risk bringing it down completely. "What kind of person stands in the middle of a park all day? Our kids are afraid to go there. We have to stay with them or drive them all the way to Brechfa to play."

From their lofty bench, the council of seven dark suits looked down upon those gathered. They added, "It certainly is strange, and we've had our police department out to investigate. Clearly, they have been inadequate in resolving the problem. We aren't quite sure why he's there or what he's doing, and none of the officers have been able to figure it out either. A concern we must address with their leader." They glanced at the police chief, who frowned as she hovered near the exit.

I stared at my fingers, imagining them to be roots, tendrils to penetrate rock and soil. I swallowed and raised my hand.

"Yes? Young lady in the back, you have something to say?" the council asked, faces pale even in the flickering orange light.

I stood and plucked at my dress, envying Thomas's jeans, Jack's dark jacket, their short hair, the stubble that would soon sprout on their chins. I felt my own smooth cheeks, folding arms over a budding chest as Jack raised an eyebrow, Thomas's knee just touching his, Jack letting it stay there.

I took a breath and said, "He is a tree. He told us."

A few chuckles bounced around the room, along with "absurd" and "ridiculous."

"Young lady," the council said, "he is clearly a man, not a tree. Whatever delusions he may have, he cannot remain a permanent fixture of our park. It simply isn't right to behave in such a manner."

"Unsightly. Frightening," some townspeople chimed in. "Unnatural."

Thomas's forearms disappeared in his pockets—how I wished I had pockets of my own—and he muttered something under his breath, shifting his leg away from Jack's.

I started to sit, but then straightened and added, "*He* says he's a tree. Wouldn't he know?"

No one answered, though the adults looked to one another, a hint of fear shading their eyes, distrust of anything that disturbed the norms settled for centuries upon this small, isolated town in the middle of the Welsh countryside.

After little more discussion, the council instituted a curfew in Grove Park that would take effect the following night. The police chief received her commission: anyone in the park between 11 PM and 6 AM must be ordered to vacate the property.

The town groundskeeper made hasty signs and posted them at the park's entrances. We considered tearing them down, but decided instead to sit with Garold when the police came. It was an opportunity to express ourselves, to lash out against the establishment, whatever that meant, to fight for something even if we didn't entirely know what exactly we were fighting for. Or perhaps we did, in some subterranean part of us; a seed had been planted, taking root in our minds. When I saw Garold, I recognized in him something I had long tried to hide within myself, a search for self-identity amidst a sense of disconnectedness, a sense of unbelonging. I kept this from the others, though. They didn't need to know. Not everything. Not just yet.

Thomas, of course, nearly stayed home, citing a stomach ache, but Jack threw pebbles at his window and promised to keep at it until Thomas finally snuck out the back. I stocked my backpack with snacks, and Jack brought a flashlight and rope so we could tie ourselves together around Garold—if it came to that.

We got there before the police, but not before the ravens, who shuffled along the edge of the park where the border blended into the forest. They croaked and flapped their wings as a crowd began to gather, spectators carrying electric lanterns. "Is that Jimmy?" Jack asked, spotting our classmate, captain of the football team.

"Yeah, I think it is," I said, waving to Jimmy who raised a hand in return.

"Come on over!" Jack called. But Jimmy ignored him, his parents clutching his shoulders.

A sudden chill bit through our clothes, and we shivered, a quick glance passing between us. "Is this really a good idea?" Thomas asked.

"Of course it is," Jack said. His hand darted like a fox, so quick I might have missed it if I hadn't been looking. Even so, I blinked and wondered if I really had seen him squeeze Thomas's hand.

"I belong here," Garold kept repeating to no one in particular, the grass at his feet now reaching past his knees, blending so thoroughly it became difficult to discern where his body ended and the earth began.

When the police arrived at 10:45 PM, they issued a warning, shining their spotlights at Garold. "As per local ordinance," the sergeant said, "Grove Park shall close to visitors at eleven each night. Sir, we are giving you a lawful order to leave now or face legal consequences." The sergeant looked at us as though just noticing we were there. "What are you kids doing? Go on, get home now. Where are your parents?" He looked to the crowd interspersed along the tree line.

"We're not leaving," Jack said. "We won't let you take him."

The sergeant shined his light in Jack's face. "Come on, now, no sense getting mixed up in this. How old are you, twelve, thirteen? You really want a police record?"

Jack dropped to the ground at Garold's feet—Thomas too, though sweat started to bead on his brow, and I followed. We leaned against Garold's legs and wrapped the rope around ourselves.

"Sarge? Should we take them all?" one of the patrol officers asked.

"Wait till they fall asleep, then we'll take the tree man. Can't be long, they'll knock out soon enough. And see if we've gotten any calls about missing children."

But we didn't fall asleep. We stayed up long after the crowd of townspeople dispersed, long after the officers finished their fourth cups of coffee, with the ravens still watching like silent sentinels. "All right kids," the sergeant finally said. "You win. Why don't you let us take you home, and we'll leave this man alone?"

"Thank God," Thomas said, starting to shrug off the rope when Jack grabbed his arm.

"Wait. First, this *man* is a *tree*. Second, how do we know you're telling the truth?" Jack asked, his eyes narrowing.

"You'll just have to trust us, kid," the sergeant sighed.

"I think we'll wait until morning when you can't make him leave. Six AM, right?"

The sergeant ground his teeth, and the standoff continued.

We took turns sleeping. The police did the same, with nothing else they could do short of ripping us bodily away. Garold stood as he always stood.

When a gray haze lightened the sky, our parents found us in the park after we didn't appear for breakfast and they discovered our empty beds. Perhaps they should've been more concerned, but it was Gwernogle after all, and nothing bad ever happened here. Jack's dad only chuckled and praised his son's rope work. "I taught him that knot," he said to the sergeant who checked his watch.

Nevertheless, Thomas's mother gasped, "What on Earth were you thinking?" She reached for his hand, but he wriggled away. "Thomas, what are you doing? Come with me this instant." She looked at Garold and frowned. "Thomas. Right now. Come with me."

My father stared at the ground, rubbing his chin.

"I'm not leaving!" I called out, and he scowled.

"Thomas, you have to go to school. Come with your mother. Come right now." Her glasses trembled dangerously on the bridge of her nose. "Stop this madness."

"Tell them to stop." Thomas nodded to the police, fingers wrapped around Jack's wrist, eyes widening as though surprised at his own boldness.

"Okay," the sergeant said.

"Really?" Thomas squeaked.

"Six AM. Curfew's over. Until tonight, anyway. We'll be back."

"And so will we!" Jack yelled between yawns.

Our parents tried to stop us. My father threatened to ground me, lock me in my room, take away my spotty internet. But I insisted I'd climb out the window. "Ashley, what's gotten into you?" he asked, running fingers through his hair. "You were always a well-behaved girl. Why this sudden change?"

"Maybe it's not so sudden," I offered, before my voice withered. *Maybe I've never felt comfortable as your little girl*, I wanted to say, *as the perfect pastor's perfect daughter. Maybe this skin isn't really my own.* But of course, I only looked down as he tapped his fingers on the counter.

Thomas's mother outlined the dangers, some more likely than others, and listed the health effects of improper sleep. But he shook his head, and said, "Jack will be there."

"You do everything with that boy," his mother said, frowning. "If he walked off a cliff, you'd follow him." And Thomas didn't deny it.

Jack's own father gave him sleeping bags and water canteens, and showed him more sophisticated knots.

Unable to contain us, our parents came on the second night of our vigil and watched on the wooden bridge beside the ravens, wary of violating the curfew themselves. When the police arrived, they brandished their nightsticks. One officer spun his like a propeller, and it whistled through the air. They tried half-heartedly to untie the rope that bound us, and Garold stiffened more than usual at their approach; but we covered the knots with our hands, our bodies, Thomas's arms wrapped around Jack's waist, and eventually the police gave up, retreating to their cruisers, where they sipped coffee and joked about worse ways to pass a night shift.

On the third night, the council of seven appeared in their raven-black suits, faces like ghouls in the lamplight. "Sergeant," they said. "Why is this man still here?" Birds cackled in the trees, a murder of crows circling over Garold's head.

The sergeant nodded towards us. "He's attracted some sympathy from the youth."

The council hovered over us like shades of Hades. "If they are a problem, Sergeant, then remove them as well," they said.

The sergeant laughed. "Right. And when the local paper runs a story about the police abducting children in the park, you lot will be the first to call for our resignation. I'd like to keep my job, thank you."

The council scowled, and they conferred with one another. Then, as one, they reached for our rope. The ravens fluttered their wings.

"I wouldn't do that," the sergeant said, tapping his nightstick.

"And why not?" the council hissed.

"Well, you see, since you're not officers of the law, if you lay a hand on these children, then that would be battery. Something I just couldn't turn my back on."

The council looked for a moment like they might do it anyway, and we held our breath, eyeing the ravens that hopped closer. Thomas grabbed Jack's arm and squeezed. But Garold rested his hands on our shoulders and stared at the council, acorn eyes boring into theirs of obsidian.

Without another word, the council of seven withdrew into the darkness, and the ravens along with them.

"Think they'll be back?" one of the officers asked.

The sergeant shrugged. "Let's hope not. Can't say I appreciate when those devils tell me how to do my work."

On the fourth night, we found a case of water by Garold when we arrived, along with a bag of chips and a container of homemade casserole. On the fifth night, our classmate Jimmy shuffled up and asked if he could join us. His parents screamed from the park's border, but he stood resolute, his back turned to them, eyes cautiously darting between Jack and Thomas. "You two, are you..." he couldn't seem to finish the sentence, but I knew what he meant. I think we all knew.

"Sit with us," I offered. "We won't turn you away. Garold certainly won't."

On the sixth night, Mr. Morton came with a notebook. "Fascinating," he'd mutter occasionally, asking us questions, trying to interview Garold who never said much, other than, "I belong here, as a tree. No, not a man. A *tree*." Mr. Morton stared, once, when Thomas's pinky overlapped with Jack's on the ground, frowning at first, but then twisting his lips in what might have been the beginning of a smile.

On the sixth night, we insisted that our parents sit with us. At first they stood a ways off, apologizing repeatedly to the police, who just sipped their coffee. But we grabbed their hands and brought them closer. We introduced them to Garold, who ever so slightly nodded his head.

"May I ask, sir, what it is you're doing here?" Thomas's mother dusted off her sleeve. Perhaps she saw the way her son's foot tapped against Jack's. Perhaps she chose to ignore it.

"I belong here," Garold rustled. "Should have been planted here instead of mother's womb. I should wear bark on branches, grow leaves, not hair. Drop acorns, not..." His lips tightened, and he tugged on his army tags until the chain nearly broke.

I fidgeted—but this night, with jeans borrowed from Thomas's wardrobe, I had something underneath, something between my skin and the scratchy wool of my father's dress. Thomas never questioned why I wanted them, when I asked for a pair, just handed them over and said I'd probably look better in them than he did.

Garold's eyes shifted like roots searching for purchase, and caught her gaze. "Do you believe that I belong?"

"Oh," Thomas's mother answered, glancing away. "I suppose we all belong, don't we? One way or another."

Garold slowly smiled.

On the seventh night, Jimmy brought the rest of the football team. They came at first to see the novelty—and because the school's star athlete told them to. But then something shifted; around Garold, we all seemed to find a sense of belonging, near this man-who-was-a-tree, where normativity began to fray around the edges—if we could accept this, what couldn't we accept?

Our nightly protest slowly transformed. People came at first to see what the whole town talked about, but then stayed for the fellowship, where conversations bonded strangers around bonfires, the community gathered with Garold at its center. Those who were more vocally inclined offered entertainment, and even the police partook of the homemade pies and dishes that went around.

Folk began asking Garold where he came from, if he had any family, but he never said much other than "I belong here." Then they started asking why he thought he was a tree.

Jack intervened, holding up a finger. "No, no, no. He doesn't *think* he's a tree. He *is* a tree."

In that moment, my heart sang. I added, "He's probably never felt comfortable in his own skin. It's not like bark. It's too soft." He closed his eyes and hummed as I spoke. "The world moves too fast for him. Trees, they take it slow. This is where he belongs. The world doesn't feel wrong, here. He doesn't feel wrong." I wound a coil of hair around my finger. "Like me."

The townspeople nodded—perhaps they didn't hear those last words lost to the wind, or didn't know quite how to process them, their heads tilted slightly to the side as they said, "That's nice," and moved on to other conversation.

A fortnight after our first vigil, Jack asked, as he stood watch over Garold—still wary of the police, still fingering the Swiss knife in his pocket—"Do you think they've finally accepted him?"

"Who?" I asked, trying to coax a shrew towards me with a handful of oats as someone in the crowd sang "*Suo Gan.*"

"The town. The adults."

Thomas shrugged, hands eternally in his pockets. "Seems like they're warming up, at the least."

"I meant, *accepted* who?"

"Oh. Garold, of course."

My thoughts flashed to the scissors sitting on my dresser back home, their gleam in the lamplight, my own visage in the mirror, the glint in Thomas's eyes when he looked at Jack, my father's preaching on Sunday. I searched the crowd for my father's face and caught him laughing with Thomas's mother, nodding in our direction, throwing us a smile and wave.

He came over, a package tucked under his arm, bringing Thomas's mother and Jack's father with him. "Hello, Garold," he said as he approached, hefting the brown paper. "We, uh... the three of us got you something." He held out the gift, but Garold made no move to accept it. So my father untied the strings, stripped off the wrappings and waved a denim jacket with embroidery like vines running down the sleeves. Garold's face brightened, even in the shadows cast by the fires, and Thomas's mother helped him shed his old skin, disturbing the squirrel perched on his shoulder.

"You didn't have to," I said to my dad. "But thanks."

He squeezed my shoulder, and that morning, before catching a moment of sleep, I slipped my hair between the shears and cut it, strands floating to the floor like leaves. When breakfast time came, I stood at the top of the steps, waiting to descend, taking a breath, remembering Garold. Each step felt like I carried a millstone, but foot by foot, I dragged myself to the table. My father looked up from his coffee mug, ran his eyes over my head, but said nothing, only swallowed once and finished his meal.

When Jack and Thomas saw me at school, they gaped for a moment, but then punched my shoulder. "New look, huh?" Jack said, his cheeks slightly reddening. "Maybe I'll try on one of your dresses tomorrow."

"Do it," I teased. "I've already got a pair of Thomas's jeans I'm going to wear."

When Garold saw me later that day, his smile cracked through leathered skin wider than I'd ever seen before, like a split in bark that could never close again. "You understand," he said, though I wasn't quite sure, this time, what he meant.

Garold's newfound smile brightened his face even as children sat under his shade to escape the sun, or swung from his arm as they might a branch, little boys climbing to sit on his shoulders beside robins and bluejays, pointing out and laughing as though they had scaled the tallest tree in the world. Ravens occasionally watched us from the edge of the park, brooding, but they never came close.

The council quietly rescinded their ordinance, and the following night, at the Treedom Rally, as our gatherings had come to be known, the police assured us Garold would be left to conduct his business in whatever manner he wished.

"I still don't trust them," Jack said, even as the townspeople cheered and congratulated Garold. "We should stay, just in case."

But we were tired—we were ready for a night of sleep in our own beds. So we didn't stay. Perhaps we should have, because the next morning, Garold was gone. His clothes remained—boots with chipmunks nestled inside, jacket spread upon the grass—and a sapling rose where he had once stood, the soil churned at its base as though someone had just planted it. The disturbed ground was oblong and the length of a man, but none of us mentioned that aloud.

Jack bent over and picked something out of the dirt. "His army tags," he said, holding them up to the sun.

We protested at the police station, but they insisted they hadn't taken him. The town council similarly held up their hands and shrugged. We tried to form a search party, but our parents said he had likely just moved on, that he must have found whatever he was looking for. No one bothered to dig up the sapling, to see what lay beneath it.

In the park, we ringed Garold's sapling with stones big enough, high enough, to mark it as sacred, a barrier against the town groundskeeper, who grumbled each time he passed our shrine. It would remain a testament to Garold, a monument, we reasoned. We would ensure Gwernogle never forgot.

Jack scratched *Garold* into one of the rocks with his knife, adding, *who is a tree*, while I left a handful of granola so the birds and squirrels would come. Thomas bowed his head and said something that might have been a prayer, though we had never taken him as spiritually inclined. I laid a hand on the bark still supple and soft and a tingle shot up my arm, up the sleeve of Thomas's shirt I had borrowed, through my body, across the jeans so wonderfully scratchy and tight on my legs. Suddenly, I knew. "He did it," I breathed. "It's him. He never left."

Jack scoffed, but then he felt the bark too, and his eyes widened. In a flash, he nodded, then hugged Thomas, pecked him quickly on the cheek. Thomas wiped his face at first, glancing around, but then touched a finger to the sapling and nodded too. It didn't make sense—not logically, anyway, not according to the laws of biology or science. But it did make sense in the same strange way that faith makes sense, even when reason or convention say otherwise.

We tried to guess what kind of tree it might be, but of course we were no experts in dendrology. The nascent green shoots might have been oak, as Jack suggested, or willow, as Thomas believed, or even maple, as I supposed. We hung Garold's tags at the sapling's peak, where they still rest to this day, never bothered by ravens. And whenever we have moments of doubt, or uncertainty, we visit Garold and climb his branches, pulling ourselves to the top where we sit beside robins and cardinals, Jack and Thomas hand in hand, my own legs clad in jeans. From that height, we look out on the town, the twinkle of new electric light shining through the old stone inn and the shrinking flock of ravens who linger on it.

See A.J. Cunder's story "Treedom" online at Metaphorosis.
If you liked it, leave a comment. Authors love that!
Remember to subscribe to our e-mail updates so you'll know when
new stories are posted.

About the story

The concept for this piece emerged from my own struggles with "fitting in," and finding acceptance as a member of the gay community. At first, Garold was meant to embody this transformation, while the children were mostly just observers—conduits between Garold and the town. But after a few rounds of edits, I realized (along with Morris) that the true heart of this story centered around the three children and their interaction with Garold— how he is able to change them—first, to accept their true selves, and second, to help a conservative town at least begin to consider (if not embrace) self-identities that disrupt deeply ingrained normative values. And I wanted the piece to accomplish this by pushing the concept of self-identity beyond LGBTQIA+ to explore what it means to know one's self even in a way no one else can. I hope, at least in some small way, this story can participate in the critical dialogue ongoing in our society that will one day produce a world of acceptance, no matter the clothes we wear, the bodies we inhabit, or the love we share.

A question for the author

Q: If your writing style were a bird, what type of bird would it be and why?

A: My first instinct when I saw this was to say "raven" because of how prominently they're featured in "Treedom". However, I posed this question to the writers group I frequently attend and one member, after careful consideration, suggested that my writing style most appropriately compares to a swan. She explained that swans are both elegant and fierce, mysterious and passionate, light and dark. I think that's a nearly perfect summation of my writing style—at the sentence level, I aim for graceful language with the power to evoke deep emotion; in terms of plot, I often find myself discovering the mysteries of a story as I write it (I seldom plan out anything in advance); and I would certainly agree that my stories tend to balance light and dark aspects, striving for a hopeful note but at the same time acknowledging the grim realities that so often face humanity.

About the author

A.J. Cunder is a Second Reader for Metaphorosis

A medievalist, a type 1 diabetic, and a cyber crime investigator, A.J. graduated from Seton Hall University with a Masters in Creative Writing after getting his Bachelors in English and Philosophy. Hobbies that occupy his spare time include sword fighting, playing the piano, learning the viola, running, hiking, spoiling his husky, and, of course, writing. He currently serves on the editorial staff of *Flash Fiction Online, Cosmic Roots & Eldritch Shores*, and *Metaphorosis*.

www.WrestlingTheDragon.com, @aj_cunder

Right Behind You

Matthew Gomez

Surface

Carlos sat in the grav-lift, the orange light of sodium lamps pushing through his closed eyelids. He imagined the light was a sunrise back home in El Salvador and that he was sitting next to his wife and daughter at their kitchen table. He smelled fried plantains and charred pupusas instead of the stale air recirculating through his exo-suit. With concentration, he could reach out and run his fingers through his wife's hair, put his hand on his daughter's tiny shoulder—a memory he cherished. One he *didn't* mind reliving again and again.

He savored the illusion until his new partner settled into the grav-lift bench opposite him, and Carlos's comms filled with the familiar, incessant crackle of a Geiger counter. At ground-level, the device emitted the quiet static of a radio losing reception. As the grav-lift surged downward, carrying Carlos and his partner deeper into the hot zone, the Geiger counter's crackle grew. The orange glow of the lights strobed as the cart picked up speed, and Carlos's imagination faltered. He was no longer in El Salvador, but heading for the reactor meltdown the cart carried them toward.

Once touted as the answer to North America's energy crisis, the underground reactor had been built close enough to the Pacific to pipe in water for cooling but far enough underground it would be sequestered from any natural disasters that might disturb its cores. In the unlikely event that something went wrong, its builders promised, the reactors would stay safe.

The promise had held for six months.

During the first seismic rumblings of the Great Quakes, managers at the reactor smiled and congratulated themselves on the facility's safety. When those rumblings grew into earth-shattering quakes, cracking the ground open like the surface of a dried lakebed, the whole western hemisphere risked radioactive poisoning. It was why Carlos and hundreds of other immigrant workers just like him now found themselves tunneling through a mountain of underground rock to install a containment barrier.

"You drill where we say, and we plug up the holes," a bored engineer had said to Carlos during orientation nearly two years ago. "Do what we say, and you'll stay safe. Before you know it, you'll be holding a green card and can put all this behind you."

Carlos, yanked from his memory of home by the Geiger counter's hissing crackle, opened his eyes in annoyance. "Turn that fucking thing off," he said in Spanish, looking through the dense glass of his visor into the brown eyes of his young partner.

The kid obediently moved his hand to his wrist console, but he paused. Sweat beaded on his forehead, his eyes wide with nerves like a rabbit surveying the sky over an open field. "The foreman told us to leave it on," he responded, his accent familiar. "Said it's a safety regulation."

"It's annoying and useless," Carlos said. "We're descending toward a nuclear meltdown. There's radiation—lots of it. Now turn it off."

The Geiger counters were one of many supposed safety protocols meant to protect the workers. They were there for show, just like the air circulators, bulky med kits, and alarms conspicuously placed in the tunnels below. If a collapse occurred or the reactor faced some unexpected explosion, none of it would save the workers. The only equipment that mattered was the exo-suits Carlos and his partner wore. With hydraulic joints, embedded lead plating, and powerful filters, they were the only thing separating the workers from the radioactive air in the tunnels.

The kid obeyed and turned off his Geiger counter. The crackle playing through Carlos's comms was replaced by the kid's rapid, shallow breathing and the whir of air rushing past their bulky exo-suits.

The sound reminded Carlos of the swelling panic he'd felt *his* first time down. The orange lamps had illuminated the tunnel ahead, but it might as well have been a black hole drawing him toward inevitable doom. Only time and repetition made things easier, but those first dozen trips down were hell. Carlos didn't feel bad about putting the kid in his place, but he needed to play nice for now, or his plan would fall apart before it really got started.

"We're going to be fine," Carlos said, working to subdue the grit in his voice. "I know it's your first time down, but I've done it hundreds of times. We'll be back surface-side before you know it."

"It doesn't seem worth it," the kid said, his voice cracking. "I shouldn't have come."

Carlos shook his head. As dangerous as the excavation work was, it was worth it. Signing up had bought him and his family temporary US citizenship, with the promise of full citizenship after he completed his contract. His wife and daughter were in family housing 1,500 miles away in Texas, safe from the violent gangs that had run them out of El Salvador. Carlos had gladly traded the risks of the excavation for the extortion he faced back home. Anything to protect his family.

"Do what I say, and you'll be fine," Carlos grunted. He hoped the confidence in his voice was enough to mask his intentions—mask the plan he'd set in motion when he selected the kid as his partner.

After so many trips down, the rebreather on Carlos's exo-suit was beginning to fail, which was a death sentence for someone that spent the bulk of each day in subterranean tunnels over a radioactive meltdown. He'd tried going to the foreman for a replacement, but he'd burned that bridge long ago, which left Carlos only one other option: take one for himself.

Finding the kid—his mark—had been easy. At the first sign of his rebreather filter failing, Carlos had started hanging around the shuttle drop-off at the main gate of the workers' camp. Every evening he'd watched new recruits spill out of their gleaming metal shuttles, looking for the crown tattoo that would ease his conscience. He didn't need to know anything else about his victim. The mark of the gang that had driven him here was enough. Carlos's whole body had trembled when he saw the kid emerge from the shuttle, the crown tattoo on his forehead peeking out from behind black bangs. He was younger than Carlos had hoped for, but the boy's hard expression conveyed the exact violence Carlos had run from. The kid was young, but that didn't make him innocent.

Carlos's wrist console beeped a warning about his rebreather filter as the grav-lift continued its descent, and he slapped it quiet with a gloved hand.

"What was that?" the kid asked.

"Your accent sounds familiar," Carlos responded, ignoring the question. "Salvadoran?"

The kid looked up, his tense expression easing. "Guatemalan."

"What's your name?"

"Miguel," the kid mumbled.

"I'm Carlos. We're going to be fine. Just breathe."

"You've really been down hundreds of times?" Miguel asked.

"It'll be two years in a few weeks, and I'll be finished."

"Guess you know what you're doing."

Carlos nodded. Playing nice with the kid took more restraint than he had expected. For the first time since Carlos had spotted Miguel, they were close enough that Carlos could reach out, wrap his reinforced fingers around Miguel's throat until his body went limp, then strip his suit of its new rebreather filter—all before they reached the bottom of the grav-lift track. But then he'd be left with a body and no way to get rid of the evidence. That wouldn't do. If he were caught, his shot at citizenship would disintegrate, so instead he clenched his jaw, gripped the edge of the cart to steady his trembling hands, and focused on the gentle sway of the grav-lift, ruminating on the real work ahead of him.

1,000 Feet

A red light flashed ahead, illuminating a reflective placard glowing through a fine coating of dust: *1,000 feet below surface.*

"Is all the housing as bad as mine, or do they stick the new guys in the worst units?" Miguel asked, tapping through a series of menus on his wrist console.

The fidgeting reminded Carlos of the way his daughter distracted herself with her favorite toy: a pink plastic horse, the joints of its limbs worn loose. The memory peeled open the hurt he felt from being away for so long and flared up the anger he'd been working to subdue. If it weren't for *Los Reyes*, the gang comprised of countless vicious punks just like Miguel, he'd be home and able to see his daughter—wrap her up in his arms until she giggled and squirmed free.

"What do you think?" Carlos spat.

Miguel looked up, his eyebrows knitted. "Sorry, just wondering."

Play nice, Carlos reminded himself, a sigh creeping past his lips. "They're all shitholes. Just enough to keep the weather out and our stink in. Everyone's too exhausted at the end of a shift to bother cleaning."

"Doesn't the foreman say anything?"

Just the mention of the foreman made Carlos's hands tighten into fists. The guy was a sociopath. When he felt particularly irritable, Carlos liked to imagine what he might do if he found himself in a locked room with the guy.

"He couldn't care less. To him and everyone else running this mess we're just bodies. They call us 'backs' when they think we're not listening."

" 'Backs'?"

Carlos twisted to the side and tapped a reinforced finger against the flexible section of exo-suit covering his back. "It's all they think we're good for in this country—we're strong and we'll do the work their poor won't touch. It's always been that way here. Ask the Chinese in the 1800s. Ask our great-grandparents and their parents, who picked crops for American stomachs. Ask *our parents*, who built the desalinization plants off the coast when the rivers dried up. Then ask yourself what the foreman thinks of you."

"I don't care what the foreman thinks as long as I get mine," Miguel said.

Typical, Carlos thought. "You should," he said. "You give your humanity to someone like the foreman, and you'll never get it back."

Carlos knew from experience. Soon after he'd started, he'd gone to the foreman to complain about a number of broken safety regulations he'd witnessed: tunnelers like himself working without scanners to get more done in less time and areas not being cordoned off properly during excavations, to name just a couple. The foreman made it clear that results were all that mattered.

"If you're that upset about how I'm running things here, you can go back to your shithole country," the foreman had said. The auto-translator box on the foreman's desk leeched the venom from his tone as it spat out the words in a monotone Spanish, but Carlos got the point. "No one's forcing you to stay here. Last thing I need is another *back* that doesn't know how to keep his fuckin' mouth shut."

Back then, Carlos had thought the foreman had to be an anomaly. Not everyone could be so careless about regulations, not with so many lives at risk. So he waited, keeping a tally of the broken safety measures until he could tell someone who would actually listen.

He'd found his chance at the end of a shift in the tunnels when he ran across a group of officials wrapping up one of their regular inspections. They were gathered at the equipment check-out stands and stood out like black flies in a bowl of crema. Their gloved fingers were too clean and their postures too upright. The heaviest thing they'd lifted that day were the tablets they scribbled on as they moved through the hot zone.

Carlos had walked up, tapped one on the shoulder, and begun the speech he'd been running through his head since his conversation with the foreman. The officials translated Carlos's statement with their tablets, nodding along as he spoke. When he finished, he noticed one of the officials shaking his head and chuckling to himself. Carlos couldn't figure out why. And it wasn't until he woke up the next morning being shaken awake by the foreman that he understood. The officials hadn't taken their findings to any regulators at higher offices of government. They'd taken it straight to the foreman.

Carlos could still remember the expression on the foreman's face as he'd leaned over him, his face blood red. Without an auto-translator, Carlos didn't understand what the foreman was muttering, but he knew it wasn't good. The foreman didn't yell, which made the even cadence of his words even more terrifying.

Carlos had hoped the foreman might eventually forget, but that was wishful thinking at best, willful ignorance at worst. That foreman's ability to hold a grudge had proved stronger than Carlos expected, and he regretted ever thinking he could make a difference.

"It's worth it, though," Miguel said, snapping Carlos back to the present. "Land of opportunity and all." The kid's optimism was an annoying reminder of how Carlos had felt when he'd signed on.

Carlos scoffed. "It better be." Suddenly he was the one breathing hard.

"You seem too smart for this."

The compliment caught Carlos off-guard. He liked it better when the kid fit the gangster image Carlos had crafted in his head. He shifted uncomfortably in the cart. "I studied history back home. Wanted to be a teacher."

"Why this, then?"

Carlos clenched his jaw, replaying for the thousandth time in his head his final interaction with *Los Reyes*—the reason he'd fled with his wife and daughter to the United States. "There weren't any other options."

"It was that bad in El Salvador?"

"We're going almost two miles underground to excavate tunnels above a nuclear meltdown. Yeah. It was really bad."

Miguel nodded.

"You know that tattoo won't do you any favors if you live long enough to get citizenship," Carlos said before the kid could ask another stupid question.

Miguel reached up, putting a gloved hand against the lead glass of his visor, his fingers massaging the spot directly over the crown. For the first time since he'd sat across from Carlos, Miguel seemed to run out of things to say.

Carlos's wrist console beeped, and he slapped it silent once more.

"Something wrong with your suit?" Miguel asked, dropping his hand to his lap.

"It's fine," Carlos lied. He'd gone to the foreman for a replacement a month ago, but as Carlos was explaining the problems with his suit, the foreman lifted a hand to silence him, took a deep breath, then leaned in close to the auto-translator.

"Damn thing seems to be on the fritz," the foreman said, his words translated into perfect Spanish. He slapped the speaker with false irritation. "Everything you're saying is coming out garbled."

The foreman flicked the power switch off, and the auto-translator went dead. He pointed a finger at Carlos. With the auto-translator off, Carlos didn't understand what the foreman said next, but the expression he wore—the sweat beading on his red face—was enough to let Carlos know he wasn't getting a new rebreather filter.

Every breath since then felt borrowed, another grain of sand dropped from the dwindling top of an hourglass. He kicked at the silt-covered bottom of the grav-lift and wondered how much radioactive dust he'd inhale when his rebreather finally stopped working. He wondered how long he'd live afterward. He wondered if he'd live long enough to see his family again if it came to that.

The exo-suit suddenly felt too small, too cramped, and Carlos's pulse throbbed in his neck. A shiver ran down his back, and he grew lightheaded as anxiety surged its way through his body. Holding his breath, Carlos looked up, afraid Miguel might have sensed something odd about the sudden silence.

Miguel was fiddling with the console on his wrist, the light from its panel illuminating the rebreather jutting from his chest— the one containing a fresh set of filters. Carlos's eyes locked onto the rebreather. Only then did his shoulders relax, and the painful knot in his chest begin to loosen.

7,000 Feet

The sub-surface air pumping into Carlos's exo-suit grew warmer the further they descended, the collapsed radioactive cores dumping heat into the network of tunnels like a raging furnace.

To pass the time and hopefully stave off his swelling anxiety, Carlos scanned his exo-suit for damage, running his fingers over the thousands of scrapes and dings that scarred its metal exterior. Despite the countless abrasions, the suit still functioned. It kept the radiation out, and its hydraulic pistons multiplied the output of his well-toned muscles. Without a new rebreather filter, though, the suit would be little more than a walking coffin, which the foreman had made clear was no concern of his. Carlos didn't need the auto-translator to know that if he died in the suit, the foreman would have a line of other "backs" eager to stuff themselves inside it.

Carlos had gone to some of the partners he'd worked with to see if they might request a new filter for him, but each attempt had been met with averted eyes and a half-hearted excuse. It wasn't that they didn't care or didn't want to help, but Carlos's status with the foreman had become well-known by that point, and helping Carlos might mean risking their own chance at citizenship —their own chance at survival. Carlos had hoped that an unspoken sense of solidarity might eventually cause one of them to change their mind, but it turned out that a little sympathy wasn't quite strong enough to loosen desperation's grip.

As they passed the 7,000-foot placard, the sign's blinking red light cast his body in a devilish glow.

"So how'd you get your crown?" Carlos asked. Just mentioning the tattoo steeled Carlos's resolve, loosened that knot in his chest a fraction more. "You have to earn it, right?"

The tattoo was enough justification for what Carlos planned to do, but he found himself thinking of his wife and daughter. If they asked him how he'd survived the mines, he'd damn well better have a better answer than, "I killed my young partner because he was a piece of shit gangster that deserved it." Carlos knew the tattoo wasn't some casual sign of affiliation with *Los Reyes*, but he'd sleep better if he had a better grasp on just how rotten Miguel really was.

Miguel looked up from the floor of the grav-lift, his eyes only briefly connecting with Carlos's. It was the same look Carlos's daughter gave him when she'd done something wrong. It was almost like Miguel was afraid of disappointing Carlos with the truth.

"Don't want to talk about it," Miguel muttered, returning his gaze to the floor.

"Oh, come on," Carlos said. "What was it? You rob a bank? Steal some poor kid's bicycle?"

"I said I don't want to talk about it," Miguel growled.

Carlos could feel Miguel reaching his tipping point. He just needed a little push. "Beat up one of your gang's rivals? Burn their house down?"

"I fucking killed someone," Miguel blurted. His tone caught Carlos off-guard. It wasn't boastful. Instead, the words seemed to barely squeeze past the kid's clenched throat.

You rat, Carlos thought. *Probably murdered some poor bastard in the street and took off before you got fingered for the act.* He shook his head and rolled his eyes. "So you ran? Afraid you'd get caught and actually have to own up to what you did?"

"Yeah, I ran," Miguel responded. "But not because I was afraid of getting caught. I ran because I didn't want to have to do it again." He looked up from the floor of the grav-lift and locked eyes with Carlos. It was hard to tell through the thick glass of his visor, but it looked like the whites of his eyes had gone red.

Just the light, Carlos thought.

"My mom died when I was little," Miguel continued. "I never knew my dad. My older brother did what he could to take care of us, but he was just a kid himself. This crown doesn't mean what you think. I know to you it just makes me a thug, but to my brother and me, it was our only ticket to food, a place to sleep, protection. And without money to pay for any of it, it had to be earned one way or another. I'm not proud of it, and if I could have figured out a way to get by without *Los Reyes*, I promise you I wouldn't have done what I did. But it's too late for that now. So here I am."

For the first time that day, Carlos didn't know how to respond, and for the briefest moment, the scorching anger he'd felt toward Miguel waned. He understood what it meant to sacrifice a part of yourself to survive. It was why he'd taken this job in the first place. Digging out the tunnels gave him a path toward a better future with his family. Without it, he'd have been left at the mercy of *Los Reyes* or whatever gang might eventually come along to take their place.

Carlos wished his brain had a console like his exo-suit. If he could, he'd shut it off to stop the thought spiral sucking him in toward its center: if Carlos and his wife had died back in El

Salvador, how would his daughter have gotten by? Would he blame her for joining a gang if it meant she would be fed and have a safe place to sleep? Of course not.

Both men fell silent as the grav-lift descended further.

Eventually the staging area, another few hundred feet down, glowed beneath a halo of lights. The sudden glare snapped Carlos out of his thoughts, reminded him of the plan he'd set in motion. The light anchored him. It renewed his sense of purpose— reminded him that it was time to act. Nothing the kid had said had changed anything. None of it made him less guilty. He was a *murderer*, after all. The person Miguel killed could have just as easily been Carlos. It could have been his wife. It could have been his *daughter*.

Carlos squeezed his hands tight enough to crack his knuckles. "When we get down, hop in line for a mag-hammer and a battery bank," he said, reciting the lines he'd scripted for himself. "I'll grab our drill."

"I should get a scanner, too, right?"

"Weren't you saying just a few minutes ago that you were glad to be with someone experienced?" Carlos asked. "If you're gonna slow me down, I can find someone else to hold your hand."

"No, no," Miguel said. "It's fine."

The grav-lift slowed its rapid descent, coming to a complete stop against a set of worn rubber bumpers at the end of the grav-track. Carlos stood, mashed a button to open the grav-lift's door, then stepped onto the staging platform. Ahead were two equipment distribution stalls. Carlos departed without a word to check out their drill and lights.

Standing in line, Carlos felt anxiety swelling in him again, his legs wobbly even with the exo-suit's hydraulic assistance. He watched Miguel approach the check-out for mag-hammers, battery banks, and scanners.

The worker handing out the equipment lifted all three onto the counter, but Miguel only scooped up the mag-hammer and battery bank. As he turned toward Carlos, the distribution worker called out, holding up the scanner.

Please, Carlos thought. *Leave it.*

Miguel shook his head at the worker and turned back toward Carlos. The worker shrugged and replaced the scanner on the rack behind him.

Carlos let out the breath he'd been holding, and he nodded at Miguel.

"We're in tunnel 67C," Carlos said as Miguel approached. "We'll take the elevator down the last few hundred feet, then get to work." Carlos signed for a drill and a pair of high-output LED lamps, and they set off toward a wide elevator platform that would carry them toward a spiderweb of connected tunnels that spread over the fractured reactor cores below.

"Guess the real work is about to start," Miguel said as he and Carlos stepped off the elevator and walked down a dimly lit feeder tunnel toward 67C.

Carlos looked down at his wrist console, the screen red with its relentless warning. "You could say that," he replied. Miguel's murder confession bubbled back into his thoughts, and the familiar anger Carlos felt toward *Los Reyes* simmered once more to life.

8,500 Feet

Carlos enjoyed the drill's unyielding vibrations. It numbed his arms up to his shoulders and drowned out the pounding of his pulse.

Before starting, he'd trained the pair of LED lamps at the craggy rock at the end of the tunnel and plotted out the holes he would drill, mapping out a constellation that would collapse at the precise moment he needed.

Without a scanner's LiDAR and sub-seismic readings feeding into his heads-up display, nothing would warn Carlos of an imminent collapse, but, more importantly, it wouldn't warn Miguel either. Carlos had only his instincts and a thousand hours of muscle memory to guide his hands.

Over and over, he buried the drill's diamond-crusted tip into the rock, watching ribbons of silt drift down as he yanked the tool free. He might as well have been drilling into his own nerves, each hole a gamble that could render his plan useless and snuff out his chances of seeing his wife and daughter again.

As usual, Carlos's thoughts drifted toward El Salvador as his hands instinctively drove the drill into the rock. It was his mind's attempt to find peace amongst the cacophony and danger of the tunnels. He pictured the home he'd left behind: the exterior the color of the sky, the terra-cotta roof gleaming red in the sun.

What should have been a happy memory always led to the same chain reaction of images. He saw the exterior of the home, then the front door, slightly ajar. Next he was striding inside, his heartbeat accelerating, then turning the corner. There, two men stood in his kitchen, guns pointed at his wife and daughter. *Los Reyes.* The Kings.

Even with his eyes focused on the wall of rock ahead of him as he drilled, Carlos could see the crowns tattooed on the men's foreheads in perfect, crystalline detail. He could see the way one of the crowns lifted as the leader of the pair—a rail-thin man with pock-marked skin and bulging veins—conveyed a final warning. With a grimace that twisted into a smile, the man explained exactly what would happen if Carlos didn't cough up the 'protection' money he owed.

"Bang," he'd said, the gun aimed at Carlos's wife, his hand jerking back with an imaginary recoil. Then he pivoted the gun toward Carlos's daughter. "Bang," and another imaginary recoil.

Carlos normally dreaded the memory's inevitable turn, but this time he welcomed it and the familiar way it strengthened his resolve and numbed his fears.

Carlos yanked the drill free of the wall and spun to face Miguel, the crown on his forehead lit with the blue glow of his exo-suit's HUD lights. "You're up," Carlos said, sweat cascading down his forehead and soaking into the undershirt he wore beneath his Tyvek coveralls. He shoved the drill against Miguel's chest hard enough to scratch the pristine paint coating the kid's refurbished exo-suit.

Miguel got that same rabbit-in-an-open-field look on his face, but he traded the mag-hammer he'd been holding for the drill without question.

Carlos pointed at the small section of wall he'd left untouched. "Start here and stay within this area." He traced a square against the rock with his finger. "I'll make sure you're good. When you finish, we'll mag-hammer the shit out of the wall and be that much closer to calling it a day."

Miguel nodded, lifted the drill, and leaned into the rock with the full force of his exo-suit.

With Miguel distracted, Carlos aimed the mag-hammer at the ribbed material covering Miguel's neck. *It'll be over quickly*, he told himself. *Painless.*

He rested his thumb next to the mag-hammer's trigger, its chiseled tip poised to pierce the soft, unexpecting flesh of his young partner. One twitch of his finger, and Carlos could steal the kid's rebreather and bury the evidence beneath a small mountain of rock.

That godawful memory of his daughter sitting at the kitchen table with a gun pointed at her head, her pink toy horse in her lap, played once more in his mind. He sucked in a breath and moved his finger over the trigger, but a sound rang out before he smashed it down.

Miguel was *laughing*.

The sound made Carlos hesitate, and instead of pressing the mag-hammer's trigger, he froze.

Miguel yanked the drill free and turned around suddenly, a smile spread across his face. "My brother would love this thing," he said.

Carlos dropped the mag-hammer to his side. "Your brother?" he asked, stumbling over the words as he feigned an inspection of the mag-hammer.

"Yeah, man," Miguel said. "He got a job doing construction a few months before I left. I thought it sounded horrible, but he said he loved the chaos of the work sites. Something about the way he and the other workers could take a bare patch of earth and create something new." He returned his attention to the wall and resumed drilling.

"Why's he not here with you, then?" Carlos asked, hoping to keep Miguel distracted. "Preferred the company of *Los Reyes* back home?"

Miguel ripped the drill out of the wall, the rock groaning with the sudden movement. "Fuck *Los Reyes*," Miguel said, slamming an armored forearm against the tunnel wall.

Another groan emanated from the rock, and Carlos instinctively took a step back, moving Miguel out of reach of the mag-hammer's tip.

"Me and my brother would be here together if it weren't for them," Miguel said through clenched teeth. "Here we may just be 'backs' but back home people like me are knives. We're weapons— used up until we're dull," his voice cracked. "Or broken." He turned once more toward Carlos and stared at him, his visor fogged with heated breaths.

Through two layers of leaded glass, Carlos inspected Miguel's face. Maybe it was the fogged visor, but the crown on his forehead looked less like ink and more like a brand—a keloid scar marking Miguel's loyalty, willing or not.

The rock overhead released a cloud of silt, and the walls of the tunnel groaned, this time loud enough for Miguel to notice. "That doesn't sound good," he muttered.

Pebbles raining on his shoulders, Carlos dropped the mag-hammer, grabbed Miguel's exo-suit, and yanked. He and the kid stumbled backward as the rock overhead collapsed with a thunderous shudder. Dust and debris blasted outward, ricocheting off Carlos's suit and smothering the yellow light of the lamps Carlos had set up.

"My god!" Miguel screamed, his legs buried beneath a massive rock and a thousand crumbling stones.

Carlos scrambled to his feet and saw Miguel through the blanketing dust. The red warning light on Carlos's wrist blinked, strobing the walls in crimson. Dust from the collapse plugged the last working portions of his rebreather filter, leaving Carlos only the stale air that remained in his suit.

"Help!" Miguel screamed, his voice rattling the speakers in Carlos's helmet. "I can't move! My legs, man! My fucking legs are stuck!"

Carlos's eyes darted between the mag-hammer he had kicked free of the collapse and the kid. *Not too late*, he thought. He snatched the mag-hammer off the ground and held it over the back of Miguel's head.

"Help me!" Miguel screamed.

Carlos tried to ignore the shrill cries. He tried to focus on what needed to be done. He tried to focus on the hope he still felt at seeing his wife and daughter again. He could end Miguel's suffering. He could take away the kid's pain—save him from another two years toiling beneath a mountain of rock. And in doing so, he could preserve his own future, the one he'd worked so hard to earn.

He breathed hard, sucking in borrowed breaths as he did his best to hold the tip of the hammer steady, ensuring it would strike true, penetrate Miguel's helmet and end the kid's suffering. If he wanted to see his family again, he just needed to pull the trigger—just like he'd done so many thousands of times over the past two years.

But as he worked up the courage to act, that same image of his home in El Salvador crept into his mind, only this time Miguel sat at the table, and instead of the gunman, Carlos himself stood in the center of the kitchen, the mag-hammer pointed at Miguel's temple.

"Fuck!" Carlos screamed, the residual air in his suit thinning. It was all he could say. Torn between self-preservation and becoming the very thing he'd been running from, he froze, unable to act.

None of the tunnel workers signed up to spend their days miles underground next to a nuclear meltdown because it sounded like good work. They were all running from something, and in a weird twist of fate, it seemed Carlos and Miguel were both running from *Los Reyes*.

The tip of the mag-hammer dipped as Carlos's vision swam, his HUD flashing red warnings about his oxygen levels. The chiseled tip hit Miguel's helmet, scraping a shallow rut in the metal, and Miguel let out a moan that snapped Carlos back into reality. "I'm sorry," Carlos muttered, though he wasn't sure whether he was directing the sentiment at Miguel, himself, or his wife and daughter.

He lifted the mag-hammer and pointed it toward the boulder pinning the kid's legs. He pressed the trigger, and the rock shattered into fragments as Carlos's visor fogged over completely. He searched for Miguel's hands, found them, and pulled. The kid screamed as he was jerked free of the debris, his legs mangled.

Carlos wheezed as he dragged Miguel toward the tunnel's mouth, the kid's screams muted as Carlos's consciousness wavered.

When they reached relative safety, the valves containing the air in Carlos's suit finally gave way, popping open with a violent hiss. The suit's fail-safes gave way as his HUD went solid red and his wrist console screeched in warning. Carlos sucked in a lungful of radioactive air, and as oxygen once again permeated his body, his thoughts turned immediately toward his wife and daughter.

Workers in the nearby tunnels emerged, running toward the dust-covered pair at the mouth of 67C.

"He saved me," Miguel croaked as the workers descended on them.

Carlos, supported by a ring of workers, stumbled toward the elevator that would carry him and Miguel to the staging area. As they moved, he heard Miguel whimpering over and over about how Carlos had rescued him.

Carlos drew in another long, quivering breath. As he exhaled, he stared at his hands through tears that welled in his eyes. He knew the kid was wrong. He'd nearly killed Miguel, maybe crippled him.

But then that same old memory came flashing back, only the gangsters were gone, and at the table sat his wife, his daughter, *and* Miguel.

The workers assisting Carlos and Miguel led them toward a waiting grav-lift at the staging area, where they eased Carlos onto the grav-lift's empty bench and laid Miguel down as gingerly as they could onto the floor. Carlos's head swam with each breath, the radiation he inhaled contaminating his cells with poison, and he knew he'd die before he saw his wife and daughter again.

As the grav-lift began its long ascent, Carlos fought off a sudden rush of nausea and leaned over Miguel. "Finish your contract and do something with your life," Carlos wheezed.

Miguel's eyes were wide with pain and panic, but he seemed to understand, though he only nodded in response.

"And the next time you're in a position to help someone, you do it, even if it hurts," Carlos continued. "Because if we don't watch each other's backs, no one else will, and you'll find yourself right back where you started: letting someone use *your* back for *their* gain."

Miguel managed another nod before squeezing his eyes shut and succumbing to the pain wracking his crushed legs.

Carlos sucked in a shuddering breath, sat back against the grav-lift's bench, and slapped his wrist console quiet for the last time. He focused on his breathing, and once more, the sodium lamps became the sunrise cresting over the hills, and the air rushing past his exo-suit became a breeze through his kitchen window.

See Matthew Gomez's story "Right Behind You" online at
Metaphorosis.
If you liked it, leave a comment. Authors love that!
Remember to subscribe to our e-mail updates so you'll know when
new stories are posted.

About the story

I taught high school English for a number of years, and during that time I wrote a series of lessons based on a story in *The Economist* called "Fields of Tears." The article describes the lengths migrant farm workers from Latin America go to in hopes of earning a better life for their families in the United States. Many of these workers not only endure a perilous journey to get to the U.S., they then suffer through tremendous hardships as part of a workforce that performs back-breaking labor to hand-harvest crops. It's a thankless job, but one that promises at least the hope of a better future. The U.S. has a history of exploiting others' desperation for our gain. For "Right Behind You," I tried to imagine what that exploitation might look like in a future where an environmental disaster has threatened the safety of the West Coast. Like harvesting crops in the present day, the nuclear disaster has created a job that even our country's most impoverished and desperate won't touch. The story evolved into an investigation of how shared suffering might act as a bridge between two people seemingly at odds. I believe compassion and empathy are our two most defining emotions as humans, and I wanted to see how those feelings might stack up against an individual's instinct for self-preservation.

A question for the author

Q: Do you write with a particular audience in mind?

A: I've tried in the past to write with a particular audience in mind, and each of those stories has failed. In *The Emotional Craft of Fiction*, Donald Maass writes, "The novelist...is not causing readers to feel as the novelist does, or as his characters do, but rather inducing for each reader a unique emotional journey through a story." That line took a lot of pressure off me as a writer by helping me realize I have no control over how a reader interprets my work. That boils down to each reader's life experiences and preferences. Now, I write to entertain myself or work through an idea I find challenging. I do my best to explore ideas in a way I find interesting, and I hope that my readers experience some of the same wonder reading my stories that I felt while writing them.

About the author

Matthew Gomez is the Podcast Editor and Host for Metaphorosis.

Matthew Gomez believes that a story's magic lies in its ability to transpose us into another being's existence, and that the empathy learned there helps us grow in uncharted ways. He serves as the podcast editor for *Metaphorosis Magazine* and is a graduate of Regis University's Mile-High MFA program. One of his earliest heartbreaks occurred when he learned his best friend had lied when he promised hoverboards, like those in *Back to the Future Part II*, would be available to the public in the mid-90's. It's still the litmus test he uses to determine whether we've made it to the future he dreamt of during his childhood.

Find him online at www.gomezwrites.com or on Twitter at @golongria.

The Unlucky Few Who Must Not Cast

J. Tynan Burke

"Hi, my name's Dennis, and I'm magic—"

Dennis stopped before the last word. It didn't apply to him, and he resented the suggestion that it did. Unfortunately, nobody had told the other people in the basement of that run-down Victorian. They looked up from a half-circle of folding chairs, eager for him to finish the line. And finish it he would: doing so was part of the meeting, which he had to attend, by Guild order, that night and nine more times that month, as punishment for his recent magic 'abuse'. Dennis took a centering breath. The air was vaguely moldy.

"...and I'm magic-dependent."

"Hi, Dennis," the basement chorused, out of sync.

Over at the sign-in table, a woman made eye contact. Henrietta, she'd said her name was. Mid-forties, short purple hair, studded collar. Compared to her, Dennis felt decidedly unhip with his Muji khakis and backpack. She gave him a thumbs up; she knew it was his first meeting. Dennis's eye twitched. If magic hadn't been forbidden at MA meetings, he would've cracked open his emergency invisibility potion. Instead he sat back down on his creaky chair, and took a sip of the awful coffee he'd gotten from a dented urn at the snack table. Was it a little late for caffeine? Sure. But he'd need it. He'd been exhausted in the weeks since Phoebe had dumped him, and the meeting was bound to be boring. He planned to stay up late doing spell research anyway.

The man next to him—and it was mostly men, in that basement—stood up. He was dressed like a contractor and shedding the dust to prove it. "My name's Sam, and I'm magic-dependent."

"Hi, Sam," Dennis muttered into his flimsy paper cup.

After everybody had said hello, the facilitator introduced a birdlike woman, "with a reading from the Codex," MA's self-help bible. He passed her a laminated page; she held it in unsteady hands. "How MA Works," she recited. "We are the unlucky few who must not cast. For us, magic is little more than a way to cheat at life. Such a road leads only to destruction. Some end up in prison; some find their bodies wracked with cramps and seizures; some die. Some overindulge and empty themselves so completely, hungry spirits come to fill the void within. The stories we share attest to all of these; they also attest to how good things can become. If you like what you hear, we beg of you to abandon casting and follow our path. You stand at a turning point. You must be fearless in pursuit of abstinence…"

Dennis wanted to scoff. None of that had ever happened to him, but the Guild still thought he belonged with these freaks, just because he'd cast a little while drafting that commodities report. The rule forbidding actuaries from using magic at work was dumb. Who cared? His boss was never going to find out, and it wasn't like he'd acted on some addictive compulsion. The spell had just been an expedient way out of a jam. That was hardly magic dependence.

The woman finished reading and handed the page back to the facilitator, who stepped into the center of the semicircle of chairs. He scratched his careful beard and said he was pleased to welcome that night's speaker, who went by the name of Shisk. Dennis clapped politely as a hulking man came to shake the facilitator's hand. Shisk looked around at his audience. He flashed a smile and tugged down on the hem of his hand-knit sweater.

"My name's Shisk," the big man said, "and I'm magic-dependent." His voice was heavy, either slightly stoned or permanently so.

The room: "Hi, Shisk."

Shisk cocked a wave. The hand he used, his left, moved oddly. Maybe it was a trick of the light. "Hey. So. Who am I, and how did I get here? I can tell you how I got here easily enough: by being a dumbass, then being responsible instead. A few of you probably know what that's like."

Polite chuckles. Dennis rolled his eyes.

"To make the story a little longer. I grew up in northwest BC. My family is Tlingit. I was seventeen when I got my first taste of *x'aséikw*, and I was hooked. *X'aséikw*, that's Tlingit for—"

Aether, Dennis thought, using the Hermetic term. Shisk finished his sentence with the nondenominational version, *mana*. Not for the first time, Dennis marveled that it could be harnessed by such diverse traditions. The Guild's chaos magicians theorized that human mystics were like blind men trying to describe an elephant: touching on some fundamental truth but failing to see its whole.

"It happened while we were getting ready for my grandpa's memorial party, arranging his stuff for a display. Drums, tools, things from his early life as an *ixt*, a shaman. I'd never put much stock in it... until I picked up one of his old ceremonial masks. What a rush!" He smiled; it faded. "The Guild found out, like they do, and set me up with a master to study shamanism, or what's left of it..."

While Shisk babbled about his training, Dennis's thoughts drifted to his own awakening. It had been similar in spirit. He'd been a freshman in college, wearing too much black and recreationally reading *Magick in Theory and Practice*. Trying out one of Crowley's rituals had sounded fun, so he had. A small water elemental had appeared in its summoning circle and begun to meander. Dennis had dropped the book in shock; eventually he'd thought to pick it back up and dismiss the creature. Not twelve hours later he'd been contacted by the Guild. They'd sworn him to secrecy and set him up with a master in the anthropology department.

The parallel with Shisk's story was no coincidence. Scooping up the accidentally-awoken was one way the Guild kept magic *sub rosa*. Dennis was also familiar with another way: the Guild monitored its members closely and intervened whenever things threatened to get out of hand. By keeping the magic world self-governing, the theory went, the Guild could avoid telling anything to the actual government. The only problem was that the restrictions could be stupid; sometimes harmless actuaries had to attend boring meetings for people with no self-control.

Shisk went on about how casting had crept into his carpentry business, and eventually taken over his life. Dennis held in a yawn, half bored, half exhausted. How was listening to this guy supposed to help him with his 'problem'? He sipped his lousy coffee, and regretted it.

"Alright," Shisk said eventually. "So that's where I was at in life. I was casting first thing when I woke up and last thing before bed. I'd jones hard for a spell whenever I was in polite company. And I was chronically low on *x'aséikw*. My hands would tremble so bad I couldn't use a saw. My feet would cramp up and stay stuck that way; sometimes I couldn't even get my shoes off. Never did get a full-on seizure, thankfully, but..."

Further evidence that Dennis was not like these people. He'd had some tremors before—who hadn't?—but nothing like what had happened to Shisk. No, Dennis always stopped with a solid amount of *aether* in the tank. Using too much was unpleasant; being half-empty made him feel half-dead. More importantly, it was dangerous, and could make him all-the-way-dead. *Aether* wasn't just fuel for casting; it was also natural protection against spirits. A mage with too little risked possession.

Aether was found in all things, though Dennis wouldn't have been surprised if it were absent from his coffee. It flowed into a caster when they ate, drank, and breathed. Methods of recharging faster were complicated or unsavory. Dennis had never cast enough to need one. Shisk, it seemed, had never been meticulous or evil enough to use one.

"But I still wasn't happy," Shisk said. "Wasting my ancestors' gift on making canoes for lawyers wasn't cutting it. I ended up doing freelance hero stuff. You know: find something wrong in the spirit world, go fix it."

Dennis sighed and rubbed his temple. A sob story from a caster with a hero complex—how *novel*. Heroism never ended well —hadn't Shisk known?

Dennis knew, and his path to learning it had been short. Like most newcomers, he'd been ready to save the world after his awakening. The feeling had lasted about three months, until one evening when he and his master had summoned the wrong spirit. The monster had almost killed them; they had beaten it back, but spent days just cleaning the ichor off the walls, and they never had gotten it all out of the carpet. And for what? If you zoomed out, getting rid of one evil spirit was nothing more than a rounding error.

Shisk's ominous story made Dennis glad that he'd had this revelation when he had. His life would have been very different without it. For starters, he might have actually belonged at this meeting. *There but for the grace of The One...*

"One day I read that a few camping groups had gone missing in the Kitlope Conservancy. This is primeval rainforest, sacred to some, and full of *jeks*—spirits. The sort of place where a missing person can be more than just lost. A quick divination showed me the spot where they'd vanished. I grabbed my toolbelt and headed out.

"Around twilight, I got to the clearing I'd identified. I recognized a threshold on one side, between two tall cedars. A bloodless prickling in my fingers and toes reminded me how little *x'aséikw* I had, but I went through anyway. I was a badass monster-hunter, right?"

Entering the spirit world with low *aether* was even stupider than everything else Shisk had described. On this side of the barriers, monsters generally had to be invited; on that side, all bets were off. Dennis leaned forward, grimly fascinated by the direction of Shisk's story. It was like a good horror movie.

"A river burbled on the other side of the threshold. In front of the river... the *jek* had the shape of a man, except his mouth was too big for his skull, and his eyes moved independently. He was humming to himself, and bending a length of raw wood. Next to him was an unfinished canoe. Its naked ribs seemed like grasping fingers." Shisk illustrated this by making a claw with his left hand. Dennis again noticed something odd about it.

"I rested my hand on the handle of my grandpa's copper dagger, and asked the *jek* about the campers. The jek frowned, and then in a blur he was on me. I stumbled and cracked my head on a rock. Saw stars, heard ringing. He rushed to stand over me, one eye on me, one darting around the clearing. 'You've made a powerful enemy, *ixt*,' he hissed, with a voice like a blade scraping over bark."

Shisk's play-by-play of the fight was brutal. If this had actually been a horror movie, Dennis would have watched from between splayed fingers. Yes, he'd fought monsters before, but he hadn't *enjoyed* it. At least the brutality wasn't senseless—Shisk had been on a rescue mission. That counted for something.

"He wore me down until my hands were so bloody I couldn't even hold the dagger. With all that blood, I'd lost nearly all my *x'aséikw*, too, so I didn't dare cast. I'd never felt worse in my life. Heavy, like my heart was pumping sludge."

Shisk frowned deeply and grunted.

"The *jek* had me pinned against a tree. He was choking me with both hands. But I had one trick left, an old piece of Tlingit lore. I snapped a chunk of sap from that tree trunk and jammed it into my gasping mouth. I mouthed an incantation and grew as sturdy as a cedar. The pressure on my neck... stopped mattering.

"I put my palms on the *jek*'s tattered shirt and willed roots and branches to grow. They tore through him. His whole body shuddered. His hands fell from my neck as he went limp. I heaved in breath after ragged breath, and my throat burned. For a while I sat on the damp leaves and panted. When I finally stood up, it was too dark to search for the campers. They were probably long dead anyway. I hung my head, and my face burned with anger. After all I'd been through, I hadn't saved anybody. I decided to head home."

Dennis felt his body deflate. Shisk had risked his life for nothing. That wasn't how stories were supposed to go, and was far more upsetting than most horror movies. He felt faintly ill.

"When I got close to the threshold, something started probing me, trying to find a way in before I left. Probably the *jek* I'd just fought—killing the skin isn't always enough. I moved as fast as I could, but not fast enough. He—the *jek*, what remained of it—had one last go at me. I don't know how long I spent fighting him inside of myself. Too long. I managed to cram his presence down into my forearm, then my hand, then…"

Shisk held up his left hand and unsnapped what Dennis had assumed was a bracelet. He peeled it from his wrist and palm; his three least important fingers came off along with it. A prosthesis. He wiggled his remaining thumb and forefinger. Dennis's nausea grew; he averted his eyes. "I'll just say it was good I still had that dagger. I put the fingers in a warded Ziploc and hauled ass to the hospital.

"I spent the next few days getting stoned and pretending it had been a carpentry accident. Pretty soon there was a knock at my door. You guessed it: a representative from the Guild. I'd been sentenced to twenty MA meetings. They thought it would give me some perspective, make me less likely to release a dangerous spirit in the future. I was pissed, but in a weird way, I was relieved, too. I obviously didn't have things under control—I'd almost become that *jek*'s next skin. I wouldn't wish that on my worst enemy, so why was I living a life where it might happen to me?"

Shisk said that his path to enlightenment had come through working the steps at MA. Dennis happily sank back into annoyed boredom; Shisk's rock-bottom had been hard to hear about, but the pseudo-religious trappings of 'the program' were easy to scorn.

At length, the shaman concluded. "So yeah, that's my story: how things were, what happened, and how they are now. If I can make it, so can you. *Yan tután, aagáa yéi kgwatee*: have faith and it shall be so. Thank you." Shisk gave the slightest bow and efficiently refastened his prosthesis. After shaking the facilitator's hand, he sat down on a front-row chair. Everyone clapped. Dennis joined them, and not only to be polite: as sermons went, it had been a good one, with a triumphant ending, and a vivid low point that lingered in his mind.

The facilitator opened the room up. People spoke for a minute or two about their own lives. None held Dennis's attention; addict-talk was boring, and all their mistakes were stereotypical. One had tried to cast his way out of gambling debt; another had developed crippling anxiety from too much divination. Instead of thinking about these people's problems, which were not his, or Shisk's story, from which he was still recovering, Dennis focused on nursing his coffee. *How is it even possible for the coffee to be this bad?* he wondered. *It seems like it would take a lot of work. What did they use, fresh scrapings from the street?*

Eventually the facilitator asked them all to stand and link hands. Sam held Dennis's left hand in a callused grip. The man on his right had clammy skin. Dennis mumbled along with a prayer that he vaguely knew: *Grant me the serenity to accept the things I cannot change, the courage to change the things I can, and the wisdom to know the difference.* Then the attendees sat again while the leaders went over administrivia about the next meeting. They collected volunteers for set-up and teardown and refreshments, and Dennis's very first MA meeting was over.

The lights rose. The room filled with the rustling of jackets and the metal noises of latches and zippers. Sitting still in the flurry of bright activity, Dennis felt nailed to his chair, not because anybody was paying attention to him, but because somebody might. He didn't like talking to strangers in the best of circumstances; he definitely didn't wish to right now.

Part of him wanted to spring to his feet and dash to Henrietta, to leave as soon as possible, to get away from this dusty and depressing basement. This urge went away when he saw somebody do just that—somebody who was a twitching wreck. Bad company to keep. With hunched shoulders, he remained seated and checked his email, waiting for Henrietta to finish signing out the other mandated attendees.

Soon it was only him and mingling stragglers. He retrieved his backpack and hoodie from under his chair, then slipped them on. On his way to Henrietta, he slunk between groups discussing happy hour plans and passages from the Codex. Once at her formica table, he produced a folded paper from his backpack and smoothed it out in front of her. She tapped the back of her pen on the gridded form, which was empty except for the first half of the first row.

"What'd you think, first-timer?" she said, looking up at him, pen poised over the page.

"Ah…" Dennis flashed a terrified smile. "Not as bad as I thought it would be?"

She gave a single *ha*. "You know, we get that a lot. Makes me wonder what people expect."

"Er." He swallowed. "Better coffee?"

"I know, right? Jenny—she's on refreshments—she means well, but, yeah. Don't worry, I won't tell." She looked around the basement, then took a crumpled pack of Lucky Strikes from her leather jacket. "Hey, you smoke?"

Dennis's eyes flickered to her pen. She still hadn't written anything. "No. I should get heading home, anyway. The cat'll want dinner."

"Oh, what's her name?"

"*His* name is Oscar."

"Why don't you come show me pictures while I burn one." She glanced at the form. "Dennis."

Dennis gave a low, mirthless chuckle, even though this hostage situation wasn't funny. "You're trying to trick me."

Henrietta smirked. "Is it working? I like to talk to all the newbies. Come on. Five minutes. You'll thank me later." She put her pen into a canvas zipper bag, which she used to weigh down the page, then walked upstairs, waving at Dennis to follow.

Blinking furiously, Dennis stared at the receding woman. *What the hell?* He entertained filling out the form himself, but he didn't know how to fake her initials. Also, it wasn't like him to cut corners; that he'd done so at work recently was the exception that proved the rule. What was he so afraid of, anyway, that he couldn't bear a five-minute chat? He groaned at himself, then hurried over the scuffed hardwood to catch her.

Thanks to the cloud cover, the night was dark and warm, even though a half-rain spat from the sky. Henrietta stopped at a tree on the front lawn. She leaned against the trunk and plucked a cigarette from the pack. She lit it with a Zippo, and the air filled with the reek of naphtha and unfiltered tobacco. Dennis scrunched his nose.

Henrietta pointed the business end of her cigarette at him. "Let me guess. You don't think you belong here."

Dennis opened, closed, opened his mouth. Apparently she didn't like to just talk to newbies, she also enjoyed haranguing them. "Is it that obvious?"

"There's a reason the Guild gives you guys sign-in sheets. Admitting you have a problem is a tough step." She blew out smoke. "Pun intended."

"Yeah." Not planning to take this first step himself, Dennis left it at that. Henrietta smoked; the silence grew heavy and awkward. He had to say something—but what? He supposed he might as well say what was on his mind. "You know, if I'm being honest... I'm not sure casting *is* my problem. I've never had the cramps or gotten possessed or anything."

To his surprise, Henrietta shrugged. The snaps on her epaulets briefly reflected a nearby sodium street light. "Hey, maybe it isn't. Not everybody here's an addict. For some people, like, casting makes their real problems worse. The community here helps them maintain their abstinence."

Dennis half-muttered, "Sort of seems like we didn't hear from any of them."

"Eh. They're not that vocal. Some of them are as embarrassed as you seem to be."

Dennis felt himself blush. Embarrassed, yes; *one of them*, no. "But I don't even have... other problems. Nothing casting makes worse, I mean."

"Hm." Henrietta looked him over, then leaned in. The smoky smell intensified. "Shisk left something out of his story, you know. A year before his life went to hell, he did a first stint in MA. Got sent here for vigilantism; some jackass was robbing houses in his neighborhood, and the cops didn't care, so he used a charm to get the guy to confess on tape.

"We all thought he had a hero complex, and a shitty attitude, too. Nothing was ever his fault. Thought he knew better than everybody else. Could've saved himself a lot of trouble if he'd stuck with the program long enough to get over himself." She rested her back against the tree again and took a leisurely drag. "What I'm trying to say is, the real problems aren't always obvious at first."

"Why would he leave that out?"

"I dunno, vanity? Pretty screwed up, right? I mean, what's the point of speaking if you aren't going to be honest."

"Yeah."

Dennis knew she was trying to manipulate him, but that didn't blunt his surprise. Shisk had had an *early warning* about this? He could have kept those fingers, if he'd only gotten over himself? A vision of the shaman's self-mutilation came to mind. Dennis's stomach ache returned.

Did he have more in common with Shisk than he'd thought? They'd both had hero complexes, however short-lived Dennis's might have been. And they'd both landed in MA because of penny-ante rule violations. It wasn't a perfect parallel, but it didn't have to be to make him anxious. Could his situation escalate like the shaman's had? What sort of violent horrors might be in his own future? Even the less tragic options weren't great; he might become an emotional cripple like the divination addict they'd heard from.

But no, no, of course he wasn't the same as these people. He and Shisk had both broken rules, but the rule Shisk had broken had made sense; Dennis had broken a stupid one. An actuary casting at work was like a driver pumping their own gas down in Oregon. Sure, it was a violation, but it didn't mean they needed

Gas Pumpers Anonymous meetings. Just like Dennis didn't need *this* meeting. He should have been at home, having dinner with Oscar. Instead he'd probably have to clean up some passive-aggressive cat vomit. He checked Henrietta's progress on her cigarette. Still half remaining. He grunted.

She held up a palm. "Alright, alright. You heard me out. Thanks. I'll finish quick. How about you tell me how you ended up here, and we can get you on the road."

Dennis sipped his coffee and grimaced. Other than his chat with the Guild rep, he hadn't talked about this with anybody. But if it would help get him home—fine. "I got caught casting at work. A divination. I'm an actuary, so I'm monitored. And here I am." He laughed bitterly. "It's a stupid rule. So I know what next quarter's PNW rainfall will be, so what?"

Henrietta's eyebrows rose. "That's actually kind of a big screw up. You might not want to hear this, but the Guild has those rules for a—"

"I *know* why we have those rules. I just think it's dumb. It's not like I was a cop setting up a pre-crime division. We're talking about lumber futures here."

She looked at him like he'd told her he had not one cat, but fifteen. "Christ, man. If every jerk-off who could read the *I Ching* felt the same way, the foundations of modern finance would crumble. Doesn't sound too bad to me, but I get why others feel different. Even if—"

"Oh come on, nobody cares about—"

"Let me finish." She paused to glare at him, then shook her head. "*Even if* this rule is totally bogus, you knew it was a rule, you knew you were monitored, you did it anyway. What gives? You don't seem like the type to break rules just because you don't like them." She waved a hand vaguely, perhaps indicating his subdued head-to-toe Muji.

"Not every rule is the same!" He pointed at her leather coat, her torn jeans. "You look like you've probably bought drugs before. Does that *mean* anything? No!"

"Maybe you need to talk to Shisk."

"Maybe I need to go home." He folded his arms.

She rolled her eyes. "Easy there, cowboy. God, listen to yourself."

The cigarette's cherry glowed between them as she took a drag. Dennis watched her face brighten and fade. She looked scared. No: worried. For him. He couldn't remember the last time somebody had looked at him that way. It gave him pause.

Listen to yourself. He took a deep breath and slowly released it while he replayed the conversation. His arms fell to his sides as he realized that Henrietta had been right to call him out. He'd been radiating anger and entitlement. He'd sounded like an excuse-making know-it-all, just like Shisk had been at his first meeting. He'd sounded, to borrow a phrase from that earlier recitation, like somebody who used magic to cheat at life. Even his body language had been juvenile and petty. But he wasn't that person—or he never used to be. If he was now, well, that was unacceptable.

"I'm sorry. Let me try again. I hadn't planned to cast that morning. I just... did. I was tired, on an unrealistic deadline... it was an easy out." He sighed; more excuses. His hands fell to his sides. "I was so exhausted. Still am. I haven't been sleeping well lately."

"What's keeping you up?"

"I'll stay up late casting some nights. I know how it sounds, but it's not like that." Henrietta raised a skeptical eyebrow. Dennis scrunched his nose again, but it was from self-consciousness, not the smoke. "I've just been sort of angry. I got—*dumped* isn't even the right word..."

The rain moved from spitting to drizzling. After the first drops struck his forehead, he put his hood up. "I'd been seeing this woman, Phoebe. Pretty casually. She got serious with somebody else, and that was that. I'm sort of mad, but not at her or anything. It just sucks. What do other guys have that I don't, you know? I work hard, I make jokes, I—" He laughed at himself, sunk his hands deep into his hoodie pockets. "I have a cute cat. I dunno. Casting is something I can do that other guys can't. So lately, a lot of nights, I've stayed up late working on a spell. Not like I'll ever be able to show it to a date. Which is silly, since it's just a modified will-o'-wisp summoning, optimized to look nice in a city... I probably sound like a loser."

He shook his head. He barely recognized himself right now. The real Dennis was neither pitiable nor an arrogant prick. Maybe he really did have some things to work out. The cost of not doing so could apparently be dire; he made a mental note to check if his insurance covered therapy. In the meantime, it was possible there were worse places to be than these meetings.

Henrietta smiled kindly. "Sounds pretty, actually." A drop of rain struck the nub of her cigarette, and hissed. She frowned at it, then flicked the remnants into the street. "Let's head back in and we'll get that form signed."

"Okay. Thanks."

He followed her into the old house, into the dingy basement, to the formica table, where his form still rested under her bag of pens. Seeing the mostly-empty sheet of paper reminded him that he'd have to spend many more hours in this musty room, sitting on a folding chair that had long since lost its padding, listening to lectures.

Henrietta crouched at the table. Her knees popped; Dennis winced. She selected a pen from her bag. After scribbling something on his form, she handed it to him. "There ya go. See you Wednesday?"

"Is that the next one? Yeah, I guess." He slipped his form into a document sleeve in his backpack. A few drops of coffee spilled from his carelessly-held cup. "Ah! Crap."

"Careful now, you don't want to waste your favorite drink."

"Ha." There really was no excuse for how bad it was. *Nobody deserves coffee like this*, he thought. *The meetings would be so much easier if we had the right refreshments. Maybe we will next time. Er, not 'we', like I'm a member, but I'm, you know, in the room, and... who am I kidding.*

"Hey," he said, "before I go. Snacks and stuff are handled by volunteers, right? What if I offered to bring... you know... *good* coffee? Wouldn't be much trouble."

Henrietta straightened and looked him over with a curious smirk. "Didn't expect *that*. You'll have to run it by Jenny. I think she's still here. Let's check the kitchen. C'mon."

A few minutes later, Dennis stepped out into the rain and hurried to his car. He opened the door to his Civic and sat on the gray cloth seat. *All Things Considered* came on when he turned the key; Audie Cornish began a story about a blight affecting California strawberries. Dennis pulled away from the curb, then mashed the volume button, killing the sound. He had a lot to think about. That word, *we*, was as good a place to start as any.

See J. Tynan Burke's story "The Unlucky Few Who Must Not Cast" online at Metaphorosis.
If you liked it, leave a comment. Authors love that!
Remember to subscribe to our e-mail updates so you'll know when new stories are posted.

About the story

Addiction treatment focuses on sin—we have programs for alcohol, drugs, sex, overeating, gambling, and so forth. Overindulging in virtuous behavior, by contrast, is called heroism. But that can have negative outcomes, too, especially in speculative fiction—how many times have Marvel heroes wrecked Manhattan, to say nothing of their own bodies? Should people like that have a program, too?

These questions first came to me a few years ago and resulted in two ideas: an accountant who is also a hobbyist wizard, and a twelve-step meeting for magic addicts. I jotted down a line and moved on: "Hi, my name's Dennis, and I'm a wizard."

This year, I finally got around to writing the second sentence, plus a few more after that. I really enjoyed exploring what such a program might look like. What sort of fallen heroes would you meet? And what would the experience be like for somebody who had been ordered to attend? Giving up a vice can be hard enough—what's it like when you're told to give up a virtue? To stop doing the one thing that makes you special?

This being a short story, I didn't have room to explore all the facets of this, but that's okay. I have bigger plans for Dennis, and so does fate.

A question for the author

Q: Duckbilled platypus – result of divine distraction, or alternate universe crossover?

A: The Aboriginal Australians have several theories on the origin of this noble monotreme. Generally, these involve a duck mating with a water-rat. This is true enough, but it leaves out that these creatures were biologically compatible only because the duck in question was from a universe where birds are mammals. The crossover event is believed to have coincided with the formation of the Chicxulub crater. It is unknown what else, if anything, crossed alongside.

About the author

J. Tynan Burke is the Assistant Editor for Metaphorosis.

J. Tynan Burke is a software engineer and writer. He lives in New York City with his husband and their enormous cat, Samwise. When he isn't typing, he plays tabletop RPGs and streams murder mysteries. His dream is to one day be an old man futzing around in the garden. You can find his stories in *Metaphorosis, Swords and Sorcery Magazine*, and various anthologies.

www.tynanburke.com, @tynanpants

The Great Contradiction

Jordan Chase-Young

Truths can be hard to accept. Long ago, few scholars believed the world was infinite. They were sure its plane had an edge, even as explorers reported continents marching without end in all directions. The world's infinitude made humankind feel insignificant—until we accepted it.

I once felt I was wiser than the ancients. Felt I could embrace any truth. But that has changed. After seeing what I have seen in the black Void above our sky, where the suns make their migrations, I know better.

I learned my lesson the year a fellow scholar asked me to help his research. Normally I would have declined. My work at the Academy of Natural Philosophy in Suyu-Paca, where I've spent most of my life, makes long absences difficult. But I had much respect for the man who sought my insight. And his offer was so generous—three silver links per day of absence—that refusal seemed absurd. Along with his letter, he sent a box of twenty silver links to prove the offer's sincerity: ten for me, ten for my department's seneschal so she might permit my leave.

"How long do you expect to be gone?" The seneschal was a thin woman slowly being digested by paperwork. She sat stiff and stark-lit in the dusty glare of her office window. "You have prentices in need of guidance, lectures I'll have to fill…"

"No more than three months, including travel." I fought the desperation in my tone, knowing she had every right to reject my leave. "But this is Wallaq Squechalwalaq, the finest scientist in the Ecumene. I doubt I'll ever have a greater opportunity to distinguish myself."

"That's all very nice, Atapua, but it's the Academy you're obliged to distinguish. You serve the Academy foremost, do you not?"

"Of course, Madam Seneschal."

"That is good." She gave me a slow look before signing my writ of leave. "I anticipate your return, knowing you'll have much to show for it."

I gave a bow of gratitude. "I won't disappoint you."

"No," she agreed. "Not if you want your contract renewed."

The day before setting out, I traded two of my new silver links for a sack of bronze ones and gave these to the poor languishing in the streets of Suyu-Paca. Another two I spent on books. Three I sent to my beloved sister, who has been caring for my mother on my birth-continent since my father died. I've long been afflicted by the delusion that sending one's family money can soothe one's guilt for neglecting it.

With the last three links, I rented the healthiest cloudstrider I could find to fly me across the Ecumene. She was a lean beast with broad wings and a long graceful trunk. I had her tusks cleaned, but I washed her brown fur myself. They say grooming cloudstriders is the best way to bond with them.

The trip took a month. I followed one of the Imperial routes, flying twelve hours a day and sleeping each night in a waytown. Miles up, each continent I passed looked as artificial as sculpture. The cities shrank the farther I flew from the core of the Ecumene, eventually becoming sparse dots.

It was hard not to be overwhelmed by the world's infinitude, knowing the Ecumene's sixteen settled continents—not to mention the hundreds of mapped but unsettled ones beyond them—comprised little more than a pebble on a floor without end. If I'd known what lay beyond that pebble, as I do now, I might have been more reluctant to travel.

But I was excited then. And desperate to show the Academy it had chosen wisely in letting me go.

When I arrived, landing a short distance from the tiny windflogged town of Far Eye, Wallaq greeted me not as the highborn I knew him to be, but as a humble scholar, lifting his pointed brown hat for a bow.

"Welcome, Atapua." His deep voice contradicted his small, slim frame. Handsome, with dark blue skin and silver spectacles, he looked as much younger than my thirty-eight as I looked older, though we were the same age almost to the day.

"Well met, Suz Squechalwalaq." I unstrapped my flying mask and gave a bow of my own.

"Wallaq," he corrected gently. "No point in first names if we don't use them."

I nodded, settling into a more casual mode. "I hope it's not untoward to admit I would have taken your offer for a much smaller sum. My admiration for your work—"

"Yes, yes, likewise." He smiled an easy smile. "We can flatter each other once your steed is stabled and we have hot food in front of us. I've toiled all day and I'm starved."

"Dinner sounds lovely," I said.

I had only a vague idea why he'd summoned me to the remotest town in the remotest continent of the Ecumene. His letter had spoken of *a project to plumb the mysteries of the world* that would require an *interplay of our various strains of expertise in logic and science*. All very cryptic.

But the town looked more suited to shellfishing than science. A stark foil to the warm, teeming city of Suyu-Paca, Far Eye sat on a chilly promontory overlooking a sea. The settlement consisted of nothing more than a dozen rickety jacals sulking beside Wallaq's stone manse. The whole populace served him, I assumed, it being too far from others to have much trade.

As we neared the manse, I caught a muffled din from one of its turret windows, a mix of gruff talk and harsh clanging like in a blacksmith's forge.

"What are you building in there, I wonder?" I asked, my curiosity briefly overcoming my manners.

He gave a casual shrug, his face betraying the tiniest flash of irritation. "Nothing you need to worry about just now."

This only stoked my curiosity, but I had enough sense not to probe.

Dinner was sublime, a large brown vegetable that locals call a forest crab. I cracked its gravied casing with small metal jaws to reach the flesh beneath, relishing each bite as Wallaq's musician, a slender Suyunen woman, played a flute by the crackling hearth.

The manse was huge but not cavernous, thanks to its compact rooms. Only the dining room felt spacious. Large windows looked onto a churning sea beneath a cloudy sky. Hundreds of books filled the walls. Numerous maps lay open on twin fogwood tables. After a sip of wine, I hazarded a guess that most of Wallaq's rooms went to waste, since one could happily spend all their time in this one.

"Correct," he said with a laugh, dismantling his meal with graceful precision. "It's all a bit much for a hermit, I'll grant. But in my defense, I plan to turn this place into an academy someday. When that time comes I'll need every room."

I raised my brow. "An academy? *Here?*"

He shrugged. "Life at the edge of civilization concentrates the mind. And once this continent is well-populated, in a few hundred years or so, this building will be the oldest around. It is good to leave one's mark in stone as well as paper, I feel."

"I suppose," I said, sponging up gravy with a bit of forest crab. I never quite understood folk who cultivated their legacies with such obsessiveness, but perhaps that was just a certain parochialism stemming from my low birth.

"You must be curious why I brought you here," he said with an air of significance.

"Not just food and banter, I trust."

"Alas."

"To be perfectly honest, Suz Sque—er, Wallaq—whatever riddles of nature you think a journeyman scholar like myself can unravel, I have failed to guess."

He pointed his crab-jaws meaningfully at me, staring over his spectacles. "Journeyman in station, perhaps, but not intellect. There, you are my equal."

I was a bit startled by this. He didn't really believe that, surely…?

"The riddle I have in store for us," he went on, "is the greatest of all riddles. The very empress of logical conundrums. Can you guess what it is?"

I shook my head, at a loss.

"I bet you can if you think on it," he said. "But that won't be necessary. Tonight is for food and sleep. Only that. I want you rested for the work ahead."

"No need to convince me," I said.

Shattered from travel, I was eager to engage his ideas—but even more eager for rest. Now that I knew he fancied me his equal —an eccentric delusion, I felt, but a flattering one—I wanted to show him only my sharpest edge.

"Play us Pemac's Fourth Jaunt, in honor of our guest," Wallaq called to the musician, and she slid into the playful piece with exuberance.

Next morning, I met Wallaq at the edge of town. We strolled into the pine forest that cowled a third of the continent, I with a walking stick tucked underarm and he with his small, jeweled hands clasped behind himself.

After a brief interrogation to ensure my sleep and breakfast had been up to his standards, he started in.

"How long did you live on Maipo, may I ask?"

The question took me a little off-guard. Though my subtly striped pink skin marks me as a tribesman of that continent, most folk assume from my Imperial dress and manner that I'm diaspora-born.

"Until fifteen," I said, "when I began to prentice at the Academy. How did you guess?"

He drew a pipe from his satchel and placed a small bit of moss in it. "One can always spot a native Maiponen from the pride they carry with them, thick as perfume." He lit the pipe and puffed it. "I ask because I once spent several months on your birth-continent, studying its flora. Don't these pines remind you of Maipo's?"

I regarded the thick, ribbed trunks and yellowish needles. "Distant relations, maybe."

He nodded thoughtfully. "It intrigues me."

"Why is that?"

"Trees move between continents with an ease animals cannot match. Even cloudstriders, blessed with flight, spread to just four continents before we tamed them. Pines thrive on far more."

I pushed away a low branch with my walking stick. "Seeds are simple vessels. They can survive on the open sea for many days."

"Yes," he said eagerly. "Animals are *not* simple. They need stable environments. Stable food, competitors, climates. Their complexity makes them fragile." He pushed up his spectacles. "Which makes me wonder, of course, about civilizations."

"Are they robust like trees," I guessed, "or fragile like animals?"

"Precisely." He gave a heavy sigh, as if confronting a notion he would rather not. "We seem to be alone in this vast world. Where are all the other civilizations? Did they reach a limit to their growth that no technology can surmount?"

I smiled. So this was the riddle he had in mind: the Great Contradiction. I should have guessed. I knew from my reading that the problem had vexed him for some time.

The question behind the Great Contradiction is simple: *Given the world's vastness, why has no other sapient race been found?*

First, some background. Countless species have been discovered in the sixteen settled continents and in the seas between them. Dozens of those species show keen intelligence. Yet none wield tools or use language as humans do. On the strength of our cleverness, humankind filled its cradle-continent of Suyu in one millennium. From there it spread to two more and filled those in the same span. From there to six others, filling those likewise. And so on. The pattern is clear. From civilization's birth, we have grown exponentially. At current rates, we will fill several hundred continents in a few more millennia. In another few, many thousand.

The riddle arises when one considers that our world, according to geologists, is several million years old. Consider how far a species such as ours could spread in that time. Theirs would be an Ecumene of staggering immensity. Yet we have seen no such thing. Why not? Are civilizations so rare, or do they collapse after a time, done in by wars or plagues or something else?

Ten scholars will give eleven explanations for the Great Contradiction, but Wallaq, I knew, had never found one satisfactory.

"Maybe civilizations are simply that rare," I speculated.

"How rare can they be if they grow exponentially?" he asked. "You've read Suz Huanya Veriyal's treatise on the fate of the world, I assume."

"She thinks the suns will gutter in ten billion years, stranding us in eternal night."

"Many agree with her estimates, including me."

"Her calculations are compelling," I admitted, "however much the thought of a finite future saddens me."

"If she is right, ten billion years await. Plenty of time to thrive. And yet, if our world is millions of years old, as also seems true, there is something deeply strange and suspicious about the timing of our race's emergence."

It took me a second to grasp where he was headed. When I did, I felt a small swell of pride at figuring it out.

"If the emergence of civilization is randomly spaced in time," I said, brushing pine needles from my poncho, "any one civilization should expect to be born near the middle of the world's lifespan."

"Yes." His delight that I could keep pace was palpable. "A straightforward application of Chezaqual's Rule of Banality: *Observers should assume they are not special.* An emergence as early as ours is wildly unlikely."

"Maybe ours is the first," I suggested.

"Or the pessimists are right," he said. "Civilizations reliably destroy themselves."

"A pleasant thought for a pleasant walk."

"I have others."

We returned to Far Eye at twilight. Though my mind was drained and we had made no progress on our subject, I was relaxed and content knowing I'd made a good impression.

"It's quite pleasant," he said, "having someone to discuss these things with. Most folk here, bless their hearts, don't have much taste for high theory."

"They're not deranged, you mean."

He nodded solemnly.

Approaching his manse, I heard that odd clangor from the turret again, but I was too spent to think much of it.

In the dining room, he showed me his collection of maps. These replenished my energy, as beautiful things do. Maps of cities and provinces, seas and continents. Maps of the entire Ecumene, painted and printed and sketched. Even a few crude efforts at charting the lands beyond. Though the atmosphere blurs the Ecumene's margins, even for those who dare skirt the Void's Edge for the highest view, explorers fill the gaps by ranging far and sharing their sketches in the Cartographer's Quarter of Suyu-Paca. Like many restless provincials, I once had ambitions of doing such work, but quickly abandoned them when I considered the merits of living past thirty.

"Have you ever wondered whether it's possible to fly above the Void's Edge?" he asked. He was stoking the hearth as I admired a delicate print of *Heaven's Glory*, one of the oldest maps known.

For a moment I thought I'd misheard. Everyone knew such a feat could not be done. The Void above our world is airless and shatteringly cold. An infinite vacuum where the world's gravitational hold on its atmosphere loses out to the collective gravity of the suns. He knew flight was impossible in vacuum. Was he testing me?

"Folk have tried," I said. "And paid the price."

He held his hands to the fire. "Maybe they went about it wrong. Imagine if we could reach that abyss above the clouds. Reach it and gaze on the world as the suns do. What would we see? Other civilizations? Things unguessably strange?"

"Well," I said, my tone dipping into gentle mockery, "if you find a cloudstrider that can fly through the Void, you should go up and find out."

He chuckled.

That night, after a bowl of salty soup and a warm slice of butterbread, I lay awake, steeped in thoughts of flying through the

Void as the suns do, millions of miles up. I imagined the world as an endless floor spangled in continents of every hue. I imagined the dark flecks of cities swelling into splotches, swelling and slowly merging into one vast metropolis.

Was this how the Ecumene would look in a million years, I wondered, an insatiable lichen of steel and stone? It seemed inevitable. The thought of such dense, hungry life made me shiver, even as it filled me with a certain grim wonder.

The days passed pleasantly. Sometimes we talked in the dining room, other times in the forest or along the coast. We circled the same ideas, hunting for new insights into the Great Contradiction. A small part of me worried that Wallaq would send me home in disappointment, leaving me nothing to show the Academy. But he was optimistic and seemed indifferent to the lack of progress. He was used to it, he said.

But I was getting itchy. I read all I could from his library, nodding off each night with a book on my chest.

Ten days in, my efforts proved worthwhile. I found a slim, unassuming volume by the scholar Suz Icholaya Inuya, whose name I knew dimly. It was a commentary on the works of the ancient scholar Reva, who made many notable predictions about the fate of civilization based on his study of history. In her book Inuya argued that such predictions were warped by the predictor's context, a bias she called Observer Blindness. A predictor is unusual, the bias said, because their existence depends upon historical accidents they cannot know. The future will not resemble the past should those accidents cease to shape events.

I bridled. If she was right, then how was any prediction possible? Her reasoning held a fatalism that threatened to unravel all efforts to solve the Great Contradiction. Yet it had merit. I granted that.

After pondering her work a bit longer, I stumbled upon an idea so interesting I almost sprang a muscle rushing to my desk. I wrote furiously before the thought could fade.

The idea was this. Suppose some span after the world's beginning, say ten million years, civilizations merge to engulf the world. Afterward, no room will remain for new civilizations to form. All of nature will have been used up. Thus anyone pondering the Great Contradiction, like myself, must inhabit that slice of cosmic history before such a phase-change has occurred.

This was the solution to the Great Contradiction.

My heart raced. The implications overwhelmed me. With some statistical juggling, my insight let me calculate not just when humankind was likely to meet other civilizations but, through parallel reasoning, how far away they should be.

Carried away by my excitement, I felt an urge to share my insight immediately. I put on my slippers and hurried to Wallaq's room, wending through a labyrinth of torchlit corridors, my head humming with adrenaline.

En route, I heard an odd, metallic tapping that seemed to come from a nearby stairwell; I assumed it was the sea wind rattling something outside the manse and went on.

Reaching Wallaq's chamber, I was disappointed to see no candlelight below his door. I had a thought to wake him. Surely he'd forgive me under the circumstances. But common sense restrained me. I would tell him tomorrow, I decided, and headed back to my room.

I paused at the stairwell, puzzled by that strange tapping. On a lark, I followed the sound to a higher level, realizing it was the din from the turret I'd been hearing. The building's thick walls had kept the noise from reaching my chamber.

As I neared the source, a shut room at the end of a corridor, I grew amazed that any stone could muffle such a racket. And more amazed that anyone would be tinkering at this hour.

Four or five voices wove through the clanging. They spoke Imperial Suyunen, so I was able to parse the few words I caught. It seemed the builders were making a machine, or several machines, but I struggled to tease out much more than that. One builder complained of a deadline; another reminded him how much they were being paid. A third mentioned the Void.

My pulse rose. What did their work have to do with the Void? Did the deadline have to do with me? Did Wallaq want the project done before I went home?

I would have listened longer, but one of the builders mentioned turning in for the night. That was my cue to return to my room.

I lay in bed for hours, pondering Wallaq's mysterious project even more than my discovery. Piecing together all I'd heard, I began to suspect what he was building.

We broke fast near a tide pool several miles up the coast. I wanted to discuss my thoughts right away, but Wallaq insisted on eating first.

We munched sour seedpods while watching the wildlife, sleek gray animals with otter bodies and cuttlefish heads. They were foraging dark strands of kelp that had tangled on the rocks. The air was cool and salty.

I was nervous. What if he found my ideas absurd? What if they were? I needed something to take back to the Academy, something to impress the seneschal. Neglecting to renew my contract had been no idle threat.

But I was getting ahead of myself. I took a breath to still my nerves.

When we finished eating, I proposed my explanation for the Great Contradiction.

Wallaq puffed his pipe in silence. My nervousness grew as the silence stretched. I wrung my hands, waiting for him to tear apart my theory. Waiting for him to realize I wasn't his equal, I was a fraud and he'd been a fool to bring me here and—

"They build them clever on Maipo," he said, nodding. "I think you may have solved it."

Sighing inwardly, I veiled my pride with calm detachment. "Writing a treatise will take time. Weeks, at least. Then there is the Academy's process of review, which my theory may not survive."

"If it is correct, we will know soon enough."

"What do you mean?"

"What I mean," he said, "is we will fly as high as needed to search those distances likely to harbor other civilizations. Thanks to your calculations of how far away they should be, we have a notion of how high we must go."

My hunch was right. "You're building a device to leave the atmosphere."

"*Devices*," he said proudly, appearing to enjoy the emotions on my face. "Shall I show you?"

"God's mercy, yes."

The first thing he showed me resembled a suit of armor with a barrel fixed to the back. Twin tubes ran from the barrel to a glass-visored helm. The builders massed at the edge of the workshop watched with prideful protectiveness while I studied their work. The craftsmanship of the steel surpassed anything I'd seen in my life.

"The armor's insulated against cold," Wallaq said, "and retains air spectacularly well. The air is stored in that barrel."

"Compressed?"

"Yes. Four and a quarter-hour's worth. One tube brings air into the helm. Another draws carbon dioxide into a chamber at the barrel's base, where a sieve of minerals traps it."

"Ingenious."

He showed the second object, a bulky canvas-and-steel harness containing a parachute and joined by ropes to several winches. He pulled a cord to make the parachute retract.

"These ropes tether the voidfarer—my term—to four attendants' cloudstriders. Once you're done surveying, the attendants winch you back into the atmosphere, where you then release your parachute for easy wrangling."

"How does one enter the Void to begin with? The air is too thin at the Edge for cloudstriders to near it."

"That's the best part."

He showed the last device, a cross between a saddle and a catapult. It too was jellyfished with ropes and winches.

"It wasn't easy, calibrating the force needed to fling one past the Edge without breaking the tethers." He twisted one of the saddle-catapult's knobs to tense the device, then pulled a lever. The catapult portion sprang upright, making the table shudder. "As you might expect, a fair number of wooden dummies are hurtling through the Void as we speak."

I shook my head in awe. "How long have you worked on all this?"

"For fifteen years, I've tested things of this kind, but only the past three have borne fruit. In a few days, the work will be done. Thanks to you, we know how high the voidfarer must rise and thus how long the tethers should be. I'll be making the inaugural journey myself."

I was startled. "If I'd known that was your plan—"

"The pressure would have hurt your concentration," he said, and he was right.

"Can't you send someone else? Someone whose death, God forbid, would not be so...?"

Tragic? Disastrous? Words failed me. There is a certain callousness in assuming anyone's death could be less terrible than anyone else's, and an extra callousness in suggesting he put another soul at risk in his stead. Yet I could not help myself, knowing what the Ecumene would lose if he perished.

He shook his head. "I cannot. I could not live with others dying for my vanity. Less altruistically, I wish to be remembered as the first soul to reach the Void. After all my struggle, I cannot let another claim that legacy."

"Ah." *Legacy. Of course.*

"Naturally," he said, waving his hand, "you will be free to make a survey of the Void as well. It is only fair."

The thought chilled me. I was intensely curious about the Void, like any scholar. But I was also a bit of a coward. I did not like to put myself in danger when I did not have to.

Disappointment came into his eyes at my hesitation, subtle but sharp enough to sting my pride. "My devices have been tested exhaustively. I assure you, they're quite safe. Are you not eager to see your ideas vindicated?"

"Yes," I said with a nervous swallow. "Of course."

He smiled and clapped my shoulder. "Good."

The evening he returned from his survey, I was deep in my treatise, my head heavy with numbers and hands smudged with ink. The sound of cloudstriders through my open window tore me from my work. I put on my boots and hurried out of the manse.

Wallaq removed his helm. His face was flushed. His eyes looked far away.

"Wine first," he said.

I did not argue.

We drank in the dining room. A servant brought tubers diced over black moss and drizzled in oil. He touched none of it. Just gazed at the darkening sea, hearthlight playing over his spectacles like an errant thought.

I felt him struggling with emotions and did not speak for some time. Finally I could not help myself. "What did you see?"

"I don't think you'll believe it," he said. "I did not, at first."

"Tell me."

He spread his small hands on the table like an augur laying out bones.

"Truthfully, I'm not sure. Only that they must be the work of a sapient race."

"*They?*"

"I will tell you. But you must promise something." His tone went low and his gaze turned grave and steady. "You must promise to believe that what I saw is what I saw, believe I am telling you the truth as I perceived it. Do you promise?"

"I promise," I said, forcing calm into my tone even as my heart banged my ribs in anticipation.

He gave a nod and looked down at his hands. "I saw tendrils."

"What?"

"Do not speak until I'm finished." I shut my mouth. "I saw tendrils, on the horizon. Black tendrils that have captured a sun."

He paused as if summoning the memory took physical effort. I learned forward slightly, the hair on my neck standing straight.

"*Digested* may be more apt," he went on. "They rise hundreds of miles above the atmosphere, these tendrils, their contours just visible in their captured sun's red light. The land at their base is paved in darkness. A great darkness that throbs with strange lightning."

He kept looking down as he spoke, as if afraid to find disbelief on my face.

"That is what I saw," he said. "Whatever race built them must hold unimaginable power. But what frightens me most is their—strangeness. They seem nothing like us, Atapua. Their works look so sterile, so cold."

At last he stared at me again, and his expression was such that I knew—simply knew—he was telling the truth.

A dozen emotions warred in me. There was joy in my vindication. Feelings of awe and wonder. There was curiosity, confusion. Most of all, dread. A dark ashplume of dread that settled over my soul in slow waves.

The scholar in me had expected this news, or something like it. The rest, the human part, had not. Had never fully absorbed the implications of my theory.

"These—tendrils." My voice was brittle at the edges. "How far away?"

"Millions of miles, at least."

"What else did you see?"

"The light of the captured sun blocks much of the horizon. I did spy other things—a mountain that pierces the atmosphere, for instance—but nothing so clearly artificial as these—these sun-eaters. Even at that height, one can only see so much."

It is rare to hear a thing which you know will change humankind forever. This was such. I considered it carefully.

The first thing that came to mind, small and selfish though it may seem, was that my contract at the Academy would never lapse now that I was tied to the most important discovery in the Ecumene's history. I would be raised to masterhood overnight, no doubt, and would never want again for respect or money. A delicious thought.

My next thought was less so. When the populace learned what Wallaq and I had discovered, how would they react? He and I were jaded scholars, not easily flustered, yet this discovery put fear in both of us. Surely ordinary folk would fare worse. Much worse.

Along with their peace of mind would go a certain innocent confidence in the rightness of their beliefs. A hundred gods would be cast down. The very gearwheels of human morale might shriek to a halt.

For the first time in my life, the fate of humankind no longer felt abstract. It felt personal.

"Do you still wish to go up there?" he asked.

I nodded. "I must see the truth, however much I fear it."

The air-suit was warm and heavy. The tube filtering my breath tasted like salty leather. The visor bent sunlight strangely, spraying brief rainbows. Too cumbersome to carry unaided, my telescope was joined by several articulated rods to my breastplate.

The saddle-catapult creaked each time my cloudstrider beat her wings, creaked and shuddered as she pushed higher into the heavens. The ropes tying my saddle-catapult to my four attendants —who flew in a wide, ragged ring around me—began to tauten as they cranked their winches.

I'd never flown as high as I was now, perhaps fifteen miles above land. The clouds had thinned to milky threads. The nearest sun, a glut of golden flame now migrating over the continent of Yaro thousands of miles to my left, outshone by several orders of magnitude the next-nearest, whose path lay countless miles outside the Ecumene.

By now my terror had faded to resignation. If I was to die, at least I would die in service to the truth.

But I was *not* going to die. Wallaq had survived. I would survive as well.

Up I climbed, until the sky's blueness grew brittle. Once my saddle-catapult's tethers were taut enough to support me, I uncoupled the saddle-catapult from my cloudstrider, who descended back toward Far Eye.

Now was the moment.

I licked my lips, bracing myself. I twisted the knob of my saddle-catapult, felt it tense, and pulled the release lever.

The Void's blackness crashed over me.

I was weightless, rising like a bullet shot into a vast night, my air-suit's own set of tethers, mercifully joined to my attendants far below, following me ever upward.

Once free of the atmosphere, I saw the world as no human but Wallaq had seen it: a bright mosaic chased with the white of clouds and the gray-blue of seas. Continents shone like topaz and amethyst and emerald.

I rose and rose until the ropes wrenched me back, and then I started falling, then rising again, my motion slowly stabilizing as my kinetic energy dissipated, leaving me held by the collective gravity of the suns. My guts did a slew of gymnastics all the while. Wallaq had warned me about this part, but it was no less unpleasant for that.

As my stomach stilled, my senses sharpened. The world's enormity filled me with a cold loneliness, a stifling vulnerability. The thought of my ropes snapping sloshed thick in my head, but I shook it away. I had to concentrate, I told myself. Had to focus or I couldn't do what was necessary.

I looked through the telescope and scanned the horizon.

After about ten minutes, I found it.

I'm not sure what I'd been expecting. Perhaps part of me hoped Wallaq had misperceived.

I dialed the aperture with gemcutter care. *There.* Countless continents away, untrammeled by atmosphere, sat a red sun tangled deep within scores of black tendrils.

My body reacted several ways at once. My pulse rose. My skin began to slicken with sweat. I prayed a Maiponen prayer I had not used in two decades of godlessness.

The tendrils were artificial. Unmistakably. Their trunks had a metallic sheen and their forking branches a flawless symmetry. The violet lightning at their roots surged in orderly grids instead of stochastic squiggles. It was like the disembodied eyeball of a dead god, cataracted with rot yet still smoldering with divine energy. A voice in me said to look away, said this was not something I was meant to see. But I could not.

I found Wallaq at his hearth, winecup in hand. He and wine had seldom been apart of late, and his slight slur suggested this was not tonight's first drink.

"Cursed together," he said, cup raised in greeting. "Cursed with the truth of our insignificance."

I am not much of a drinker, but for once I understood that timeless thirst for oblivion. I poured a cup and sat beside him.

"It was more incredible than I expected, and more terrible," I said.

"Do you regret it?"

I shook my head. "Yet the sight will haunt me, Wallaq. For a long time."

"As it will me."

I could not sleep for two nights.

What I saw in the Void changed me. In my religious youth, the high god of the Maiponen faith had seemed too distant to matter in worldly affairs, and so I was free to imagine that humankind determined its fate, a freedom I carried happily into adulthood. It gave me comfort. A sense of purpose.

Now I knew the truth. Gods were no myth. Humankind was not the cynosure of reality. It was only a small—perhaps transient—participant.

What will befall humankind when it meets the sun-eaters? I wondered with fear in my marrow. When the ambits of both civilizations converged, in who knew how many centuries, would there be war? Mere devourment? What happens when a god meets an insect?

I could not begin to guess, no matter how hard I tried, and this tortured the part of me that yearned to know all.

I finished my treatise a few days sooner than hoped. Wallaq helped me revise it a dozen times, scrawling notes in each draft, smoothing the language. I knew it was the most important thing I'd ever write. Maybe the most important thing *anyone* would ever write. Yet I felt detached from it. Stripped to cool spareness, my words failed to touch a tenth of the import of what I sought to explain.

Words are dead things. Some truths can only be seen. Yet words were all I had.

Done with the work, I had my first deep sleep in days. I did not look forward to leaving Far Eye, not a bit, but I had struggled long and hard with the treatise and I was glad to have it behind me.

The night before I left, we feasted. We ate butterbread bowls brimming with molten beans, crackers tucked in mashed spicecorn, plump mauve vegetables marinated to soupy softness.

We had devil's dowry, a red Yaronen fudge laced with a subtle euphoric. We drank and talked deep into the night. My pleasure was tinged with sadness, knowing my taste of the highborn's life would soon be over, along with my new friendship.

A servant opened a finely wrought folding-case on the dining table. Inside was a long chain of silver links. I'd never seen so much money in one place.

"Thank you," I told Wallaq. "Thank you."

He waved aside my bows of gratitude. "You earned every mote. Truthfully, after all your help, I should be paying you double."

"There's always time to repent."

He smiled. "Good try."

We clinked cups and drank. He'd saved his best wine for last.

"I'll miss your company," he said. "It will be hideously dull around here without our discussions."

"I'm sure you'll be plenty busy fending off scholars when they come swarming to verify our discovery," I said.

He winced at the thought. "Or those who've come to vent their hatred over it. No doubt I'll have to quadruple my security. Are you concerned for your safety?"

I shook my head. "Only worried for the Ecumene's sanity. Worried what will become of faith and purpose, what will become of folks' trust in the Empress to protect them, what will become of the things that hold a civilization intact."

"We're scholars, not priests," he said testily. "Our loyalty is to truth, not the comfort of three billion souls. Best not forget that."

This rankled me. Was he so distant from ordinary suffering that he could not appreciate the pain our discovery would bring?

"*Your* loyalty may be to truth," I said as calm as I could, mindful of the emotions my wine was trying to draw from me. "Mine is to civilization."

"The two are not at odds," he said.

"Perhaps, in this case, they are."

He frowned. "What are you suggesting, precisely? That publishing this treatise would be a mistake?"

I laughed. Wallaq, I saw then, was the emotional equivalent of a child. Not in any simple or disparaging sense—merely in the sense that he could not appreciate any considerations outside his appetites, which in his case were wholly intellectual. He was a child, yes, who ate knowledge for breakfast, lunch, and dinner, and to whom morality was a bowl of tasteless vegetables. I knew such people at the Academy, of course, though none half so intelligent or resourceful, so it had been easy to overlook this tendency in him.

He'd been wrong to suggest I was his equal. I could never be his equal, as I did not have the childlike singlemindedness that his cast of genius requires.

"What I am saying," I said flatly, "is that publishing the treatise *might very well* be a mistake. What I am saying is that I might spare us both a good deal of misery by—well, throwing the damned thing into the fire."

I gave the roaring hearth a small salute with my winecup.

His face showed no amusement. "You're drunk, friend. Don't say such nonsense."

"I'm serious." My annoyance was bubbling to anger. I set down my cup, intending to walk to the table where my treatise lay, but he must have sensed this because he placed a gentle hand on my arm before I could stand.

"Listen," he said. "You underestimate people." His hold was surprisingly firm for such a small man. "The truth is inevitable. If you were to burn that treatise, which of course you won't, it would only be a matter of years before others learn what we've learned. Don't you see? You cannot burn the truth, Atapua. But people will adapt, as they always have."

His soft voice held reassurance. His face was calm, understanding. Yet there was a marked tension in him, as if he were ready to do anything to stop me from burning that document.

He was right, as he so often was. He was right. I could not have burned the treatise no matter how drunk I got. I was proud of my work, unreasonably so, even as I feared it.

"Yes," I sighed, relaxing a little. "People will adapt."

I did not wholly believe it, but it was not beyond possibility either. People accept many painful truths. Mortality, for instance. Injustice. Why couldn't they accept the truth of the sun-eaters?

Perhaps.

See Jordan Chase-Young's story "The Great Contradiction" online at Metaphorosis.
If you liked it, leave a comment. Authors love that!
Remember to subscribe to our e-mail updates so you'll know when new stories are posted.

About the story

Earlier this year, my friend Robin Hanson shared a provocative paper exploring the possibility that humankind's early emergence in cosmic history, and the apparent absence of other civilizations in the universe, may be a selection effect due to most of the universe's future being under alien control (https://arxiv.org/abs/2102.01522). I puzzled over how to turn this insight into a story and finally settled on a fantasy parable, as I felt that would be easier to fit into a few thousand words. The Ecumene is one of many SFF settings that've been collecting dust in my head, so I was grateful to have a story to set in it.

The most challenging aspect of the tale was plugging in concepts like the Fermi Paradox, Copernican principle, and selection effects while keeping the language accessible and the pacing smooth. I ended up trimming a lot of Atapua's analysis to avoid bogging down the piece. I also fleshed out Atapua's emotional world more and more with each draft, hoping to capture the complex emotions that scientists can have upon reaching a breakthrough with ambiguous consequences.

Though the setting is fantasy, the story is pure SF; it's about the fun and often scary ordeal of uncovering a difficult truth about reality. I share some of Atapua's anxieties about that process, but I tend to side with Wallaq's view that people are good at adapting to hard truths. What about you?

A question for the author

Q: Can beautiful things be funny?

A: Humor's a funny thing. Though many writers say humor's tougher to write than drama, funny stories have always been harder to sell than dark ones. If I asked you to name the most beautiful story ever written, I bet you'd pick a drama, maybe even a tragedy. Beauty and darkness feel oddly close, whereas humor seems somehow more frivolous. Hence attempts to call comics "graphic novels" to make them more respectable.

Where do these associations come from? Maybe humor is mainly about incongruencies in the world, such as paradoxes in language or social relations, whereas beauty hinges more on congruency, elegance, symmetry, order. Humor may also be time-serving and culture-bound, beauty timeless and universal. Still, it's a rare masterpiece that doesn't have a dollop of mirth to lessen the gloom, and nature, the greatest masterpiece of all, is often wickedly funny. Look at a blobfish lately?

About the author

Jordan Chase-Young is the Proofreader for Metaphorosis.

Jordan Chase-Young is an American SFF writer living in Australia with his wife and their stable of cyborgized battle koalas. He's kind of obsessed with the future: What will it look like? Where will it lead? His first published story, "Shards", appeared in the July 2020 issue of *Metaphorosis*. Since then, his stories have appeared in *Unidentified Funny Objects 8*, *The Colored Lens*, *McCoy's Monthly*, and the Zombies Need Brains anthology *When Worlds Collide*.

ebookofthenewsun.wordpress.com, @jachaseyoung

December

Orla, Always

Thomas Ha

She raised her head to listen for the rustle of his whispers.

It was always the same muttered words that she could never fully comprehend, followed by the sound of his hands—those callused, filth-crusted fingers tapping across the surface of the cellar door, feeling the wood for the lock and handle.

Even in the pitch of the underground, she could smell the crisp morning and knew to shut her eyes as searing white light spilled in around him, waiting for the creak of the door to seal in the darkness again, then for the pounding of his footfalls down the stone steps. She sensed the moment when he settled in the chair across from her bed, the clatter of his lantern on the ground telling her it was safe to look at him if she wanted.

But Orla could never raise her eyes to his.

Something about the sagging skin and darkened lines of his face bittered the back of her tongue with bile. Every time he visited, it seemed to Orla that he'd aged more than she remembered—shocks of gray sprouting at his temples and speckling the stubble of his beard, and the dewiness of his disheveled brow that told her that the simplest tasks were beginning to tire him more than before. It meant that the day she would be free of him was fast approaching, and if she were quiet and careful enough, she just might find the right moment to take that freedom.

Until then, she waited calmly, taking the bowl of stew he had brought her and drinking from one of its unchipped edges.

"I've been thinking," Orla said, pacing herself between mouthfuls. "About the last time we went for a walk, out there."

She watched him shift like he was struggling to hear her, or maybe to see her clearly in the mix of shadow and light, and because it disturbed her to look at his face, Orla in turn focused, as she often did, on his throat, just to the side of the point of swallowing, where the hint of a pulse quivered in the lantern's glow.

"I thought it'd be nice, one of these days, if we could walk again." She put the bowl on the floor when she was finished. "Maybe through the village, away from the Erst Field, even? Wherever the king's watchmen will allow us to go. It's just...been so long since I've seen the outside."

He said nothing, but she knew his mind was beginning to turn, that he had a fondness for their walks and craved the idea of a time when he didn't keep her locked away.

"You could tie my hands with rope," she went on. "And bind yourself to me with the other end. I won't run this time. I promise." She pushed her mouth to smile and forced her voice higher, to set him at ease.

And while he seemed to consider the notion, lost somewhere in his thoughts, or perhaps remembering something else from before, Orla felt under the wool and straw beneath her for the shard that she kept, the one she had wrenched free from the wooden bed frame during the quiet hours of the day when he disappeared.

It had taken countless cuts and splinters across the soft pads of her hands to pry apart the cracks in the grain in just the right way, until she had a fragment that she could wield. But now it was as if she could almost feel the light air outside enveloping her face, chilly and waiting, just for her. She squeezed the wood fragment in her throbbing, blistered hand and thought of the vast openness above her again and nothing between her and home.

The great, dark rock that would take her home.

"So?" she asked hopefully. "Can we walk together again?"

He did not move, or even blink, and he barely whispered the word.

"No."

Orla jumped from the bed and plunged the shard into his throat, and she allowed herself to look at him then, to take in the bare anguish that twisted across his face.

And she grinned, even as he roared and threw her against the stone wall.

She grinned, until she realized that she had missed.

That, aged and tired and hulking though he was, he had moved, just barely, catching the wood in the sinewy muscle just above his collar bone, where it protruded now as the blood spread under his shirt, hovering near the pulse in his throat, but not close enough.

The rage that flashed in his eyes, in that instant, frightened her deeply. It was an old anger she had rarely seen, that was reserved for the worst of things, but never, before, for her.

It was there now.

It might have been only a glimmer, but she knew that he would grab her by the neck and bash her against the stones.

So Orla crawled. She clambered backward, bending her limbs in the new ways as she moved to the ceiling, retreating to the corner, aloft where he could not pull her down. And though she was terrified, she dared not show it, instead widening the opening of her jaw.

She felt her second tongue squeeze its way through the canal of her throat and unfurl onto the wall, slapping wetly across the stones beneath her and dangling between them. She arched its end so that he could clearly see the curve of its barbs and would hesitate to reach for her, unless he wanted to feel her slice deep, flowing gashes across his arms.

No, he wouldn't dare try to hurt her now when she was like this.

He could only stand below, staring, so small in the lantern light, holding his wound and grunting in pain through his clenched teeth.

"Let me go *home*," she cried.

He looked at her strangely, pathetically, before turning to take the bowl, his heavy footfalls thumping again up each of the steps. He paused one last time to peer at her from the glow of his lantern across the dark space between them.

Then she shut her eyes as white flooded in from the open cellar door.

Brian sat for a time in the house, touching the wooden fragment embedded near his neck. He pulled steadily, sliding the shard out of his muscle bit by bit, blood dripping onto his shoulder and chest before he applied pressure with a cloth.

He tried to think of nothing else as he cleaned the wound, but he kept imagining Orla, and her disquieting excitement as she leapt, that glee as she sank the shard into him, and the moment after, however brief, when he almost lashed out in return.

He wondered if Orla's mother could have kept the girl calm, but that only let in more unbidden thoughts. Brian rose to leave, even as his wound continued to bleed through the dressing.

He could only stay so long in those empty rooms.

The gray morning outside provided just enough sharpness to revive him, his breath misting as he stared at the cobblestones of the main road of Codladh village, until his eyes eventually met the figure of a man hunched in the doorway of another home.

The man looked back at Brian, his hands caked black with soil from working through the night. Brian could tell that he'd also just emerged from his cellar, and like all of the parents in Codladh, had come up just a bit darker in his face. Brian thought to say something, perhaps ask about the dig or how the other parents were doing, but the man's front door had already slid shut, just as the noise began.

It carried across the village, like the heavy echoing of giant bells that Brian had once heard in the cities—at least, that's how the noise always sounded to him. Others heard horses screaming, as if they'd been lashed, or the feverish rise of locusts chittering in the summer. But for Brian, it was only the bells, and when they came, he whispered the words he always said under his breath as they clanged, words repeated again and again to carry his mind through the moment, until the silence finally settled in around his ears again.

The morning chill remained for a while longer, and Brian squinted at the flashes of sun peeking through the dark sheets of clouds, until, eventually, a horse clopped near, its ears twitching from the flies gathering around its glossy, black body.

The king's soldier on its back leaned forward in his saddle and stared at Brian carefully, his clear eyes peering out above the cloth that covered his nose and mouth.

"Bit of trouble?" He spoke with a youthful, quavering voice and pointed to a few dots of blood that had seeped through Brian's bandage.

"No trouble."

The soldier cleared his throat.

"On with you, then."

Brian and his escort took the quickest path to the Erst Field, around the village's edge and along the curve of the main road. He ignored the soldiers lined around Codladh Square and positioned between the houses, their stares following him and all the other villagers who were going about their day with their heads bowed. The king's men had come to treat this like an ordinary plague town, wary of desperate runners who might break their barricade, but the truth was that no man or woman in Codladh was going to run.

Brian made it a point to nod to his neighbors as he passed, and he could tell each one was searching his face for signs of what might come of the dig. They looked to him for answers, now, because of what little they knew of his life before he came to the village.

When he first arrived those years ago, as an outsider, before Orla's mother took him in, when he still carried his experiences like poison, the people of Codladh had been distant with him, as they should have been.

But as time passed, and he learned to let his anger go, when Orla was born, he assumed, though he couldn't identify a particular moment, the others seemed to think of him more as one of their own. And he almost forgot that they had ever seen him as anything else.

Now, though, they needed that other part of him. They needed the outsider to tell them if this might be the day they finally buried the stone.

Everyone in Codladh knew they were almost to the end, now that the pit they had constructed had become quarry-like, deep and wide and buttressed by all manner of wooden framing, to the point where it was almost impossible to see all the way down to the bottom.

But Brian kept his expression impassive as ever, understanding that they all needed to guard themselves from hoping for too much or too little, that losing that balance would hurt the village worse than any affliction.

He continued beyond the edge of Codladh, where he would, on most days, walk the quarter mile to the flats and take up his post at the dig. But today he heard something he recognized coming just beyond the tall grass, almost muffled by the heaviness in the air, and he found himself heading toward it, neither hurrying nor slowing his pace.

"You! Where are you—Wait!"

His young escort called from his horse with increasing urgency as Brian kept walking further from the road. And when it was clear that Brian wasn't turning around, the escort followed, over a slope and down to a patchwork of dewy grass and muck, where they found a circle of men gathered, each of them in the dull leather uniform of the king's army, laughing as they stood around a covered tumbrel.

The group of soldiers jeered and chattered to one another until they gradually turned to see Brian come upon them. There was a flicker of uncertainty across the group—some of their hands floating down to their hilts and changing their stances—but that dissipated when they realized he was only a villager, and a few of their expressions, what he could see above the cloth strips covering their mouths, took a different cast.

Brian ignored them, looking beyond their figures and between the bars of the tumbrel and barely making out the slinking shape of an afflicted boy held captive in the cart.

The boy was no more than fourteen, pressing his shivering body against one of the corners of the cart, his arms wrapped around the wooden slats. The flaking cracks forming around the folds of his mouth hinted at muscles beginning to change their shape, and the whorls of skin that covered what were once his eyes left only shrunken pinholes to take in and shut out the light.

The afflicted boy sank further from the reach of the men, and through his torn clothing Brian could see the exposed lumps of bone growing on either side of the boy's ribs, the beginnings of the smaller arms that some of the other Codladh children grew in their final stages.

"*Home*," the boy rasped, mucus dripping from the corner of his lips.

It was only a second, but Brian thought back to Orla—how there were moments, more and more frequent, when the cadence and lilt of her voice became unrecognizable that way—moments when she believed she was speaking but only made that same rasping, barking noise.

Brian studied the boy's face, noticing the small cuts where the child had been prodded.

"Move on," one of the men nearest to the tumbrel said. He seemed older than the others and had the serious affect of someone with authority.

"*Home.*"

Brian looked to the older soldier and spoke so that everyone could hear him. "This boy...His name is Liam," he said. "Liam Conroy." He stepped forward, and because he was taller than most men, he cast a shadow that tended to make others attentive.

"His family lives on the far side of the square by the fallen wych elm," Brian continued. "His father is the apothecary, and his mother, Rosemary, tends to swine. They're good people, who care very much for their son."

Some of the soldiers shifted uneasily.

"*Home.*"

"You don't...have to do anything more than this," Brian went on. "He's just a child."

The older soldier stared and touched the cloth over his mouth. "You keep on with your work, and we will with ours." He looked at the escort on horseback, as if to indicate that he'd best see Brian on his way, but the younger soldier seemed unsure what to do.

Brian closed his hand, and something small in him stirred, thinking of what could happen if he pressed the men.

He knew the soldiers looked at the parents, including Brian, with a queasy disdain. It didn't matter that Codladh was made of hardworking men and women, apothecaries and swineherds who loved their children dearly. That love alone lacked any real power, any strength, which was the only attribute of meaning to a soldier.

All they saw in the villagers were hollowed, pitiful creatures barely capable of digging in the fields, and the king's men despised them all the more for it.

Even so, Brian still knew the innerworkings of soldiers' minds, especially restless, overeager ones like these, and he felt there were other ways that this could go if he approached them with something of consequence, something that they comprehended.

"If this is the way it's to be, I understand," he said evenly, slowly, so that they had to lean into the words to follow him. "But...who do I say is responsible when the Thinling asks? I assume you." Brian gestured at the markings on the older man's pauldron, half-obscured by his wool cloak, and the soldier blinked rapidly.

"The Thinling?" He touched his shoulder, and the tenor of his voice changed.

"Yes. He's observing the dig, and we're meant to speak shortly."

The older man briefly turned to the escort on horseback, who gave the slightest nod, then he swallowed and scratched his ear before finally responding. "If that's true...that the Thinling's here... You can already see, this one is..."

"Still meant for the Thinling to study," Brian finished, without raising his voice. "And he doesn't like losing subjects for study. I can tell you that."

The murmuring among the men seemed to die in their throats. Some things had changed in the infantry over the years, but the palpable chill among the footmen at the mention of the Thinling was the same as it ever had been.

The older soldier looked at no one in particular, and Brian could see his halted breathing from the movement of the cloth on his face. "If that's how...if that's how the Thinling says he wants things, we'll follow that, of course." He waved to the men behind him, and a few lifted the rails of the tumbrel up from the mud.

"Of course," Brian repeated.

"By the wych elm, you said?"

Brian nodded.

The men began dragging the tumbrel toward Codladh, the large wheels wobbling through the inches of mud. The older soldier stopped at the slope, giving Brian a look before taking his leave, less of anger and more searching, like he was trying to understand why Brian's bearing wasn't quite like the others in Codladh.

But Brian's gaze stayed only on the boy who clutched the bars and looked back at him ponderously with the dark holes of what had once been his eyes, until the cart and the men eventually disappeared over the hill.

"And he arrives."

The Thinling called out as Brian and his escort approached the canvas tent. The king's physician rose from a planning table set outside, his unusually skinny frame stretching impossibly upward as he stood, tall in a way that always reminded Brian of a reflection distorted in cracked glass. On the table in front of him, the bloody remains of an animal streamed over the edges, seeping plops of wet mass onto the dirt, and the Thinling held up his hands, long, slender fingers doused in a fierce red that dripped to his elbows as he smiled.

The escort hesitated, his black horse slowing to a halting clop as they reached the end of the road, shaking its head anxiously at the smell of the blood.

Brian looked up at the young man reassuringly. "You've done your part now and don't need to be here for this."

The soldier's eyes darted away from the figure of the Thinling, and when he lowered the cloth over his mouth, revealing his smooth, beardless face, Brian realized the escort couldn't have been much older than Orla.

"Are you sure...you want to be alone?" the boy asked, a genuine concern tinging his voice under the trembling, reminding Brian vaguely of other men he knew who followed the king's flag.

"I'll be fine, son. Thank you. Go back to the others."

Brian reached up his hand, and the soldier clasped it. "May He bless the roads before you," the young man intoned.

"And may all the dark things die," Brian finished.

He watched the soldier trot his horse hurriedly to the path and away, then he turned back to the tent where the Thinling waited.

Simon Wayn, the name by which Brian had known the Thinling when they'd first met during the campaigns, grinned with large, unnaturally white teeth. The footmen back then had whispered that he was born of something unholy, and Brian wondered if there was some truth in the rumor, because Simon's face was just as it had been decades ago, like porcelain untouched by time.

They had first met outside a field tent not unlike this one, when Brian was barely old enough to hold a blade, still dark-haired and lean and without the weight in his heart he'd later carry, and he'd looked at the Thinling directly and without hesitation, even then, providing the latest reports on field movements that the physician had requested.

"*Do you not fear me, soldier?*" the pale man had asked him all those years ago, his unsettling eyes studying Brian's expression carefully.

"*No,*" Brian said simply, maybe foolishly in retrospect.

"*But surely you must find me strange? Something other than normal to someone like you, at least?*" he pressed, almost as though interrogating him.

"*There is, I think, nothing strange, or even normal for that matter, sir,*" Brian swallowed. "*Only what we know, and take for granted, and that we have yet to know, and fear.*"

And something about the answer seemed to please Simon in just the right way, because he gave the first of many smiles to Brian, chilling and practiced, that Brian would learn signaled a request to follow.

"*Tell me, young man. What do you know of the creatures that come from the otherworld?*"

The memory, and those words in particular, lingered with Brian in the present as the Thinling extended a blood-covered hand, unaware that there was anything curious in the gesture. Brian shook it, looking down at the limbless, open carcass on the table between them, its skin flayed completely from the weeping, pink muscle, and its lungs and heart churning slowly, the only sign it was somehow still barely alive.

The Thinling plucked a small sac from the body and held it up for a moment, then sucked it delicately into his mouth. He invited Brian to take a piece of his choosing, but Brian held up a hand to decline.

"The dig site," Brian said, looking away and waiting until the Thinling was done chewing. "Everything to your expectations, I hope?"

Simon licked his fingertips before dabbing his mouth with a handkerchief. "Very much so, I'd say," he returned to the bloody remains and tossed aside what seemed to be the wound cord of intestines onto the ground. "The pit will be deep enough soon, possibly today."

"And then we can begin?"

Simon looked up.

"Oh yes. And then we can begin."

Brian stared at the blighted expanse of the Erst Field in front of them, his eyes drawn across the flat plateau to the tall, jagged figure of the Slaking Stone, which was what the Thinling had come to call the dark rock over the course of his study. It stood ominously alone in the middle of the land and was, by Brian's estimation, at least the size of a fortified castle turret, stretching fifty feet or more into the air and growing ever so slightly with each day that passed.

Brian didn't need to look on it long, because he had seen every detail of its angular, obsidian body in his mind every day since it came to their village.

That creeping dawn when it first appeared—when men harrowing the soil stumbled upon it and called all of Codladh to see—the faithful had claimed it was a Godsent artifact, or some kind of blessing crystal from the old folktales, bestowing good fortune to the village.

But Brian, who stood far back from others in the crowd at the Erst Field that day, had already known.

He'd seen enough in his younger days to recognize an otherworldly creature like this one.

And so Brian sent his first letters to the king's court immediately, doing his best to describe the dark rock: its measurements, its properties, his assumption that its elemental fundament was perhaps of the earth, given its appearance. It had been some time since he had contacted the capital, years since he left to begin his quieter life in Codladh, but he hadn't known where else to turn with something of this nature. *Send men,* he had written, *because it won't be long before it begins to prey on the minds of the people living here.* But, even then, he couldn't have anticipated how quickly the sickness would fall on Codladh after that.

It had started with a noise.

A booming, like the clang of a bell deeper than any he'd heard before, a noise so penetrating it entered his mind and covering his ears did nothing to dampen it. It was so painful that it woke him suddenly in the night and caused him to stumble through the dark, searching for Orla, but finding her nowhere in their home. His shouts were soon joined by others outside as he wandered into the road. Fathers, mothers, were screaming their children's names, unable to find them in their beds or around their houses. He went with the throng of others, floating lanterns glowing in the night as they all moved outward from the village, until, of course, among the waves of wheat that still grew in the Erst Field at the time, they saw the boys and girls of Codladh gathered in a ring around the Slaking Stone, hands outstretched.

Brian still remembered Orla standing in her night shirt, her eyes half closed, sleepily smiling at her father.

"*What's wrong?*" Orla had whispered as Brian clutched her to his chest. "*What's wrong?*"

Brian closed his hand tightly as he stared at the stone and thought of her.

"How is the girl?" Simon asked, bringing Brian out of his memories as he looked back from the field. The Thinling inserted his fingers back into the body before him, exploring the cavernous spaces under the ribs.

"The same," Brian answered.

"Really?" Simon tilted his head one way and then the other, lifting another organ and prodding it with thin fingertips. "She should be well along, I would think. If you'd like me to take a look —"

"No!" Brian said, then softened his voice. "It's fine. We're fine."

Simon's eyes rested on the patches of blood near the collar of Brian's shirt, where his injury had seeped over the course of the morning.

Brian touched it and cleared his throat. "Fine, I said."

The Thinling's face was unreadable, but he returned to pulling apart the carcass, and Brian let out a small breath.

"My men have finished the sledge," Simon nodded to the other end of the Erst Field, and Brian could barely see the large platform of planks and wheels that had been constructed. "Once the Slaking Stone's dragged over to the pit, we can bury it, finally, just as we discussed."

The method for killing the creature had been worked out between them in the early months, before the king's army could redirect men from the Mist Bridges to the countryside for support. Brian had written more urgent letters when the affliction started showing itself in earnest, only in the children for some reason.

It was only ever in the children.

The boys and girls began forgetting things, becoming agitated at the mention of their names, lashing out when others got too close. And every time the noise from the stone rang through the village, whether day or night, the children turned their heads toward the Erst Field, like animals hearing a call.

Home.

Brian recalled Orla's face, twisted and distorted in a way he'd never seen it, raging as he shut the cellar doors on her, because there was no other way to keep her from being drawn to the rock in the middle of the night.

"*Let me go home! Let me go!*" she screamed. He had felt the pressure of her hands beating against the other side of the bouncing wood, stronger than ever before, and pushed back with all his might. Brian had wept that first time, bolting the cellar door shut, the sound of screeching metal joining the inhuman wailing coming from below.

The Thinling had his theories about what was happening to the children. *The form this otherworlder has taken—I don't believe it's even rock. What you describe seems more like the cocoon of a metamorph to my mind,* Simon wrote. His first letters to Brian were warm, eager to connect over the subject of otherworlders, almost blithely unaware of the pain Brian and his neighbors were suffering. *Something else, something worse, is being birthed from within the Slaking Stone.*

The Thinling believed young ones, being the most vulnerable and persuadable in thought, were the ideal candidate for the rock to subsume, and that their transformation aided its development. Maybe the vile barbs and limbs, the violent tendencies, the inexorable draw of the children to the Erst Field, were meant to serve the stone in its defense while it gestated. Or maybe the physical alterations were echoes of the form the otherworlder itself was going to take next, and the changes were a side effect of its deep hold on the children's minds.

Simon's correspondence appended ink illustrations of what the dark rock might contain, nightmarish studies of many-limbed creatures with dripping carapaces and segmented bodies, things that Brian could hardly believe the Thinling could stand to envision, let alone reproduce.

But regardless of the cause or meaning of the transformations in the children, the men and women of Codladh did everything they could think of to treat or reverse them. Tonics, leeches, sweat baths, but nothing productive came of it, and the children grew steadily worse. Several parents tried leaving Codladh with their young ones in tow, hoping that distance from the dark rock would bring them to their senses. But they all found they couldn't go more than a mile before the children started screaming and writhing in pain, as if their innards were being raked by glass.

Others turned to destroying the stone itself, as if they had the means for such a thing—setting fire to the field or slinging pickaxes and blades to crack it apart. But the dark exterior of the otherworlder remained completely unmarred, no matter what was done.

That's because its affinity isn't of the earth, Simon had written after a number of further exchanges. *The way its sound flows, its control over the children within a distance. It's of the air, I'd wager. That's how the transformative affliction works through them.* Brian could see the Thinling's excitement in the flourishes of the ink. *So to kill it, we will have to take that air away.*

Simon's letter enclosed a diagram, a side view of a pit roughly a hundred feet deep. He drew ladders, support platforms, and timber to keep the walls of the pit stable. And above the hole, Simon had designed a set of beams and pulleys, spidering down with ropes and buckets, so that men at the mouth of the pit could set aside the soil sent up to them by the diggers.

As always, Simon thought of every last detail.

And, as he had in years past, Brian took the Thinling's plans and organized the work to make them real, acting as the hand to Simon's thoughts, building and executing the contraptions that the Thinling designed in his madness.

In doing so, Brian recalled, familiarly more than fondly, the time he had previously spent as one of the king's Cullers after that fateful first meeting with Simon outside of that tent—a service as one of the men selected by the Thinling to identify, study, entrap, and destroy otherworldly things that invaded from beyond the Mist Bridges.

It was a part of himself he had all but smothered, and he felt a kind of misery and, if he were being honest with himself, perhaps a small fervor, in having to surface it again. But no matter what he was feeling or not feeling about the past, Brian, like the rest of Codladh, would do whatever was necessary to see this through.

The fathers and mothers whose families were affected by the affliction volunteered for the dig site first, taking up the shovels and buckets to carve out the ditch just beyond the field. The rest of the untouched, either too young or too old for children of their own, began providing supplies for the village's project.

And now, after weeks and months of toiling, here they stood, finally on the cusp of destroying the Stone.

The Thinling drew back his lips, flashing his red-stained teeth with the eagerness he always showed when they reached this moment before they hunted an otherworlder down.

"There is just...one more thing, Brian," he said, pulling vigorously at the carcass. "The sledgemen haven't been able to approach the Slaking Stone as of late. It keeps filling the field with that...noise when anyone gets close. The pain it causes at that distance is unbearable, or so my men tell me." He laughed, and held up a round, black piece of tissue from the animal that Brian did not recognize. "But...I've been working on something to help with that."

The Thinling reached into the drawers of the planning table. He brought up a wineskin with one hand, removing the cap with his teeth and holding it under Brian's nose.

The odor made him draw back and gasp from the sharpness of it.

"Dwale?" Brian coughed, vaguely remembering the burning stench from the battlefield, when the physicians would drench wounds and make men drink it before they went under the knife.

The Thinling nodded. "Barrow swine gall, henbane, opium and a few other touches." He picked up the round black flesh and squeezed it over the opening of the wineskin, letting a stream of dark juice spill into the pouch before capping it again. "If we can apply enough of this to the creature's body—fill some of the cracks and narrows of it with the dwale—it will sleep so deeply that its noises will subside for several days, at least. That will give us the time we need to drag it to the pit and put it to rest, once and for all. If...someone can get to it, that is."

Simon looked pointedly at Brian, and he understood what he was asking of him, having been tasked like this many times before. Brian had always been Simon's favorite to use for kills like these, because the Thinling believed that the otherworlders came from an unstable plane of the intangible. And while they took a strange pleasure in forming in this physical world, twisting and reshaping things for their own amusement, they were ultimately, at their core, creatures of the mind. So it took people of equanimity, of unshakable thought and heart like Brian, to defeat them. Or those were just the lies the Thinling told to lure others into his work; Brian supposed that he would never really know.

And truthfully, it mattered little to Brian in the moment, as he took the wineskin from the Thinling's long fingers and squeezed the pouch.

"We all still wonder, at court, you know," Simon brushed his pale hair from his eyes with bloody fingers. "Whether you might return to this someday. After all, there's not much in a place like this for men like us, is there?"

Brian hesitated, thinking of what he might say to the Thinling in response. He wondered, momentarily, if he could perhaps make the Thinling understand why he had left the Cullers all those years ago, how he had found more meaning in this place than in any of the hunts or battles or marches under the king's flag.

But he knew Simon was too set in his views, about men he used for fodder and about villages like these, and Brian realized it wouldn't make any difference in the end.

So he remained silent, nodding in thanks for the dwale before moving beyond the table.

"And may all the dark things die," Simon smiled.

"And may all the dark things die," Brian answered, heading toward the destitute flatland, where the Slaking Stone waited.

The moment Brian stepped onto the field, he felt the deep, clanging noise begin. The sound overtook him and flooded deep into his stomach, almost as if the stone understood what was coming and was trying, instinctively, to push it away.

The ringing in Brian's ears gradually began to shift in sensation to something he had never experienced, like the touches of insects crawling somewhere behind his eyes and down into the soft point at the back of his throat, choking him from within.

He ignored the feeling—believing it was the stone trying to disturb and unsettle him—and resisted his body's instincts to gag or tear at himself. Instead, he continued, step by step, across the field.

The closer he came, the larger the otherworlder loomed, and he could see more clearly, along the base of the rock, the stone-fused bodies of the children who had escaped their cellars to what they had told their tearful parents was "*Home,*" this skeletal embrace that absorbed their changed blood and flesh, until only pieces of them lining the rock remained. Simon believed that by drinking them, the creature was softening its shell, preparing to emerge in its next form when enough of their bodies had merged.

Brian tried not to look at the faces pressed to the black surface as he walked ahead.

Another booming sound filled his head then, and he fell, drops of blood raining from his nose onto the deadened soil. The world swayed, like everything was pulling away under him, and he had to shut his eyes before he could rise to his feet.

The stone was in his thoughts now, he knew, as he reached the midpoint of the Erst Field, because it began to invade his vision with impossible figures, the way otherworlders sometimes liked to do. He could see shadows of men walking in the field that he gradually realized were echoes of dead and dying things he had seen long ago when he fought for the king, in distant lands near the base of the Mist Bridges, where the otherworlders stalked freely, like merciless lords, bending the people they encountered to their will to become mindless servants who would slaughter others in their name. Dripping limbs, arrow-filled faces, men with severed fingers, scraping at his boots.

But Brian walked ahead, forcing the shapes to fade to blurs in the corners of his vision as he advanced toward the stone, relegating those violent shades to his memories again.

The booming grew to an aching roar as he got even closer, just within reach, and an immense pressure squeezed somewhere inside of him. He felt he was sinking into the freezing blackness of the sea, weighted chains around his neck, and he collapsed wholly, unable to bring himself to rise.

A burning spread through Brian's lungs as the world began to whirl, and he almost felt he might succumb to panic. But he reminded himself that, like all else, these feelings were illusory, and he turned his mind to his breathing, concentrating on its rhythm, until he found his center of balance again.

The spinning subsided, and he found purchase with his fingers, lifting himself just enough to dig his elbows into the soil and steady his knees.

Then, finally, he stood at the Slaking Stone, observing the blur of his own body reflected in its glassy surface, and the relentless hollow noise softened to a dull and distant hum. The creature couldn't speak, as far as they knew, but at this close distance, Brian could sense, as much as he could in any other injured, living thing, that, more than anything else in that moment, it was afraid.

There were sudden flickers of images bursting in Brian's thoughts that he believed to be the stone seeping further into his head—images of the king's soldiers, dragging the Slaking Stone to the sledge, and casting its body deep, down, decisively, into the pit Codladh had made. Cascading sheets of earth pounded on top of it in the hole, over and over, until all light was blocked out from above, and the stone felt nothing but a black, crushing weight.

And then it showed him the children, showed him Orla, screaming in the cellars across the village, crying out like they were being pressed down and strangled by something unseen.

Brian held his breath.

He saw Orla huffing rapidly, her cheek against the stone floor, until her breathing slowed to a deflated stop, and her wet eyes looked on lifelessly ahead.

The message from the Slaking Stone was clear.

If you kill me, they will die.

Brian had known otherworlders to bargain like this, close to the end. They were never any different than men in that way, no matter how they tried to disguise it. But whether the stone was lying to save itself or telling the truth about what its death would do, it made no meaningful difference, Brian knew. All that mattered, all that ever mattered, was whether Brian did everything he could for Orla and the others, while there was still time.

Brian looked back at the jagged planes of dark rock, unblinking, and decided, if they were somehow connected in this way, that he would try to show it something else.

He concentrated on the image of Orla, as she was before she became sick, when she smiled sweetly and rested her cheek on his chest when she embraced him. He recalled her stumbling as a young girl on the shores of the Codladh river, giggling as she slipped on the smooth stones and regained her balance, cold water dripping from her chin as she laughed.

And he imagined Orla's mother, years before she passed. He remembered when she had taken him in, when he was weary and first found his way to the village, and she cared for him until he remembered how to care for himself. He remembered how he finally learned to sleep by her side through the night without waking. How she sat near the crackling fireplace, gently touching her swelling, pregnant belly. And how, later, she held their child in the crook of her arm—that pink face barely peeking out from the folds of blankets—and she whispered the words, those same words, that Brian still repeated to himself under his breath each day. *"My sweet girl."*

This, Brian thought, sending his intentions to the dark rock, not knowing whether it could feel any fraction of what Brian had felt, if it could even understand what he was showing it.

This is forever. No matter what may come. No matter what happens to her. No matter what happens to me.

This is forever. Do you understand?

And in the seconds after, there was nothing Brian felt from the rock in return—no image, or pain, or form of retort—just an overwhelming sense of bewilderment over the memories.

Because, of course, the creature would never comprehend any of what Brian felt, not really. Much like the Thinling, and the king's soldiers, and any of the others who might sneer at everything a village like Codladh was and had to offer, they would never, could never, understand the meaning and power in these ordinary things.

In that moment, Brian realized, above all, he pitied them for it.

He opened the wineskin and poured the dwale across the cracks of the Slaking Stone, watching the liquid spread and sink into the crevices. And he felt a shuddering, a dimming of the otherworlder deep within his mind as it sank into a darkness from which it would never emerge, before a silence, heavy and welcome, finally fell over the field.

Orla turned back and looked at the cellar door.

She heard nothing and was unsure what she had been listening for.

In fact, she was almost certain that the door she was seeing wasn't real and that she'd long since fallen asleep, because she could still sense her body, ungainly and leaden and almost unfamiliar, pressed against the bed, in the dark, as her mind continued to drift.

But the cellar door in her dream, the one in front of her now, opened as if it were always meant to lead her away, out into a gray afternoon where the sun's warmth seemed determined to stay out of reach. And somewhere, beyond the door and a village square and an unmarked field, Orla imagined a pit, strange and unnatural, stretching so far and so deep that it could swallow a mountain.

And she saw a man there, pacing toward the chasm—a man Orla knew well, somehow, she was all but sure. His heavily-lined face, creased brow, those downturned shoulders, it all meant something to her, even if she couldn't grasp it just then.

She watched as he passed a group of villagers working pulleys at the mouth of the pit, buckets rising and falling in rhythm, and he descended the ladder to the first platform, then another, to the next. And things grew dimmer around him as he went further below, until there was only a distant circle of stifled light above, cut by the wood support beams like a fractured window to a world that didn't seem to exist.

Near him, one of the other men, with eyes sleepless and dark, handed him a shovel, and he turned to take up a position between the rest of them.

She watched as he bent low and scraped and bent low and scraped—his muscle and bone seeming to spread something of a chill, but the heat from a fresh wound near his neck throbbing, keeping him moving and reaching.

Again and again.

Filling the bucket closest to him, he whispered softly in time with the scraping of the metal sliding into the dirt.

Again and again.

"*My sweet girl*," he said, almost in recitation, like he knew no one would hear him.

"*My sweet girl.*"

Something about the words felt familiar—as if she'd heard them every day of her life, whispered in her ear, or at her bedside, or through the cellar door.

"*My sweet girl*," the man said, as he reached and pulled the dirt from the ground, his fingers mottled with blisters and blood and dirt.

Again and again.

"*My sweet girl.*"

And above them in the distance, she saw a black, jagged rock, larger than any of the houses in the village, larger than anything Orla remembered seeing, dragged on a massive sledge over to the pit's open mouth by dozens of oxen and men. As it neared the site, the diggers emerged, slowly climbing the scaffolds and ladders to the edge. They joined together in the shouting and shoving, straining and screaming, some doing their best to hold back tears as it took everything in all of them to move the rock.

The villagers gave the wheeled sledge one final push, down and over into the hole, and there was a thunderous echo that seemed to shake the world as the dark thing plummeted into the emptiness below. It crashed through the wide beams and tangle of rope and pulleys, and soil ruptured and spilled from the unstable sides of the pit as the cavernous hole partially swallowed itself, the stone finally disappearing from sight in the waves of all that shadow and earth.

Orla watched the men and women standing there above the chasm, their faces breaking with a pained relief, and she drifted across those people, one by one, their names and other little recollections of them seeping slowly back to her. Until she found that man again, the one she'd recognized from before, now standing at the pit's edge with the rest.

Her thoughts stayed with him as he looked down into the darkness, at a deep nothing beneath him, his fingers still reaching below slightly, out of instinct and habit borne of hours and days and weeks of all that digging.

And somehow, Orla knew, even when she woke shortly after, confused and in pain, looking up at the cellar door, still closed.

She knew, even as she felt her senses return, and her body began to seem less strange and separate, joining again with her mind, as if they'd never been apart.

She knew that her father would be waiting somewhere, at the other side of the door.

And no matter what happened next, he would still be there, reaching out for her, always.

See Thomas Ha's story "Orla, Always" online at Metaphorosis.
If you liked it, leave a comment. Authors love that!
Remember to subscribe to our e-mail updates so you'll know when
new stories are posted.

About the story

I mainly wanted to write about losing a loved one to an influence beyond your control, the pain and animosity that can accompany that kind of gradual loss, and your inability (especially if you're a parent estranged from a child) to let go of the hope that you'll reconnect, which can be risky, if not outright dangerous. I've written other stories with similar themes, and they do not always end well. This one arguably does, depending on your view of the ending.

I also wanted to create a stark fantasy world with a traditional good versus evil construct (i.e. the king's army and the otherworlders), but where both sides are brutal, and where it's really ordinary people, like Codladh's villagers, with their devotion and resilience, who make a difference. Instead of a bombastic battle to win the day, I wanted to write a less common kind of conflict where physical violence was not necessarily the key.

And lastly, I just really wanted something weird. Knights versus aliens was my original concept. Something humans might think of as demonic or hellish but is actually quite strange and difficult for people to understand and confront—a sentient rock or a mystical disease, instead of a horned monster. The otherworlders are never confirmed as aliens, but I imagine them as interdimensional creatures of some kind, with motives that are almost beyond comprehension. What I was interested in exploring was, how do good, ordinary people, with everything to lose, endure and survive in the face of something like that?

A question for the author

Q: How has your writing evolved over time?

A: I'm working on being more judicious with my writing. I have a tendency to over-explain my characters and their motivations, so I'm learning to trust my readers more by paring some of that back. Similarly, while my stories vary in genre and style, I'm beginning to home in on subjects that matter to me personally, so I think a kind of consistency is slowly forming in a small body of work. But, like many folks, I am still very much a work in progress, so I have a lot yet to figure out.

About the author

Thomas Ha is a former attorney turned stay-at-home father who enjoys writing speculative fiction during the rare moments when all of his kids are napping at the same time. Thomas grew up in Honolulu and, after a decade plus of living in the northeast, now resides in Los Angeles.

thomashawrites.com, @ThomasHaWrites

Dry Season

Caite Sajwaj

The Ozarks haven't seen rain in nearly five years. All the well-to-do folks from Springfield to Fayetteville moved away after the first year. Now, the tourists are gone, and the lake's dried up to nothing more than a craterous puddle. In the town of Sunrise Beach, Missouri, the children ride sleds down the parched shore. They dig in the sand for bones and beer tabs and lost jewelry.

It's June. Before the dry season, the town would've been packed to the gills with drunk tourists. They'd spill onto the streets from every restaurant and dive bar and pool hall, reeking of beer and Banana Boat tanning oil. But, this year, there are no tourists.

At Redhead's Pizzeria, Janie Rivas, who isn't a redhead but a brunette, stands behind the cash register, vigorously chewing a stick of Big Red. Janie's lived in Sunrise Beach all her life. She doesn't particularly mind the lack of tourists, though she could use the tips. Two weeks ago, Janie got her acceptance letter from the University of Washington, and the cost of living in Seattle isn't anything to sneeze at. But her only customers today are the remaining three city counselors and they've never left more than 10%. So, instead of refilling their water glasses, Janie just listens to their conversation.

"What if it never rains again?" Myrna Fairway asks. Myrna owns Gator's Waterfront Grill. Her last customer was a young man passing through on his way to Denver, and he didn't even order anything, just asked to use her bathroom.

"It has to rain sometime," Lou Conaway says. He's 83, and he's spent his whole life in Sunrise Beach. To Lou, the last five years are nothing, a pothole on an otherwise smooth road.

"Well, *when* is sometime, Lou?" asks Mayor Cobb. "The town is dying. Hell, we don't even have a beach anymore! We have to do something *now*." Cobb works in the post office. His annual mayoral salary is $1, but there's something about that title—*mayor*. He's afraid he'll soon be mayor of nothing.

"What're we supposed to do?" Lou asks. "This is *the weather* we're talking about."

"You know very well what we're supposed to do," Myrna says quietly.

Lou curses.

"She's right," Mayor Cobb says. "We have to make an offering."

They take a vote, but it's just a formality. Myrna and Mayor Cobb have been on the city council together for three decades, and the only time they've broken ranks is when Myrna voted to rename Main Street "Sunrise Street," and Mayor Cobb voted to rename it after himself. But this isn't about vanity. This is about survival. And so, Janie listens to them decide, 2-1, that the town of Sunrise Beach will make an offering, whatever that is.

The next day, Mayor Cobb issues a proclamation and the townspeople gather at the docks. Janie isn't among them. She's tethered to one of the beams, watching dawn sunlight gleam off the ancient remains of broken beer bottles, still half-buried in the lakebed. Sun-bleached driftwood juts from the sand, like the bones of a monstrous sea creature or the pillars of a long-lost temple. Janie is still wearing her work-shirt from the pizzeria.

The townspeople watch and wait. Soon, the dry season will be over, and the air will hum with the sounds of motorboats and churning water. At one point, a man shouts, "I think I felt a drop!" But it's only sweat that dripped from his forehead. An hour later, there's still no rain. The sky is the clear, bright blue of a gas fire. Eventually, the crowd begins to thin. The citizens of Sunrise Beach have lives to get back to. They have morning shifts starting soon. They have children that need to be dropped off at daycare. And they expected something exciting to happen, something *spectacular* —a torrential downpour of Old Testament proportions, perhaps. But offerings are not miracles. Offerings take time, and the people of Sunrise Beach have grown bored. One by one, they file away, until only Janie is left.

She stares out across the lake bed. The dirt is dry and brittle and laced with shallow fissures, like a crust of brown bread split in the oven. Morning turns to midday and, still, the rain doesn't come. *This is all bullshit*, Janie thinks. Just superstition. Any minute now, the city council will realize they've made a huge mistake. "Sorry for the trouble," they'll say, and give Janie a nice chunk of change so she doesn't go running her mouth. She'll move to Washington like she planned. There are no droughts in Washington. Then, she feels it, cold and sharp as a bullet. *Rain.*

It comes slow at first, then fast. Water pools at the bottom of the lake, settling into the cracks and creases in the dirt. Janie starts to cry, but she doesn't call for help. The townspeople will be here soon enough, and it won't be to help her. No, they'll flock to the shore to chant and cheer and dance in the rain. Some of the children have never even *seen* rain before. Their parents will bring them outside to stomp in the puddles.

Janie writhes and shimmies, trying to slip from her bindings. When that doesn't work, she jerks and screams and kicks the ancient wooden beams of the dock. But this dock has stood over a hundred years, and it'll likely stand for a hundred more. Janie, by her best estimates, won't last more than a few hours. She wonders if she'll end up drowning to death or if whatever it is she's an offering to will eat her. She guesses it depends how quickly the water reaches neck level, and for how long it stays there. Either way, it won't be pretty.

Defeated, she slumps backward and closes her eyes. In her mind, she tries to go somewhere else. Washington. She conjures the scent of pine and sea salt, the sound of waves slapping rocky shores, the hum of public buses. And just when she has it, something...*slurps.*

Janie keeps her eyes squeezed shut, imagining some Cthulhu-like creature rising from the muddy lake bed, tentacles writhing, rows of teeth gnashing, ready to gobble her up and fulfill the unholy contract. There's another *slurp*, closer now. Janie's stomach twists. Her fingers tremble.

"Hey," a voice says.

Janie's eyes snap open, lashes dripping rainwater. A man is standing there, slurping a Sonic Route 44 like he's at a backyard barbeque and not the bottom of a flooding lake. He's wearing cargo shorts and a Pabst Blue Ribbon t-shirt. The man takes another loud, lingering drink.

"Who're you?" she sputters through the rain. A small part of her hopes this stranger is here to save her, but a bigger part knows better than to hope.

The man studies her, gnawing absently at the red straw in his drink. His eyes are the color of a brewing storm.

"I'm the Lake God," he says finally. If Janie weren't tethered to a piece of wood at the bottom of the lake, she wouldn't believe for a second that this guy is god of anything; he looks like he works at a bait shop. But she *is* tethered to a piece of wood at the bottom of the lake, so she figures he's probably telling the truth.

"I'm the offering," Janie replies.

Rain is still pouring violently from the sky. Every drop that hits Janie's skin feels like a shot from a pellet gun. The Lake God takes another long drink and shoves his free hand in his pocket.

"Yeah," he sighs. "Sure looks like it."

Janie says nothing. Her wrists feel like the skin's been rubbed off them and her eyes sting from the rain. The only thing keeping her from collapsing into a puddle is the rope tethering her to the beam. She doesn't want to die for this shithole town, and she *definitely* doesn't want to play human sacrifice to a god that can't even muster some goddamn enthusiasm about it.

The Lake God steps closer, still chewing on his straw. He smells like soil and pond scum, like algae washed ashore and left to rot in the sun.

"So, what's a young thing like you doing here?" he asks. "Thought it'd be one of the older ones. You know, for efficiency's sake." The Lake God shakes his head like he can't believe it.

"I was going to leave," Janie says. "I was moving to Seattle for school next month. I was going to be a hydrologist." She doesn't know why she keeps rambling. Maybe she's having one of those moments that people sometimes have right before they die, when they're compelled to confess their darkest secrets and dearest wishes.

"That's a damn shame. Seattle's a real nice place. Best cup of coffee I've ever had."

"Well, too bad I won't have a chance to try it," Janie says dryly.

The Lake God asks for her name. She tells him. *Janie Rivas. Nice to meet you.* She imagines she's at freshman orientation, introducing herself to her class, instead of at the bottom of a lake, introducing herself to a reluctant God.

"Well, listen, Janie. This is mighty awkward, but this whole —" the Lake God gestures at her bindings "—*human sacrifice* business isn't much to my taste anymore."

The sky is a dark, miasmic gray. The rain is falling so hard and fast that Janie can barely keep her eyes open. Her clothes are heavy and cold on her slick skin.

"Then why's this the first time it's rained in five years?" Janie asks, panting.

A shadow, like a storm cloud, passes over the Lake God's face. A great burst of lightning forks across the sky and a surge of rainfall pours down, heavy as the slap of an ocean wave. The Lake

God stands immovable at the bottom of the lake, now the eye of a hurricane. Janie cries out. The water is rising, reaching up like the hands of the dead beckoning for her to come down and join them. And then, as quickly as it started, the rain stops. The wind holds its breath. The water lapping at Janie's knees goes still. The Lake God looks at her with eyes the color of a starless sky. He chews on his straw some more, thoughtfully. His Pabst Blue Ribbon shirt is curiously dry.

"Janie," he says finally, "How 'bout you and I talk this over some place where you aren't in imminent peril of drowning?"

"Sounds swell," says Janie.

The Lake God, inexplicably, drives an old Ford Bronco, and with it, he drives them to a gas station halfway between Sunrise Beach and the next ghost town. The rain has stopped and the air smells strangely of damp hot dogs. All but one gas pump are covered with faded yellow bags that say, "Out of Order." The Lake God buys them each a clownishly large soda and they sit outside on the curb, talking for a long time.

"So, you've been on vacation for five years?" Janie asks.

"Well," he says, "I was Lake God for a lot longer than that." Even gods, it seems, tire eventually. But the Lake God assures Janie that he took precautions. Or, at least, he thought he did. His cousin from Lake Tahoe was supposed to check in on the place every so often. "Guess this is why they say not to mix family and business," he grumbles.

"What now?" Janie asks. Part of her hopes he'll smite the town of Sunrise Beach with a terrible flood, a freak superstorm the likes of which the world has never seen. A larger part just wants to forget this nasty business, order a large pizza, and take a long, hot shower.

"Well," says the Lake God. "I s'pose I could stick around to take care of the lake, but then what if someone gets it in their head to offer up another poor soul next time there's a drought?"

"If you were around to take care of the lake, there wouldn't be another drought," Janie points out.

The Lake God stabs his straw further into his drink, muddling the crushed ice at the bottom. Above them, the clouds swirl, tinged the same stormy gray as his eyes.

"I never liked being tied down." He says the words with a strange sort of resignation, like he's been tasked with the cosmic equivalent of cleaning the toilet.

They sit in silence, watching the clouds brew dark storms in their underbellies. A gust of wind swirls through the parking lot, kicking up puffs of dirt.

Janie sighs. She doesn't miss the tourists, but she sure does hate to see the place she grew up gone to shit. That's why she decided to go to Seattle to become a hydrologist in the first place. She'd find untapped groundwater, or engineer some genius irrigation system to restore the lake. But now... if she'd known it was as easy as being a Lake God, she might've checked what the course load for that particular field of study looked like.

"What if someone else took care of the lake? Someone other than your cousin, I mean," Janie says.

The Lake God rubs his chin. Overhead, the clouds still. "Well now, Janie," he says. "Isn't that an idea?"

When Janie shows back up in town later that day, the people of Sunrise Beach give her a wide berth. If it weren't raining, they'd probably drag her back down to the bottom of the lake, but it *is* raining, so they let her stay. Still, no one knows quite what to say to her. Some of the townspeople feel guilty, but for most of them, it's just awkward. Yeah, it's great that the Lake God spared her, but does she have to rub it in their faces? A few people work up the courage to ask questions.

"What happened down there, Janie?"

"Did you see him?"

"What did he say?"

Whenever these questions come, Janie just shrugs. She keeps to herself. She watches a lot of Netflix and, occasionally, goes for a swim in the lake. When it's not raining, that is.

There are whispers that maybe the Lake God didn't spare Janie. Maybe she just made a deal with him. The good people of Sunrise Beach are afraid. On the day Janie leaves for Seattle, Myrna Fairway and Lou Conaway of the Sunrise Beach City Council resign, and Mayor Cobb skips town entirely. The people burn down the City Hall as their own kind of offering and hope that's the end of it. No one is harmed, and the citizens of Sunrise Beach are steadfast in their silence about what exactly happened and *who* is responsible.

Janie, of course, won't hear about this until months later, when she returns to Sunrise Beach over fall break, accompanied by a man that smells of wet soil and algae. In Washington, Janie's learned of drainage-basin management and agricultural water balance and flood forecasting. She's pleased to find that, after all that, summoning rains comes quite naturally.

After graduation, the man that was once the Lake God claps her on the back as they say their farewells. When Janie asks where he plans to go, he says, "Somewhere without any damn lakes, that's for sure!"

When Janie returns to Sunrise Beach for good, the tourists return as well, filling every restaurant and dive bar and pool hall. The townspeople still don't know what to say to Janie, or whether they should say anything at all. At first, they're too afraid to let their children splash in puddles, let alone swim in the lake. But, after five years of steady rain, their fears grow dull and they grow bored, so they pull the tarps off their fishing boats. They pack their coolers with beer and hard seltzers. The cautious ones buy their children life jackets. They convince themselves that if one of them had been chosen as the offering, Janie would've stood in the crowd, watching and waiting and saying nothing, just like they did.

Janie lets the townsfolk think what they will. Her blood has long since turned to water, and with it, any rage she felt ebbed away like a wave receding from the shore.

See Caite Sajwaj's story "Dry Season" online at Metaphorosis.
If you liked it, leave a comment. Authors love that!
Remember to subscribe to our e-mail updates so you'll know when
new stories are posted.

About the story

When I started writing "Dry Season", the one thing I knew for sure was that it'd be set in Lake of the Ozarks during a very extended drought. The plot only started to develop during the pandemic, when tourism completely dried up. For a place like Sunrise Beach, which is so small it's technically a village and has an economy that relies almost completely on tourism, that was devastating. When things get that dire, people often appeal to their deity of choice. And, there it was: the inciting incident of the story.

Next came the characters, and the rest of the story is more theirs than mine.

First, the people of Sunrise Beach, who are presented as a sort of collective consciousness. This was inspired by the chorus of the Maids in Margaret Atwood's "The Penelopiad" (though the townsfolk of Sunrise Beach are certainly guilty where the Maids were not). It's also an unintended reference to groupthink—surprise!

The Lake God, was originally intended to be this sort of primordial, eldritch beast. In his present form, he's more a distillation of Lake of the Ozarks given human form. That decision was completely spontaneous. Honestly, it was less a decision and more, "Well, there he is." His character is, rather unexpectedly, very precious to me, and I hope you all enjoy him.

Now, Janie, is very different than any protagonist I've ever written in that we aren't privy to many of her thoughts. She's really a reflection of my own somewhat complicated relationship with being from a rural town. Clearly, she both loves and loathes Sunrise Beach, and, like many of us that both love and loathe our hometowns, she's developed a bit of a savior complex about it. Hey, if she ends up unhappy in her new role, she can always find someone else to take over, right?

A question for the author

Q: Do you have a garden? Have you ever grown your own food?

A: I'm what you might call "in between" gardens right now. We recently moved and I was only able to bring along some herbs and two potted tomato plants. Now, I'm in the process of planning a new garden that will make much better use of space and produce a lot more food. My hope is that we'll be able to grow enough food to share with our neighbors and local food pantry. We'll plant a flower garden to feed our pollinator friends too, of course!

About the author

Caite Sajwaj writes ghost stories and tall tales inspired by the urban fringe areas of the Midwest. When not writing, she enjoys gardening, craft cocktails, and befriending the neighborhood crows. She lives in Lawrence, Kansas, with her husband and their rescue dog, Josie.

caitesajwaj.com, @CaiteSajwaj

Stand or Fall

David Whitmarsh

Ilyas Bardakci was dead, but he hadn't stopped breathing, hadn't stopped moving, hadn't stopped thinking. He had no chance, no hope, no idea where in the void of interstellar space his ship had emerged. The radiation pulse from the nuke that had torn through his flesh had burned through half the ship's systems. That was the price he'd paid for hesitating. Wavering between solidarity and vengeance, he'd left it too late and jumped blind.

The reactor was down. Backup power was enough to keep the air pumping, the lights on, and the remaining instruments running, at least for a few hours. If life support lasted long enough, the radiation sickness would certainly kill him, but he wasn't dead yet, unlike those he'd left behind. Thinking of them fed the rage and the rage beat down the rising nausea. His fingers danced over the controls. Telescopes and sensors on the hull of the tiny vessel twisted on their mounts, searching for bearings of the brightest stars. Tentative spectral matches scrolled up the display: Sirius, Muphrid, Denebola. Calculations converged on an answer: he was twenty-eight light-years from the Muphrid system where he'd started.

For Ilyas, the jump had happened in the blink of an eye, but during that timeless instant twenty-eight years had elapsed. Twenty-eight years since everyone and everything he had known had perished. The habitats, stations, planet-side cities, a hundred and forty million people. All gone. Twenty-eight light-years behind him, twenty-eight years in the past. Celeste had been right: fighting was futile, and he had lost her because of his refusal to listen.

With no reactor, he could jump again only as far as the residual charge in the drive allowed. A search of the almanac revealed the colony closest to his crippled vessel: GJ430.1, HIP 56238, a star so insignificant it was nameless, known only by numbers from ancient catalogues; so dim it was barely a star at all. No major planets, two balls of rock smaller than Earth's moon, and a meagre smattering of asteroids, yet people lived there, and it was less than three light-years from his current position.

In the placid emptiness of the interstellar void he had time to check the calculations. With the autopilot dead, he had to point the vessel by hand and eye towards his target and set the displacement to the required range.

Another instant, another three years. His telescope found the single habitat cylinder, Thurlina, twenty kilometres long, four in diameter, turning its slow dance close around the dim red star. The docking complex at the sunlit axis held a handful of kinetic in-system tugs and freighters, nothing with interstellar capability. Population seven hundred thousand according to the almanac, a pacific society, friendly, welcoming, but a cultural and industrial backwater. The almanac was sixty years out of date.

His hand, beginning to blister from the radiation burns, lifted the cover from the mayday alarm. He passed out before he could press it.

Weight pressed him down on a soft bed. Muted footsteps paced around his dreams.

Celeste.

No. Celeste had given up the fight long ago. The soft footsteps faded and he slid from delirium to darkness.

A soft bed, a softly-lit windowless room. Ilyas tried to speak, but his throat was dry. He raised his arm to test the strength of the gravity that held him down, but learned only his own weakness. Wires snaked out from under the bedclothes to the monitors by the bedside. Thin tubes red with blood penetrated the pale blotchy skin of his arm.

"Water," he mumbled, and blacked out again.

Grey eyes peered at him from above the mask, wisps of ash-blond hair escaping from the edge of the cap.

"Awake, hey?" A female voice. "You're better off sleeping through this part." She turned from him and her arms moved but he couldn't see what her hands were doing. A few clicks, a beep. The room receded and his eyelids closed of their own accord.

Celeste waited for him, sitting out on the balcony of their small apartment, the light of the sun-tube bright on her bare arms.

She looked up from the book she was reading. "How did it go? Did you save anyone?"

No. They're all dead, he tried to answer, but his mouth was too dry.

Celeste laid down the book. "But you got away. You're alive. Don't waste that." She raised her right hand to stroke his cheek, red blood dripping from the gash along her wrist. "I'm sorry, sweetheart."

Sorry for what she had done, or for what he had? Ilyas couldn't tell.

"Stand or Fall! Stand or Fall!" Ilyas had shouted with the rest of them as they stood in the great hall. On the giant screen above the stage, they cheered as the demolition charges rippled through the evacuation fleet. They cheered again when the image of the expanding cloud of debris was replaced by Marshal Petro's stern face.

"How do you feel today, Ilyas?" The same grey eyes, the same ash-blond hair, but no cap, no mask. Young, pretty, like the daughter he'd never had. Her hair was short, neat. No cosmetics, no jewellery except a thin chain around her neck that hung down beneath her blouse.

"Thirsty," he croaked.

She held the cup with one hand and raised his head with the other while he grasped the straw between his lips. Cold water flooded his mouth, the sweetest thing he had ever tasted.

"Slowly," she said. "Not too much."

He swallowed and relaxed to allow his head to be lowered back to the pillow. "How long?"

"You've been here three weeks. A tug pulled you in to the dock after your jump triggered the sensors."

"Thank the crew for me."

"No crew. Automated. We've a lot of automation in Thurlina." She smiled like it was a joke. "When you're a little stronger you'll see. For now you need to rest, and you are not my only patient."

On her way out she paused to look back at him. "I'm Mila. Mila Kraft." The door closed and her soft footsteps faded to silence. Silence that drew on and on until Ilyas fell asleep again.

For a few minutes, the ablative dust clouds had done their job. The Enemy's hypervelocity projectiles blasted to plasma as they collided with the fine grains, but the shock waves carved openings in the clouds faster than they could be replenished. For years, the people of Muphrid had worked to build those defences but they brought only minutes of respite. The projectiles, simple fragments of iron each weighing a few grams but travelling close to the speed of light, tore into the orbital habitats, stations, and cities, each piece with the energy of a small nuclear device. Hundreds of them, thousands, millions.

Ilyas and his squadron waited to defend against the second wave of the attack. By the time it came they were defending expanding clouds of dust and debris and craters glowing red.

Ilyas lay wide awake in the soft bed in the softly lit room. A faint hissing and burbling from the machine pumping his blood had been the only sound since the gentle machine that washed and wiped and dressed him had left the room with motors whirring. That had been ten minutes ago, or an hour, or two. He searched for his anger, but it was weak, as he was.

Footsteps approached, the door opened. Dr Mila Kraft entered with her sad smile. A trolley followed her in on silent wheels.

"Good morning, Ilyas."

"Doctor."

She raised the head of the bed so he sat upright and summoned a machine from the corner of the room, one with jointed cermel arms and fine grippers. The hissing and burbling of the blood pump faded out.

"This may sting a little." She watched as the machine disconnected the blood-filled tubes from his arm. Gentle pressure, and the thick needles were withdrawn, a dressing applied. A dull ache, nothing more.

She lifted the cover from the trolley that had followed her in. A rich spicy smell filled the room. His mouth watered, his stomach tightened painfully.

"You came from Muphrid," she said as she lifted the tray from the trolley. "The mechs pulled the log from your vessel."

"Yes."

"We picked up the last transmission from Muphrid a little while before you arrived. I'm so sorry." She laid the tray across his lap. He picked up the spoon and dipped it into the dark orange liquid. "Take it slow. The treatment you've had has been... intensive. It'll take time for your system to settle down."

"OK." His hand shook as he raised the spoon.

"Can you manage?"

"Think so." Warm, thick, flavours of coriander and cumin and other spices unfamiliar. Ilyas closed his eyes and absorbed the taste, the texture.

"Your vessel wasn't designed for interstellar flight."

It was a statement, not a question. The spoon paused on its way back to the bowl. "A weapons control platform. The drive was originally from a long-range scoutship, adapted for multiple short jumps on a single charge. I was trying to make a sub-second jump, a hundred thousand kilometres to escape a missile. It detonated early and the radiation scrambled my flight controls. I jumped nearly thirty light-years."

"I'm sorry," she said. "I shouldn't distract you. Eat."

When the bowl was empty she placed the tray back on the trolley and sent it away. As it left the room a chair rolled in to take its place.

"Swing your legs out." She took his upper arm and elbow and eased him to a standing position. His legs shook as she turned and lowered him into the chair. Hard to judge in his weakened state but the spin of the habitat gave a gravity close to standard. Even so, she supported him and lowered him into the chair with practised ease.

She walked beside his chair along the long echoing corridor. Ilyas squinted against the bright light from the window at the end.

"You really believed you could hold off the Enemy at Muphrid?"

"We did."

"Even after what happened to the Sol system, to Earth?"

"A lack of commitment, Marshal Petro said. Everywhere before us put more effort into running away than trying to fight. No one ran from Muphrid."

"Why not?"

"We didn't let them." Ten years of martial law after Petro seized power, all the considerable industrial capacity of the Muphrid system had been dedicated to defence. No effort wasted on evacuation ships. Those under construction or not yet departed had been destroyed as a demonstration of resolve. They'd taken the drives out first, though. The scoutship drives went into weapons control platforms like Ilyas's ship, the colony ship drives into the rail-gun and missile batteries. Except one; Marshal Petro had kept one of those drives for his own use: a yacht, mobile presidential palace, centre of government, military headquarters.

A means of escape.

Now the anger rose. Two hundred thousand people could have escaped on the evacuation fleet. Two hundred thousand out of a hundred and forty million. Ilyas's anger was not directed at the Enemy, the Enemy was impersonal, implacable, like the tides that ripped apart a sun as it spiralled into a neutron star. No one knew where the Enemy came from or why they sought the extinction of the human species. A plague of machines spreading from star to star killing everyone, destroying everything, they were like a force of nature. Anger at them was pointless.

His anger, his hatred, he held solely for Marshal Petro, who had misled him, misled all of them, before finally betraying them. Through all the years since the evacuation fleet was blown up Ilyas had convinced himself it had been the right thing to do. He had had to believe it, had to believe that Celeste had been wrong to do as she did. "Stand or fall," he muttered through clenched teeth.

The window at the end of the corridor looked out onto the townscape of Thurlina, lengthways along the cylindrical habitat, a jumble of white-walled buildings and narrow streets broken up with small greens, broad parklands, trees. To right and left the ground curved up, fading into the blue-grey of a sunlit haze. Along the axis high above, the sun-tube glared with the bright yellow-white of Earth's sun. Familiar yet strange. His own home habitat was twice the size, with taller buildings, ziggurat shaped apartment blocks reaching up towards the sun-tube. Some of the larger buildings here in Thurlina had one or more narrow towers or pointed spires, each bearing on its wall or pinnacle the cross and crescent symbol of the Syntheist faith.

"I came from Muphrid." Ilyas looked up at Mila. "We followed the Humanist Covenant."

She stood still beside him, unperturbed by his observation. "Don't be concerned, Ilyas. Our faith isn't like some sects. Church and Covenant have lived in harmony in Thurlina since the colony was founded."

A small bird with a yellow breast, shades of delicate blue on the wings and head, and a dark band across the eyes sang in the high branches of a tree some metres from the window. It stood out sharply against the green leaves. Nothing else moved. Thurlina was home to seven hundred thousand people, according to his almanac, but the almanac was sixty years out of date. There had been no interstellar ships in the docks when he arrived, no way for anyone to escape when the Enemy reached here.

"My ship was damaged," he said, "but the drive was intact." A single-seater, someone in Thurlina was bound to claim it for themselves, to get away before the Enemy came here, too.

"The mechs are doing what they do when they find something broken. They're fixing it."

"What will happen to it?"

She touched her hand to his shoulder. "You can leave when it's ready, when you're well enough."

The lift took them down to the ground floor, and the chair rolled across a wide entrance lobby: white walls, shining floor, the light of the sun-tube pouring in through tall glass windows. No one stood behind the reception desk, no one sat in the low couches of the waiting area. Nothing moved except a small spider mech working its way across the expanse of glass, cleaning away unseen dirt. Glass doors slid silently aside to allow them into the grassed grounds around the hospital. Ilyas had not seen so much green space in over a decade, since before they'd built the flight training facility over his local park, the same facility where he had enlisted. Ilyas's chair rolled beside Mila along the path and round the side of the building to a row of modest single-storey houses. The light was fading, the glare of the sun-tube diminishing, the shadowy patchwork of streets and buildings becoming visible overhead on the far side of the cylinder.

"This is yours." Mila led him up a path to the third door. "Kitchen, bedroom, living area. There's a gym at the back. You can cook for yourself or order in. Eat and drink small amounts, often, until your stomach is used to food again. Gentle exercise; just stand and sit a few times today. You'll soon get your strength back."

An aurocular lay on the living room table. She picked it up and handed it to him. "Anything you need, just ask, or call me. I'll be back in a couple of hours to check on you."

The aurocular was a commonplace design, hooking over the ears and resting on the brow. The earpieces slipped into place and the lasers projected their image into his eyes. A few blinks, a few words and he was looking at a 3D projection of what had once been settled space, a rough globe of stars centred on Sol. Nu Phoenicis, the first to fall to the Enemy, lay at the surface on one side. Zosma almost diametrically opposite. Most of the stars shone as white dots. Those that had been settled, but now known to be lost to the Enemy, were red. Green denoted those where humanity still survived — doubtless some of those had fallen, but news travelled slowly on starships or laser beams, percolating through settled space at the speed of light. The globe, a hundred light-years across, was speckled with red. Green stars clustered in a lens-shaped region roughly centred on the axis between Sol and Zosma.

Ilyas zoomed in on the region around this system, GJ430.1. Muphrid glowed red, having fallen thirty years before. The Enemy's usual pattern would have them consolidate their position in one system for between one and five years, rebuilding their arsenal to assault the next, jumping at light speed. Years yet before they would reach here from Muphrid, but Muphrid was not the nearest red star. Ilyas drilled down into the details of Gliese 3649, a small research station seven years away: contact had been lost two years before.

It might be ten years before the Enemy arrived from Muphrid. It could be tomorrow if they came from Gliese 3649.

On his own two feet, Ilyas made it into the kitchen and stood, legs shaking, elbows on the countertop to take his weight, while he waited for a prepared concoction of pasta, tomato, and mycoprotein to heat through. After the meal he shuffled into the hallway and down to the bathroom. The absence of hair when he unzipped caught him by surprise. The radiation, or the treatment. He ran his hand over his scalp — a fine stiff fuzz rippled beneath his fingers. A look in the mirror revealed a gaunt face with skin raw pink stretched tight and a uniform dark shadow of emerging hair on his scalp. His fingers explored the sharp boundary at the temple where the receding edge had formerly given him a pronounced widow's peak.

Raised voices outside dragged him from his reflection. He stumbled out from the bathroom to the front door and grasped a handrail for support. Just outside the next dwelling, a woman sat in a wheelchair. Hair short and white, face filled with deep creases. Her hand curled claw-like on the arm of the chair. Mila Kraft crouched facing her, speaking too softly to hear.

"No! Leave me alone! Sinner!" the old woman shouted. Her chair wheeled around and carried her into her house. Mila stood, facing the door for a moment, then turned and walked away.

Another of Mila's patients. Ilyas made his way indoors and returned to the lounge, to the aurocular, to the globe of green and red dots. Amongst the green, the most populous system was Denebola. A system rich with natural resources and a mature industrial base eighteen years from Thurlina. The latest news from Denebola was of a construction programme for a fleet of colony ships to travel a thousand light years or more into the beyond, to find a new home far from settled space, far from the Enemy.

No guarantees. No one knew where the Enemy came from. They might be anywhere out there, or they might continue their expansion to reach the refugees in a thousand years. But to be lucky, you have to survive, to stay in the game until the next roll of the dice.

Nearer than Denebola lay Zosma, less than seven years away. Less well developed but with settlements on one of a pair of binary planets and in the space around. A cultural melange of evacuees from throughout settled space. It was questionable whether they had the capacity to build the drives for a large colony ship, like the drive in Marshal Petro's yacht, but the hull, the robotics and industrial base for a new colony, those were easy to build. If Petro had gone there, he could bargain with them for the resources to rebuild his yacht into a colony ship. He might save a thousand people, maybe more. At Muphrid they might have saved two hundred thousand. Ilyas's anger seethed

Denebola and Zosma were the two systems to which Petro might have fled. Others were too small, too hostile, or too close to the curving plane of the Enemy's advance. If Ilyas followed Petro to Zosma, he would only be three years behind him; Thurlina lay almost on the straight-line route from Muphrid. Denebola was closer to Muphrid than Thurlina was. By the time Ilyas could reach Denebola it would be nearly fifty years since the fall of Muphrid, thirty since Petro could have arrived there, and probably at least ten since it was overrun by the Enemy.

Ilyas's anger congealed to cold purpose. He would go to Zosma, three years behind Petro, find him and exact the justice he deserved. He would require luck, that Petro would not have already completed his colony ship and escaped to the beyond, that Ilyas could get close enough to him to take his revenge, but luck had favoured Ilyas so far: the jump from Muphrid had landed him close to Thurlina, Mila Kraft had saved his life, and his ship would be returned to him. Luck had favoured Ilyas Bardakci, as long as he could avoid thinking about what he had lost.

A brief spell in the gym, every machine set to the lightest of the stone weights on their cords, then Ilyas was hungry again, ravenous. A knock at the door interrupted him half-way through his second plate of assorted vegetables with a slab of some cultured protein.

Mila's brow furrowed when he opened the door, still chewing "Don't overdo it, Ilyas, you'll make yourself sick."

She sat him down in the lounge, strapped a monitor on his arm and slipped an aurocular on her brow to read it. Her eyes were drawn to the space over the coffee table where his virtual projection of the star map hung.

"They'll be here soon," he said. "The Enemy."

"I know." She lowered her eyes. "Your pulse, blood pressure are good. You must be feeling a little stronger already. I should explain the treatment you've received."

"My almanac said seven hundred thousand people lived here, but that was sixty years ago. How many are there now?"

"Three."

"Three hundred thousand?"

"No." She peered at him from under the brow of the aurocular. "Three. Including you."

Ilyas stared in silence at her waiting eyes, taking it in. Seven hundred thousand.

"How?"

"A hundred years ago we heard of the loss of Nu Phoenicis. A far away tragedy, all we could do was hold those who suffered and died in our prayers. Then as the years went by and more systems fell, the church council realised that one day they would reach us here. The council resolved that when they did, there should be no one for them to kill." She slipped her aurocular off. "Sixty years ago, we stopped having children."

"Many families at Muphrid did have children. They had faith in Marshal Petro. They had hope for the future."

"Not you?"

Ilyas's eyes ranged unseeing from Mila, to the living room window, to his own hands clasped in his lap. "I had faith, but Celeste, my wife, she wouldn't have children unless we could leave. Then... I lost her."

"Lost her?"

Ten years, and the pain of it was still so sharp he couldn't talk about it.

"Marshal Petro never asked the children at Muphrid whether we should stand and fight." He raised his head and met Mila's eyes. "You stopped having children sixty years ago? There should be tens, hundreds of thousands of people still here."

"This system is poor in resources. The population long ago reached the limit that we could support, so there were few children. Afterwards, we stripped the system bare of metals to build what ships we could, scavenged from those we already had and sent them out to the beyond to find a new life. We were able to build enough to send away everyone with a subjective age under fifty. The rest have all lived out their lives in peace here. Only Isolde is left."

Isolde. His neighbour. "And you. How long since you came back?"

"Back? I've never been away."

"You're young. You said there were no children born in the last sixty years. I assumed you'd gained years from relativity."

A half-smile, a nod of understanding. "Almost no children. Biology is hard to tame, Ilyas. Accidents happen. I *was* born after the last ship left."

Birds were singing with the brightening of the sun-tube when Ilyas woke from a deep, dreamless sleep. His muscles sang with a gentle tension and his joints tingled with the need to move. He pulled the cover aside and briskly stood, marched into the bathroom, urinated, washed. The mirror showed him a face thin rather than gaunt, a body taut and slender rather than famished. That thought awakened his appetite and he stepped smartly around the wheelchair in the hallway, heading for the kitchen.

Bread, hummus, dried fruits, and a crunchy biscuit of insect protein took the edge off enough for the desire to move, walk, run, jump, shout to override his hunger.

Ilyas stepped out of his front door and ran. He ran along the path that led back around to the front of the hospital building and out of the grounds, past stone pillars and into a maze of narrow winding streets. On either hand, stone walls with closed doors and vacant windows. On corners, plate glass of cafés, shops, hairdressers, each one pristine, shining, ready to greet its next customer. Looking back the way he had come, the five-storey facade of the hospital dominated the houses. Behind it, the slope of the habitat's end cap rose up, a patchwork of greens and browns cut through with spiral paths, fading into a white haze as it curved to vertical.

Street after street looped in long curves to new streets, all different but all the same, until one bend opened up onto a wide park. Rabbits grazed on grassland dotted with trees and cut by a lake that curved gently around the habitat's circumference. In the middle of a low, arching, wooden bridge over the lake Ilyas stopped, gasping for breath. Sweat ran down his face and stung his eyes. The scene around him darkened. His eyes filled with thickening shadows and his legs buckled beneath him.

Before the lockdown, Celeste had wanted them to flee Muphrid, to try and secure a place on a departing ship, any ship, going anywhere.

"Treat the world as it is!" she'd shouted, "You're deluding yourself, Ilyas, you can't fight the Enemy!"

Ilyas expected her to leave him the day he went to the great hall to cheer on the demolition of the evacuation fleet. She did, in her own way. He returned to a silent apartment, to her naked form lying motionless in a bath of crimson water. When he had reached for her hand he sliced open his own palm on the shard of glass she held, his blood mingling with hers.

"Stand or fall," he murmured.

"What was that, Ilyas?" Mila Kraft was sitting by his bedside.

"What happened?"

"You fainted. I did tell you not to overdo it." She held out a glass of pale liquid. "Drink this."

He shuffled up the bed to sit upright, took the glass, and drank. Cool, sweet. "I felt so... alive."

She took the empty glass from him. "How old are you, Ilyas?"

"I was born twenty-five eighty CE, eighty-nine years ago, and I've lived about fifty-seven of those." Thirty-two years in all spent in the timeless instants of light-speed travel, almost all of that in the journey from Muphrid.

She leaned forward, elbows on knees and reached out to take his hand. She held it palm uppermost. The scar that had crossed his palm was gone.

"You are eighty-nine elapsed years old, fifty-seven subjective. You were close to death when you came here, Ilyas. I don't know how much radiation you'd received, but many times a fatal dose."

"I guess I'll need to worry about cancers..."

"No, you won't. Didn't your almanac tell you about Thurlina's specialisation in medical science? I did a full-body tissue regeneration. You've lost a lot of weight with flushing out the dead and damaged cells but you now have a biological age of twenty-five."

The lost scar, restored sharpness of vision. The taut flesh, the once-receding hair now regrowing. Mila sat, still holding his hand in hers, her hand and his both with clear, unblemished skin.

"What you said about your birth being an accident. Was that true, or are you really..."

She let go the hand. "True enough. I'm older than I look, but not that old. I was born after the last starship left. As the youngest, I would have to care for the last ones, so I trained as a doctor and I gave myself the treatments that the older generation denied themselves. The same as I had to give you to save your life."

"So, I could live another eighty years, subjective?"

"One step at a time, Ilyas. Let's get you well, first."

She gave him an exercise programme and dietary advice and left him with strict instructions not to exceed the boundaries she'd laid down.

"Walk before you run," she said. "Tomorrow we'll go for a gentle walk."

After a shower and another light meal, Ilyas rested. In the evening, as the sun-tube dimmed, he ventured out to take the short stroll that Mila's programme allowed him.

"Are you another one?" A quavering voice called out from the shadowed porch of the adjacent house.

Ilyas ambled up the path and crouched down before the seated figure. "Another what, Isolde?" She was old, wrinkles joined to creases and wrapped into folds of sagging skin beneath thin, curled hair. A straggle of stiff grey hairs struggled from her upper lip.

"Damned impertinence. Using my name without giving one in return."

"Ilyas." He offered his hand.

Isolde *harrumphed*, flicked the joystick, and her chair wheeled around and into her house.

"The mechs have some questions about your ship." The light of the sun-tube sparkled on the lake as they walked, Mila's hand on Ilyas's arm to steady him.

"What kind of questions?"

"They'd like to replace some of the damaged metal components with composites. Metals are scarce here."

"That's OK."

They walked a dozen paces in silence.

"There's something else," Mila said. She stopped and turned to face him. "They said there was a range limiter. It was restricted to jumps no more than a light-day, but it had been bypassed."

Ilyas fixed his gaze on the trees on the lake's far shore.

"Treat the world as it is, Ilyas, not how you wish it were. That applies to your own self as much as the world about you. To move on, to heal, you have to reconcile yourself to what happened. Your escape from Muphrid wasn't an accident, was it?"

A dozen heartbeats, two long breaths Ilyas kept his eyes on the trees. "Ten years before the Enemy came to Muphrid, Marshal Petro ordered the destruction of the evacuation fleet. There would be no way out for any of us. I took my place in the squadron thinking that if Petro were wrong, I'd die with everyone else when the Enemy came." One more deep breath and he looked Mila in the eyes. "A short while before the end, a colleague, an engineer, told me about the limiter and how to bypass it. All the ships built on drives salvaged from the evacuation fleet had them except Marshal Petro's yacht. If the defence failed, he could get away, he and his family. We were *all* supposed to stay. Stand or fall, victory or death."

Ilyas turned away and folded his arms. "When I found out about Petro's yacht, I swore he would pay if the defence failed. I don't know that he got away, but if he did, I intend to find him."

Petro must have gone to Zosma. At Zosma he would have had leverage, a starship drive that could power a colony ship. At Denebola, he would have been one more desperate refugee.

She took his arm again and they walked on in silence. They crossed the bridge over the lake and sat at one of a dozen empty tables outside a cafe. A mech served them fresh salad with a pale oily fish.

"How long could this last?" he asked. "If the Enemy didn't come."

"Who knows? The habitat shell would last indefinitely. The mechs repair and replace themselves; everything is recycled."

"But the Enemy will come."

She didn't answer.

"What will you do, you and Isolde?"

She looked at him. "We always knew some us might be alive when the Enemy came. We have implants. When the sensors detect the Enemy's approach, that will trigger the implants and release a drug."

In every system, the attack took the same form. The first thing the sensors would detect would be the gravity waves as the Enemy's forces jumped to the system's outer reaches. Within hours, the hail of hypervelocity projectiles would shatter or vaporise anything fixed, or too big to move quickly. Finally, the missiles would come, jumping into the inner system to seek and destroy anything that remained and mop up survivors. Ilyas's mission had been to direct the rail guns to defend against the missiles, but just as the hail of hypervelocity projectiles had overwhelmed the protective shields of dust, so the missiles had kept coming and coming. Too many, too fast for the defences.

"My wife, Celeste, she took her own life after the evacuation fleet was destroyed."

"I can understand that." Mila reached out to rest her hand on his. "But our faith doesn't allow us to intentionally take a life, even our own. The implant releases a sedative so we'll be asleep when the Enemy strikes."

"My ship, if the mechs stripped out the sensors, the weapons control systems, boosted the life support, they might make room for two."

She closed her eyes and raised her face to the sky. "I used to dream of what I would do if I were away from here. The life I could lead... friends... lovers... children."

She drew her hand away. "All my life I've known I would be here until the end, caring for my elders. I can't change now. I can't leave Isolde."

"Nineteen days." Ilyas set his empty wine glass down. "Why do you have a feast every nineteen days?"

Mila raised and tilted the bottle towards him. He nodded and she poured. "Syntheism is a fusion of all the old religions. The nineteen-day feast is a tradition we inherited from the Bahá'í."

Isolde sat hunched in her chair, but with a grin on her face and a sparkle in her eyes. "Itself a mongrel faith," she cackled.

"And the Covenant is just Buddhism without spirituality." Mila retorted.

That set Isolde laughing again, and Mila joined her. They were both in their finery. Isolde wore a fine quilted jacket in dark greens and maroons, embroidered in gold thread. Gold, here where metals of any kind were more precious than anywhere. Gold too, the cross and crescent pendant that hung from Mila's neck, framed by her low-cut dress.

"Why 'sinners', Isolde?" Ilyas took a sip from his glass. "What sin have we committed?"

Mila grinned and rolled her eyes.

Isolde pointed her crooked finger at Mila, then Ilyas. "Look at you both, in the full flush of youth. What of the penance!"

"Penance?"

Mila pushed her plate away. "A penance for our hubris. We have affronted God and his prophets with our desire for eternal youth, and so we should allow ourselves to grow old and die a natural death before the Enemy comes. But Isolde, that oath was made before I was born. I'm not bound by the promises of my elders."

"Bah! That's Covenant talk. You were raised in the faith."

"And you were raised in the Covenant, Isolde. Atheists."

"*Atheist* defines us by what we are not," Ilyas said, catching Isolde's eye. "What we *are* is humanists," they choroused.

"But Isolde," Ilyas continued. "you're Covenant, yet you still followed the faith's edict to grow old?"

Isolde paused, the laughter fell from her eyes. "You and I both know that gods are fairy tales for the credulous, young man, but solidarity with your community is an essential part of humanity. How would I have felt if I'd stayed young and beautiful while my friends and neighbours all withered with age?"

Ilyas nodded. "Covenant solidarity played a big part for us at Muphrid."

Isolde's hand banged the table with surprising ferocity. "Yet you forgot the Covenant's first precept! *Treat the world as it is, not as you wish it were!*" Her needle-sharp eyes bored into Ilyas. "Year after year I saw the news feeds coming from Muphrid. That charlatan Petro told you what you wanted to hear, and you all lapped it up. And what about the fifth precept: *Disdain those who concur. Honour those who dissent.* Were there no dissenting voices?"

Celeste. She had been a dissenting voice.

"Isolde..." Mila reached out to touch Isolde's arm and she jerked it angrily away.

"It's alright, Mila." Ilyas said. "Petro had a valid argument, Isolde. Everyone before us had spent their resources on running, not fighting. Petro's crime was to run away himself."

"Still you deceive yourself. For every one who could have left, hundreds would be left behind. Petro played on your secret fears. You would rather no one was saved than be left behind yourself. He was a devil of your own making." Isolde backed her chair from the table. "I'm tired, Mila. Help me to my bed."

Ilyas cleared the table — the mechs would have done it, but it kept him busy while Mila helped Isolde. He waited for her outside the door. A clear night revealed the tracery of street lights on the habitat's far side, with dark patches of parks, all cut through with the arrow-straight silhouette of the darkened sun-tube.

Disdain those who concur. Honour those who dissent. The dissenters at Muphrid were all silenced, or had silenced themselves, like Celeste.

"Isolde's asleep." Mila appeared at his elbow. "She was sharp tonight." Her hand reached for his.

"Tomorrow." He clasped his hands behind his back. "I'd like to go to my ship."

Mila cast her eyes down. "OK. I understand."

Before bed, Ilyas sat alone in his living room gazing through the aurocular. At the star map, and through the eyes of Thurlina's sensors that waited patiently for the coming of the Enemy.

His dreams that night took him back to Muphrid, where he wandered the empty streets past the flight school, through abandoned parks and into the echoing emptiness of the great hall, finally climbing the stairs to his apartment on the fourth floor of the ziggurat. He found Celeste reading her book, lying in the bath of crimson water.

"You're too late," she said.

"Too late for what?"

"You killed us all, now it's time."

"Why do you say that. Why say that *I* killed everyone?"

"Look in the mirror."

Ilyas felt the presence of the mirror behind him, the mirrored door of the small cabinet over the sink. He didn't want to turn, didn't want to look.

"Look in the mirror!"

Her words compelled him, unwilling, he turned. A familiar face stared back; thick grey hair, broad features, stern expression. Marshal Petro.

"Now," Celeste's voice reverberated from the bathroom tiles. "It's time."

Ilyas woke to the sound of a distant siren. He slipped on the aurocular to see Thurlina's sensors scintillating with gravity waves from every direction. The Enemy was here. Only hours remained before the hail of hypervelocity projectiles would shatter the habitat's silicate shell. He rose from his bed, washed and dressed, and made his way out into the dim light of night. In the adjacent dwelling, Isolde's frail form lay still as stone in her bed. Her implant had fulfilled its intended purpose and spared her pain, the stilling of her weak heart an unfortunate side effect.

He sat a moment with her, replaying her words of the previous evening. *Honour those who dissent.*

In the next house, Mila breathed softly in her sleep. He touched her hand. "Mila," he whispered, but she did not stir. In the darkness of her bedroom Ilyas searched for his anger but found only the image of Marshal Petro's face staring at him from the mirror in his dream.

A word to Ilyas's aurocular summoned a transit car which took him the short distance from the hospital to the end cap before rising up the slope into the open between fields and vineyards. Quickly, the climb steepened until it ascended the vertical face to the axis, weight declining to nothing, then out through the hub into windowless passages, a maze of pressurised tubes that spidered out from the axis to the zero-g docks, workshops, and freight and passenger terminals.

It stopped in an embarkation hall. Long glass windows on one side looked out on the aged and pitted outer wall of the habitat's end-cap, its motion barely visible as it turned beneath. The docks extended out past the window on the other side: lattices of struts with clamps and docking ports, all empty but the one where Ilyas's ship sat. Tiny, patched and battered, but whole.

The weight of his burden had slowed him on the walk from Mila's dwelling to the transit, and the inertia of it made him clumsy as he manoeuvred without gravity along the tube to the docking port. Ilyas squeezed through the open hatch and into the cramped cockpit. A systems check showed the reactor on-line, the ship ready, the range-limit still disabled. He prepared a navigation program so that when he began the launch sequence the hatch would close, the clamps release. A short spurt from the thrusters and the ship would clear the dock and make the jump to the Zosma system. Seven years would elapse; the blink of an eye in subjective time.

Little time remained, but enough for the burden that waited in the access tube. A few moments and he was finished. Ilyas reached across the cramped space of the cockpit to press the button to begin the launch sequence. As the hatch closed he made his way back to the embarkation hall to watch the departure through the long window.

This time, he would treat the world as it was. What did it matter where Petro had fled, if he had escaped at all? Ilyas had constructed an impeccable chain of logic that would lead him to Zosma, as impeccable as the logic of defending Muphrid had been. Petro had been Ilyas's own creation. His, and all those who had stood in the great hall with him.

This time, someone would be saved, someone would survive at least until the next roll of the dice. In seven years elapsed, hours subjective, the sedative would wear off and Mila Kraft would awaken in the cockpit of his ship looking out at the colonies at Zosma.

"Stand or fall." Ilyas folded his arms and waited.

See David Whitmarsh's story "Stand or Fall" online at Metaphorosis. If you liked it, leave a comment. Authors love that! Remember to subscribe to our e-mail updates so you'll know when new stories are posted.

About the story

This story began life as an exercise in filling the backstory of a character in an as yet unpublished novel that follows the fate of two thousand refugees who escape the Enemy's attack on Zosma, one of the last of humanity's settled systems. Mila Kraft, who is sent by Ilyas to Zosma at the end of this story, is one of the main characters; a doctor who is older than she looks, and follows the syntheist faith but is sympathetic to the Covenant. I started by thinking about how she acquired all those attributes.

The Enemy's assault on humanity lies in the past in the novel, forming part of the background. Writing this story gave me a chance to play with ideas about how different societies, isolated from each other by the light-speed limit on travel and communication, would react in different ways to the inexorable advance on an invincible enemy.

The first draft almost wrote itself in just a few days. The mechanics of the story came together easily, but it has taken many revisions and much valued feedback from others to develop and clarify Ilyas's arc.

A question for the author

Q: Q: What's better: writing or having written?

A: Writing, by far. I get great pleasure from creating new worlds, working them out in more detail than ever reaches the page, then populating them with characters that I move through the arcs of their stories. Once having written, it's just time to move onto the next thing. Better than having written, is having been read.

About the author

David Whitmarsh is a rehabilitated software engineer who now spends his days playing acoustic blues badly and writing. David lives in West Sussex with his wife, two cats and a varying subset of his four adult children.

@whitmarshdj

Gatekeepers

Douglas DiCicco

Now she'd never get to finish her book, Elsie thought. She'd just gotten to the good bit when her train derailed.

"So what happens now?" she asked Osiris. "You weigh my heart against a feather?"

"Not personally, no," Osiris answered. "Too many dead people these days. The gatekeepers handle that now. I just get the process started."

Osiris reached into Elsie's chest and pulled out her heart. It was more colorful than Elsie would have guessed, much more luminous. Her heart was a whirl of metallic sheens and colorful glows.

"What did you love most in life?" Osiris asked, eyes on the heart.

"Stories," Elsie answered.

Osiris smiled and pressed the heart into Elsie's hands. It squelched with disconcerting wetness.

"I'd start there." Osiris pointed down one of the countless corridors stretching endlessly into the dark in every direction. Like all the others, it was lined with shadowy figures, each standing before a flickering portal. "Third on the left. Best of luck."

Elsie followed the directions. She felt her heartbeat quicken in her hands. She was nervous.

The third shade on the left hovered before a portal to an endless library. Up close, Elsie could smell tea and paper wafting through.

"Do you seek to take your eternal rest in my realm?" the shade asked.

"I think so?" Elsie answered. She wasn't quite certain how all this worked.

The answer seemed to be enough for the shade. It took Elsie's heart from her and held it up to the light. It turned the heart from side to side, then upside down. The shade shook its head disapprovingly. "No, no. I'm sorry. This won't do at all."

"Why not?" Elsie frowned.

"See this bit here?" The shade tapped at a silver bit on the heart's underside. It produced a quiet metallic ping. "Dragon scale. Or some other mythical creature. Doesn't matter." The shade passed the heart back, handling it like a scrap of rotten fish it was eager to be rid of. "If it's part of your heart, I can't let you pass."

"Why does that matter?" Elsie asked.

The shade sighed. "Because this is the portal to the Realm of Literary Readers," it answered. "Literary," the shade repeated the word, emphasizing each and every syllable. "This is a place for the souls of serious readers of serious works."

"I like serious literature," Elsie insisted.

"Yes, but you also like dragons. Or something just as bad. Something that smacks of genre," the shade said. "I'm sorry, but there's no place for you in my realm. Try the Realm of Fantasy Readers." It stretched out a shadowy limb. "Down that way, fifth on the right."

Elsie took the advice and presented her heart to the shade guarding the portal to the Realm of Fantasy Readers. It was just as unimpressed as the first shade had been. "No, I'm sorry. I don't think this is the place for you."

"The last one I spoke with thought it was," Elsie said. "They said there's a dragon scale on my heart."

"What, this?" The new shade poked at the heart's silver bit. "Oh, no. That's no dragon scale. No, looks like chrome to me. You probably want the Realm of Cyberpunk Readers. Back the way you came. Second on your left."

The guardian of the Realm of Cyberpunk Readers was no more receptive to Elsie's heart. "The hearts of true cyberpunk aficionados are wrought of naught but chrome and bleed naught but code. Look, you've got this much larger dark patch right here." It prodded a particularly squishy portion of the heart. "I'd try Horror Readers."

The shade at the portal to the Realm of Horror Readers weighed Elsie's heart and found it too light. The guardian of the Realm of Comedy Readers weighed it again, and found it too heavy. Her heart was too cold for Erotica, too hot for Cozy Mysteries. Elsie's heart was too old-fashioned for Science Fiction, too modern for Alternate History.

"Have you tried the Realm of Literary Readers?" suggested the shade guarding the Realm of Thriller Readers, after a rejection full of misdirection and shocking twists.

Elsie slumped against the wall, knees against her chest, clutching her heart tightly. She had wandered the endless halls for what felt like an eternity. She felt no closer to finding the place she belonged. Each of the realms had something which drew her in, but the shades barred her way at every turn.

"Still here?"

Elsie looked up to see Osiris offering her a hand. She took it and got back to her feet. "I don't belong anywhere," she said, barely holding back tears.

Osiris smiled gently. "Which stories were your favorites?"

Elsie considered the question for a moment. "The ones I told myself."

"Ah." Osiris gave Elsie's hand a gentle squeeze. "Come with me."

Osiris led her to a portal guarded by a squat and smoky shade.

"Try this one." Osiris suggested.

Elsie stepped forward. She could hear the scribbling of pens and the clacking of typewriters echoing from the portal. She smelled good coffee and cheap whisky. She glimpsed untidy desks overflowing with crumpled notes and obscure reference tomes. The portal beckoned to her like none of the others had.

"Do you seek to take your eternal rest here, in the Realm of Writers?" the shade asked, holding out a shadowy tendril.

"Yes." Elsie said, handing over her heart.

The shade inspected the heart. The parade of rejections had drained Elsie's heart of much of the energy and vigor it once possessed. It was a dark, shriveled thing now, hard and bitter, like an especially withered raisin.

"It certainly looks like a writer's heart," the shade said. It placed the heart on a shelf beside the portal. "Thank you for your interest in the Realm of Writers. You can expect an answer in six to eight weeks."

Elsie sat before the shade and waited. She waited, and waited, and waited. Six weeks passed. Then eight. Then twelve. It was somewhere around half a year when the shade finally picked her heart off the shelf, eyeballed it for a moment, then tossed it back to Elsie.

"Thank you for your submission to the Realm of Writers." The shade sounded very rehearsed. "Unfortunately, your heart does not meet our realm's needs at the present moment."

"What?" Elsie cried. She'd really thought this would be the one.

"We receive many quality hearts of the recently deceased," the shade continued. "I'm afraid your heart didn't quite win me over. I wish you the best of luck finding another placement for your eternal soul."

Elsie sat there a moment, stunned, staring at the withered lump her heart had become. She had no idea what to do now, where to go. This was the only place that had felt right for her, and now it was closed off. Not knowing what else to do, she got back to her feet and prepared to resume what felt like a futile search.

"Didn't like this one after all?" Osiris was back.

"I don't belong here either," Elsie said, holding back tears.

Osiris arched an eyebrow. "Says who?"

Elsie pointed to the shade in front of the portal.

"Ah." Osiris smiled. "You know... they're only as strong as you let them be."

Elsie watched the shade for a moment. When she turned back to Osiris, they had already disappeared.

She looked down at the heart in her hands. She saw a flicker of light somewhere deep in the core. A spark that hadn't quite been snuffed out. She turned back to the portal and marched forward.

"You again." The shade seemed both surprised and mildly annoyed. "I'm sorry, I can't provide personal feedback on each and every heart I examine. If you'd like to try again with a new core personal identity, maybe something a little more mainstream, I'd be happy to review another submission."

Elsie ignored the shade and kept moving toward the portal. Her heart glowed brighter.

"Wait!" The shade moved to block Elsie from the portal. "You can't go in. You aren't a real writer. I haven't approved you yet."

Elsie held up her heart. The light shone straight through the shade. She walked through it, ignoring the guardian's wailing as she entered the portal.

"This time..." Elsie said as the light enveloped her. "I'm going to write my own ending."

See Douglas DiCicco's story "Gatekeepers" online at Metaphorosis.
If you liked it, leave a comment. Authors love that!
Remember to subscribe to our e-mail updates so you'll know when new stories are posted.

About the story

The world of fiction is full of gatekeepers, from editors of major publications to social media trolls who take it upon themselves to police who counts as a "real" fan of their genre. This can be demoralizing not only to writers, but to readers. This story came from taking that problem to an extreme, and thinking about the ways people can respond to it.

A question for the author

Q: Do you have any pets? Do they influence your writing?

A: I have no pets at the moment, but I've had many over the years: a dog, three cats, two parakeets. Like any part of the family, pets shape your whole view of the world. That can't help but influence your writing.

About the author

Douglas DiCicco is an author of speculative fiction living in Clovis, California. He has worked as an attorney, a teacher, and a Renaissance Faire performer.

@CiccoDouglas

Tides

Ailsa Bristow

The woman stood at the edge of a cliff, suspended halfway between sky and sea. At her back, beyond the rocky outcrop, was the ancient cottage, shutters clattering with the ocean breeze.

She breathed the world in. There had been a storm last night, and the world was salt-scrubbed clean. She watched the sun begin to roll over the horizon, painting the sky in hazy yellows and soft pinks. It was a day for starting over.

She began to walk. Her legs were still stiff, foreign things, and she stumbled a little at first, but soon found her stride. She tried not to think about the old man she'd left behind in the cottage. In the inside pocket of the windbreaker he'd loaned her was a thick roll of green bills that she'd found in a kitchen drawer that morning.

She walked. The skin on her hands blackened with dirt that she stooped to gather by the fistful for no other reason than to inhale its foreign fragrance. She walked, letting the roar of the sea grow more distant with every step. The land seemed quiet until she trained herself to listen for the furtive creatures burrowing in the earth and to hear the wind singing in the trees. From time to time, she spotted the dim shapes of squat buildings in the distance. She avoided them, her stomach clenching as she remembered the way the old man's eyes had crinkled as he smiled.

Perhaps it was better not to risk getting too close to other strangers.

She walked.

As she walked, she gathered new words, fragments of overheard stories, questions. Her days were loose. She might rest beneath the shade of a beech tree for hours or run as fast as she could just to feel the way the wind tugged at her hair. She slept in barns and in hollows and, once, in the bed of a pick-up truck, where the blankets she found felt like a gift, just for her. She slipped among the people whose words she ate up, who shared food with her, always a passer-by. She thought she might keep herself safe, that way.

When she arrived in the city it was airless, choked with dust and fumes. She almost turned around and walked straight back the way she had come, ready to give up on whatever impulse had brought her this far. Only curiosity forced her feet forward.

She wanted more stories. She wanted answers.

There were words for what she'd done. She was a runaway, a fugitive, a thief. But none of the words seemed to fit right; they cut tight against her skin.

She had been seeking solid ground for a long time. Not even the ocean had been wide or deep enough to contain her restless heart.

Her mother, her voice crashing and roaring, had told her: "This is who you are. This is where you belong."

Though it had never been spoken between them, she knew her mother was lying. Or at least, she wasn't telling the whole truth. There was another world she belonged to. It didn't matter that the ocean was her home, her inheritance. It was also her prison.

Without meaning to, she had found the beach—colliding fragments of all that made her: salt, shadow, stillness. She was transmogrified; fresh bone grazing against socket; new skin tested by sharp rocks. Her untested lungs had choked on cooling air.

Her mother roared in fury as her wayward daughter scrambled along the beach. Wave after wave lashed her legs, tried to pull her back in. She had dug her fingers into the grit and damp of the sand. Her hands had found rocks, a way to tether herself to the land. When the old man found her, she was still clinging to them, the skin on her palms red and raw.

The old man had lived his whole life by the sea. She could smell it on him. He ought to have known enough stories to warn him away from beautiful young women washed up on the shore. Still, he had covered her with his jacket, and offered her his hand, and she had taken it, pulling herself up and away from the sand, the stone, the water.

She tried not to think of how much of herself she might have left behind.

The cottage was ancient—too few windows, and all of them small—but comfortable enough. In the kitchen, plates and bowls were stacked on every surface; spoiling fruit spilled out of a bowl, but the fridge was bare and empty.

"Sorry," the old man said, with a vague wave of the hand. "Since my wife died, I've not had much company."

He'd fumbled through the cupboards, at last pulling out a battered box of pasta and a dusty jar of sauce.

"I'm sorry," she said. "About your wife."

His jaw tightened. "S'alright," he mumbled, but she could read the grief in his face: the way his eyes seemed to look just past her when he spoke, the rumpled shirt, the hollows of his cheeks.

"Tell me a story," she said, and, as they sat down to eat the pasta he had cooked until flaccid, he had.

There was a young man, lived round these parts. Fisherman by trade. Cut him open and his veins would have run with salt water, that's right. He knew the water like a husband knows his wife. Knew just by looking at the water when a squall was coming. Knew never to set sail on a Friday, knew never to tempt the winds by whistling when at sea. Knew the sea for a goddess, and a fearsome one at that, and knew enough not to scoff at the devotions the older men made as they set sail, even though they were good Christians when they set foot back on the land.

And the young man fell in love with sea. Even when he was not out to fish, he would journey out in his boat, to admire the glimmer of sunlight upon the waves. When the water was calm, he'd let the little boat drift, and let his fingers run back and forth through the icy waters, a caress. When a storm blew, he roared along with the sea, his heart thrumming.

And the sea, in her own way, loved him too. Loved the solidity of him, loved his quick-quick energy. Loved his youth and his wonder, loved the startling blue of his eyes.

One day, a storm caught the young fisherman off-guard—the swelling waves tugged him in towards a sandbar, tossed the boat over jagged rocks.

The fisherman ought to have died, but the sea, well, she scooped him up. Carried him to a cove and forced herself—at great cost—to join him on the shore, so she could pump the water from his lungs. Kept his frozen body warm with her own body, pressed a kiss to his raw and bloody lips.

She had waited, unwilling to speak lest she break the story's spell, but the man's voice had faded and drifted. The light outside the cottage died and the *plink plink plink* of rain against glass filled the silence between them.

"And?" she asked when she could bear it no longer. "What happened next?"

The old man startled, blinked at her as if he'd forgotten she was there. His hand grazed the rough stubble on his chin.

"The story ends the way all stories about love must end," the man said, his smile wry. "Tragedy and loss." He'd shifted abruptly out of his chair, began to gather the plates from dinner. She hurried to help him; her hands clumsy as she dried the heavy pan. When the task was done, the old man stood staring at his hands, pruned by the dish water. He didn't look up, but when he spoke it was clearly: "Still, better to have loved and lost. Better to have loved and lost."

The city invited strangers. She noticed the way the people moved through it and left only the barest of traces. A damp palm print on a revolving door, the lingering smell of perfume in a bathroom stall.

The city was a place to disappear into; a place where she could have a life of her own making.

She became skilled at getting by. She learned how to take favours without giving up too much of herself. Learned the city's rhythm, grew used to the heat of so many bodies pressed up against one another. Learned how, sometimes, if she looked into someone's eyes for just the right amount of time, they would forget what she'd neglected to pay for. They always sent her off with a smile.

Still, it didn't matter how far she had travelled from the ocean. She woke sometimes to the sound of crashing waves. The water in her bathroom sink ran thick with salt, coating the basin with crystals. When she walked down the grey city streets, seagulls as lost as she was cried out, *come home, home come home, come, come.*

A man with eyes the colour of moss approached her in a bar.

"Adam," he said, sticking out his hand. She couldn't help but smile at his boyish bravado. She gave him a name, let him buy her a drink.

He asked her where home was.

"That's a complicated question," she said, and he nodded as if he understood. He told her about the place where he grew up. The landlocked mountains where rock hemmed in the sky. He told her about driving up mist-skirted highways, passing trees standing sentinel.

"A place like that gets in your bones," he said. "I'll never leave it."

He had a habit of running his hand through his brown hair, leaving it sticking out in every direction. He shook his head and gave a wry laugh. "I think I've had one too many," he said, tipping his empty glass.

"No," she said. "No, I know exactly what you mean." Her eyes slid away. "I'd love to see the mountains, someday."

They left together, drunk and laughing. She let him into her damp basement apartment. Her eyes followed his as he took in the bare walls, the single bed, the wilting flowers on the kitchen counter.

"How long did you say you'd been here?"

She didn't answer, and when she kissed him, he tasted of pine.

Adam fit into her life in ways she hadn't known she needed. Together, they painted her apartment. She spent hours agonizing over paint chips until she at last selected a white called *fresh start*. Adam laughed. He arrived at her door week after week with his arm full of plants—cacti, palms, rubber plants, succulents, spider plants—until her apartment brimmed with green.

"Things even you can't kill," he said with a grin.

He cooked her breakfast and as she ate, he read her the headlines, his face reddening as he unspooled all the trouble in the world.

She asked him for a story, and he laughed, asked "What *kind* of story?" and looked baffled when she shrugged and said, "Any kind of story." He sat in silent thought for a minute. When he began to speak, his dark brows pinched together in concentration.

When I was a kid, my dad couldn't work out how he ended up with a wimp like me. I'd cry at anything: a dead raccoon at the side of the road, the thought of puppies being separated from their mothers, a harsh word from a kid at school. My mom called me sensitive *but, my dad… well. He wanted to protect me, I guess. Signed me up for judo, got me into weightlifting, gave me my first sip of beer when I was 12 years old. He loved me in his own way, I think.*

So anyway, when I was sixteen, dad and I went on a camping trip. It was the thing we'd always shared. We loved the crisp mountain air, loved bathing in still, crystal clear lakes. We'd spend our days hiking, gathering firewood, making camp, maybe fishing. At night, my dad would whittle and tell me all about his dad, his childhood, the kind of things we never normally talked about.

On the last night, he told me he was sick. There wasn't much that could be done, he said. A few months, maybe half a year. And I cried. Of course I did, as if I were splitting into a million pieces. He hugged me tight, and I could smell the salt-sweat of his skin, the lingering sunscreen, the sweet mildewy scent of his clothes. His hands were rough, and red, and he gripped me so hard it was as though he thought he could hold me together through sheer force of will. He held me until I had nothing more in me, until I was empty and stunned.

It was a clear night, the stars sprawled out across the velvet sky. My dad still held me close.

Finally, he said, "You can't care this much, son. You can't keep living life with your heart on your sleeve. The world'll destroy you if you care too much."

I didn't know what to say to that and so I said nothing. Six weeks later, he was dead.

Adam worked as a government relations officer at a large non-profit. As they spent more time together, her space began to fill with briefing papers and glossy reports, printouts of statistical models, survey data sets. He dressed every morning in his grey dress pants and when she saw him in the evenings his tie was always loose, his shirt sleeves rolled up. He'd seemed baffled when she told him that she worked odd jobs—catering shifts and office temp work, mostly—couldn't understand her lack of drive, ambition.

"Maybe I've had enough of ambition for one lifetime," she'd said. "Maybe I want to paint on a smaller canvas."

The truth was, she liked to be anonymous, forgettable. She sailed through galas and parties, tray of canapes balanced in one hand, offering guests an impassive smile. All the while, her mind floated away.

In her new life, she was slow, dreamy. She lost hours gathering stories, imagining new possibilities. She wrote herself into many different futures: a house with Adam, two kids and a dog; a lonely mountaintop cabin where she would paint and write; a bustling farmhouse, full of friends and guests, honeysuckle creeping up the walls.

"You have enough energy for the both of us," she'd tell Adam with a playful nudge. "You change the world. I'm just trying to live in it."

Still, it rankled. To spend time with Adam was to be recruited into his causes. Housing accessibility and playground regeneration. Traffic calming and environmental justice. Once, she even found him furiously typing on a neighbourhood Facebook page, dedicated to saving the local Starbucks.

Her burbling laugh had been cut short by the look on his face. It was the most accessible coffee shop in the area, he'd told her, lonely young moms used it, it was a safe place for homeless people. "Community spaces *matter*," he'd said, his cheeks stained red.

One morning she woke to find his face bathed in the blue light from his phone. His hair was matted to one side of his head, and she could trace the lines of the pillow creases across his cheeks. He propped himself up on an elbow, thrust the phone at her. "Look at this," he demanded. She stared at the image of a beached whale, its body swollen and grotesque against the white sand.

She looked away. "Do you have to—"

"This is *happening*," he said. "Right here, right now. It's our duty to look. To do something."

She rolled out of bed, backed away from him and the photo he was still brandishing at her. "What are you doing? This isn't *doing* anything," she spat.

She'd left as he continued to lecture her, picking up her bag and slamming the door shut behind her. She didn't return until the sun began to bruise in the sky.

Adam was sat there on the steps that led up to her apartment, eyes rimmed with red, stubble skimming his chin.

She waited as he pushed himself up, ran a hand through his wild hair. Everything they'd said and everything they'd left unsaid hung between them.

And then he closed the space between them, pulled her into a tight embrace. "Don't you ever do that again; do you hear me?" His voice was thick with his too-ready tears. "I thought—"

But she didn't let him finish, pressed her mouth against his lips. As they made their way back into the apartment, she thought about the yoke of belonging to someone; of the obligation that came from holding another person's happiness between your hands.

Despite everything, they *were* happy. Her happiness was physical, solid, lodged beneath her ribcage. Happiness was a kind of pain. Adam's eyes, his smile, his hand grazing hers—her happiness tended to be a sharp-clawed thing that seemed to press against her ribs. She was afraid—if she let her happiness loose, would it crack her open? Would it gut her?

In the cool blue light of a morning, she thought about ending things. She could form the words so easily, knew how his face would crumple, knew how he would fight back the tears. Would he be gentle in the face of heartbreak? Would he shout and slam the door on their life together? When he told the story to their friends would he cast her as the villain?

Sleepy, he rolled over in the bed, pulled her into his body. His eyes blinked open.

"What's this?" he asked, brushing a thumb over her damp cheeks.

"I just..." The words lodged in her throat. How could she tell him all the ways she'd fought to get free, only to find herself clutching him?

"I don't want to leave you," she choked out.

Adam searched her face, his gaze gentle. He planted a kiss on her forehead, rested his chin there. "So don't," he said, as if it were that simple. Her body shook with the force of a sadness that needed to crash over rocks.

"You don't understand," she whispered. "Where I come from... I'll never leave there. I'll always being going back there. And that means..."

He cupped her chin in his palms. "Means you'll have to leave me?"

She nodded; her throat too closed for words.

He considered her. "You talk as if there's no choices to be made, love."

Her mother's voice echoed on her tongue. "I'm flighty, selfish. I'll never settle down, never take things seriously."

Adam pulled back. His thumb gently nudged her chin until she met his gaze. "That's not you. That's not who you are." He was close enough for his breath to warm her skin. "You can promise me right now. Whatever choices we make, we'll make them together."

Pine and salt, leaves rustling and the crash of waves. Her thoughts tangled, but he didn't release her from his arms and so she nodded. "I promise."

Days passed, weeks passed, months passed, and she stayed.

She and Adam moved into to a house with a garden that she did not know how to tend. They visited farmer's markets, they argued over who had or had not taken out the garbage, they filled their house with the laughter and shouting of friends who believed that a good argument over wine would be enough to put the world to rights.

And Adam grew used to the way the gulls would line up along their back fence every morning.

They were building a life, she thought, day by day. She had never realized it would be so ordinary, so tedious, so beautiful.

They stretched out on their deck on a late July night, the plum sky shimmering with the light of the city. Heat pounded like a pulse through them. Adam rolled a joint as she sipped a glass of cool earthy wine.

They sank back into the pillows and blankets they'd pulled outside. They talked about taking a trip to the mountains—she'd still never seen the place where he was born.

Silence fell between them.

"You'll make a wonderful mother, one day."

His palm pressed against her thigh. She flinched but did not pull away.

"You don't want to?"

"No—I mean—I haven't really thought about it yet."

He rolled her onto her side so he could cradle her in his arms. "So... Think about it."

The story was almost too easy to write. Stacks of laundry. Toys underfoot. Counting steps and hopping over the cracks in the sidewalk. Naming all the animals in the city park zoo. Green eyes that would promise endless summer. A laugh that could crack a day wide open.

She could see it all.

She kissed him before she could say all that was in her heart.

The night breeze whispered *come home*. Water dripping from taps calling *come, come, come*. The gulls, once silent, began to caw, ever more insistent, *come home, home, home*. She tried to ignore it, but the message echoed across water as wide as continents, and over the windswept land.

Thin-lipped newscasters delivered the solemn news that the ocean was dying. Fish washed up rotting on the shoreline. The water stank of sulphur. Children foolish enough to splash in wading pools, lakes, or even puddles, appeared in emergency rooms, their skin blistering and black. There was no explanation; something had gone wrong. Adam read her the stories over their breakfast coffees until she at last begged him to stop.

"We have a duty," he said, frowning.

An argument years in the making echoed between them.

Rain drummed against the windows, *come home*. The wind howled, *come home*. She tossed in the bed, trying to sleep through the clamour of a storm until she heard in a roll of thunder the message she had been trying to ignore. *Your mother is dead. Come home.*

She forgot to eat. Her eyes, once deep blue, turned dishwater grey. Sentences, thoughts drifted away from her.

"What is it?" Adam asked her. He tried being gentle, but when he couldn't reach her the words became an accusation. "What's going on with you?"

It wasn't that she didn't want to tell him. It was that anytime she tried to fishhook the words up through her mouth, she found only breath and silence.

Come home, come home.

She dreamed of the old man, pictured the way he stood staring at his hands in the basin of soapy dishwater. *Better to have loved and lost*, he'd said. But he'd also told her all love stories ended in tragedy and loss.

She considered the weight of a lifetime of waiting.

Remembered the fractured sadness in the old man's deep blue eyes.

She woke to the sheets soaked and reeking of brine. Ice cold water flooded the lungs that were made for land and not sea. There was no seawall to hold the waters back; her body screamed at the shock and then turned numb.

She lurched from the bed, her breath rasping. Adam stumbled after her.

"What's happening?" His green eyes were wide as she began slinging her belongings into a backpack. "What's going on?"

She blinked up at him through salt-water tears. She forced the words out through numb lips. "I can't. I can't anymore."

His face shuttered.

He stood at the door as she struggled down the steps with the bag of things she knew she would not need for long.

He stood on the front step, rain soaking through his t-shirt, plastering his dark hair to his skull. She wanted to be strong enough to walk away without a backward glance, but she couldn't help herself. One last look.

His mouth twisted. "I suppose I should thank you," he said, his voice trembling. "You tried to warn me once, didn't you?" His fists clenched and she knew she had to listen to what came next.

She didn't have to wait for long. He heaved a breath, and she noticed his eyes full of tears he was fighting not to shed. Then, turning slightly to one side, no longer looking at her, he said, "Go then. I should've known all along that you're too selfish to love me back."

An old man approached from the distance.

"So, you're back," he said.

Tears slid down her face.

The old man knelt beside her and drew her close. She inhaled his warmth, the tang of his body. She pressed into his solid, human form. Her borrowed body shook—there was so much she must leave behind.

"Tell me a story," she said, her words thick with tears.

And so, he did. The story of the restless goddess of the sea who'd fallen in love with a mortal man. The child she'd borne him. The life they'd tried to make together, wedged between water, rock, and sky.

"It never could last. When she realized what would happen to the seas if she left them forever..." His voice cracked; his eyes turned misty. "She had a duty. She had to return to her home."

She swallowed the words down, let them seep into her marrow.

"Life had to go on, you understand. The man, he married, and the sea..." He kept his eye on the crashing waves. "The sea is the sea. She moves according to a pattern of tides."

She was silent for a while, listening to the barely perceptible flutter in her belly. "I thought I could belong here," she said. "But I think I always knew I'd return to the sea one day." Her voice was the crash of waves against rock.

"She loved you, you know," he said. "Would be proud to see the woman you've become."

The old man held her for one last breath, and then gently let her go.

She let herself go, unpicking sinew from bone, atom from atom. *I have a duty*, she whispered, as she stretched herself thin, until she became a net spread across the ocean. She pictured Adam's face, serious and pale, his eyebrows bunched over those green eyes. But the water needed her more. And so she let the currents pull her under, sinking and bobbing, until there was no difference between her and the waves that carried her.

See Ailsa Bristow's story "Tides" online at Metaphorosis.
If you liked it, leave a comment. Authors love that!
Remember to subscribe to our e-mail updates so you'll know when new stories are posted.

About the story

I wrote the first draft of "Tides" in 2017. In its first iterations, it was very closely focused on the unnamed protagonist. I'm interested in questions of fate and free will, what we inherit vs. what we choose for ourselves. I wanted to explore a tense relationship between mother and daughter, and explore the urge to rebel against familial duty. And, because my brain is my brain, the idea of a fairytale or myth made the most sense to me.

I've always been fascinated by the sea: I remember being told once that growing up in the UK you're never more than 60 miles from the ocean. I love its beauty and respect its power; and I love the stories and legends that shape the way we look at the sea. I don't think using the idea of the sea as a personified being was a conscious choice, but something that just clicked for me.

As the story grew and changed under multiple revisions I know that many other themes that interest me worked their way into the story. Both the protagonist and Adam have left their homes, and I look at the way they try to make a new home together in a place that neither of them belong to. I can see a lot of my own climate anxiety and feelings of powerlessness come through in Adam—the question that echoes beneath this story is, perhaps, what are we willing to sacrifice in order to do the right thing? Adam says all the right words, but it is the protagonist who ultimately gives up the things she has fought for so fiercely.

As a writer, I love working on the stories that feel like a mystery to me as they are being written. The process of revising this story has been a process of getting clearer and clearer about who these characters are, and why they make the choices they make. That these characters continue to live and breathe in my imagination, four years after they first took root there, seems to me part of the magic of being a writer.

A question for the author

Q: What is the first/most recent book that you lost sleep reading/thinking about?

A: I read Erin Morgenstern's *The Starless Sea* earlier this year and it's stayed with me. I loved how Morgenstern created this rich, vivid fantasy world that also tells us so much about our own world and what it means to be human. And I definitely did some writerly swooning over some of the sentences in that book! I highly recommend it, if you haven't already read it.

About the author

Ailsa Bristow is a British writer who grew up living at least half her time in the stories she created. Now she lives in Toronto, with her partner and their idiosyncratic but much loved cat, Steve. She continues to spend most of her time dreaming of other worlds.

www.ailsabristow.ca, @AilsaBristow

Copyright

Title information

Metaphorosis 2021

ISBN: 978-1-64076-217-6 (e-book)
ISBN: 978-1-64076-218-3 (paperback)
ISBN: 978-1-64076-219-0 (hardcover)

Copyright

"The Nocturnals II" © 2021, Mariah Montoya

"Singot" © 2021, E.C. Fuller
"Souls Like Sea Glass" © 2021, Josie Smith
"Free Hugs" © 2021, Jennifer Shelby
"The Art of Unpicking Stitches" © 2021, Jennifer Hudak
"The Nocturnals III" © 2021, Mariah Montoya

"A Wizard Comes to Shorehaven" © 2021, L.J. Wetherby
"The Waves In Which We Drown" © 2021, Rubella Dithers
"Rapunzel Dreams of Elephants" © 2021, Rachel Delaney Craft
"The Nocturnals IV" © 2021, Mariah Montoya

"Tumbler" © 2021, B. Morris Allen
"Till All the Hundred Summers Pass" © 2021, J.A. Legg
"A Seedling in the Dark" © 2021, Eleanor R. Wood
"The Nocturnals V" © 2021, Mariah Montoya
"Ennui Tea" © 2021, Ivy Grimes

"The Tick of the Clock" © 2021, J.C. Pillard
"Genesis" © 2021, Lisa Short
"Tell the Crows I'm Home" © 2021, Laurel Beckley
"The Azurian Shield" © 2021, Karl El-Koura

"Treedom" © 2021, A.J. Cunder
"Right Behind You" © 2021, Matthew Gomez
"The Unlucky Few Who Must Not Cast" © 2021, J. Tynan Burke
"The Great Contradiction" © 2021, Jordan Chase-Young

"Orla, Always" © 2021, Thomas Ha
"Dry Season" © 2021, Caite Sajwaj
"Stand or Fall" © 2021, David Whitmarsh
"Gatekeepers" © 2021, Douglas DiCicco
"Tides" © 2021, Ailsa Bristow

Authors also retain copyrights to all other material in the anthology.

Works of fiction

This book contains works of fiction. Characters, dialogue, places, organizations, incidents, and events portrayed in the works are fictional and are products of the author's imagination or used fictitiously. Any resemblance to actual persons, places, organizations, or events is coincidental.

All rights reserved

Moral rights asserted

Each author whose work is included in this book has asserted their moral rights, including the right to be identified as the author of their respective work(s).

Publisher

a magazine of speculative fiction

Metaphorosis Magazine is an imprint of
Metaphorosis Publishing
Neskowin, OR, USA

www.metaphorosis.com

"Metaphorosis" is a registered trademark.

Discounts available

Substantial discounts are available for educational institutions, including writing workshops. Discounts are also available for quantity purchases. For details, contact Metaphorosis at metaphorosis.com/about

Metaphorosis Publishing

Metaphorosis offers beautifully written science fiction and fantasy. Our imprints include:

Metaphorosis Magazine

Plant Based Press

Verdage

Help keep Metaphorosis running at
Patreon.com/metaphorosis

See more about some of our books on the following pages.

Metaphorosis
a magazine of speculative fiction

Metaphorosis is an online speculative fiction magazine dedicated to quality writing. We publish an original story every week, along with author bios, interviews, and notes on story origins. Come and see us online at magazine.Metaphorosis.com

We publish monthly print and e-book issues, as well as yearly Best of and Complete anthologies.

plant
based
press

Vegan-friendly science fiction and fantasy, including an annual anthology of the year's best SFF stories.

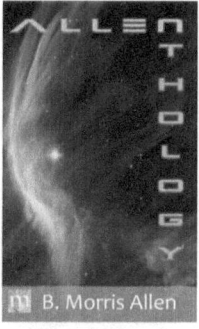

Susurrus

A darkly romantic story of magic, love, and suffering.

Allenthology: Volume I

A quarter century of SFF from B. Morris Allen, including the full contents of the collections *Tocsin, Start with Stones,* and *Metaphorosis.*

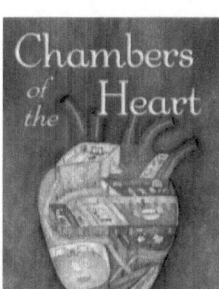

Chambers of the Heart

A heart that's a bulding, a dog that's a program, a woman who's sinking irretrievably — stories about love, loss, and motion. A collection of speculative stories from author and editor B. Morris Allen.

Best Vegan Science Fiction & Fantasy
2016-2020

The best vegan-friendly science fiction and fantasy stories from each year. Great SFF that just doesn't happen to include meat-eating, hunting, horse-riding, etc.

Verdage

Science fiction and fantasy books for writers – full of great stories, but with an additional focus on the craft of speculative fiction writing.

Reading 5X5 x2

Duets

How do authors' voices change when they collaborate?

A round-robin of five talented science fiction and fantasy authors collaborating with each other and writing solo.

Including stories by Evan Marcroft, David Gallay, J. Tynan Burke, L'Erin Ogle, and Douglas Anstruther.

Score

an SFF symphony

What if stories were written like music? *Score* is an anthology of varied stories arranged to follow an emotional score from the heights of joy to the depths of despair – but always with a little hope shining through.

Reading 5X5

Five stories, five times

Twenty-five SFF authors, five base stories, five versions of each – see how different writers take on the same material, with stories in contemporary and high fantasy, soft and hard SF, and a mysterious 'other' category.

Reading 5X5

Writers' Edition

All the stories from the regular, readers' edition, plus two extra stories, the story seed, and authors' notes on writing. Over 100 pages of additional material specifically aimed at writers.

www.ingramcontent.com/pod-product-compliance
Lightning Source LLC
Chambersburg PA
CBHW050606110726
47899CB00001B/1